THE
MOTE
IN
GOD'S
EYE

Larry Niven and Jerry Pournelle

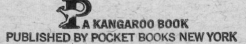

A KANGAROO BOOK
PUBLISHED BY POCKET BOOKS NEW YORK

Distributed in Canada by PaperJacks Ltd., a Licensee
of the trademarks of Simon & Schuster, a division of
Gulf+Western Corporation.

THE MOTE IN GOD'S EYE

Simon & Schuster edition published 1974

POCKET BOOK edition published October, 1975

8th printing...........April, 1977

This POCKET BOOK edition includes every word contained in
the original, higher-priced edition. It is printed from brand-new
plates made from completly reset, clear, easy-to-read type.
POCKET BOOK editions are published by
POCKET BOOKS,
a division of Simon & Schuster, Inc.,
A GULF+WESTERN COMPANY
Trademarks registered in the United States
and other countries.
In Canada distributed by PaperJacks Ltd.,
330 Steelcase Road, Markham, Ontario.

ISBN: 0-671-80107-4.
Library of Congress Catalog Card Number: 74-10723.

Printed in Canada.

To Marilyn and Roberta,
who put up with us while we wrote this;
and to Lurton and Ginny,
who made us do the job over again.

DRAMATIS PERSONAE

RODERICK HAROLD, Lord Blaine, Commander, Imperial
Space Navy

ARKLEY KELLEY, Gunner, Imperial Marines, and Blaine
family retainer

ADMIRAL SIR VLADIMIR RICHARD GEORGE PLEKHANOV,
Vice Admiral Commanding Imperial Navy Forces, New
Chicago, and Acting Governor General, New Chicago

CAPTAIN BRUNO CZILLER, Imperial Space Navy, Master
of INSS *MacArthur*

COMMANDER JOHN CARGILL, ISN, First Lieutenant of
MacArthur

COMMANDER JOCK (SANDY) SINCLAIR, ISN, Chief Engineer of *MacArthur*

MIDSHIPMAN HORST STALEY, ISN, senior midshipman
aboard INSS *MacArthur*

MIDSHIPMAN JONATHON WHITBREAD, ISN

KEVIN RENNER, Sailing Master Lieutenant, Imperial
Space Navy Reserve

LADY SANDRA LIDDELL LEONOVNA BRIGHT FOWLER, B.A.,
M.S., doctoral candidate in anthropology, Imperial University of Sparta

HIS EXCELLENCY HORACE HUSSEIN BURY, Trader and
Magnate; Chairman of the Board, Imperial Autonetics
Company, Ltd.

MIDSHIPMAN GAVIN POTTER, ISN

FLEET ADMIRAL HOWLAND CRANSTON, Commander-in-
Chief, His Majesty's Forces Beyond the Coal Sack

HIS IMPERIAL HIGHNESS RICHARD STEFAN MERRILL, Viceroy for His Majesty's Dominions Beyond the Coal Sack

DR. ANTHONY HORVATH, Minister of Science for Trans-
Coalsack Sector

DR. JACOB BUCKMAN, Astrophysicist

FATHER DAVID HARDY, Chaplain-Captain, Imperial Space
Navy Reserve

ADMIRAL LAVRENTI KUTUZOV, Vice Admiral Commanding His Majesty's Expedition Beyond Murcheson's Eye

SENATOR BENJAMIN BRIGHT FOWLER, Majority Leader and Member of Privy Council

DR. SIGMUND HOROWITZ, Professor of Xenobiology, University of New Scotland

HERBERT COLVIN, onetime Captain of Space Forces of the Republic of Union, and onetime master of Union cruiser *Defiant*

CHRONOLOGY

1969	Neil Armstrong sets foot on Earth's Moon.
1990	Series of treaties between United States and Soviet Union creates the CoDominium.
2008	First successful interstellar drive tested. Alderson Drive perfected.
2020	First interstellar colonies. Beginning of Great Exodus.
2040	CoDominium Bureau of Relocation begins mass out-system shipment of convicts. Colonization of Sparta and St. Ekaterina.
2079	Sergei Lermontov becomes Grand Admiral of CoDominium Space Navy.
2103	Great Patriotic Wars. End of the CoDominium. Exodus of the Fleet.
2110	Coronation of Lysander I of Sparta. Fleet swears loyalty to the Spartan throne. Marriage of dynasties produces union between Sparta and St. Ekaterina.
2111	Formation Wars begin.
2250	Leonidas I proclaims Empire of Man.
2250–2600	Empire of Man enforces interstellar peace.
2450	Jasper Murcheson explores region beyond the Coal Sack. Terraforming of New Scotland.
2603	Secession Wars begin. Growth of Sauron supermen. St. Ekaterina nearly destroyed.
2640	Secession Wars continue. Dark Ages in many systems. Effective termination of First Empire. Sauron supermen exterminated.
2800	Interstellar trade ceases. Piracy and brigandage. Dark Ages.
2862	Coherent light from the Mote reaches New Scotland.
2870	Effective end of Secession Wars.

And why beholdest thou the mote that is in thy brother's eye, but considerest not the beam that is in thine own eye?

MATTHEW 7 : 3

THE
MOTE
IN
GOD'S
EYE

Prologue

"Throughout the past thousand years of history it has been traditional to regard the Alderson Drive as an unmixed blessing. Without the faster than light travel Alderson's discoveries made possible, humanity would have been trapped in the tiny prison of the Solar System when the Great Patriotic Wars destroyed the CoDominium on Earth. Instead, we had already settled more than two hundred worlds.

"A blessing, yes. We might now be extinct were it not for the Alderson Drive. But unmixed? Consider. The same tramline effect that colonized the stars, the same interstellar contacts that allowed the formation of the First Empire, allow interstellar war. The worlds wrecked in two hundred years of Secession Wars were both settled and destroyed by ships using the Alderson Drive.

"Because of the Alderson Drive we need never consider the space between the stars. Because we can shunt between stellar systems in zero time, our ships and ships' drives need cover only interplanetary distances. We say that the Second Empire of Man rules two hundred worlds and all the space between, over fifteen million cubic parsecs . . .

"Consider the true picture. Think of myriads of tiny bubbles, very sparsely scattered, rising through a vast black sea. We rule some of the bubbles. Of the waters we know nothing . . ."

—from a speech delivered by Dr. Anthony Horvath at the Blaine Institute, A.D. 3029.

PART ONE

THE CRAZY EDDIE PROBE

1 · *Command*

A.D. 3017

"Admiral's compliments, and you're to come to his office right away," Midshipman Staley announced.

Commander Roderick Blaine looked frantically around the bridge, where his officers were directing repairs with low and urgent voices, surgeons assisting at a difficult operation. The gray steel compartment was a confusion of activities, each orderly by itself, but the overall impression was of chaos. Screens above one helmsman's station showed the planet below and the other ships in orbit near *MacArthur,* but everywhere else the panel covers had been removed from consoles, test instruments were clipped into their insides, and technicians stood by with color-coded electronic assemblies to replace everything that seemed doubtful. Thumps and whines sounded through the ship as somewhere aft the engineering crew worked on the hull.

The scars of battle showed everywhere, ugly burns where the ship's protective Langston Field had overloaded momentarily. An irregular hole larger than a man's fist was burned completely through one console, and now two technicians seemed permanently installed in the system by a web of cables. Rod Blaine looked at the black stains

1

that had spread across his battle dress. A whiff of metal vapor and burned meat was still in his nostrils, or in his brain, and again he saw fire and molten metal erupt from the hull and wash across his left side. His left arm was still bound across his chest by an elastic bandage, and he could follow most of the previous week's activities by the stains it carried.

And I've only been aboard an hour! he thought. With the Captain ashore, and everything a mess. I can't leave now! He turned to the midshipman. "Right away?"

"Yes, sir. The signal's marked urgent."

Nothing for it, then, and Rod would catch hell when the Captain came back aboard. First Lieutenant Cargill and Engineer Sinclair were competent men, but Rod was Exec and damage control was his responsibility, even if he'd been away from *MacArthur* when she took most of the hits.

Rod's Marine orderly coughed discreetly and pointed to the stained uniform. "Sir, we've time to get you more decent?"

"Good thinking." Rod glanced at the status board to be sure. Yes, he had half an hour before he could take a boat down to the planet's surface. Leaving sooner wouldn't get him to the Admiral's office any quicker. It would be a relief to get out of these coveralls. He hadn't undressed since he was wounded.

They had to send for a surgeon's mate to undress him. The medic snipped at the armor cloth embedded in his left arm and muttered. "Hold still, sir. That arm's cooked good." His voice was disapproving. "You should have been in sick bay a week ago."

"Hardly possible," Rod answered. A week before, *MacArthur* had been in battle with a rebel warship, who'd scored more hits than she ought to have before surrendering. After the victory Rod was prize master in the enemy vessel, and there weren't facilities for proper treatment there. As the armor came away he smelled something worse than week-old sweat. Touch of gangrene, maybe.

"Yessir." A few more threads were cut away. The synthetic was as tough as steel. "Now it's gonna take surgery, Commander. Got to cut all that away before the regeneration stimulators can work. While we got you in sick bay we can fix that nose."

"I like my nose," Rod told him coldly. He fingered the slightly crooked appendage and recalled the battle when it was broken. Rod thought it made him look older, no bad thing at twenty-four standard years; and it was the badge of an earned, not inherited, success. Rod was proud of his family background, but there were times when the Blaine reputation was a bit hard to live up to.

Eventually the armor was cut loose and his arm smeared with Numbitol. The stewards helped him into a powder-blue uniform, red sash, gold braid, epaulettes; all wrinkled and crushed, but better than monofiber coveralls. The stiff jacket hurt his arm despite the anesthetic until he found that he could rest his forearm on the pistol butt.

When he was dressed he boarded the landing gig from *MacArthur*'s hangar deck, and the coxswain let the boat drop through the big flight elevator doors without having the spin taken off the ship. It was a dangerous maneuver, but it saved time. Retros fired, and the little winged flyer plunged into atmosphere.

NEW CHICAGO: Inhabited world, Trans-Coalsack Sector, approximately 20 parsecs from Sector Capital. The primary is an F9 yellow star commonly referred to as Beta Hortensis.

The atmosphere is very nearly Earth-normal and breathable without aids or filters. Gravity is 1.08 standard. The planetary radius is 1.05, and mass is 1.21 Earth-standard, indicating a planet of greater than normal density. New Chicago is inclined at 41 degrees with a semi-major axis of 1.06 AU, moderately eccentric. The resulting variations in seasonal temperatures have confined the inhabited areas to a relatively narrow band in the south temperate zone.

There is one moon at normal distance, commonly called Evanston. The origin of the name is obscure.

New Chicago is 70 percent seas. Land area is mostly mountainous with continuing volcanic activity. The extensive metal industries of the First Empire period were nearly all destroyed in the Secession Wars; reconstruction of an industrial base has proceded satisfactorily since New Chicago was admitted to the Second Empire in A.D. 2940.

Most inhabitants reside in a single city which bears the same name as the planet. Other population centers are widely scattered, with none having a population over 45,000. Total planet population was reported as 6.7 million in the census of 2990. There are iron mining and smelting towns in the mountains, and extensive agricultural settlements. The planet is self-sufficient in foodstuffs.

New Chicago possesses a growing merchant fleet, and is located at a convenient point to serve as a center of Trans-Coalsack interstellar trade. It is governed by a governor general and a council appointed by the Viceroy of Trans-Coalsack Sector, there is an elected assembly, and two delegates have been admitted to the Imperial Parliament.

Rod Blaine scowled at the words flowing across the screen of his pocket computer. The physical data were current, but everything else was obsolete. The rebels had changed even the name of their world, from New Chicago to Dame Liberty. Her government would have to be built all over again. Certainly she'd lose her delegates; she might even lose the right to an elected assembly.

He put the instrument away and looked down. They were over mountainous country, and he saw no signs of war. There hadn't been any area bombardments, thank God.

It happened sometimes: a city fortress would hold out with the aid of satellite-based planetary defenses. The Navy had no time for prolonged sieges. Imperial policy was to finish rebellions at the lowest possible cost in lives—but to finish them. A holdout rebel planet might be reduced to glittering lava fields, with nothing surviving but a few cities lidded by the black domes of Langston Fields; and what then? There weren't enough ships to transport food across interstellar distances. Plague and famine would follow.

Yet, he thought, it was the only possible way. He had sworn the Oath on taking the Imperial commission. Humanity must be reunited into one government, by persuasion or by force, so that the hundreds of years of Secession Wars could never happen again. Every Imperial officer had seen what horrors those wars brought; that was why the academies were located on Earth instead of at the Capital.

As they neared the city he saw the first signs of battle. A ring of blasted lands, ruined outlying fortresses, broken concrete rails of the transportation system; then the almost untouched city which had been secure within the perfect circle of its Langston Field. The city had taken minor damage, but once the Field was off, effective resistance had ceased. Only fanatics fought on against the Imperial Marines.

They passed over the ruins of a tall building crumpled over by a falling landing boat. Someone must have fired on the Marines and the pilot hadn't wanted his death to be for nothing . . .

They circled the city, slowing to allow them to approach the landing docks without breaking out all the windows. The buildings were old, most built by hydrocarbon technology, Rod guessed, with strips torn out and replaced by more modern structures. Nothing remained of the First Empire city which had stood here.

When they dropped onto the port on top of Government House, Rod saw that slowing hadn't been required. Most city windows were smashed already. Mobs milled in the streets, and the only moving vehicles were military convoys. Some people stood idly, others ran in and out of shops. Gray-coated Imperial Marines stood guard behind electrified riot fences around Government House. The flyer landed.

Blaine was rushed down the elevator to the Governor General's floor. There wasn't a woman in the building, although Imperial government offices usually bristled with them, and Rod missed the girls. He'd been in space a long time. He gave his name to the ramrod-straight Marine at the receptionist's desk and waited.

He wasn't looking forward to the coming interview, and spent the time glaring at blank walls. All the decorative paintings, the three-d star map with Imperial banners floating above the provinces, all the standard equipment of a governor general's office on a Class One planet, were gone, leaving ugly places on the walls.

The guard motioned him into the office. Admiral Sir Vladimir Richard George Plekhanov, Vice Admiral of the Black, Knight of St. Michael and St. George, was seated at the Governor General's desk. There was no sign of His Excellency Mr. Haruna, and for a moment Rod thought the Admiral was alone. Then he noticed Captain Cziller, his immediate superior as master of *MacArthur*, standing by the window. All the transparencies had been knocked out, and there were deep scratches in the paneled walls. The displays and furniture were gone. Even the Great Seal —crown and spaceship, eagle, sickle and hammer—was missing from above the duralplast desk. There had never in Rod's memory been a duralplast desk in a governor general's office.

"Commander Blaine reporting as ordered, sir."

Plekhanov absently returned the salute. Cziller didn't look around from the window. Rod stood at stiff attention while the Admiral regarded him with an unchanging expression. Finally: "Good morning, Commander."

"Good morning, sir."

"Not really. I suppose I haven't seen you since I last visited Crucis Court. How is the Marquis?"

"Well when I was last home, sir."

The Admiral nodded and continued to regard Blaine with a critical look. He hasn't changed, Rod thought. An enormously competent man, who fought a tendency to fat by exercising in high gravity. The Navy sent Plekhanov when hard fighting was expected. He's never been known to excuse an incompetent officer, and there was a gunroom rumor that he'd had the Crown Prince—now Emperor—stretched over a mess table and whacked with a spatball paddle back when His Highness was serving as a midshipman in *Plataea*.

"I have your report here, Blaine. You had to fight your way to the rebel Field generator. You lost a company of Imperial Marines."

"Yes, sir." Fanatic rebel guardsmen had defended the generator station, and the battle had been fierce.

"And just what the devil were you doing in a ground action?" the Admiral demanded. "Cziller gave you that captured cruiser to escort our assault carrier. Did you have orders to go down with the boats?"

"No, sir."

"I suppose you think the aristocracy isn't subject to Navy discipline?"

"Of course I don't think that, sir."

Plekhanov ignored him. "Then there's this deal you made with a rebel leader. What was his name?" Plekhanov glanced at the papers. "Stone. Jonas Stone. Immunity from arrest. Restoration of property. Damn you, do you imagine that every naval officer has authority to make deals with subjects in rebellion? Or do you hold some diplomatic commission I'm not aware of, Commander?"

"No, sir." Rod's lips were pressed tightly against his teeth. He wanted to shout, but he didn't. To hell with Navy tradition, he thought. I won the damned war.

"But you do have an explanation?" the Admiral demanded.

"Yes, sir."

"Well?"

Rod spoke through tightening throat muscles. "Sir. While commanding the prize *Defiant,* I received a signal from the rebel city. At that time the city's Langston Field was intact, Captain Cziller aboard *MacArthur* was fully engaged with the satellite planetary defenses, and the main body of the fleet was in general engagement with rebel forces. The message was signed by a rebel leader. Mr. Stone promised to admit Imperial forces into the city on condition that he obtain full immunity from prosecution and restoration of his personal property. He gave a time limit of one hour, and insisted on a member of the aristocracy as guarantor. If there were anything to his offer, the war would end once the Marines entered the city's Field generator house. There being no possibility of consultation with higher authority, I took the landing force down myself and gave Mr. Stone my personal word of honor."

Plekhanov frowned. "Your word. As Lord Blaine. Not as a Navy officer."

"It was the only way he'd discuss it, Admiral."

"I see." Plekhanov was thoughtful now. If he disavowed Blaine's word, Rod would be through, in the Navy, in government, everywhere. On the other hand, Admiral Plekhanov would have to explain to the House of Peers. "What made you think this offer was genuine?"

"Sir, it was in Imperial code and countersigned by a Navy intelligence officer."

"So you risked your ship—"

"Against the chance of ending the war without destroying the planet. Yes, sir. I might point out that Mr. Stone's message described the city prison camp where they were keeping the Imperial officers and citizens."

"I see." Plekhanov's hands moved in a sudden angry gesture. "All right. I've no use for traitors, even one who helps us. But I'll honor your bargain, and that means I have to give official approval to your going down with the landing boats. I *don't* have to like it, Blaine, and I don't. It was a damn fool stunt."

One that worked, Rod thought. He continued to stand at attention, but he felt the knot in his guts loosen.

The Admiral grunted. "Your father takes stupid chances. Almost got us both killed on Tanith. It's a bloody wonder your family's survived through eleven marquises, and it'll be a bigger one if you live to be twelfth. All right, sit down."

"Thank you, sir." Rod said stiffly, his voice coldly polite.

The Admiral's face relaxed slightly. "Did I ever tell you your father was my commanding officer on Tanith?" Plekhanov asked conversationally.

"No, sir. He did." There was still no warmth in Rod's voice.

"He was also the best friend I ever had in the Navy, Commander. His influence put me in this seat, and he asked to have you under my command."

"Yes, sir." I knew that. Now I wonder why.

"You'd like to ask me what I expected you to do, wouldn't you, Commander?"

Rod twitched in surprise. "Yes, sir."

"What would have happened if that offer *hadn't* been genuine? If it had been a trap?"

"The rebels might have destroyed my command."

"Yes." Plekhanov's voice was steely calm. "But you thought it worth the risk because you had a chance to end the war with few casualties on either side. Right?"

"Yes, sir."

"And if the Marines were killed, just what would my fleet have been able to do?" The Admiral slammed both fists against the desk. "I'd have had no choices at all!" he roared. "Every week I keep this fleet here is another chance for outies to hit one of our planets! There'd have been no time to send for another assault carrier and more Marines. If you'd lost your command, I'd have blasted this planet into the stone age, Blaine. Aristocrat or no, don't you *ever* put anyone in that position again! Do you understand me?"

"Yes, sir . . ." He's right. But— What good would the Marines have been with the city's Field intact? Rod's shoulders slumped. Something. He'd have done something. But what?

"It turned out well," Plekhanov said coldly. "Maybe you were right. Maybe you weren't. You do another stunt like that and I'll have your sword. Is that understood?" He lifted a printout of Rod's service career. "Is *MacArthur* ready for space?"

"Sir?" The question was asked in the same tone as the threat, and it took Rod a moment to shift mental gears. "For space, sir. Not a battle. And I wouldn't want to see her go far without a refit." In the frantic hour he'd spent aboard, Rod had carried out a thorough inspection, which was one reason he needed a shave. Now he sat uncomfortably and wondered. *MacArthur*'s captain stood at the window, obviously listening, but he hadn't said a word. Why didn't the Admiral ask *him?*

As Blaine wondered, Plekhanov made up his mind. "Well? Bruno, you're Fleet Captain. Make your recommendation."

Bruno Cziller turned from the window. Rod was startled: Cziller no longer wore the little silver replica of *MacArthur* that showed him to be her master. Instead the comet and sunburst of the Naval Staff shone on his breast, and Cziller wore the broad stripes of a brevet admiral.

"How are you, Commander?" Cziller asked formally. Then grinned. That twisted lopsided grin was famous through *MacArthur.* "You're looking all right. At least from the right profile you do. Well, you were aboard an hour. What damage did you find?"

Confused, Rod reported the present condition of *Mac-Arthur* as he'd found her, and the repairs he'd ordered. Cziller nodded and asked questions. Finally: "And you conclude she's ready for space, but not war. Is that it?"

"Yes, sir. Not against a capital ship, anyway."

"It's true, too. Admiral, my recommendation. Commander Blaine is ready for promotion and we can give him *MacArthur* to take for refit to New Scotland, then on to the Capital. He can take Senator Fowler's niece with him."

Give him *MacArthur?* Rod heard him dimly, wonderingly. He was afraid to believe it, but here was the chance to show Plekhanov and everyone else.

"He's young. Never be allowed to keep that ship as a first command," Plekhanov said. "Still and all, it's probably the best way. He can't get in too much trouble going to Sparta by way of New Caledonia. She's yours, Captain." When Rod said nothing, Plekhanov barked at him. "You. Blaine. You're promoted to captain and command of *MacArthur.* My writer will have your orders in half an hour."

Cziller grinned one-sided. "Say something," he suggested.

"Thank you, sir. I— I thought you didn't approve of me."

"Not sure I do," Plekhanov said. "If I had any choice you'd be somebody's exec. You'll probably make a good marquis, but you don't have the Navy temperament. I don't suppose it matters, the Navy's not your career anyway."

"Not any more, sir," Rod said carefully.

It still hurt inside. Big George, who filled a room with barbells when he was twelve and was built like a wedge before he was sixteen—his brother George was dead in a battle halfway across the Empire. Rod would be planning his future, or thinking wistfully about home, and the memory would come as if someone had pricked his soul with a needle. Dead. George?

George should have inherited the estates and titles. Rod had wanted nothing more than a Navy career and the chance to become Grand Admiral someday. Now—less than ten years and he'd have to take his place in Parliament.

"You'll have two passengers," Cziller said. "One you've met. You do know Lady Sandra Bright Fowler, don't you? Senator Fowler's niece."

"Yes, sir. I hadn't seen her for years, but her uncle dines at Crucis Court quite often . . . then I found her in the prison camp. How is she?"

"Not very good," Cziller said. His grin vanished. "We're packing her home, and I don't have to tell you to handle with care. She'll be with you as far as New Scotland, and all the way to the Capital if she wants. That's up to her. Your other passenger, though, that's a different matter."

Rod looked up attentively. Cziller looked to Plekhanov, got a nod, and continued, "His Excellency, Trader Horace Hussein Bury, Magnate, Chairman of the Board of Imperial Autonetics, and something big in the Imperial Traders Association. He stays with you all the way to Sparta, and I mean he *stays* aboard your ship, do you understand?"

"Well, not exactly, sir," Rod answered.

Plekhanov sniffed. "Cziller made it clear enough. We think Bury was behind this rebellion, but there's not enough evidence to put him in preventive detention. He'd appeal to the Emperor. All right, we'll send him to Sparta to make his appeal. As the Navy's guest. But who do I send him with, Blaine? He's worth millions. More. How many men would turn down a whole planet for a bribe? Bury could offer one."

"I—yes, sir," Rod said.

"And don't look so damned shocked," Plekhanov barked. "I haven't accused any of my officers of corruption. But the fact is, you're richer than Bury. He can't even *tempt* you. It's my main reason for giving you command of *MacArthur*, so I don't have to worry about our wealthy friend."

"I see. Thank you anyway, sir." And I *will* show you it was no mistake.

Plekhanov nodded as if reading Blaine's thoughts. "You might make a good Navy officer. Here's your chance. I need Cziller to help govern this planet. The rebels killed the Governor General."

"Killed Mr. Haruna?" Rod was stunned. He remembered the wrinkled old gentleman, well over a hundred when he came to Rod's home— "He's an old friend of my father's."

"He wasn't the only one they killed. They had the heads strung up on pikes outside Government House. Somebody thought that'd make the people fight on longer. Make 'em afraid to surrender to us. Well, they have reason to be afraid now. Your deal with Stone. Any other conditions?"

"Yes, sir. It's off if he refuses to cooperate with Intelligence. He has to name all the conspirators."

Plekhanov looked significantly at Cziller. "Get your men on that, Bruno. It's a start. All right, Blaine, get your ship fixed up and scoot." The Admiral stood; the interview was over. "You'll have a lot to do, Captain. Get to it."

2 • The Passengers

Horace Hussein Chamoun al Shamlan Bury pointed out the last of the articles he would take with him and dismissed the servants. He knew they would wait just outside his suite, ready to divide the wealth he was leaving behind, but it amused him to make them wait. They would be all the happier for the thrill of stealing.

When the room was empty he poured a large glass of wine. It was poor quality stuff brought in after the blockade, but he hardly noticed. Wine was officially forbidden on Levant, which meant that the hordes of winesellers foisted off anything alcoholic on their customers, even wealthy ones like the Bury family. Horace Bury had never developed any real appreciation for expensive liquors. He bought them to show his wealth, and for entertaining; but for himself anything would do. Coffees were a different matter.

He was a small man, as were most of the people of Levant, with dark features and a prominent nose, dark, burning eyes and sharp features, quick gestures, and a violent temper that only his intimate associates suspected. Alone now, he permitted himself a scowl. There was a printout from Admiral Plekhanov's writers on the desk, and he easily translated the formally polite phrases inviting him to leave New Chicago and regretting that no civilian passage would be available. The Navy was suspicious, and he felt a cold knot of rage threaten to engulf him despite the wine. He was outwardly calm, though, as he sat at the desk and ticked off points on his fingers.

What had the Navy on him? There were the suspicions of Naval Intelligence, but no evidence. There was the usual hatred of the Navy for Imperial Traders, compounded, he thought, because some of the Navy staff were Jews, and all Jews hated Levantines. But the Navy could have no real evidence or he wouldn't be going aboard *MacArthur* as a guest. He'd be in irons. That meant Jonas Stone still kept his silence.

He ought to keep silence. Bury had paid him a hundred thousand crowns with a promise of more. But he had no confidence in Stone: two nights before, Bury had seen certain men on lower Kosciusko Street and paid them fifty thousand crowns, and it shouldn't be long until Stone was silent forever. Let him whisper secrets in his grave.

Was there anything else undone? he wondered. No. What would come would come, glory be to Allah . . . He grimaced. That kind of thinking came naturally, and he despised himself for a superstitious fool. Let his father praise Allah for his accomplishments; fortune came to the man who left nothing to chance; as he had left few things undone in his ninety standard years.

The Empire had come to Levant ten years after Horace was born, and at first its influence was small. In those days Imperial policies were different and the planet came into the Empire with a standing nearly equal to more advanced worlds. Horace Bury's father soon realized Imperialism could be made to pay. By becoming one of those the Imperials used to govern the planet, he had amassed immense wealth: he'd sold audiences with the governor, and hawked justice like cabbages in the market place, but always carefully, always leaving others to face the wrath of the hard-nosed men of the Imperial service.

His father was careful with investments, and he'd used his influence to have Horace Hussein educated on Sparta. He'd even given him a name suggested by an Imperial Navy officer; only later did they learn that Horace was hardly common in the Empire and was a name to be laughed at.

Bury drowned the memory of early days in the Capital schools with another beaker of wine. He'd learned! And now he'd invested his father's money, and his own. Horace Bury wasn't someone to laugh at. It had taken thirty years, but his agents had located the officer who'd given him that name. The stereographs of his agony were hidden in Bury's home on Levant. He'd had the last laugh.

Now he bought and sold men who laughed at him, as he bought votes in Parliament, bought ships, and had almost bought this planet of New Chicago. And by the Prophet—blast!—by damn he'd own it yet. Control of New Chicago would give his family influence here beyond the Coal Sack, here where the Empire was weak and new planets were found monthly. A man might look to—to anything!

The reverie had helped. Now he summoned his agents, the man who'd guard his interests here, and Nabil, who would accompany him as a servant on the warship. Nabil, a small man, much smaller than Horace, younger than he looked, with a ferret face that could be disguised many ways, and skills with dagger and poison learned on ten planets. Horace Hussein Bury smiled. So the Imperials would keep him prisoner aboard their warships? So long as there were no ships for Levant, let them. But when they were at a busy port, they might find it harder to do.

For three days Rod worked on *MacArthur*. Leaking tankage, burned-out components, all had to be replaced. There were few spares, and *MacArthur*'s crew spent hours in space cannibalizing the Union war fleet hulks in orbit around New Chicago.

Slowly *MacArthur* was put back into battleworthy condition. Blaine worked with Jack Cargill, First Lieutenant and now Exec, and Commander Jock Sinclair, the Chief Engineer. Like many engineering officers, Sinclair was from New Scotland. His heavy accent was common among Scots throughout space. Somehow they had preserved it as a badge of pride during the Secession Wars, even on planets where Gaelic was a forgotten language. Rod privately suspected that the Scots studied their speech off duty so they'd be unintelligible to the rest of humanity.

Hull plates were welded on, enormous patches of armor stripped from Union warships and sweated into place. Sinclair worked wonders adapting New Chicago equipment for use in *MacArthur,* until he had built a patchwork of components and spares that hardly matched the ship's original blueprints. The bridge officers worked through the nights trying to explain and describe the changes to the ship's master computer.

Cargill and Sinclair nearly came to blows over some of the adaptations, Sinclair maintaining that the important thing was to have the ship ready for space, while the First Lieutenant insisted that he'd never be able to direct combat repairs because God Himself didn't know what had been done to the ship.

"I dinna care to hear such blasphemy," Sinclair was saying as Rod came into range. "And is it nae enough that *I* ken wha' we hae done to her?"

"Not unless you want to be cook too, you maniac tinker! This morning the wardroom cook couldn't operate the coffeepot! One of your artificers took the microwave heater. Now by God you'll bring that back . . ."

"Aye, we'll strip it oot o' number-three tank, just as soon as you find me parts for the pump it replaces. Can you no be happy, man? The ship can fight again. Or is coffee more important?"

Cargill took a deep breath, then started over. "The ship can fight," he said in what amounted to baby talk, "until somebody makes a hole in her. Then she has to be fixed. Now suppose I had to repair this," he said, laying a hand on something Rod was almost sure was an air adsorber-converter. "The damned thing looks half-melted now. How would I know what was damaged? Or if it were damaged at all? Suppose . . ."

"Man, you wouldna' hae troubles if you did nae fash yoursel' wi . . ."

"Will you stop that? You talk like everybody else when you get excited!"

"That's a damn lie!"

But at that point Rod thought it better to step into view. He sent the Chief Engineer to his end of the ship and Cargill forward. There would be no settling their dispute until *MacArthur* could be thoroughly refitted in New Scotland's Yards.

Blaine spent a night in sick bay under orders from the surgeon lieutenant. He came out with his arm immobile in a tremendous padded cast like a pillow grafted on him. He felt mean and preternaturally alert for the next few days; but nobody actually laughed out loud in his hearing.

On the third day after taking command Blaine held ship's inspection. All work was stopped and the ship given spin. Then Blaine and Cargill went over her.

Rod was tempted to take advantage of his recent experience as *MacArthur*'s Exec. He knew all the places where a lazy executive officer might skimp on the work. But it was his first inspection, the ship only just under repair from battle damage, and Cargill was too good an officer to let something pass that he could possibly have corrected. Blaine took a leisurely tour, checking the important gear but otherwise letting Cargill guide him. As he did, he mentally resolved not to let this be a precedent. When there was more time, he'd go over the ship and find out everything.

A full company of Marines guarded the New Chicago space port. Since the city's Langston Field generator had fallen there had been no resurgence of hostilities. Indeed, most of the populace seemed to welcome the Imperial forces with an exhausted relief more convincing than parades and cheering. But the New Chicago revolt had reached the Empire as a stunning surprise; a resurgence would be no surprise at all.

So Marines patrolled the space port and guarded the Imperial boats, and Sally Fowler felt their eyes as she walked with her servants through hot sunlight toward a boat-shaped lifting body. They didn't bother her. She was Senator Fowler's niece; she was used to being stared at.

Lovely, one of the guards was thinking. *But no expression. You'd think she'd be happy to be out of that stinking prison camp, but she doesn't look it.* Perspiration dripped steadily down his ribs, and he thought, *She doesn't sweat. She was carved from ice by the finest sculptor that ever lived.*

The boat was big, and two-thirds empty. Sally's eyes took in two small dark men—Bury and his servant, and no doubt about which was which—and four younger men showing fear, anticipation, and awe. The mark of New Chicago's outback was on them. New recruits, she guessed.

She took one of the last seats at the back. She was not in a conversational mood. Adam and Annie looked at her with worried expressions, then took seats across the aisle. They knew.

"It's good to be leaving," said Annie.

Sally didn't respond. She felt nothing at all.

She'd been like this ever since the Marines had burst into the prison camp. There had been good food, and a hot bath, and clean clothes, and the deference of those about her . . . and none of it had reached her. She'd felt nothing. Those months in the prison camp had burned something out of her. Perhaps permanently, she thought. It bothered her remotely.

When Sally Fowler left the Imperial University at Sparta with her master's degree in anthropology she had persuaded her uncle that instead of graduate school she should travel through the Empire, observe newly conquered provinces, and study primitive cultures first hand. She would even write a book.

"After all," she had insisted, "what can I learn here? It's out there beyond the Coal Sack that I'm needed."

She had a mental image of her triumphant return, publications and scholarly articles, winning a place for herself in her profession rather than passively waiting to be married off to some young aristocrat. Sally fully intended to marry, but not until she could start with more than her inheritances. She wanted to be something in her own right, to serve the realm in ways other than bearing it sons to be killed in warships.

Surprisingly, her uncle had agreed. If Sally had known more of people instead of academic psychology she might have realized why. Benjamin Bright Fowler, her father's younger brother, had inherited nothing, had won his place as leader of the Senate by sheer guts and ability. With no children of his own, he thought of his brother's only surviving child as his daughter, and he had seen enough young girls whose only importance was their relatives and their money. Sally and a classmate had left Sparta with Sally's servants, Adam and Annie, headed for the provinces and the study of primitive human cultures that the Navy was forever finding. Some planets had not been visited by starships for three hundred years and more, and the wars had so reduced their populations that savagery returned.

They were on their way to a primitive colony world, with a stopover at New Chicago to change ships, when the revolution broke out. Sally's friend Dorothy had been outside the city that day, and had never been found. The Union Guards of the Committee of Public Safety had dragged Sally from her hotel suite, stripped her of her valuables, and thrown her into the camp.

In the first days the camp was orderly. Imperial nobility, civil servants, and former Imperial soldiers made the camp safer than the streets of New Chicago. But day after day the aristocrats and government officials were taken from the camp and never seen again, while common criminals were added to the mixture. Adam and Annie found her somehow, and the other inhabitants of her tent were Imperial citizens, not criminals. She had survived first days, then weeks, finally months of imprisonment beneath the endless black night of the city's Langston Field.

At first it had been an adventure, frightening, unpleasant, but no worse. Then the rations had been reduced, and reduced again, and the prisoners began to starve. Near the end the last signs of order had disappeared. Sanitary regulations were not enforced. Emaciated corpses lay stacked by the gates for days before the death squads came for them.

It had become an unending nightmare. Her name was posted at the gate: the Committee of Public Safety wanted her. The other camp inmates swore that Sally Fowler was dead, and since the guards seldom entered the compound she was saved from whatever fate had overtaken other members of governing families.

As conditions became worse, Sally found a new inner strength. She tried to set an example for others in her tent. They looked to her as their leader, with Adam as her prime minister. When she cried, everyone was afraid. And so, at age twenty-two standard years, her dark hair a tangled mess, her clothes filthy and torn and her hands coarse and dirty, Sally could not even throw herself into a corner and weep. All she could do was endure the nightmare.

Into the nightmare had come rumors of Imperial battleships in the sky above the black dome—and rumors that the prisoners would be slaughtered before the ships could break through. She had smiled and pretended not to believe it could happen. Pretended? A nightmare was not real.

Then the Marines had crashed through, led by a big

blood-covered man with the manners of the Court and one arm in a sling. The nightmare had ended then, and Sally waited to wake up. They'd cleaned her, fed her, clothed her—why didn't she wake up? Her soul felt wrapped in cotton.

Acceleration was heavy on her chest. The shadows in the cabin were sharp as razors. The New Chicago recruits crowded at the windows, chattering. They must be in space. But Adam and Annie watched her with worried eyes. They'd been fat when first they saw New Chicago. Now the skin of their faces hung in folds. She knew they'd given her too much of their own food. Yet they seemed to have survived better than she.

I wish I could cry, she thought. I ought to cry. For Dorothy. I kept waiting for them to tell me Dorothy had been found. Nothing. She disappeared from the dream.

A record voice said something she didn't try to catch.

Then the weight lifted from her and she was floating.

Floating.

Were they actually going to let her go?

She turned abruptly to the window. New Chicago glowed like any Earthlike world, its distinctive patterns unreadable. Bright seas and lands, all the shades of blue smeared with the white frosting of cloud. Dwindling. As it shrank, she stared out, hiding her face. Nobody should see that feral snarl. In that moment she could have ordered New Chicago burned down to bedrock.

After inspection, Rod conducted Divine Worship on the hangar deck. They had only just finished the last hymn when the midshipman of the watch announced that the passengers were coming aboard. Blaine watched the crew scurry back to work. There would be no free Sundays while his ship wasn't in fighting trim, no matter what service traditions might say about Sundays in orbit. Blaine listened as the men went past, alert for signs of resentment. Instead he heard idle chatter, and no more than the expected grumbling.

"All right, I know what a mote is," Stoker Jackson was saying to his partner. "I can understand getting a mote in me eye. But how in God's Name can I get a *beam* there? You tell me that, now, how can a beam get in a man's eye and him not know it? Ain't reason."

"You're absolutely right. What's a beam?"

"What's a beam? Oh ho, you're from Tabletop, aren't you? Well, a beam is sawn wood—wood. It comes from a tree. A tree, that's a *great, big . . .*"

The voices faded out. Blaine made his way quickly back to the bridge. If Sally Fowler had been the only passenger he would have been happy to meet her at the hangar deck, but he wanted this Bury to understand their relationship immediately. It wouldn't do for him to think the captain of one of His Majesty's warships would go out of his way to greet a Trader.

From the bridge Rod watched the screens as the wedge-shaped craft matched orbit and was winched aboard, drifting into *MacArthur* between the great rectangular wings of the hangar doors. His hand hovered near the intercom switches. Such operations were tricky.

Midshipman Whitbread met the passengers. Bury was first, followed by a small dark man the Trader didn't bother to introduce. Both wore clothing reasonable for space, balloon trousers with tight ankle bands, tunics belted into place, all pockets zipped or velcroed closed. Bury seemed angry. He cursed his servant, and Whitbread thoughtfully recorded the man's comments, intending to run them through the ship's brain later. The midshipman sent the Trader forward with a petty officer, but waited for Miss Fowler himself. He'd seen pictures of her.

They put Bury in the Chaplain's quarters, Sally in the First Lieutenant's cabin. The ostensible reason she got the largest quarters was that Annie, her servant, would have to share her cabin. The menservants could be bunked down with the crew, but a woman, even one as old as Annie, couldn't mingle with the men. Spacers off-planet long enough develop new standards of beauty. They'd never bother a senator's niece, but a housekeeper would be something else. It all made sense, and if the First Lieutenant's cabin was next to Captain Blaine's quarters, while the Chaplain's stateroom was a level down and three bulkheads aft, nobody was going to complain.

"Passengers aboard, sir," Midshipman Whitbread reported.

"Good. Everyone comfortable?"

"Well, Miss Fowler is, sir. Petty Officer Allot showed the Trader to his cabin . . ."

"Reasonable." Blaine settled into his command seat. Lady Sandra—no, she preferred Sally, he remembered—hadn't looked too good in the brief moments he'd seen her in the prison camp. The way Whitbread talked, she'd recovered a bit. Rod had wanted to hide when he first recognized her striding out of a tent in the prison camp. He'd been covered with blood and dirt—and then she'd come closer. She'd walked like a lady of the Court, but she was gaunt, half-starved, and great dark circles showed under her eyes. And those eyes. Blank. Well, she'd had two weeks to come back to life, and she was free of New Chicago forever.

"I presume you'll demonstrate acceleration stations for Miss Fowler?" Rod asked.

"Yes, sir," Whitbread replied. And null grav practice too, he thought.

Blaine regarded his midshipman with amusement. He had no trouble reading his thoughts. Well, let him hope, but rank hath its privileges. Besides, he knew the girl, he'd met her when she was ten years old.

"Signal from Government House," the watch reported.

Cziller's cheerful, careless voice reached him. "Hello, Blaine! Ready to cast off?" The Fleet Captain was slouched bonelessly in a desk chair, puffing on an enormous and disreputable pipe.

"Yes, sir." Rod started to say something else, but choked it off.

"Passengers settled in all right?" Rod could have sworn his former captain was laughing at him.

"Yes, sir."

"And your crew? No complaints?"

"You know damned well— We'll manage, sir." Blaine choked back his anger. It was difficult to be angry at

Cziller, after all he'd given him his ship, but blast the man! "We're not overcrowded, but she'll space."

"Listen, Blaine, I didn't strip you for fun. We just don't have the men to govern here, and you'll get crew before any get to us. I've sent you twenty recruits, young locals who think they'll like it in space. Hell, maybe they will. I did."

Green men who knew nothing and would have to be shown every job, but the petty officers could take care of that. Twenty men would help. Rod felt a little better.

Cziller fussed with papers. "And I'll give you back a couple squads of your Marines, though I doubt if you'll find enemies to fight in New Scotland."

"Aye aye, sir. Thank you for leaving me Whitbread and Staley." Except for those two, Cziller and Plekhanov had stripped off every midshipman aboard, and many of the better petty officers as well. But they had left the very best men. There were enough for continuity. The ship lived, although some berths looked as if she'd lost a battle.

"You're welcome. She's a good ship, Blaine. Odds are the Admiralty won't let you keep her, but you may get lucky. *I've* got to govern a planet with my bare hands. There's not even money! Only Republic scrip! The rebels took all the Imperial crowns and gave out printed paper. How the blazes are we going to get real money in circulation?"

"Yes, sir." As a full captain, Rod was in theory equal in rank to Cziller. A brevet appointment to admiral was for courtesy only, so that captains senior to Cziller could take orders from him as Fleet Captain without embarrassment. But a naval promotion board had yet to pass on Blaine's admission to post rank, and he was young enough to worry about the coming ordeal. Perhaps in six weeks' time he would be a commander again.

"One point," said Cziller. "I just said there's no money on the planet, but it's not quite true. We have some *very* rich men here. One of them is Jonas Stone, the man who let your Marines into the city. He says he was able to hide his money from the rebels. Well, why not? He was one of them. But we've found an ordinary miner dead drunk with a fortune in Imperial crowns. He won't say where he got the money, but we think it was from Bury."

"Yes, sir."

"So watch His Excellency. OK, your dispatches and new crewmen will be aboard within the hour." Cziller glanced at his computer. "Make that forty-three minutes. You can boost out as soon as they're aboard." Cziller pocketed the computer and began tamping his pipe. "Give my regards to MacPherson at the Yards, and keep one thing in mind: if the work on the ship drags, and it will, don't send memos to the Admiral. It only gets MacPherson mad. Which figures. Instead, bring Jamie aboard and drink scotch with him. You can't put away as much as he can, but trying to do it'll get you more work than a memo."

"Yes, sir," Rod said hesitantly. He suddenly realized just how unready he was to command *MacArthur*. He knew the technical stuff, probably better than Cziller, but the dozens of little tricks that you could learn only through experience . . .

Cziller must have been reading his mind. It was an ability every officer under him had suspected. "Relax, Captain. They won't replace you before you get to the Capital, and you'll have had a lot of time aboard *Old Mac* by then. And don't spend your time boning the board exams, either. It won't do you a bit of good." Cziller puffed at the huge pipe and let a thick stream of smoke pour from his mouth. "You've work to do, I won't keep you. But when you get to New Scotland, make a point of looking at the Coal Sack. There's few sights in the galaxy to equal it. The Face of God, some call it." Cziller's image faded, his lopsided smile seeming to remain on the screen like the Cheshire cat's.

3 · *Dinner Party*

MacArthur accelerated away from New Chicago at one standard gravity. All over the ship crewmen worked to change over from the down-is-outboard orientation of orbit when spin furnished the gravity to the up-is-forward of powered flight. Unlike merchant ships, which often coast long distances from inner planets to the Alderson Jump points, warships usually accelerate continuously.

Two days out from New Chicago, Blaine held a dinner party.

The crew brought out linens and candelabra, heavy silver plate and etched crystal, products of skilled craftsmen on half a dozen worlds; a treasure trove belonging, not to Blaine, but to *MacArthur* herself. The furniture was all in place, taken from its spin position around the outer bulkheads and remounted on the after bulkheads—except for the big spin table, which was recessed into what was now the cylindrical wardroom wall.

That curved dining table had bothered Sally Fowler. She had seen it two days ago, when *MacArthur* was still under spin and the outer bulkhead was a deck, likewise curved. Now Blaine noted her moment of relief as she entered via the stairwell.

He remarked its absence in Bury, who was affable, very much at ease, and clearly enjoying himself. He had spent time in space, Blaine decided. Possibly more time than Rod.

It was Blaine's first opportunity to meet the passengers formally. As he sat in his place at the head of the table, watching the stewards in spotless dress white bring in the first course, Blaine suppressed a smile. *MacArthur* had everything except food.

"I'm much afraid the dinner's not up to the furnishings," he told Sally. "But we'll see what we find." Kelley and the stewards had conferred with the chief petty officer cook all afternoon, but Rod didn't expect much.

There was plenty to eat, of course. Ship's fodder: bio-plast, yeast steaks, New Washington corn plant; but Blaine had had no chance to lay in cabin stores for himself on New Chicago, and his own supplies had been destroyed in the battle with the rebel planetary defenses. Captain Cziller had of course removed his own personal goods. He'd also managed to take the leading cook and the number-three turret gunner who'd served as captain's cook.

The first dish was brought in, an enormous platter with a heavy cover that looked like beaten gold. Golden dragons chased each other around the perimeter, while the good fortune hexagrams of the *I Ching* floated benignly above them. Fashioned on Xanadu, the dish and cover were worth the price of one of *MacArthur*'s gigs. Gunner Kelley stood behind Blaine, imperious in dress whites and scarlet sash, the perfect major-domo. It was difficult to recognize him as the man who could make new recruits faint from his chewing out, the sergeant who had led *MacArthur*'s Marines in battle against the Union Guard. Kelley lifted the cover with a practiced flourish.

"Magnificent!" Sally exclaimed. If she was only being polite, she carried it off well, and Kelley beamed. A pastry replica of *MacArthur* and the black-domed fortress she had fought, every detail sculpted more carefully than an art treasure in the Imperial Palace, lay revealed on the platter. The other dishes were the same, so that if they hid yeast cake and other drab fare, the effect was of a banquet. Rod managed to forget his concern and enjoy the dinner.

"And what will you be doing now, my lady?" Sinclair asked. "Hae you been to New Scotland before?"

"No, I was supposed to be traveling professionally, Commander Sinclair. It wouldn't be flattering to your homeland for me to have visited there, would it?" She smiled, but there were light-years of blank space behind her eyes.

"And why would nae we be flattered from a visit by you? There's nae place in the Empire that would no think itself honored."

"Thank you—but I'm an anthropologist specializing in

primitive cultures. New Scotland is hardly that," she assured him. The accent sparked professional interest. *Do they really talk that way in New Scotland? The man sounds like something from a pre-Empire novel.* But she thought that very carefully, not looking at Sinclair as she did. She could sense the engineer's desperate pride.

"Well said," Bury applauded. "I seem to have met a number of anthropologists lately. Is it a new specialty?"

"Yes. Pity there weren't more of us earlier. We've destroyed all that was good in so many places we've taken into the Empire. We hope never to make those mistakes again."

"I suppose it must be something of a shock," said Blaine, "to be brought into the Empire, like it or not, without warning—even if there weren't any other problems. Perhaps you should have stayed on New Chicago. Captain Cziller said he was having trouble governing the place."

"I couldn't." She looked moodily down at her plate, then glanced up with a forced smile. "Our first rule is that we must be sympathetic toward the people we study. And I hate that place," she added with venomous sincerity. The emotion felt good. Even hatred was better than—emptiness.

"Aye," Sinclair agreed. "Anyone would, being kept in prison camp for months."

"Worse than that, Commander. Dorothy disappeared. She was the girl I came with. She just—vanished." There was a long silence, and Sally was embarrassed. "Please, don't let me spoil our party."

Blaine was searching for something to say when Whitbread gave him his opportunity. At first Blaine saw only that the junior midshipman was doing something under the edge of the table—but what? Tugging at the tablecloth, testing its tensile strength. And earlier he'd been looking at the crystal. "Yes, Mr. Whitbread," Rod said. "It's very strong."

Whitbread looked up, flushing, but Blaine didn't intend to embarrass the boy. "Tablecloth, silverware, plates, platters, crystal, all have to be fairly durable," he told the company at large. "Mere glassware wouldn't last the first battle. Our crystal is something else. It was cut from the wind screen of a wrecked First Empire reentry vehicle. Or so I was told. It's certain we can't make such materials any longer. The linen isn't really linen, either; it's an artificial fiber, also First Empire. The covers on the platters are crystal-iron electroplated onto beaten gold."

"It was the crystal I noticed first," Whitbread said diffidently.

"So did I, some years ago." Blaine smiled at the middies. They were officers, but they were also teen-age boys, and Rod could remember his days in the gun room. More courses were brought, to mix with shop talk scaled down for laymen, as Kelley orchestrated the dinner. Finally the table was clear except for coffee and wines.

"Mr. Vice," Blaine said formally.

Whitbread, junior to Staley by three weeks, raised his glass. "Captain, my lady. His Imperial Majesty." The officers lifted their glasses to their sovereign, as Navy men had done for two thousand years.

"You'll let me show you around my homeland," Sinclair asked anxiously.

"Certainly. Thank you, but I don't know how long we'll be there." Sally looked expectantly to Blaine.

"Nor I. We're to put in for a refit, and how long that takes is up to the Yards."

"Well, if it's not too long, I'll stay with you. Tell me, Commander, is there much traffic from New Scotland to the Capital?"

"More than from most worlds this side of the Coal Sack, though that's nae saying a lot. Few ships with decent facilities for carrying passengers. Perhaps Mr. Bury can say more; his liners put into New Scotland."

"But, as you say, not to carry passengers. Our business is to disrupt interstellar trade, you know." Bury saw quizzical looks. He continued, "Imperial Autonetics is the business of transporting robotic factories. Whenever we can make something on a planet cheaper than others can ship it in, we set up plants. Our main competition's the merchant carriers."

Bury poured himself another glass of wine, carefully selecting one that Blaine had said was in short supply. (It *must* be a good one; otherwise the scarcity wouldn't have bothered the Captain.) "That's why I was on New Chicago when the rebellion broke out."

Nods of acceptance from Sinclair and Sally Fowler; Blaine with his posture too still and face too blank; Whitbread nudging Staley—*Wait'll I tell you*—gave Bury most of what he wanted to know. Suspicions, but nothing confirmed, nothing official. "You have a fascinating vocation," he told Sally before the silence could stretch. "Tell us more, won't you? Have you seen many primitive worlds?"

"None at all," she said ruefully. "I know about them only from books. We would have gone on to visit Harlequin, but the rebellion—" She stopped.

"I was on Makassar once," said Blaine.

She brightened instantly. "There was a whole chapter on that one. Very primitive, wasn't it?"

"It still is. There wasn't a big colony there to begin with. The whole industrial complex was smashed down to bedrock in the Secession Wars, and nobody visited the place for four hundred years. They had an Iron Age culture by the time we got there. Swords. Mail armor. Wooden seagoing sailing ships."

"But what were the people like?" Sally asked eagerly. "How did they live?"

Rod shrugged, embarrassed. "I was only there a few days. Hardly time enough to get the feel of a world. Years ago, when I was Staley's age. I remember mostly looking for a good tavern." After all, he wanted to add, I'm not an anthropologist.

The conversation drifted on. Rod felt tired, and looked for a polite opportunity to bring the dinner to a close. The others seemed rooted to their seats.

"Ye study cultural evolution," Sinclair was saying earnestly, "and perhaps that's wise. But could we nae have physical evolution as well? The First Empire was verra large and sparsely spread, with room enough for almost anything. May we no find somewhere, off in some neglected corner of the old Empire, a planet full o' supermen?"

Both midshipmen looked suddenly alert. Bury asked, "What would physical evolution of humans bring, my lady?"

"They used to teach us that evolution of intelligent beings wasn't possible," she said. "Societies protect their weaker members. Civilizations tend to make wheel chairs and spectacles and hearing aids as soon as they have the tools for them. When a society makes war, the men generally have to pass a fitness test before they're *allowed* to risk their lives. I suppose it helps win the war." She smiled. "But it leaves precious little room for the survival of the fittest."

"But suppose," Whitbread suggested, "suppose a culture were knocked even further back than Makassar? All the way to complete savagery: clubs and fire. There'd be evolution then, wouldn't there?"

Three glasses of wine had overcome Sally's black mood, and she was eager to talk of professional matters. Her uncle often told her she talked too much for a lady, and she tried to watch herself, but wine always did it to her—wine and a ready audience. It felt good, after weeks of nothingness.

"Certainly," she said. "Until a society evolved. You'd have natural selection until enough humans got together to protect each other from the environment. But it isn't long enough. Mr. Whitbread, there is a world where they practice ritual infanticide. The elders examine children and kill the ones who don't conform to their standards of perfection. It's not evolution, exactly, but you might get some results that way—except that it hasn't been long enough."

"People breed horses. And dogs," Rod observed.

"Yes. But they haven't got a new species. Ever. And societies can't keep constant rules long enough to make any real changes in the human race. Come again in a million years— Of course there were the deliberate attempts to breed supermen. Like Sauron System."

Sinclair grunted. "Those beasties," he spat. " 'Twas they

started the Secession Wars and nearly killed the lot o' us."
He stopped suddenly as Midshipman Whitbread cleared
his throat.

Sally jumped into the lull. "That's another system I
can't be sympathetic with. Although they're Empire loyal-
ists now . . ." She looked around. Everyone had a strange
look, and Sinclair was trying to hide his face behind a
tilted wineglass. Midshipman Horst Staley's angular face
might have been carved from stone. "What's the matter?"
she asked.

There was a long silence. Finally Whitbread spoke.
"Mr. Staley is from Sauron System, my lady."

"I—I'm sorry," Sally blurted. "I guess I really put my
foot in it, didn't I? Really, Mr. Staley, I'm . . ."

"If my young gentlemen can't take that much pressure, I
don't need them in my ship," Rod said. "And you weren't
the only one to put your foot in it." He looked significantly at Sinclair. "We don't judge men by what their home
worlds did hundreds of years ago." *Damn*. That sounds
stilted. "You were saying about evolution?"

"It—it ought to be pretty well closed off for an intelligent species," she said. "Species evolve to meet the environment. An intelligent species changes the environment
to suit itself. As soon as a species becomes intelligent, it
should stop evolving."

"A pity we don't have any others for comparison,"
Bury said easily. "Only a few fancied ones." He told a
long story about an improbably intelligent octopoid meeting a centaur, and everyone laughed. "Well, Captain, it
was a fine dinner," Bury ended.

"Yes." Rod stood and offered Sally his arm, and the
others scrambled to their feet. She was quiet again as he
escorted her through the corridor to her cabin, and only
polite as they parted. Rod went back to the bridge. More
repairs had to be recorded into the ship's brain.

4 • *Priority OC*

Hyperspace travel can be strange and frustrating.

It takes an immeasurably short time to travel between stars: but as the line of travel, or tramline, exists only along one critical path between each pair of stars (never quite a straight line, but close enough to visualize it so) and the end points of the paths are far from the distortions in space caused by stars and large planetary masses, it follows that a ship spends most of its time crawling from one end point to another.

Worse than that, not every pair of stars is joined by tramlines. Pathways are generated along lines of equipotential thermonuclear flux, and the presence of others stars in the geometric pattern can prevent the pathway from existing at all. Of those links that do exist, not all have been mapped. They are difficult to find.

MacArthur's passengers found that travel aboard an Imperial warship was akin to imprisonment. The crew had duties to perform and repairs to make even when off watch. The passengers had each other's company, and what social life Navy routine would permit. There was no place for the entertainment facilities that luxury liners would carry.

It was boring. By the time *MacArthur* was ready for her last Jump, the passengers saw their arrival in New Caledonia as a release from jail.

NEW CALEDONIA: Star system behind the Coal Sack with F8 primary star catalogued as Murcheson A. The distant binary, Murcheson B, is not part of the New Caledonia system. Murcheson A has six planets in five orbits, with four inner planets, a relatively wide gap containing the debris of an unformed planet, and two outer planets in a Trojan relationship. The four inner planets are named Conchobar, New Ireland, New Scotland, and Fomor, in their order from the sun which is known locally

32

as Cal, or Old Cal, or the Sun. The middle two planets are inhabited, both terraformed by First Empire scientists after Jasper Murcheson, who was related to Alexander IV, persuaded the Council that the New Caledonian system would be the proper place to establish an Imperial university. It is now known that Murcheson was primarily interested in having an inhabited planet near the red supergiant known as Murcheson's Eye, and as he was not satisfied with the climate of New Ireland demanded the terraforming of New Scotland as well.

Fomor is a relatively small planet with almost no atmosphere and few interesting features. It does, however, possess several fungi which are biologically related to other fungi found in the Trans-Coalsack Sector, and their manner of transmission to Fomor has stimulated an endless controversy in the *Journal of the Imperial Society of Xenobiologists*, since no other life forms native to New Caledonia exist.

The two outer planets occupy the same orbit and are named Dagda and Mider in keeping with the system's Celtic mythological nomenclature. Dagda is a gas giant, and the Empire maintains fuel stations on the planet's two moons, Angus and Brigit. Merchant ships are cautioned that Brigit is a Navy base and may not be approached without permission.

Mider is a cold metal ball, extensively mined, and troublesome to cosmologists because its manner of formation does not appear to conform to either of the two major contending theories of planetary origin.

New Scotland and New Ireland, the only inhabited planets of the system, had extensive atmospheres of water vapor and methane when discovered, but no free oxygen. Biological packages in massive quantities transformed them into inhabitable worlds at considerable cost; toward the end of the project Murcheson lost his influence in the Council but by then the investment was so high that the project was carried on to completion. In less than a hundred years of intensive effort the domed colonies became open colonies, one of the most triumphant accomplishments of the First Empire.

Both worlds were partially depopulated during the Secession Wars, with New Ireland joining the rebel forces while New Scotland remained staunchly loyalist. After interstellar travel was lost in the Trans-Coalsack Sector, New Scotland continued the struggle until its rediscovery by the Second Empire. As a consequence, New Scotland is the Trans-Coalsack Sector Capital.

MacArthur shuddered and dropped into existence beyond the orbit of Dagda. For long moments her crew sat at their hyperspace transition stations, disoriented, fighting to overcome the confusion that always follows instantaneous travel.

Why? One branch of physics at the Imperial University on Sigismund contends that hyperspace travel requires, not zero time, but transfinite time, and that this produces the characteristic confusion of both men and computer equipment. Other theories suggest that the Jump produces stretching or shrinking of local space, affecting nerves and computer elements alike; or that not all parts of the ship appear at the same time; or that inertia and mass vary on a subatomic level after transition. No one knows, but the effect is real.

"Helmsman," Blaine said thickly. His eyes slowly focused on the bridge displays.

"Aye aye, sir." The voice was numbed and uncomprehending, but the crewman automatically responded.

"Set a course for Dagda. Get her moving."

"Aye aye." In the early days of hyperspace travel, ship's computers had tried to accelerate immediately after popout. It didn't take long to find out that computers were even more confused than men. Now all automatic equipment was turned off for transition. Lights flashed on Blaine's displays as crewmen slowly reactivated *MacArthur* and checked out their systems.

"We'll put her down on Brigit, Mr. Renner," Blaine continued. "Make your velocity match. Mr. Staley, you will assist the Sailing Master."

"Ave aye, sir." The bridge came back to life. Crewmen stirred and returned to duties. Stewards brought coffee after acceleration and gravity returned. Men left hyperspace stations to return to patrol duties, while *MacArthur*'s artificial eyes scanned space for enemies. The trouble board flashed green as each station reported successful transition.

Blaine nodded in satisfaction as he sipped his coffee. It was always like this, and after hundreds of transitions he still felt it. There was something basically *wrong* with instantaneous travel, something that outraged the senses, something the mind wouldn't accept at a level below thought. The habits of the Service carried men through; these too were ingrained at a level more basic than intellectual functions.

"Mr. Whitbread, my compliments to the Chief Yeoman of Signals and please report us in to Fleet Headquarters on New Scotland. Get our course and speed from Staley, and you can signal the fuel station on Brigit that we're coming in. Inform Fleet of our destination."

"Aye aye, sir. Signal in ten minutes, sir?"

"Yes."

Whitbread unbuckled from his command seat behind the Captain and walked drunkenly to the helm station. "I'll need full engine power for a signal in ten minutes, Horst." He made his way from the bridge, recovering rapidly. Young men usually did, which was one reason for having young officers in command of the ships.

"NOW HEAR THIS," Staley announced. The call sounded through the ship. "NOW HEAR THIS. END OF ACCELERATION IN TEN MINUTES. BRIEF PERIOD OF FREE FALL IN TEN MINUTES."

"But why?" Blaine heard. He looked up to see Sally Fowler at the bridge entranceway. His invitation to the passengers to come to the bridge when there was no emergency had worked out fine: Bury hardly ever made use of the privilege. "Why free fall so soon?" she asked.

"Need the power to make a signal," Blaine answered. "At this distance it'll use up a significant part of our engine power to produce the maser beam. We could overload the engines if we had to, but it's standard to coast for messages if there's no real hurry."

"Oh." She sat in Whitbread's abandoned chair. Rod swiveled his command seat to face her, wishing again that someone would design a free fall outfit for girls that didn't cover so much of their legs, or that brief shorts would come back into fashion. Right now skirts were down to calves on Sparta, and the provinces copied the Capital. For shipboard wear the designers produced pantaloon things, comfortable enough, but baggy . . .

"When do we get to New Scotland?" she asked.

"Depends on how long we stay off Dagda. Sinclair wants to do some outside work while we're dirtside." He took out his pocket computer and wrote quickly with the attached stylus. "Let's see, we're about one and a half billion kilometers from New Scotland, that's uh, make it a hundred hours to turnover. About two hundred hours' travel time, plus what we spend on Dagda. And the time it takes to get to Dagda, of course. That's not so far, about twenty hours from here."

"So we'll still be a couple of weeks at least," she said. "I thought once we got here we'd—" She broke off, laughing. "It's silly. Why can't you invent something that lets you Jump around in interplanetary space? There's something faintly ridiculous about it, we went five light years in no time at all, now it takes weeks to get to New Scotland."

"Tired of us so soon? It's worse than that, really. It takes an insignificant part of our hydrogen to make a Jump— Well, it isn't trivial, but it's not a lot compared to what it'll take getting to New Scotland. I don't have enough fuel aboard to go direct, in fact not in less than a year, but there's more than enough to make a Jump. All *that* takes is enough energy to get into hyperspace."

Sally snared a cup of coffee from the steward. She was learning to drink Navy coffee, which wasn't like anything else in the Galaxy. "So we just have to put up with it," she said.

"Afraid so. I've been on trips where it was faster to drive over to another Alderson point, make a Jump, move around in the new system, Jump somewhere else, keep doing that until you come back to the original system at a different place—do all that and it would still be faster than merely to sail across the original system in normal space. But not this time, the geometry isn't right."

"Pity," she laughed. "We'd see more of the universe for the same price." She didn't say she was bored; but Rod thought she was, and there wasn't much he could do about it. He had little time to spend with her, and there weren't many sights to see.

"NOW HEAR THIS. STAND BY FOR FREE FALL." She barely had time to strap herself in before the drive cut out.

Chief Yeoman of Signals Lud Shattuck squinted into his aiming sight, his knobby fingers making incredibly fine adjustments for such clumsy appendages. Outside *MacArthur*'s hull, a telescope hunted under Shattuck's guidance until it found a tiny dot of light. It hunted again until the dot was perfectly centered. Shattuck grunted in satisfaction and touched a switch. A maser antenna slaved itself to the telescope while the ship's computer decided where the dot of light would be when the message arrived. A coded message wound off its tape reel, while aft *MacArthur*'s engines fused hydrogen to helium. Energy rode out through the antenna, energy modulated by the thin tape in Shattuck's cubicle, reaching toward New Scotland.

Rod was at dinner alone in his cabin when the reply arrived. A duty yeoman looked at the heading and shouted for Chief Shattuck. Four minutes later Midshipman Whitbread knocked at his captain's door.

"Yes," Rod answered irritably.

"Message from Fleet Admiral Cranston, sir."

Rod looked up in irritation. He hadn't wanted to eat alone, but the wardroom had invited Sally Fowler to dinner—it was their turn, after all—and if Blaine had invited himself to dine with his officers, Mr. Bury would have come too. Now even this miserable dinner was interrupted. "Can't it wait?"

"It's priority OC, sir."

"A hot flash for us? OC?" Blaine stood abruptly, the protein aspic forgotten. "Read it to me, Mr. Whitbread."

"Yes, sir. MACARTHUR FROM IMPFLEETNEW SCOT. OC OC 8175—"

"You may omit the authentication codes, Midshipman. I assume you checked them out."

"Yes, sir. Uh, anyway, sir, date, code . . . MESSAGE BEGINS YOU WILL PROCEED WITH ALL POSSIBLE SPEED REPEAT ALL POSSIBLE SPEED TO BRIGIT FOR REFUELING WITH PRIORITY DOUBLE A ONE STOP YOU WILL REFUEL IN MINIMUM POSSIBLE TIME STOP PARAGRAPH

"MACARTHUR WILL THEN PROCEED TO—uh, sir, it gives some coordinate points in the New Cal system—OR ANY OTHER VECTOR YOUR CHOICE TO INTERCEPT AND INVESTIGATE MYSTERIOUS OBJECT ENTERING NEW CALEDONIA SYSTEM FROM NORMAL SPACE REPEAT NORMAL SPACE STOP OBJECT PROCEEDS ALONG GALACTIC VECTOR—uh, it gives a course from the general direction of the Coal Sack, sir—AT A SPEED OF APPROXIMATELY SEVEN PERCENT VELOCITY OF LIGHT STOP OBJECT IS DECELERATING RAPIDLY STOP IMPERIAL UNIVERSITY ASTRONOMERS SAY SPECTRUM OF INTRUDER IS SPECTRUM OF NEW CAL SUN BLUE SHIFTED STOP OBVIOUS CONCLUSION THAT INTRUDER IS POWERED BY LIGHT SAIL STOP PARAGRAPH

"IMPERIAL UNIVERSITY ASTRONOMERS CERTAIN OBJECT IS ARTIFACT CONSTRUCTED BY INTELLIGENT BEINGS STOP FYI NO KNOWN HUMAN COLONIES AT APPARENT ORIGIN OF INTRUDER STOP PARAGRAPH

"CRUISER LERMONTOV DISPATCHED TO ASSIST BUT CANNOT ARRIVE TO MATCH VELOCITY WITH INTRUDER UNTIL SEVENTYONE HOURS AFTER MINIMUM TIME MACARTHUR VELOCITY MATCH WITH OBJECT STOP PROCEED WITH CAUTION STOP YOU ARE TO ASSUME INTRUDER IS HOSTILE UNTIL OTHERWISE ASSURED STOP YOU ARE ORDERED TO USE CAUTION BUT DO NOT INITIATE HOSTILITIES REPEAT DO NOT INITIATE HOSTILITIES STOP

"BREAK BREAK GO GET IT CZILLER STOP WISH I WAS OUT THERE STOP GODSPEED STOP CRANSTON BREAK MESSAGE ENDS AUTHENTICATION—uh, that's it, sir." Whitbread was breathless.

"That's it. That's quite a lot of it, Mr. Whitbread." Blaine fingered the intercom switch. "Wardroom."

"Wardroom aye aye, Captain," Midshipman Staley answered.

"Get me Cargill."

The First Lieutenant sounded resentful when he came on. Blaine was intruding on his dinner party. Rod felt an inner satisfaction for doing it. "Jack, get to the bridge. I want this bird moving. I'll have a minimum time course to land us on Brigit, and I mean minimum. You can run the tanks, but get us there fast."

"Aye aye, sir. Passengers aren't going to like it."

"Rape the— Uh, my compliments to the passengers, and this is a Fleet emergency. Too bad about your dinner party, Jack, but get your passengers into hydraulic beds and move this ship. I'll be on the bridge in a minute."

"Yes, sir." The intercom went silent for a moment, then Staley's voice hooted through the ship. "NOW HEAR THIS. NOW HEAR THIS. STAND BY FOR PROLONGED ACCELERATION ABOVE TWO GRAVITIES. DEPARTMENT HEADS SIGNAL WHEN SECURED FOR INCREASED ACCELERATION."

"OK," Blaine said. He turned to Whitbread. "Punch that damned vector designation into the computer and let's see where the hell that intruder comes from." He realized he was swearing and made an effort to calm down. Intruders—aliens? Good God, what a break! To be in command of the first ship to make contact with aliens . . . "Let's just see where they're from, shall we?"

Whitbread moved to the input console next to Blaine's desk. The screen swam violently, then flashed numbers.

"Blast your eyes, Whitbread, I'm not a mathematician! Put it on a graph!"

"Sorry, sir." Whitbread fiddled with the input controls again. The screen became a black volume filled with blobs and lines of colored light. Big blobs were stars colored for type, velocity vectors were narrow green lines, acceleration vectors were lavender, projected paths were dimly lit red curves. The long green line—

Blaine looked at the screen in disbelief, then laid his finger along the knot in his nose. "From the Mote. Well, I will be go to hell. From the Mote, in normal space." There was no known tramline to the intruder's star. It hung in isolation, a yellow fleck near the supergiant Murcheson's Eye. Visions of octopoids danced in his head.

Suppose they were hostile? he thought suddenly. If *Old Mac* had to fight an alien ship, she'd need more work. Work they'd put off because it ought to be done in orbit, or dirtside, and now they'd have to do it at two plus gee. But it was *MacArthur*'s baby—and his. Somehow they'd do it.

5 · *The Face of God*

Blaine made his way quickly to the bridge and strapped himself into the command chair. As soon as he was settled he reached for the intercom unit. A startled Midshipman Whitbread looked out of the screen from the Captain's cabin.

Blaine gambled. "Read it to me, Mister."

"Uh—sir?"

"You have the regs open to the standing orders on alien contact, don't you? Read them to me, please." Blaine remembered looking them up, long ago, for fun and curiosity. Most cadets did.

"Yes, sir." Visibly, Whitbread wondered if the Captain had been reading his mind, then decided that it was the Captain's prerogative. This incident would start legends. " 'Section 4500: First contact with nonhuman sentient beings. Note: Sentient beings are defined as creatures which employ tools and communication in purposeful behavior. Subnote: Officers are cautioned to use judgment in applying this definition. The hive rat of Makassar, as an example, employs tools and communication to maintain its nest, but is not sentient.

" 'Section One: Upon encounter with sentient nonhuman beings, officers will communicate the existence of such aliens to nearest Fleet command. All other objectives will be considered secondary to this accomplishment. Section Two: After the objective described in section one is assured, officers will attempt to establish communication with the aliens, provided however that in so doing they are not authorized to risk their command unless so ordered by higher authority. Although officers will not initiate hostilities it must be assumed that nonhuman sentient creatures may be hostile. Section Three—' "

Whitbread was cut off by the final acceleration warning. Blaine nodded acknowledgment to the middie and settled back in his couch. The regulations weren't likely to be much use anyway. They mostly dealt with initial contact without prior warning, and here Fleet command pretty well knew *MacArthur* was going out to intercept an alien vessel.

Ship's gravity edged upward, slowly enough to give the crew time to adjust, a full minute to rise to three gravities. Blaine felt two hundred sixty kilos settling into his acceleration couch. Throughout the ship men would be moving with the wary attention one gives to lifting weights, but it was not a crippling acceleration. Not for a young man. For Bury it would be rough, but the Trader would be all right if he stayed in his gee bed.

Blaine felt very much at ease in his contoured armchair. It had headrest and fingertip controls, lapboard, power swiveling so that the entire bridge was in view without effort, even a personal relief tube. Warships are designed for long periods of high gravity.

Blaine fiddled with his screen controls to produce a 3-d graph overhead. He cut in the privacy switch to hide his doodles from the rest of the crew. Around him the bridge officers attended to their duties, Cargill and Sailing Master Renner huddled together near the astrogation station, Midshipman Staley settled next to the helmsman ready to assist if needed but mostly there to learn how to handle the ship. Blaine's long fingers moved over the screen controls.

A long green velocity line, a short lavender vector pointing in the opposite direction—with a small white ball between. So. The intruder had come straight from the direction of the Mote and was decelerating directly into the New Cal system . . . and it was somewhat bigger than

Earth's Moon. A ship-sized object would have been a dimensionless point.

A good thing Whitbread hadn't noticed that. There'd be gossip, tales to the crew, panic among the new hands . . . Blaine felt the metallic taste of fear himself. My God, it was *big*.

"But they'd have to have something that big," Rod muttered. Thirty-five light years, through normal space! There never had been a human civilization that could manage such a thing. Still—how did the Admiralty expect him to "investigate" it? Much less "intercept" it? Land on it with Marines?

What in Hannigan's Hell was a light sail?

"Course to Brigit, sir," Sailing Master Renner announced.

Blaine snapped up from his reverie and touched his screen controls again. The ship's course appeared on his screen as a pictorial diagram below tables of figures. Rod spoke with effort. "Approved." Then he went back to the impossibly large object on his view screen. Suddenly he took out his pocket computer and scribbled madly across its face. Words and numbers flowed across the surface, and he nodded . . .

Of course light pressure could be used for propulsion. In fact *MacArthur* did exactly that, using hydrogen fusion to generate photons and emitting them in an enormous spreading cone of light. A reflecting mirror could use outside light as propulsion and get twice the efficiency. Naturally the mirror should be as large as possible, and as light, and ideally it should reflect all the light that fell on it.

Blaine grinned to himself. He had been nerving himself to attack a spacegoing planet with his half-repaired battle cruiser! Naturally the computer had pictured an object that size as a globe. In reality it was probably a sheet of silvered fabric thousands of kilometers across, attached by adjustable shrouds to the mass that would be the ship proper.

In fact, with an albedo of one— Blaine sketched rapidly. The light sail would need about eight million square kilometers of area. If circular, it would be about three thousand klicks across . . .

It was using light for thrust, so . . . Blaine called up the intruder's deceleration, matched it to the total reflected light, divided . . . so. Sail and payload together massed about 450 thousand kilograms.

That didn't sound dangerous.

In fact, it didn't sound like a working spacecraft, not one that could cross thirty-five light years in normal space. The alien pilots would go mad with so little room—unless they were tiny, or *liked* enclosed spaces, or had spent the past several hundred years living in inflated balloons with filmy, lightweight walls . . . no. There was too little known and too much room for speculation. Still, there was nothing better to do. He fingered the knot on his nose.

Blaine was about to clear the screens, then thought again and increased the magnification. He stared at the result for a long time, then swore softly.

The intruder was heading straight into the sun.

MacArthur decelerated at nearly three gravities directly into orbit around Brigit; then she descended into the protective Langston Field of the base on the moonlet, a small black dart sinking toward a tremendous black pillow, the two joined by a thread of intense white. Without the Field to absorb the energy of thrust, the main drive would have burned enormous craters into the snowball moon.

The fueling station crew rushed to their tasks. Liquid hydrogen, electrolized from the mushy ice of Brigit and distilled after liquefaction, poured into *MacArthur*'s tankage complexes. At the same time Sinclair drove his men outside. Crewmen swarmed across the ship to take advantage of low gravity with the ship dirtside. Boatswains screamed at supply masters as Brigit was stripped of spare parts.

"Commander Frenzi requests permission to come aboard, sir," the watch officer called.

Rod grimaced. "Send him up." He turned back to Sally Fowler, seated demurely in the watch midshipman's seat.

"But don't you understand, we'll be accelerating at high gees all the way to intercept. You *know* what that feels like now. Besides, it's a dangerous mission!"

"Pooh. Your orders were to take me to New Scotland," she huffed. "They said nothing about stranding me on a snowball."

"Those were general orders. If Cziller'd known we'd have to fight, he'd never have let you aboard. As captain of this ship, it's my decision, and I say I'm not about to take Senator Fowler's niece out to a possible battle."

"Oh." She thought for a moment. The direct approach hadn't worked. "Rod. Listen. Please. You see this as a tremendous adventure, don't you? How do you think I feel? Whether those are aliens or just lost colonists trying to find the Empire again, this is *my* field. It's what I was trained for, and I'm the only anthropologist aboard. You *need* me."

"We can do without. It's too dangerous."

"You're letting Mr. Bury stay aboard."

"Not letting. The Admiralty specifically ordered me to keep him in my ship. I don't have discretion about him, but I do about you and your servants—"

"If it's Adam and Annie you're worried about, we'll leave them here. They couldn't take the acceleration anyway. But I can take anything you can, Captain My Lord Roderick Blaine. I've seen you after a hyperspace Jump, dazed, staring around, not knowing what to do, and I was able to leave my cabin and walk up here to the bridge! So don't tell me how helpless I am! Now, are you going to let me stay here, or . . ."

"Or what?"

"Or nothing, of course. I know I can't threaten you. Please, Rod?" She tried everything, including batting her eyes, and that was too much, because Rod burst out laughing.

"Commander Frenzi, sir," the Marine sentry outside the bridge companionway announced.

"Come in, Romeo, come in," Rod said more heartily than he felt. Frenzi was thirty-five, a good ten years older than Blaine, and Rod had served under him for three months of the most miserable duty he could ever recall. The man was a good administrator but a horrible ship's officer.

Frenzi peered around the bridge, his jaw thrust forward. "Ah. Blaine. Where's Captain Cziller?"

"On New Chicago," Rod said pleasantly. "I'm master of *MacArthur* now." He swiveled so that Frenzi could see the four rings on each sleeve.

Frenzi's face became more craggy. His lips drooped. "Congratulations." Long pause. "Sir."

"Thanks, Romeo. Still takes getting used to myself."

"Well, I'll go out and tell the troops not to hurry about the fueling, shall I?" Frenzi said. He turned to go.

"What the hell do you mean, not to hurry? I've got a double-A-one priority. Want to see the message?"

"I've seen it. They relayed a copy through my station, Blaine—uh, Captain. But the message makes it clear that Admiral Cranston thinks Cziller is still in command of *MacArthur*. I respectfully suggest, sir, that he would not have sent this ship to intercept a possible alien if he knew that her master was—was a young officer with his first command. Sir."

Before Blaine could answer, Sally spoke. "I've seen the message, Commander, and it was addressed to *MacArthur*, not Cziller. And it gives the *ship* refueling priority . . ."

Frenzi regarded her coldly. "*Lermontov* will be quite adequate for this intercept, I think. If you'll excuse me, Captain, I must get back to my station." He glared at Sally again. "I didn't know they were taking females out of uniform as midshipmen."

"I happen to be Senator Fowler's niece and aboard this ship under Admiralty orders, Commander," she told him sternly. "I am astonished at your lack of manners. My family is not accustomed to such treatment, and I am certain my friends at Court will be shocked to find that an Imperial officer could be so rude."

Frenzi blushed and looked around wildly. "My apologies, my lady. No insult intended, I assure you . . . I was merely surprised we don't very often see girls aboard warships certainly not young ladies as attractive as you I beg your pardon . . ." His voice trailed off, still without punctuation, as he withdrew from the bridge.

"Now why couldn't you react like that?" Sally wondered aloud.

Rod grinned at her, then jumped from his seat. "He'll signal Cranston that I'm in command here! We have—what, about an hour for a message to get to New Scotland, another for it to get back." Rod stabbed at the intercom controls. "ALL HANDS. THIS IS THE CAPTAIN. LIFT-OFF IN ONE HUNDRED TWENTY-FIVE MINUTES. LIFT-OFF IN ONE HUNDRED TWENTY-FIVE MINUTES. IF YOU'RE NOT ABOARD WE'LL LEAVE YOU BEHIND."

"That's the way," Sally shouted as encouragement. "Let him send his messages." While Blaine turned to hurry his crew along, she left the bridge to go hide in her cabin.

Rod made another call. "Commander Sinclair. Let me know if there's any delay out there." If Frenzi slowed him down, Blaine just might be able to get him shot. He'd certainly try . . . long ago he'd daydreamed of having Frenzi shot.

The reports came in. Cargill came onto the bridge with a sheaf of transfer orders and a satisfied look. *MacArthur*'s boatswains, copies of the priority message in hand, had gone looking for the best men on Brigit.

New crew and old hands swarmed around the ship, yanking out damaged equipment and hurriedly thrusting in spares from Brigit's supply depot, running checkout procedures and rushing to the next job. Other replacement parts were stored as they arrived. Later they could be used to replace Sinclair's melted-looking jury rigs . . . if anyone could figure out how. It was difficult enough telling what was inside one of those standardized black boxes. Rod spotted a microwave heater and routed it to the wardroom; Cargill would like that.

When the fueling was nearly finished, Rod donned his pressure suit and went outside. His inspection wasn't needed, but it helped crew morale to know that the Old Man was looking over everyone's shoulder. While he was out there, Rod looked for the intruder.

The Face of God stared at him across space.

The Coal Sack was a nebular mass of dust and gas, small as such things go—twenty-four to thirty light years thick—but dense, and close enough to New Caledonia to block off a quarter of the sky. Earth and the Imperial Capital, Sparta, were forever invisible on its other side. The spreading blackness hid most of the Empire, but it made a fine velvet backdrop for two close, brilliant stars.

Even without that backdrop, Murcheson's Eye was the brightest star in the sky—a great red giant thirty-five light years distant. The white fleck at one edge was a yellow dwarf companion star, smaller and dimmer and less interesting: the Mote. Here the Coal Sack had the shape of a hooded man, head and shoulders; and the off-centered red supergiant became a watchful, malevolent eye.

The Face of God. It was a famous sight throughout the Empire, this extraordinary view of the Coal Sack from New Cal. But standing here in the cold of space it was different. In a picture it looked like the Coal Sack. Here it was real.

And something he couldn't see was coming at him out of the Mote in God's Eye.

6 • *The Light Sail*

One gravity only—with queasy sensations as *MacArthur* lined up on her proper interception course. Elastic webbing held him in the acceleration chair during these few moments of changing but normal gravity—minutes, Rod suspected, that he'd soon look back on with wistful longing.

Kevin Renner had been mate of an interstellar trading vessel before joining *MacArthur* as her sailing master. He was a lean man with a narrow face, and he was ten years older than Blaine. As Rod steered his acceleration chair up behind him, Renner was matching curves in a view screen; and his self-satisfied grin was not the expression of a Navy man.

"Got our course, Lieutenant Renner?"

"Yes, sir," Kevin Renner said with relish. "Right into the sun at four gees!"

Blaine gave in to the desire to call his bluff. "Move her."

The warning alarms sounded and *MacArthur* accelerated. Crew and passengers felt their weight settle gradually deeper into beds and chairs and couches, and they nerved themselves for several days of weighing far too much.

"You were joking, weren't you?" Blaine asked.

The Sailing Master looked at him quizzically. "You knew we were dealing with a light-sail propulsion system, sir?"

"Naturally."

"Then look here." Renner's nimble fingers made a green curve on the view screen, a parabola rising sharply at the right. "Sunlight per square centimeter falling on a light sail decreases as the square of the distance from the star. Acceleration varies directly as the sunlight reflected from the sail."

"Of course, Mr. Renner. Make your point."

Renner made another parabola, very like the first, but in blue. "The stellar wind can also propel a light sail. Thrust varies about the same way. The important difference is that the stellar wind is atomic nuclei. They stick where they hit the sail. The momentum is transferred directly—and it's all radial to the sun."

"You can't tack against it," Blaine realized suddenly. "You can tack against the light by tilting the sail, but the stellar wind always thrusts you straight away from the sun."

"Right. So, Captain, suppose you were coming into a system at 7 percent of the speed of light, God forbid, and you wanted to stop. What would you do?"

"Drop all the weight I could," Blaine mused. "Hmm. I don't see how it'd be a problem. They must have launched the same way."

"I don't think they did. They're moving too fast. But pass that for a minute. What counts is they're moving too fast to *stop* unless they get very close to the sun, very close indeed. The intruder is in fact diving right into the sun. Probably it will tack hard after the sunlight has decelerated it enough . . . provided the vessel hasn't melted and the shrouds haven't parted or the sail ripped. But it is such a close thing that they simply have to skydive; they have no choice."

"Ah," said Blaine.

"One need hardly mention," Renner added, "that when we match course with them, we too will be moving straight toward the sun . . ."

"At 7 percent of the speed of light?"

"At 6. The intruder will have slowed somewhat by then. It will take us one hundred twenty-five hours, doing four gees most of the way, slowing somewhat near the end."

"That's going to be hard on everybody," Blaine said. And suddenly he wondered, belatedly, if Sally Fowler had in fact gotten off. "Especially the passengers. Couldn't you give me an easier course?"

"Yes, sir," Renner said instantly. "I can pull alongside in one hundred and seventy hours without ever going over two and a half gees—and save some fuel too, because the probe will have more time to slow down. The course we're on now gets us to New Ireland with dry tanks, assuming we take the intruder under tow."

"Dry tanks. But you liked this course better." Rod was learning to dislike the Sailing Master and his grin that constantly implied that the Captain had forgotten something crucial and obvious. "Tell me why," he suggested.

"It occurred to me the intruder might be hostile."

"Yes. So?"

"If we were to match courses with him and he disabled the engines . . ."

"We'd be falling into the sun at 6 percent of light speed. Right. So you match us up as far from Cal as possible, to leave time to do something about it."

"Yessir. Exactly."

"Right. You're enjoying this, aren't you, Mr. Renner?"

"I wouldn't have missed it for anything, sir. What about you?"

"Carry on, Mr. Renner." Blaine guided his acceleration chair to another screen and began checking the Sailing Master's course. Presently he pointed out that the Sailing Master could give them nearly an hour at one gee just before intercept, thereby giving everyone a chance to recuperate. Renner agreed with idiot enthusiasm and went to work on the change.

"I can use friends aboard my ship," Captain Cziller used to tell his midshipmen, "but I'd sell them all for a competent sailing master." Renner was competent. Renner was also a smartass; but that was a good bargain. Rod would settle for a competent smartass.

At four gravities nobody walked, nobody lifted anything. The black box replacements in the hold stayed there while *MacArthur* ran on Sinclair's makeshifts. Most of the crew worked from their cots, or from mobile chairs, or didn't work at all.

In crew sections they played elaborate word games, or speculated on the coming encounter, or told stories. Half the screens on the ship showed the same thing: a disc like the sun, with Murcheson's Eye behind it and the Coal Sack as background.

The telltales in Sally's cabin showed oxygen consumption. Rod said words of potent and evil magic under his breath. He almost called her then, but postponed it. He called Bury instead.

Bury was in the gee bath: a film of highly elastic mylar over liquid. Only his face and hands showed above the curved surface. His face looked old—it almost showed his true age.

"Captain, you chose not to put me off on Brigit. Instead, you are taking a civilian into possible combat. Might I ask why?"

"Of course, Mr. Bury. I supposed it would be most inconvenient for you to be stranded on a ball of ice with no assured transportation. Perhaps I was mistaken."

Bury smiled—or tried to. Every man aboard looked twice his age, with four times gravity pulling down on the skin of his face. Bury's smile was like weight lifting. "No, Captain, you were not mistaken. I saw your orders in the wardroom. So. We are on our way to meet a non-human spacecraft."

"It certainly looks that way."

"Perhaps they will have things to trade. Especially if they come from a nonterrestrial world. We can hope. Captain, would you keep me posted on what is happening?"

"I will probably not have the time," Blaine said, choosing the most civil of several answers that occurred to him.

"Yes, of course, I didn't mean personally. I only want access to information on our progress. At my age I dare not move from this rubber bathtub for the duration of our voyage. How long will we be under four gees?"

"One hundred and twenty-five hours. One twenty-four, now."

"Thank you, Captain." Bury vanished from the screen.

Rod rubbed thoughtfully at the knot on his nose. Did Bury know his status aboard *MacArthur*? It couldn't be important. He called Sally's cabin.

She looked as if she hadn't slept in a week or smiled in years. Blaine said, "Hello, Sally. Sorry you came?"

"I told you I can take anything you can take," Sally said calmly. She gripped the arms of her chair and stood up. She let go and spread her arms to show how capable she was.

"Be careful," Blaine said, trying to keep his voice steady. "No sudden moves. Keep your knees straight. You can break your back just sitting down. Now stay erect, but reach behind you. Get both the chair arms in your hands before you try to bend at the waist——"

She didn't believe it was dangerous, not until she started to sit down. Then the muscles in her arms knotted, panic flared in her eyes, and she sat much too abruptly, as if *MacArthur*'s gravity had *sucked* her down.

"Are you hurt?"

"No," she said. "Only my pride."

"Then you stay in that chair, damn your eyes! Do you see me standing up? You do not. And you won't!"

"All right." She turned her head from side to side. She was obviously dizzy from the jolt.

"Did you get your servants off?"

"Yes. I had to trick them—they wouldn't have gone without my baggage." She laughed an old woman's laugh. "I'm wearing everything I own until we get to New Caledonia."

"Tricked them, did you? The way you tricked me. I should have had Kelley *put* you off." Rod's voice was bitter. He knew he looked twice his age, a cripple in a wheel chair. "All right, you're aboard. I can't put you off now."

"But I may be able to help. I am an anthropologist." She winced at the thought of trying to get up again. "Can I get you on the intercom?"

"You'll get the middie of the watch. Tell him if you really need to talk to me. But, Sally—this is a warship. Those aliens may not be friendly. For God's sake remember that; my watch officers haven't time for scientific discussion in the middle of a battle!"

"I know that. You might give me credit for a little sense." She tried to laugh. "Even if I don't know better than to stand up at four gees."

"Yeah. Now do me another favor. Get into your gee bath."

"Do I have to take my clothes off to use it?"

Blaine couldn't blush; there wasn't enough blood flowing to his head. "It's a good idea, especially if you've got buckles. Turn off the vision pickup on the phone."

"Right."

"And be careful. I could send one of the married ratings to help—"

"No, thank you."

"Then wait. We'll have a few minutes of lower gee at intervals. Don't get out of that chair alone in high gee!"

She didn't even look tempted. One experience was enough.

"Lermontov's calling again," Whitbread announced.

"Forget it. Don't acknowledge."

"Aye aye, sir. Do not acknowledge."

Rod could guess what the cruiser wanted. *Lermontov* wanted first crack at the intruder—but *MacArthur's* sister ship wouldn't even get close to the aliens before the approach to the sun was just too close. Better to intercept out where there was some room.

At least that's what Rod told himself. He could trust Whitbread and the communications people; *Lermontov's* signals wouldn't be in the log.

Three and a half days. Two minutes of 1.5 gee every four hours to change the watch, grab forgotten articles, shift positions; then the warning horns sounded, the jolt meters swung over, and too much weight returned.

At first *MacArthur's* bow had pointed sixty degrees askew of Cal. They had to line up with the intruder's course. With that accomplished, *MacArthur* turned again. Her bow pointed at the brightest star in the heavens.

Cal began to grow. He also changed color, but minutely. No one would notice that blue shift with the naked eye. What the men did see in the screens was that the brightest star had become a disc and was growing hourly.

It didn't grow brighter because the screens kept it constant; but the tiny sun disc grew ominously larger, and it lay directly ahead. Behind them was another disc of the same color, the white of an F8 star. It, too, grew hourly larger. *MacArthur* was sandwiched between two colliding suns.

On the second day Staley brought a new midshipman up to the bridge, both moving in traveling acceleration chairs. Except for a brief interview on Brigit, Rod hadn't met him: Gavin Potter, a sixteen-year-old boy from New Scotland. Potter was tall for his age; he seemed to hunch in upon himself, as if afraid to be noticed.

Blaine thought Potter was merely being shown about the ship; a good idea, since if the intruder turned out hostile, the boy might have to move about *MacArthur* with total familiarity—possibly in darkness and variable gravity.

Staley obviously had more in mind. Blaine realized they were trying to get his attention. "Yes, Mr. Staley?"

"This is Midshipman Gavin Potter, sir," Staley said. "He's told me something I think you ought to hear."

"All right, go ahead." Any diversion from high gravity was welcome.

"There was a church in our street, sir. In a farm town on New Scotland." Potter's voice was soft and low, and he spoke carefully so that he blotted out all but a ghostly remnant of the brogue that made Sinclair's speech so distinctive.

"A church," Blaine said encouragingly. "Not an orthodox church, I take it—"

"No, sir. A Church of Him. There aren't many members. A friend and I snuck inside once, for a joke."

"Did you get caught?"

"I know I'm telling this badly, sir. The thing is— There was a big blowup of an old holo of Murcheson's Eye against the Coal Sack. The Face of God, just like on postcards. Only, only it was different in this picture. The Eye was very much brighter than now, and it was blue-green, not red. With a red dot at one edge."

"It could have been a portrait," Blaine suggested. He took out his pocket computer and scrawled "Church of Him" across its face, then punched for information. The box linked with the ship's library, and information began to roll across its face. "It says the Church of Him believes that the Coal Sack, with that one red eye showing, really is the Face of God. Couldn't they have retouched it to make the eye more impressive?" Rod continued to sound interested; time enough to say something about wasting his time when the middies were through. If they were wasting time . . .

"But—" said Potter.

"Sir—" said Staley, leaning too far forward in his chair.

"One at a time. Mr. Staley?"

"I didn't just ask Potter, sir. I checked with Commander Sinclair. He says his grandfather told him the Mote was once brighter than Murcheson's Eye, and bright green. And the way Gavin's describing that holo—well, sir, stars don't radiate all one color. So—"

"All the more reason to think the holo was retouched. But it is funny, with that intruder coming straight out of the Mote . . ."

"Light," Potter said firmly.

"Light sail!" Rod shouted in sudden realization. "Good thinking." The whole bridge crew turned to look at the Captain. "Renner! Did you say the intruder is moving faster than it ought to be?"

"Yes, sir," Renner answered from his station across the bridge. "If it was launched from a habitable world circling the Mote."

"Could it have used a battery of laser cannon?"

"Sure, why not?" Renner wheeled over. "In fact, you could launch with a small battery, then add more cannon as the vehicle got farther and farther away. You get a terrific advantage that way. If one of the cannon breaks down you've got it right there in your system to repair it."

"Like leaving your motor home," Potter cried, "and you still able to use it."

"Well, there are efficiency problems. Depending on how tight the beam can be held," Renner answered. "Pity you couldn't use it for braking, too. Have you any reason to believe—"

Rod left them telling the Sailing Master about the variations in the Mote. For himself, he didn't particularly care. His problem was, what would the intruder do now?

It was twenty hours to rendezvous when Renner came to Blaine's post and asked to use the Captain's screens. The man apparently could not talk without a view screen connected to a computer. He would be mute with only his voice.

"Captain, look," he said, and threw a plot of the local stellar region on the screen. "The intruder came from here. Whoever launched it fired a laser cannon, or a set of laser cannon—probably a whole mess of them on asteroids, with mirrors to focus them—for about forty-five years, so the intruder would have a beam to travel on. The beam and the intruder both came straight in from the Mote."

"But there'd be records," Blaine said. "Somebody would have seen that the Mote was putting out coherent light."

Renner shrugged. "How good are New Scotland's records?"

"Let's just see." It took only moments to learn that astronomical data from New Scotland were suspect, and no such records were carried in *MacArthur*'s library because of that. "Oh, well. Let's assume you're right."

"But that's the point: it's not right, Captain," Renner protested. "You see, it *is* possible to turn in interstellar space. What they should have done—"

The new path left the Mote at a slight angle to the first. "Again they coast most of the way. At this point" —where the intruder would have been well past New Cal—"we charge the ship up to ten million volts. The background magnetic field of the Galaxy gives the ship a half turn, and it's coming toward the New Caledonia system *from behind*. Meanwhile, whoever is operating the beam has turned it off for a hundred and fifty years. Now he turns it on again. The probe uses the beam for braking.

"You sure that magnetic effect would work?"

"It's high school physics! And the interstellar magnetic fields have been well mapped, Captain."

"Well, then, why didn't they use it?"

"I don't *know,*" Renner cried in frustration. "Maybe they just didn't think of it. Maybe they were afraid the lasers wouldn't last. Maybe they didn't trust whoever they left behind to run them. Captain, we just don't know enough about them."

"*I* know that, Renner. Why get in such a sweat about it? If our luck holds, we'll just damn well ask them."

A slow, reluctant smile broke across Renner's face. "But that's cheating."

"Oh, go get some sleep."

Rod woke to the sound of the speakers: "GRAVITY SHIFT IN TEN MINUTES. STAND BY FOR CHANGE TO ONE STANDARD GRAVITY IN TEN MINUTES."

Blaine smiled—*one gravity!*—and felt the smile tighten. One hour to match velocities with the intruder. He activated his watch screens, to see a blaze of light fore and aft. *MacArthur* was sandwiched between two suns. Now Cal was as large as Sol seen from Venus, but brighter;

Cal was a hotter star. The intruder was a smaller disc, but brighter still. The sail was concave.

It was effort merely to use the intercom. "Sinclair."

"Engineering, aye aye, Captain."

Rod was pleased to see that Sinclair was in a hydraulic bed. "How's the Field holding, Sandy?"

"Verra well, Captain. Temperature steady."

"Thank you." Rod was pleased. The Langston Field absorbed energy; that was its basic function. It absorbed even the kinetic energy of exploding gas or radiation particles, with an efficiency proportional to the cube of the incoming velocities. In battle, the hellish fury of hydrogen torpedoes, and the concentrated photon energies of lasers, would strike the Field and be dispersed, absorbed, contained. As the energy levels increased, the Field would begin to glow, its absolute black becoming red, orange, yellow, climbing up the spectrum toward the violet.

That was the basic problem of the Langston Field. The energy had to be radiated away; if the Field overloaded, it would release all the stored energy in a blinding white flash, radiating inward as well as outward. It took ship's power to prevent that—and that power was added to the Field's stored energies as well. When the Field grew too hot, ships died. Quickly.

Normally a warship could get hellishly near a sun without being in mortal danger, her Field never growing hotter than the temperature of the star plus the amounts added to maintain control of the Field. Now, with a sun before and another behind, the Field could radiate only to the sides—and that had to be controlled or *MacArthur* would experience lateral accelerations. The sides were getting narrower and the suns bigger and the Field hotter. A tinge of red showed on Rod's screens. It wasn't an impending disaster, but it had to be watched.

Normal gravity returned. Rod moved quickly to the bridge and nodded to the watch midshipman. "General quarters. Battle stations."

Alarms hooted through the ship.

* * *

For 124 hours the intruder had shown no awareness of *MacArthur*'s approach. It showed none now; and it drew steadily closer.

The light sail was a vast expanse of uniform white across the aft screens, until Renner found a small black dot. He played with it until he had a large black dot, sharp edged, whose radar shadow showed it four thousand kilometers closer to *MacArthur* than the sail behind it.

"That's our target, sir," Renner announced. "They probably put everything in one pod, everything that wasn't part of the sail. One weight at the end of the shrouds to hold the sail steady."

"Right. Get us alongside it, Mr. Renner. Mr. Whitbread! My compliments to the Yeoman of Signals, and I want to send messages in clear. As many bands as he can cover, low power."

"Yes, sir. Recording."

"Hello, light-sail vessel. This is Imperial Ship *MacArthur*. Give our recognition signals. Welcome to New Caledonia and the Empire of Man. We wish to come alongside. Please acknowledge. Send that in Anglic, Russian, French, Chinese, and anything else you can think of. If they're human there's no telling where they're from."

Fifteen minutes to match. Ship's gravity changed, changed again as Renner began to match velocities and positions with the intruder's cargo pod instead of the sail.

Rod took a moment to answer Sally's call. "Make it fast, Sally. If you please. We're under battle conditions."

"Yes, Rod, I know. May I come to the bridge?"

"Afraid not. All seats occupied."

"I'm not surprised. Rod, I just wanted to remind you of something. Don't expect them to be simple."

"I beg your pardon?"

"Just because they don't use Alderson Drive, you'll expect them to be primitive. Don't. And even if they were primitive, primitive doesn't mean simple. Their techniques and ways of thought may be *very* complex."

"I'll keep it in mind. Anything else? OK, hang on, Sally. Whitbread, when you've got no other duties, let Miss Fowler know what's going on." He closed the intercom from his mind and looked at the stern screen even as Staley shouted.

The intruder's light sail was rippling. Reflected light ran across it in great, ponderous, wavy lines. Rod blinked but it didn't help; it is very difficult to see the shape of a distorted mirror. "That could be our signal," Rod said. "They're using the mirror to flash—"

The glare became blinding, and all the screens on that side went dead.

The forward scanners were operative and recording. They showed a wide white disc, the star New Caledonia, very close, and approaching very fast, 6 percent of the velocity of light; and they showed it with most of the light filtered away.

For a moment they also showed several odd black silhouettes against that white background. Nobody noticed, in that terrible moment when *MacArthur* was burned blind; and in the next moment the images were gone.

Kevin Renner spoke into the stunned silence: "They didn't have to shout," he complained.

"Thank you, Mr. Renner," Rod said icily. "Have you other, perhaps more concrete suggestions?"

MacArthur was moving in erratic jolts, but the light sail followed her perfectly. "Yes, sir," Renner said. "We'd do well to leave focus of that mirror."

"Damage control, Captain," Cargill reported from his station aft. "We're getting a lot of energy into the Field. Too much and damned fast, with none of it going anywhere. If it were concentrated it would burn holes in us, but the way it washes across, we can hold maybe ten minutes."

"Captain, I'll steer around behind the sail," Renner said. "At least we've got sun-side scanners, and I can remember where the pod was—"

"Never mind that. Take us through the sail," Rod ordered.

"But we don't know—"

"That was an order, Mr. Renner. And you're in a Navy ship."

"Aye aye, sir."

The Field was brick red and growing brighter; but red wasn't dangerous. Not for a while.

As Renner worked the ship, Rod said casually, "You may be assuming the aliens are using unreasonably strong materials. Are you?"

"It's a possibility, sir." *MacArthur* jolted; she was committed now. Renner seemed to be bracing himself for a shock.

"But the stronger the materials are, Mr. Renner, the thinner they will spread them, so as to pick up the maximum amount of sunlight for the weight. If they have very strong thread they will weave it thin to get more square kilometers per kilo, right? Even if meteors later get a few square km of sail, well, they still made a profit, didn't they? So they'll make it just strong enough."

"Yes, sir," Renner sang. He was driving at four gees, keeping Cal directly astern; he was grinning like a thief, and he was no longer bracing himself for the crash.

Well, I convinced him, Rod thought; and braced himself for the crash.

The Langston Field was yellow with heat.

Then, suddenly, the sunward scanners showed black except for the green-hot edge of *MacArthur*'s own Field, and a ragged blazing silhouette of white where *MacArthur* had ripped through the intruder's sail.

"Hell, we never felt it!" Rod laughed. "Mr. Renner. How long before we impact the sun?"

"Forty-five minutes, sir. Unless we do something about it."

"First things first, Mr. Renner. You keep us matched up with the sail, and right here." Rod activated another circuit to reach the Gunnery Officer. "Crawford! Put some light on that sail and see if you can find the shroud connections. I want you to cut the pod off that parachute before they fire on us again!"

"Aye aye, sir." Crawford seemed happy at the prospect.

There were thirty-two shrouds in all: twenty-four around the edge of the circular fabric mirror and a ring of eight nearer the center. Conical distortions in the fabric told where they were. The back of the sail was black; it flashed to vapor under the pinpoint attack of the forward laser batteries.

Then the sail was loose, billowing and rippling as it floated toward *MacArthur*. Again the ship swept through, as if the light sail were so many square kilometers of tissue paper . . .

And the intruder's pod was falling loose toward an F8 sun.

"Thirty-five minutes to impact," Renner said without being asked.

"Thank you, Mr. Renner. Commander Cargill, take the con. You will take that pod in tow."

And Rod felt a wild internal glee at Renner's astonishment.

7 • *The Crazy Eddie Probe*

"But—" said Renner and pointed at Cal's growing image on the bridge screens. Before he could say anything else *MacArthur* leaped ahead at six gees, no smooth transition this time. Jolt meters swung wildly as the ship hurtled straight toward the looming sun.

"Captain?" Through the roaring blood in his ears Blaine heard his exec call from the after bridge. "Captain, how much damage can we sustain?"

It was an effort to speak. "Anything that'll get us home," Rod gasped.

"Roger." Cargill's orders sounded through the intercom. "Mr. Potter! Is hangar deck clear to vacuum? All shuttles stowed?"

"Yes, sir." The question was irrelevant under battle conditions, but Cargill was a careful man.

"Open the hangar doors," Cargill ordered. "Captain, we might lose the hangar deck hatches."

"Rape 'em."

"I'm bringing the pod aboard fast, no time to match velocities. We'll take damage—"

"You have the con, Commander. Carry out your orders." There was a red haze on the bridge. Rod blinked, but it was still there, not in the air but in his retinas. Six gravities was too much for sustained effort. If anyone fainted—well, they'd miss all the excitement.

"Kelley!" Rod barked. "When we turn ship, take the Marines aft and stand by to intercept anything coming out of that pod! And you'd better move fast. Cargill won't hold acceleration."

"Aye aye, sir." Six gravities and Kelley's gravel rasp was the same as ever.

The pod was three thousand kilometers ahead, invisible even to the clearest vision, but growing steadily on the bridge screens, steadily but slowly, much too slowly, even as Cal seemed to grow too fast.

Four minutes at six gravities. Four minutes of agony, then the alarms hooted. There was a moment of blessed relief. Kelley's Marines clattered through the ship, diving in the low, shifting gravity as *MacArthur* turned end for end. There wouldn't be acceleration couches back there where the Marines would cover hangar deck. Webbing straps to suspend the men in corridors, others in the hangar space itself hung like flies in a spider web, weapons ready— ready for what?

The alarms sounded, and jolt meters swung again as *MacArthur* braked toward the pod. Rod turned his screen controls with an effort. There was hangar deck, cold and dark, the fuzzy outline of the inner surface of the ship's defensive field an impossible black. Good, he thought. No significant heat storage. Plenty of capacity to take up the rotational energy of the pod if it had any, slow down the impact to something that *MacArthur* might be able to handle.

Eight minutes at six gees, the maximum the crew would be able to stand. Then the intruder was no longer ahead as *MacArthur* turned and fell toward it sidewise. The crushing acceleration ended, then there was low side thrust as Cargill fired the port batteries to slow their headlong rush to the pod.

It was cylindrical, with one rounded end, tumbling through space. As it turned Rod saw that the other end was jagged with a myriad of projections—thirty-two projections? But there should have been shrouds trailing from those knobs, and there was nothing.

It was moving up to *MacArthur* far too fast, and it was too big to fit in the hangar deck. The thing was massive, too damn massive! And there was nothing to brake with to the sides but the port batteries!

It was *here*. Hangar deck camera showed the rounded end of the intruder, dull and metallic, pushing through the Langston Field, slowing, the rotation stopping, but still it moved relative to *MacArthur*. The battle cruiser surged sidewise, terribly, throwing the crew against their harness straps, while the rounded end of the pod grew and grew and—CRUNCH!

Rod shook his head to clear it of the red mist which had formed again. "Get us out of here. Mr. Renner, take the con!"

Jolt meters swung before the acceleration alarms; Renner must have set up the course in advance and slapped the keys the instant he was given control. Blaine peered at the dials through the crimson mist. Good, Renner wasn't trying anything fancy; just blast lateral to *MacArthur*'s course and let the sun whip her around. Were they accelerating in the plane of Cal's planets? Be tricky to rendezvous with *Lermontov* for hydrogen. If they couldn't bring *Mac* in on this pass, she'd have dry tanks . . . fuzzily Blaine touched display controls and watched as the main computer showed a course plot. Yes. Renner had set it up properly, and fast work too.

Let him do it, Rod thought. Renner's competent, better astrogator than I am. Time to inspect the ship. What happened to her when we took that thing aboard? But all the screens covering that area were blank, cameras burned off or smashed. Outside it wasn't much better. "Fly her blind, Mr. Renner," Blaine ordered. "Cameras would just boil off anyway. Wait until we're moving away from Cal."

"Damage report, Skipper."

"Go ahead, Commander Cargill."

"We've got the intruder clamped in with the hangar doors. It's jammed in solid, I don't think we can rattle it around with normal acceleration. I don't have a full report, but that hangar deck will never be the same, sir."

"Anything major, Number One?"

"No, sir. I could give you the whole list—minor problems, things jarred loose, equipment failed under impact stress—but it boils down to this: if we don't have to fight, we're in good shape."

"Fine. Now see what you can get me from the Marines. The com lines to Kelley's station seem to be out."

"Aye aye, sir."

Somebody would have to move around at six gees to carry out that order, Blaine thought. Hope to God he can do it in a travel chair. A man might just slither along under that strain, but he wouldn't be good for much afterwards. Was it worth it? For probably negative information? But suppose it wasn't negative . . .

"Marine Corporal Pietrov reporting to Captain, sir." Thick accent of St. Ekaterina. "No activity from intruder, sir."

"Cargill here, Captain," another voice added.

"Yes."

"Do you need Kelley? Mr. Potter was able to get a line to Pietrov without leaving his scooter, but there's a problem if he has to go further."

"Pietrov's fine, Number One. Good work, Potter. Corporal, can you see Mr. Kelley? Is he all right?"

"The Gunner's waved at me, sir. He is on duty in number-two air lock."

"Good. Report any activity by intruder immediately, Corporal." Blaine switched off as the warning horns sounded again. Fifty kilos lifted from his chest as the ship's acceleration eased. Tricky thing, this, he thought. Got to balance between getting too close to Cal and cooking the crew, and just killing everybody from the gee stress.

At his station forward, one of the helmsmen leaned against the padding of his couch. His partner leaned against him to touch helmets. For an instant they cut their mikes while Quartermaster's Mate First Class Orontez spoke to his partner. "My brother wanted me to help him with his wet-ranch on Aphrodite and I thought it was too goddamn dangerous. So I joined the flipping Navy."

"Commander Sinclair, have we enough energy for a report to Fleet?"

"Aye, Skipper, the engines hold verra well indeed. Yon object is nae so massive as we thought, and we've hydrogen to spare."

"Good." Blaine called the communications room to send out his report. Intruder aboard. Cylinder, ratio of axes four to one. Uniform metallic in appearance but close inspection impossible until acceleration eases off. Suggest *Lermontov* attempt to recover the sail, which would decelerate rapidly with no pod ahead of it. Estimated time of arrival, New Scotland . . . suggest *MacArthur* put into orbit around uninhabited moon of New Scotland. No evidence of life or activity aboard alien, but . . .

It was a very large "but," Rod thought. Just what was that thing? Had it fired on him deliberately? Was it under command, or what kind of robot could pilot it across light years of normal space? What would it, whoever or whatever was commanding it, think of being stuffed into the hangar deck of a battle cruiser, cut loose from its shrouds . . . Hell of an undignified end to thirty-five light years of travel.

And there was nothing he could do to find out. Nothing at all. *MacArthur*'s situation wasn't so critical, Renner had her well under control; but neither Blaine nor Cargill could leave his station, and he wasn't about to send junior officers to investigate that thing.

"Is it over?" Sally's voice was plaintive. "Is everything all right?"

"Yes." Rod shuddered involuntarily as he thought of

what might have happened. "Yes, it's aboard and we've seen nothing about it other than its size. It won't answer signals." Now why did he feel a little twinge of satisfaction because she'd just have to wait like the rest of them?

MacArthur plunged on, whipping around Cal so close that there was a measurable drag from the corona; but Renner's astrogation was perfect and the Field held nicely. They waited.

At two gravities Rod could leave the bridge. He stood with an effort, transferred to a scooter, and started aft. The elevators let him "down" as he moved through the ship, and he stopped at each deck to note the alert crewmen still at their posts despite being at general quarters too long. *MacArthur* had to be the best ship in the Navy . . . and he'd keep her that way!

When he reached Kelley's position at the air lock to hangar deck, there was still nothing new.

"You can see there's hatches or something there, sir," Kelley said. He pointed with a flash. As the light flicked up the alien craft Rod saw the ruins of his boats crushed against the steel decks.

"And it's done nothing?"

"Not one thing, Captain. It come in, whapped against the decks—like to threw me into a bulkhead; that thing didn't come in fast but she come down *hard*. Then, nothing. My files, me, the middies who keep swarming around here, none of us seen a thing, Cap'n."

"Just as well," Rod muttered. He took out his own light and played it on the enormous cylinder. The upper half vanished into the uniform black of the Field.

His light swept across a row of conical knobs; each a meter in diameter and three times that in length. He searched, but there was nothing there—no tag ends of the shrouds which ought to be hanging from them, no visible opening in the knob through which the shroud could have been reeled. Nothing.

"Keep watching it, Kelley. I want continuous surveillance." Captain Rod Blaine went back to the bridge with no more information than he'd had before and sat staring at his screens. Unconsciously his hand moved to rub the bridge of his nose.

Just what in God's name *had* he caught?

8 • *The Alien*

Blaine stood rigidly at attention before the massive desk. Fleet Admiral Howland Cranston, Commander-in-Chief of His Majesty's forces beyond the Coal Sack, glared across a rose-teak desk whose exquisite carvings would have fascinated Rod if he'd been at liberty to examine them. The Admiral fingered a thick sheaf of papers.

"Know what these are, Captain?"

"No, sir."

"Requests that you be dismissed from the Service. Half the faculty at Imperial University. Couple of padres from the Church and one Bishop. Secretary of the Humanity League. Every bleeding heart this side of the Coal Sack wants your scalp."

"Yes, sir." There didn't seem to be anything else to say. Rod stood at stiff attention, waiting for it to be over. What would his father think? Would anyone understand?

Cranston glared again. There was no expression in his eyes at all. His undress uniform was shapeless. Miniatures of a dozen decorations told the story of a commander who'd ruthlessly driven himself and his subordinates beyond any hope of survival.

"The man who fired on the first alien contact the human race ever made," Cranston said coldly. "Crippled their probe. You know we only found one passenger, and he's *dead?* Life-system failure, maybe." Cranston fingered the sheaf of papers and viciously thrust them away. "Damned civilians, they always end up influencing the Navy. They leave me no choice.

"All right. Captain Blaine, as Fleet Admiral of this Sector I hereby confirm your promotion to captain and assign you to command of His Majesty's battle cruiser *MacArthur*. Now sit down." As Rod dazedly looked for a chair, Cranston grunted. "That'll show the bastards. Try to tell me how to run my command, will they? Blaine, you're the luckiest officer in the Service. A board would have confirmed your promotion anyway, but without this you'd never have kept that ship."

"Yes. Sir." It was true enough, but that couldn't keep the note of pride out of Rod's voice. And *MacArthur* was his— "Sir? Have they found out anything about the probe? Since we left the probe in orbit I've been busy in the Yards getting *MacArthur* refitted."

"We've opened it, Captain. I'm not sure I believe what we found, but we've got inside the thing. We found this." He produced an enlarged photograph.

The creature was stretched out on a laboratory table. The scale beside it showed that it was small, 1.24 meters from top of head to what Rod at first thought were shoes, then decided were its feet. There were no toes, although a ridge of what might have been horn covered the forward edges.

The rest was a scrambled nightmare. There were two slender right arms ending in delicate hands, four fingers and two opposed thumbs on each. On the left side was a single massive arm, virtually a club of flesh, easily bigger than both right arms combined. Its hand was three thick fingers closed like a vise.

Cripple? Mutation? The creature was symmetrical below where its waist would have been; from the waist up it was—different.

The torso was lumpy. The musculature was more complex than that of men. Rod could not discern the basic bone structure beneath.

The arms—well, they made a weird kind of sense. The elbows of the right arms fitted too well, like nested plastic cups. Evolution had done that. The creature was not a cripple.

The head was the worst.

There was no neck. The massive muscles of the left shoulder sloped smoothly up to the top of the alien's head. The left side of the skull blended into the left shoulder and was much larger than the right. There was no left ear and no room for one. A great membranous goblin's ear decorated the right side, above a narrow shoulder that would have been almost human except that there was a similar shoulder below and slightly behind the first.

The face was like nothing he had ever seen. On such a head it should not even have been a face. But there were two symmetrical slanted eyes, wide open in death, very human, somehow oriental. There was a mouth, expressionless, with the lips slightly parted to show points of teeth.

"Well, how do you like him?"

Rod answered, "I'm sorry it's dead. I can think of a million questions to ask it— There was only this one?"

"Yes. Only him, inside the ship. Now look at this."

Cranston touched a corner of his desk to reveal a recessed control panel. Curtains on the wall to Rod's left parted and the room lights dimmed. A screen lighted uniformly white.

Shadows suddenly shot in from the edges, dwindled as they converged toward the center, and were gone, all in a few seconds.

"We took that off your sun-side cameras, the ones that weren't burned off. Now I'll slow it down."

Shadows moved jerkily inward on a white background. There were half a dozen showing when the Admiral stopped the film.

"Well?"

"They look like—like that," said Rod.

"Glad you think so. Now watch." The projector started again. The odd shapes dwindled, converged, and disappeared, not as if they had dwindled to infinity, but as if they had evaporated.

"But that shows passengers being ejected from the probe and burned up by the light sail. What sense does that make?"

"It doesn't. And you can find forty explanations out at the university. Picture's not too clear anyway. Notice how distorted they were? Different sizes, different shapes. No way to tell if they were alive. One of the anthropologist

types thinks they were statues of gods thrown out to protect them from profanation. He's about sold that theory
to the rest of 'em, except for those who say the pictures
were flawed film, or mirages from the Langston Field, or
fakes."

"Yes, sir." That didn't need comment, and Blaine made
none. He returned to his seat and examined the photograph again. A million questions . . . if only the pilot were
not dead . . .

After a long time the Admiral grunted, "Yeah. Here's
a copy of the report on what we found in the probe. Take
it somewhere and study it, you've got an appointment
with the Viceroy tomorrow afternoon and he'll expect you
to know something. Your anthropologist helped write that
report, you can discuss it with her if you want. Later on
you can go look at the probe, we're bringing it down today." Cranston chuckled at Blaine's surprised look. "Curious about why you're getting this stuff? You'll find out.
His Highness has plans and you're going to be part of
them. We'll let you know."

Rod saluted and left in bewilderment, the TOP SECRET
report clutched under his arm.

The report was mostly questions.

Most of the probe's internal equipment was junk, fused
and melted clutters of plastic blocks, remains of integrated
circuitry, odd strips of conducting and semiconducting
materials jumbled together in no rational order. There
was no trace of the shroud lines, no gear for reeling them
in, no apertures in the thirty-two projections at one end of
the probe. If the shrouds were all one molecule it might
explain why they were missing; they would have come
apart, changed chemically, when Blaine's cannon cut them.
But how had they controlled the sail? Could the shrouds
somehow be made to contract and relax, like a muscle?

An odd idea, but some of the intact mechanisms were
just as odd. There was no standardization of parts in the
probe. Two widgets intended to do almost the same job
could be subtly different or wildly different. Braces and

mountings seemed hand carved. The probe was as much a sculpture as a machine.

Blaine read that, shook his head, and called Sally. Presently she joined him in his cabin.

"Yes, I wrote that," she said. "It seems to be true. Every nut and bolt in that probe was designed separately. It's less surprising if you think of the probe as having a religious purpose. But that's not all. You know how redundancy works?"

"In machines? Two gilkickies to do one job. In case one fails."

"Well, it seems that the Moties work it both ways."

"Moties?"

She shrugged. "We had to call them something. The Motie engineers made two widgets do one job, all right, but the second widget does two other jobs, and some of the supports are also bimetallic thermostats and thermoelectric generators all in one. Rod, I barely understand the words. Modules: human engineers work in modules, don't they?"

"For a complicated job, of course they do."

"The Moties don't. It's all one piece, everything working on everything else. Rod, there's a fair chance the Moties are brighter than we are."

Rod whistled. "That's . . . frightening. Now, wait a minute. They'd have the Alderson Drive, wouldn't they?"

"I wouldn't know about that. But they have some things we don't. There are biotemperature superconductors," she said, rolling it as if she'd memorized the phrase, "painted on in strips."

"Then there's this." She reached past him to turn pages. "Here, look at this photo. All the little pebbly meteor holes."

"Micrometeorites. It figures."

"Well, nothing larger than four thousand microns got through the meteor defense. Only nobody ever found a meteor defense. They don't have the Langston Field or anything like it."

"But—"

"It must have been the sail. You see what that means?

The autopilot attacked us because it thought *MacArthur* was a meteor."

"What about the pilot? Why didn't—"

"No. The alien was in frozen sleep, as near as we can tell. The life-support systems went wrong about the time we took it aboard. We killed it."

"That's definite?"

Sally nodded.

"Hell. All that way it came. The Humanity League wants my head on a platter with an apple in my mouth, and I don't blame them. Aghhhh . . ." A sound of pain.

"Stop it," Sally said softly.

"Sorry. Where do we go from here?"

"The autopsy. It fills half the report." She turned pages and Rod winced. Sally Fowler had a stronger stomach than most ladies of the Court.

The meat of the Motie was pale; its blood was pink, like a mixture of tree sap and human blood. The surgeons had cut deep into its back, exposing the bones from the back of the skull to where the coccyx would have been on a man.

"I don't understand. Where's the spine?"

"There is none," Sally told him. "Evolution doesn't seem to have invented vertebrae on Mote Prime."

There were three bones in the back, each as solid as a leg bone. The uppermost was an extension of the skull, as if the skull had a twenty-cm handle. The joint at its lower end was at shoulder level; it would nod the head but would not turn it.

The main backbone was longer and thicker. It ended in a bulky, elaborate joining, partly ball-and-socket, at about the small of the back. The lower backbone flared into hips and sockets for the thighs.

There was a spinal cord, a major nervous connective line, but it ran ventral to the backbones, not through them.

"It can't turn its head," Rod said aloud. "It has to turn at the waist. That's why the big joint is so elaborate. Right?"

"That's right. I watched them test that joint. It'll turn the torso to face straight backward. Impressed?"

Rod nodded and turned the page. In that picture the surgeons had exposed the skull.

Small wonder the head was lopsided. Not only was the left side of the brain larger, to control the sensitive, complexly innervated right arms; but the massive tendons of the left shoulder connected to knobs on the left side of the skull for greater leverage.

"All designed around the arms," Sally said. "Think of the Motie as a toolmaker and you'll see the point. The right arms are for the fine work such as fixing a watch. The left arm lifts and holds. He could probably lift one end of an air car with the left hand and use the right arms to tinker with the motors. And that idiot Horowitz thought it was a mutation!" She turned more pages. "Look."

"Right, I noticed that myself. The arms fit too well." The photographs showed the right arms in various positions, and they could not be made to get in each other's way. The arms were about the same length when extended; but the bottom arm had a long forearm and short humerus, whereas in the top arm the forearm and humerus were about the same length. With the arms at the alien's side, the fingertips of the top arm hung just below the bottom arm's wrist.

He read on. The alien's chemistry was subtly different from the human but not wildly so, as anyone might have expected from previous extraterrestrial biology. All known life was sufficiently similar that some theorists held to spore dispersion through interstellar space as the origin of life everywhere. The theory was not widely held, but it was defensible, and the alien would not settle the matter.

Long after Sally left, Rod was still studying the report. When he was finished, three facts stuck in his mind:

The Motie was an intelligent toolmaker.

It had traveled across thirty-five light years to find human civilization.

And Rod Blaine had killed it.

9 • *His Highness Has Decided*

The Viceregal Palace dominated New Scotland's only major city. Sally stared in admiration at the huge structure and excitedly pointed out the ripple of colors that changed with each motion of the flyer.

"How did it get that effect?" she asked. "It doesn't seem like an oil film."

"Cut from good New Scot rock," Sinclair answered. "You've nae seen rock like this before. There was nae life here until the First Empire seeded the planet; yon palace is rock wi' all the colors just as it boiled out of the interior."

"It's beautiful," she told him. The Palace was the only building with open space around it. New Scotland huddled in small warrens, and from the air it was easy to see circular patterns like growth rings of a tree circle making the construction of larger field generators for protection of the city. Sally asked, "Wouldn't it be simpler to make a city plan using right angles now?"

"Simpler, aye," Sinclair answered. "But we've been through two hundred years of war, lass. Few care to live wi' nae Field for protection—not that we do no trust the Navy and Empire," he added hastily. "But 'tis no easy to break habits that old. We'd rather stay crowded and ken we can fight."

The flyer circled in to rest on the scarred lava roof of the Palace. The streets below were a bustle of color, tartans and plaids, everyone jostling his neighbor in the narrow streets. Sally was surprised to see just how small the Imperial Sector Capital was.

Rod left Sally and his officers in a comfortable lounge and followed starched Marine guides. The Council Chamber was a mixture of simplicity and splendor, walls of unadorned rock contrasting with patterned wool carpets and tapestries. Battle banners hung from high rafters.

The Marines showed Rod to a seat. Immediately in

front of him was a raised dais for the Council and its attendants, and above that the viceregal throne dominated the entire chamber; yet even the throne was overshadowed by an immense solido of His Most Royal and Imperial Highness and Majesty, Leonidas IX, by Grace of God Emperor of Humanity. When there was a message from the Throne world the image would come alive, but now it showed a man no more than forty dressed in the midnight black of an Admiral of the Fleet, unadorned by decorations or medals. Dark eyes stared at and through each person in the chamber.

The chamber filled rapidly. There were Sector Parliament members, military and naval officers, scurrying civilians attended by harried clerks. Rod had no idea what to expect, but he noted jealous glances from those behind him. He was by far the most junior officer in the front row of the guest seats. Admiral Cranston took a seat two places to Blaine's left and nodded crisply to his subordinate.

A gong sounded. The Palace major-domo, coal black, symbolic whip thrust into his belted white uniform, came onto the platform above them and struck the stage with his staff of office. A line of men filed into the room to take their places on the dais. The Imperial Councilors were less impressive than their titles, Rod decided. Mostly they seemed to be harried men—but many of them had the same look as the Emperor's portrait, the ability to look beyond those in the chamber to something that could only be guessed at. They sat impassively until the gong was struck again.

The major-domo took a pose and struck the stage three times with his staff. "HIS MOST EXCELLENT HIGHNESS STEFAN YURI ALEXANDROVITCH MERRILL, VICEROY TO HIS IMPERIAL MAJESTY FOR THE REALM BEYOND THE COAL SACK. MAY GOD GRANT WISDOM TO HIS MAJESTY AND HIS HIGHNESS."

Everyone scrambled to his feet. As Rod stood he thought of what was happening. It would be easy to be cynical. After all, Merrill was only a man; His Imperial Majesty was only a man. They put their trousers on one leg at a time. But they held responsibility for the destiny of the human race. The Council could advise them. The Senate could debate. The Assembly could shout and demand. Yet when all the conflicting demands were heard, when all the advice was pondered, someone had to act in the name of mankind . . . No, the ceremonial entrance wasn't exaggerated. Men who had that kind of power should be reminded of it.

His Highness was a tall, lanky man with bushy eyebrows. He wore the dress uniform of the Navy, sunbursts and comets on his breast, decorations earned in years of service to the Realm. When he reached his throne, he turned to the solido above it and bowed. The major-domo led the pledge of allegiance to the Crown before Merrill took his seat and nodded to the Council.

Duke Bonin, the elderly Lord President of the Council, stood at his place at the center of the big table. "My lords and gentlemen. By order of His Highness the Council meets to consider the matter of the alien vessel from the Mote. This may be a long session," he added with no trace of sarcasm.

"You all have before you the reports of our investigation of the alien ship. I can summarize them in two significant points: the aliens have neither the Alderson Drive nor the Langston Field. On the other hand, they appear to have other technologies considerably in advance of anything the Empire has ever had—and I include in that the First Empire."

There were gasps in the chamber. The First Empire was held in almost mystical reverence by many Imperial governors and most subjects. Bonin nodded significantly. "We now consider what we must do. His Excellency Sir Traffin Geary, Sector Minister for External Affairs."

Sir Traffin was nearly as tall as the Viceroy, but the resemblance ended there. Instead of His Highness' trim, athletic figure, Sir Traffin was shaped like a barrel. "Your Highness, my lords and gentlemen. We have sent a courier to Sparta and another will be dispatched within the week. This probe was slower than light, and launched well over a hundred years ago. We need do nothing about it for a few months. I propose that we make preparations here for an expedition to the Mote, but otherwise wait for instructions from His Majesty." Geary jutted his under lip truculently as he looked around the Council Chamber. "I suspect this comes as a surprise to many of you who know my temperament, but I think it wise to give this matter extended thought. Our decision may affect the destiny of the human race."

There were murmurs of approval. The President nodded to the man at his left. "My Lord Richard MacDonald Armstrong, Sector Minister of War."

In contrast to the bulk of Sir Traffin, the War Minister was almost diminutive, his features small to match his body, not finely chiseled, so that there was an impression of softness in the face. Only the eyes were hard, with a look to match those of the portrait above him.

"I full well understand the views of Sir Traffin," Armstrong began. "I do not care for this responsibility. It is great comfort to us to know that on Sparta the wisest men of the race will backstop our failures and mistakes."

Not much New Scot to his accent, Rod thought. Only a trace, but the man was obviously a native. Wonder if they can all talk like the rest of us when they have to?

"But we may not have the time," Armstrong said softly. "Consider. One hundred and thirteen years ago, as best our records show, the Mote glowed so brightly that it outshone Murcheson's Eye. Then one day it went out. That would no doubt be when the probe was ready to turn end for end and begin deceleration into our system. The lasers that launched that thing had been on a long time. The builders have had a hundred and fifty years at least to develop new technology. Think of that, my lords. In a hundred and fifty years, men on Earth went from windpowered warships to a landing on Earth's Moon. From gunpowder to hydrogen fusion. To a level of technology which might have built that probe—and in no more than a hundred and fifty years after *that,* had the Alderson Drive, the Field, ten interstellar colonies, and the Co-Dominium. Fifty years later the Fleet left Earth to found the First Empire. That is what a hundred and fifty years can be to a growing race, my lords. And that's what we're faced with, else they'd have been here before.

"I say we can't afford to wait!" The old man's voice lashed out to fill the chamber. "Wait for word from Sparta? With all respect to His Majesty's advisers, what can they tell us that we won't know better than they? By the time they can reply we'll have sent more reports. Perhaps things will have changed here and their instructions will make no sense. God's teeth, it's better to make our own mistakes!"

"Your recommendation?" the Council President asked dryly.

"I have already ordered Admiral Cranston to assemble all the warships we can spare from occupation and patrol duties. I have sent to His Majesty a most urgent request that additional forces be assigned to this sector. Now I propose that a naval expedition go to the Mote and find out what's happening there while the Yards convert enough vessels to be sure that we can destroy the alien home worlds if necessary."

There were gasps in the chamber. One of the Council members rose hurriedly to demand recognition.

"Dr. Anthony Horvath, Minister of Science," the President announced.

"Your Highness, my lords, I am speechless," Horvath began.

"Would to God you were," Admiral Cranston muttered at his seat to Rod's left.

Horvath was an elderly, carefully dressed man with precise gestures and every word spoken just so, as if he intended to say just that and no more. He spoke quietly but every word carried through the room perfectly. "My lords, there is nothing threatening about this probe. It carried only one passenger, and it has had no opportunity to report to those who sent it." Horvath looked significantly at Admiral Cranston. "We have seen absolutely no signs that the aliens have faster-than-light technology, nor the slightest hint of danger, yet My Lord Armstrong speaks of assembling the Fleet. He acts as if all humanity were threatened by one dead alien and a light sail! Now I ask you, is this reasonable?"

"What is your proposal, Dr. Horvath?" the President asked.

"Send an expedition, yes. I agree with Minister Armstrong that it would be pointless to expect the Throne to issue detailed instructions from that great distance in time. Send a Navy ship if it makes everyone more comfortable. But staff it with scientists, foreign office personnel, representatives of the merchant class. Go in peace as they came in peace, don't treat these aliens as if they were outie pirates! There won't ever be an opportunity like this again, my lords. The first contact between humans and intelligent aliens. Oh, we'll find other sentient species, but we'll never find a first one again. What we do here will be in our history forever. Do not make a blot on that page!"

"Thank you, Dr. Horvath," the President said. "Are there other comments?"

There were. Everyone spoke at once until order was established at last. "Gentlemen, we must have a decision," Duke Bonin said. "What is the advice you wish to offer His Highness? Do we send an expedition to the Mote or no?"

That was settled quickly. The military and science groups easily outnumbered Sir Traffin's supporters. Ships would be sent as soon as feasible.

"Excellent." Bonin nodded. "And perhaps the character of the expedition? Shall it be naval or civil?"

The major-domo struck the stage with his staff. Every head turned toward the high throne where Merrill had sat impassively through the debate. "I thank the Council, but I shall need no advice concerning this final matter," the Viceroy said. "Since the question concerns the safety of the Realm there can be no problem of sector prerogatives involved." The stately address was spoiled as Merrill ran his fingers through his hair. He dropped his hand hurriedly to his lap as he realized what he was doing. A thin smile came to his face. "Although I suspect the Council's advice might be the same as my own. Sir Traffin, would your group favor a purely scientific expedition?"

"No, Your Highness."

"And I think we need not ask My Lord Minister of War for his opinion. Dr. Horvath's group would be out-voted in any event. As planning an expedition of this nature requires something less than the full Council, I will see Dr. Horvath, Sir Traffin, My Lord Armstrong, and Admiral Cranston in my office immediately. Admiral, is the officer you spoke of here?"

"Yes, Your Highness."

"Bring him with you." Merrill stood and strode from the throne so quickly that the major-domo had no chance to do his ceremonial office. Belatedly he struck the stage with his staff and faced the Imperial portrait. "IT IS HIS HIGHNESS' PLEASURE THAT THIS COUNCIL BE DISMISSED. MAY GOD GRANT WISDOM TO HIS HIGHNESS. GOD SAVE THE EMPEROR."

As the others left the Chamber, Admiral Cranston took Rod's arm and led him through a small door by the stage. "What'd you think of all this?" Cranston asked.

"Orderly. I've been in Council meetings on Sparta where I thought they'd come to blows. Old Borin knows how to run a meeting."

"Yeah. You understand this political crap, don't you? Better'n I do, anyway. You may be a better choice than I thought."

"Choice for what, sir?"

"Isn't it pretty obvious, Captain? His Nibs and I decided last night. You're going to take *MacArthur* to the Mote."

10 • *The Planet Killer*

Viceroy Merrill had two offices. One was large, ornately furnished, decorated with gifts and tributes from a score of worlds. A solido of the Emperor dominated the wall behind a desk of Samualite teak inlaid with ivory and gold, flowering carpets of living grasses from Tabletop provided soft footing and air purification, and tri-v cameras were invisibly recessed into New Scot rock walls for the convenience of newsmen covering ceremonial events.

Rod had only a brief glance at His Highness' place of splendor before he was led through it to a much smaller room of almost monastic simplicity. The Viceroy sat at a huge duroplast desk. His hair was a tangled mess. He had opened the collar of his uniform tunic and his dress boots stood against the wall.

"Ah. Come in, Admiral. See you brought young Blaine. How are you, boy? You won't remember me. Only time we met you were, what, two years old? Three? Damned if I can remember. How's the Marquis?"

"Very well, Your Highness. I'm sure he would send—"

"Course, of course. Good man, your father. Bar's right over there." Merrill picked up a sheaf of papers and glanced quickly through the pages, turning them so rapidly they were a blur. "About what I thought." He scrawled a signature on the last page; the out basket coughed and the papers vanished.

"Perhaps I should introduce Captain Blaine to . . ." Admiral Cranston began.

"Course, of course. Careless of me. Dr. Horvath, Minister Armstrong, Sir Traffin, Captain Blaine, *MacArthur*. Marquis of Crucis' boy, you know."

"MacArthur." Dr. Horvath said it contemptuously. "I see. If Your Highness will excuse me, I can't think why you'd want *him* here."

"Can't, eh?" Merrill asked. "Use some logic, Doctor. You know what the meeting's about, right?"

"I can't say I care for the conclusion I get, Your Highness. And I still see no reason why this—militaristic fanatic should be part of planning an expedition of such vast importance."

"Is this a complaint against one of my officers, sir?" Admiral Cranston snapped. "If so, may I ask you—"

"That will do," Merrill drawled. He tossed another thick packet of papers into the out basket and thoughtfully watched it vanish. "Dr. Horvath, suppose you state your objections and be done with it." It was impossible to tell whom Merrill intended his thin smile for.

"My objections are obvious enough. This young man may have engaged the human race in war with the first intelligent aliens we've ever found. The Admiralty has not seen fit to cashier him, but I will strenuously object to his having any further contact with the aliens. Sir, don't you appreciate the *enormity* of what he's done?"

"No, sir, I dinna see the point," War Minister Armstrong interjected.

"But that ship came thirty-five light years. Through normal space. Over a hundred and fifty years in flight! An achievement that the First Empire couldn't match. And for what? To be crippled at its destination, fired on, stuffed into the hold of a battleship and ferried to—" The Science Minister ran out of breath.

"Blaine, did you fire on the probe?" Merrill asked.

"No, Your Highness. It fired on us. My orders were to intercept and inspect. After the alien vessel attacked my ship, I cut it loose from the light sail it was using as a weapon."

"Leaving you no choice but to take it aboard or let it burn up," Sir Traffin added. "Good work, that."

"But unnecessary if the probe hadn't been crippled," Horvath insisted. "When it fired on you why didn't you have the good sense to get behind the sail and follow it? Use the sail as a shield! You didn't need to kill it."

"That thing fired on an Imperial warship," Cranston exploded. "And you think one of my officers would—"

Merrill held up his hand. "I'm curious, Captain. Why didn't you do what Dr. Horvath suggested?"

"I—" Blaine sat rigidly for a moment, his thoughts whirling. "Well, sir, we were low on fuel and pretty close to Cal. If I'd kept pace with the probe I'd have ended up out of control and unable to keep station on it at all, assuming that *MacArthur*'s Drive didn't burn up the sail anyway. We needed the velocity to get back out of Cal's gravity well . . . and my orders were to intercept." He stopped for a moment to finger his broken nose.

Merrill nodded. "One more question, Blaine. What did you think when you were assigned to investigate an alien ship?"

"I was excited at the chance of meeting them, sir."

"Gentlemen, he doesn't sound like an unreasoning xenophobe to me. But when his ship was attacked, he defended her. Dr. Horvath, had he actually fired on the probe itself —which was surely the easiest way to see that it didn't damage his ship—I would personally see that he was dismissed as unfit to serve His Majesty in any capacity whatever. Instead he carefully cut the probe loose from its weapon and at great risk to his own ship took it aboard. I like that combination, gentlemen." He turned to Armstrong. "Dickie, will you tell them what we've decided about the expedition?"

"Yes, Your Highness." The War Minister cleared his throat. "Two ships. The Imperial battleship *Lenin* and the battle cruiser *MacArthur*. *MacArthur* will be modified to suit Dr. Horvath's requirements and will carry the civilian personnel of this expedition. That is to include scientists, merchants, Foreign Office people, and the missionary contingent His Reverence demands, in addition to a naval crew. All contact with the alien civilization will be conducted by *MacArthur*."

Merrill nodded in emphasis. "Under no circumstances will *Lenin* take aliens aboard or place herself in danger of capture. I want to be sure we get some information back from this expedition."

"Bit extreme, isn't it?" Horvath asked.

"No, sir." Sir Traffin was emphatic. "Richard is primarily concerned that the aliens have no opportunity to obtain either the Langston Field or the Alderson Drive from us, and I am in full agreement."

"But if they—suppose they capture *MacArthur*?" Horvath asked.

Admiral Cranston exhaled a stream of blue pipe smoke. "Then *Lenin* will blast *MacArthur* out of space."

Blaine nodded. He'd already figured that out.

"Take a good man to make that decision," Sir Traffin observed. "Who are you sending in *Lenin*?"

"Admiral Lavrenti Kutuzov. We sent a courier ship for him yesterday."

"The Butcher!" Horvath set his drink on the table and turned in fury to the Viceroy. "Your Highness, I protest! Of all the men in the Empire there's not a worse choice! You must know that Kutuzov was the man who—who sterilized Istvan. Of all the paranoid creatures in the— Sir, I beg you to reconsider. A man like that could— Don't you understand? These are intelligent aliens! This could be the greatest moment in all history, and you want to send off an expedition commanded by a subhuman who thinks with his reflexes! It's insane."

"It would be more insane to send an expedition commanded by the likes of yourself," Armstrong replied. "I dinna mean it as an insult, Doctor, but you see aliens as friends, you look to the opportunities. You dinna see the dangers. Perhaps my friends and I see too many o' them, but I'd rather be wrong my way than yours."

"The Council . . ." Horvath protested feebly.

"Not a matter for the Council," Merrill stated. "Matter of Imperial Defense. Safety of the Realm and all that, you know. Be a neat question just how much the Imperial Parliament on Sparta has to say about it. As His Majesty's representative in this sector, I've already decided."

"I see." Horvath sat in dejection for a moment, then brightened. "But you said that *MacArthur* would be modified to suit the scientific requirements. That we can have a full scientific expedition."

Merrill nodded. "Yes. Hope we won't have anything for Kutuzov to do. Up to your people to see to it he doesn't have to take action. Just there as a precaution."

Blaine cleared his throat carefully.

"Speak up, laddie," Armstrong said.

"I was wondering about my passengers, sir."

"Course, of course," Merrill answered. "Senator Fowler's niece and that Trader fellow. Think they'd want to go along?"

"I know Sally—Miss Fowler will," Rod answered. "She's turned down two chances to get to Sparta, and she's been going to Admiralty headquarters every day."

"Anthropology student," Merrill murmured. "If she wants to go, let her. Won't do any harm to show the Humanity League we aren't sending a punitive expedition, and I can't think of a better way to make that obvious. Good politics. What about this Bury fellow?"

"I don't know, sir."

"See if he wants to go," Merrill said. "Admiral, you haven't got a suitable ship headed for the Capital, have you?"

"Nothing I'd want to trust that man in," Cranston answered. "You saw Plekhanov's report."

"Yes. Well, Dr. Horvath wanted to take Traders. I'd think His Excellency would welcome the opportunity to be there . . . just tell him one of his competitors could be invited. Ought to do it, eh? Never saw a merchant yet who wouldn't go through hell to get an edge on the competition."

"When will we leave, sir?" Rod asked.

Merrill shrugged. "Up to Horvath's people. Lot of work to do, I expect. *Lenin* ought to be here in a month. It'll pick up Kutuzov on the way. Don't see why you can't go as soon after that as you think *MacArthur* is ready."

11 • *The Church of Him*

At a hundred and fifty kilometers an hour the monorail car moved with a subdued hissing sound. The Saturday crowd of passengers seemed to be enjoying themselves in a quiet way. They did little talking. In one clump near the back a man was sharing a flask around. Even this group wasn't noisy; they only smiled more. A few well-behaved children at window seats craned their necks to see out, pointed, and asked questions in incomprehensible dialect.

Kevin Renner behaved in much the same fashion. He leaned sideways with his head against the clear plastic window, the better to see an alien world. His lean face bore an uncomplicated smile.

Staley was on the aisle, apparently sitting at attention. Potter sat between them.

The three were not on leave; they were off duty and could be recalled via their pocket computers. Artificers at the New Scotland Yards were busy scraping the boats off the walls of *MacArthur*'s hangar deck and making other, more extensive repairs under Sinclair's supervision. Sinclair might need Potter, in particular, at any moment; and Potter was their native guide. Perhaps Staley was remembering this; but his rigid posture was no sign of discomfort. He was enjoying himself. He always sat that way.

Potter was doing most of the talking and all the pointing. "Those twin volcanoes; d'ye see them, Mr. Renner? D'ye see yon boxlike structures near the peak of each one? They're atmosphere control. When yon volcanoes belch gas, the maintenance posts fire jets of tailored algae into the air steam. Without them our atmosphere would soon be foul again."

"Un. You couldn't have kept them going during the Secession Wars. How did you manage?"

"Badly."

The landscape was marked by queer sharp lines. Here there was the green patchwork quilt of cultivated fields, there a lifeless landscape, almost lunar but for the softening of erosion. It was strange to see a broad river meandering unconcerned from cultivation to desert. There were no weeds. Nothing grew wild. The forest grove they were passing now had the same sharp borders and orderly arrangement as the broad strips of flower beds they had passed earlier.

"You've been on New Scotland for three hundred years," said Renner. "Why is it still like this? I'd think there'd be topsoil by now, and scattered seeds. Some of the land would have gone wild."

"How often does it happen that cultivated land turns to wild life on a colony world? For aye our history the people hae spread faster than the topsoil." Potter suddenly sat up straight. "Look ahead. We're coming into Quentin's Patch."

The car slowed smoothly. Doors swung up and a handful of passengers filtered out. The Navy men moved away with Potter in the lead. Potter was almost skipping. This was his home town.

Renner stopped suddenly. "Look, you can see Murcheson's Eye in daylight!"

It was true. The star was high in the east, a red spark just visible against blue sky.

"Can't make out the Face of God, though."

Heads turned to look at the Navy men. Potter spoke softly. "Mr. Renner, you must not call it the Face of God on this world."

"Huh? Why not?"

"A Himmist would call it the Face of Him. They do not refer directly to their God. A good Church member does not believe that it is anything but the Coal Sack."

"They call it the Face of God everywhere else. Good Church member or not."

"Elsewhere in the Empire there are no Himmists. If ye'll walk this way, we should reach the Church of Him before dark."

Quentin's Patch was a small village surrounded by wheat fields. The walkway was a broad stream of basalt with a ripple to its surface, as if it were a convenient lava flow. Renner guessed that a ship's drive had hovered here long ago, marking out the walkways before any buildings were erected. The surface bore a myriad of spreading cracks. With the two- and three-story houses now lining both sides, the walk could hardly be repaired in the same manner.

Renner asked, "How did the Himmists get started?"

"Legend has it," Potter said, and stopped. "Aye, it may not be all legend. What the Himmists say is that one day the Face of God awoke."

"Um?"

"He opened His single eye."

"That would figure, if the Moties were actually using laser cannon to propel a light sail. Any dates on that?"

"Aye." Potter thought. "It happened during the Secession Wars. The war did us great damage, you know. New Scotland remained loyal to the Empire, but New Ireland did not. We were evenly matched. For fifty years or there-abouts we fought each other, until there were nae inter-stellar ships left and nae contact with the stars at all. Then, in 2870, a ship fell into the system. 'Twas the *Ley Crater,* a trading ship converted for war, with a working Langston Field and a hold full of torpedoes. Damaged as she was, she was the most powerful ship in New Caledonia System; we had sunk that low. With her aid we destroyed the New Irish traitors."

"That was a hundred and fifty years ago. You told it like you lived through it."

Potter smiled. "We take our history verra personally here."

"Of course," said Staley.

"Ye asked for dates," said Potter. "The university rec-ords do no say. Some o' the computer records were scrambled by war damage, ye know. Something happened to the Eye, that's sure, but it must have happened late in the war. It would not have made that big an impression, ye ken."

"Why not? The Face of—the eye is the biggest, bright-est thing in your sky."

Potter smiled without mirth. "Not during the war. I hae read diaries. People hid under the university Langston Field. When they came out they saw the sky as a battle-field, alive with strange lights and the radiations from ex-ploding ships. It was only after the war ended that people began to look at the sky. Then the astronomers tried to study what had happened to the Eye. And then it was that Howard Grote Littlemead was stricken with divine inspira-tion."

"He decided that the Face of God was just what it looked like."

"Aye, that he did. And he convinced many people. Here we are, gentlemen."

The Church of Him was both imposing and shabby. It was built of quarried stone to withstand the ages, and it had done so; but the stone was worn, sandblasted by storms; there were cracks in the lintel and cornices and elsewhere; initials and obscenities had been carved into the walls with lasers and other tools.

The priest was a tall, round man with a soft, beaten look to him. But he was unexpectedly firm in his refusal to let them in. It did no good when Potter revealed himself as a fellow townsman. The Church of Him and its priests had suffered much at the hands of townsmen.

"Come, let us reason together," Renner said to him. "You don't really think we mean to profane anything, do you?"

"Ye are nae believers. What business hae ye here?"

"We only want to see the picture of the Co—of the Face of Him in its glory. Having seen this, we depart. If you won't let us in, we may be able to force you by going through channels. This is Navy business."

The priest looked scorn. "This is New Scotland, not one o' yer primitive colonies wi' nae government but blasphemin' Marines. 'Twould take the Viceroy's orders to force yer way here. And ye're but tourists."

"Have you heard of the alien probe?"

The priest lost some of his assurance. "Aye."

"We believe it was launched by laser cannon. From the Mote."

The priest was nonplused. Then he laughed long and loud. Still laughing, he ushered them in. He would say no word to them, but he led them over the chipped tiles through an entry hall and into the main sanctuary. Then he stood aside to watch their faces.

The Face of Him occupied half the wall. It looked like a huge holograph. The stars around the edge were slightly blurred, as would be the case with a very old holograph. And there was the holograph sense of looking into infinity.

The Eye in that Face blazed pure green, with terrifying intensity. Pure green with a red fleck in it.

"My God!" Staley said, and hastily added, "I don't mean it the way it sounds. But—the *power!* It'd take the industrial might of an advanced world to put out that much light from thirty-five light years away!"

"I thought I had remembered it bigger than it was," Potter whispered.

"Ye see!" the priest crowed. "And ye think that could hae been a natural phenomenon! Well, hae ye seen enough?"

"Yah," said Renner, and they left.

They stopped outside in the failing sunlight. Renner was shaking his head. "I don't blame Littlemead a damn bit," he said. "The wonder is he didn't convince everyone on the planet."

"We're a stubborn lot," said Potter. "Yon squinting silhouette in the night sky may hae been too obvious, too . . ."

"Here I am, stupid!" Renner suggested.

"Aye. New Scots dinna like being treated as dullards, not even by Him."

Remembering the decayed building with its shabby interior, Renner said, "The Church of Him seems to have fallen on evil days since Littlemead saw the light."

"Aye. In 2902 the light went out. One hundred and fifteen years ago. That event was verra well documented. 'Twas the end o' astronomy here until the Empire returned."

"Did the Mote go out suddenly?"

Potter shrugged. "None know. It must hae happened around the other side o' the world, you see. Ye must hae noticed that civilization here is but a spreading patch on a barren world. Mr. Renner. When the Coal Sack rose that night it rose like a blinded man. To the Himmists it must hae seemed that God had gone to sleep again."

"Rough on them?"

"Howard Grote Littlemead took an overdose of sleeping pills. The Himmists say he hastened to meet his God."

"Possibly to demand an explanation," said Renner. "You're very quiet, Mr. Staley."

Horst looked up grim-faced. "They can build laser cannon that fill the sky. And we're taking a military expedition there."

12 · *Descent into Hell*

It was just possible to assemble everyone on hangar deck. The closed launching hatch doors—repaired, but obviously so—were the only open space large enough for the ship's company and the scientific personnel to gather, and it was crowded even there. The hangar compartment was stuffed with gear: extra landing craft, the longboat and the cutter, crated scientific equipment, ship's stores, and other crates whose purpose even Blaine didn't know. Dr. Horvath's people insisted on carrying nearly every scientific instrument used in their specialties on the chance that it might be useful; the Navy could hardly argue with them, since there were no precedents for an expedition of this kind.

Now the huge space was packed to overflowing. Viceroy Merrill, Minister Armstrong, Admiral Cranston, Cardinal Randolph, and a host of lesser officials stood confusedly about while Rod hoped that his officers had been able to complete preparations for the ship's departure. The last days had been a blur of unavoidable activities, mostly social, with little time for the important work of preparing his ship. Now, waiting for the final ceremonies, Rod wished he'd got out of Capital social life and stayed aboard his ship like a hermit. For the next year or so he'd be under the command of Admiral Kutuzov, and he suspected that the Admiral was not wholly pleased with his subordinate ship commander. The Russian was conspicuously absent from the ceremonies on *MacArthur*'s hangar doors.

No one had missed him. Kutuzov was a massive, burly man with a heavy sense of humor. He looked like something out of a textbook of Russian history and talked the same way. This was partially due to his upbringing on St. Ekaterina, but mostly through his own choice. Kutuzov spent hours studying ancient Russian customs and adopted many of them as part of the image he projected. His flag-

91

ship bridge was decorated with icons, a samovar of tea bubbled in his cabin, and his Marines were trained in what Kutuzov hoped were fair imitations of Cossack dances.

Navy opinion on the man was universal: highly competent, rigidly faithful to any orders given him, and so lacking in human compassion that everyone felt uncomfortable around him. Because the Navy and Parliament officially approved of Kutuzov's action in ordering the destruction of a rebel planet—the Imperial Council had determined that the drastic measure had prevented the revolt of an entire sector—Kutuzov was invited to all social functions; but no one was disappointed when he refused his invitations.

"The main problem is yon loony Russian customs," Sinclair had offered when *MacArthur*'s officers were discussing their new admiral.

"No different from the Scots," First Lieutenant Cargill had observed. "At least he doesn't try to make us all understand Russian. He speaks Anglic well enough."

"Is that meant to say we Scots dinna speak Anglic?" Sinclair demanded.

"I'll let you guess." But then Cargill thought better of it. "Of course not, Sandy. Sometimes when you get excited I can't understand you, but . . . here, have a drink."

That, thought Rod, had been something to see, Cargill trying his best to be friendly with Sinclair. Of course the reason was obvious. With the ship in New Scotland's Yards under the attention of Yardmaster MacPherson's crews, Cargill was at pains not to irritate the Chief Engineer. He might end up with his cabin removed—or worse.

Viceroy Merrill was saying something. Rod snapped out of his reverie and strained to listen in the confused babble of sounds.

"I said, I really don't see the point to all this, Captain. Could have had all this ceremony on the ground—except for your blessing, Your Reverence."

"Ships have left New Scotland without my attentions before," the Cardinal mused. "Not, perhaps, on a mission quite so perplexing to the Church as this one. Well, that will be young Hardy's problem now." He indicated the expedition chaplain. David Hardy was nearly twice Blaine's age, and his nominal equal in rank, so that the Cardinal's reference had to be relative.

"Well, are we ready?"

"Yes, Your Eminence." Blaine nodded to Kelley.

"SHIP'S COMPANY, ATTEN—SHUT!" The babble stilled, trailing off rather than being cut off as it would if there weren't civilians aboard.

The Cardinal took a thin stole from his pocket, kissed the hem, and placed it over his neck. Chaplain Hardy handed him the silver pail and asperger, a wand with a hollow ball at the end. Cardinal Randolph dipped the wand in the pail and shook water toward the assembled officers and crew. "Thou shalt purge me, and I shall be clean. Thou shalt wash me and I shall be whiter than snow. Glory be to the Father, the Son, and the Holy Ghost."

"As it was in the beginning, is now and ever shall be, worlds without end, amen." Rod found himself responding automatically. Did he believe in all that? Or was it only good for discipline? He couldn't decide, but he was glad the Cardinal had come. *MacArthur* might need all the benefits she could get . . .

The official party boarded an atmosphere flyer as warning horns sounded. *MacArthur*'s crew scrambled to leave hangar deck, and Rod stepped into an air-lock chamber. Pumps whined to empty the hangar space of air, then the great double doors opened. Meanwhile, *MacArthur* lost her spin as the central flywheels whirred. With only naval people aboard, an atmosphere craft might be launched through the doors under spin, dropping in the curved—relative to *MacArthur*—trajectory induced by the Coriolis effect, but with the Viceroy and the Cardinal lifting out that was out of the question. The landing craft lifted gently at 150 cm/sec until it was clear of the hangar doors.

"Close and seal," Rod ordered crisply. "Stand by for acceleration." He turned and launched himself in null gravity toward his bridge. Behind him telescoping braces opened across the hangar deck space—guy wires and struts, braces of all kinds—until the hollow was partly filled. The design of a warship's hangar space is an intricate specialty, since spotting boats may have to be launched at a moment's notice, yet the vast empty space needs to be braced against possible disaster. Now with the extra boats of Horvath's scientists in addition to the full complement of *MacArthur*'s own, hangar deck was a maze of ships, braces, and crates.

The rest of the ship was as crowded. In place of the usual orderly activity brought on by acceleration warning, *MacArthur*'s corridors were boiling with personnel. Some of the scientists were half in battle armor, having confused acceleration warning with battle stations. Others stood in critical passageways blocking traffic and unable to decide where to go. Petty officers screamed at them, unable to curse the civilians and also unable to do anything else.

Rod finally arrived at the bridge, while behind him officers and boatswains shamefacedly worked to clear the passageways and report ready for acceleration. Privately Blaine couldn't blame his crew for being unable to control the scientists, but he could hardly ignore the situation. Moreover, if he excused his staff, they would have no control over the civilians. He couldn't really threaten a Science Minister and his people with anything; but if he were hard enough on his *own* crew, the scientists might cooperate in order to spare the spacers . . . It was a theory worth trying, he thought. As he glanced at a tv monitor showing two Marines and four civilian lab technicians in a tangle against the after messroom bulkhead, Rod silently cursed and hoped it would work. Something had to.

"Signal from flag, sir. Keep station on *Redpines*."

"Acknowledge, Mr. Potter. Mr. Renner, take the con and follow the number-three tanker."

"Aye aye, sir." Renner grinned. "And so we're off. Pity the regulations don't provide for champagne at a time like this."

"I'd think you'd have your hands full, Mr. Renner. Admiral Kutuzov insists we keep what he calls a proper formation."

"Yes, sir. I discussed that with *Lenin*'s Sailing Master last night."

"Oh." Rod settled back in his command chair. It would be a difficult trip, he thought. All those scientists aboard. Dr. Horvath had insisted on coming himself, and he was going to be a problem. The ship was so swarming with civilians that most of *MacArthur*'s officers were doubled up in cabins already too small; junior lieutenants slung hammocks in the gun room with midshipmen; Marines were packed into recreation quarters so that their barracks rooms could be stuffed with scientific gear. Rod was beginning to wish that Horvath had won his argument with Cranston. The scientist had wanted to take an assault carrier with its enormous bunk spaces.

The Admiralty had put a stop to that. The expedition would consist of ships able to defend themselves and those only. The tankers would accompany the fleet to Murcheson's Eye, but they weren't coming to the Mote.

In deference to the civilians, the trip was at 1.2 gee. Rod suffered through innumerable dinner parties, mediated arguments between scientists and crew, and fended off attempts by Dr. Buckman the astrophysicist to monopolize Sally's time.

First Jump was routine. The transfer point to Murcheson's Eye was well located. New Caledonia was a magnificent white point source in the moment before *MacArthur* Jumped. Then Murcheson's Eye was a wide red glare the size of a baseball held at arm's length.

The fleet moved inward.

Gavin Potter had traded hammocks with Horst Staley. It had cost him a week's labor doing two men's laundry, but it had been worth it. Staley's hammock had a view port.

Naturally the port was beneath the hammock, in the cylindrical spin floor of the gun room. Potter lay face down in the hammock to look through the webbing, a gentle smile on his long face.

Whitbread was face up in his own hammock directly across the spin floor from Potter. He had been watching Potter for several minutes before he spoke.

"Mr. Potter."

The New Scot turned only his head. "Yes, Mr. Whitbread?"

Whitbread continued to watch him, contemplatively, with his arms folded behind his head. He was quite aware that Potter's infatuation with Murcheson's Eye was none of his damned business. Incomprehensible, Potter remained polite. How much needling would he take?

Entertaining things were happening aboard *MacArthur*, but there was no way for midshipmen to get to them. An off-duty middie must make his own entertainment.

"Potter, I seem to remember you were transferred aboard *Old Mac* on Dagda, just before we went to pick up the probe." Whitbread's voice was a carrying one. Horst Staley, who was also off duty, turned over in what had been Potter's bunk and gave them his attention. Whitbread noticed without seeming to.

Potter turned and blinked. "Yes, Mr. Whitbread. That's right."

"Well, *somebody* has to tell you, and I don't suppose anyone else has thought of it. Your first shipboard mission involved diving right into an F8 sun. I hope it hasn't given you a bad impression of the Service."

"Not at all. I found it exciting," Potter said courteously.

"The point is, diving straight into a sun is a rare thing in the Service. It doesn't happen every trip. I thought someone ought to tell you."

"But, Mr. Whitbread, are we no about to do exactly that?"

"Hah?" Whitbread hadn't expected that.

"No ship of the First Empire ever found a transfer point from Murcheson's Eye to the Mote. They may no have wanted it badly, but we can assume they tried somewhat," Potter said seriously. "Now, I have had verra little experience in space, but I am not uneducated, Mr. Whitbread. Murcheson's Eye is a red supergiant, a big, empty star, as big as the orbit of Saturn in Sol System. It seems reasonable that the Alderson Point to the Mote is within yon star if it exists. Does it not?"

Horst Staley rose up on an elbow. "I think he's right. It would explain why nobody ever plotted the transfer point. They all knew where it was—"

"But nobody wanted to go look. Yes, of *course* he's right," Whitbread said in disgust. "And that's just where we're going. Whee! Here we go again."

"Exactly," said Potter; and smiling gently, he turned on his face again.

"It's most unusual," Whitbread protested. "Doubt me if you must, but I assure you we don't go diving into stars more than two out of three trips." He paused. "And even that's too many."

The fleet slowed to a halt at the fuzzy edge of Murcheson's Eye. There was no question of orbits. At this distance the supergiant's gravity was so feeble that it would have taken years for a ship to fall into it.

The tankers linked up and began to transfer fuel.

An odd, tenuous friendship had grown between Horace Bury and Buckman, the astrophysicist. Bury had sometimes wondered about it. What did Buckman want with Bury?

Buckman was a lean, knobby, bird-boned man. From the look of him he sometimes forgot to eat for days at a time. Buckman seemed to care for nobody and nothing in what Bury considered the real universe. People, time, power, money, were only the means Buckman used to explore the inner workings of the stars. Why would he seek the company of a merchant?

But Buckman liked to talk, and Bury at least had the time to listen. *MacArthur* was a beehive these days, frantically busy and crowded as hell. And there was room to pace in Bury's cabin.

Or, Bury speculated cynically, he might like Bury's coffee. Bury had almost a dozen varieties of coffee beans, his own grinder, and filter cones to make it. He was quite aware of how his coffee compared with that in the huge percolators about the ship.

Nabil served them coffee while they watched the fuel transfer on Bury's screen. The tanker fueling *MacArthur* was hidden, but *Lenin* and the other tanker showed as two space-black elongated eggs, linked by a silver umbilicus, silhouetted against a backdrop of fuzzy scarlet.

"It should not be that dangerous," said Dr. Buckman. "You're thinking of it as a descent into a sun, Bury. Which it is, technically. But that whole vast volume isn't all that much more massive than Cal or any other yellow dwarf. Think of it as a red-hot vacuum. Except for the core, of course; *that's* probably tiny and very dense.

"We'll learn a great deal going in," he said. His eyes were alight, focused on infinity. Bury, watching him sidewise, found the expression fascinating. He had seen it before, but rarely. It marked men who could not be bought in any coin available to Horace Bury.

Bury had no more practical use for Buckman than Buckman had for Bury. Bury could relax with Buckman, as much as he could relax with anybody. He liked the feeling.

He said, "I thought you would already know everything about the Eye."

"You mean Murcheson's explorations? Too many records have been lost, and some of the others aren't trustworthy. I've had my instruments going since the Jump. Bury, the proportion of heavy particles in the solar wind is amazingly high. And helium—tremendous. But Murcheson's ships never went into the Eye itself, as far as we know. That's when we'll *really* learn things." Buckman frowned. "I hope our instruments can stand up to it. They have to poke through the Langston Field, of course. We're likely to be down in that red-hot fog for some considerable time, Bury. If the Field collapses it'll ruin everything."

Bury stared, then laughed. "Yes, Doctor, it certainly would!"

Buckman looked puzzled. Then, "Ah. I see what you

mean. It would kill us too, wouldn't it? I hadn't thought of that."

Acceleration warnings sounded. *MacArthur* was moving into the Eye.

Sinclair's thick burr sounded in Rod's ear. "Engineering report, Captain. All systems green. Field holding verra well, 'tis nae so warm as we feared."

"Good," Blaine replied. "Thanks, Sandy." Rod watched the tankers receding against the stars. Already they were thousands of kilometers away, visible only through the telescopes as bright as points of light.

The next screen showed a white splotch within a red fog: *Lenin* leading into the universal red glare. *Lenin's* crew would search for the Alderson point—if there were such a point.

"Still, 'tis certain the Field will leak inward sooner or later," Sinclair's voice continued. "There's no place for the heat to go, it must be stored. 'Tis no like a space battle, Captain. But we can hold wi' no place to radiate the accumulated energy for at least seventy-two hours. After that—we hae no data. No one has tried this loony stunt before."

"Yes."

"Somebody should have," Renner said cheerfully. He had been listening from his post on the bridge. *MacArthur* was holding at one gee, but it took attention: the thin photosphere was presenting more resistance than expected. "You'd think Murcheson would have tried it. The First Empire had better ships than ours."

"Maybe he did," Rod said absently. He watched *Lenin* move away, breaking trail for *MacArthur,* and felt an unreasonable irritation. *MacArthur* should have gone first . . .

The senior officers slept at their duty stations. There wasn't much anyone could do if the Field soaked up too much energy, but Rod felt better in his command seat. Finally it was obvious that he wasn't needed.

A signal came from *Lenin* and *MacArthur* cut her engines. Warning horns sounded, and she came under spin until other hoots signaled the end of unpleasant changes in gravity. Crew and passengers climbed out of safety rigging.

"Dismiss the watch below," Rod ordered.

Renner stood and stretched elaborately. "That's that, Captain. Of course we'll have to slow down as the photosphere gets thicker, but that's all right. The friction slows us down anyway." He looked at his screens and asked questions with swiftly moving fingers. "It's not as thick as, say, an atmosphere out there, but it's a lot thicker than a solar wind."

Blaine could see that for himself. *Lenin* was still ahead, at the outer limit of detection, and her engines were off. She was a black splinter in the screens, her outlines blurred by four thousand kilometers of red-hot fog.

The Eye thickened around them.

Rod stayed on the bridge another hour, then persuaded himself that he was being unfair. "Mr. Renner."

"Yes, sir?"

"You can go off watch now. Let Mr. Crawford take her."

"Aye aye, sir." Renner headed for his cabin. He'd reached the conclusion that he wasn't needed on the bridge fifty-eight minutes before. Now for a hot shower, and some sleep in his bunk instead of the conning chair . . .

The companionway to his cabin was jammed, as usual. Kevin Renner was pushing his way through with single-minded determination when someone lurched hard against him.

"Dammit! Excuse me," he snarled. He watched the miscreant regain his feet by hanging onto the lapels of Renner's uniform. "Dr. Horvath, isn't it?"

"My apologies." The Science Minister stepped back and brushed at himself ineffectually. "I haven't gotten used to spin gravity yet. None of us have. It's the Coriolis effect that throws us off."

"No. It's the elbows," Renner said. He regained his habitual grin. "There are six times as many elbows as people aboard this ship, Doctor. I've been counting."

"Very funny, Mr.—Renner, isn't it? Sailing Master Renner. Renner, this crowding bothers my personnel as much as yours. If we could stay out of your way, we would. But we can't. The data on the Eye have to be collected. We may never have such a chance again."

"I know, Doctor, and I sympathize. Now if you'll—" Visions of hot water and clean bedding receded as Horvath clutched at his lapels again.

"Just a moment, please." Horvath seemed to be making up his mind about something. "Mr. Renner, you were aboard *MacArthur* when she captured the alien probe, weren't you?"

"Hoo Boy, I sure was."

"I'd like to talk to you."

"Now? But, Doctor, the ship may need my attention at any moment—"

"I consider it urgent."

"But we're cruising through the photosphere of a star, as you may have noticed." *And I haven't had a hot shower in three days, as you may also have noticed* . . . Renner took a second look at Horvath's expression and gave up. "All right, Doctor. Only let's get out of the passageway."

Horvath's cabin was as cramped as anything on board, except that it had walls. More than half of *MacArthur*'s crew would have considered those walls an undeserved luxury. Horvath apparently did not, from the look of disgust and the muttered apologies as they entered the cabin.

He lifted the bunk into the bulkhead and dropped two chairs from the opposite wall. "Sit down, Renner. There are things about that interception that have been bothering me. I hope I can get an unbiased view from you. You're not a regular Navy man."

The Sailing Master did not bother to deny it. He had been mate on a merchant ship before, and would skipper one when he left the Navy with his increased experience; and he could hardly wait to return to the merchant service.

"So," said Horvath, and sat down on the very edge of

the foldout chair. "Renner, was it absolutely necessary to attack the probe?"

Renner started to laugh.

Horvath took it, though he looked as if he had eaten a bad oyster.

"All right," said Renner. "I shouldn't have laughed. You weren't there. Did you know the probe was diving into Cal for maximum deceleration?"

"Certainly, and I appreciate that you were too. But was it really that dangerous?"

"Dr. Horvath, the Captain surprised me twice. Utterly. When the probe attacked, I was trying to take us around the edge of the sail before we were cooked. Maybe I'd have got us away in time and maybe not. But the Captain took us *through* the sail. It was brilliant, it was something *I* should have thought of, and I happen to think the man's a genius. He's also a suicidal maniac."

"What?"

On Renner's face was retrospective dread. "He should *never* have tried to pick up the probe. We'd lost too much time. We were about to ram a star. I wouldn't have *believed* we could pick up the damned thing so fast . . ."

"Blaine did that himself?"

"No. He gave the job to Cargill. Who's better at tight high-grav maneuvers than anybody else aboard. That's the point, Doctor. The Captain picked the best man for the job and got out of the way."

"And you would have run for it?"

"Forthrightly and without embarrassment."

"But he picked it up. Well." Horvath seemed to taste something bad. "But he also fired on it. The first—"

"It shot first."

"That was a meteor defense!"

"So what?"

Horvath clamped his lips.

"All right, Doctor, try this. Suppose you left your car on a hill with the brakes off and the wheels turned the wrong way, and suppose it rolled down the hill and killed four people. What's your ethical position?"

"Terrible. Make your point, Renner."

"The Moties are at least as intelligent as we are. Granted? OK. They built a meteor defense. They had an obligation to see to it that it did not fire on neutral space craft."

Horvath sat there for what seemed a long time, while Kevin Renner thought about the limited capacity of the hot-water tanks in officers' country. That bad-taste expression was natural to Horvath, Renner saw; the lines in his face fell into it naturally and readily. Finally the Science Minister said, "Thank you, Mr. Renner."

"You're welcome." Renner stood.

An alarm sounded.

"Oh, Lord. That's me." Renner dashed for the bridge.

They were deep within the Eye: deep enough that the thin starstuff around them showed yellow. The Field indicators showed yellow too, but with a tinge of green.

All this Renner saw as he glanced around at half a dozen screens on the bridge. He looked at the plots on his own screens; and he did not see the battleship. *"Lenin's* Jumped?"

"Right," Midshipman Whitbread said. "We're next, sir." The red-haired middie's grin seemed to meet at the back of his head.

Blaine sailed into the bridge without touching the companionway sides. "Take the con, Mr. Renner. The pilot ought to be at your station now."

"Aye aye, sir." Renner turned to Whitbread. "I relieve you." His fingers danced across the input keys, then he hit a line of buttons even as the new data flowed onto his screen. Alarms went off in rapid succession: JUMP STATIONS, BATTLE STATIONS, HEAVY ACCELERATION WARNING. *MacArthur* prepared herself for the unknown.

PART TWO

THE CRAZY EDDIE POINT

---

13 • *Look Around You*

She was the first to find the intruders.

She had been exploring a shapeless mass of stony asteroid that turned out to be mostly empty space. Some earlier culture had carved out rooms and nooks and tankages and storage chambers, then fused the detritus into more rooms and chambers, until the mass was a stone beehive. It had all happened very long ago, but that was of no interest to her.

In later ages meteoroids had made dozens of holes through the construct. Thick walls had been gradually thinned so that air might be chemically extracted from the stone. There was no air now. There was no metal anywhere. Dry mummies, and stone, stone, little else and nothing at all for an Engineer.

She left via a meteoroid puncture; for all the air locks had been fused shut by vacuum welding. A long time after that someone had removed their metal working parts.

After she was outside, she saw them, very far away, a tiny glimmer of golden light against the Coal Sack. It was worth a look. Anything was worth a look.

The Engineer returned to her ship.

Telescope and spectrometer failed her at first. There were two of the golden slivers, and some bulk inside each of them, but something was shutting out her view of the masses inside. Patiently the Engineer went to work on her instruments, redesigning, recalibrating, rebuilding, her hands working at blinding speed guided by a thousand Cycles of instincts.

There were force fields to be penetrated. Presently she had something that would do that. Not well, but she could see large objects.

She looked again.

Metal. Endless, endless metal.

She took off immediately. The call of treasure was not to be ignored. There was little of free will in an Engineer.

Blaine watched a flurry of activity through a red fog as he fought to regain control of his traitor body after return to normal space. An all-clear signal flashed from *Lenin,* and Rod breathed more easily. Nothing threatened, and he could enjoy the view.

It was the Eye he saw first. Murcheson's Eye was a tremendous ruby, brighter than a hundred full moons, all alone on the black velvet of the Coal Sack.

On the other side of the sky, the Mote was the brightest of a sea of stars. All systems looked this way at breakout: a lot of stars, and one distant sun. To starboard was a splinter of light, *Lenin,* her Langston Field radiating the overload picked up in the Eye.

Admiral Kutuzov made one final check and signaled Blaine again. Until something threatened, the scientists aboard *MacArthur* were in charge. Rod ordered coffee and waited for information.

At first there was maddeningly little that he hadn't already known. The Mote was only thirty-five light years from New Scotland, and there had been a number of observations, some dating back to Jasper Murcheson himself. A G2 star, less energetic than Sol, cooler, smaller and a bit less massive. It showed almost no sunspot activity at the moment, and the astrophysicists found it dull.

Rod had known about the gas giant before they started. Early astronomers had deduced it from perturbations in the Mote's orbit around the Eye. They knew the gas giant planet's mass and they found it almost where they expected, seventy degrees around from them. Heavier than Jupiter, but smaller, much denser, with a degenerate matter core. While the scientists worked, the Navy men plotted courses to the gas giant, in case one or the other warship should need to refuel. Scooping up hydrogen by ramming through a gas giant's atmosphere on a hyperbolic orbit was hard on ships and crew but a lot better than being stranded in an alien system.

"We're searching out the Trojan points now, Captain," Buckman told Rod two hours after breakout.

"Any sign of the Mote planet?"

"Not yet." Buckman hung up.

Why was Buckman concerned with Trojan points? Sixty degrees ahead of the giant planet in its orbit, and sixty degrees behind, would be two points of stable equilibrium, called Trojan points after the Trojan asteroids that occupy similar points in Jupiter's orbit. Over millions of years they ought to have collected dust clouds and clusters of asteroids. But why would Buckman bother with these?

Buckman called again when he found the Trojans. "They're packed!" Buckman gloated. "Either this whole system is cluttered with asteroids from edge to edge or there's a new principle at work. There's more junk in Mote Beta's Trojans than has ever been reported in another system. It's a wonder they haven't all collected to form a pair of moons—"

"Have you found the habitable planet yet?"

"Not yet," said Buckman, and faded off the screen. That was three hours after breakout.

He called back half an hour later. "Those Trojan point asteroids have *very* high albedos, Captain. They must be thick with dust. That might explain how so many of the larger particles were captured. The dust clouds slow them down, then polish them smooth—"

"Dr. Buckman! There is an inhabited world in this system and it is vital that we find it. These are the first intelligent aliens—"

"Dammit, Captain, we're looking! We're looking!" Buckman glanced to one side, then withdrew. The screen was blank for a moment, showing only a badly focused shot of a technician in the background.

Blaine found himself confronting Science Minister Horvath, who said, "Please excuse the interruption, Captain. Do I understand you are not satisfied with our search methods?"

"Dr. Horvath, I have no wish to intrude on your prerogatives. But you've taken over all my instruments, and I keep hearing about asteroids. I wonder if we're all looking for the same thing?"

Horvath's reply was mild. "This is not a space battle, Captain." He paused. "In a war operation, you would know your target. You would probably know the ephemeris of the planets in any system of interest—"

"Hell, survey teams find planets."

"Ever been on one, Captain?"

"No."

"Well, think about the problem we face. Until we located the gas giant and the Trojan asteroids we weren't precise about the plane of the system. From the probe's instruments we have deduced the temperature the Moties find comfortable, and from *that* we deduce how far from their sun their planet should be—and we still must search out a toroid a hundred and twenty million kilometers in radius. Do you follow me?"

Blaine nodded.

"We're going to have to search that entire region. We know the planet isn't hidden behind the sun because we're above the plane of the system. But when we finish photographing the system we have to examine this enormous star field for the one dot of light we want."

"Perhaps I was expecting too much."

"Perhaps. We're all waiting as fast as we can." He smiled—a spasm that lifted his whole face for a split second—and vanished.

Six hours after breakout Horvath reported again. There was no sign of Buckman. "No, Captain, we haven't found the inhabited planet. But Dr. Buckman's time-wasting observations have identified a Motie civilization. In the Trojan points."

"They're inhabited?"

"Definitely. Both Trojan points are seething with microwave frequencies. We should have guessed from the high albedos of the larger bodies. Polished surfaces are a natural product of civilization—I'm afraid Dr. Buckman's people think too much in terms of a dead universe."

"Thank you, Doctor. Is any of that message traffic for us?"

"I don't think so, Captain. But the nearest Trojan point is below us in this system's plane—about three million kilometers away. I suggest we go there. From the apparent density of civilization in the Trojan points it may be that the inhabited planet is not the real nexus of Motie civilization. Perhaps it is like Earth. Or worse."

Rod was shocked. He had found Earth herself shocking, not all that many years ago. New Annapolis was kept on Manhome so that Imperial officers would know just how vital was the great task of the Empire.

And if men had not had the Alderson Drive before Earth's last battles, and the nearest star had been thirty-five light years away instead of four— "That's a horrible thought."

"I agree. It's also only a guess, Captain. But in any event there is a viable civilization nearby, and I think we should go to it."

"I—just a moment." Chief Yeoman Lud Shattuck was at the bridge companionway gesturing frantically at Rod's number-four screen.

"We used the message-sending locator scopes, Skipper," Shattuck shouted across the bridge. "Look, sir."

The screen showed black space with pinhole dots of stars and a blue-green point circled by an indicator lighting-ring. As Rod watched, the point blinked, twice.

"We've found the inhabited planet," Rod said with satisfaction. He couldn't resist. "We beat you to it, Doctor."

After all the waiting, it was as if everything broke at once.

The light was first. There might have been an Earthlike

world behind it; there probably was, for it was in the doughnut locus Horvath was searching. But the light hid whatever was behind it, and it wasn't surprising that the communications people had found it first. Watching for signals was their job.

Cargill and Horvath's team worked together to answer the pulses. *One, two, three, four* blinked the light, and Cargill used the forward batteries to send *five, six, seven.* Twenty minutes later the light sent *three one eight four eleven,* repeated, and the ship's brain ground out: *Pi,* base twelve. Cargill used the computer to find *e* to the same base and replied with that.

But the true message was, *We want to talk to you.* And *MacArthur's* answer was, *Fine.* Elaborations would have to wait.

And the second development was already in.

"Fusion light," said Sailing Master Renner. He bent close over his screen. His fingers played strange, silent music on his control board. "No Langston Field. Naturally. They're just enclosing the hydrogen, fusing it and blasting it out. A plasma bottle. It's not as hot as our drives, which means lower efficiency. Red shift, if I'm reading the impurities right . . . it must be aimed away from us."

"You think it's a ship coming to meet us?"

"Yessir. A small one. Give us a few minutes and I'll tell you its acceleration. Meanwhile, we assume an acceleration of one gee . . ." Renner's fingers had been tapping all the while ". . . and get a mass of thirty tons. Later we'll readjust that."

"Too big to be a missile," Blaine said thoughtfully. "Should we meet him halfway, Mr. Renner?"

Renner frowned. "There's a problem. He's aiming at where we are now. We don't know how much fuel he's got, or how bright he is."

"Let's ask, anyway. Eyes! Get me Admiral Kutuzov."

The Admiral was on his bridge. Blurs out of focus behind him showed activity aboard *Lenin.* "I've seen it, Captain," Kutuzov said. "What do you want to do about it?"

"I want to go meet that ship. But in case it can't change

course or we can't catch it, it will come here, sir. *Lenin* could wait for it."

"And do what, Captain? My instructions are clear. *Lenin* is to have nothing to do with aliens."

"But you could send out a boat, sir. A gig, which we'll pick up with your men. Sir."

"How many boats do you think I have, Blaine? Let me repeat my instructions. *Lenin* is here to protect secret of Alderson Drive and Langston Field. To accomplish task we will not only not communicate with aliens, we will not communicate with you when message might be intercepted."

"Yes, sir." Blaine stared at the burly man on the screen. Didn't he have a shred of curiosity? Nobody could be that much of a machine . . . or could he? "We'll go to the alien ship, sir. Dr. Horvath wants to anyway."

"Very good, Captain. Carry on."

"Yes, sir." Rod cut off the screen with relief, then turned to Renner. "Let's go make first contact with an alien, Mr. Renner."

"I think you just did that," said Renner. He glanced nervously at the screens to be sure the Admiral was gone.

Horace Bury was just leaving his cabin—on the theory that he might be less bored somewhere else—when Buckman's head popped out of a companionway.

Bury changed his mind at once. "Dr. Buckman! May I offer you coffee?"

Protuberant eyes turned, blinked, focused. "What? Oh. Yes, thank you, Bury. It might wake me. There's been so much to do—I can only stay a moment—"

Buckman dropped into Bury's guest chair, limp as a physician's display skeleton. His eyes were red; his eyelids drooped at half-mast. His breathing was too loud. The stringy muscle tissue along his bare arm drooped. Bury wondered what an autopsy would show if Buckman were to die at this moment: exhaustion, malnutrition, or both?

Bury made a difficult decision. "Nabil, some coffee. With cream, sugar, and brandy for Dr. Buckman."

"Now, Bury, I'm afraid that during working hours—

Oh, well. Thank you, Nabil." Buckman sipped, then gulped. "Ah! That's good. Thank you, Bury, that ought to wake me."

"You seemed to need it. Normally I would never adulterate good coffee with distilled spirits. Dr. Buckman, have you been eating?"

"I don't remember."

"You haven't. Nabil, food for our guest. Quickly."

"Bury, we're so busy, I really haven't time. There's a whole solar system to explore, not to mention the jobs for the Navy—tracing neutrino emissions, tracking that damned light—"

"Doctor, if you were to die at this moment, many of yours notes would never be written down, would they?"

Buckman smiled. "So theatrical, Bury. But I suppose I can spare a few minutes. All we're doing now is waiting for that signal light to go off."

"A signal from the Mote planet?"

"From Mote Prime, yes, at least it came from the right place. But we can't see the planet until they turn off the laser, and they *won't*. They talk and talk, and for what? What can they tell us if we don't speak a common language?"

"After all, Doctor, how can they tell us *anything* until they teach us their language? I presume that's what they're trying to do now. Isn't anyone working on that?"

Buckman gave a feral snarl. "Horvath has all the instruments feeding information to Hardy and the linguists. Can't get any decent observations of the Coal Sack—and no one's ever been this close to it before!" His look softened. "But we can study the Trojan asteroids."

Buckman's eye took on *that* look, the focus on infinity. "There' are too many of them. And not enough dust. I was wrong, Bury; there's not enough dust to capture so many rocks, or to polish them either. The Moties probably did the polishing, they must be all *through* those rocks, the neutrino emissions are *fantastic*. But how did so many *rocks* get captured?"

"Neutrino emissions. That means a fusion technology."

Buckman smiled. "One of a high order. Thinking of trade possibilities?"

"Of course. Why else would I be here?" And I would be here even if the Navy had not made it clear that the alternative was a formal arrest . . . but Buckman wouldn't know that. Only Blaine did. "The higher their civilization, the more they'll have to trade." And the harder they'd be to cheat; but Buckman wouldn't be interested in such things.

Buckman complained, "We could move so much faster if the Navy didn't use our telescopes. And Horvath lets them! Ah, good." Nabil entered, pushing a tray.

Buckman ate like a starved rat. Between mouthfuls he said, "Not that all the Navy's projects are totally without interest. The alien ship—"

"Ship?"

"There's a ship coming to meet us. Didn't you know?"

"No."

"Well, its point of departure is a large, stony asteroid well outside the main cluster. The point is, it's very light. It must have a very odd shape, unless there are gas bubbles all through the rock, which would mean—"

Bury laughed outright. "Doctor, surely an alien space craft is more interesting than a stony meteorite!"

Buckman looked startled. "Why?"

The slivers turned red, then black. Clearly the things were cooling; but how had they become hot in the first place?

The Engineer had stopped wondering about that when one of the slivers came toward her. There were power sources inside the metal bulks.

And they were self-motivated. What were they? Engineers, or Masters, or senseless machinery? A Mediator on some incomprehensible task? She resented the Mediators, who could so easily and so unreasonably interfere with important work.

Perhaps the slivers were Watchmakers; but more likely they contained a Master. The Engineer considered running, but the approaching bulk was too powerful. It ac-

celerated at 1.14 gravities, nearly the limit of her ship. There was nothing for an Engineer to do but meet it.

Besides . . . all that metal! In useful form, as far as she could tell. The Clusters were full of metal artifacts, but in alloys too tough to convert.

All that metal.

But it must meet her, not the other way around. She had not the fuel or the acceleration. She worked out turnover points in her head. The other would do the same, of course. Luckily the solution was unique, assuming constant acceleration. There would be no need for communication.

Engineers were not good at communication.

14 • *The Engineer*

The alien ship was a compact bulk, irregular of shape and dull gray in color, like modeling clay molded in cupped hands. Extrusions sprouted at seeming random: a ring of hooks around what Whitbread took for the aft end; a thread of bright silver girdling its waist; transparent bulges fore and aft; antennae in highly imaginative curves; and dead aft, a kind of stinger: a spine many times the length of the hull, very long and straight and narrow.

Whitbread coasted slowly inward. He rode a space-to-space taxi, the cabin a polarized plastic bubble, the short hull studded with "thruster clusters"—arrays of attitude jets. Whitbread had trained for space in such a vehicle. Its field of view was enormous; it was childishly easy to steer; it was cheap, weaponless, and expendable.

And the alien could see him inside. *We come in peace, with nothing hidden*—assuming its alien eyes could see through clear battle plastic.

"That spine generates the plasma fields for the drive," his communicator was saying. There was no screen, but the voice was Cargill's. "We watched it during deceleration. That spiggot device beneath the spine probably feeds hydrogen into the fields."

"I'd better stay out of its way," said Mr. Whitbread.

"Right. The field intensity would probably wreck your instruments. It might affect your nervous systems too."

The alien ship was very close now. Whitbread fired bursts to slow himself. The attitude jets sounded like popcorn popping.

"See any signs of an air lock?"

"No, sir."

"Open your own air lock. Maybe that will get the idea across."

"Aye aye, sir." Whitbread could see the alien through the forward bubble. It was motionless, watching him, and it looked very like the photographs he had seen of the dead one in the probe. Jonathon Whitbread saw a neckless, lopsided head, smooth brown fur, a heavy left arm gripping something, two slender right arms moving frantically fast, doing things out of his field of vision.

Whitbread opened his air lock. And waited.

At least the Motie hadn't started shooting yet.

The Engineer was captivated. She hardly noticed the tiny vehicle nearby. There were no new principles embodied there. But the big ship!

It had a strange field around it, something the Engineer had never believed possible. It registered on half a dozen of the Engineer's instruments. To others the force envelope was partly transparent. The Engineer knew enough about the warship already to scare the wits out of Captain Blaine if he'd known. But it was not enough to satisfy an Engineer.

All that gadgetry! And metal!

The small vehicle's curved door was opening and closing now. It flashed lights on and off. Patterns of electromagnetic force radiated from both vehicles. The signals meant nothing to an Engineer.

It was the ship's gadetry that held her attention. The Field itself, its properties intriguing and puzzling, its underlying principles a matter of guesswork. The Engineer was

*ready to spend the rest of her life trying. For one look at
the generator she would have died. The big ship's motive
force was different from any fusion plant the Engineer had
ever heard of; and its workings seemed to use the properties of that mysterious force envelope.*

How to get aboard? How to get through that envelope?

*The intuition that came was rare for an Engineer. The
small craft . . . was it trying to talk to her? It had come
from the large craft. Then . . .*

*The small craft was a link to the larger ship, to the force
envelope and its technology and the mystery of its sudden
appearance.*

*She had forgotten danger. She had forgotten everything
in the burning urge to know more about that field. The
Engineer opened her air-lock door and waited to see what
would happen.*

"Mister Whitbread, your alien is trying to use probes on
MacArthur," Captain Blaine was saying, "Commander
Cargill says he has them blocked. If that makes the alien
suspicious, it can't be helped. Has he tried any kind of
probe on you?"

"No, sir."

Rod frowned and rubbed the bridge of his nose. "You're
sure?"

"I've been watching the instruments, sir."

"That's funny. You're smaller, but you're close. You'd
think he—"

"The air lock!" Whitbread snapped. "Sir, the Motie's
opened his air lock."

"I see it. A mouth opened in the hull. Is that what you
mean?"

"Yessir. Nothing coming out. I can see the whole cabin
through that opening. The Motie's in his control cabin—
permission to enter, sir?"

"Hmm. OK. Watch yourself. Stay in communication.
And good luck, Whitbread."

Jonathon sat a moment, nerving himself. He had half
hoped the Captain would forbid it as too dangerous. But
of course midshipmen are expendable . . .

Whitbread braced himself in the open air lock. The alien ship was very close. With the entire ship watching him, he launched himself into space.

Part of the alien's hull had stretched like skin, to open into a kind of funnel. A strange way to build an air lock, thought Whitbread. He used backpack jets to slow himself as he drifted straight into the funnel, straight toward the Motie, who stood waiting to receive him.

The alien wore only its soft brown fur and four thick pads of black hair, one in each armpit and one at the groin. "No sign of what's holding the air in, but there's *got* to be air in there," Whitbread told the mike. A moment later he knew. He had run into invisible honey.

The air lock closed against his back.

He almost panicked. Caught like a fly in amber, no forward, no retreat. He was in a cell 130 cm high, the height of the alien. It stood before him on the other side of the invisible wall, blank-faced, looking him over.

The Motie. It was shorter than the other, the dead one in the probe. Its color was different: there were no white markings through the brown fur. There was another, subtler, more elusive difference . . . perhaps the difference between the quick and the dead, perhaps something else.

The Motie was not frightening. Its smooth fur was like one of the Doberman pinschers Whitbread's mother used to raise, but there was nothing vicious or powerful-looking about the alien. Whitbread would have liked to stroke its fur.

The face was no more than a sketch, without expression, except for a gentle upward curve of the lipless mouth, a sardonic half-smile. Small, flat-footed, smooth-furred, almost featureless— It looks like a cartoon, Whitbread thought. How could he be afraid of a cartoon?

But Jonathon Whitbread was crouched in a space much too small for him, and the alien was doing nothing about it.

The cabin was a crowded patchwork of panels and dark crevasses, and tiny faces peered at him from the shadows. Vermin! The ship was infested with vermin. Rats? Food supply? The Motie did not seem disturbed as one flashed into the open, then another, more dancing from cover to cover, crowding close to see the intruder.

They were *big* things. Much bigger than rats, much smaller than men. They peered from the corners, curious but timid. One dodged close and Whitbread got a good look. What he saw made him gasp. It was a tiny Motie!

It was a difficult time for the Engineer. The intruder's entry should have answered questions, but it only raised more.

What was it? Big, big-headed, symmetrical as an animal, but equipped with its own vehicle like an Engineer or a Master. There had never been a class like this. Would it obey or command? Could the hands be as clumsy as they looked? Mutation, monster, sport? What was it for?

Its mouth was moving now. It must be speaking into a communications device. That was no help. Even Messengers used language.

Engineers were not equipped to make such decisions; but one could always wait for more data.

Engineers had endless patience.

"There's air," Whitbread reported. He watched the tell-tales that showed in a mirror just above his eye level. "Did I mention that? I wouldn't want to try breathing it. Normal pressure, oxygen around 18 percent, CO_2 about 2 percent, enough helium to register, and—"

"Helium? That's odd. Just how much?"

Whitbread switched over to a more sensitive scale and waited for the analyzer to work. "Around 1 percent. Just under."

"Anything else?"

"Poisons. SO_2, carbon monoxide, nitrous oxides, ketones, alcohols, and some other stuff that doesn't read out with this suit. The light blinks yellow."

"Wouldn't kill you fast, then. You could breathe it a while and still get help in time to save your lungs."

"That's what I thought," Whitbread said uneasily. He began loosening the dogs holding down his faceplate.

"What does that mean, Whitbread?"

"Nothing, sir." Jonathon had been doubled over far too long. Every joint and muscle screamed for surcease. He had run out of things to describe in the alien cabin. And the thrice-damned Motie just *stood* there in its sandals and its faint smile, watching, watching . . .

"Whitbread?"

Whitbread took a deep breath and held it. He lifted the faceplate against slight pressure, looked the alien in the eye, and screamed all in one breath, *"Will* you for God's sake turn off that damned force field!" and snapped the faceplate down.

The alien turned to his control board and moved something. The soft barrier in front of Whitbread vanished.

Whitbread took two steps forward. He straightened up a half-inch at a time, feeling the pain and hearing the creaking of unused joints. He had been crouched in that cramped space for an hour and a half, examined by half a dozen twisted Brownies and one bland, patient alien. He hurt!

He had trapped cabin air under his faceplate. The stink caught at his throat, so that he stopped breathing; then self-consciously he sniffed at it in case anyone wanted to know what it was.

He smelled animals and machines, ozone, gasoline, hot oil, halitosis, old sweat socks burning, glue, and things he had never smelled before. It was unbelievably rich—and his suit was removing it, thank God.

He asked, "Did you hear me yell?"

"Yes, and so did everyone in this ship," said Cargill's voice. "I don't think there's a man aboard who isn't following you, unless it's Buckman. Any result?"

"He turned off the force field. Right away. He was just waiting for me to remind him.

"And I'm in the cabin now. I told you about the repairs? It's *all* repairs, all hand made, even the control panels. But it's all well done, nothing actually in the way, for a Motie, that is. Me, I'm too big. I don't dare move.

"The little ones have all disappeared. No, there's one peeping out of a corner. The big one is waiting to see what I do. I wish he'd stop that."

"See if he'll come back to the ship with you—"

"I'll try, sir."

The alien had understood him before, or seemed to, but it did not understand him now. Whitbread thought furiously. Sign language? His eye fell on something that *had* to be a Motie pressure suit.

He pulled it from its rack, noting its lightness: no weaponry, no armor. He handed it to the alien, then pointed to *MacArthur* beyond the bubble.

The alien began dressing at once. In literally seconds it was in full gear, in a suit that, inflated, looked like ten beach balls glued together. Only the gauntlets were more than simple inflated spheres.

It took a transparent plastic sack from the wall and reached suddenly to capture one of the ⅓-meter-high miniatures. He stuffed it into the sack headfirst while the miniature wriggled, then turned to Whitbread and rushed at the middle with lightning speed. It had reached behind Whitbread with two right hands and was already moving away when Whitbread reacted: a violent and involuntary *yip!*

"Whitbread? What's hapening? Answer me!" Another voice in the background of Whitbread's suit said crisply, "Marines, stand by."

"Nothing, Commander Cargill. It's all right. No attack, I mean. I think the alien's ready to go—no, it isn't. It's got two of the parasites in a plastic sack, and it's inflating the sack from an air spiggot. One of the little beasts was on my back. I never felt it.

"Now the alien's making something. I don't understand what's keeping it. It *knows* we want to go to *MacArthur*— it put on a pressure suit."

"What's it doing?"

"It's got the cover off the control panel. It's rewiring things. A moment ago it was squeezing silver toothpaste in a ribbon along the printed circuitry. I'm only telling you what it *looks* like, of course. YIPE!"

"Whitbread?"

The midshipman was caught in a hurricane. Arms and legs flailing, he snatched frantically for something, *any-*

thing solid. He was scraped along the side of the air lock, reached and found nothing to grasp. Then night and stars whirled past him.

"The Motie opened the air lock," he reported. "No warning. I'm outside, in space." His hands used attitude jets to stop his tumbling. "I think he let all the breathing air out. There's a great fog of ice crystals around me, and —Oh, Lord, it's the Motie! No, it isn't, it's not wearing a pressure suit. There goes another one."

"They must be the little ones," Cargill said.

"Right. He's killed all the parasites. He probably has to do it every so often, to clear them out. He doesn't know how long he'll be aboard *MacArthur* and he doesn't want them running wild. So he's evacuated the ship."

"He should have warned you."

"Damn right he should! Excuse me, sir."

"Are you all right, Whitbread?" A new voice. The Captain's.

"Yessir. I'm approaching the alien's ship. Ah, here he comes now. He's jumping for the taxi." Whitbread stopped his approach and turned to watch the Motie. The alien sailed through space like a cluster of beach balls, but graceful, graceful. Within a transparent balloon fixed to its torso, two small, spidery figures gestured wildly. The alien paid them no attention.

"A perfect jump," Whitbread muttered. "Unless—he's cutting it a bit fine. Jesus!" The alien was still decelerating as it flew through the taxi door, dead centered, so that it never touched the edges. "He must be awfully sure of his balance."

"Whitbread, is that alien inside your vehicle? Without you?"

Whitbread winced at the bite in the Captain's voice. "Yes, sir. I'm going after him."

"See you do, Mister."

The alien was at the pilot's station, studying the controls intensely. Suddenly it reached out and began to turn the quick fasteners at the panel's edge. Whitbread yelped and rushed up to grab the alien's shoulder. It paid no attention.

Whitbread put his helmet against the alien's. "Leave

that to hell alone!" he shouted. Then he gestured to the passenger's saddle. The alien rose slowly, turned, and straddled the saddle. It didn't fit there. Whitbread took the controls gratefully and began to maneuver the taxi toward *MacArthur*.

He brought the taxi to a stop just beyond the neat hole Sinclair had opened in *MacArthur*'s Field. The alien ship was out of sight around the bulk of the warship. Hangar deck was below, and the midshipman yearned to take the gig through under her own power, to demonstrate his ability to the watching alien, but he knew better. They waited.

Suited spacers came up from the hangar deck. Cables trailed behind them. The spacers waved. Whitbread waved back, and seconds later Sinclair started the winches to tug the gig down into *MacArthur*. As they passed the hangar doors more cables were made fast to the top side of the gig. These pulled taut, slowing the taxi, as the great hangar doors began to close.

The Motie was watching, its entire body swiveling from side to side, reminding Whitbread of an owl he had once seen in a zoo on Sparta. Amazingly, the tiny creatures in the alien's bag were also watching; they aped the larger alien. Finally they were at rest, and Whitbread gestured toward the air lock. Through the thick glass he could see Gunner Kelley and a dozen armed Marines.

There were twenty screens in a curved array in front of Rod Blaine, and consequently every scientist aboard *MacArthur* wanted to sit near him. As the only possible way to settle the squabbles, Rod ordered the ship to battle stations and the bridge cleared of all civilian personnel. Now he watched as Whitbread climbed aboard the gig.

Through the camera eye mounted on Whitbread's helmet Blaine could see the alien seated in the pilot's chair, its image seeming to grow as the middie rushed toward it. Blaine turned to Renner. "Did you see what it did?"

"Yah. Sir. The alien was— Captain, I'd swear it was trying to take the gig's controls apart."

"So would I." They watched in frustration as Whitbread

piloted the gig toward *MacArthur*. Blaine couldn't blame the boy for not looking around at his passenger while trying to steer the boat, but . . . best leave him alone. They waited while the cables were made fast to the gig and it was winched down into *MacArthur*.

"Captain!" It was Staley, midshipman of the watch, but Rod could see it too. Several screens and a couple of minor batteries were trained on the gig, but the heavy stuff was all aimed at the alien ship; and it had come to life.

A streamer of blue light glowed at the stern of the alien craft. The color of Cherenkov radiation, it flowed parallel to the slender silver spine at the tail. Suddenly there was a line of intense white light beside it.

"Yon ship's under way, Captain," Sinclair reported.

"God damn it to hell!" His own screens showed the same thing, also that the ship's batteries were tracking the alien craft.

"Permission to fire?" the gunnery officer asked.

"No!" But what was the thing up to? Rod wondered. Time enough when Whitbread got aboard, he supposed. The alien ship couldn't escape. And neither would the alien.

"Kelley!"

"Sir!"

"Squad to the air lock. Escort Whitbread and that thing to the reception room. Politely, Gunner. Politely, but make sure it doesn't go anywhere else."

"Aye aye, Captain."

"Number One?" Blaine called.

"Yes, sir," Cargill answered.

"You were monitoring Whitbread's helmet camera the entire time he was in that ship?"

"Yes, sir."

"Any chance there was another alien aboard?"

"No, sir. There wasn't room. Right, Sandy?"

"Aye, Captain," Sinclair answered. Blaine had activated a com circuit to both the after bridge and the engine room. "Not if that beastie were to carry fuel too. And we saw nae doors."

"There wasn't any air-lock door either, until it opened,"

Rod reminded him. "Was there anything that might have been a bathroom?"

"Captain, did we nae see the w.c.? I took the object on port side near the air lock to be such."

"Yeah. Then that thing's on autopilot, would you both agree? But we didn't see him program it."

"We saw him practically rebuild the controls, Captain," Cargill said. "My Lord! Do you think that's how they control . . ."

"Seems verra inefficient, but the beastie did nae else that could hae been the programming of an autopilot," Sinclair mused. "And 'twas bloody quick about it, sir. Captain, do ye think it *built* an autopilot?"

There was a glare on one of Rod's screens. "Catch that? A blue flare in the alien ship's air lock. Now what was that for?"

"To kill yon vermin?" Sinclair asked.

"Hardly. The vacuum would have done," Cargill answered.

Whitbread came onto the bridge and stood stiffly in front of Blaine's command chair. "Reporting to Captain, sir."

"Well done, Mr. Whitbread," Rod said. "Uh—have you any ideas about those two vermin he brought abroad? Such as why they're here?"

"No, sir—courtesy? We might want to dissect one?"

"Possibly. If we knew what they were. Now take a look at that." Blaine pointed at his screens.

The alien ship was turning, the white light of its drive drawing an arc on the sky. It seemed to be heading back to the Trojan points.

And Jonathon Whitbread was the only man alive who had ever been inside. As Blaine released the crew from action stations, the red-haired midshipman was probably thinking that the ordeal was over.

15 · Work

The Engineer's mouth was wide and lipless, turned up at the corners. It looked like a half-smile of gentle happiness, but it was not. It was a permanent fixture of her cartoon face.

Nonetheless, the Engineer was happy.

Her joy had grown and grown. Coming through the Langston Field had been a new experience, like penetrating a black bubble of retarded time. Even without instruments, that told her something about the Field. She was more eager than ever to see that generator.

The ship within the bubble seemed unnecessarily crude, and it was rich, rich! There were parts in the hangar deck that seemed unattached to anything else, mechanisms so plentiful that they didn't have to be used! And many things she could not understand at a glance.

Some would be structural adaptations to the Field, or to the mysterious drive that worked from the Field. Others must be genuinely new inventions to do familiar things, new circuits, at least new to an unsophisticated Engineer miner. She recognized weapons, weapons on the big ship, weapons on the boats in the hangar space, personal weapons carried by the aliens clustered around the other side of the air lock.

This did not surprise her. She had known this new class were givers of orders, not takers of orders. Naturally they would have weapons. They might even have Warriors.

The double-door air lock was too complex, too easy to jam, primitive, and wasteful of metals and materials. She was needed here, she could see that. The new class must have come here to get her, there couldn't be any Engineers aboard the ship if they used things like this. She started to take the mechanism apart, but the stranger pulled at her arm and she abandoned the idea. She didn't have the tools anyway, and she didn't know what it would be lawful

124

to use to make the tools. There would be time for all
that . . .

A lot of others, much like the first one, clustered around
her. They wore strange coverings, most of it alike, and
carried weapons, but they didn't give orders. The stranger
kept trying to talk to her.

Couldn't they see she wasn't a Mediator? They were not
too bright, this primitive new class. But they were givers of
orders. The first one had shouted a clear command.

And they couldn't speak Language.

The situation was remarkably free of decisions. An Engineer need only go where she was led, repair and redesign
where the opportunity arose, and wait for a Mediator. Or a
Master. And there was so much to do, so much to do . . .

The petty officers' lounge had been converted into a
reception room for alien visitors. The petty officers had to
take over one of the Marine messes, doubling the joeys
into the other. All over the ship adjustments had to be
made to accommodate the swarms of civilians and their
needs.

As a laboratory the lounge might lack something, but it
was secure, and had plenty of running water, wall plugs,
hot plates, and refreshment facilities. At least there was
nothing to smack of the dissection table.

After some argument it had been decided not to attempt
to build furniture to fit the aliens. Anything they built
would only accommodate the passenger aboard the probe,
and *that* seemed absurd.

There were plenty of tv pickups, so that although only a
few key personnel were allowed in the lounge, nearly
everyone aboard the ship could watch. Sally Fowler waited
with the scientists, and she was determined to win the
Motie's trust. She didn't care who was watching or what
it would take to do that.

As it turned out, the Motie's trust was easy to come by.
She was as trustful as a child. Her first move on coming
out of the air lock was to tear open the plastic sack containing the miniatures and give it to the first hand that
reached for it. She never bothered about them again.

She went where she was led, walking between the Marines until Sally took her by the hand at the reception room door, and everywhere she went she looked about, her body swiveling like an owl's head. When Sally let go, the Motie simply stood and waited for further instructions, watching everyone with that same gentle smile.

She did not seem to understand gestures. Sally and Horvath and others tried to talk to the Motie, with no result. Dr. Hardy, the Chaplain linguist, drew mathematical diagrams and nothing happened. The Motie did not understand and was not interested.

She was interested in tools, though. As soon as she was inside she reached for Gunner Kelley's sidearm. At a command from Dr. Horvath the Marine reluctantly unloaded the weapon and let her handle one of the cartridges before surrendering the gun. The Motie took it completely apart, to Kelley's annoyance and everyone else's amusement, then put it back together again, correctly, to Kelley's amazement. She examined the Marine's hand, bending the fingers to the limit and working them in their joints, using her own fingers to probe the muscles and the complex bones of the wrist. She examined Sally Fowler's hand in the same way for comparison.

The Motie took tools from her belt and began to work on the grip of the pistol, building it up with plastic squeezed from a tube.

"The little ones are female," one of the biologists announced. "Like the big one."

"A female asteroid miner," Sally said. Her eyes took on a faraway look. "If they use females in a hazardous job like that, they're going to have a culture a lot different from the Empire's." She regarded the Motie speculatively. The alien smiled back.

"We would be better occupied in learning what it eats," Horvath mused. "It doesn't seem to have brought a food supply, and Captain Blaine informs me that its ship has departed for parts unknown." He glanced at the miniature Moties, who were moving about on the big table originally used for spatball. "Unless those are a food supply."

"We'd best not try cooking them just yet," Renner announced from near the door. "They could be children. Immature Moties."

Sally turned suddenly and half gasped before regaining her scientific detachment. Not that she'd be part of cooking anything before she knew what it was.

Horvath spoke. "Mr. Renner, why is *MacArthur*'s Sailing Master concerning himself with an investigation of extraterrestrial anatomy?"

"The ship's at rest, the Captain secured from general quarters, and I'm off duty," Renner said. He conveniently neglected to mention the Captain's standing orders about crew getting in the scientists' way. "Are you ordering me out?"

Horvath thought about it. On the bridge, so did Rod Blaine, but he didn't like Horvath much anyway. The Science Minister shook his head. "No. But I think your suggestion about the small aliens was frivolous."

"Not at all. They could lose the second left arm the way we lose our baby teeth." One of the biologists nodded agreement. "What other differences are there? Size?"

"Ontogeny recapitulates phylogeny," someone said. Someone else said, "Oh, shut up."

The alien gave Kelley back his sidearm and looked around. Renner was the only naval officer in the room, and the alien went up to him and reached for his pistol. Renner unloaded the weapon and handed it over, then submitted to the same meticulous examination of his hand. This time the Motie worked much faster, its hands moving with almost blinding speed.

"Me, I think they're monkeys," Renner said. "Ancestors to the intelligent Moties. Which could mean you were right, too. There are people who eat monkey meat on a dozen planets. But we can hardly risk it yet."

The Motie worked on Renner's weapon, then laid it on the table. Renner picked it up. He frowned, for the flat butt had been built up into curving ridges which were now as hard as the original plastic. Even the trigger had been built up. Renner shifted the piece in his hand, and suddenly it was perfect. Like part of his hand, and it aimed itself.

He savored it for a moment, and noted that Kelley had already reloaded and holstered his own sidearm after a puzzled look. The pistol was perfect, and Renner would hate to lose it; no wonder the Marine hadn't spoken. The Sailing Master handed the piece to Horvath.

The elderly Science Minister took the pistol. "Our visitor seems to know tools," he said. "I don't know guns, of course, but the weapon seems well tailored to the human hand."

Renner took it back. Something nagged him about Horvath's comment. It lacked enthusiasm. Could the gun have fit his own hand better than Horvath's?

The Motie looked around the lounge, swiveling at the torso, staring at each of the scientists, then at other equipment, looking and waiting, waiting.

One of the miniatures sat cross-legged in front of Renner, also watching and waiting. It seemed totally unafraid. Renner reached to scratch it behind the ear, the *right* ear. Like the big Motie, it had no left ear; shoulder muscles for the upper left arm depended from the top of the head. But it seemed to enjoy the scratching, Renner carefully avoided the ear itself, which was large and fragile.

Sally watched, wondering what to do next, and wondering also what bothered her about Renner's performance. Not the incongruity of a ship's officer scratching the ear of what seemed to be an alien monkey, but something else, something about the ear itself . . .

16 · *Idiot Savant*

Dr. Buckman was on duty in the observation room when the blinding laser signal from the inner system went out.

There was a planet there all right, about the size of Earth, with a distorting fringe of transparent atmosphere. He nodded in satisfaction; that was a lot of detail to see at this distance. The Navy had good equipment and they used it well. Some of the petty officers would make good astronomical assistants; pity they were wasted here . . .

What was left of his astronomy section went to work analyzing data from observations of the planet, and Buckman called Captain Blaine.

"I wish you'd get me back some of my men," he complained. "They're all standing around the lounge watching the Motie."

Blaine shrugged. He could hardly order the scientists around. Buckman's management of his department was his own affair. "Do the best you can, Doctor. Everyone's curious about the alien. Even my Sailing Master, who's got no business down there at all. What have you got so far? Is it a terrestrial planet?"

"In a manner of speaking. A touch smaller than Earth, with a water-oxygen atmosphere. But there are traces in the spectrum that have me intrigued. The helium line is very strong, far too strong. I suspect the data."

"A strong helium line? One percent or thereabouts?"

"It would be if the reading were correct, but frankly— Why did you say that?"

"The breathing air in the Motie ship was 1 percent helium, with some rather odd components; I think your reading is accurate."

"But, Captain, there's *no way* a terrestrial planet could hold that much helium! It *has* to be spurious. Some of the other lines are even worse."

"Ketones? Hydrocarbon complexes?"

"Yes!"

"Dr. Buckman, I think you'd better have a look at Mr. Whitbread's report on the atmosphere in the Motie ship. You'll find it in the computer. And take a neutrino reading, please."

"That won't be convenient, Captain."

"Take it anyway," Rod told the stubborn, bony face on the intercom screen. "We need to know the state of their industry."

Buckman snapped, "Are you trying to make war on them?"

"Not yet," Blaine answered; and let it go at that. "While

you've got the instruments set up, take a neutrino reading on the asteroid the Motie ship came from. It's quite a way outside the Trojan point cluster, so you won't have a problem with background emissions."

"Captain, this will interfere with my work!"

"I'll send you an officer to help out." Rod thought rapidly. "Potter. I'll give you Mr. Potter as an assistant." Potter should like that. "This work is necessary, Dr. Buckman. The more we know about them, the more easily we can talk to them. The sooner we can talk to them, the sooner we can interpret their own astronomical observations." That ought to get him.

Buckman frowned. "Why, that's true. I hadn't thought of that at all."

"Fine, Doctor." Rod clicked off before Buckman could voice a further protest. Then he turned to Midshipman Whitbread in the doorway. "Come in and sit down, Mr. Whitbread."

"Thank you, sir." Whitbread sat. The chairs in the Captain's watch cabin were netting on a steel frame, lightweight but comfortable. Whitbread perched on the very edge of one. Cargill handed him a coffee cup, which he held in both hands. He looked painfully alert.

Cargill said, "Relax, boy."

Nothing happened.

Rod said, "Whitbread, let me tell you something. Everyone on this ship wants to pick your brain, not later, but *now.* I get first crack because I'm Captain. When we're finished, I'll turn you over to Horvath and his people. When they're finished with you, if ever, you'll go off watch. You'll think then that you're about to get some sleep, but no. The gun room will want the whole story. They'll be coming off watch at staggered intervals, so you'll have to repeat everything half a dozen times. Are you getting the picture?"

Whitbread was dismayed—as he ought to have been.

"Right, then. Set your coffee down on the niche. Good. Now slide back until your spine touches the chair back. Now relax, dammit! Close your eyes."

For a wonder, Whitbread did. After a moment he smiled blissfully.

"I've got the recorder off," Blaine told him—which wasn't true. "We'll get your formal report later. What I want now is facts, impressions, anything you want to say. My immediate problem is whether to stop that Motie ship."

"Can we? Still? Sir?"

Blaine glanced at Cargill. The First Lieutenant nodded. "It's only half an hour away. We could stop it any time in the next couple of days. No protective Field, remember? And the hull looked to be flimsy enough through your helmet camera. Two minutes from the forward batteries would vaporize the whole ship, no sweat."

"Or," Blaine said, "we could catch up with it, knock out its drive, and take it in tow. The Chief Engineer would give a year's salary to take that electromagnetic fusion system apart. So would the Imperial Traders' Association; that thing's perfect for asteroid mining."

"I'd vote against that," Whitbread said with his eyes closed. "If this were a democracy. Sir."

"It isn't, and the Admiral's inclined to grab that Motie ship. So are some of the scientists, but Horvath's against it. Why are you?"

"It would be the first hostile act, sir. I'd avoid that right up until the Moties tried to destroy *MacArthur*." Whitbread opened his eyes. "Even then, wouldn't the Field scare them off? We're in their home system, Captain, and we did come to see if we could get along with them—at least I think we did, sir."

Cargill chuckled. "Sounds just like Dr. Horvath, doesn't he, Skipper?"

"Besides, sir, what is the Motie ship doing that might interfere with us?"

"Going home alone, probably with a message."

"I don't think there was a message, sir. He didn't do anything that might have been writing, and he didn't *talk* at all."

"She," Blaine told him. "The biologists say the Motie

is female. Both of the little ones are too, and one is pregnant."

"Pregnant. Should I have noticed that, sir?"

Blaine grinned. "What would you have looked for? And where? You didn't even notice that all the little ones have four arms each."

"*Four—?*"

"Never mind that, Mr. Whitbread. You saw no messages, but then you didn't know the Motie was programming—or building—an autopilot until the ship took off. And an empty ship is a message all by itself. We ready for visitors, Jack?"

Cargill nodded. "And if we're not, you can bet *Lenin* is."

"Don't count on too much help from *Lenin*, Number One. Kutuzov thinks it might be interesting to see what kind of account of herself *MacArthur* could give against the Moties. He might not do anything but watch, then run for home."

"Is that—that doesn't sound much like the Admiral, sir," Cargill protested.

"It sounds like him if you'd overheard the fight he had with Dr. Horvath. Our Minister of Science keeps telling the Admiral to keep out of the way, and Kutuzov is about to take him at his word." Blaine turned to his midshipman. "You don't have to spread this around the gun room either, Whitbread."

"No, sir."

"Now, while we've got the time, let's see what you can remember about that Motie ship." Blaine touched controls and several views of the alien craft appeared on his wall screens. "This is what the computer knows so far," Rod explained. "We've mapped some of the interior already. There was no shielding from our probes, nothing to hide, but that doesn't make it all that easy to understand."

Blaine took up a light pointer. "These areas held liquid hydrogen. Now there was heavy machinery *here;* did you see any of it?"

"No, sir, but that back panel looked as if it would roll up."

"Good." Blaine nodded and Cargill sketched it in with the screen stylus.

"Like that?" the First Lieutenant asked. "Fine." He touched the record button. "Now, we know there was quite a lot of hydrogen fuel hidden away. And that drive of theirs ionizes, heats, and enriches the hydrogen with hot carbon vapor. It takes a lot of machinery to do that. Where was it?"

"Sir, shouldn't the Chief Engineer be here?"

"He *should* be here, Mr. Whitbread. Unfortunately there are about ten things happening at once on this ship, and Commander Sinclair is needed elsewhere. He'll get his chance at you soon enough——Jack, let's not forget the Mote design philosophy. We keep looking for separate mechanisms to do each job, but on that probe, everything did four or five overlapping things at once, so to speak. It could be we're looking for too much machinery."

"Yes, sir—but, Captain, no matter how you slice it, that ship had to perform a minimum number of functions. *Had* to. And we can't find equipment enough for half of them."

"Not with our technology, anyway," Blaine said thoughtfully. Then he grinned, a young man's broad and impertinent grin. "We may be looking for a combination microwave oven, fuel ionizer, and sauna. OK, now the alien herself. Your impressions, Whitbread. Is it *that* intelligent?"

"She didn't understand anything I said. Except that one time, when I screamed 'Turn off the force field!' She understood that right away. Otherwise nothing."

"You've edited that a bit, lad," Cargill said. "But never mind. What do you think, boy? Does the alien understand Anglic? Is she faking?"

"I don't know. She didn't even understand my gestures, except once. That was when I handed her her own suit—and that's a pretty pointed hint, sir."

"She may simply be stupid," Rod said.

"She's an asteroid miner, Captain," Cargill said slowly. "That's fairly certain. At least that's an asteroid miner's ship. The hooks and clamps at the stern have to be for hanging on durable cargo, like ore and air-bearing rock."

"So?" Blaine prompted.

"I've known some asteroid miners, Skipper. They tend to be stubborn, independent, self-reliant to the point of eccentricity, and close-mouthed. They'll trust each other with their lives, but not with their women or property. And they forget how to talk out there; at least it seems that way."

They both looked hopefully at Whitbread, who said, "I don't know, sir. I just don't know. She's not stupid. You should have seen her hands moving around in the guts of the instrument panel, rewiring, making new circuits, recalibrating half a dozen things at once, it looked like. Maybe—maybe our sign language just doesn't work. I don't know why."

Rod pushed a finger along the knot in his nose. "It might be surprising if it did work," he said thoughtfully. "And this is one example of a completely alien race. If we were aliens and picked up an asteroid miner, what conclusions would we draw about the Empire?" Blaine filled his coffee cup, then Whitbread's. "Well, Horvath's team is more likely to come up with something than we are. They have the Motie to work with."

Sally Fowler watched the Motie with a feeling of deep frustration. "I can't decide whether she's stupid or I am. Did you see what happened when I drew her a diagram of the Pythagorean Theorem?"

"Uh huh." Renner's grin was no help at all. "She took your pocket computer apart and put it back together again. She didn't draw anything. She's stupid in some ways, though," he said more seriously. "Meaning no insult to our eminently trustworthy selves, she's too damned trusting. Maybe she's low on survival instincts."

Sally nodded and watched the Motie at work.

"She's a genius at building things," Renner said. "But she doesn't understand language, gestures, or pictures. Could the bloody alien be a genius and a moron at the same time?"

"Idiot savant," Sally murmured. "It happens with humans, but it's quite rare. Imbecile children with the ability to extract cube roots and do logarithms in their heads. Mathematical whizzes who can't buckle their shoes."

"It's a difference in perceptions." Horvath had been engaged in a more thorough study of the small Moties. "One has to *learn* that a picture is a picture. Your drawings— Good God, what's it doing now?"

Someone screamed in the companionway.

Ostensibly Cargill was delivering Whitbread to the scientists. Actually, he had no doubt that Whitbread could have found his way to the wardroom where they had brought the Moties while artificers built a cage for the miniatures in the petty officers' lounge. But Jack Cargill was curious.

Halfway through the companionway he caught his first sight of the alien. It was disassembling the wardroom coffee maker—an act of malice made all the more diabolical by the innocence of her smile.

She cringed away at Cargill's yell—and the First Lieutenant saw that it was too late. Tiny screws and parts were scattered across the table. The alien had broken the percolator tube, possibly to analyze the soldering technique. Bits of the timing mechanism were neatly arrayed. The Motie had pulled the cylindrical shell open along its welded seam.

Cargill found that the Science Minister had him by the arm. "You're frightening the alien," Horvath said in a low voice. "Go away, please."

"Doctor, have the goodness to tell me—"

"Elsewhere." Horvath propelled him to the other end of the room. Cargill glimpsed the miniature aliens squatting on the games table, surrounded by members of the life sciences group and by samples from the galley: grain, bread, carrots and celery, defrosted raw and cooked meat. "Now," said Horvath. "What do you mean by barging into—"

"That monster ruined the wardroom coffee maker!"

"We're lucky," Midshipman Whitbread said irreverently. "She was trying to take apart the number-four air lock mechanism until I stopped her."

"All she's interested in is tools." Horvath was pointedly ignoring Cargill's agitation. "For once I even agree with Admiral Kutuzov. The alien must not be allowed to see the Alderson Drive or the Field generators. She seems able to deduce what a thing is for and how it works almost without touching it."

"Never mind that!" Cargill said. "Couldn't you have given the Motie something else to play with? That coffee maker is half repairs anyway. Nobody could figure out how it's made since Sandy Sinclair finished with it. And the Motie's broken some of the parts."

"If they were that easy to break, they can probably be fixed," Horvath said soothingly. "Look, we can give you one of the urns from the labs, or have one of our techs— Ah, Miss Fowler, has the alien calmed down? Now, Mr. —Whitbread? We're glad you're here; we've been waiting for you, as the only man to have actually communicated with the alien. Here, Commander Cargill, please stay away from the Motie—"

But Cargill was halfway across the room. The alien cringed a bit, but Cargill stayed well out of her reach. He glowered at her as he considered his coffee maker. It had been reassembled.

The Motie pulled away from Sally Fowler. She found a conical plastic container, filled it with tap water, and used it to fill the coffee maker. One of the wardroom stewards sniggered.

The Motie poured in two containers of water, inserted the grounds basket, and waited.

The amused steward looked to Cargill, who nodded. The messboy dug out the tin of ground coffee, used the measuring spoon, and started the urn. The alien watched closely all the while. So did one of the miniatures, despite the distraction of a biologist waving a carrot in her face. "It did that before, watched me make the coffee, sir," the steward said. "Thought it might want some, but the scientists didn't offer it none."

"We may have a godawful mess here in a minute, Ernie.

Stand by to clean up." Cargill turned to Sally. "How good is that monster at putting things together again?"

"Quite good," Sally told him. "She fixed my pocket computer."

The percolator bubbled, and the water in the indicator tube turned brown. Cargill hesitantly poured a cup and tasted. "Why, that's all right," he said. He handed the cup to the Motie.

She tasted the black, bitter brew, squawled, and threw the cup at the bulkhead.

Sally led Whitbread into the wardroom pantry. "You made the Motie understand you. How?"

"It was only that once," Whitbread said. "I've been wondering if I made a mistake. Could she have decided to let me loose about the time I opened my helmet and screamed?"

Sally scowled. "She just *stands* there. She doesn't even seem to know we're *trying* to talk to her. And she never tries to talk back . . ." She dropped her voice, muttering mostly to herself. "It is a basic characteristic of intelligent species that they attempt to communicate. Whitbread, what's your first name?"

Whitbread was startled. "Jonathon, my lady."

"All right, Jonathon, I'm Sally. As man to woman, Jonathon, what in blazes am I doing wrong? Why won't she try to talk to me?"

"Well, Sally," Whitbread said tentatively. He liked the taste of the name. And she wasn't more than a couple of years older than he was— "Sally, I could think of half a dozen reasons. Maybe she reads minds."

"What would that have to do with—"

"She wouldn't know about language, would she? What you're trying to teach wouldn't make sense. Maybe she can only read *our* minds when we're screaming mad, like I was."

"Or Commander Cargill was—" Sally said thoughtfully. "She did move away from the coffee maker. But not for long. No, I don't believe it."

"Neither do I. I think she's lying."

"Lying?"

"Playing dumb. She doesn't know what to tell us, so she tells us nothing. Plays for time. She is interested in our machinery. This gives her time to learn about it."

Sally nodded slowly. "One of the biologists had the same idea. That she's waiting for instructions, and learning as much as she can until they come— Jonathon, how would we catch her at it?"

"I don't think we do," Whitbread said slowly. "How would you catch an intelligent mouse playing dumb, if you'd never seen a mouse and neither had anyone else?"

"Blazes. Well, we'll just have to keep on trying." She frowned, thinking of the Motie's performance with the coffee maker, then gave Whitbread a long, thoughtful look. "You're exhausted. Go get some sleep, there's nothing you need to tell us right away, is there?"

"No." Whitbread yawned. There was a scampering sound behind him and they both turned quickly, but there was nothing there. "Speaking of mice," Whitbread said.

"How can they live on a steel ship?" Sally asked.

Whitbread shrugged. "They come aboard with the food supplies, even in personal gear. Once in a while we evacuate portions of the ship, move the crew around, and open up to space, to control them, but we never get them all. This trip, with all the extra personnel aboard, we haven't even been able to do that."

"Interesting." Sally nodded. "Mice can live almost anywhere humans can—you know, there are probably as many mice in the galaxy as people? We've carried them to nearly every planet. Jonathon, are the miniatures *mice?*"

Whitbread shrugged. "She certainly didn't care about them. Killed all but two—but why bring two aboard? And a randomly selected two at that."

Sally nodded again. "We watched her catch them." She laughed suddenly. "And Mr. Renner was wondering if they were baby Moties! Get to sleep, Jonathon. We'll see you in ten hours or so."

17 · *Mr. Crawford's Eviction*

Midshipman Jonathon Whitbread reached his hammock much sooner than he had expected. He sagged blissfully into the netting and closed his eyes . . . and opened one, feeling other eyes upon him.

"Yes, Mr. Potter," he sighed.

"Mr. Whitbread, I would be obliged if you would talk to Mr. Staley."

It was not what he expected. Whitbread opened his other eye. "Uh?"

"Something's upset him. You know how he is, he won't complain, he'd rather die. But he walks around like a robot, hardly speaks to anyone except politely. He eats alone . . . you've known him longer than I have, I thought you might find out why."

"All right, Potter. I'll try. When I wake up." He closed his eyes. Potter was still there. "In eight hours, Potter. It can't be *that* urgent."

In another part of *MacArthur* Sailing Master Renner tossed fitfully in a stateroom not much larger than his bunk. It was the Third Lieutenant's berth, but two scientists had Renner's cabin, and the Third had moved in with a Marine officer.

Renner sat up suddenly in the darkness, his mind hunting for something that might have been a dream. Then he turned on the light and fumbled with the unfamiliar intercom panel. The rating who answered showed remarkable self-control: he didn't scream or anything. "Get me Miss Sally Fowler," Renner said.

The rating did, without comment. *Must be a robot,* Renner thought. He knew how he looked.

Sally was not asleep. She and Dr. Horvath had just finished installing the Motie in the Gunnery Officer's cabin. Her face and voice as she said "Yes, Mr. Renner?" somehow informed Renner that he looked like a cross between a man and a mole—a remarkable feat of nonverbal communication.

Renner skipped it. "I remembered something. Have you got your pocket computer?"

"Certainly." She took it out to show him.

"Please test it for me."

Her face a puzzled mask, Sally drew letters on the face of the flat box, wiped them, scrawled a simple problem, then a complex one that would require the ship's computer to help. Then she called up an arbitrary personal data file from ship's memory. "It works all right."

Renner's voice was thick with sleep. "Am I crazy, or did we watch the Motie take that thing apart and put it back together again?"

"Certainly. She did the same with your gun."

"But a *pocket computer?*" Renner stared. "You know that's impossible, don't you?"

She thought it was a joke. "No, I didn't."

"Well, it is. Ask Dr. Horvath." Renner hung up and went back to sleep.

Sally caught up with Dr. Horvath as he was turning into his cabin. She told him about the computer.

"But those things are one big integrated circuit. We don't even try to repair them . . ." Horvath muttered other things to himself.

While Renner slept, Horvath and Sally woke the physical sciences staff. None of them got much sleep that night.

"Morning" on a warship is a relative thing. The morning watch is from 0400 to 0800, a time when the human species would normally sleep; but space knows nothing of this. A full crew is needed on the bridge and in the engine rooms no matter what the time. As a watchkeeping officer, Whitbread stood one watch in three, but *MacArthur's* orderly quarter bill was confused beyond repair. He had both the morning and forenoon watches off, eight glorious hours of sleep; yet, somehow, he found himself awake and in the warrant officers' mess at 0900.

"There's nothing wrong with me," Horst Staley protested. "I don't know where you got that idea. Forget it."

"OK," Whitbread said easily. He chose juice and cereal and put them on his tray. He was just behind Staley in the cafeteria line, which was natural enough since he had followed Staley in.

"Though I appreciate your concern," Staley told him. There was no trace of emotion in the voice.

Whitbread nodded agreeably. He picked up his tray and followed Staley's unnaturally straight back. Predictably, Staley chose an empty table. Whitbread joined him.

In the Empire were numerous worlds where the dominant races were white caucasian. On such worlds the pictures on Navy enlistment posters always looked like Horst Staley. His jaw was square, his eyes icy blue. His face was all planes and angles, bilaterally symmetrical, and without expression. His back was straight, his shoulders broad, his belly was flat and hard and ridged with muscle. He contrasted sharply with Whitbread, who would fight a weight problem all his life, and was at least slightly rounded everywhere.

They ate in silence, a long breakfast. Finally, too casually, Staley asked, as if he had to ask, "How went your mission?"

Whitbread was ready. "Rugged. The worst hour and a half the Motie spent staring at me. Look." Whitbread stood. He twisted his head sideways and let his knees sag and shoulders slump, to fit him into an invisible coffin 130 cm high. "Like this, for an hour and a half." He sat down again. "Torture, I tell you. I kept wishing they'd picked you."

Staley flushed. "I did volunteer."

Bull's-eye. "It was my turn. You were the one who accepted *Defiant*'s surrender, back off New Chicago."

"And let that maniac steal my bomb!"

Whitbread put his fork down. "Oh?"

"You didn't know?"

"Of course not. Think Blaine would spread it all over the ship? You did come back a bit shaken after that mission. We wondered why."

"Now you know. Some jackass tried to renege. *Defiant*'s captain wouldn't let him, but he might have." Staley rubbed his hands together, painfully hard. "He snatched the bomb away from me. And I let him! I'd have given anything for the chance to—" Staley stood up suddenly, but Whitbread was quick enough to catch him by the arm.

"Sit down," he said. "I can tell you why you weren't picked."

"I suppose you can read the Captain's mind?" They kept their voices low by tacit consent. *MacArthur*'s interior partitions were all sound-absorbent anyway, and their voices were very clear, if soft.

"Second-guessing officers is good practice for a middie," said Whitbread.

"Why, then? Was it because of the bomb?"

"Indirectly. You'd have been tempted to prove yourself. But even without that, you're too much the hero, Horst. Perfect physical shape, good lungs—ever meet an admiral with a soft voice?—utter dedication, and no sense of humor."

"I do too have a sense of humor."

"No, you don't."

"I don't?"

"Not a trace. The situation didn't call for a hero, Horst. It called for someone who didn't mind being made ridiculous in a good cause."

"You're kidding. Damn, I never know when you're kidding."

"Now would be a poor time. I'm not making fun of you, Horst. Listen, I shouldn't *have* to explain this. You watched it all, didn't you? Sally told me I was on all the intercom screens, live, in color and 3D."

"You were." Staley smiled briefly. "We should have had a view of your face. Especially when you started swearing. We got no warning at all. The view jumped a bit, then you screamed at the alien, and everybody cracked up."

"What would you have done?"

"Not that. I don't know. Followed orders, I guess." The

icy eyes narrowed. "I wouldn't have tried to shoot my way out, if that's what you're thinking."

"Maybe a second of cutting laser into the control panel? To kill the force field?"

"Not without orders."

"What about the sign language? I spent some time making gestures, hoping the alien would understand me, but it never did."

"We couldn't see that. What about it?"

"I told you," Whitbread said. "The mission took someone willing to make a fool of himself in a good cause. Think about how often you heard people laugh at me while I was bringing back the Motie."

Staley nodded.

"Now forget them and think about the Motie. What about her sense of humor? Would you like a Motie laughing at you, Horst? You might never be sure if she was or wasn't; you don't know what it looks like or sounds like—"

"You're being ridiculous."

"All anyone knew was that the situation called for someone to find out whether the aliens were willing to talk to us. It didn't need someone to uphold the Imperial honor. Plenty of time for that after we know what we're facing. There'll be room for heroes, Horst. There always is."

"That's reassuring," said Staley. He had finished breakfast. Now he stood and walked out fast, with his back very straight, leaving Whitbread wondering.

Oh, well, Whitbread thought. I tried. And just maybe . . .

Luxury in a warship is relative.

Gunnery Officer Crawford's stateroom was the size of his bed. When the bed was up, he had room to change clothes and a small sink to brush his teeth. To lower the bed for sleeping he had first to step into the corridor; and being tall for a Navy man, Crawford had learned to sleep curled up.

A bed and a door with a lock on it, instead of a hammock or one tier of many bunks: luxury. He would have fought to keep it; but he had lost the toss. Now he bunked in *MacArthur*'s cutter while an alien monster occupied his quarters.

"She's only a little more than a meter tall, of course she fits," Sally Fowler said judiciously. "Still, it's only a tiny room. Do you think she can stand it? Otherwise we'll have to keep her in the lounge."

"I saw the cabin of her ship. It wasn't any bigger. She can stand it," Whitbread said. It was too late to try sleeping in the gun room, and he was supposed to tell the scientists everything he knew: at least that ought to work if Cargill asked why he'd been pestering Sally. "I suppose you've got someone watching her through the intercom?"

She nodded. Whitbread followed her into the scientists' lounge. Part of the room had been screened off with wire netting and the two miniatures were in there. One was nibbling at a head of cabbage, using four arms to hold it to her chest. The other, her abdomen swollen with pregnancy, was playing with a flashlight.

Just like a monkey, Whitbread thought. It was the first chance he'd had to look at the miniatures. Their fur was thicker, and mottled brown and yellow where the large one was uniformly soft brown. The four arms were nearly alike, five fingers on the left hands and six on the rights; but the arms and fingers were identically slender, identically jointed. Yet the muscles of the upper left shoulder were anchored to the top of the skull. Why, if not for greater strength and leverage?

He was delighted when Sally led him to a small corner table away from where the biosciences people were scratching their heads and arguing loudly. He got coffee for both of them and asked her about the strange musculature of the miniatures; it wasn't what he'd really like to talk to her about, but it was a start . . .

"We think it's vestigial," she said. "They obviously don't need it; the left arms aren't sized for heavy work anyway."

"Then the little ones aren't monkeys! They're an offshoot of the big ones."

"Or they're both an offshoot of something else. Jonathon, we've got more than two classifications already. Look." She turned to the intercom screen and a view of the Motie's room appeared.

"She seems happy enough," said Whitbread. He grinned at what the Motie had been doing. "Mr. Crawford isn't going to like what she's done to his bunk."

"Dr. Horvath didn't want to stop her. She can fiddle with anything she likes as long as it isn't the intercom."

Crawford's bunk had been shortened and contoured. The contours were exceedingly strange, not only because of the complex joints in the Motie's back, but also because she apparently slept on her side. The mattress had been cut and sewn, the underlying steel bent and twisted. Now there were grooves for two right arms and a pit for a projecting hipbone and a high ridge to serve as a pillow—

"Why would she sleep only on her right side?" Whitbread asked.

"Maybe she'd rather defend herself with her left, if she happened to be surprised in her sleep. The left is so much stronger."

"Could be. Poor Crawford. Maybe she's expecting him to try and cut her throat some night." He watched the alien at work on the overhead lamp. "She does have a one-track mind, doesn't she? We could get some good out of this. She might improve something."

"Perhaps. Jonathon, did you study sketches of the dissected alien?"

She sounded like a schoolmistress. She was old enough to be one, too; but much too pretty, Whitbread thought. He said, "Yes, ma'am."

"Do you see any differences?"

"The color of the fur is different. But that's nothing. The other one was in suspended animation for hundreds of years."

"Anything else?"

"The other one was taller, I think. I wouldn't swear."

"Look at her head."

Whitbread frowned. "I don't see it."

Sally used her pocket computer. It hummed slightly, indicating that it was in communication with the main ship's memory. Somewhere in *MacArthur* a laser moved across holographic lines. The ship's memory held everything humanity knew of Moties—such as it was. It found the information Sally asked for and sent it to her pocket computer; a sketch appeared on the face of the flat box.

Whitbread studied the sketch, then looked to the screen and the Motie. "Her forehead. It slopes!"

"That's what we thought, Dr. Horvath and I."

"It's not easy to see. The Motie's head is so flinking lopsided anyway."

"I know. But it's there. We think there's a difference in the hands, too, but it's very small." Sally frowned and three short grooves appeared between brown eyes. She'd cut her hair short for space, and the frown and short hair made her look very efficient. Whitbread didn't like it. "That gives us three different kinds of Motie," she said. "And only four Moties. That's a high mutation rate, wouldn't you say?"

"I . . . wouldn't be surprised." Whitbread remembered the history lessons Chaplain Hardy had held for the midshipmen during the trip out. "They're trapped in this system. Bottled up. If they had an atomic war, they'd have to live with it afterwards, wouldn't they?" He thought of Earth and shuddered.

"We haven't seen any evidence of atomic wars."

"Except the mutation rate."

Sally laughed. "You're arguing in circles. Anyway, it doesn't hold up. None of these three types is a cripple, Jonathon. They're all very well adapted, all healthy—except the dead one, of course, and she hardly counts. They wouldn't choose a cripple to pilot the probe."

"No. So what's the answer?"

"You saw them first, Jonathon. Call the one in the probe Type A. What was the relationship between Types B and C?"

"I don't know."

"But you saw them together."

"It didn't make sense. The little ones stayed out of the big one's way, at first, and the big one let them alone.

Then I signaled the big one that I wanted her to go with me to *MacArthur*. She forthwith picked the first two little ones that came to hand, made sure they were safe, and killed the rest without warning!"

Whitbread paused, thinking of the whirlwind that had blown him out the Motie ship air lock. "So you tell me. What are the little ones? Pets? Children? But she *killed* them. Vermin? Why save two of them? Food animals? Have you tried that?"

Sally grimaced. It was almost a snarl, remarkable on her pretty face, an expression she would never have worn on any social occasion. "Tried what? Fricassee one of the little beasts and offer it to the big one? Be reasonable."

The alien in Crawford's room poured a handful of—some kind of seed—and ate it. "Popcorn," said Sally. "We tried it on the little ones first. Maybe *that's* what they were for, food testers."

"Maybe."

"She eats cabbage too. Well, she won't starve, but she may die of vitamin deficiencies. All we can do is watch and wait— I suppose we'll go to the alien's home planet pretty soon. In the meantime, Jonathon, you're the only man who's seen the Motie ship. Was the pilot's seat contoured? I only got a glimpse of it through your helmet camera."

"It was contoured. In fact, it fitted her like a glove. I noticed something else. The control board ran along the right side of the seat. For right hands only . . ."

He remembered a great deal about the mining ship, as it turned out. It kept him in Lady Sally's enjoyable company until he had to go on watch. But none of it was particularly useful.

Whitbread had no sooner taken his station on the bridge than Dr. Buckman called for the Captain.

"A ship, Blaine," Buckman said. "From the inhabitable world, Mote Prime. We didn't find it because it was hidden by that damned laser signal."

Blaine nodded. His own screens had shown the Motie

ship nine minutes before. Chief Shattuck's crew wasn't about to let civilians keep a better watch than the Navy.

"It will reach us in about eighty-one hours," Buckman said. "It's accelerating at point eight seven gees, which is the surface gravity of Mote Prime by some odd coincidence. It's spitting neutrinos. In general it behaves like the first ship, except that it's far more massive. I'll let you know if we get anything else."

"Fine. Keep an eye on it, Doctor." Blaine nodded and Whitbread cut the circuit. The Captain turned to his exec. "Let's compare what we know with Buckman's file, Number One."

"Aye aye, sir." Cargill toyed with the computer controls for a few minutes. "Captain?"

"Yes?"

"Look at the starting time. That alien ship got under way in not much more than an hour after we broke out."

Blaine whistled to himself. "Are you sure? That gives ten minutes to detect us, another ten for us to dee them, and forty minutes to get ready and launch. Jack, what kind of ship launches in forty minutes?"

Cargill frowned. "None I ever heard of. The Navy *could* do it, keep a ship with a full crew on ready alert . . ."

"Precisely. I think that's a warship coming at us, Number One. You'd better tell the Admiral, then Horvath. Whitbread, get me Buckman."

"Yes?" The astrophysicist looked harried.

"Doctor, I need everything your people can get about that Motie ship. Now. And would you give some thought to their rather strange acceleration?"

Buckman studied the numbers Blaine sent down to his screen. "This seems straightforward enough. They launched from Mote Prime or a closely orbiting moon forty minutes after we arrived. What's the problem?"

"If they launched that fast, it's almost certainly a warship. We'd like to believe otherwise."

Buckman was annoyed. "Believe what you like, but you'll ruin the math, Captain. Either they launched in forty minutes, or . . . well, you could start the Motie vehicle something over two million kilometers this side of

Mote Prime; that would give them more time . . . but I don't believe it."

"No more do I. I want you to satisfy yourself about this, Dr. Buckman. What could we assume that would give them more time to launch?"

"Let me see . . . I'm not used to thinking in terms of rocketry, you know. Gravitational accelerations are more my field, if you'll pardon the pun. Hmmm." Buckman's eyes went curiously blank. For a moment he looked like an idiot. "You'd have to assume a period of coasting. And a much higher acceleration in the launching mechanism. Much higher."

"How long to coast?"

"Several hours for every hour you want to give them to make up their minds. Captain, I don't understand your problem. Why can't they have launched a scientific survey ship in forty minutes? Why assume a warship? After all, *MacArthur* is both, and it took you an unreasonably long time to launch. I was ready days early."

Blaine turned him off. I'll break his scrawny neck, he told himself. They'll court-martial me, but I'll claim justifiable homicide. I'll subpoena everyone who knew him. They're *bound* to let me off. He touched keys. "Number One, what have you got?"

"They launched that ship in forty minutes."

"Which makes it a warship."

"So the Admiral thinks, sir. Dr. Horvath wasn't convinced."

"Neither am I, but we'll want to be ready for them. And we'll want to know more about Moties than Horvath's people are learning from our passenger. Number One, I want you to take the cutter and get over to that asteroid the Motie came from. There's no sign of activity there, so it should be safe enough—and I want to know just what the Motie was *doing* there. It might give us a clue."

18 · *The Stone Beehive*

Horace Bury watched the foot-high Moties playing behind the wire screen. "Do they bite?" he asked.

"They haven't yet," Horvath answered. "Not even when the biotechs took blood samples." Bury puzzled him. Science Minister Horvath considered himself a good judge of people—once he'd left science and gone into politics he'd had to learn fast—but he couldn't fathom Bury's thought processes. The Trader's easy smile was only a public face; behind it, remote and emotionless, he watched the Moties like God judging a dubious creation.

Bury was thinking, My but they're ugly. What a shame. They'd be useless as house pets, unless— He checked himself and stepped forward to reach through a gap in the netting large enough for an arm but not a Motie.

"Behind the ear," Horvath suggested.

"Thank you." Bury wondered if one would come to investigate his hand. The thin one came, and Bury scratched her behind the ear, carefully, for the ear looked fragile and delicate. But she seemed to enjoy it.

They'd make terrible pets, Bury thought, but they'd sell for thousands each. For a while. Before the novelty wore off. Best to hit every planet simultaneously. If they breed in captivity, and if we can keep them fed, and if I sell out before people stop buying— "Allah be—! She took my watch!"

"They love tools. You may have noticed that flashlight we gave them."

"Never mind that, Horvath. How do I get my watch back? In Allah's— How did the catch come unfastened?"

"Reach in and take it. Or let me." Horvath tried. The enclosure was too big, and the Motie didn't want to give up the watch. Horvath dithered. "I don't want to disturb them too much."

"Horvath, that watch is worth eight hundred crowns! It not only tells the time and the date, but—" Bury paused.

"Come to that, it's also shockproof. We advertise that any shock that will stop a Chronos will also kill the owner. She probably can't hurt it much."

The Motie was examining the wrist watch in a sober, studious manner. Bury wondered if others would find that manner captivating. No house pet behaved like that. Not even cats.

"You have cameras on them?"

"Of course," said Horvath.

"My firm may want to buy this sequence. For advertising purposes." That's one thing, Bury thought. Now there was a Motie ship coming here, and Cargill taking the cutter somewhere. He'd never get anywhere pumping Cargill, but Buckman was going. There might be returns from the coffee the astrophysicist drank after all . . .

The thought saddened him obscurely.

The cutter was the largest of the vehicles in hangar deck. She was a lifting body, with a flat upper surface that fitted flat against one wall of hangar deck. She had her own access hatches, to join the cutter's air locks to the habitable regions of *MacArthur* because hangar deck was usually in vacuum.

There was no Langston Field generator aboard the cutter, and no Alderson Drive. But her drive was efficient and powerful, and her fuel capacity was considerable, even without strap-on tanks. The ablative shielding along her nose was good for one (1) reentry into a terrestrial atmosphere at up to 20 km/sec, or many reentries if they could be taken more slowly. She was designed for a crew of six, but would carry more. She could go from planet to planet, but not between stars. History had been made again and again by space craft smaller than *MacArthur*'s cutter.

There were half a dozen men bunking in her now. One had been kicked out to make room for Crawford when Crawford was kicked out of his own stateroom by a three-armed alien.

Cargill smiled when he saw that. "I'll take Crawford," he decided. "Be a shame to move him again. Lafferty as coxswain. Three Marines . . ." He bent over his crew list. "Staley as midshipman." He'd welcome a chance to prove himself, and was steady enough under orders.

The cutter's interior was clean and polished, but there was evidence of Sinclair's oddball repairs along the port wall where *Defiant's* lasers had flashed through the ablative shielding; even at the long distances from which the cutter engaged, the damage had been severe.

Cargill spread his things out in the only enclosed cabin space and reviewed his flight plan options. Over that distance they could go at three gees all the way. In practice, it might be one gee over and five back. Just because the rock didn't have a fusion plant didn't mean it was uninhabited.

Jack Cargill remembered the speed with which the Motie had rebuilt his big percolator. Without even knowing what coffee was supposed to taste like! Could they be *beyond* fusion? He left his gear and put on a pressure suit, a skintight woven garment that was just porous enough to allow sweat to pass; it was a self-regulating temperature control, and with the tightly woven fabric to assist, his own skin was able to stand up to space. The helmet attached to a seal at the collar. In combat heavy armor would go over the whole mess, but this was good enough for inspections.

From the outside there was no evidence of damage or repair. Part of the heat shield hung below the cutter's nose like a great shovel blade, exposing the control room blister, windows, and the snout of the cutter's main armament: a laser cannon.

In battle the cutter's first duty was to make observations and reports. Sometimes she'd try to sneak in on a torpedo run on a blinded enemy warship. Against Motie ships with no Field, that cannon would be more than enough.

Cargill inspected the cutter's weapons with more than usual thoroughness. Already he feared the Moties. In this he was almost alone; but he would not be so forever.

* * *

The second alien ship was larger than the first, but estimates of its mass had a high finagle factor, depending on the acceleration (known), fuel consumption (deduced from drive temperature), operating temperature (deduced from the radiation spectrum, whose peak was in the soft x-ray region) and efficiency (pure guesswork). When it was all folded together the mass seemed much too small: about right for a three-man ship.

"But they aren't men," Renner pointed out. "Four Moties weigh as much as two men, but they don't need as much room. We don't know what they're carrying for equipment, or armament, or shielding. Thin walls don't seem to scare them, and that lets them build bigger cabins—"

"All right." Rod cut him off. "If you don't know, just say so."

"I don't know."

"Thank you," Rod said patiently. "Is there anything you *are* sure of?"

"Oddly enough, there is, sir. Acceleration. It's been constant to three significant figures since we spotted the ship. Now that's odd," Renner said. "Normally you fool with the drive to keep it running at peak, you correct minor errors in course . . . and if you leave it alone, there's still variation. To keep the acceleration that constant they must be constantly fiddling with it."

Rod rubbed the bridge of his nose. "It's a signal. They're telling us exactly where they're going."

"Yes, sir. Right here. They're saying to wait for them." Renner wore that strange, fierce grin. "Oh, we know something else, Captain. The ship's cross-sectional profile has decreased since we sighted it. Probably they've ditched some fuel tanks."

"How did you get that? Don't you have to have the target transit the sun?"

"Usually, yes. Here it blocks the Coal Sack. There's enough light bouncing off the Coal Sack to give us a good estimate of that ship's cross-sectional area. Haven't you noticed the colors in the Coal Sack, Captain?"

"No." Blaine rubbed at his nose again. "Throwaway

fuel tanks doesn't make them sound like a warship, does it? But it's no guarantee. All it really tells us is that they're in a hurry."

Staley and Buckman occupied the rear seats in the cutter's triangular control cabin. As the cutter pulled away at one gee, Staley watched *MacArthur*'s Field close behind them. Against the black of the Coal Sack the battle cruiser seemed to go invisible. There was nothing to look at but the sky.

Half that sky was Coal Sack, starless except for a hot pink point several degrees in from the edge. It was as if the universe ended here. Like a wall, Horst thought.

"Look at it," said Buckman, and Horst jumped. "There are people on New Scotland who call it the Face of God. Superstitious idiots!"

"Right," said Horst. Superstitions were silly.

"From here it doesn't look at all like a man, and it's ten times as magnificent! I wish my sister's husband could see it. He belongs to the Church of Him."

Horst nodded in the semidarkness.

From any of the known human worlds, the Coal Sack was a black hole in the sky. One would expect it to be black here. But now that Horst's eyes were adjusting, he saw traces of red glowing within the Coal Sack. Now the nebular material showed like layer after layer of gauzy curtains, or like blood spreading in water. The longer he looked, the deeper he could see into it. Eddies and whorls and flow patterns showed light years deep in the vacuum-thin dust and gas.

"Imagine, *me* stuck with a Himmist for a brother-in-law! I've tried to educate the fool," Buckman said energetically, "but he just won't listen."

"I don't think I've ever seen a more beautiful sky. Dr. Buckman, is all that light coming from Murcheson's Eye?"

"Doesn't seem possible, does it? We've tried to find other sources, fluorescence, UV stars deep in the dust, like that. If there were masses in there we'd have found them with mass indicators. Staley, it's not *that* unlikely. The Eye isn't that far from the Coal Sack."

"A couple of light years."

"Well, what of it? Light travels farther than that, given a free path!" Buckman's teeth glowed in the faint multi-colored light of the control panel. "Murcheson lost a golden opportunity by not studying the Coal Sack when he had the chance. Of course he was on the wrong side of the Eye, and he probably didn't venture very far from the breakout point . . . and it's our luck, Staley! There's never been an opportunity like this! A thick interstellar mass, and a red supergiant right at the edge for illumination! Look, look along my arm, Staley, to where the currents flow toward that eddy. Like a whirlpool, isn't it? If your captain would stop twiddling his thumbs and give me access to the ship's computer, I could prove that that eddy is a protostar in the process of condensation! Or that it isn't."

Buckman had a temporary rank higher than Staley's, but he was a civilian. In any case, he shouldn't be talking about the Captain that way. "We do use the computer for other things, Dr. Buckman."

Buckman let go of Staley's arm. "Too damned many." His eyes seemed lost; his soul was lost in that enormous veil of red-lit darkness. "We may not need it, though. The Moties must have been observing the Coal Sack for all their history; hundreds of years, maybe thousands. Especially if they've developed some such pseudoscience as astrology. If we can talk to them . . ." He trailed off.

Staley said, "We wondered why you were so eager to come along."

"What? Do you mean jaunting off with you to see this rock? Staley, I don't care what the Motie was using it for. I want to know why the Trojan points are so crowded."

"You think there'll be clues?"

"Maybe, in the composition of the rock. We can hope so."

"I may be able to help you there," Staley said slowly. "Sauron—my home—has an asteroid belt and mining industries. I learned something about rock mining from my uncles. Thought I might be a miner myself, once." He stopped abruptly, expecting Buckman to bring up an unpleasant subject.

Buckman said, "I wonder what the Captain expects to find there?"

"He told me that. We know just one thing about that rock," said Staley. "A Motie was interested in it. When we know why, we'll know something about Moties."

"Not very much," Buckman growled.

Staley relaxed. Either Buckman didn't know why Sauron was infamous, or . . . no. Tactful? Buckman? Not hardly.

The Motie pup was born five hours after *MacArthur's* cutter left for the asteroid. The birth was remarkably doglike, considering the mother's distant relationship to dogs; and there was only the one pup, about the size of a rat.

The lounge was very popular that day, as crew and officers and scientists and even the Chaplain found an excuse to drop by.

"Look how much smaller the lower left arm is," said Sally. "We were right, Jonathan. The little ones are derived from the big Moties."

Someone thought of leading the large Motie down to the lounge. She did not seem the least interested in the new miniature Motie; but she did make sounds at the others. One of them dug Horace Bury's watch out from under a pillow and gave it to her.

Rod watched the activities around the Motie pup when he could. It seemed very highly developed for a newborn; within hours of its birth it was nibbling at cabbages, and it seemed able to walk, although the mother usually carried it with one set of arms. She moved rapidly and was hardly hampered by it at all.

Meanwhile, the Motie ship drew nearer; and if there was any change in its acceleration, it was too small for *MacArthur* to detect.

"They'll be here in seventy hours," Rod told Cargill via laser message. "I want you back in sixty. Don't let Buckman start anything he can't finish within the time limit. If you contact aliens, tell me fast—and don't try to talk to them unless there's no way out."

"Aye aye, Skipper."

"Not my orders, Jack. Kutuzov's. He's not happy about this excursion. Just look that rock over and get back."

The rock was thirty million kilometers distant from *MacArthur*, about a twenty-five-hour trip each way at one gee. Four gravities would cut that in half. Not enough, Staley thought, to make it worthwhile putting up with four gees.

"But we could go at 1.5 gee, sir," he suggested to Cargill. "Not only would the trip be faster, but we'd get tired faster. We wouldn't move around so much. The cutter wouldn't seem so crowded."

"That's brilliant," Cargill said warmly. "A brilliant suggestion, Mr. Staley."

"Then we'll do it?"

"We will not."

"But—why not, sir?"

"Because I don't like plus gees. Because it uses fuel, and if we use too much *MacArthur* may have to dive into the gas giant to get us home. Never waste fuel, Mr. Staley. You may want it someday. And besides, it's a nitwit idea."

"Yes, sir."

"Nitwit ideas are for emergencies. You use them when you've got nothing else to try. If they work, they go in the Book. Otherwise you follow the Book, which is largely a collection of nitwit ideas that worked." Cargill smiled at Staley's puzzled look. "Let me tell you about the one *I* got in the Book . . ."

For a midshipman it was always school time. Staley would hold higher ranks than this one, if he had the ability, and if he lived.

Cargill finished his story and looked at the time. "Get some sleep, Staley. You'll have the con after turnover."

From a distance the asteroid looked dark, rough, and porous. It rotated once in thirty-one hours; oddly slow, according to Buckman. There was no sign of activity: no motion, no radiation, no anomalous neutrino flux. Horst Staley searched for temperature variations but there were none.

"I think that confirms it," he reported. "The place must be empty. A life form that evolved on Mote Prime would need heat, wouldn't it, sir?"

"Yes."

The cutter moved in. Stippling which had made the rock look porous at a distance became pocks, then gaping holes of random size. Meteors, obviously. But so many?

"I told you the Trojan points were crowded," Buckman said happily. "Probably the asteroid passes through the thick of the Trojan cluster regularly . . . only, give me a close-up of that big pock there, Cargill."

Two powers higher, and the screen was half filled by a black pit. Smaller pits showed around it.

"No sign of a crater rim," Cargill said.

"Noticed that, did you? Damn thing's hollow. *That's* why the density is so low. Well, it's not inhabited now, but it must have been once. They even went to the trouble of giving it a comfortable rotation." Buckman turned. "Cargill, we'll want to search through that thing."

"Yes, but not you. A Navy crew will board the rock."

"This is my field of competence, damn it!"

"Your safety's mine, Doctor. Lafferty, take us around the rock."

The back of the asteroid was one enormous cup-shaped crater.

"Pocked with little craters . . . but they are craters. Not holes," said Cargill. "Doctor, what do you make of that?"

"I can't imagine. Not if it's a natural formation—"

"It was moved!" Staley exclaimed.

"Oddly enough, just what I was thinking," Cargill said. "The asteroid was moved using thermonuclear devices, exploding the bombs progressively in the same crater to channel the blast. It's been done before. Get me a radiation reading, Midshipman."

"Aye aye, sir." He left, and returned in a minute. "Nothing, sir. It's cold."

"Really?" Cargill went to check that for himself. When

he finished he looked at his instruments and frowned. "Cold as a pirate's heart. If they used bombs, they must have been goddamn clean. That shouldn't surprise me."

The cutter circled farther around the flying mountain.

"That could be an air lock. There." Staley pointed at a raised cap of stone surrounded by an archery target in faded orange paint.

"Right, but I doubt if we'd get it open. We'll go in through one of the meteor holes. Still . . . we'll look it over. Lafferty, take us in."

In their reports they called it Beehive Asteroid. The rock was all many-sided chambers without floors linked by channels too small for men, all choked with dried asymmetrical mummies. Whatever miracles the builders had made, artificial gravity was not one of them. The corridors went in all directions; the larger chambers and storage rooms were studded everywhere with knobs for hand holds, anchor points for lines, storage niches.

The mummies floated everywhere, thin and dried, with gaping mouths. They varied from a meter to a meter and a half in height. Staley chose several and sent them back to the cutter.

There was machinery too, all incomprehensible to Staley and his men, all frozen fast by vacuum cementing. Staley had one of the smaller machines torn from the wall. He chose it for strangeness, not potential use; none of the machines was complete. "No metal," Staley reported. "Stone flywheels and things that look like they might be integrated circuits—ceramics with impurities, that kind of thing. But very little metal, sir."

They moved on at random. Eventually they reached a central chamber. It was gigantic, and so was the machine that dominated it. Cables that might have been power superconductors led from the wreck, convincing Staley that this was the asteroid's power source; but it showed no trace of radiation.

They worked through narrow passages between incomprehensible blocks of stone, and found a large metallic box.

"Cut into that," Staley ordered.

Lafferty used his cutting laser. They stool around watching the narrow green beam do nothing to the silvery casing. Staley wondered: where was the energy going? Could they be pumping power into it, somehow? Warmth on his face hinted at the answer.

He took a thermometer reading. The casing was just less than red-hot, all over. When Lafferty turned off the laser the casing cooled rapidly; but it maintained the same temperature at every point.

A *superconductor of heat*. Staley whistled into his suit mike and wondered if he could find a smaller sample. Then he tried using pliers on the casing—and it bent like tin. A strip came away in the pliers. They tore sheets off with their gauntleted hands.

It was impossible to map the Beehive with its tight, curving corridors. It was hard to tell where they were; but they marked their paths as they went, and used proton-beam instruments to measure distances through walls.

The corridor walls were eggshell thin throughout the interior. They were not much thicker outside. Beehive Asteroid could not have been a safe place to live.

But the wall beneath the crater was many meters thick.

Radiation, Staley thought. There must have been residual radiation. Otherwise they would have carved this wall out the way they did all the others, to make room for themselves.

There must have been a wild population explosion here.

And then something killed them all off.

And now there was no radiation at all. How long ago did it all happen? The place was covered with small meteor holes; scores of holes in the walls. How long?

Staley looked speculatively at the small, heavy Motie artifact Lafferty and Sohl were manhandling through the corridor. Vacuum cementing—and the wandering of elementary particles across an interface. That might tell *MacArthur*'s civilian scientists just how long Beehive Asteroid had been abandoned; but already he knew one thing. It was *old*.

19 • *Channel Two's Popularity*

Chaplain David Hardy watched the miniatures only through the intercom because that way he wasn't involved in the endless speculations on what Moties were. It was a question of scientific interest to Horvath and his people; but to Chaplain Hardy there was more than intellectual curiosity at stake. It was his job to determine if Moties were human. Horvath's scientists only wondered if they were intelligent.

The one question preceded the other, of course. It was unlikely that God had created beings with souls and no intelligence; but it was quite possible that He had created intelligent beings with no souls, or beings whose salvation was brought about by ways entirely different from those of mankind. They might even be a form of angel, although an unlikelier-looking set of angels would be hard to imagine. Hardy grinned at the thought and went back to his study of the miniatures. The big Motie was asleep.

The miniatures weren't doing anything interesting at the moment either. It wasn't necessary for Hardy to watch them continuously. Everything was holographed anyway, and as *MacArthur*'s linguist, Hardy would be informed if anything happened. He was already certain the miniatures were neither intelligent nor human.

He sighed deeply. What is man that Thou art mindful of him, O Lord? And why is it my problem to know what place Moties have in Thy plan? Well, that at least was straightforward. Second-guessing God is an old, old game. On paper he was the best man for the job, certainly the best man in Trans-Coalsack Sector.

Hardy had been fifteen years a priest and twelve years a Navy chaplain, but he was only beginning to think of it as his profession. At age thirty-five he had been a full professor at the Imperial University on Sparta, an expert in ancient and modern human languages and the esoteric art

161

called linguistic archeology. Dr. David Hardy had been happy enough tracing the origins of recently discovered colonies lost for centuries. By studying their languages and their words for common objects he could tell what part of space the original colonists had come from. Usually he could pinpoint the planet and even the city.

He liked everything about the university except the students. He had not been particularly religious until his wife was killed in a landing boat crash; then, and he was not sure even yet how it happened, the Bishop had come to see him, and Hardy had looked long and searchingly at his life —and entered a seminary. His first assignment after ordination had been a disastrous tour as chaplain to students. It hadn't worked, and he could see that he was not cut out for a parish priest. The Navy needed chaplains, and could always use linguists . . .

Now, at age fifty-two, he sat in front of an intercom screen watching four-armed monsters playing with cabbages. A Latin crossword puzzle lay on the desk at his left hand, and Hardy played idly with it. *Domine, non——— sum . . .*

"*Dignis,* of course." Hardy chuckled to himself. Precisely what he had said when the Cardinal gave him the assignment of accompanying the Mote expedition. "Lord, I am not worthy . . ."

"None of us is, Hardy," the Cardinal had said. "But then we're not worthy of the priesthood either, and that's more presumption than going out to look at aliens."

"Yes, my lord." He looked at the crossword puzzle again. It was more interesting than the aliens at the moment.

Rod Blaine would not have agreed, but then the Captain didn't get as many chances to watch the playful little creatures as the Chaplain did. There was work to do but for now it could be neglected. His cabin intercom buzzed insistently, and the miniatures vanished to be replaced by the smooth round face of his clerk. "Dr. Horvath insists on speaking with you."

"Put him on," said Rod.

As usual, Horvath's manner was a study in formal cordiality. Horvath must be getting used to getting along with men he could not allow himself to dislike. "Good morning, Captain. We have our first pictures of the alien ship. I thought you'd like to know."

"Thank you, Doctor. What coding?"

"They're not filed yet. I have them right here." The image split, Horvath's face on one half, and a blurred shadow on the other. It was long and narrow, with one end wider than the other, and it seemed to be translucent. The narrow end terminated in a needle spine.

"We caught this picture when the alien made mid-course turnover. Enlargement and noise eliminators gave us this and we won't have better until it's alongside." Naturally, Rod thought. The alien ship would now have its drive pointed toward *MacArthur*.

"The spine is probably the Motie fusion drive." An arrow of light sprang into the picture. "And these formations at the front end— Well, let me show you a density pattern."

The density pattern showed a pencil-shaped shadow circled by a row of much wider, almost invisible toroids. "See? An inner core, rigid, used for launching. We can guess what's in there: the fusion motor, the air and water regeneration chamber for the crew. We've assumed that this section was launched via linear accelerator at high thrust."

"And the rings?"

"Inflatable fuel tanks, we think. Some of them are empty now, as you can see. They may have been kept as living space. Others were undoubtedly ditched."

"Uh huh." Rod studied the silhouette while Horvath watched him from the other side of the screen. Finally Rod said, "Doctor, these tanks couldn't have been on the ship when it was launched."

"No. They may have been launched to meet the core section. Without passengers, they could have been given a much higher thrust."

"In a linear accelerator? The tanks don't look metallic."

"Er—no. They don't seem to be metallic."

"The fuel *has* to be hydrogen, right? So how could those have been launched?"

"We . . . don't know." Horvath hesitated again. "There may have been a metal core. Also ditched."

"Um. All right. Thank you."

After some thought, Rod put the pictures on the intercom. Nearly everything went on the intercom, which served as library, amusement center, and communications for *MacArthur*. In intervals between alerts, or during a battle, one channel of the intercom might show—anything. Canned entertainments. Chess tournaments. Spatball games between the champions of each watch. A play, if the crew had *that* much time on their hands—and they did, sometimes, on blockade duty.

The alien ship was naturally the main topic of conversation in the wardroom.

"There are shadows in yon hollow doughnuts," Sinclair stated. "And they move."

"Passengers. Or furniture," Renner said. "Which means that at least these first four sections are being used as living space. That could be a *lot* of Moties."

"Especially," Rod said as he entered, "if they're as crowded as that mining ship was. Sit down, gentlemen. Carry on." He signaled to a steward for coffee.

"One for every man aboard *MacArthur*," Renner said. "Good thing we've got all this extra room, isn't it?"

Blaine winced. Sinclair looked as if the next intercom event might star the Chief Engineer and the Sailing Master, fifteen rounds . . .

"Sandy, what do you think of Horvath's idea?" Renner asked. "I don't care much for his theory of launching the fuel balloons with a metal core. Wouldn't metal shells around the tanks be better? More structural support. Unless . . ."

"Aye?" Sinclair prompted. Renner said nothing.

"What is it, Renner?" Blaine demanded.

"Never mind, sir. It was a real blue-sky thought. I should learn to discipline my mind."

"Spill it, Mr. Renner."

Renner was new to the Navy, but he was learning to recognize that tone. "Yessir. It occurred to me that hydrogen is metallic at the right temperature and pressure. If those tanks were *really* pressurized, the hydrogen would carry a current—but it would take the kind of pressures you find at the core of a gas giant planet."

"Renner, you don't *really* think—"

"No, of course not, Captain. It was just a thought."

Renner's oddball idea bothered Sandy Sinclair well into the next watch. Engineer officers normally stand no watches on the bridge, but Sinclair's artificers had just finished an overhaul of the bridge life-support systems and Sinclair wanted to test them. Rather than keep another watch officer in armor while the bridge was exposed to vacuum, Sandy took the watch himself.

His repairs worked perfectly, as they always did. Now, his armor stripped off, Sinclair relaxed in the command chair watching the Moties. The Motie program had tremendous popularity throughout the ship, with attention divided between the big Motie in Crawford's stateroom and the miniatures. The big Motie had just finished rebuilding the lamp in her quarters. Now it gave a redder, more diffused light, and she was cutting away at the length of Crawford's bunk to give herself nearly a square meter of working space. Sinclair admired the Motie's work; she was deft, as sure of herself as anyone Sinclair had ever seen. Let the scientists debate, Sandy thought; that beastie was *intelligent*.

On Channel Two, the miniatures played. People watched them even more than the big Motie; and Bury, watching everyone watch the little Moties, smiled to himself.

Channel Two caught Sinclair's eye and he looked away from the big Motie, then suddenly sat bolt upright. The miniatures were having sexual intercourse. "Get that off the intercom!" Sinclair ordered. The signal rating looked pained, but switched the screen so that Channel Two went blank. Moments later, Renner came onto the bridge.

"What's the matter with the intercom, Sandy?" he asked.

"There is nothing wrong with the intercom," Sinclair said stiffly.

"There is too. Channel Two is blank."

"Aye, Mr. Renner. 'Tis blank at my orders." Sinclair looked uncomfortable.

Renner grinned. "And who did you think would object to the—ah, program?" he asked.

"Mon, we will nae show dirty pictures aboard this ship —and with a chaplain aboard! Not to mention the lady."

The lady in question had been watching Channel Two also, and when it faded Sally Fowler put down her fork and left the mess room. Beyond that point she practically ran, ignoring the looks of those she passed. She was puffing when she reached the lounge—where the miniature Moties were still in *flagrante delicto*. She stood beside the cage and watched them for almost a minute. Then she said, not to anyone in particular, "The last time anyone looked, those two were both female."

Nobody said anything.

"They change sex!" she exclaimed. "I'll bet it's pregnancy that triggers it. Dr. Horvath, what do you think?"

"It seems likely enough," Horvath said slowly. "In fact . . . I'm almost sure the one on top was the mother of the little one." He seemed to be fighting off a stutter. Definitely he was blushing.

"Oh, good heavens," said Sally.

It had only just occurred to her what she must have looked like. Hurrying out of the mess room the moment the scene went off the intercom. Arriving out of breath. The Trans-Coalsack cultures had almost universally developed intense prudery within their cultures . . .

And she was an Imperial lady, hurrying to see two aliens make love, so to speak.

She wanted to shout, to explain. It's important! This change of sex, it must hold for all the Moties. It will affect their life styles, their personalities, their history. It shows that young Moties become nearly independent at fantastically low wages . . . Was the pup weaned already, or did the "mother," now male, secrete milk even after the sex change? This will affect everything about Moties, *everything*. It's crucial. That's why I hurried—

Instead, she left. Abruptly.

20 • *Night Watch*

For a wonder the gun room was quiet. With three junior lieutenants crammed in among six middies, it was usually a scene of chaos. Potter sighed thankfully to see that everyone was asleep except Jonathon Whitbread. Despite his banter, Whitbread was one of Potter's friends aboard *MacArthur*.

"How's astronomy?" Whitbread asked softly. The older midshipman was sprawled in his hammock. "Hand me a bulb of beer, will you, Gavin?"

Potter got one for himself too. "It's a madhouse down there, Jonathon. I thought it would be better once they found Mote Prime, but it isn't."

"Hm. Mapping a planet's no more than routine for the Navy," Whitbread told him.

"It might be routine for the Navy, but this is my first deep space cruise. They have me doing most of the work while they discuss new theories I can't understand. I suppose you'd say it's good training?"

"It's good training."

"Thank you." Potter gulped beer.

"It doesn't get any more fun, either. What have you got so far?"

"Quite a bit. There is one moon, you know, so getting the mass was straightforward. Surface gravity about 870 cm/sec square."

"Point 87 standard. Just what the Motie-probe's accelerating. No surprises there."

"But they are in the atmosphere," Potter said eagerly. "And we've mapped the civilization centers. Neutrinos, roiled air columns above fusion plants, electromagnetics—

they're everywhere, on every continent and even out into the seas. That planet's *crowded*." Potter said it in awe. He was used to the sparseness of New Scotland. "We've got a map, too. They were just finishing the globe when I left. Would you like to see it?"

"Sure." Whitbread unstraped from his web hammock. They climbed down two decks to scientist country. Most of the civilians worked in the relatively high gravity areas near the outer surface of *MacArthur*, but bunked nearer the ship's core.

The 120-cm globe was set up in a small lounge used by the astronomy section. During action stations the compartment would be occupied by damage-control parties and used for emergency-repair assemblies. Now it was empty. A chime announced three bells in the last watch.

The planet was mapped completely except for the south pole, and the globe indicated the planet's axial tilt. *MacArthur*'s light-amplifying telescopes had given a picture much like any Earth-type planet: deep and varied blues smeared with white frosting, red deserts, and white tips of mountains. The films had been taken at various times and many wave lengths so that the cloud covers didn't obscure too much of the surface. Industrial centers marked in gold dotted the planet.

Whitbread studied it carefully while Potter poured coffee from Dr. Buckman's Dewar flask. Buckman, for some reason, always had the best coffee in the ship—at least the best that middies had access to.

"Mr. Potter, why do I get the feeling that it looks like Mars?"

"I wouldn't know, Mr. Whitbread. What's a Mars?"

"Sol Four. Haven't you ever been to New Annapolis?"

"I'm Trans-Coalsack, remember."

Whitbread nodded. "You'll get there, though. But I guess they skip part of the training for colonial recruits. It's a pity. Maybe the Captain can arrange it for you. The fun thing is that last training mission, when they make you calculate an emergency minimum fuel landing on Mars, and then *do* it with sealed tanks. You have to use the atmosphere to brake, and since there isn't very damned much of it, you almost have to graze the ground to get any benefit."

"That sounds like fun, Mr. Whitbread. A pity I have a dentist appointment that day——"

Whitbread continued to stare at the globe while they sipped coffee. "It bothers me, Gavin. It really does. Let's go ask somebody."

"Commander Cargill's still out at the Beehive." As First Lieutenant, Cargill was officially in charge of midshipman training. He was also patient with the youngsters, when many other officers were not.

"Maybe somebody will still be up," Whitbread suggested. They went forward toward the bridge, and saw Renner with flecks of soap on his chin. They did not hear him cursing because he now had to share a head with nine other officers.

Whitbread explained his problem. "And it looks like Mars, Mr. Renner. But I don't know why."

"Beats me," Renner said. "I've never been anywhere near Sol." There was no reason for merchant ships to go closer to Sol than the orbit of Neptune, although as the original home of humanity Sol was centrally located as a transfer point to other and more valuable systems. "Never heard anything good about Mars, either. Why is it important?"

"I don't know. It probably isn't."

"But you seem to think it is."

Whitbread didn't answer.

"There's something peculiar about Mote Prime, though. It looks like any random world in the Empire, except—— Or is it just because I know it's covered with alien monsters? Tell you what, I'm due for a glass of wine with the Captain in five minutes. Just let me get my tunic and you come along. We'll ask him."

Renner darted into his stateroom before Whitbread and Potter could protest. Potter looked at his companion accusingly. Now what kind of trouble had he got them into?

Renner led them down the ladders into the high-gravity tower where the Captain's patrol cabin was. A bored Marine sat at the desk outside Blaine's quarters. Whitbread recognized him—reputedly, Sergeant Maloney's vacuum still, located somewhere forward of the port torpedo room, made the best Irish Mist in the fleet. Maloney strove for quality, not quantity.

"Sure, bring the middies in," Blaine said. "There's not much to do until the cutter gets back. Come in, gentlemen. Wine, coffee, or something stronger?"

Whitbread and Potter settled for sherry, although Potter would have preferred Scotch. He had been drinking it since he was eleven. They sat in small folding chairs which fitted into dogs scattered around the deck of Blaine's patrol cabin. The observation ports were open and the ship's Field off, so *MacArthur*'s bulk hovered above them. Blaine noted the middies' nervous glances and smiled. It got to everybody at first.

"What's the problem?" Blaine asked. Whitbread explained.

"I see. Mr. Potter, would you get that globe on my intercom? Thank you." Rod studied the image on the screen. "Hm. Normal-looking world. The colors are off, somehow. Clouds look—well, dirty. Not surprising. There's all kinds of crud in the atmosphere. You'd know that, Mr. Whitbread."

"Yes, sir." Whitbread wrinkled his nose. "Filthy stuff."

"Right. But it's the helium that's driving Buckman up the bulkhead. I wonder if he's figured it out yet? He's had several days . . . Dammit, Whitbread, it *does* look like Mars. But why?"

Whitbread shrugged. By now he was sorry he'd raised the subject.

"It's hard to see the contours. It always is." Absently Rod carried his coffee and Irish Mist over to the intercom screen. Officially he didn't know where the Irish Mist came from. Kelley and his Marines always saw that the Captain had plenty, though. Cziller had liked slivovitz, and *that* had strained Maloney's ingenuity to the breaking point.

Blaine traced the outline of a small sea. "You can't tell land from sea, but the clouds always look like permanent formations . . ." He traced it again. "That sea's almost a circle."

"Yah. So's this one." Renner traced a faint ring of islands, much larger than the sea Blaine had studied. "And this—you can only see part of the arc." This was on land, an arc of low hills.

"They're *all* circles," Blaine announced. "Just like Mars. That's it. Mars has been circling through Sol's asteroid belt for four billion years. But there aren't that many asteroids in this system, and they're all in the Trojan points."

"Sir aren't most of the circles a bit small for that?" Potter asked.

"So they are, Mr. Potter. So they are."

"But what would it mean?" Whitbread said aloud. He meant it mostly for himself.

"Another mystery for Buckman," Blaine said. "He'll love it. Now, let's use the time more constructively. I'm glad you brought the young gentlemen, Mr. Renner. I don't suppose you both play bridge?"

They did, as it happened, but Whitbread had a string of bad luck. He lost nearly a full day's pay.

The game was ended by the return of the cutter. Cargill came immediately to the Captain's quarters to tell about the expedition. He had brought information, a pair of incomprehensible Motie mechanisms now being offloaded in hangar deck, and a torn sheet of gold-metallic stuff which he carried himself with thick gloves. Blaine thanked Renner and the middies for the game and they took the thinly veiled hint, although Whitbread would have liked to stay.

"I'm for my bunk," Potter announced. "Unless—"

"Yes?" Whitbread prompted.

"Would it nae be a bonny sight if Mr. Crawford were to see his stateroom now?" Potter asked mischievously.

A slow grin spread across Jonathon Whitbread's plump features. "It would indeed, Mr. Potter. It would indeed. Let's hurry!"

It was worth it. The midshipmen weren't alone in the debriefing rooms off hangar deck when a signal rating, prompted by Whitbread, tuned in the stateroom.

Crawford didn't disappoint them. He would have committed xenocide, the first such crime in human history, if he hadn't been restrained by his friends. He raved so much that the Captain heard about it, and as a result Crawford went directly from patrol to standing the next watch.

Buckman collected Potter and scurried to the astronomy lab, sure that the young middie had created chaos. He was pleasantly surprised at the work accomplished. He was also pleased with the coffee waiting for him. That flask was *always* full, and Buckman had come to expect it. He knew that it was somehow the work of Horace Bury.

Within half an hour of the cutter's arrival, Bury knew of the sheet of golden metal. Now that was something odd—and potentially quite valuable. The ancient-looking Motie machines might be equally so— If he could only get access to the cutter's computer! But Nabil's skills didn't include that one.

Ultimately there would be coffee and conversation with Buckman, but that could wait, that could wait. And tomorrow the Motie ship would arrive. No question about it, this was going to be a very valuable expedition—and the Navy thought they were punishing him by keeping him away from his business! True, there would be no growth without Bury to supervise it and drive his underlings on, but it wouldn't suffer much either; and now, with what he would learn here, Imperial Autonetics might become the most powerful firm in the Imperial Traders' Association. If the Navy thought the ITA made trouble for them now, wait until it was controlled by Horace Bury! He smiled slyly to himself. Nabil, seeing his master's smile, hunched nervously and tried to be inconspicuous.

Below in hangar deck Whitbread was put to work along with everyone else who had wandered there. Cargill had brought back a number of items from the Stone Beehive, and they had to be uncrated. Whitbread was ingenious enough to volunteer to assist Sally before Cargill gave him another job.

They unloaded skeletons and mummies for the anthropology lab. There were doll-sized miniatures, very fragile, that matched the live miniatures in the petty officers' lounge. Other skeletons, which Staley said were very numerous in the Beehive, matched the Motie miner now bunked in Crawford's stateroom.

"Hah!" cried Sally. They were unpacking still another mummy.

"Uh?" Whitbread asked.

"This one, Jonathon. It matches the one in the Motie probe. Or does it? The forehead slope is wrong . . . but of course they'd pick the most intelligent person they could find as emissary to New Caledonia. This is a first contact with aliens for them too."

There was a small, small-headed mummy, only a meter long, with large, fragile hands. The long fingers on all three hands were broken. There was a dry hand which Cargill had found floating free, different from anything yet found: the bones strong and straight and thick, the joints large. "Arthritis?" Sally wondered. They packed it carefully away and went on to the next box, the remains of a foot which had also been floating free. It had a small, sharp thorn on the heel, and the front of the foot was as hard as a horse's hoof, quite sharp and pointed, unlike the other Motie foot structures.

"Mutations?" Sally said. She turned to Midshipman Staley, who had also been drafted for striking the cargo below. "You say the radiation was all gone?"

"It was dead cold, uh—Sally," said Staley. "But it must have been a hell of a radiation at one time."

Sally shivered. "I wonder just now much time we're talking about. Thousands of years? It would depend on how clean those bombs they used to propel the asteroid were."

"There was no way of telling," Staley answered. "But that place *felt* old, Sally. Old, old. The most ancient thing I can compare it to is the Great Pyramid on Earth. It felt older than that."

"Um," she said. "But that's no *evidence,* Horst."

"No. But that place was *old.* I know it."

Analysis of the finds would have to wait. Just unloading and storing took them well into the first watch, and everyone was tired. It was 0130, three bells in the first watch, when Sally went to her cabin and Staley to the gun room. Jonathon Whitbread was left alone.

He had drunk too much coffee in the Captain's cabin and he was not tired. He could sleep later. In fact he would have to, since the Motie ship would pull alongside *MacArthur* during the forenoon watch; but that was nine hours away, and Whitbread was young.

MacArthur's corridors glowed with half the lights of the ship's day. They were nearly empty, with the stateroom doors all closed. The ever present human voices that drifted in every corridor during *MacArthur*'s day, interfering with each other until no single voice could be heard, had given way to—silence.

The tension of the day remained, though. *MacArthur* would never be at rest while in the alien system. And out there, invisible, her screens up and her crew standing double watches, was the great cylindrical bulk of *Lenin*. Whitbread thought of the huge laser cannon on the battleship: many would be trained on *MacArthur* right now.

Whitbread loved night watches. There was room to breathe, and room to be alone. There was company too, crewmen on watch, late-working scientists—only this time everyone seemed to be asleep. Oh, well, he could watch the miniatures on the intercom, have a final drink, read a little, and go to sleep. The nice thing about the first watch was that there would be unoccupied labs to sit in.

The intercom screen was blank when he dialed the Moties. Whitbread scowled for a second—then grinned and strolled off toward the petty officers' lounge.

Be it admitted: Whitbread was expecting to find two miniature Moties engaged in sexual congress. A midshipman must find his own entertainment, after all.

He opened the door—and something shot between his feet and out, a flash of yellow and brown. Whitbread's family had owned dogs. It gave him certain trained reflexes. He jumped back, fast, slammed the door to keep anything else from getting out, then looked down the corridor.

He saw it quite clearly in the instant before it dodged

into the crew galley area. One of the miniature Moties; and the shape above its shoulders had to be the pup.

The other adult must still be in the petty officers' lounge. For a moment Whitbread hesitated. He had caught dogs by moving after them *immediately*. It was in the galley —but it didn't know him, wasn't trained to his voice— and damn it, *it wasn't a dog*. Whitbread scowled. This would be no fun at all. He went to an intercom and called the watch officer.

"Jee Zuss Christ," said Crawford. "All right, you say one of the goddamn things is still in the lounge? Are you sure?"

"No, sir. I haven't actually looked in there, but I only spotted one."

"*Don't* look in there," Crawford ordered. "Stay by the door and don't let *anyone* in there. I'll have to call the Captain." Crawford scowled. The Captain might well bite his head off, being called out of bed because a pet had got loose, but the standing orders said any activities by aliens must be reported to the Captain immediately.

Blaine was one of those fortunate people who can come awake instantly without transition. He listened to Crawford's report.

"All right, Crawford, get a couple of Marines to relieve Whitbread and tell the midshipman to stand by. I'll want his story. Turn out another squad of Marines and wake up the cooks. Have them search the galley." He closed his eyes to think. "Keep the lounge sealed until Dr. Horvath gets down there." He switched off the intercom. Have to call Horvath, Rod thought.

And have to call the Admiral. Best to postpone *that* until he knew what had happened. But it couldn't be put off long. He pulled on his tunic before calling the Science Minister.

"They got *loose*? How?" Horvath demanded. The Science Minister was *not* one of those fortunate people. His eyes were wounds. His thin hair went in all directions at once. He worked his mouth, clearly not satisfied with the taste.

"We don't know," Rod explained patiently. "The camera was off. One of my officers went to investigate." That'll do for the scientists, anyway. Damned if I'm going to let a bunch of civilians roast the kid. If he's got lumps coming, I'll give 'em myself. "Doctor, we'll save time if you'll come down to the lounge area immediately."

The corridor outside the lounge was crowded. Horvath in a rumpled red-silk dressing gown; four Marines, Leyton, the junior officer of the watch, Whitbread, Sally Fowler dressed in a bulky housecoat but with her face well scrubbed and her hair in a bandanna. Two cooks and a petty officer cook, all muttering as they rattled pans in the galley, were searching for the Motie while more Marines looked around helplessly.

Whitbread was saying, "I slammed the door and looked down the corridor. The other one *could* have gone the other way—"

"But you think he's still in there."

"Yessir."

"All right, let's see if we can get in there without letting him out."

"Uh—do they bite, Cap'n?" a Marine corporal asked. "We could issue the men some gauntlets."

"That won't be necessary," Horvath assured them. "They have never bitten anyone."

"Yessir," the corporal said. One of his men muttered, "They said that about hive rats, too," but no one paid any attention. Six men and a woman formed a semicircle around Horvath as he prepared to open the door. They were tense, grim, the armed Marines ready for anything. For the first time Rod felt a wild urge to laugh. He choked it down. But that poor, tiny beast—

Horvath went through the door quickly. Nothing came out.

They waited.

"All right," the Science Minister called. "I can see it. Come on in, one at a time. It's under the table."

The miniature watched them slide through the door, one by one, and surround it. If it were waiting for an opening, it never saw one. When the door was shut and seven men and a woman ringed its refuge, it surrendered. Sally cradled it in her arms.

"Poor little thing," she crooned. The Motie looked around, obviously frightened.

Whitbread examined what was left of the camera. It had shorted out, somehow. The short had maintained itself long enough for metal and plastic to fuse and drip, leaving a stench not yet removed by *MacArthur*'s air plant. The wire netting just behind the camera had melted too, leaving a large hole. Blaine came over to examine the wreckage.

"Sally," Rod asked. "Could they have been intelligent enough to *plan* this?"

"No!" said Sally and Horvath, forcefully, in chorus. "The brain's too small," Dr. Horvath amplified.

"Ah," Whitbread said to himself. But he did not forget that the camera had been inside the netting.

Two communications division artificers were summoned to patch the hole. They welded new netting over it, and Sally put the miniature back in its cage. The artificers brought in another video camera, which they mounted *outside* the netting. No one made any comment.

The search went on through the watch. No one found the female and the pup. They tried getting the big Motie to help, but she obviously didn't understand or wasn't interested. Finally, Blaine went back to his cabin to sleep for a couple of hours. When he woke the miniatures were still missing.

"We could set the ferrets after them," Cargill suggested at breakfast in the wardroom. A leading torpedoman kept a pair of the cat-sized rodents and used them to keep the forecastle clear of mice and rats. The ferrets were extremely efficient at that.

"They'd kill the Moties," Sally protested. "They aren't dangerous. Certainly no more dangerous than rats. We can't kill them!"

"If we don't find them pretty soon, the Admiral's going to kill *me*," Rod growled, but he gave in. The search continued and Blaine went to the bridge.

"Get me the Admiral," he told Staley.

"Aye aye, sir." The midshipman spoke into the com circuit.

A few moments later Admiral Kutuzov's craggy bearded features came onto the screen. The Admiral was on his bridge, drinking tea from a glass. Now that Rod thought of it, he had never spoken to Kutuzov when he *wasn't* on the bridge. When did he sleep? Blaine reported the missing Moties.

"You still have no idea what these miniatures are, Captain?" Kutuzov demanded.

"No, sir. There are several theories. The most popular is that they're related to the Moties the same way that monkeys are related to humanity."

"That is interesting, Captain. And I suppose these theories explain why there are monkeys on asteroid mining ship? And why this miner brought two monkeys aboard your war vessel? I have not noticed that we carry monkeys, Captain Blaine."

"No, sir."

"The Motie probe arrives in three hours," Kutuzov muttered. "And the miniatures escaped last night. This timing is interesting, Captain. I think those miniatures are spies."

"Spies, sir?"

"Spies. You are told they are not intelligent. Perhaps true, but could they memorize? That does not seem to me impossible. You have told me of mechanical abilities of large alien. It ordered miniatures to return that Trader's watch. Captain, under no circumstances may adult alien be allowed contact with miniatures which have escaped. Nor may any large alien do so. Is that understood?"

"Yes, sir . . ."

"You want reason?" the Admiral demanded. "If there is any chance at all that those beasts could learn secrets of Drive and Field, Captain . . ."

"Yes, sir. I'll see to it."

"See that you do, Captain."

Blaine sat for a moment staring at the blank screen, then glanced across at Cargill. "Jack, you shipped with the Admiral once, didn't you? What's he really like under all that legendary image?"

Cargill took a seat near Blaine's command chair. "I was only a middie when he was Captain, Skipper. Not too close a relationship. One thing, we all respected him. He's the toughest officer in the service and he doesn't excuse anyone, especially not himself. But if there are battles to be fought, you've got a better chance of coming back alive with the Tsar in command."

"So I've heard. He's won more general fleet actions than any officer in the service, but Jesus, what a tough bastard."

"Yes, sir." Cargill studied his captain closely. They had been lieutenants together not long before, and it was easier to talk to Blaine than it would be with an older CO. "You've never been on St. Ekaterina, have you, Skipper?"

"No."

"But we've got several crewmen from there. *Lenin* has more, of course. There's an unholy high percentage of Katerinas in the Navy, Skipper. You know why?"

"Only vaguely."

"They were settled by the Russian elements of the old CoDominium fleet," Cargill said. "When the CD fleet pulled out of Sol System, the Russkis put their women and children on Ekaterina. In the Formation Wars they got hit bad. Then the Secession Wars started when Sauron hit St. Ekaterina without warning. It stayed loyal, but . . ."

"Like New Scotland," Rod said.

Cargill nodded enthusiastically. "Yes, sir. Imperial loyalist fanatics. With good reason, given their history. The only peace they've ever seen has been when the Empire's strong."

Rod nodded judiciously, then turned back to his screens. There was one way to make the Admiral happy. "Staley," Blaine snapped. "Have Gunner Kelley order all Marines to search for the escaped Moties. They are to shoot on sight. Shoot to disable, if possible, but shoot. And have those ferrets turned loose in the galley area."

21 • *The Ambassadors*

As the Motie ship made its final approach, all details of its construction remained hidden by the flaring drive. *MacArthur* watched with screens up and charged. A hundred kilometers away, *Lenin* watched too.

"Battle stations, Mr. Staley," Blaine ordered softly.

Staley grasped the large red handle which now pointed to Condition Two and moved it all the way clockwise. Alarms trilled, then a recorded trumpet sang "To Arms!," rapid notes echoing through steel corridors.

"NOW HEAR THIS. NOW HEAR THIS. BATTLE STATIONS, BATTLE STATIONS. CONDITION RED ONE."

Officers and crew rushed to action stations—gun crews, talkers, torpedomen, Marines. Shipfitters and cooks and storekeepers became damage-control men. Surgeon's mates manned emergency aid stations throughout the ship—all quickly, all silently. Rod felt a burst of pride. Cziller had given him a taut ship, and by God they *still* were taut.

"COM ROOM REPORTS CONDITION RED ONE," the bridge talker announced. The quartermaster's mate third class said words given him by someone else, and all over the ship men rushed to obey, but he gave no orders of his own. He parroted words that would send *MacArthur* leaping across space, fire laser cannon and launch torpedoes, attack or withdraw, and he reported results that Blaine probably already knew from his screens and instruments. He took no initiative and never would, but through him the ship was commanded. He was an all-powerful mindless robot.

"GUNNERY STATIONS REPORT CONDITION RED ONE."

"MARINE COMMANDER REPORTS CONDITION RED ONE."

"Staley, have the Marines not on sentry duty continue the search for those missing aliens," Blaine ordered.

"Aye aye, sir."

"DAMAGE CONTROL REPORTS CONDITION RED ONE."

The Motie ship decelerated toward *MacArthur,* the fusion flame of its drive a blaze on the battle cruiser's screens. Rod watched nervously. "Sandy, how much of that drive could we take?"

"It's nae too hot, Captain," Sinclair reported through the intercom. "The Field can handle all of that for twenty minutes or more. And 'tis nae focused, Skipper, there'd be nae hot spots."

Blaine nodded. He'd reached the same conclusion, but it was wise to check when possible. He watched the light grow steadily.

"Peaceful enough," Rod told Renner. "Even if it is a warship."

"I'm not so sure it is one, Captain." Renner seemed very much at ease. Even if the Motie should attack he'd be more a spectator than a participant. "At least they've aimed their drive flame to miss. Courtesy counts."

"The hell it does. That flames *spreads*. Some of it is spilling onto our Langston Field, and they can observe what it does to us."

"I hadn't thought of that."

"MARINES REPORT CIVILIANS IN CORRIDORS, B DECK BULKHEAD TWENTY."

"God damn it!" Blaine shouted. "That's astronomy. Get those corridors cleared!"

"It'll be Buckman," Renner grinned. "And they'll have their troubles getting him to his stateroom . . ."

"Yeah. Mr. Staley, tell the Marines to put Buckman in his cabin even if they have to frogmarch him there."

Whitbread grinned to himself. *MacArthur* was in free fall, all her spin gone. Now how would the Marines frogmarch the astrophysicist in that?

"TORPEDO ROOMS REPORT CONDITION RED ONE. TORPE-DOES ARMED AND READY."

"One of the leading cooks thinks he saw a miniature," Staley said. "The Marines are on the way."

The alien ship drew closer, her drive a steady white blaze. She was cutting it very fine, Blaine thought. The deceleration hadn't changed at all. They obviously trusted *everything*—their drives, their computers, sensors . . .

"ENGINE ROOM REPORTS CONDITION RED ONE. FIELD AT MAXIMUM STRENGTH."

"The Marines have Dr. Buckman in his stateroom," Staley said. "Dr. Horvath is on the intercom. He wants to complain."

"Listen to him, Staley. But not for long."

"GUNNERY REPORTS ALL BATTERIES LOCKED ONTO ALIEN CRAFT. LOCKED ON AND TRACKING."

MacArthur was at full alert. All through the ship her crew waited at action stations. All nonessential equipment located near the ship's hull had been sent below.

The tower containing Blaine's patrol cabin stuck out of the battle cruiser's hull like an afterthought. For spin gravity it was conveniently far from the ship's axis, but in a battle it would be the first thing shot off. Blaine's cabin was an empty shell now, his desk and the more important gear long since automatically raised into one of the null-gravity recreation areas.

Every idle compartment at the ship's core was jammed, while the outer decks were empty, cleared to make way for damage-control parties.

And the Motie ship was approaching fast. She was still no more than a brightening light, a fusion jet fanning out to splash *MacArthur*'s Langston Field.

"GUNNERY REPORTS ALIEN SHIP DECELERATING AT POINT EIGHT SEVEN ZERO GRAVITIES."

"No surprises," said Renner sotto voce.

The light expanded to fill the screen—and then dimmed. Next moment the alien ship was sliding precisely alongside the battle cruiser, and its drive flame was already off.

It was as if the vessel had entered an invisible dock predetermined six days ago. The thing was at rest relative to *MacArthur*. Rod saw shadows moving within the inflated rings at its fore end.

Renner snarled, an ugly sound. His face contorted. "Goddamn show-offs!"

"Mr. Renner, control yourself."

"Sorry, sir. That's the most astounding feat of astrogation I've ever heard of. If anyone tried to tell me about it, I'd call him a liar. Who do they think they are?" Renner was genuinely angry. "Any astrogator-in-training that tried a stunt like that would be out on his tail, if he lived through the crash."

Blaine nodded. The Motie pilot had left no margin of error at all. And— "I was wrong. That couldn't possibly be a warship. *Look* at it."

"Yah. It's as fragile as a butterfly. I could crush it in my hand."

Rod mused a moment, then gave orders. "Ask for volunteers. To make first contact with that ship, alone, using an unarmed taxi. And . . . keep Condition Red One."

There were a good many volunteers.

Natural Mr. Midshipman Whitbread was one of them. And Whitbread had done it before.

Now he waited in the taxi. He watched the hangar doors unfolding through his polarized plastic faceplate.

He had done this before. The Motie miner hadn't killed him, had she? The black rippled. Sudden stars showed through a gap in the Langston Field.

"That's big enough," Cargill's voice said in his right ear. "You may launch, Mr. Whitbread. On your way—and Godspeed."

Whitbread fired thruster clusters. The taxi rose, floated through the opening into starry space and the distant glare of Murcheson's Eye. Behind him the Langston Field closed. Whitbread was sealed outside.

MacArthur was a sharply bounded region of supernatural blackness. Whitbread circled it at leisure. The Mote flashed bright over the black rim, followed by the alien ship.

Whitbread took his time. The ship grew slowly. Its core was as slender as a spear. Functional marking showed along its sides: hatch covers, instrument ports, antennae, no way to tell. A single black square fin jutted from near the midpoint: possibly a radiator surface.

Within the broad translucent doughnuts that circled the

fore end he could see moving shapes. They showed clearly enough to arouse horror: vaguely human shadows twisted out of true.

Four toroids, and shadows within them all. Whitbread reported, "They're using all their fuel tanks for living space. They can't expect to get home without our help."

The Captain's voice: "You're sure?"

"Yes, sir. There could be an inboard tank, but it wouldn't be very large."

He had nearly reached the alien craft. Whitbread slowed to a smooth stop just alongside the inhabited fuel tanks. He opened his air-lock door.

A door opened immediately near the fore end of the metal core. A Motie stood in the oval opening; it wore a transparent envelope. The alien waited.

Whitbread said, "Permission to leave the—"

"Granted. Report whenever convenient. Otherwise, use your own judgment. The Marines are standing by, Whitbread, so don't yell for help unless you *mean* it. They'll come fast. Now good luck."

As Cargill's voice faded, the Captain came on again. "Don't take any serious risks, Whitbread. Remember, we want you back to report."

"Aye aye, sir."

The Motie stepped gracefully out of his way as Whitbread approached the air lock. It left the Motie standing comically on vacuum, its big left hand gripping a ring that jutted out from the hull. "There's stuff poking out all over," Whitbread said into his mike. "This thing *couldn't* have been launched from inside an atmosphere."

He stopped himself in the oval opening and nodded at the gently smiling alien. He was only half sardonic as he asked formally, "Permission to come aboard?"

The alien bowed from the waist—or perhaps it was an exaggerated nod? The joint in its back was below the shoulders. It gestured toward the ship with the two right arms.

The air lock was Motie-sized, cramped. Whitbread found three recessed buttons in a web of silver streamers.

Circuitry. The Motie watched his hesitation, then reached past him to push first one, then another.

The lock closed behind him.

The Mediator stood on emptiness, waiting for the lock to cycle. She wondered at the intruder's queer structure, at the symmetry and the odd articulation of its bones. Clearly the thing was not related to known life. And its home ship had appeared in what the Mediator thought of as the Crazy Eddie point.

She was far more puzzled at its failure to work out the lock circuitry without help.

It must be here in the capacity of a Mediator. It had to be intelligent. Didn't it? Or would they send an animal first? No, certainly not. They couldn't be that alien; it would be a deadly insult in any culture.

The lock opened. She stepped in and set it cycling. The intruder was waiting in the corridor, filling it like a cork in a bottle. The Mediator took time to strip off her pressure envelope, leaving her naked. Alien as it was, the thing might easily assume she was a Warrior. She must convince the creature that she was unarmed.

She led the way toward the roomier inflated sections. The big, clumsy creature had trouble moving. It did not adapt well to free fall. It stopped to peer through window panels into sections of the ship, and examined mechanisms the Browns had installed in the corridor . . . why would an intelligent being do that?

The Mediator would have liked to tow the creature, but it might take that as an attack. She must avoid that at all costs.

For the present, she would treat it as a Master.

There was an acceleration chamber: twenty-six twisted bunks stacked in three columns, all similar in appearance to Crawford's transformed bunk; yet they were not quite identical, either. The Motie moved ahead of him, graceful as a dolphin. Its short pelt was a random pattern of curved brown and white stripes, punctuated by four patches of thick white fur at the groin and armpits. Whitbread found it beautiful. Now it had stopped to wait for him—impatiently, Whitbread thought.

He tried not to think about how thoroughly he was trapped. The corridor was unlighted and claustrophobically narrow. He looked into a line of tanks connected by pumps, possibly a cooling system for hydrogen fuel. It would connect to that single black fin outside.

Light flashed on the Motie.

It was a big opening, big enough even for Whitbread. Beyond: dim sunlight, like the light beneath a thunderstorm. Whitbread followed the Motie into what had to be one of the toroids. He was immediately surrounded by aliens.

They were all identical. That seemingly random pattern of brown and white was repeated on every one of them. At least a dozen smiling lopsided faces ringed him at a polite distance. They chattered to each other in quick squeaky voices.

The chattering stopped suddenly. One of the Moties approached Whitbread and spoke several short sentences that might have been in different languages, though to Whitbread they were all meaningless.

Whitbread shrugged, theatrically, palms forward.

The Motie repeated the gesture, instantly, with incredible accuracy. Whitbread cracked up. He sprawled helplessly in free fall, arms folded around his middle, cackling like a chicken.

Blaine spoke in his ear, his voice sober and metallic. "All right, Whitbread, everyone else is laughing too. The question is—"

"Oh, no! Sir, am I on the intercom again?"

"The question is, what do the Moties think you're doing?"

"Yessir. It was the third arm that did it." Whitbread had sobered. "It's time for my strip-tease act, Captain. Please take me off that intercom . . ."

The telltale at his chin was yellow, of course. Slow poison; but this time he wasn't going to breath it. He took a deep breath, undogged, and lifted his helmet. Still holding his breath, he took SCUBA gear from an outside patch of his suit and fitted the mouthpiece between his teeth. He turned on the air; it worked fine.

Leisurely he began to strip. First came the baggy coverall that contained the suit electronics and support gear. Then he unsnapped the cover strips that shielded the zippers, and opened the tight fabric of the pressure suit itself. The zippers ran along each limb and up the chest; without them it would take hours to get in and out of a suit, which looked like a body stocking or a leotard. The elastic fibers conformed to every curve of his musculature, as they had to, to keep him from exploding in vacuum; with their support, his own skin was in a sense his pressure suit, and his sweat glands were the temperature-regulating system.

The tanks floated free in front of him as he struggled out of the suit. The Moties moved slowly, and one—a Brown, no stripes, identical to the miner aboard *MacArthur*—came over to help.

He used the all-purpose goop in his tool kit to stick his helmet to the translucent plastic wall. Surprisingly it did not work. The brown Motie recognized his difficulty instantly. He (she, it) produced a tube of something and dabbed it on Whitbread's helmet; now it stuck. Jonathon faced the camera toward him, and stuck the rest of his suit next to it.

Humans would have aligned themselves with their heads at the same end, as if they must define an up direction before they could talk comfortably. The Moties were at all angles. They clearly didn't give a damn. They waited, smiling.

Whitbread wriggled the rest of the way out of his suit, until he wore nothing at all.

The Moties moved in to examine him.

The Brown was startling among all the brown-and-white patterns. It was shorter than the others, with slightly bigger hands and an odd look to the head; as far as Whitbread could tell, it was identical to the miner. The others looked like the dead one in the Motie light-sail probe.

The brown one was examining his suit, and seemed to be doing things to the tool kit; but the others were prodding at him, seeking the musculature and articulations of his body, looking for places where prodding would produce reflex twitching and jumping.

Two examined his teeth, which were clenched. Others traced his bones with their fingers: his ribs, his spine, the shape of his head, his pelvis, the bones of his feet. They palpated his hands and moved the fingers in ways they were not meant to go. Although they were gentle enough, it was all thoroughly unpleasant.

The chattering rose to a crescendo. Some of the sounds were so shrill they were nearly inaudible shrieks and whistles, but behind them were melodious mid-range tones. One phrase seemed to be repeated constantly in high tenor. Then they were all behind him, showing each other his spine. They were very excited about Whitbread's spine. A Motie signaled him by catching his eye and then hunching back and forth. The joints jutted as if its back were broken in two places. Whitbread felt queasy watching it, but he got the idea. He curled into fetal position, straightened, then curled up again. A dozen small alien hands probed his back.

Presently they backed away. One approached and seemed to invite Whitbread to explore his (her, its) anatomy. Whitbread shook his head and deliberately looked away. That was for the scientists.

He received his helmet and spoke into the mike. "Ready to report, sir. I'm not sure what to do next. Shall I try to get some of them to come back to *MacArthur* with me?"

Captain Blaine's voice sounded strained. "Definitely not. Can you get outside their ship?"

"Yes, sir, if I have to."

"We'd rather you did. Report on a secure line, Whitbread."

"Uh—yes, sir." Jonathon signaled the Moties, pointed to his helmet and then to the air lock. The one who had been conducting him around nodded. He climbed back into his suit with help from the brown Motie, dogged the fastenings and attached his helmet. A Brown-and-white led him to the air lock.

There was no convenient place outside to attach the

safety line, but after a glance his Motie escort glued a hook onto the ship's surface. It did not look substantial, that hook. Jonathon worried about it briefly. Then he frowned. Where was the ring the Motie had held when Whitbread first approached? It was gone. Why?

Oh, well. *MacArthur* was close. If the hook broke off they would come get him. Gingerly he pushed away from the Motie ship until he hung in empty space. He used his helmet sights to line up exactly with the antenna protruding from *MacArthur's* totally black surface. Then he touched the SECURITY stud with his tongue.

A thin beam of coherent light stabbed out from his helmet. Another came in from *MacArthur,* following his own into a tiny receptable set into the helmet. A ring around that receptacle stayed in darkness; if there were any spillover the tracking system on *MacArthur* would correct it or, if the spill touched still a third ring around Whitbread's receiving antenna, cut off communication entirely.

"Secure, sir," he reported. He let an irritated but puzzled note creep into his voice. After all, he thought, I'm entitled to a *little* expression of opinion. Aren't I?

Blaine answered immediately. "Mr. Whitbread, the reason for this security is not merely to make you uncomfortable. The Moties do not understand our language now, but they can make recordings; and later they will understand Anglic. Do you follow me?"

"Why—yes sir." Ye gods, the Old Man was really thinking ahead.

"Now, Mr. Whitbread, we cannot allow any Motie aboard *MacArthur* until we have disposed of the problem of the miniatures, and we will do nothing to let the Moties know we have such a problem. Is that understood?"

"Yes, sir."

"Excellent. I am sending a boatload of scientists your way—now that you've broken the ground, so to speak. By the way, well done. Before I send the others, have you further comments?"

"Um. Yes, sir. First, there are two children aboard. I

saw them clinging to the backs of adults. They're bigger than miniatures, and colored like the adults."

"More evidence of peaceful intent," Blaine said. "What else?"

"Well, I didn't get a chance to count them, but it looks like twenty-three Brown-and-whites and two brown asteroid-miner types. Both of the children were with the Browns. I've been wondering why."

"Eventually we'll be able to ask them. All right, Whitbread, we'll send over the scientists. They'll have the cutter. Renner, you on?"

"Yes, sir."

"Work out a course. I want *MacArthur* fifty kilometers from the Motie ship. I don't know what the Moties will do when we move, but the cutter'll be over there first."

"You're moving the ship, sir?" Renner asked incredulously. Whitbread wanted to cheer but restrained himself.

"Yes."

Nobody said anything for a long moment.

"All right," Blaine capitulated. "I'll explain. The Admiral is very concerned about the miniatures. He thinks they might be able to talk about the ship. We've orders to see that the escaped miniatures have no chance to communicate with an adult Motie, and one klick is just a bit close."

There was more silence.

"That's all, gentlemen. Thank you, Mr. Whitbread," Rod said. "Mr. Staley, inform Dr. Hardy that he can get aboard the cutter any time."

"Well, you're on," Chaplain Hardy thought to himself. He was a round, vague man, with dreamy eyes and red hair just beginning to turn gray. Except for conducting the Sunday worship services he had deliberately stayed in his cabin during most of the expedition.

David Hardy was not unfriendly. Anyone could come to his cabin for coffee, a drink, a game of chess, or a long talk, and many did. He merely disliked people in large numbers. He could not get to know them in a crowd.

He also retained his professional inclination not to discuss his work with amateurs and not to publish results until enough evidence was in. That, he told himself, would be impossible now. And what *were* the aliens? Certainly they were intelligent. Certainly they were sentient. And certainly they had a place in the divine scheme of the universe. But what?

Crewmen moved Hardy's equipment aboard the cutter. A tape library, several stacks of children's books, reference works (not many; the cutter's computer would be able to draw on the ship's library; but David still liked *books,* impractical as they were). There was other equipment: two display screens with sound transducers, pitch references, electronic filters to shape speech sounds, raise or lower pitch, change timbre and phase. He had tried to stow the gear himself, but First Lieutenant Cargill had talked him out of it. Marines were expert at the task, and Hardy's worries about damage were nothing compared to theirs; if anything broke they'd have Kelley to contend with.

Hardy met Sally in the air lock. She was not traveling light either. Left to herself, she'd have taken *everything,* even the bones and mummies from the Stone Beehive; but the Captain would only allow her holographs, and even those were hidden until she could learn the Moties' attitude toward grave robbers. From Cargill's description of the Beehive, the Moties had no burial customs, but that was absurd. *Everyone* had burial customs, even the most primitive humans.

She could not take the Motie miner, either, or the remaining miniature, which had become female again. And the ferrets and Marines were searching for the other miniature and the pup (and *why* had it run away with the other miniature, not its mother?). She wondered if the fuss she had made about Rod's orders to the Marines might be responsible for the ease with which she won her place on the cutter. She knew she wasn't really being fair to Rod. He had his orders from the Admiral. But it was wrong! The miniatures weren't going to hurt anyone. It took a paranoid to fear them.

She followed Chaplain Hardy into the cutter's lounge. Dr. Horvath was already there. The three of them would be the first scientists aboard the alien ship, and she felt a surge of excitement. There was so much to learn!

An anthropologist—she thought of herself as fully qualified now, and certainly there was no one to dispute it—a linguist, and Horvath, who had been a competent physicist before going into administration. Horvath was the only useless one in the group, but with his rank he was entitled to the seat if he demanded it. She did not think the same description applied to herself, although half the scientists aboard *MacArthur* did.

Three scientists, a coxswain, two able spacers, and Jonathon Whitbread. No Marines, and no weapons aboard. Almost, the excitement was enough to cover the fear that welled up from somewhere in her insides. They had to be unarmed, of course; but she would have felt better, all the same, if Rod Blaine had been aboard. And that was impossible.

Later there would be more people on the cutter. Buckman with a million questions once Hardy cracked the communications problem. The biologists would come in force. A Navy officer, probably Crawford, to study the Motie weapons. An engineering officer. Anyone, but not the Captain. It was unlikely that Kutuzov would allow Rod Blaine to leave his ship no matter how peaceful they might find the Moties.

She was suddenly homesick. On Sparta she had a home, Charing Close, and within minutes was the Capital. Sparta was the center of civilization—but she seemed to be living in a series of space craft of diminishing sizes, with the prison camp thrown in for variety. When she graduated from the university she had made a decision: she would be a person, not an ornament to some man's career. Right now, though, there was much to be said for being an ornament, especially for the right man, only— No. She must be her own woman.

There was a crash couch and a curved instrument board at one end of the cutter's lounge. It was the fire-control bridge—some lounge! But there were also couches and recessed tables for games and dining.

"Have you been through this boat?" Horvath was asking her.

"I beg your pardon?" Sally answered.

"I said, 'Have you been through this boat?' It has gun emplacements all over it. They took out the works, but they left enough to show there were guns. Same with the torpedoes. They're gone, but the launch ports are still there. What kind of embassy ship is this?"

Hardy looked up from a private reverie. "What would you have done in the Captain's place?"

"I'd have used an unarmed boat."

"There aren't any," Hardy replied softly. "None you could live on, as you'd know if you spent any time on hangar deck." Chapel was held on hangar deck, and Horvath had not attended. That was his business, but no harm in reminding him.

"But it's so obviously a disarmed warship!"

Hardy nodded. "The Moties were bound to discover our terrible secret sooner or later. We are a warlike species, Anthony. It's part of our nature. Even so, we arrive in a complete disarmed fighting vessel. Don't you think that's a significant message for the Moties?"

"But this is so important to the Empire!"

David Hardy nodded assent. The Science Minister was right, although the Chaplain suspected he had the wrong reasons.

There was a slight lurch, and the cutter was on her way. Rod watched on the bridge screens and felt helpless frustration. From the moment the cutter came alongside the Motie vessel, one of Crawford's batteries would be locked onto her—and Sally Fowler was aboard the frail, disarmed ship.

The original plan had the Moties coming aboard *MacArthur*, but until the miniatures were found that was impossible. Rod was glad that his ship would not be host to the aliens. I'm learning to think paranoid, he told himself. Like the Admiral.

Meanwhile, there was no sign of the miniatures, Sally wasn't speaking to him, and everyone else was edgy.

"Ready to take over, Captain," Renner said. "I relieve you, sir."

"Right. Carry on, Sailing Master."

Acceleration alarms rang, and *MacArthur* moved smoothly away from the alien vessel—and away from the cutter, and Sally.

22 • *Word Games*

The shower: a plastic bag of soapy water with a young man in it, the neck of the bag sealed tight around the man's neck. Whitbread used a long-handled brush to scratch himself everywhere he itched, which was everywhere. There was pleasure in the pulling and stretching of muscles. It was so flinking small in the Motie ship! So claustrophobic-cramped!

When he was clean he joined the others in the lounge.

The Chaplain and Horvath and Sally Fowler, all wearing sticky-bottomed falling slippers, all aligned in the up direction. Whitbread would never have noticed such a thing before. He said, "Science Minister Horvath, I am to place myself under your orders for the time being."

"Very well, Mr. . . . Whitbread." Horvath trailed off. He seemed worried and preoccupied. They all did.

The Chaplain spoke with effort. "You see, none of us really knows what to do next. We've never contacted *aliens* before."

"They're friendly. They wanted to talk," said Whitbread.

"Good. Good, but it leaves me entirely on the hook." The Chaplain's laugh was all nerves. "What was it like, Whitbread?"

He tried to tell them. Cramped, until you got to the plastic toroids . . . fragile . . . no point in trying to tell the Moties apart except the Browns were somehow different from the Brown-and-whites . . . "They're unarmed," he told them. "I spent three hours exploring that ship.

There's no place aboard that they could be hiding big weapons."

"Did you get the impression they were guiding you away from anything?"

"No—oo."

"You don't sound very certain," Horvath said sharply.

"Oh it isn't that, sir. I was just remembering the tool room. We wound up in a room that was all tools, walls and floor and ceiling. A couple of walls had simple things on them: hand drills, ripsaws with odd handles, screws and a screwdriver. Things I could recognize. I saw nails and what I think was a hammer with a big flat head. It all looked like a hobby shop in somebody's basement. But there were some really complex things in there, too, things I couldn't figure at all."

The alien ship floated just outside the forward window. Inhuman shadows moved within it. Sally was watching them too . . . but Horvath said dryly, "You were saying that the aliens were *not herding* you."

"I don't think they led me *away* from anything. I'm sure I was led *to* that tool room. I don't know why, but I think it was an intelligence test. If it was, I flunked."

Chaplain Hardy said, "The only Motie we've questioned so far doesn't understand the simplest gestures. Now you tell me that these Moties have been giving you intelligence tests—"

"And interpreting gestures. Amazingly quick to understand them, in fact. Yes, sir. They're *different*. You saw the pictures."

Hardy wound a strand of his thinning red hair around a knobby finger and tugged gently. "From your helmet camera? Yes, Jonathon. I think we're dealing with two kinds of Moties. One is an idiot savant and doesn't talk. The other . . . talks," he finished lamely. He caught himself playing with his hair and smoothed it back into place. "I hope I can learn to talk back."

They're all dreading it, Whitbread realized. Especially Sally. And even Chaplain Hardy, who never gets upset about anything. All dreading that first move.

Horvath said, "Any other impressions?"

"I keep thinking that ship was designed for free fall. There are sticky strips all over. Inflated furniture likewise. And there are short passages joining the toroids, as wide as the toroids themselves. Under acceleration they'd be like open trap doors with no way around them."

"That's strange," Horvath mused. "The ship was under acceleration until four hours ago."

"Exactly, sir. The joins must be new." The thought hit Whitbread suddenly. Those joins must be new . . .

"But that tells us even more," Chaplain Hardy said quietly. "And you say the furniture is at all angles. We all saw that the Moties didn't care how they were oriented when they spoke to you. As if they were peculiarly adapted to free fall. As if they *evolved* there . . ."

"But that's impossible," Sally protested. "Impossible but—you're right, Dr. Hardy! Humans *always* orient themselves. Even the old Marines who've been in space all their lives! But nobody can evolve in free fall."

"An old enough race could," Hardy said. "And there are the nonsymmetric arms. Evolutionary advancement? It would be well to keep the theory in mind when we talk to the Moties." If we can talk to them, he added to himself.

"They went crazy over my backbone," Whitbread said. "As if they'd never seen one." He stopped. "I don't know whether you were told. I stripped for them. It seemed only fair that they . . . know what they're dealing with." He couldn't look at Sally.

"I'm not laughing," she said. "I'm going to have to do the same thing."

Whitbread's head snapped up. *"What?"*

Sally chose her words with care; remember provincial mores, she told herself. She did not look up from the deck. "Whatever Captain Blaine and Admiral Kutuzov choose to hide from the Moties, the existence of two human sexes isn't one of them. They're entitled to know how we're made, and I'm the only woman aboard *MacArthur*."

"But you're Senator Fowler's niece!"

She did smile at that. "We won't tell them." She stood

up immediately. "Coxswain Lafferty, we'll be going now." She turned back, very much the Imperial lady, even to her stance, which gave no sign that she was in free fall. "Jonathon, thank you for your concern. Chaplain, you may join me as soon as I call." And she went.

A long time later Whitbread said, "I wondered what was making everyone so nervous."

And Horvath, looking straight ahead, said, "She insisted."

Sally called the cutter when she arrived. The same Motie who had greeted Whitbread, or an identical one, bowed her aboard in a courtly fashion. A camera on the taxi picked that up and caused the Chaplain to lean forward sharply. "That half-nod is very like you, Whitbread. He's an excellent mimic."

Sally called again minutes later, by voice alone. She was in one of the toroids. "There are Moties all around me. A lot of them are carrying instruments. Hand-sized. Jonathon, did—"

"Most of them didn't have anything in their hands. These instruments, what do they look like?"

"Well, one looks like a camera that's been half taken apart, and another has a screen like an oscilloscope screen." Pause. "Well, here goes. Fowler out." Click.

For twenty minutes they knew nothing of Sally Fowler. Three men fidgeted, their eyes riveted to a blank intercom screen.

When she finally called, her voice was brisk. "All right, gentlemen, you may come over now."

"I'm on." Hardy unstrapped and floated in a slow arc to the cutter air lock. His voice, too, was brisk with relief. The waiting was ended.

There was the usual bustle of bridge activities around Rod, scientists looking at the main view screens, quartermasters securing from *MacArthur*'s fifty-kilometer move. To keep occupied Rod was having Midshipman Staley run through a simulated Marine assault on the Motie ship. All purely theoretical, of course; but it did help keep

Rod from brooding about what was happening aboard the alien vessel. The call from Horvath was a welcome distraction, and Rod was ebulliently cordial as he answered.

"Hello, Doctor! How are things going?"

Horvath was almost smiling. "Very well, thank you, Captain. Dr. Hardy is on his way to join Lady Sally. I sent your man Whitbread along."

"Good." Rod felt tension pain where it had settled above and between his shoulder blades. So Sally had got through that . . .

"Captain, Mr. Whitbread mentioned a tool room aboard the alien ship. He believes that he was being tested for his tool-using ability. It strikes me that the Moties may be judging us all on that ability."

"Well they might. Making and using tools is a basic—"

"Yes, yes, Captain, but none of us are toolmakers! We have a linguist, an anthropologist, an administrator—me —and some Navy warriors. The joke is on us, Captain. We spent too much consideration on learning about Moties. None on impressing them with *our* intelligence."

Blaine considered that. "There are the ships themselves . . . but you have a point, Doctor. I'll send you someone. We're bound to have someone aboard who can do well on such a test."

When Horvath was off the screen, Rod touched the intercom controls again. "Kelley, you can take half your Marines off alert now."

"Aye aye, Captain." The Gunner's face showed no signs of emotion, but Rod knew just how uncomfortable battle armor was. The entire Marine force of *MacArthur* was wearing it on full alert in hangar deck.

Then, thoughtfully, Blaine called Sinclair. "It's an unusual problem, Sandy. We need someone who's generally good with tools and willing to go aboard the Motie ship. If you'll pick me some men, I'll ask for volunteers."

"Never mind, Captain. I'll go myself."

Blaine was shocked. "*You,* Sandy?"

"Aye and why not, Captain? Am I no skilled with tools? Can I no fix anything that ever worked in the first place? My laddies can handle aye that could go wrong wi' *MacArthur*. I've trained them well. Ye will no miss me . . ."

"Hold on a minute, Sandy."

"Aye, Captain?"

"OK. Anybody who'd do well in a test will know the Field and Drive. Even so, maybe the Admiral won't let you go."

"There's nae another aboard who'll find out *everything* about yon beasties' ship, Captain."

"Yeah—OK, get the surgeon's approval. And give me a name. Whom shall I send if you can't go?"

"Send Jacks, then. Or Leigh Battson, or any of my lads but Thumbs Menchikov."

"Menchikov. Isn't he the artificer who saved six men trapped in the after torpedo room during the battle with *Defiant?*"

"Aye, Captain. He's also the laddie who fixed your shower two weeks before that battle."

"Oh. Well, thanks, Sandy." He rang off and looked around the bridge. There was really very little for him to do. The screens showed the Motie ship in the center of *MacArthur*'s main battery fire pattern; his ship was safe enough from anything the alien vessel could do, but now Sally would be joined by Hardy and Whitbread . . . He turned to Staley. "That last was very good. Now work out a rescue plan assuming that only half the Marines are on ready alert."

Sally heard the activity as Hardy and Whitbread were conducted aboard the Motie ship, but she barely glanced around when they appeared. She had taken the time to dress properly, but grudged the necessity, and in the dim and filtered Motelight she was running her hands over the body of a Brown-and-white, bending its (her) elbow and shoulder joints and tracing the muscles, all the while dictating a running monologue into her throat mike.

"I conclude they are another subspecies, but closely related to the Browns, perhaps closely enough to breed true. This must be determined by genetic coding, when we take samples back to New Scotland where there is proper equipment. Perhaps the Moties know, but we should be careful about what we ask until we determine what taboos exist among Moties.

"There is obviously no sex discrimination such as exists in the Empire; in fact the predominance of females is remarkable. One Brown is male and cares for both pups. The pups are weaned, or at least there is no obvious sign of a nursing female—or male—aboard.

"My hypothesis is that, unlike humanity after the Secession Wars, there is no shortage of mothers or childbearers, and thus there is no cultural mechanism of overprotectiveness such as survives within the Empire. I have no theory of why there are no pups among the Brown-and-whites, although it is possible that the immature Moties I observe are the issue of Brown-and-whites and the Browns serve as child trainers. There is certainly a tendency to have the Browns do all the technical work.

"The difference in the two types is definite if not dramatic. The hands are larger and better developed in the Brown, and the forehead of the Brown slopes back more sharply. The Brown is smaller. Question: Which is better evolved as a tool user? The Brown-and-white has a slightly larger brain capacity, the Brown has better hands. So far every Brown-and-white I have seen is female, and there is one of each sex of Brown: is this accident, a clue to their culture, or something biological? Transcript ends. Welcome aboard, gentlemen."

Whitbread said, "Any trouble?"

Her head was in a plastic hood that sealed around her neck like a Navy shower bag; she was obviously not used to nasal respirators. The bag blurred her voice slightly. "None at all. I certainly learned as much as they did from the um, er, orgy. What's next?"

Language lessons.

There was a word: *Fyunch(click)*. When the Chaplain pointed at himself and said "David," the Motie he was looking at twisted her lower right arm around into the same position and said "Fyunch(click)," making the click with her tongue.

Fine. But Sally said, "My Motie had the same name, I think."

"Do you mean I've picked the same alien?"

"No, I don't think so. And I *know* Fyunch(click)"—she said it carefully, making the click with her tongue, then ruined the effect by giggling—"isn't the word for Motie. I've tried that."

The Chaplain frowned. "Perhaps all proper names sound alike to us. Or we may have the word for *arm*," he said seriously. There was a classic story about that, so old that it probably came from preatomic days. He turned to another Motie, pointed at himself, and said, "Fyunch-(click)?" His accent was nearly perfect, and he didn't giggle.

The Motie said, "No."

"They picked that up quickly," said Sally.

Whitbread tried it. He swam among the Moties, pointing to himself and saying "Fyunch(click)?" He obtained four perfectly articulated *Nos* before an inverted Motie tapped him on the kneecap and said, "Fyunch(click)? Yes."

So: there were three Moties who would say "Fyunch-(click)" to a human. Each to a different human, and not to the others. So?

"It may mean something like 'I am assigned to you,'" Whitbread suggested.

"Certainly one hypothesis," Hardy agreed. A rather good one, but there were insufficient data—had the boy made a lucky guess?

Moties crawled around them. Some of the instruments they carried might have been cameras or recorders. Some instruments made noises when the humans spoke; others extruded tape, or made wiggly orange lines on small screens. The Moties gave some attention to Hardy's own instruments, especially the male Brown mute, who disassembled Hardy's oscilloscope and put it back together again before his eyes. The images on it seemed brighter, and the persistence control worked much better, he thought. Interesting. And only the Browns did things like that.

The language lessons had become a group effort. It was a game now, this teaching of Anglic to Moties. Point and say the word, and the Moties would generally remember it. David Hardy gave thanks.

The Moties kept fiddling with the insides of their instruments, tuning them, or sometimes handing them to a Brown with a flurry of bird whistles. The range of their own voices was astonishing. Speaking Motie, they ranged from bass to treble in instants. The pitch was part of the code, Hardy guessed.

He was aware of time passing. His belly was a vast emptiness whose complaints he ignored with absent-minded contempt. Chafe spots developed around his nose where the respirator fitted. His eyes smarted from Motie atmosphere that got under his goggles, and he wished he'd opted for either a helmet or a plastic sack like Sally's. The Mote itself was a diffused bright point that moved slowly across the curved translucent wall. Dry breathing air was slowly dehydrating him.

These things he felt as passing time, and ignored. A kind of joy was in him. David Hardy was fulfilling his mission in life.

Despite the uniqueness of the situation, Hardy decided to stick to traditional linguistics. There were unprecedented problems with *hand, face, ears, fingers.* It developed that the dozen fingers of the right hands had one collective name, the three thick fingers of the left another. The ear had one name flat and another erect. There was no name for *face,* although they picked up the Anglic word immediately, and seemed to think it a worthwhile innovation.

He had thought that his muscles had adjusted to free fall; but now they bothered him. He did not put it down to exhaustion. He did not know where Sally had disappeared to, and the fact did not bother him. This was a measure of his acceptance of both Sally and the Moties as colleagues; but it was also a measure of how tired he was. Hardy considered himself enlightened, but what Sally would have called "overprotectiveness of women" was deeply ingrained in the Imperial culture—especially so in the monastic Navy.

It was only when his air gave out that the others could persuade Hardy to go back to the cutter.

Their supper was plain, and they hurried through it to compare notes. Mercifully the others left him alone until he'd eaten, Horvath taking the lead in shushing everyone although he was obviously the most curious of the lot. Even though the utensils were designed for free-fall conditions, none of the others were used to long periods of zero gravity, and eating took new habits that could be learned only through concentration. Finally Hardy let one of the crewmen remove his lap tray and looked up. Three eager faces telepathically beamed a million questions at him.

"They learn Anglic well enough," David said. "I wish I could say the same for my own progress."

"They work at it," Whitbread wondered. "When you give them a word, they keep using it, over and over, trying it out in sentences, trying it out on everything around whatever you showed them—I never saw anything like it."

"That's because you didn't watch Dr. Hardy very long," Sally said. "We were taught that technique in school, but I'm not very good at it."

"Young people seldom are." Hardy stretched out to relax. That void had been filled. But it was embarrassing —the Moties were better at his job than he was. "Young people usually haven't the patience for linguistics. In this case, though, your eagerness helps, since the Moties are directing your efforts quite professionally. By the way, Jonathon, where did you go?"

"I took my Fyunch(click) outside and showed him around the taxi. We ran out of things to show the Moties in their own ship and I didn't want to bring them here. Can we do that?"

"Certainly." Horvath smiled. "I've spoken to Captain Blaine and he leaves it to our judgment. As he says, there's nothing secret on the cutter. However, I'd like there to be something a little special—some ceremony, wouldn't you think? After all, except for the asteroid miner the Moties have never visited a human ship."

Hardy shrugged. "They make little enough of our coming aboard their craft. You want to remember, though, unless the whole Motie race is fantastically gifted at languages—a hypothesis I reject—they've had their special ceremony before they lifted off their planet. They've put language specialists aboard. I wouldn't be surprised to discover that our Fyunch(click)s are the Motie equivalent of full professors."

Whitbread shook his head. The others looked at him, and finally he spoke. He was rather proud of having worked out a technique to let a junior officer interrupt the others. "Sir, that ship left the Mote planet only *hours*—maybe less than one hour—after *MacArthur* appeared in their system. How would they have time to gather specialists?"

"I hadn't known that," Hardy said slowly. "But these *must* be specialists of some kind. What use would such fantastic linguistic abilities be among the general population? And fantastic is not too strong a word. Still and all, we've managed to puzzle them slightly, or did the rest of you notice?"

"The tool room?" Sally asked. "I guess that's what you'd call it, although I don't think I'd have figured it out if Jonathon hadn't given me the clue first. They took me there just after I left you, Dr. Hardy, and they didn't seem puzzled to me. I noticed you stayed a lot longer than I did, though."

"What did you do there?" David asked.

"Why nothing. I looked at all the gadgetry. The whole place was covered with junk—by the way, those wall clamps weren't substantial enough to take real gravity, I'm sure of that. They *must* have built that room after they got here. But anyway, since there wasn't anything I could understand I didn't pay much attention to the place."

Hardy folded his hands in an attitude of prayer, then looked up embarrassed. He'd got into that habit long before he entered the priesthood, and somehow could never break himself of it; but it indicated concentration, not reverence. "You did nothing, and they were not curious about it." He thought furiously for long seconds. "Yet I asked the names of the equipment, and spent quite a long time there, and my Fyunch(click) seemed very surprised. I could be misinterpreting the emotion, but I really think my interest in the tools unsettled them."

"Did you try to use any of the gadgets?" Whitbread asked.

"No. Did you?"

"Well, I played around with some of the stuff . . ."

"And were they surprised or curious about that?"

Jonathon shrugged. "They were all watching me all the time. I didn't notice anything different."

"Yes." Hardy folded his hands again, but this time didn't notice he was doing it. "I think there is something odd about that room and the interest they showed in our interest in it. But I doubt that we'll know why until Captain Blaine sends over his expert. Do you know who's coming?"

Horvath nodded. "He's sending Chief Engineer Sinclair."

"Hmmm." The sound was involuntary. The others looked at Jonathon Whitbread, who grinned slowly. "If the Moties were puzzled by *you,* sir, just think what'll go through their heads when they hear Commander Sinclair talk."

On a Navy warship men do not maintain an average weight. During the long idle periods those who like to eat amuse themselves by eating. They grow fat. But men who can dedicate their lives to a cause—including a good percentage of those who will remain in the Navy—tend to forget about eating. Food cannot hold their attention.

Sandy Sinclair looked straight ahead of himself as he sat rigid on the edge of the examining table. It was this way with Sinclair: he could not look a man in the eye while he was naked. He was big and lean, and his stringy muscles were much stronger than they looked. He might have been an average man given a skeleton three sizes too large.

A third of his surface area was pink scar tissue. Sharp metal flying out of an explosion had left that pink ridge across his short ribs. Most of the rest had been burned into him by puffs of flame or droplets of metal. A space battle left burns, if it left a man alive at all.

The doctor was twenty-three, and cheerful. "Twenty-four years in service, eh? Ever been in a battle?"

Sinclair snapped, "You'll hae your own share o' scars if ye stay wi' the Navy long enough."

"I believe you, somehow. Well, Commander, you're in admirable shape for a man in his forties. You could handle a month of free fall, I think, but we'll play safe and drag you back to *MacArthur* twice a week. I don't suppose I have to tell you to keep up on the free-fall exercises."

Rod Blaine called the cutter several times the next day, but it was evening before he could get anyone besides the pilot. Even Horvath had gone aboard the Motie ship.

Chaplain Hardy was exhausted and jubilant, with a smile spread across his face and great dark circles under his eyes. "I'm taking it as a lesson in humility, Captain. They're far better at my job—well, at linguistics, anyway —than I am. I've decided that the fastest way to learn their language will be to teach them Anglic. No human throat will ever speak their language—languages?—without computer assistance."

"Agreed. It would take a full orchestra. I've heard some of your tapes. In fact, Chaplain, there wasn't much else to do."

Hardy smiled. "Sorry. We'll try to arrange more frequent reporting. By the way, Dr. Horvath is showing a party of Moties through the cutter now. They seem particularly interested in the drive. The brown one wants to take things apart, but the pilot won't let him. You did say there were secrets on this boat."

"Certainly I said that, but it might be a bit premature to let them fool with your power source. What did Sinclair say about it?"

"I don't know, Captain." Hardy looked puzzled. "They've had him in that tool room all day. He's still in there."

Blaine fingered the knot on his nose. He was getting the information he needed, but Chaplain Hardy hadn't been exactly whom he wanted to talk to. "Uh, how many Moties are there aboard your ship?"

"Four. One for each of us: myself, Dr. Horvath, Lady Sally, and Mr. Whitbread. They seem to be assigned as mutual guides."

"Four of them." Rod was trying to get used to the idea. The cutter wasn't a commissioned vessel, but it was one of His Majesty's warships, and somehow having a bunch of aliens aboard was—nuts. Horvath knew the risks he was taking. "Only four? Doesn't Sinclair have a guide?"

"Oddly enough, no. A number of them are watching him work in the tool room, but there was no special one assigned to him."

"And none for the coxswain or the spacers on the cutter?"

"No." Hardy thought a moment. "That is odd, isn't it? As if they class Commander Sinclair with the unimportant crewmen."

"Maybe they just don't like the Navy."

David Hardy shrugged. Then, carefully, he said, "Captain, sooner or later we'll have to invite them aboard *MacArthur.*"

"I'm afraid that's out of the question."

Hardy sighed. "Well, that's why I brought it up now, so that we could thrash it out. They've shown that they trust us, Captain. There's not a cubic centimeter of their embassy ship that we haven't seen, or at least probed with instruments. Whitbread will testify that there's no sign of weaponry aboard. Eventually they're going to wonder what guilty secrets we're hiding aboard."

"I'm going to tell you, Are there Moties within earshot?"

"No. And they haven't learned Anglic *that* well anyway."

"Don't forget they *will* learn, and don't forget recorders. Now, Chaplain, you've got a problem—about Moties and Creation. The Empire has another. For a long time we've talked about the Great Galactic Wizards showing up and deciding whether to let the humans join, right? Only it's the other way around, isn't it? We've got to decide whether to let the Moties out of their system, and until that's decided we don't want them to see the Langston Field generators, the Alderson Drive, our weapons . . . not even just how much of *MacArthur* is living space, Chaplain. It would give away too much about our capabilities. We've a lot to hide, and we'll hide it."

"You're treating them as enemies," David Hardy said gently.

"And that's neither your decision nor mine, Doctor. Besides, I've got some questions I want answered before I decide that the Moties are nothing more than steadfast friends." Rod let his gaze go past the Chaplain, and his eyes focused a long way off. I'm not sorry it's not my decision, he thought. But ultimately they're going to ask me. As future Marquis of Crucis, if nothing else.

He had known the subject would come up, and would again; and he was ready. "First, why did they send us a ship from Mote Prime? Why not from the Trojan cluster? It's much closer."

"I'll ask them when I can."

"Second, why four Moties? It may not be important, but I'd like to know why they assigned one to each of you scientists, one to Whitbread, and none to any of the crew."

"They were right, weren't they? They set guides on the four people most interested in teaching them—"

"Exactly. How did they know? Just for example, how could they have known Dr. Horvath would be aboard? And the third question is, what are they building *now?*"

"All right, Captain." Hardy looked unhappy, not angry. He was and would be harder to refuse than Horvath . . . partly because he was Rod's confessor. And the subject would come up again. Rod was sure of that.

23 • *Eliza Crossing the Ice*

During the weeks that followed *MacArthur* was a bustle of activity. Every scientist worked overtime after each data transmission from the cutter, and every one of them wanted Navy assistance *immediately*. There was also the problem of the escaped miniatures, but this had settled to a game, with *MacArthur* losing. In the mess room it was even money that they were both dead, but no bodies were found. It worried Rod Blaine, but there was nothing he could do.

He also allowed the Marines to stand watches in normal uniform. There were no threats to the cutter, and it was ridiculous to keep a dozen men uncomfortable in battle armor. Instead he doubled the watch keeping surveillance around *MacArthur,* but no one—or no thing—tried to approach, escape, or send messages. Meanwhile the biologists went wild over clues to Motie psychology and physiology, the astronomy section continued to map Mote Prime, Buckman dithered whenever anyone else used the astronomical gear, and Blaine tried to keep his overcrowded ship running smoothly. His appreciation of Horvath grew every time he had to mediate a dispute between scientists.

There was more activity aboard the cutter. Commander Sinclair had gone aboard and been immediately taken to the Motie ship. Three days passed before a Brown-and-white began following Sinclair around, and it was a peculiarly quiet Motie. It did seem interested in the cutter's machinery, unlike the others who had assigned themselves to a human. Sinclair and his Fyunch(click) spent long hours aboard the alien ship, poking into corners, examining everything.

"The lad was right about the tool room," Sinclair told Blaine during one of his daily reports. "It's like the nonverbal intelligence tests BuPers worked up for new recruits. There are things wrong wi' some o' the tools, and 'tis my task to put them right."

"Wrong how?"

Sinclair chuckled, remembering. He had some difficulty explaining the joke to Blaine. The hammer with the big, flat head would hit a thumb every time. It needed to be trimmed. The laser heated too fast . . . and that was a tricky one. It had generated the wrong frequency of light. Sinclair fixed it by doubling the frequency—somehow. He also learned more about compact lasers than he'd ever known before. There were other tests like that. "They're good, Captain. It took ingenuity to come up wi' some of the testing gadgets wi'out giving away more than they did. But they canna keep me from learning about their ship . . . Captain, I already ken enough to redesign the ship's boats to be more efficient. Or make millions o' crowns designing miner ships."

"Retiring when we go back, Sandy?" Rod asked; but he grinned widely to show he didn't mean it.

In the second week, Rod Blaine also acquired a Fyunch(click).

He was both dismayed and flattered. The Motie looked like all the others: brown-and-white markings, a gentle smile in a lopsided face just high enough above the deck that Rod could have patted her on the head—if he'd ever seen the Motie face to face, which he never would.

Each time he called the cutter she was there, always eager to see Blaine and talk to him. Each time he called, her Anglic was better. They would exchange a few words, and that was that. He didn't have *time* for a Fyunch(click), or a need for one either. Learning Motie language wasn't his job—from the progress made, it wasn't *anyone's* job— and he only saw her through a phone link. What use was a guide he would never meet?

"They seem to think you're important," was Hardy's dead-pan answer.

It was something to think about while he presided over his madhouse of a ship. And the alien didn't complain at all.

*   *   *

The month's flurry of activity hardly affected Horace Bury. He received no news at all from the cutter, and had nothing to contribute to the scientific work on the ship. Alert to rumors, which were always helpful, he waited for news to filter down through the grapevine; but not very much did. Communications with the cutter seemed to stop with the bridge, and he had no real friends among the scientists other than Buckman. Blaine had given up putting everything on the intercom. For the first time since he left New Chicago, Bury felt imprisoned.

It bothered him more than it should have, although he was introspective enough to know why. All his life he had tried to control his environment as far as he could reach: around a world, across light years of space and decades of time—or throughout a Navy battle cruiser. The crew treated him as a guest, but not as a master; and anywhere he was not master, he was a prisoner.

He was losing money, too. Somewhere in the restricted sections of *MacArthur,* beyond the reach of all but the highest ranking scientists, physicists were studying the golden stuff from the Stone Beehive. It took weeks of effort to pick up the rumor that it was a superconductor of heat.

That would be priceless stuff, and he knew he must obtain a sample. He even knew how it might be done, but forced himself to idleness. Not yet! The time to steal his sample would be just before *MacArthur* docked in New Scotland. Ships would be waiting there despite the cost, not only a ship openly acknowledging him as owner, but at least one other. Meanwhile, listen, find out, know what else he should have when he left *MacArthur.*

He had several reports on the Stone Beehive to crosscheck against each other. He even tried to gain information from Buckman; but the results were more amusing than profitable.

"Oh, forget the Stone Beehive," Buckman had exclaimed. "It was *moved* into place. It's no damned use at all. The Beehive's got nothing to do with the formation of the Trojan point clusters, and the Moties have messed up the internal structure to the point where you can't tell *any-thing* about the original rock . . ."

So. The Moties could and did make superconductors of heat. And there were always the little Moties. He enjoyed the search for the escaped miniatures. Naturally most of the Navy personnel were silently rooting for the underdog, the fleeing miniature and the child, Eliza crossing the ice. And the miniature was winning. Food disappeared from odd places: staterooms, lounges, everywhere but the kitchen itself. The ferrets could find no scent. How could the miniatures have made truce with the ferrets? Bury wondered. Certainly the aliens were . . . alien, yet the ferrets had had no trouble scenting them the first night.

Bury enjoyed the hunt, but . . . He took the lesson: a miniature was harder to catch than to keep. If he expected to sell many as pets he had better sell them in foolproof cages. Then there was the matter of acquiring a breeding pair. The longer the miniatures remained free, the less grew Bury's chances of persuading the Navy that they were harmless, friendly pets.

But it was fun seeing the Navy look foolish. Bury rooted for both sides, and practiced patience; and the weeks went on.

While six Fyunch(click)s bunked aboard the cutter, the rest of the Moties worked. The interior of the alien ship changed like dreams; it was different every time any-one went aboard. Sinclair and Whitbread made a point of touring it periodically to see that no weapons were built; perhaps they would have known and perhaps not.

One day Hardy and Horvath stopped by the Captain's watch cabin after an hour in *MacArthur*'s exercise rooms.

"The Moties have a fuel tank coming," Horvath told Rod. "It was launched at about the same time as their own ship, by linear accelerator, but in a fuel-saving orbit. It should arrive in two weeks."

"So that's what it is." Blaine and his officers had worried about that silent object coasting at leisure toward their position.

"You knew about it? You might have mentioned it to us."

"They'll need to retrieve it," Blaine speculated. "Hmm. I wonder if one of my boats might get it for them. Would they let us do that?"

"I see no reason why not. We'll ask," said David Hardy. "One more thing, Captain."

Rod knew something tricky was coming. Horvath had Dr. Hardy ask for all the things Rod might refuse.

"The Moties want to build an air-lock bridge between the cutter and the embassy ship," Hardy finished.

"It's only a temporary structure and we need it." Horvath paused. "It's only a hypothesis, you understand, but, Captain, we now think that every structure is only temporary to them. They must have had high-gee couches at takeoff, but they're gone now. They arrived with no fuel to take them home. They almost certainly redesigned their life-support system for free fall in the three hours following their arrival."

" 'And this too shall pass away,' " Hardy added helpfully. "But the idea doesn't bother them. They seem to like it."

"It's a major departure from human psychology," Horvath said earnestly. "Perhaps a Motie would never try to design anything permanent at all. There will be no sphinx, no pyramids, no Washington Monument, no Lenin's Tomb."

"Doctor, I don't like the idea of joining the two ships."

"But, Captain, we *need* something like this. People and Moties are constantly passing back and forth, and they have to use the taxi every time. Besides, the Moties have already started work—"

"May I point out that if they join those two ships, you and everyone aboard will thenceforth be hostage to the Moties' good will?"

Horvath was ruffled. "I'm sure the aliens can be trusted, Captain. We're making very good progress with them."

"Besides," Chaplain Hardy added equably, "we're hostage *now*. There was never a way to avoid the situation. *MacArthur* and *Lenin* are our protection, if we need protection. If two battleships don't scare them—well, we knew the situation when we boarded the cutter."

Blaine ground his teeth. If the cutter was expendable, the cutter's personnel were not. Sinclair, Sally Fowler, Dr. Horvath, the Chaplain—*MacArthur's* most valuable people were living aboard the cutter. Yet the Chaplain was clearly right. They were all subject to murder at any moment, save for the risk of *MacArthur's* vengeance.

"Tell them to go ahead," Rod said. The air-lock bridge would not increase the danger at all.

The lock was begun as soon as Rod gave permission. A tube of thin metal, flexibly jointed, jutting from the hull of the Motie ship, it snaked toward them like a living creature. Moties swarmed around it in fragile-seeming suits. As seen from the cutter's main port, they might almost have been men—almost.

Sally's eyes blurred as she watched. The lighting was strange—dim Motelight and space-black shadows, and occasional flares of artificial light, everything reflected from the bright, curved metal surface. The perspective was all wrong, and it gave her a headache.

"I keep wondering where they're getting the metal," said Whitbread. He sat near her, as he usually did when they were both between jobs. "There wasn't any spare mass aboard the ship, not the first time I went through it and not now. They must be tearing their ship apart."

"That would fit," said Horvath.

They had gathered around the main window after dinner, with tea and coffee bulbs in their hands. The Moties had become tea and chocolate fanciers; they could not stomach coffee. Human, Motie, human, Motie, they circled the window on the horseshoe-shaped free-fall bench. The Fyunch(click)s had learned the human trick of aligning themselves all in the same direction.

"Look how fast they work," Sally said. "The bridge seems to grow before your very eyes." Again her eyes tried to cross. It was as if many of the Moties were working farther back, well behind the others. "The one marked with the orange strips must be a Brown. She seems to be in charge, don't you think?"

"She's also doing most of the work," said Sinclair.

"That makes an odd kind of sense," said Hardy. "If she knows enough to give the orders, she must be able to do the work better than any of the others, too, wouldn't you think?" He rubbed his eyes. "Am I out of my mind, or are some of those Moties smaller than others?"

"It does look that way," said Sally.

Whitbread stared at the bridge builders. Many of the Moties seemed to be working a long way *behind* the embassy ship—until three of them passed in front of it. Carefully he said, "Has anyone tried watching this through the scope? Lafferty, get it on for us, will you?"

In the telescope screen it was shockingly clear. Some of the Motie workmen were tiny, small enough to crawl into any crevice. And they had four arms each.

"Do—do you often use those creatures as workmen?" Sally asked her Fyunch(click).

"Yes. We find them very useful. Are there not—equal —creatures in your ships?" The alien seemed surprised. Of all the Moties, Sally's gave the impression of being most often surprised at the humans. "Do you think Rod will be worried?"

"But what are they?" Sally demanded. She ignored the question the Motie had asked.

"They are—workers," the Motie answered. "Useful— animals. You are surprised because they are small? Yours are large, then?"

"Uh, yes," Sally answered absently. She looked to the others. "I think I'd like to go see these—animals—close up. Anyone want to come along?" But Whitbread was already getting into his suit, and so were the others.

"Fyunch(click)," said the alien.

"God Almighty!" Blaine exploded. "Have they got you answering the phones now?"

The alien spoke slowly, with care for enunciation. Her grammar was not perfect, but her grasp of idiom and inflection was freshly amazing every time she spoke. "Why not? I talk well enough. I can remember a message. I can use the recorder. I have little to do when you are not available."

"I can't help that."

"I know." With a touch of complacence the alien added, "I startled a rating."

"God's teeth, you startled *me*. Who's around?"

"Coxswain Lafferty. All the other humans are absent. They have gone to look at the—tunnel. When it is finished the ratings will not have to go with them when they wish to visit the other ship. Can I pass on a message?"

"No, thanks, I'll call back."

"Sally should be back soon," said Blaine's Motie. "How are you? How goes the ship?"

"Well enough."

"You always sound so cautious when you speak of the ship. Am I stepping on Navy secrets? It-ss not the ship that concerns me, Rod. I'm Fyunch(click) to you. It means considerably more than just *guide*." The Motie gestured oddly. Rod had seen her do that before, when she was upset or annoyed.

"Just what does Fyunch(click) mean?"

"I am assigned to you. You are a project, a master-work. I am to learn as much about you as there is to know. I am to become an expert on you, My Lord Roderick Blaine, and you are to become a field of study to me. It-ss not your gigantic, rigid, badly designed ship that interest-ss me, it-ss your attitudes toward that ship and the humans aboard, your degree of control over them, your interess-t in their welfare, et cetera."

How would Kutuzov handle this? Break contact? Hell. "Nobody likes being watched. Anyone would feel a bit uncomfortable being studied like that."

"We guessed you would take it that way. But, Rod, you're here to study us, are-unt you? Surely we are entitled to study you back."

"You have that right." Rod's voice was stiff despite himself. "But if someone becomes embarrassed while you're talking to him, that's probably the reason."

"God damn it to hell," said Blaine's Motie. "You are

the first intelligent beings we've ever met who are-unt relatives. Why should you expect to be comfortable with us?" She rubbed the flat center of her face with her upper right forefinger, then dropped her hand as if embarrassed. It was the same gesture she'd used a moment before.

There were noises off screen. Blaine's Motie said, "Hang on a moment. Okay, it-ss Sally and Whitbread." Her voice rose. "Sally? The Captain's on screen." She slid out of the chair. Sally Fowler slid in. Her smile seemed forced as she said, "Hello, Captain. What's new?"

"Business as usual. How goes it at your end?"

"Rod, you look flustered. It's a strange experience, isn't it? Don't worry, she can't hear us now."

"Good. I'm not sure I like an alien reading my mind that way. I don't suppose they really read minds."

"They say not. And they guess wrong sometimes." She ran a hand through her hair, which was in disarray, perhaps because she had just doffed a pressure suit helmet. "Wildly wrong. Commander Sinclair's Fyunch(click) wouldn't talk to him at first. They thought he was a Brown; you know, an idiot carpenter type. How are you doing with the miniatures?"

That was a subject they'd both learned to avoid. Rod wondered why she'd brought it up. "The loose ones are still loose. No sign of them. They might even have died somewhere we wouldn't find them. We've still got the one that stayed behind. I think you'd better have a look at her, Sally, next time you're over. She may be sick."

Sally nodded. "I'll come over tomorrow. Rod, have you been watching the alien work party?"

"Not particularly. The air lock seems almost finished already."

"Yes . . . Rod, they've been using trained miniatures to do part of the work."

Rod stared stupidly.

Sally's eyes shifted uneasily. "Trained miniatures. In pressure suits. We didn't know there were any aboard. I suppose they must be shy; they must hide when humans are aboard. But they're only animals, after all. We asked."

"Animals." OhmyGod. What would Kutuzov say?

"Sally, this is important. Can you come over tonight and brief me? You and anyone else who knows anything about this."

"All right. Commander Sinclair is watching them now. Rod, it's really fantastic how well the little beasts are trained. And they can get into places where you'd have to use jointed tools and spy eyes."

"I can imagine. Sally, tell me the truth. Is there the slightest chance the miniatures are intelligent?"

"No. They're just trained."

"Just trained." And if there were any alive aboard *MacArthur* they'd have explored the ship from stem to stern. "Sally, is there the slightest chance that any of the aliens can hear me now?"

"No. I'm using the earphone, and we haven't allowed them to work on our equipment."

"So far as you know. Now listen carefully, then I want to talk privately to everyone else on that cutter, one at a time. Has anyone said anything—anything at all—about there being miniatures loose aboard *MacArthur?*"

"No-oo. You told us not to, remember? Rod, what's wrong?"

What's wrong. "For God's sake, *don't* say anything about the loose miniatures. I'll tell the others as you put them on. And I want to see all of you, everyone except the cutter's regular crew, tonight. It's time we pooled our knowledge about Moties, because I'm going to have to report to the Admiral tomorrow morning." He looked almost pale. "I guess I can wait that long."

"Well, of course you can," she said. She smiled enchantingly, but it didn't come off very well. She didn't think she'd ever seen Rod so concerned, and it upset her. "We'll be over in an hour. Now here's Mr. Whitbread, and please, Rod, stop worrying."

24 · *Brownies*

MacArthur's wardroom was crowded. All the seats at the main table were taken by officers and scientists and there were others around the periphery. At one bulkhead the communications people had installed a large screen, while the mess stewards got in the artificers' way as they delivered coffee to the assembled company. Everyone chattered, carefree, except Sally. She remembered Rod Blaine's worried face, and she couldn't join in the happy reunion.

Officers and ratings stood as Rod came into the wardroom. Some of the civilians stood likewise; others pretended not to see the Captain; and a few looked at him, then looked away, exploiting their civilian status. As Rod took his place at the head of the table he muttered, "At ease," then sat carefully. Sally thought he looked even more worried than before.

"Kelley."

"Sir!"

"Is this room secure?"

"As near as we can make it, sir. Four files outside and I looked into the duct works."

"What is this?" Horvath demanded. "Just who do you think you are guarding against?"

"Everyone—and every thing—not here, Doctor." Rod looked at the Science Minister with eyes that showed both command and pleading. "I must tell you that everything discussed here will be classified Top Secret. Do each and all of you waive the reading of the Imperial Regulations on disclosure of classified information?"

There was muttered assent. The cheery mood of the group had suddenly vanished.

"Any dissents? Let the record show there were none. Dr. Horvath, I am given to understand that three hours ago you discovered that the miniatures are highly trained animals capable of technical work performed under command. Is that correct?"

"Yes. Certainly. It was quite a surprise, I can tell you! The implications are enormous—if we can learn to direct them, they would be fabulous additions to our capabilities."

Rod nodded absently. "Is there any chance that we could have known that earlier? Did anyone know it? Anyone at all?"

There was a confused babble but no one answered. Rod said, carefully and clearly, "Let the record show there was no one."

"What is this record you keep speaking of?" Horvath demanded. "And why are you concerned about it?"

"Dr. Horvath, this conversation will be recorded and duly witnessed because it may be evidence in a court-martial. Quite possibly mine. Is that clear enough?"

"What— Good heavens!" Sally gasped. "Court-martial? You? Why?"

"The charge would be high treason," Rod said. "I see most of my officers aren't surprised. My lady, gentlemen, we have strict orders from the Viceroy himself to do nothing to compromise any Imperial military technology, and in particular to protect the Langston Field and Alderson Drive from Motie inspection. In the past weeks animals capable of learning that technology and quite possibly of passing it on to other Moties have roamed my ship at will. *Now* do you understand?"

"I see." Horvath showed no signs of alarm, but his face grew thoughtful. "And you have secured this room— Do you really believe the miniatures can understand what we say?"

Rod shrugged. "I think it possible they can memorize conversations and repeat them. But are the miniatures still alive? Kelley?"

"Sir, there haven't been any signs of them for weeks. No raids on food stores. Ferrets haven't turned up a thing but a bloody lot of mice. I think the beasties are dead, Captain."

Blaine rubbed his nose, then quickly drew his hand

away. "Gunner, have you ever heard of 'Brownies' aboard this ship?"

Kelley's face showed no surprise. In fact it showed nothing. "Brownies, Captain?"

"Rod, have you lost your mind?" Sally blurted. Everyone was looking at her, and some of them didn't seem friendly. Oh boy, she thought, I've stuck my foot in it. Some of them know what he's talking about. Oh boy.

"I said Brownies, Gunner. Have you ever heard of them?"

"Well, not officially, Captain. I will say some of the spacers seem lately to believe in the Little People. Couldn't see any harm in it meself." But Kelley looked confused. He had heard of this and he hadn't reported it, and now the Captain, *his* Captain, might be in trouble over it . . .

"Anyone else?" Rod demanded.

"Uh—sir?"

Rod had to strain to see who was speaking. Midshipman Potter was near the far wall, almost hidden by two biologists. "Yes, Mr. Potter?"

"Some of the men in my watch section, Captain—they say that if ye leave some food—grain, cereals, mess leftovers, anything at all—in the corridors or under your bunk along with something that needs fixing, it gets fixed." Potter looked uncomfortable. It was obvious he thought he was reporting nonsense. "One of the men called them 'Brownies.' I thought it a joke."

Once Potter had spoken there were a dozen others. Even some of the scientists. Microscopes with smoother focusing operations than the best things ever made by Leica Optical. A handmade lamp in the biology section. Boots and shoes customized to individual feet. Rod looked up at that one.

"Kelley. How many of your troops have sidearms individualized like yours and Mr. Renner's?"

"Uh—I don't know, sir."

"I can see one from here. You, man, Polizawsky, how did you come by that weapon?"

The Marine stammered. He wasn't used to speaking to officers, certainly not the Captain, and *most* certainly not the Captain in an ugly mood. "Uh, well, sir, I leaves my weapon and a bag o' popcorn by my bunk and next morning it's done, sir. Like the others said, Captain."

"And you didn't think this unusual enough to report to Gunner Kelley?"

"Uh—sir—uh, some of the others, we thought maybe, uh, well, the Surgeon's been talking about hallucinations in space, Captain, and we, uh—"

"Besides, if you reported it I might stop the whole thing," Rod finished for him. Oh, God damn it to hell! How was he going to explain all this? Busy, too busy arbitrating squabbles with the scientists— But the fact stood out. He'd neglected his naval duties, and with what outcome?

"Aren't you taking all this too seriously?" Horvath asked. "After all, Captain, the Viceroy's orders were given before we knew much about Moties. Now, surely, we can see they aren't dangerous, and they certainly aren't hostile."

"Are you suggesting, Doctor, that we put ourselves in the position of countermanding an Imperial Directive?"

Horvath looked amused. His grin spread slowly across his face. "Oh no," he said. "I don't even imply it. I only suggest that if and when—when, really, it's inevitable— that policy is changed, all this will seem a trifle silly, Captain Blaine. Childish in fact."

"Be damned to you!" Sinclair exploded. "That's nae way to talk to the Captain, mon!"

"Gently, Sandy," First Lieutenant Cargill interjected. "Dr. Horvath, I take it you've never been involved in military intelligence? No, of course not. But you see, in intelligence work we have to go by capabilities, not by intentions. If a potential enemy *can* do something to you, you have to prepare for it, without regard to what you think he *wants* to do."

"Exactly," Rod said. He was glad of the interruptions. Sinclair was still fuming at his end of the table, and it wouldn't take much to make him explode again. "So first we have to find out what the potential of the miniatures is. From what I've seen of the air-lock construction, plus what we gather about the 'Brownies,' that's quite high."

"But they're only animals," Sally insisted. She looked at the fuming Sinclair, the sardonically smiling Horvath, and Rod's worried face. "You don't understand. This business with tools—well, *yes,* they're good with tools, but it's not *intelligence.* Their heads are too small. The more brain tissue they use for this instinct to make tools work, the more they have to give up. They've virtually no sense of smell or taste. They're very nearsighted. They've less sense of language than a chimpanzee. Their space perception is good, and they can be trained, but they don't make tools, they only fix or change things. Intelligence!" she exploded. "What intelligent being would have custom-formed the grip on Mr. Battson's toothbrush?

"As for spying on us, how could they? Nobody could have trained them for it. They were randomly selected in the first place." She looked around at their faces, trying to judge if she was getting through.

"You're really sure the escaped miniatures are alive?" The voice was hearty, tinged with New Scot accent. Rod looked across to Dr. Blevins, a colonial veterinarian drafted into the expedition. "My own miniature is dying, Captain. Nothing I can do about it. Internal poisoning, glandular deterioration—the symptoms seem to be similar to old age."

Blaine shook his head slowly. "I wish I could think so, Doc, but there are too many Brownie stories in this ship. Before this meeting I talked to some of the other chiefs, and it's the same on the lower decks. Nobody wanted to report it because first, we'd think they were crazy, and second, the Brownies were too useful to risk losing. Now, for all of Gunner Kelley's Irish folk tales, there have never been any Little People on Navy ships—it has to be the miniatures."

There was a long silence. "What harm are they doing, anyway?" Horvath asked. "I'd think some Brownies would be an asset, Captain."

"Hah." That didn't need comment in Rod's opinion. "Harm or good, immediately after this meeting we will sterilize this ship. Sinclair, have you arranged to evacuate hangar deck?"

"Aye, Captain."

"Then do it. Open it to space, and see all the compartments in there are opened to space. I want that hangar deck *dead*. Commander Cargill, see that the essential watch crew are in battle armor. *Alone* in their battle armor, Number One. The rest of you give some thought to whatever equipment you have that can't stand hard vacuum. When hangar deck's done, Kelley's Marines will help you get that into hangar deck; then we depressurize the rest of the ship. We're going to put an end to Brownies once and for all."

"But"—"Hey, that's silly"—"My cultures will *die*"—"Goddamn regular Navy bastards are always"—"Can he do that?"—"Aye aye, Captain"—"What the hell does he think he's—"

"Tenn-*shut!*" Kelley's roar cut through the babble.

"Captain, do you really have to be so vicious about it?" Sally asked.

He shrugged. "I think they're cute too. So what? If I don't order it done, the Admiral will anyway. Now, are we all agreed that the miniatures aren't spies?"

"Not deliberate ones," Renner said. "But, Captain, do you know about the incident with the pocket computer?"

"No."

"The big Motie took Miss Fowler's pocket computer apart. And put it back together again. It works."

"Uh." Rod made a sour face. "But that was the big brown Motie."

"Which can talk to the little Moties. It made the miniatures give Mr. Bury his watch back," Renner said.

"I've got the crew alerted, Captain," Cargill reported. He was standing by the wardroom intercom. "I didn't tell anyone anything. The crew thinks it's a drill."

"Good thinking, Jack. Seriously, everyone, what's the objection to killing off these vermin? The big Motie did the same thing, and if, as you say, they're only animals, there must be plenty more of them. We won't be upsetting the big Moties one whit. Will we?"

"Well, no-oo," said Sally. "But—"

Rod shook his head decisively. "There are plenty of reasons for killing them, and I haven't heard any for keeping them around. We can take that as settled, then."

Horvath shook his head. "But it's all so drastic, Captain. Just what do we think we're protecting?"

"The Alderson Drive, directly. Indirectly, the whole Empire, but mainly the Drive," Cargill said seriously. "And don't ask me why I think the Empire needs protecting from Moties. I don't know, but—I think it does."

"You won't save the Drive. They've already *got* that," Renner announced. He gave them all a lopsided smile as everyone in the room swiveled toward him.

"What?!" Rod demanded. "How?"

"Who's the bloody traitor?" Sinclair demanded. "Name the scum!"

"Whoa! Hold it! Stop already!" Renner insisted. "They already *had* the Drive, Captain. I only learned an hour ago. It's all recorded, let me show you." He stood and went to the big screen. Images flashed across it until Renner found the place he wanted. He turned to the watchful group.

"It's nice to be the center of attention—" Renner cut off at the sight of Rod's glare. "This is a conversation between, uh, *my* Motie and myself. I'll use split screen to show you both sides of it." He touched the controls and the screen sprang to life: Renner on *MacArthur*'s bridge, his Fyunch(click) in the Motie embassy ship. Renner ran it at high speed until he found precisely what he wanted.

"You might have come from anywhere," said Renner's Motie. "Though it seems more likely that you came from a nearby star, such as—well, I can point to it." Stellar images showed on a screen behind the Motie; screens within screens. She pointed with the upper right arm. The star was New Caledonia. "We know that you have an instantaneous drive, because of where you appeared."

Renner's image sat forward. "Where we appeared?"

"Yes. You appeared precisely in the . . ." Renner's Motie seemed to search for a word. Visibly, she gave up. "Renner, I must tell you of a creature of legend."

"Say on." Renner's image dialed for coffee. Coffee and stories, they went together.

"We will call him Crazy Eddie, if you like. He is a . . . he is like me, sometimes, and he is a Brown, an idiot savant tinker, sometimes. Always he does the wrong things for excellent reasons. He does the same things over and over, and they always bring disaster, and he never learns."

There were small sounds of whispering in *MacArthur's* wardroom. Renner's image said, "For instance?"

Renner's Motie's image paused to think. It said, "When a city has grown so overlarge and crowded that it is in immediate danger of collapse . . . when food and clean water flow into the city at a rate just sufficient to feed every mouth, and every hand must work constantly to keep it that way . . . when all transportation is involved in moving vital supplies, and none is left over to move people out of the city should the need arise . . . then it is that Crazy Eddie leads the movers of garbage out on strike for better working conditions."

There was considerable laughter in the wardroom. Renner's image grinned and said, "I think I know the gentleman. Go on."

"There is the Crazy Eddie Drive. It makes ships vanish."

"Great."

"Theoretically it should be an instantaneous drive, a key to throw the universe wide open. In practice it makes ships vanish forever. The drive has been discovered and built and tested many times, and always it makes ships vanish forever with everyone aboard, but only if you use it right, mind. The ship must be in just the right place, a place difficult to locate exactly, with the machinery doing just what the theoreticians postulate it must, or nothing will happen at all."

Both Renners were laughing now. "I see. And we appeared in this point, the Crazy Eddie point. From which you deduce that we have solved the secret of the Crazy Eddie Drive."

"You got it."

"And what does that make us?"

The alien parted its lips in a smile disturbingly sharklike, disturbingly human . . . Renner gave them a good look at that smile before he turned it off.

There was a long silence, then Sinclair spoke. "Well, that's plain enough, is it not? They ken the Alderson Drive but not the Langston Field."

"Why do you say that, Commander Sinclair?" Horvath asked. Everyone tried to explain it to him at once, but the Chief Engineer's burr easily carried through the babble.

"Yon beasties' ships vanish, but only at the correct place, aye? So they ken the Drive. But they never see the ships back home, because they coom into normal space in yon red star. 'Tis plain as a pikestaff."

"Oh." Horvath nodded sadly. "With nothing to protect them— After all, it *is* the inside of a star, isn't it?"

Sally shuddered. "And your Motie said they'd tried it often." She shuddered again. Then: "But, Mr. Renner— none of the other Moties ever talk about astrogation or anything like that. *Mine* told me about 'Crazy Eddie' as if he were around only in primitive times—a lost legend."

"And *mine* spoke of Crazy Eddie as an engineer always using tomorrow's capital to fix today's problems," Sinclair blurted.

"Anyone else?" Rod prompted.

"Well—" Chaplain David Hardy looked embarrassed. His plump face was almost beet-red. "My Motie says Crazy Eddie founds religions. Weird, very logical, and singularly inappropriate religions."

"Enough," Rod protested. "I seem to be the only one whose Motie has never mentioned Crazy Eddie." He looked thoughtful. "We can all agree that the Moties do have the Drive, but not the Field?"

They all nodded. Horvath scratched his ear for a moment, then said, "Now that I remember the history of Langston's discovery, it's no surprise that the Moties don't have the Field. I'm amazed they have the Drive itself, although its principles *can* be deduced from astrophysical research. The Field, though, was a purely accidental invention."

"Given that they know it exists, then what?" Rod asked.

"Then— I don't know," Horvath said.

There was complete silence in the room. An ominous silence. Finally the bubble burst. Sally was laughing.

"You all look so deadly serious," she protested. "Suppose they have both Drive and Field? There's only the one planet full of Moties. They aren't hostile, but even if they were, do you really think they would be a threat to the Empire? Captain, what could *Lenin* do to the Mote planet right now, all by itself, if Admiral Kutuzov gave the order?"

The tension broke. Everyone smiled. She was right, of course. The Moties didn't even have warships. They didn't have the Field, and if they invented it, how would they learn space-war tactics? Poor peaceful Moties, what challenge could they be to the Empire of Man?

Everyone except Cargill. He wasn't smiling at all as he said, quite seriously, "I just don't know, my lady. And I really wish I did."

Horace Bury was not invited to the conference, although he knew of it. Now, while it was still going on, a Marine guard came to his cabin and politely, but very firmly, ushered him out of it. The guard would not say where he was taking Bury, and after a while it was obvious he did not know.

"The Gunner, he says to stay with you and be ready to take you to where the rest of them is, Mr. Bury."

Bury slyly examined the man. What would this one do for a hundred thousand crowns? But then, it wasn't necessary. Not at the moment. Surely Blaine wasn't going to have him shot. For a moment Bury was frightened. Could they have made Stone talk, back on New Chicago?

By Allah, no one was safe— Absurd. Even if Stone had told everything, there were and could be no messages to *MacArthur* from the Empire. They were as effectively sealed off as the Moties.

"You are to stay with me. Does your officer say where I am to go?"

"Not right now, Mr. Bury."

"Then take me to Dr. Buckman's laboratory. Why not? We will both be more comfortable."

The private thought about it. "OK, come on."

Bury found his friend in an ugly mood. "Pack everything that can't stand hard vacuum," Buckman was muttering. "Get everything that can ready for it. No reason. Just do it." He poked at gadgetry. He had already packed a good deal in boxes and big plastic bags.

Bury's own tension may have showed. Senseless orders, a guard outside the door . . . he was feeling like a prisoner again. It took him quite a while to calm Buckman down. Finally the astrophysicist slumped into a chair and lifted a cup of coffee. "Haven't seen you much," he said. "Been busy?"

"There is really very little for me to do in this ship. Few tell me anything," Bury said equably—and that took self-control. "Why must you be ready for hard vacuum here?"

"Hah! I don't know. Just do it. Try to call the Captain, he's in conference. Try to complain to Horvath, and *he's* in conference. If they aren't available when you need them, just what use are they, anyway?"

Sounds came through from the corridor outside: heavy things were being moved. What could it be about? Sometimes they evacuated ships to get rid of rats . . .

That was it! They were killing off the miniatures! Allah be praised, he had acted in time. Bury smiled widely in relief. He had a better idea of the value of the miniatures since the night he had left a box of *bhaklavah* next to the open faceplate of his personal pressure suit. He'd almost lost it all.

To Buckman he said, "How did you make out in the Trojan point asteroids?"

Buckman looked startled. Then he laughed. "Bury, I haven't thought about that problem in a month. We've been studying the Coal Sack."

"Ah."

"We've found a mass in there . . . probably a protostar. And an infrared source. The flow patterns in the Coal Sack are fantastic. As if the gas and dust were viscous . . . of course it's the magnetic fields that make it act like that. We're learning wonderful things about the dynamics of a dust cloud. When I think of the time I wasted on those Trojan point rocks . . . when the whole problem was so trivial!"

"Well, go on, Buckman. Don't leave me hanging."

"Uh? Oh, I'll show you." Buckman went to the intercom and read out a string of numbers.

Nothing happened.

"That's funny. Some idiot must have put a RESTRICTED on it." Buckman closed his eyes, recited another string of numbers. Photographs appeared on the screen. "Ah. There!"

Asteroids tumbled on the screen, the pictures blurred and jumpy. Some were lopsided, some almost spherical, many marked with craters . . .

"Sorry about the quality. The near Trojans are a good distance away . . . but all it took was time and *MacArthur*'s telescopes. Do you see what we found?"

"Not really. Unless . . ." All of them had craters. At least one crater. Three long, narrow asteroids in succession . . . and each had a deep crater at one end. One rock twisted almost into a cashew shape; and the crater was at the inside of the curve. Each asteroid in the sequence had a big deep crater in it; and always a line through the center would have gone through the rock's center of mass.

Bury felt fear and laughter rising in him. "Yes, I see. You found that every one of those asteroids had been moved into place artificially. Therefore you lost interest."

"Naturally. When I think that I was expecting to find some new cosmic principle—" Buckman shrugged. He swallowed some coffee.

"I don't suppose you told anyone?"

"I told Dr. Horvath. Why, do you suppose he put the RESTRICTED designation on it?"

"It may be. Buckman, how much energy do you think it would take to move such a mass of rocks around?"

"Why, I don't know. A good deal, I think. In fact . . ." Buckman's eyes glowed. "An interesting problem. I'll let you know after this idiocy is over." He turned back to his gear.

Bury sat where he was, staring at nothing. Presently he began to shiver.

"I appreciate your concern for the safety of the Empire, Admiral," Horvath said. He nodded sagely at the glowering figure on *MacArthur*'s bridge screen. "Indeed I do. The fact remains, however, that we either accept the Moties' invitation or we might as well go home. There's nothing more to learn out here."

"You, Blaine. You agree with that?" Admiral Kutuzov's expression was unchanged.

Rod shrugged. "Sir, I have to take the advice of the scientists. They say that we've got about all we're going to get from this distance."

"You want to take *MacArthur* into orbit around the Mote planet, then? That is what you recommend? For the record?"

"Yes, sir. Either that or go home, and I don't think we know enough about the Moties simply to leave."

Kutuzov took a long, slow breath. His lips tightened.

"Admiral, you have your job, I have mine," Horvath reminded him. "It's all very well to protect the Empire against whatever improbable threat the Moties pose, but I must exploit what we can learn from Motie science and technology. That, I assure you, isn't trivial. They're so far advanced in some respects that I—well, I haven't any words to describe it, that's all."

"Exactly." Kutuzov emphasized the word by pounding the arm of the command chair with his closed fists. "They have technology beyond ours. They speak our language and you say we will never speak theirs. They know the Alderson effect, and now they know Langston Fields exist. Perhaps, Dr. Horvath, we should go home. Now."

"But—" Horvath began.

"And yet," Kutuzov continued. "I would not like to fight war with these Moties without knowing more about them. What are planetary defense? Who governs Moties? I notice for all your work you cannot answer that question. You do not even know who is commanding that ship of theirs."

"True." Horvath nodded vigorously. "It's a very strange situation. Sometimes I honestly think they don't have a commander, but on the other hand they do seem to refer back to their ship for instructions sometimes . . . and then there's the sex matter."

"You play games with me, Doctor?"

"No, no," Horvath said with irritation. "It's quite straightforward. All of the Brown-and-whites have been female since their arrival. In addition, the brown female has become pregnant and has given birth to a brown-and-white pup. Now it's a male."

"I know of sex changes in aliens. Perhaps one Brown-and-white was male until shortly before embassy ship arrived?"

"We thought of that. But it seems more likely that the Brown-and-whites haven't been breeding because of population pressure. They all stay female—they may even be mules, since a Brown is mother of one. Crossbreed between the Brown and something else? That would point to a something else aboard the embassy ship."

"They got an admiral aboard their ship," Kutuzov said positively. "Just as we do. I knew it. What do you tell them when they ask of me?"

Rod heard a snort behind him and guessed that Kevin Renner was strangling. "As little as possible, sir," Rod said. "Only that we're subject to orders from *Lenin*. I don't think they know your name, or if there's one man or a council aboard."

"Just so." The Admiral almost smiled. "Just what you know about their command, da? You watch, they got an admiral aboard that ship, and he's decided he wants you closer to their planet. Now my problem is, do I learn more by letting you go than he learns by getting you there?"

Horvath turned away from the screen and sent a pleading look to Heaven, Its Wonders, and All the Saints. How could he deal with a man like that, the look asked.

"Any sign of little Moties?" Kutuzov asked. "Have you

still Brownies aboard His Imperial Majesty's General Class battle cruiser *MacArthur?*"

Rod shuddered at the heavy sarcasm. "No, sir. We evacuated hangar deck and opened everything in it to space. Then I put all *MacArthur*'s passengers and crew into hangar deck and opened up the ship. We fumigated the plant rooms with ciphogene, poured carbon monoxide through all the vents, opened to space again, and after we came back from hangar deck we did the same thing there. The miniatures are dead, Admiral. We have the bodies. Twenty-four of them, to be exact, although we didn't find one of them until yesterday. It was pretty ripe after three weeks . . ."

"And there are no signs of Brownies? Or of mice?"

"No, sir. Rats, mice, and Moties—all dead. The other miniature, the one we had caged—it's dead too, sir. The vet thinks it was old age."

Kutuzov nodded. "So that problem is solved. What of adult alien you have aboard?"

"It's sick," Blaine said. "Same symptoms as the miniature had."

"Yes, that's another thing," Horvath said quickly. "I want to ask the Moties what to do for the sick miner, but Blaine won't let me without your permission."

The Admiral reached somewhere off screen. When he faced them again he held a glass of tea which he blew on noisily. "The others know you have this miner aboard?"

"Yes," Horvath said. When Kutuzov glared, the Science Minister continued quickly, "They seem to have always known it. None of us told them, I'm sure of that."

"So they know. Have they asked for the miner? Or to see it?"

"No." Horvath frowned deeply again. His voice was incredulous. "No, they haven't. In fact, they haven't shown the least concern about the miner, no more than they might have for the miniatures—you'll have seen the pictures of the Moties evacuating *their* ship, Admiral? They have to kill off the little beasts too. The things must breed like hive rats." Horvath paused, his brow wrinkled even more deeply. Then, abruptly, "Anyway, I want to ask the others what to do for the sick miner. We can't just let it die."

"That might be best for all," Kutuzov mused. "Oh, very well, Doctor. Ask them. It is hardly admitting anything important about Empire to tell them we do not know proper diet for Moties. But if you ask and they insist on seeing that miner, Blaine, you will refuse. If necessary, miner will die—tragically and suddenly, by accident, but die. Is that clearly understood? It will not talk to other Moties, not now and not ever."

"Aye aye, sir." Rod sat impassively in his command chair. Now, do I agree with that? he thought. I should be shocked, but—

"Do you still wish to ask under those circumstances, Doctor?" Kutuzov asked.

"Yes. I expected nothing else from you anyway." Horvath's lips were pressed tightly against his teeth. "We now have the main question: the Moties have invited us to take orbit around their planet. Why they have done so is a matter for interpretation. I think it is because they genuinely want to develop trade and diplomatic relations with us, and this is the logical way we should go about it. There is no evidence for any other view. You, of course, have your own theories . . ."

Kutuzov laughed. It was a deep, hearty laugh. "Actually, Doctor, I may believe same as you. What has that to do with anything? Is my task to keep Empire safe. What I believe has no importance." The Admiral stared coldly into the screens. "Very well. Captain, I give you discretion to act in this situation. However, you will first arm torpedo-destruct systems for your ship. You understand that *MacArthur* cannot be allowed to fall into Motie hands?"

"Yes, sir."

"Very well. You may go, Captain. We will follow in *Lenin*. You will transmit records of all information you obtain every hour—and you understand that if there is threat to your ship, I will not attempt to rescue you if there is any possibility of danger to *Lenin*? That my first duty is to return with information including, if this is so, how you were killed?" The Admiral turned so that he gazed directly at Horvath. "Well, Doctor, do you still want to go to Mote Prime?"

"Of course."

Kutuzov shrugged. "Carry on, Captain Blaine. Carry on."

MacArthur's towboats had retrieved an oil-drum-shaped cylinder half the size of the Motie embassy ship. It was very simple: a hard, thick shell of some foamed material, heavy with liquid hydrogen, spinning slowly, with a bleeder valve at the axis. Now it was strapped to the embassy ship aft the toroidal living spaces. The slender spine meant to guide the plasma flow for the fusion drive had been altered too, bent far to the side to direct the thrust through the new center of mass. The embassy ship was tilted far back on her drive, like a smaller but very pregnant woman trying to walk.

Moties—Brown-and-whites, guided by one of the Browns—were at work disassembling the air-lock bridge, melting it down, and reshaping the material into ring-shaped support platforms for the fragile toroids. Others worked within the ship, and three small brown-and-white shapes played among them. Again the interior changed like dreams. Free-fall furniture was reshaped. Floors were slanted, vertical to the new line of thrust.

There were no Moties aboard the cutter now; they were all at work; but contact was maintained. Some of the midshipmen took their turns doing simple muscle work aboard the embassy ship.

Whitbread and Potter were working in the acceleration chamber, moving the bunks to leave room for three smaller bunks. It was a simple rewelding job, but it took muscle. Perspiration collected in beads inside their filter helmets, and soaked their armpits.

Potter said, "I wonder what a man smells like to a Motie? Dinna answer if you find the question offensive," he added.

" 'Tis a bit hard to say," Potter's Motie answered. "My duty it is, Mr. Potter, to understand everything about my

Fyunch(click). Perhaps I fit the part too well. The smell of clean sweat wouldna offend me even if ye had nae been working in our own interest. What is it ye find funny, Mr. Whitbread?"

"Sorry. It's the accent."

"What accent is that?" Potter wondered.

Whitbread and Whitbread's Motie burst out laughing. "Well, it *is* funny," said Whitbread's Motie. "You used to have trouble telling us apart."

"Now it's the other way around," Jonathon Whitbread said. "I have to keep counting hands to know if I'm talking to Renner or Renner's Motie. Give me a hand here, will you, Gavin? . . . And Captain Blaine's Motie. I have to keep shaking myself out of the *Attention* position, and then she'll say something and I'll snap right back into it. She'll give orders like she's master of the cutter, and we'll obey, and then she'll say, 'Just a minute, Mister,' and order us to forgive her. It's confusing."

"Even so," said Whitbread's Motie, "I wonder sometimes whether we've really got you figured out. Just because I can imitate you doesn't mean I can understand you . . ."

" 'Tis our standard technique, as old as the hills, as old as some mountain ranges. It works. What else can we do, Jonathon Whitbread's Fyunch(click)?"

"I wondered, that's all. These *people* are so versatile. We can't match all of your abilities, Whitbread. You find it easy to command and easy to obey; how can you do both? You're good with tools—"

"So are you," said Whitbread, knowing it was an understatement.

"But we tire easily. You're ready to go on working, aren't you? We're not."

"Um."

"And we aren't good at fighting . . . Well, enough of that. We play your part in order to understand you, but you each seem to play a thousand parts. It makes things difficult for an honest, hardworking bug-eyed monster."

"Who told you about bug-eyed monsters?" Whitbread exclaimed.

"Mr. Renner, who else? I took it as a compliment—that he would trust my sense of humor, that is."

"Dr. Horvath would kill him. We're supposed to be tippy-toe careful in our relationship with aliens. Don't offend taboos, and all that."

"Dr. Horvath," Potter said. "I am reminded that Dr. Horvath wanted us to ask you something. Ye know that we have a Brown aboard *MacArthur.*"

"Sure. A miner. Her ship visited *MacArthur,* then came home empty. It was pretty obvious she'd stayed with you."

"She's sick," Potter said. "She has been growing worse. Dr. Blevins says it has the marks of a dietary disease, but he has nae been able to help her. Hae you any idea what it is that she might lack?"

Whitbread thought he knew why Horvath had not asked *his* Motie about the Brown; if the Moties demanded to see the miner, they must be refused on orders from the Admiral himself. Dr. Horvath thought the order was stupid; he would never be able to defend it. Whitbread and Potter were not called upon to try. Orders were orders.

When the Moties did not answer at once, Jonathon said, "Between them the biologists have tried a lot of things. New foods, analysis of the Brown's digestive fluids, x-rays for tumor. They even changed the atmosphere in her cabin to match the Mote Prime atmosphere. Nothing works. She's unhappy, she whines, she doesn't move around much. She's getting thin. Her hair is coming out."

Whitbread's Motie spoke in a voice gone oddly flat. "You haven't any idea what might be wrong with her?"

"No," said Whitbread.

It was strange and uncomfortable, the way the Moties were looking at them. They seemed identical now, floating half-crouched, anchored by hand holds: identical pose, identical markings, identical faint smiles. Their individual identities didn't show now. Perhaps it *was* all a pose—

"We'll get you some food," Potter's Motie said, suddenly. "You may hae guessed right. It may be her diet."

Both Moties left. Presently Whitbread's Motie returned with a pressure bag that contained grain and plum-sized fruits and a chunk of red meat. "Boil the meat, soak the grain, and give her the fruit raw," she said. "And test the ionization in her cabin air." She ushered them out.

The boys boarded an open scooter to return to the cutter. Presently Potter said, "They behaved verra strangely. I canna but think that something important happened a minute ago."

"Yah."

"Then what was it?"

"Maybe they think we've been mistreating the Brown. Maybe they wonder why we won't bring her here. Maybe the other way around: they're shocked that we take so much trouble for a mere Brown."

"And perhaps they were tired and we imagined it." Potter fired thruster clusters to slow the scooter.

"Gavin. Look behind us."

"Not now. I must see to the safety o' my command." Potter took his time docking the scooter, then looked around.

More than a dozen Moties had been working outside the ship. The bracing for the toroids was conspicuously unfinished . . . but the Moties were all streaming into the air lock.

The Mediators came streaming into the toroid, bouncing gently from the walls in their haste to get out of each other's way. Most of them showed in one way or another that they were Fyunch(click) to aliens. They tended to underuse their lower right arms. They wanted to line themselves with their heads pointing all in the same direction.

The Master was white. The tufts at her armpits and groin were long and silky, like the fur of an Angora cat. When they were all there, the Master turned to Whitbread's Motie and said, "Speak."

Whitbread's Motie told of the incident with the midshipmen. "I'm certain they meant it all," she concluded.

To Potter's Motie the Master said, "Do you agree?"

"Yes, completely."

There was a panicky undercurrent of whispers, some in Motie tongues, some in Anglic. It cut off when the Master said, "What did you tell them?"

"We told them the disease might well be a dietary deficiency—"

There was shocked human-sounding laughter among the Mediators, none at all among the few who had not yet been assigned Fyunch(click)s.

"—and gave them food for the Engineer. It will not help, of course."

"Were they fooled?"

"Difficult to tell. We are not good at lying directly. It is not our specialty," said Potter's Motie.

A buzz of talk rose in the toroid. The Master allowed it for a time. Presently she spoke. "What can it mean? Speak of this."

One answered. "They cannot be so different from us. They fight wars. We have heard hints of whole planets rendered uninhabitable."

Another interrupted. There was something graceful, human-feminine, in the way she moved. It seemed grotesque to the Master. "We think we know what causes humans to fight. Most animals on our world and theirs have a surrender reflex that prevents one member of a species from killing another. Humans use weapons instinctively. It makes the surrender reflex too slow."

"But it was the same with us, once," said a third. "Evolution of the Mediator mules put an end to that. Do you say that humans do not have Mediators?"

Sally Fowler's Motie said, "They have nothing that is bred for the task of communicating and negotiating between potential enemies. They are amateurs at everything, second-best at everything they do. Amateurs do their negotiating. When negotiations break down, they fight."

"They are amateurs at playing Master, too," one said. Nervously she stroked the center of her face. "They take turns at playing Master. In their warships they station Marines *between* fore and aft, in case the aft sections should wish to become masters of the ship. Yet, when *Lenin* speaks, Captain Blaine obeys like a Brown. It is," she said, "difficult to be Fyunch(click) to a part-time Master."

"Agreed," said Whitbread's Motie. "Mine is not a Master, but will be someday."

Another said, "Our Engineer has found much that needs improvement in their tools. There is now no class to fit Dr. Hardy—"

"Stop this," said the Master, and the noise stopped. "Our concern is more specific. What have you learned of their mating habits?"

"They do not speak of this to us. Learning will be difficult. There seems to be only one female aboard."

"ONE female?"

"To the best that we can learn."

"Are the rest neuters, or are most neuters?"

"It would seem that they are not. Yet the female is not pregnant, has not been pregnant at any time since our arrival."

"We must learn," said the Master. "But you must also conceal. A casual question. It must be asked very carefully, to reveal as little as possible. If what we suspect is true—can it be true?"

One said, "All of evolution is against it. Individuals that survive to breed must carry the genes for the next generation. How, then—?"

"They are alien. Remember, they are alien," said Whitbread's Motie.

"We must find out. Select one among you, and formulate your question, and select the human you will ask. The rest of you must avoid the subject unless the aliens introduce it."

"I think we must conceal nothing." One stroked the center of her face as if for reassurance. "They are alien. They may be the best hope we have ever had. With their help we may break the ancient pattern of the Cycles."

The Master showed her surprise. "You will conceal the crucial difference between Man and ourselves. They will not learn of it."

"I say we must not!" cried the other. "Listen to me! They have their own ways—they solve problems, al-

*ways—" The others converged on her. "No, listen! You
must listen!"*

"Crazy Eddie," the Master said wonderingly. "Confine
her in comfort. We will need her knowledge. No other
must be assigned to her Fyunch(click), since the strain has
driven her mad."

Blaine let the cutter lead *MacArthur* to Mote Prime at
.780 gee. He was acutely aware that *MacArthur* was an
alien warship capable of devastating half the Motie planet,
and did not like to think of what weaponry might be
trained on her by uneasy Moties. He wanted the embassy
ship to arrive first—not that it would really help, but it
might.

The cutter was almost empty now. The scientific personnel were living and working aboard *MacArthur,* reading endless data into the computer banks, cross-checking
and codifying, and reporting their findings to the Captain
for transmission to *Lenin.* They could have reported directly, of course, but there are many privileges to rank.
MacArthur's dinner parties and bridge games tended to
become discussion groups.

Everyone was concerned about the brown miner. She
became steadily worse, eating as little of the food provided by the Moties as she had of *MacArthur*'s provi-
sions. It was frustrating, and Dr. Blevins tried endless
tests with no results. The miniatures had waxed fat and
fecund while loose aboard *MacArthur,* and Blevins wondered if they had been eating something unexpected, like
missile propellant, or the insulation from cables. He offered her a variety of unlikely substances, but the Brown's
eyesight grew dim, her fur came out in patches, and she
howled. One day she stopped eating. The next she was
dead.

Horvath was beside himself with fury.

Blaine thought it fitting to call the embassy ship. The
gently smiling Brown-and-white that answered could only
be Horvath's Motie, although Blaine would have been
hard-pressed to say how he knew. "Is my Fyunch(click)

available?" Rod 'asked. Horvath's Motie made him uncomfortable.

"I'm afraid not, Captain."

"All right. I called to report that the Brown we had
aboard this ship is dead. I don't know how much it means
to you, but we did our best. The entire scientific staff of
MacArthur tried to cure her."

"I'm sure of that, Captain. It doesn't matter. May we
have the body?"

Rod considered it a moment. "I'm afraid not." He
couldn't guess what the Moties could learn from the
corpse of an alien that had never communicated when
alive; but perhaps he was learning from Kutuzov. Could
there have been microtattooing below the fur . . . ? And
why weren't the Moties more concerned about the Brown?
That was something he certainly couldn't ask. Best to be
thankful they weren't upset. "Give my regards to my
Fyunch(click)."

"I have bad news also," said Horvath's Motie. "Captain, you no longer have a Fyunch(click). She has gone
mad."

"What?" Rod was more shocked than he would have
believed. "Mad? Why? How?"

"Captain, I don't imagine you can grasp what a strain
it has been for her. There are Moties who give orders and
there are Moties who make and fix tools. We are neither:
we communicate. We can identify with a giver of orders
and it is no strain, but an *alien* giver of orders? It was too
much. She— How shall I put it? Mutiny. Your word is
mutiny. We have none. She is safe and under confinement,
but it is best for her that she does not speak with aliens
again."

"Thank you," Rod said. He watched the gently smiling
image fade from the screen and did nothing more for five
minutes. Finally he sighed and began dictating reports for
Lenin. He worked alone and it was as if he had lost a
part of himself and was waiting for it to come back.

PART THREE

MEET CRAZY EDDIE

26 • *Mote Prime*

MOTE PRIME: Marginally habitable world in the Trans-Coalsack Sector. Primary: G2 yellow dwarf star approximately ten parsecs from the Trans-Coalsack Sector Capital New Caledonia. Generally referred to as the Mote in Murcheson's Eye (*q.v.*) or the Mote. Mass 0.91 Sol; luminosity 0.78 Sol.

Mote Prime has a poisonous atmosphere breathable with the aid of commercial or standard Navy issue filters. *Contraindicated* for heart patients or where emphysema problems exist. Oxygen: 16 percent. Nitrogen: 79.4 percent. CO_2: 2.9 percent. Helium: 1 percent. Complex hydrocarbons including ketones: 0.7 percent.

Gravity: 0.780 standard. The planetary radius is 0.84, and mass is 0.57 Earth standard; a planet of normal density. Period: 0.937 standard years, or 8,750.005 hours. The planet is inclined at 18 degrees with semimajor axis of 0.93 AU (137 million kilometers). Temperatures are cool, poles uninhabitable and covered with ice. Equatorial and tropical regions are temperate to hot. The local day is 27.33 hours.

There is one moon, small and close. It is asteroidal in origin and the back side bears the characteristic indented crater typical of planetoids in the Mote system. The moon-based fusion generator and power-beaming station are critical sources for the Mote Prime civilization.

Topography: 50 percent ocean, not including extensive ice caps. Terrain is flat over most of the land area. Mountain ranges are low and heavily eroded. There are few forests. Arable lands are extensively cultivated.

The most obvious features are circular formations which are visible everywhere. The smallest are eroded to the limits of detection, while the largest can be seen only from orbit.

Although the physical features of Mote Prime are of some interest, particularly to ecologists concerned with the effects of intelligent life on planetography, the primary interest in the Mote centers on its inhabitants . . .

Two scooters converged at the cutter and suited figures climbed aboard. When both humans and Moties had checked over the ship, the Navy ratings who had brought her to orbit gratefully turned her over to the midshipmen and returned to *MacArthur*. The middies eagerly took their places in the control cabin and examined the landscape below.

"We're to tell you that all contact with you will be through this ship," Whitbread told his Motie. "Sorry, but we can't invite you aboard *MacArthur*."

Whitbread's Motie gave a very human shrug to express her opinion of orders. Obedience posed no strain on either her or her human. "What will you do with the cutter when you leave?"

"It's a gift," Whitbread told her. "Maybe you'll want it for a museum. There are things the Captain *wants* you to know about us—"

"And things he wants to conceal. Certainly."

From orbit the planet was all circles: seas, lakes, an arc of a mountain range, the line of a river, a bay . . . There was one, eroded and masked by a forest. It would have been undetectable had it not fallen exactly across a line of mountains, breaking the backbone of a continent as a man's foot breaks a snake. Beyond, a sea the size of the Black Sea showed a flattish island in the exact center.

"The magma must have welled up where the asteroid tore the crust open," said Whitbread. "Can you imagine the *sound* it must have made?"

Whitbread's Motie nodded.

"No wonder you moved all the asteroids out to the Trojan points. That was the reason, wasn't it?"

"I don't know. Our records are-unt complete from that long ago. I imagine the asteroids must have been easier to mine, easier to make a civilization from, once they were lumped together like that."

Whitbread remembered that the Beehive had been stone cold without a trace of radiation. "Just how long ago did all this happen?"

"Oh, at least ten thousand years. Whitbread, how old are your oldest records?"

"I don't know. I could ask someone." The midshipman looked down. They were crossing the Terminator—which was a series of arcs. The night side blazed with a galaxy of cities. Earth might have looked this way during the CoDominium; but the Empire's worlds had never been so heavily populated.

"Look ahead." Whitbread's Motie pointed to a fleck of flame at the world's rim. "That's the transfer ship. Now we can show you our world."

"I think your civilization must be a lot older than ours," said Whitbread.

Sally's equipment and personal effects were packed and ready in the cutter's lounge, and her minuscule cabin seemed bare and empty now. She stood at the view port and watched the silver arrowhead approach *MacArthur*. Her Motie was not watching.

"I, um, I have a rather indelicate question," Sally's Fyunch(click) said.

Sally turned from the view port. Outside, the Motie ship had come alongside and a small boat was approaching from *MacArthur*. "Go ahead."

"What do you do if you don't want children yet?"

"Oh, dear," said Sally, and she laughed a little. She was the only woman among nearly a thousand men—and in a male-oriented society. She had known all this before she came, but still she missed what she thought of as girl talk. Marriage and babies and housekeeping and scandals: they were part of civilized life. She hadn't known how big a part until the New Chicago revolt caught her up, and she missed it even more now. Sometimes in desperation she had talked recipes with *MacArthur's* cooks as a poor substitute, but the only other feminine-oriented mind within light years was—her Fyunch(click).

"Fyunch(click)," the alien reminded her. "I wouldn't raise the subject but I think I ought to know—do you have children aboard *MacArthur?*"

"Me? No!" Sally laughed again. "I'm not even married."

"Married?"

Sally told the Motie about marriage. She tried not to skip any basic assumptions. It was sometimes hard to remember that the Motie was an alien. "This must sound a bit weird," she finished.

" 'Come, I will conceal nothing from you,' as Mr. Renner would say." The mimicry was perfect, including gestures. "I think your customs are strange. I doubt that we'll adopt many of them, given the differences in physiology."

"Well—*yes.*"

"But you marry to raise children. Who raises children born without marriage?"

"There are charities," Sally said grimly. Her distaste was impossible to disguise.

"I take it *you've* never . . ." The Motie paused delicately.

"No, of course not."

"How not? I don't mean *why* not, I mean *how?*"

"Well—you know that men and women have to have sexual relations to make a baby, the same as you—I've examined you pretty thoroughly."

"So that if you aren't married you just don't—get together?"

"That's right. Of course, there are pills a woman can take if she likes men but doesn't want to take the consequences."

"Pills? How do they work? Hormones?" The Motie seemed interested, if somewhat detached.

"That's right." They had discussed hormones. Motie physiology employed chemical triggers also, but the chemicals were quite different.

"But a proper woman doesn't use them," Sally's Motie suggested.

"No."

"When will you get married?"

"When I find the right man." She thought for a moment, hesitated, and added, "I may have found him already." And the damn fool may already be married to his ship, she added to herself.

"Then why don't you marry him?"

Sally laughed. "I don't want to jump into anything. 'Marry in haste, repent at leisure.' I can get married any time." Her trained objectivity made her add, "Well, any time within the next five years. I'll be something of a spinster if I'm not married by then."

"Spinster?"

"People would think it odd." Curious now, she asked, "What if a Motie doesn't want children?"

"We don't have sexual relations," Sally's Motie said primly.

There was an almost inaudible *clunk* as the ground-to-orbit ship secured alongside.

The landing boat was a blunt arrowhead coated with ablative material. The pilot's cabin was a large wrap-around transparency, and there were no other windows. When Sally and her Motie arrived at the entryway, she was startled to see Horace Bury just ahead of her.

"You're going down to the Mote, Your Excellency?" Sally asked.

"Yes, my lady." Bury seemed as surprised as Sally. He entered the connecting tube to find that the Moties had employed an old Navy trick—the tube was pressurized with a lower pressure at the receiving end, so that the passengers were wafted along. The interior was surprisingly large, with room for all: Renner, Sally Fowler, Chaplain Hardy—Bury wondered if they would ship him back up to *MacArthur* every Sunday—Dr. Horvath, Midshipmen Whitbread and Staley, two ratings Bury did not recognize—and alien counterparts for all but three of the humans. He noted the seating arrangements with an amusement that only partly covered his fears: four abreast, with a Motie seat beside each of the human seats. As they strapped in he was further amused. They were one short.

But Dr. Horvath moved forward into the control cabin and took a seat next to the brown pilot. Bury settled into the front row, where seats were only two abreast—and a Motie took the other. Fear surged into his throat. Allah is merciful, I witness that Allah is One— *No!* There was nothing to fear and he had done nothing dangerous.

And yet—he was here, and the alien was beside him, while behind him on *MacArthur,* any accident might bring the ship's officers to discover what he had done to his pressure suit.

A pressure suit is the most identity-locked artifact a man of space can own. It is far more personal than a pipe or a toothbrush. Yet others had exposed their suits to the ministrations of the unseen Brownies. During the long voyage to Mote Prime, Commander Sinclair had examined the modifications the Brownies had made.

Bury had waited. Presently he learned through Nabil that the Brownies had doubled the efficiency of the recycling systems. Sinclair had returned the pressure suits to their owners—and begun modifying the officers' suits in a similar fashion.

One of the air tanks on Bury's suit was now a dummy. It held half a liter of pressurized air and two miniatures in suspended animation. The risks were great. He might be caught. The miniatures might die from the frozen-sleep drugs. Someday he might need air that was not there. Bury had always been willing to take risks for sufficient profit.

When the call came, he had been certain he was discovered. A Navy rating had appeared on his room screen, said, "Call for you, Mr. Bury," smiled evilly, and switched over. Before he could wonder Bury found himself facing an alien.

"Fyunch(click)," said the alien. It cocked its head and shoulders at him. "You seem confused. Surely you know the term."

Bury had recovered quickly. "Of course. I was not aware that any Motie was studying me." He did not like the idea at all.

"No, Mr. Bury, I have only just been assigned. Mr. Bury, have you thought of coming to Mote Prime?"

"No, I doubt that I would be allowed to leave the ship."

"Captain Blaine has given permission, if you-urr willing. Mr. Bury, we would deeply appreciate your comments regarding the possibilities for trade between the Mote and the Empire. It seems likely we would both profit."

Yes! Beard of the Prophet, an opportunity like that— Bury had agreed quickly. Nabil could guard the hidden Brownies.

But now, as he sat aboard the landing boat, it was difficult to control his fears. He looked at the alien beside him.

"I am Dr. Horvath's Fyunch(click)," the Motie said. "You should relax. These boats are well designed."

"Ah," said Bury, and he relaxed. The worst was hours away. Nabil had by now safely removed the dummy tank into *MacArthur*'s main air lock with hundreds of others, and it would be safe. The alien ship was undoubtedly superior to similar human craft, if for no other reason than the Moties' desire to avoid risk to the human ambassadors. But it was not the trip down that kept fear creeping into his throat until it tasted bright and sharp like new copper—

There was a slight lurch. The descent had begun.

To everyone's surprise it was dull. There were occasional shifts in gravity but no turbulence. Three separate times they felt almost subliminal *clunks,* as of landing gear coming down—and then there was a rolling sensation. The ship had come to rest.

They filed out into a pressurized chamber. The air was good but scentless, and there was nothing to see but the big inflated structure around them. They looked back at the ship and stared unashamedly.

It was gull-winged now, built like a glider. The edges of the crazy arrowhead had sprouted a bewildering variety of wings and flaps.

"That was quite a ride," Horvath said jovially as he came to join them. "The whole vehicle changes shape. There aren't any hinges on the wings—the flaps come out as if they were alive! The jet scoops open and closes like mouths! You really should have seen it. If Commander Sinclair ever comes down we'll have to give him the window seat," he chortled. He did not notice the glares.

An inflated air lock opened at the far end of the building, and three brown-and-white Moties entered. Fear rose in Bury's throat again as they separated, one joining each of the Navy ratings, while the other came directly to Bury.

"Fyunch(click)," it said.

Bury's mouth was very dry.

"Don't be afraid," said the Motie. "I can't read your mind."

It was definitely the wrong thing to say if the Motie wanted Bury at ease. "I'm told that is your profession."

The Motie laughed. "It's my profession, but I can't *do* it. All I will ever know is what you show me." It didn't sound at all as Bury sounded to himself. It must have studied humans in general; only that.

"You're male," he noticed.

"I am young. The others were female by the time they reached *MacArthur*. Mr. Bury, we have vehicles outside and a place of residence for you nearby. Come and see our city, and then we can discuss business." It took his arm in two small right arms, and the touch was very strange. Bury let himself be led to the air lock.

"Don't be afraid. I can't read your mind," it had said, reading his mind. On many rediscovered worlds of the First Empire there were rumors of mind readers, but none had ever been found, praise the mercy of Allah. This thing

claimed that it was not; and it was very alien. The touch was not abhorrent, although people of Bury's culture hated to be touched. He had been among far too many strange customs and peoples to worry about his childhood prejudices. But this Motie was reassuringly strange—and Bury had never heard of *anybody's* Fyunch(click) acting that way. Was it *trying* to reassure him?

Nothing could have lured him but the hope of profit —profit without ceiling, without limit, profit from merely looking around. Even the terraforming of the New Caledonia worlds by the First Empire had not shown the industrial power that must have moved the asteroids to Mote Beta's Trojan points.

"A good commercial product," the Motie was saying, "should not be bulky or massive. We should be able to find items scarce here and plentiful in the Empire, or vice versa. I anticipate great profit from your visit . . ."

They joined the others in the air lock. Large windows showed the airfield. "Blasted show-offs," Renner muttered to Bury. When the Trader looked at him quizzically, Renner pointed. "There's city all around, and the airport's got not one meter of extra space."

Bury nodded. Around the tiny field were skyscrapers, tall and square-built, jammed close together, with only a single belt of green running out of the city to the east. If there were a plane crash it would be a disaster—but the Moties didn't build planes to crash.

There were three ground cars, limousines, two for passengers and one for luggage, and the human seats took up two-thirds of the room in each. Bury nodded reflectively. Moties didn't mind being crowded together. As soon as they took their seats the drivers, who were Browns, whipped the cars away. The vehicles ran soundlessly, with a smooth feeling of power, and there was no jolt at all. The motors were in the hubs of the tall balloon tires, much like those of cars on Empire worlds.

Tall, ugly buildings loomed above them to shoulder out the sky. The black streets were wide but very crowded, and the Moties drove like maniacs. Tiny vehicles passed each other in intricate curved paths with centimeters of clearance. The traffic was not quite silent. There was a steady low hum that might have been all the hundreds of motors sounding together, and sometimes a stream of high-pitched gibberish that might have been cursing.

Once the humans were able to stop wincing away from each potential collision, they noticed that all the other drivers were Browns, too. Most of the cars carried a passenger, sometimes a Brown-and-white, often a pure White. These Whites were larger than the Brown-and-whites, and their fur was very clean and silky—and they were doing all the cursing as their drivers continued in silence.

Science Minister Horvath turned back to the humans in the seats behind him. "I had a look at the buildings as we came down—roof gardens on every one of them. Well, Mr. Renner, are you glad you came? We were expecting a Navy officer, but hardly you."

"It seemed most reasonable to send me," Kevin Renner said. "I was the most thoroughly available officer aboard, as the Captain put it. I won't be needed to chart courses for a while."

"And that's why they sent you?" Sally asked.

"No, I think what really convinced the Captain was the way I screamed and cried and threatened to hold my breath. Somehow he got the idea I really wanted to come. And I did." The way the navigating officer leaned forward in his seat reminded Sally of a dog sticking its head out of a car window into the wind.

They had only just noticed the walkways that ran one floor up along the edges of the buildings, and they could not see the pedestrians well at all. There were more Whites, and Brown-and-whites, and . . . others.

Something tall and symmetrical came walking like a giant among the Whites. Three meters tall it must have been, with a small, earless head that seemed submerged beneath the sloping muscles of the shoulders. It carried a massive-looking box of some kind under each of two arms. It walked like a juggernaut, steady and unstoppable.

"What's *that?*" Renner asked.

"Worker," Sally's Motie replied. "Porter. Not very intelligent . . ."

There was something else Renner strained to see, for its fur was rust-red, as if it had been dipped in blood. It was the size of his own Motie, but with a smaller head, and as it raised and flexed its right hands it showed fingers so long and delicate that Renner thought of Amazon spiders. He touched his Fyunch(click)'s shoulder and pointed. "And that?"

"Physician. Emm Dee," Renner's Motie said. "We're a differentiated species, as you may have gathered by now. They're all relatives, so to speak . . ."

"Yah. And the Whites?"

"Givers of orders. There was one aboard ship, as I'm sure you know."

"Yah, we guessed that." The Tsar had, anyway. What else was he right about?

"What do you think of our architecture?"

"Ugly. Industrial hideous," said Renner. "I knew your ideas of beauty would be different from ours, but—on your honor. Do you *have* a standard of beauty?"

"Come, I will conceal nothing from you. We do, but it doesn't resemble yours. And I still don't know what you people see in arches and pillars—"

"Freudian symbolism," Renner said firmly. Sally snorted.

"That's what Horvath's Motie keeps saying, but I've never heard a coherent explanation," Renner's Motie said. "Meanwhile, what do you think of your vehicles?"

The limousines were radically different from the two-seaters that zipped past them. No two of the two-seaters were alike either—the Moties did not seem to have discovered the advantages of standardization. But all the other vehicles they had seen were tiny, like a pair of motorcycles, while the humans rode in low-slung streamlined vehicles with soft curves bright with polish.

"They're beautiful," said Sally. "Did you design them just for us?"

"Yes," her Motie replied. "Did we guess well?"

"Perfectly. We're most flattered," Sally said. "You must have put considerable expense into . . . this . . ." She trailed off. Renner turned to see where she was looking, and gasped.

There had been castles like this in the Tyrolean Alps of Earth. They were still there, never bombed, but Renner had only seen copies on other worlds. Now a fairy-tale castle, graceful with tall spires, stood among the square buildings of the Motie city. At one corner a reaching minaret was circled by a thin balcony.

"What *is* that place?" Renner asked.

Sally's Motie answered. "You will stay there. It is pressurized and self-enclosed, with a garage and cars for your convenience."

Horace Bury spoke into the admiring silence. "You are most impressive hosts."

From the first they called it the Castle. Beyond question it had been designed and built entirely for them. It was large enough for perhaps thirty people. Its beauty and luxury were in the tradition of Sparta—with a few jarring notes.

Whitbread, Staley, Sally, Drs. Hardy and Horvath— they knew their manners. They kept firm rein on their laughter as their Fyunch(click)s showed them about their respective rooms. Able Spacers Jackson and Weiss were awed to silence and wary of saying something foolish. Horace Bury's people had rigid traditions of hospitality; aside from that, he found all customs strange except on Levant.

But Renner's people respected candor; and candor, he had found, made life easier for everyone. Except in the Navy. In the Navy he had learned to keep his mouth shut. Fortunately his Fyunch(click) held views similar to his own.

He looked about the apartment assigned him. Double bed, dresser, large closet, a couch and coffee table, all vaguely reminiscent of the travelogues he had shown the Moties. It was five times the size of his cabin aboard *Mac-Arthur*.

"Elbow room," he said with great satisfaction. He

sniffed. There was no smell at all. "You do a great job of filtering the planet's air."

"Thanks. As for the elbow room—" Renner's Motie wiggled all her elbows. "We should need more than you, but we don't."

The picture window ran from floor to ceiling, wall to wall. The city towered over him; most of the buildings in view were taller than the Castle. Renner found that he was looking straight down a city street toward a magnificent sunset that was all the shades of red. The pedestrian level showed a hurrying horde of colored blobs, mostly Reds and Browns, but also many Whites. He watched for a time, then turned back.

There was an alcove near the head of his bed. He looked into it. It held a dresser and two odd-looking pieces of furniture that Renner recognized. They resembled what the Brown had done to the bed in Crawford's stateroom.

He asked, "Two?"

"We will be assigned a Brown."

"I'm going to teach you a new word. It's called 'privacy.' It refers to the human need—"

"We know about privacy." The Motie did a double take. "You aren't suggesting it should apply between a man and his Fyunch(click)!"

Renner nodded solemnly.

"But . . . but . . . Renner, do you have any respect for tradition?"

"Do I?"

"No. Dammit. All right, Renner. We'll sling a door there. With a lock?"

"Yah. I might add that the rest probably feel the same way, whether they say so or not."

The bed, the couch, the table showed none of the familiar Motie innovations. The mattress was a bit too firm, but what the hell. Renner glanced into the bathroom and burst out laughing. The toilet was a free-fall toilet, somewhat changed from those in the cutter; it had a gold flush, carved into the semblance of a dog's head. The bathtub was . . . strange.

"I've got to try that bathtub," said Renner.

"Let me know what you think. We saw some pictures of bathtubs in your travelogues, but they looked ridiculous, given your anatomy."

"Right. Nobody's ever designed a decent bathtub. There weren't any toilets in those pictures, were there?"

"Oddly enough, there weren't."

"Mmm." Renner began sketching. When he had finished, his Motie said, "Just how much water do these use?"

"Quite a lot. Too much for space craft."

"Well, we'll see what we can do."

"Oh, and you'd better hang another door between the bathroom and the living room."

"*More* privacy?"

"Yah."

Dinner that night was like a formal dinner in Sally's old home on Sparta, but weirdly changed. The servants—silent, attentive, deferential, guided by the host who in deference to rank was Dr. Horvath's Motie—were Laborers a meter and a half tall. The food was from *MacArthur*'s stores—except for an appetizer, which was a melonlike fruit sweetened with a yellow sauce. "We guarantee it nonpoisonous," said Renner's Motie. "We've found a few foods we can guarantee, and we're looking for more. But you'll have to take your chances on the taste." The sauce killed the melon's sour taste and made it delicious.

"We can use this as a trade item," said Bury. "We would rather ship the seeds, not the melon itself. Is it hard to grow?"

"Not at all, but it requires cultivation," said Bury's Motie. "We'll give you the opportunity to test the soil. Have you found other things that might be worth trading?"

Bury frowned and looked down at his plate. Nobody had remarked on those plates. They were gold: plates, silverware, even the wine goblets, though they were shaped like fine crystal. Yet they couldn't *be* gold, because they didn't conduct heat; and they were simple copies of the plastic free-fall utensils aboard *MacArthur*'s cutter, even to the trademarks stamped on the edges.

Everyone was waiting for his answer. Trade possibilities would profoundly affect the relationship between Mote and Empire. "On our route to the Castle I looked for signs of luxuries among you. I saw none but those designed specifically for human beings. Perhaps I did not recognize them."

"I know the word, but we deal very little in luxuries. We—I speak for the givers of orders, of course—we put more emphasis on power, territory, the maintenance of a household and a dynasty. We concern ourselves with providing a proper station in life for our children."

Bury filed the information: *"We speak for the givers of orders."* He was dealing with a servant. No. An agent. He must keep that in mind, and wonder how binding were his Fyunch(click)'s promises. He smiled and said, "A pity. Luxuries travel well. You will understand my problem in finding trade goods when I tell you that it would hardly be profitable to buy gold from you."

"I thought as much. We must see if we can find something more valuable."

"Works of art, perhaps?"

"Art?"

"Let me," said Renner's Motie. She switched to a high-pitched, warbling language, talked very fast for perhaps twenty seconds, then looked about at the assembled company. "Sorry, but it was quicker that way."

Bury's Motie said, "Quite so. I take it you would want the originals?"

"If possible."

"Of course. To us a copy is as good as the original. We have many museums; I'll arrange some tours."

It developed that everyone wanted to go along.

When they returned from dinner, Whitbread almost laughed when he saw there was now a door on the bathroom. His Motie caught it and said, "Mr. Renner had words to say about privacy." She jerked a thumb at the door that now closed off her alcove.

"Oh, that one wasn't necessary," said Whitbread. He was not used to sleeping alone. If he woke in the middle of the night, who would he talk to until he fell asleep again?

Someone knocked on the door. Able Spacer Weiss—from Tabletop, Whitbread recalled. "Sir, may I speak with you privately?"

"Right," said Whitbread's Motie, and she withdrew to the alcove. The Moties had caught on to privacy fast. Whitbread ushered Weiss into the room.

"Sir, we've got sort of a problem," Weiss said. "Me and Jackson, that is. We came down to help out, you know, carrying luggage and cleaning up and like that."

"Right. You won't be doing any of that. We've each been assigned an Engineer type."

"Yes, sir, but it's more than that. Jackson and me, we've been assigned a Brown each too. And, and—"

"Fyunch(click)s."

"Right."

"Well, there are certain things you can't talk about." Both ratings were stationed in hangar deck and wouldn't know much about Field technology anyway.

"Yes, sir, we know that. No war stories, nothing about ship's weapons or drive."

"All right. Aside from that, you're on vacation. You're traveling first class, with a servant and a native guide. Enjoy it. Don't say anything the Tsar would hang you for, don't bother to ask about the local red-light district, and don't worry about the expense. Have a ball, and hope they don't send you up on the next boat."

"Aye aye, sir." Weiss grinned suddenly. "You know? This is why I joined the Navy. Strange worlds. This is what the enlistment men promised us."

" 'Golden cities far . . .' Me too."

Afterwards Whitbread stood by the picture window. The city glowed with a million lights. Most of the tiny cars had disappeared, but the streets were alive with huge, silent trucks. The pedestrians had slacked off somewhat. Whitbread spotted something tall and spindly that ran among the Whites as if they were stationary objects. It dodged around a huge Porter type and was gone.

27 • *The Guided Tour*

Renner was up before dawn. The Moties chose and set out clothing for him while he was bathing in the remarkable tub. He let their choice stand. He would indulge them; they might be the last nonmilitary servants he would ever have. His sidearm was discreetly laid out with his clothing, and after a lot of thought, Renner buckled it under a civilian jacket woven from some marvelous shining fibers. He didn't want the weapon, but regulations were regulations . . .

The others were all at breakfast, watching the dawn through the big picture window. It came on like sunset, in all the shades of red. Mote Prime's day was a few hours too long. At night they would stay up longer; they would sleep longer in the mornings and still be up at dawn.

Breakfast featured large, remarkably egg-shaped boiled eggs. Inside the shell it was as if the egg came pre-scrambled, with a maraschino cherry buried off-center. Renner was told that the cherry thing was not worth eating, and he didn't try.

"The Museum is only a few blocks from here." Dr. Horvath's Motie rubbed her right hands briskly together. "Let's walk. You'll want warm clothes, I think."

The Moties all had that problem: which pair of hands to use to imitate human gestures? Renner expected Jackson's Motie to go psychotic. Jackson was left-handed.

They walked. A cold breeze whipped them from around corners. The sun was big and dim; you could look directly at it this early in the day. Tiny cars swarmed six feet below them. The smell of Mote Prime air seeped faintly through the filter helmets, and so did the quiet hum of cars and the fast jabber of Motie voices.

The group of humans moved among crowds of Moties of all colors—and were ignored. Then a group of white-furred pedestrians turned a corner and lingered to examine them. They chattered in musical tones and stared curiously.

Bury seemed uncomfortable; he stayed within the group as much as he could. He doesn't want eye tracks all over him, Renner decided. The Sailing Master found himself being examined by a very pregnant White, the bulge of her child high up above the complexities of the major joint in her back. Renner smiled at her, squatted on his heels, and turned his back to her. His Fyunch(click) sang in low tones, and the White moved closer, then half a dozen white Moties were running a dozen small hands over his vertebrae.

"Right! A little lower," said Renner. "OK, scratch right there. Ahh." When the Whites had moved on, Renner stretched his long legs to catch up with the tour. His Motie trotted alongside.

"I trust I will not learn your irreverence," his Fyunch-(click) said.

"Why not?" Renner asked seriously.

"When you are gone there will be other work for us. No, do not be alarmed. If you are capable of satisfying the Navy, I can have no more trouble keeping the givers of orders happy." There was an almost wistful tone, Renner thought—but he wasn't sure. If Moties had facial expressions, Renner hadn't learned them.

The Museum was a good distance ahead of them. Like other buildings it was square-built, but its face was glass or something like it. "We have many places that fit your word 'museum,'" Horvath's Motie was saying, "in this and other cities. This one was closest and specializes in painting and sculpture."

A juggernaut loomed over them, three meters tall, and another meter beyond that because of the cargo on its head. It—she, Renner noted from the long, shallow bulge of pregnancy high on her abdomen. The eyes were soft animal eyes, without awareness, and she caught up with them and passed, never slowing.

"Carrying a child doesn't seem to slow a Motie down," Renner observed.

Brown-and-white shoulders and heads turned toward him. Renner's Motie said, "No, of course not. Why should it?"

Sally Fowler took up the task. She tried carefully to explain just how useless pregnant human females were. "It's one reason we tend to develop male-oriented societies. And—" She was still lecturing on childbirth problems when they reached the Museum.

The doorway would have caught Renner across the bridge of his nose. The ceilings were higher; they brushed his hair. Dr. Horvath had to bend his head.

And the lighting was a bit too yellow.

And the paintings were placed too low.

Conditions for viewing were not ideal. Aside from that, the colors in the paints themselves were off. Dr. Horvath and his Motie conversed with animation following his revelation that blue plus yellow equals green to a human eye. The Motie eye was designed like a human eye, or an octopus eye, for that matter: a globe, an adaptable lens, receptor nerves along the back. But the receptors were different.

Yet the paintings had impact. In the main hall—which had three-meter ceilings and was lined with larger paintings—the tour stopped before a street scene. Here a Brown-and-white had climbed on a car and was apparently haranguing a swarm of Browns and Brown-and-whites, while behind him the sky burned sunset-red. The expressions were all the same flat smile, but Renner sensed violence and looked closer. Many of the crowd carried tools, always in their left hands, and some were broken. The city itself was on fire.

"It's called 'Return to Your Tasks.' You'll find that the Crazy Eddie theme recurs constantly," said Sally's Motie. She moved on before she could be asked to explain further.

The next painting in line showed a quasi-Motie, tall and thin, small-headed, long-legged. It was running out of a forest, at the viewer. Its breath trailed smoky-white behind it. "The Message Carrier," Hardy's Motie called it.

The next was another outdoor scene: a score of Browns and Whites eating around a blazing campfire. Animal eyes gleamed red around them. The whole landscape was dark red; and overhead Murcheson's Eye gleamed against the Coal Sack.

"You can't tell what they're thinking and feeling from looking at them, can you? We were afraid of that," said Horvath's Motie. "Nonverbal communication. The signals are different with us."

"I suppose so," said Bury. "These paintings would all be salable, but none especially so. They would be only curiosities . . . though quite valuable as such, because of the huge potential market and the limited source. But they do not communicate. Who painted them?"

"This one is quite old. You can see that it was painted on the wall of the building itself, and—"

"But what kind of Motie? Brown-and-whites?"

There was impolite laughter among the Moties. Bury's Motie said, "You will never see a work of art that was not made by a Brown-and-white. Communication is our specialty. Art is communication."

"Does a White never have anything to say?"

"Of course. He has a Mediator say it for him. We translate, we communicate. Many of these paintings are arguments, visually expressed."

Weiss had been trailing along, saying nothing. Renner noticed. Keeping his voice down, he asked the man, "Any comments?"

Weiss scratched his jaw. "Sir, I haven't been in a museum since grade school . . . but aren't some paintings made just to be pretty?"

"Um."

There were only two portraits in all the halls of paintings. Brown-and-whites both, they both showed from the waist up. Expression in the Moties must show in body language, not faces. These portraits were oddly lighted and their arms were oddly distorted. Renner thought them evil.

"Evil? No!" said Renner's Motie. "That one caused the Crazy Eddie probe to be built. And this was the designer of a universal language, long ago."

"Is it still used?"

"After a fashion. But it fragmented, of course. Languages do that. Sinclair and Potter and Bury don't speak the same language you do. Sometimes the sounds are similar, but the nonverbal signals are very different."

Renner caught up with Weiss as they were about to enter the hall of sculpture. "You were right. In the Empire there are paintings that are just supposed to be pretty. Here, no. Did you notice the difference? No landscape without Moties *doing* something in it. Almost no portraits, and those two were slanted pictures. In fact, *everything's* slanted." He turned to appeal to his Motie. "Right? Those pictures you pointed out, done before your civilization invented the camera. *They* weren't straight representations."

"Renner, do you know how much work goes into a painting?"

"I've never tried. I can guess."

"Then can you imagine anyone going to that much trouble if he doesn't have something to say?"

"How about 'Mountains are pretty'?" Weiss suggested.

Renner's Motie shrugged.

The statues were better than the paintings. Differences in pigment and lighting did not intrude. Most did show Moties; but they were more than portraits. A chain of Moties of diminishing size, Porter to three Whites to nine Browns to twenty-seven miniatures? No, they were all done in white marble and had the shape of decision makers. Bury regarded them without expression and said, "It occurs to me that I will need interpretations of any of these before I could sell them anywhere. Or even give them as gifts."

"Inevitably so," said Bury's Motie. "This, for instance, illustrates a religion of the last century. The soul of the parent divides to become the children, and again to become the grandchildren, ad infinitum."

Another showed a number of Moties in red sandstone. They had long, slender fingers, too many on the left hand, and the left arm was comparatively small. Physicians? They were being killed by a thread of green glass that swept among them like a scythe: a laser weapon, held by something offstage. The Moties were reluctant to talk about it. "And unpleasant event in history," said Bury's Motie, and that was that.

Another showed fighting among a few marble Whites and a score of an unrecognizable type done in red sandstone. The red ones were lean and menacing, armed with more than their share of teeth and claws. Some weird machine occupied the center of the melee. "Now that one is interesting," said Renner's Motie. "By tradition, a Mediator—one of our own type—may requisition any kind of transportation he needs, from any decision maker. Long ago, a Mediator used his authority to order a time machine built. I can show you the machine, if you will travel to it; it is on the other side of this continent."

"A working time machine?"

"Not working, Jonathon. It was never completed. His Master went broke trying to finish it."

"Oh." Whitbread showed his disappointment.

"It was never tested," said the Motie. "The basic theory may be flawed."

The machine looked like a small cyclotron with a cabin inside . . . it almost made sense, like a Langston Field generator.

"You interest me strangely," Renner said to his Motie. "You can requisition any transportation, any time?"

"That's right. Our talent is communication, but our major task is stopping fights. Sally has lectured us on your, let's say, your racial problems involving weapons and the surrender reflex. We Mediators evolved out of that. We can explain one being's viewpoint to another. Noncommunication can assume dangerous proportions sometimes —usually just before a war, by one of those statistical flukes that make you believe in coincidence. If one of us

can always get to transportation—or even to telephones
or radios—war becomes unlikely."

There were awed expressions among the humans. "Ve-
e-erry nice," said Renner. Then, "I was wondering
whether you could requisition *MacArthur*."

"By law and tradition, yes. In practice, don't be a
fool."

"OK. These things fighting around the time machine—"

"Legendary demons," Bury's Motie explained. "They
defend the structure of reality."

Renner remembered ancient Spanish paintings dating
from the time of the Black Plague in Europe, paintings of
living men and women being attacked by the revived and
malevolent dead. Next to the white Moties these red sandstone things had that impossibly lean, bony look, and a
malevolence that was almost tangible.

"And why the time machine?"

"The Mediator felt that a certain incident in history
had happened because of a lack of communication. He
decided to correct it." Renner's Motie shrugged—with her
arms; a Motie couldn't lift her shoulders. "Crazy Eddie.
The Crazy Eddie probe was like that. A little more work-
able, maybe. A watcher of the sky—a meteorologist, plus
some other fields—found evidence that there was life on
a world of a nearby star. Right away this Crazy Eddie
Mediator wanted to contact them. He tied up enormous
amounts of capital and industrial power, enough to affect
most of civilization. He got his probe built, powered by a
light sail and a battery of laser cannon for—"

"This all sounds familiar."

"Right. The Crazy Eddie probe was in fact launched
toward New Caledonia, much later, and with a different
pilot. We've been assuming you followed it home."

"So it worked. Unfortunately the crew was dead, but it
reached us. So why are you still calling it the Crazy Eddie
probe? Oh, never mind," said Renner. His Motie was
chortling.

Two limousines were waiting for them outside the
Museum and a stairs had been erected leading down to

street level. Tiny two-seater cars zipped around the obstruction without slowing down, and without collisions.

Staley stopped at the bottom. "Mr. Renner! Look!"

Renner looked. A car had stopped alongside a great blank building; for there were no curbs. The brown chauffeur and his white-furred passenger disembarked, and the White walked briskly around the corner. The Brown disengaged two hidden levers at the front, then heaved against the side of the car. It collapsed like an accordian, into something half a meter wide. The Brown turned and followed the white Motie.

"They fold up!" Staley exclaimed.

"Sure they do," said Renner's Motie. "Can you imagine the traffic jam if they didn't? Come on, get in the cars."

They did. Renner said, "I wouldn't ride in one of those little death traps for Bury's own petty-cash fund."

"Oh, they're safe. That is," said Renner's Motie, "it isn't the *car* that's safe, it's the *driver*. Browns don't have much territorial instinct, for one thing. For another, they're always fiddling with the car, so nothing's ever going to fail."

The limousine started off. Browns appeared behind them and began removing the stairs.

The buildings around them were always square blocks, the streets a rectangular grid. To Horvath the city was clearly a made city, not something that had grown naturally. Someone had laid it out and ordered it built from scratch. Were they all like this? It showed none of the Browns' compulsion to innovate.

And yet, he decided, it did. Not in basics, but in such things as street lighting. In places there were broad electroluminescent strips-along the buildings. In others there were things like floating balloons, but the wind did not move them. Elsewhere, tubes ran along the sides of the streets, or down the center; or there was nothing at all that showed in the daytime.

And those boxlike cars—each was subtly different, in the design of the lights or the signs of repairs or the way the parked cars folded into themselves.

The limousines stopped. "We're here," Horvath's Motie

announced. "The zoo. The Life Forms Preserve, to be more exact. You'll find that it is arranged more for the convenience of the inhabitants than for the spectators."

Horvath and the rest looked about, puzzled. Tall rectangular buildings surrounded them. There was no open space anywhere.

"On our left. The building, gentlemen, the building! Is there some law against putting a zoo inside a building?"

The zoo, as it developed, was six stories tall, with ceilings uncommonly high for Moties. It was difficult to tell just how high the ceilings were. They looked like sky. On the first floor it was open blue sky, with drifting clouds and a sun that stood just past noon.

They strolled through a steamy jungle whose character changed as they moved. The animals could not reach them, but it was difficult to see why not. They did not seem aware of being penned up.

There was a tree like a huge bullwhip, its handle planted deep in the earth, its lash sprouting clusters of round leaves where it coiled around the trunk. An animal like a giant Motie stood flat-footed beneath it, staring at Whitbread. There were sharp, raking talons on its two right hands, and tusks showed between its lips. "It was a variant of the Porter type," said Horvath's Motie, "but never successfully domesticated. You can see why."

"These artificial environments are astounding!" Horvath exclaimed. "I've never seen better. But why not build part of the zoo in the open? Why make an environment when the real environment is already there?"

"I'm not sure why it was done. But it seems to work out."

The second floor was a desert of dry sand. The air was dry and balmy, the sky baby blue, darkening to yellow-brown at the horizon. Fleshy plants with no thorns grew through the sand. Some were the shape of thick lily pads. Many bore the marks of nibbling teeth. They found the beast that had made the tooth marks, a thing like a nude white beaver with square protruding teeth. It watched them tamely as they passed.

On the third floor it was raining steadily. Lightning

flashed, illusory miles away. The humans declined to enter, for they had no rain gear. The Moties were half angry, half apologetic. It had not occurred to them that rain would bother humans; they liked it.

"It's going to keep happening, too," Whitbread's Motie predicted. "We study you, but we don't know you. You're missing some of the most interesting plant forms too. Perhaps another day when they have the rain turned off . . ."

The fourth floor was not wild at all. There were even small round houses on distant illusory hills. Small, umbrella-shaped trees grew red and lavender fruits beneath a flat green disc of foliage. A pair of proto-Moties stood beneath one of these. They were small, round, and pudgy, and their right arms seemed to have shrunk. They looked at the tour group with sad eyes, then one reached up for a lavender fruit. Its left arm was just long enough.

"Another unworkable member of our species," said Horvath's Motie. "Extinct now except in life forms preserves." He seemed to want to hurry them on. They found another pair in a patch of melons—the same breed of melon the humans had eaten for dinner, as Hardy pointed out.

In a wide, grassy field a family of things with hooves and shaggy coats grazed placidly—except for one that stood guard, turning constantly to face the visitors.

A voice behind Whitbread said, "You're disappointed. Why?"

Whitbread looked back in surprise. "Disappointed? No! It's fascinating."

"My mistake," said Whitbread's Motie. "I think I'd like a word with Mr. Renner. Care to trail along?"

The party was somewhat spread out. Here there was no chance of getting lost, and they all enjoyed the feel of grass beneath their feet: long, coiled green blades, springier than an ordinary lawn, much like the living carpets in houses of the aristocracy and the wealthier traders.

Renner looked amiably about when he felt eyes on him. "Yes?"

"Mr. Renner, it strikes me that you're a bit disappointed in our zoo."

Whitbread winced. Renner frowned. "Yah, and I've been trying to figure it out. I shouldn't feel this way. It's a whole alien world, all compacted for our benefit. Whitbread, you feel it too?"

Whitbread nodded reluctantly.

"Hah! That's it. It's an alien world, all compacted for our benefit, right? How many zoos have you seen on how many worlds?"

Whitbread counted in his head. "Six, including Earth."

"And they were all like this one, except that the illusion is better. We were expecting something a whole order of magnitude different. It isn't. It's just another alien world, except for the intelligent Moties."

"Makes sense," said Whitbread's Motie. Perhaps her voice was a little wistful, and the humans remembered that the Moties had never seen an alien world. "Too bad, though," the Motie said. "Staley's having a ball. So are Sally and Dr. Hardy, but they're professionals."

But the next floor was a shock.

Dr. Horvath was first out of the elevator. He stopped dead. He was in a city street. "I think we have the wrong . . . door . . ." he trailed off. For a moment he felt that his mind was going.

The city was deserted. There were a few cars in the streets, but they were wrecks, and some showed signs of fire. Several buildings had collapsed, filling the street with mountains of rubble. A moving mass of black chittered at him and moved away in a swarm, away and into dark holes in a slope of broken masonry, until there were none left.

Horvath's skin crawled. When an alien hand touched his elbow he jumped and gasped.

"What's the matter, Doctor? Surely you have animals evolved for cities."

"No," said Horvath.

"Rats," said Sally Fowler. "And there's a breed of lice that lives only on human beings. But I think that's all."

"We have a good many," said Horvath's Motie. "Perhaps we can show you a few . . . though they're shy."

At a distance the small black beasts were indistinguishable from rats. Hardy snapped a picture of a swarm that was scrambling for cover. He hoped to develop a blowup later. There was a large, flattish beast, almost invisible until they were right in front of it. It was the color and pattern of the brick it was clinging to.

"Like a chameleon," Sally said. Then she had to explain chameleons.

"There's another," Sally's Motie said. She pointed out a concrete-colored animal clinging to a gray wall. "Don't try to disturb it. It has teeth."

"Where do they get their food?"

"Roof gardens. Though they can eat meat. And there's an insectivore . . ." She led them to a "rooftop" two meters above street level. There were grain and fruit trees gone riot, and a small, armless biped that fired a coiled tongue over a meter long. It looked as if it had a mouthful of walnuts.

Bitter cold met them on the sixth floor. The sky was leaden gray. Snow blew in flurries across an infinity of icy tundra. Hardy wanted to stay, for there was considerable life in that cold hell; bushes and tiny trees growing through the ice, a large, placid thing that ignored them, a furry, hopping snowshoe rabbit with dish-shaped ears and no front legs. They almost had to use force to get Hardy out; but he would have frozen in there.

Dinner was waiting for them at the Castle: ship's stores, and slices of a flat green Motie cactus 75 cm across and 3 thick. The red jelly inside tasted almost meaty. Renner liked it, but the others couldn't eat it at all. The rest they ate like starved men, talking animatedly between mouthfuls. It must have been the extra-long day that made them so hungry.

Renner's Motie said, "We have some idea what a tourist wants to see in a strange city, at least we know what you show in your travel films. Museums. The place of government. Monuments. Unique architecture. Perhaps the shops and night clubs. Above all, the way of life of the native." She gestured deprecatingly. "We've had to omit some of this. We don't have any night clubs. Too little alcohol doesn't do anything to us. Too much kills. You'll get a chance to hear our music, but frankly, you won't like it.

"Government is Mediators meeting to talk. It might be anywhere. The decision makers live where they like, and they generally consider themselves bound by the agreements of their Mediators. You'll see some of our monuments. As for our way of life, you've been studying that for some time."

"What about the way of life of a White?" Hardy asked. Then his mouth opened in a bone-cracking yawn.

"He's right," Hardy's Motie broke in. "We should be able to see a giver of orders' family residence at work. It may be that we can get permission—" The alien broke into a high gabble.

The Moties considered. Sally's Motie said, "It should be possible. We'll see. In the meantime, let's call it a day."

For the time change had caught the humans. Doctors Horvath and Hardy yawned, blinked, looked surprised, made their excuses, and departed. Bury was still going strong. Renner wondered what rotation his planet had. He himself had had enough spacegoing training to adapt to any schedule.

But the party was breaking up. Sally said her good nights and went upstairs, swaying noticeably. Renner suggested folk singing, got no response, and quit.

A spiral stair ran up the tower. Renner turned off into a corridor, following his curiosity. When he reached an air lock he realized that it must lead to the balcony, the flat ring that circled the tower. He did not care to try the Mote Prime air. He wondered if the balcony was meant to be used at all . . . and then thought of a ring encircling a slender tower, and wondered if the Moties were playing games with Freudian symbolism.

Probably they were. He continued to his room.

Renner thought at first he was in the wrong room. The color scheme was striking: orange and black, quite different from the muted pale browns of this morning. But the pressure suit on the wall was his, his design and rank markings on the chest. He looked about him, trying to decide whether he liked the change.

It was the only change—no, the room was warmer. It had been too cold last night. On a hunch, he crossed the room and checked the Moties' sleeping alcove. Yes, it was chilly in there.

Renner's Motie leaned against the doorjamb, watching him with the usual slight smile. Renner grinned shamefacedly. Then he continued his inspection.

The bathroom—the toilet was different. Just as he had sketched it. Wrong; there wasn't any water in it. And no flush.

What the hell, there was only one way to test a toilet.

When he looked, the bowl was sparkling clean. He poured a glass of water into it and watched it run away without leaving a drop. The bowl was a frictionless surface.

Have to mention this to Bury, he thought. There were bases on airless moons, and worlds where water, or energy for recycling it, was scarce. Tomorrow. He was too sleepy now.

The rotation period of Levant was 28 hours, 40.2 minutes. Bury had adjusted well enough to *MacArthur*'s standard day, but it is always easier to adjust to a longer day than to a shorter.

He waited while his Fyunch(click) sent their Brown for coffee. It made him miss Nabil . . . and wonder if the Brown had more of Nabil's skills. He had already seriously underestimated the power of the Brown-and-whites. Apparently his Motie could commandeer any vehicle on Mote Prime, whether or not it had been built yet; even so, he was an agent for someone Bury had never seen. The situation was complex.

The Brown returned with coffee and another pot, something that poured pale brown and did not steam. "Poisonous? Very likely," his Fyunch(click) said. "The pollutants might harm you, or the bacteria. It's water, from outside."

It was not Bury's habit to come too quickly to business.

An overeager businessman, he felt, was easily gulled. He was not aware of the thousands of years of tradition behind his opinion. Accordingly he and his Motie liaison talked of many things . . . " 'Of shoes and ships and sealing wax, of cabbages and kings,' " he quoted, and he identified all of these, to his Motie's evident interest. The Motie was particularly interested in the various forms of human government.

"But I don't think I should read this Lewis Carroll," he said, "until I know considerably more of human culture."

Eventually Bury raised the subject of luxuries again.

"Luxuries. Yes, I agree, in principle," said Bury's Motie. "If a luxury travels well, it can pay for itself merely in diminished fuel costs. That must be true even with your Crazy Eddie Drive. But in practice there are restrictions between us."

Bury had already thought of a few. He said, "Tell me of them."

"Coffee. Teas. Wines. I presume you deal in wines also?"

"Wine is forbidden to my religion." Bury dealt indirectly in the transfer of wines from world to world, but he could not believe the Moties would want to deal in wines.

"It doesn't matter. We could not tolerate alcohol, and we do not like the taste of coffee. The same would probably apply to your other luxury foods, though they may be worth a try."

"And you do not yourselves deal in luxuries?"

"No. In power over others, in safety, in durability of customs and dynasties . . . as usual, I speak for the givers of orders. We deal in these, for their benefit, but we also deal in diplomacy. We trade durable goods and necessities, skills— What do you think of our works of art?"

"They would sell at good prices, until they became common. But I think our trade will be more in ideas, and designs."

"Ah?"

"The frictionless toilet, and the principle behind it. Various superconductors, which you fabricate more efficiently than we. We found a sample in an asteroid. Can you duplicate it?"

"I'm sure the Browns will find a way." The Motie waved a languid hand. "There will be no problem here. You certainly have much to offer. Land for instance. We will want to buy land for our embassies."

Probably that would be offered gratis, Bury thought. But to this race land would be literally priceless; without the humans they could never have more than they had at the moment. And they would want land for settlements. This world was crowded. Bury had seen the city lights from orbit, a field of light around dark oceans. "Land," he agreed, "and grain. There are grains that grow beneath suns like yours. We know that you can eat some of them. Might they grow here more efficiently than yours? Bulk food would never be shipped at a profit, but seeds may be."

"You may also have ideas to sell us."

"I wonder. Your inventiveness is enormous and admirable."

The Motie waved a hand. "I thank you. But we have not made everything there is to make. We have our own Crazy Eddie Drive, for example, but the force field generator that protects—"

"If I should be shot, you would lose the only merchant in this system."

"Allah's— I mean to say, are your authorities really so determined to guard their secrets?"

"Perhaps they will change their minds when they know you better. Besides, I'm not a physicist," Bury said blandly.

"Ah. Bury, we have not exhausted the subject of art. Our artists have a free hand and ready access to materials, and very little supervision. In principle the exchange of art between Mote and Empire would facilitate communication. We have never yet tried to aim our art at an alien mind."

"Dr. Hardy's books and education tapes contain many such works of art."

"We must study them." Bury's Motie sipped contemplatively at his dirty water. "We spoke of coffees and wines. My associates have noticed—how shall I put it?—a strong cultural set toward wines, among your scientists and Navy officers."

"Yes. Place of origin, dates, labels, ability to travel in free fall, what wines go with what foods." Bury grimaced. "I have listened, but I know nothing of this. I find it annoying and expensive that some of my ships must move under constant acceleration merely to protect a wine bottle from its own sediments. Why can they not simply be centrifuged on arrival?"

"And coffees? They all drink coffee. Coffee varies according to its genetics, soil, climate, method of roasting. I know this is so. I have seen your stores."

"I have much greater variety aboard *MacArthur*. Yes . . . and there is variety among coffee drinkers. Cultural differences. On an American-descended world like Tabletop they would not touch the oily brew preferred in New Paris, and they find the brew of Levant much too sweet and strong."

"Ah."

"Have you heard of Jamaica Blue Mountain? It grows on Earth itself, on a large island; the island was never bombed, and the mutations were weeded out in the centuries following the collapse of the CoDominium. It cannot be bought. Navy ships carry it to the Imperial Palace on Sparta."

"How does it taste?"

"As I told you, it is reserved for the Royal—" Bury hesitated. "Very well. You know me that well. I would not pay such a price again, but I do not regret it."

"The Navy misjudges your worth because you lack knowledge of wines." Bury's Motie did not seem to be smiling. Its bland expression was a Trader's: it matched Bury's own. "Quite foolish of them, of course. If they knew how much there was to learn about coffee—"

"What are you suggesting?"

"You have stores aboard. Teach them about coffee. Use your own stores for the purpose."

"My stores would not last a week among the officers of a battle cruiser!"

"You would show them a similarity between your culture and theirs. Or do you dislike that idea? No, Bury, I am not reading your mind. You dislike the Navy; you tend to exaggerate the differences between them and you. Perhaps they think the same way?"

"I am not reading your mind." Bury suppressed the fury building in him—and at that moment he saw it. He knew why the alien kept repeating that phrase. It was to keep him off balance. In a trading situation.

Bury smiled broadly. "A week's worth of good will. Well, I will try your suggestion when we are back in orbit and I dine aboard *MacArthur*. Allah knows they have much to learn about coffee. Perhaps I can even teach them how to use their percolators correctly."

28 • *Kaffee Klatsch*

Rod and Sally sat alone in the Captain's patrol cabin. The intercom screens were off, and the status board above Rod's desk showed a neat pattern of green lights. Rod stretched his long legs out and sipped at his drink. "You know, this is about the first time we've had alone together since we left New Caledonia. It's nice."

She smiled uncertainly. "But we don't have very long —the Moties are expecting us to come back, and I've got dictating to do . . . How much longer can we stay in the Mote system, Rod?"

Blaine shrugged. "Up to the Admiral. Viceroy Merrill wanted us back as soon as possible, but Dr. Horvath wants to learn more. So do I. Sally, we *still* don't have anything significant to report! We don't *know* whether the Moties are a threat to the Empire or not."

"Rod Blaine, will you stop acting like a Regular Navy officer and be yourself? There is not one shred of evidence that the Moties are hostile. We haven't seen any signs of weapons, or wars, or anything like that—"

"I know," Rod said sourly. "And that worries me. Sally, have you ever heard of a human civilization that didn't have soldiers?"

"No, but Moties aren't human."

"Neither are ants, but they've got soldiers— Maybe you're right, I'm catching it from Kutuzov. Speaking of which, he wants more frequent reports. You know that every scrap of data gets transmitted raw to *Lenin* inside an hour? We've even sent over samples of Motie artifacts, and some of the modified stuff the Brownies worked on . . ."

Sally laughed. Rod looked pained for a moment, then joined her. "I'm sorry, Rod. I know it must have been painful to have to tell the Tsar that you had Brownies on your ship—but it *was* funny!"

"Yeah. Funny. Anyway, we send everything we can to *Lenin*—and you think *I'm* paranoid? Kutuzov has everything inspected in space, then sealed into containers filled with ciphogene and parked *outside* his ship! I think he's afraid of contamination." The intercom buzzed. "Oh, damn." Rod turned to the screen. "Captain here."

"Chaplain Hardy to see you, Captain," the Marine sentry announced. "With Mr. Renner and the scientists."

Rod sighed and gave Sally a helpless look. "Send them in and send in my steward. I imagine they'll all want a drink."

They did. Eventually everyone was seated, and his cabin was crowded. Rod greeted the Mote expedition personnel, then took a sheaf of papers from his desk. "First question: Do you need Navy ratings with you? I understand they've nothing to do."

"Well, there's no harm in their being there," Dr. Horvath said. "But they do take up room the scientific staff could use."

"In other words, no," Rod said. "Fine. I'll let you decide which of your people to replace them with, Dr. Horvath. Next point: Do you need Marines?"

"Good heavens, no," Sally protested. She looked quickly to Horvath, who nodded. "Captain, the Moties are so far from being hostile, they've built the Castle for us. It's magnificent! Why can't you come down and *see* it?"

Rod laughed bitterly. "Admiral's orders. For that matter, I can't let any officer who knows how to construct a Langston Field go down." He nodded to himself. "The Admiral and I agree on one point: If you do need help, two Marines won't be any use—and giving the Moties a chance to work that Fyunch(click) thing on a pair of warriors doesn't seem like a good idea. That brings up the next point. Dr. Horvath, is Mr. Renner satisfactory to you? Perhaps I should ask him to leave the room while you reply."

"Nonsense. Mr. Renner has been very helpful. Captain, does your restriction apply to my people? Am I forbidden to take, say, a physicist to Mote Prime?"

"Yes."

"But Dr. Buckman is counting on going. The Moties have been studying Murcheson's Eye and the Coal Sack for a long time . . . how long, Mr. Potter?"

The midshipman squirmed uncomfortably before answering. "Thousands of years, sir," he said finally. "Only . . ."

"Only what, Mister?" Rod prompted. Potter was a bit shy, and he'd have to outgrow that. "Speak up."

"Yes, sir. There are gaps in their observations, Captain. The Moties hae never mentioned the fact, but Dr. Buckman says it is obvious. I would hae said they sometimes lose interest in astronomy, but Dr. Buckman can nae understand that."

"He wouldn't," Rod laughed. "Just how important are those observations, Mr. Potter?"

"For astrophysics, perhaps verra important, Captain. They hae been watching yon supergiant for aye their history as it passed across the Coal Sack. 'Twill go supernova and then become a black hole—and the Moties say they know when."

Midshipman Whitbread laughed. Everyone turned to stare at him. Whitbread could hardly control his features. "Sorry, sir—but I was there when Gavin told Buckman

about that. The Eye will explode in A.D. 2,774,020 on
April 27 between four and four-thirty in the morning,
they say. I thought Dr. Buckman was going to strangle
himself. Then he started doing his own checking. It took
him thirty hours—"

Sally grinned. "And he almost killed the Fyunch(click)
doing it," she added. "Had Dr. Horvath's Motie translat-
ing for him when his own came apart."

"Yes, but he found out they were right," Whitbread
told them. The midshipman cleared his throat and mim-
icked Buckman's dry voice. "Damned close, Mr. Potter.
I've got the mathematics and observations to prove it."

"You're developing a talent for acting, Mr. Whitbread,"
First Lieutenant Cargill said. "Pity your work in astrogation doesn't show a similar improvement. Captain, it seems
to me that Dr. Buckman can get everything he needs here.
There's no reason for him to go to the Motie planet."

"Agreed. Dr. Horvath, the answer is no. Besides—do
you *really* want to spend a week cooped up with Buckman? You needn't answer that," he added quickly. "Whom
will you take?"

Horvath frowned for a moment. "De Vandalia, I suppose."

"Yes, please," Sally said quickly. "We *need* a geologist.
I've tried digging for rock samples, and I didn't learn a
thing about the make-up of Mote Prime. There's nothing
but ruins made up of older ruins."

"You mean they don't have rocks?" Cargill asked.

"They have rocks, Commander," she answered. "Gran-
ite and lava and basalts, but they aren't where whatever
formed this planet put them. They've all been *used*, for
walls, or tiles, or roofs. I did find cores in a museum, but
I can't make much sense out of them."

"Now wait a minute," said Rod. "You mean you go out
and dig at random, and wherever you dig you find what's
left of a city? Even out in the farm lands?"

"Well, there wasn't time for many digs. But where I
did dig, there was always something else underneath. I
never knew when to stop! Captain, there was a city like
A.D. 2000 New York under a cluster of adobe huts with-

out plumbing. I think they had a civilization that collapsed, perhaps two thousand years ago."

"That would explain the observation lapses," Rod said. "But—they seem brighter than that. Why would they let a civilization collapse?" He looked to Horvath, who shrugged.

"I have an idea," Sally said. "The contaminants in the air—wasn't there a problem with pollution from internal combustion engines on Earth sometime during the CoDominium? Suppose the Moties had a civilization based on fossil fuels and ran out? Mightn't they have dropped back into an Iron Age before they developed fusion power and plasma physics again? They seem to be awfully short on radioactive ores."

Rod shrugged. "A geologist could help a lot, then—and he has far more need to be on the spot than Dr. Buckman does. I take it that's settled, Dr. Horvath?"

The Science Minister nodded sourly. "But I still don't like this Navy interference with our work. You tell him, Dr. Hardy. This must stop."

The Chaplain linguist looked surprised. He had sat at the back of the room, saying nothing but listening attentively. "Well, I have to agree that a geologist will be more useful on the surface than an astrophysicist, Anthony. And—Captain, I find myself in a unique position. As a scientist I cannot approve of all these restrictions placed on our contact with the Moties. As representative of the Church I have an impossible task. And as a Navy officer —I think I have to agree with the Admiral."

Everyone turned toward the portly Chaplain in surprise. "I am astonished, Dr. Hardy," Horvath said. "Have you seen the smallest evidence of warlike activities on Mote Prime?"

Hardy folded his hands carefully and spoke across the tops of his fingertips. "No. And that, Anthony, is what concerns me. We know the Moties *do* have wars: the Mediator class was evolved, possibly consciously evolved, to stop them. I do not think they always succeed. So why are the Moties hiding their armaments from us? For the same reason we conceal ours, is the obvious answer, but consider: we do not conceal the fact that we *have* weapons, or even what their general nature is. Why do they?"

"Probably ashamed of them," Sally answered. She winced at the look on Rod's face. "I didn't really mean it *that* way—but they *have* been civilized longer than we have, and they might be embarrassed by their violent past."

"Possibly," Hardy admitted. He sniffed his brandy speculatively. "And possibly not, Sally. I have the impression the Moties are hiding something important—and hiding it right under our noses, so to speak."

There was a long silence. Horvath sniffed loudly. Finally the Science Minister said, "And how could they do that, Dr. Hardy? Their government consists of informal negotiations by representatives of the givers of orders class. Every city seems to be nearly autonomous. Mote Prime hardly has a planetary government, and you think they're able to conspire against us? It is not very reasonable."

Hardy shrugged again. "From what we have seen, Dr. Horvath, you are certainly correct. And yet I cannot rid myself of the impression that they are hiding something."

"They showed us everything," Horvath insisted. "Even givers of orders' households, where they don't normally have visitors."

"Sally was just getting to that before you came in," Rod said quickly. "I'm fascinated—how does the Motie officer class live? Like the Imperial aristocracy?"

"That's a better guess than you might think," Horvath boomed. Two dry martinis had mellowed him considerably. "There were many similarities—although the Moties have an entirely different conception of luxuries from ours. Some things in common, though. Land. Servants. That sort of thing." Horvath took another drink and warmed to his subject.

"Actually, we visited two households. One lived in a skyscraper near the Castle. Seemed to control the entire building: shops, light industry, hundreds of Browns and Reds and Workers and—oh, dozens of other castes. The other one, though, the agriculturist, was very like a country baron. The work force lived in long rows of houses, and in between the row houses were fields. The 'baron' lived in the center of all that."

Rod thought of his own family home. "Crucis Court used to be surrounded by villages and fields—but of course all the villages were fortified after the Secession Wars. So was the Court, for that matter."

"Odd you should say that," Horvath mused. "There was a sort of square fortified shape to the 'barony' too. Big atrium in the middle. For that matter, all the residential skyscrapers have no windows on the lower floors, and big roof gardens. Quite self-sufficient. Looked very military. We don't have to report that impression to the Admiral, do we? He'd be sure we'd discovered militaristic tendencies."

"Are you so sure he'd be wrong?" Jack Cargill asked. "From what I've heard, every one of those givers of orders has a self-sufficient fortress. Roof gardens. Brownies to fix all the machinery—too bad we can't tame some of them to help Sinclair." Cargill noted his captain's black look and hurriedly added, "Anyway, the agriculturist might have a better chance in a fight, but both those places sound like forts. So do all the other residential palaces I've heard about."

Dr. Horvath had been struggling to control himself, while Sally Fowler attempted without success to hide her amusement. Finally she laughed. "Commander Cargill, the Moties have had space travel and fusion power for *centuries*. If their buildings still have a fortress look, it must be traditional—there's no possible purpose! You're the military expert, just how would building your house that way help you against modern weapons?"

Cargill was silenced, but his expression showed he wasn't convinced.

"You say they try to make their houses self-sufficient?" Rod asked. "Even in the city? But that *is* silly. They'd still have to bring in water."

"It rained a lot," said Renner. "Three days out of six."

Rod looked at the Sailing Master. Was he serious?

"Did you know there are left-handed Moties?" Renner

continued. "Everything reversed. Two six-fingered left hands, one massive right arm, and the swelling of the skull is on the right."

"It took me half an hour to notice," Whitbread laughed. "The new Motie behaved just like Jackson's old one. He must have been briefed."

"Left-handed," said Rod. "Why not?" At least they'd changed the subject. The stewards brought in lunch and everyone fell to. When they finished it was time to leave for the Mote.

"A word with you, Mr. Renner," Rod said as the Sailing Master was about to go. He waited until everyone but Cargill was gone. "I need an officer down there, and you're the one senior man that I can spare who meets the Admiral's restrictions. But although you've no weapons but your sidearms, and no Marines, that's a military expedition, and if it comes to it, you're in charge."

"Yes, sir," Renner said. He sounded puzzled.

"If you had to shoot a man or a Motie, could you do it?"

"Yes, sir."

"You answered that very quickly, Mr. Renner."

"I thought it over very slowly, some time past, when I knew I was joining the Navy. If I had decided I was incapable of shooting anyone, I'd have had to make damned sure the Captain knew it."

Blaine nodded. "Next question. Can you recognize the need for military action in time to do something? Even if what you do is hopeless?"

"I think so. Captain, can I bring up something else? I do want to go back, and—"

"Speak your piece, Mr. Renner."

"Captain, your Fyunch(click) went mad."

"I'm aware of that," Captain Blaine said coldly.

"I think the Tsar's hypothetical Fyunch(click) would go mad much faster. What you want is the one officer aboard this ship who is least inclined to the military way of thinking."

"Get aboard, Mr. Renner. And good luck."

"Aye aye, sir." Renner made no attempt to hide his lopsided grin as he left the cabin.

"He'll do, Captain," Cargill said.

"I hope so, Number One. Jack, do you think it was our *military* manner that drove my Motie crazy?"

"No, sir." Cargill seemed positive.

"Then what did?"

"Captain, I don't know. I don't know a lot of things about those bug-eyed monsters. There's only one thing I *am* sure of, and that is they're learning more about us than we are about them."

"Oh, come on, Number One. They take our people anywhere they ask to go. Sally says they're bending over backwards—well, for them, that isn't so hard to do—but anyway, she says they're very cooperative. Not hiding a thing. You've always been scared of the Moties, haven't you? Any idea why?"

"No, Captain." Cargill looked closely at Blaine and decided that his boss wasn't accusing him of funk. "I just don't like the feel of this." He glanced at his pocket computer to note the time. "I've got to hurry, Skipper. I'm supposed to help Mr. Bury with that coffee business."

"Bury— Jack, I've been meaning to speak to you about him. His Motie lives on the embassy ship now. Bury's moved to the cutter. What do they talk about?"

"Sir? They're supposed to be negotiating trade deals—"

"Sure, but Bury knows a lot about the Empire. Economy, industry, general size of the Fleet, how many outies we've got to deal with, you name it and he'd probably know it."

Cargill grinned. "He hasn't let his right hand know how many fingers there are on the left, Captain. What's he going to give the Motie for free? Besides, I've sort of made sure he won't say anything you wouldn't approve of."

"Now how did you do that?"

"I told him we'd bugged every inch of the cutter, sir." Cargill's grin broadened. "Sure, he knows we can't listen to every one of those bugs every time, but—"

Rod returned the grin. "I expect that'll work. OK,

you'd better move along to the Kaffee Klatsch—you sure you don't mind helping with this?"

"Hell, Skipper, it was my idea. If Bury can show the cooks how to make better coffee during combat alerts, I might even change my opinion of him. Just why is he being kept a prisoner on this ship, anyway?"

"Prisoner? Commander Cargill—"

"Skipper, everybody in the crew knows there's something funny about that man's being aboard. The grapevine has it he's implicated in the New Chicago revolt and you're hanging onto him for the Admiralty. That's about right, isn't it?"

"Somebody's doing a lot of talking, Jack. Anyway, I can't say anything about it."

"Sure. You've got your orders, Skipper. But I notice you aren't trying to deny it. Well, it figures. Your old man is richer than Bury—I wonder how many Navy people might be for sale? It scares me, having a guy who could buy a whole planet as our prisoner." Cargill moved quickly through the companionway to the main crew kitchen.

The night before, the dinner party conversation had somehow turned to coffee, and Bury had lost his usual bored detachment when he spoke at length on the subject. He had told them of the historic Mocha-Java blend still grown in places like Makassar, and the happy combination of pure Java and the *grua* distilled on Prince Samual's World. He knew the history of Jamaica Blue Mountain although, he'd said, not its taste. As dessert was ending he suggested a "coffee tasting" in the manner of a wine-tasting party.

It had been an excellent ending to an excellent dinner, with Bury and Nabil moving like conjurors among filter cones and boiling water and hand-lettered labels. All the guests were amused, and it made Bury a different man somehow; it had been hard to think of him as a connoisseur of any kind.

"But the basic secret is to keep the equipment truly

clean," he had said. "The bitter oils of yesterday's coffee will accumulate in the works, especially in percolators."

It had ended with Bury's offer to inspect *MacArthur*'s coffee-making facilities the next day. Cargill, who thought coffee as vital to a fighting ship as torpedoes, accepted happily. Now he watched as the bearded Trader examined the large percolator and gingerly drew a cup.

"The machine is certainly well kept," he said. "Very well kept. Absolutely clean, and the brew is not reheated too often. For standard coffee, this is excellent, Commander."

Puzzled, Jack Cargill drew a cup and tasted it. "Why, that's better than the stuff the wardroom gets."

There were sidelong glances among the cooks. Cargill noticed them. He noticed something else, too. He ran a finger along the side of the percolator and brought it away with a brown, oil stain.

Bury repeated the gesture, sniffed at his finger, and touched the tip of his tongue to it. Cargill tasted the oil in his hand. It was like all the bad coffee he had ever swallowed for fear of falling asleep on duty. He looked again at the percolator and stared at the spigot handle.

"Miniatures," Cargill growled. "Take that damned thing apart."

They emptied the machine and disassembled it—as far as it would go. Parts made to unscrew were now a fused unit. But the secret of the magic percolator seemed to be selective permeability in the metal shell. It would pass the older oils.

"My company would like to purchase that secret from the Navy," said Bury.

"We'd like to have it to sell. OK, Ziffren, how long has this been going on?"

"Sir?" The petty officer cook seemed to be thinking. "I don't know, sir. Maybe two months."

"Was it this way *before* we sterilized the ship and killed off the miniatures?" Cargill demanded.

"Uh, yessir," the cook said. But he said it hesitantly, and Cargill left the mess with a frown.

Cargill made his way to Rod's cabin. "I think we've got Brownies again, Skipper." He told why.

"Have you talked to Sinclair?" Rod asked. "Jesus, Number One, the Admiral will go out of his mind. Are you sure?"

"No, sir. But I intend to find out. Skipper, I'm *positive* we looked everywhere when we cleaned out the ship. Where could they have hidden?"

"Worry about that when you know we've got them. OK, take the Chief Engineer and go over this ship again, Jack. And make damned sure this time."

"Aye aye, Skipper."

Blaine turned to the intercom screens and punched inputs. Everything known about miniatures flashed across the screen. There was not very much.

The expedition to Mote Prime had seen thousands of the miniatures throughout Castle City. Renner's Motie called them "Watchmakers," and they functioned as assistants to the brown "Engineers." The big Moties insisted the Watchmakers were not intelligent but inherited an ability to tinker with tools and equipment, as well as the typical Motie instinct of obedience to the higher castes. They required training, but the adult Watchmakers took care of most of that. Like other subservient castes they were a form of wealth, and the ability to support a large household of Watchmakers, Engineers, and other lower forms was one measure of the importance of a Master. This last was a conclusion of Chaplain Hardy, and not definitely confirmed.

An hour passed before Cargill called. "We've got 'em, Skipper," the First Lieutenant said grimly. "The B-deck air adsorber-converter—remember that half-melted thing Sandy repaired?"

"Yes."

"Well, it doesn't stick out into the corridor any more.

Sandy says it can't possibly work, and he's digging into it now—but it's enough for me. We've got 'em."

"Alert the Marines, Number One. I'm going to the bridge."

"Aye aye, sir." Cargill turned back to the air maker. Sinclair had the cover off and was muttering to himself as he examined the exposed machinery.

The guts had changed. The casing had been reshaped. The second filter Sinclair had installed was gone, and the remaining filter had been altered beyond recognition. Goop seeped from one side into a plastic bag that bulged with gas; the goop was highly volatile.

"Aye," Sinclair muttered. "And the other typical signs, Commander Cargill. Screw fastenings fused together. Missing parts and the rest."

"So it's Brownies."

"Aye," Sinclair nodded. "We thought we'd killed the lot months ago—and my records show this was inspected last week. 'Twas normal then."

"But where did they hide?" Cargill demanded. The Chief Engineer was silent. "What now, Sandy?"

Sinclair shrugged. "I'd say we look to hangar deck, sir. 'Tis the place least used aboard this ship."

"Right." Cargill punched the intercom again. "Skipper, we're going to check hangar deck—but I'm afraid there's no question about it. There are live Brownies aboard this ship."

"Do that, Jack. I've got to report to *Lenin*." Rod took a deep breath and gripped the arms of his command chair as if he were about to enter combat. "Get me the Admiral."

Kutuzov's burly features swam on the screen. Rod reported in a rush of words. "I don't know how many, sir," he finished. "My officers are searching for additional signs of the miniatures."

Kutuzov nodded. There was a long silence while the Admiral stared at a point over Blaine's left shoulder. "Captain, have you followed my orders concerning communications?" he asked finally.

"Yes, sir. Constant monitoring of all emissions to and from *MacArthur*. There's been nothing."

"Nothing so far as we know," the Admiral corrected. "We must assume nothing, but it is possible that these creatures have communicated with other Moties. If they have, we no longer have any secrets aboard *MacArthur*. If they have not— Captain, you will order the expedition to return to *MacArthur* immediately, and you will prepare to depart for New Caledonia the instant they are aboard. Is this understood?"

"Aye aye, sir," Blaine snapped.

"You do not agree?"

Rod pondered for a moment. He hadn't thought beyond the screams he'd get from Horvath and the others when they were told. And, surprisingly, he did agree. "Yes, sir. I can't think of a better course of action. But suppose I can exterminate the vermin, sir?"

"Can you *know* you have done that, Captain?" Kutuzov demanded. "Nor can I know it. Once away from this system we can disassemble *MacArthur* piece by piece, with no fear that they will communicate with others. So long as we are here, that is constant threat, and it is risk I am not prepared to take."

"What do I tell the Moties, sir?" Rod asked.

"You will say there is sudden illness aboard your vessel, Captain. And that we are forced to return to Empire. You may tell them your commander has ordered it and you have no other explanation. If later explanations are necessary, Foreign Office will have time to prepare them. For now, this will do."

"Yes, sir." The Admiral's image faded. Rod turned to the watch officer. "Mr. Crawford, this vessel will be leaving for home in a few hours. Alert the department heads, and then get me Renner on Mote Prime."

A muted alarm sounded in the Castle. Kevin Renner looked up sleepily to see his Motie at the intercom screen that formed inside one of the decorative paintings on the wall.

"The Captain wants you," the Motie said.

Renner glanced at his pocket computer. It was almost noon on *MacArthur* but the middle of the night in Castle City. He climbed sleepily to his feet and went to the screen. The expression on Blaine's face brought him to full alert. "Yes, Skipper?"

"There's a small emergency aboard, Mr. Renner. You'll have to ask the Moties to send up all our personnel. Yourself included."

"Dr. Horvath won't want to come, sir," Renner said. His mind raced furiously. There was something very wrong here, and if he could read it, so could the Moties.

Blaine's image nodded. "He'll have to nonetheless, Mister. See to it."

"Yes, sir. What about our Moties?"

"Oh, they can come up to the cutter with you," Blaine said. "It's not all *that* serious. Just an OC matter."

It took a second for that to sink in. By the time it did, Renner was in control of himself. Or hoped he was. "Aye aye, Captain. We're on the way."

He went back to his bunk and sat carefully on the edge. As he put on his boots he tried to think. The Moties couldn't possibly know the Navy's code designations, but OC meant top military priority . . . and Blaine had been far too casual when he had said that.

OK, he thought. The Moties know I'm acting. They have to. There's a military emergency out there somewhere, and I'm to get the hostages off this planet without letting the Moties know it. Which means the Moties *don't* know there's a military emergency, and that doesn't make sense.

"Fyunch(click)," his Motie reminded him. "What is the matter?"

"I don't know," Renner replied. Quite honestly.

"And you do not want to know," the Motie said. "Are you in trouble?"

"Don't know that either," Renner said. "You heard the Captain. Now how do I go about getting everybody moving in the middle of the night?"

"You may leave that to me," said Renner's Motie.

*   *   *

The hangar deck was normally kept in vacuum. The doors were so huge that a certain amount of leakage was inevitable. Later, Cargill would supervise as hangar deck was put under pressure; but for now he and Sinclair carried out their inspection in vacuum.

Everything seemed in order, nothing out of place as they entered. "Now," said Cargill. "What would you fiddle with if you were a miniature Motie?"

"I would put the boats on the hull and use the hangar deck as a fuel tank."

"There are ships like that. Be a big job for a swarm of Brownies, though." Cargill strolled out onto the hangar doors. He wasn't sure what he was looking for, and was never sure why he looked down at his feet. It took him a moment to realize that something was wrong.

The crack that separated the two huge rectangular doors . . .

. . . wasn't there.

Cargill looked about him, bewildered. There was nothing. The doors were part of the hull. The hinge motors, weighing several tons apiece, had vanished.

"Sandy?"

"Aye?"

"Where are the doors?"

"Why, y're standing on them, ye bloody— I don't believe it."

"They've sealed us in. Why? How? How could they work in vacuum?"

Sinclair ran back to the air lock. The air-lock door controls— "The instruments read green," said Sinclair. "Everything's fine, as far as *they* know. If the Brownies can fool instruments, they could have had the hangar deck under pressure until just before we arrived."

"Try the doors." Cargill swung up onto one of the retractable bracings.

"The instruments show the doors opening. Still opening . . . complete." Sinclair turned around. Nothing. A vast expanse of beige-painted floor, as solid as any part of the hull.

He heard Cargill curse. He saw Cargill swing down

from the huge retractable brace and drop onto what had been a hangar door. He saw Cargill drop through the floor as if it had been the surface of a pond.

They had to fish Cargill out of the Langston Field. He was chest deep in formless black quicksand, and sinking, his legs very cold, his heart beating very slowly. The Field absorbed all motion.

"I should have got my head into it," he said when he came round. "That's what all the manuals say. Get my brain to sleep before my heart slows down. But God's teeth! How could I think?"

"What happened?" Sinclair asked.

Cargill's mouth opened, closed, opened again. He managed to sit up. "There aren't words. It was like a miracle. It was like I was walking on water when they took away my sainthood. Sandy, it was really the damnedest thing."

"It looked a mite peculiar too."

"I bet. You see what they did, don't you? The little bastards are redesigning *MacArthur!* The doors are still there, but the ships can go through them now. In an emergency you don't even have to evacuate hangar deck."

"I'll tell the Captain," Sinclair said. He turned to the intercom.

"Where the hell did they hide?" Cargill demanded. The engineering ratings who had pulled him out stared blankly. So did Sinclair. "Where? Where didn't we look?"

His legs still felt cold. He massaged them. On the screen he could see Rod Blaine's pained expression. Cargill struggled to his feet. As he did, alarms hooted through the ship.

"NOW HEAR THIS. INTRUDER ALERT. ALL COMBAT PERSONNEL WILL DON BATTLE ARMOR. MARINES REPORT TO HANGAR DECK WITH HAND WEAPONS AND BATTLE ARMOR."

"The guns!" Cargill shouted.

"I beg your pardon?" Sinclair said. Blaine's image focused on the First Lieutenant.

"The guns, Skipper! We did not look in the guns. Damn, I'm a bloody fool, did anyone think of the guns?"

"It may be," Sinclair agreed. "Captain, I request that you send for the ferrets."

"Too late, Chief," Blaine said. "There's a hole in their cage. I already checked."

"God damn," Cargill said. He said it reverently. "God damn them." He turned to the armed Marines swarming onto hangar deck. "Follow me." He was through treating the miniatures as escaped pets, or as vermin. As of now they were enemy boarders.

They rushed forward to the nearest turret. A startled rating jumped from his post as the First Lieutenant, Chief Engineer, and a squad of Marines in battle armor crammed into his control room.

Cargill stared at the instrument board. Everything seemed normal. He hesitated in real fear before he opened the inspection hatch.

The lenses and focus rings were gone from Number 3 Battery. The space inside was alive with Brownies. Cargill jumped back in horror—and a thread of laser pulse splashed against his battle armor. He cursed and snatched a tank of ciphogene from the nearest Marine and slammed it into the gap. It wasn't necessary to open the stopcock.

The tank grew hot in his hand, and one laser beam winked through and past him. When the hissing died he was surrounded by yellow fog.

The space inside 3 Battery was thick with dead miniatures and filthy with bones. Skeletons of rats, bits of electronic gear, old boots—and dead Brownies.

"They kept a herd of rats in there," Cargill shouted. "Then they must have outgrown the herd and eaten them all. They've been eating each other—"

"And the other batteries?" Sinclair said in wonder. "We'd best be hasty."

There was a scream from the corridor outside. The Navy rating who'd been displaced from his post fell to the deck. A bright red stain appeared at his hip. "In the ventilator," he shouted.

A Marine corporal tore at the grating. Smoke flashed from his battle armor and he jumped back. "Nipped me, by God!" He stared incredulously at a neat hole in his shoulder as three other Marines fired hand lasers at a rapidly vanishing shape. Somewhere else in the ship an alarm sounded.

Cargill grabbed an intercom. "Skipper—"

"I know," Blaine said quickly. "Whatever you did has them stirred up all over the ship. There are a dozen fire fights going on right now."

"My God, sir, what do we do?"

"Send your troops to Number 2 Battery to clean that out," Blaine ordered. "Then get to damage control." He turned to another screen. "Any other instructions, Admiral?"

The bridge was alive with activity. One of the armored helmsmen jumped from his seat and whirled rapidly. "Over there!" he shouted. A Marine sentry pointed his Brownie-altered weapon helplessly.

"You are not in control of your vessel," Kutuzov said flatly.

"No, sir." It was the hardest thing Blaine had ever had to say.

"CASUALTIES IN CORRIDOR TWENTY," the bridge talker announced.

"Scientist country," Rod said. "Get all available Marines into that area and have them assist the civilians into pressure suits. Maybe we can gas the whole ship—"

"Captain Blaine. Our first task is to return to Empire with maximum information."

"Yes, sir—"

"Which means civilians aboard your vessel are more important than a battle cruiser." Kutuzov was calm, but his lips were tight with distaste. "Of second priority are Motie artifacts not yet transferred to Lenin. Captain, you will therefore order all civilians off your vessel. I will have Lenin's boats outside our protective field. You will have two reliable officers accompany civilians. You will then secure any Motie artifacts you think important for shipment to Lenin. You may attempt to regain control of your vessel in so far as that is consistent with these orders—but you will also act swiftly, Captain, because at first sign of any transmission from your vessel other than through secure circuit direct to me, I will blast *MacArthur* out of space."

Blaine nodded coldly. "Aye aye, sir."

"We understand each other, then." The Admiral's expression didn't change at all. "And Godspeed, Captain Blaine."

"What about my cutter?" Rod asked. "Sir, I have to talk to the cutter . . ."

"I will alert the cutter personnel, Captain. No. There will be no transmission from your ship."

"Aye aye, sir." Rod looked around his bridge. Everyone was staring wildly about. The Marines' weapons were drawn, and one of the quartermasters was fussing over a fallen companion.

Jesus, can I trust the intercom? Rod wondered. He shouted orders to a runner and waved three Marines to accompany the man.

"Signal from Mr. Renner, sir," the bridge talker announced.

"Don't acknowledge," Blaine growled.

"Aye aye, sir. Do not acknowledge."

The battle for *MacArthur* raged on.

30 • Nightmare

There were a dozen humans and two Brown-and-whites aboard the cutter. The other ground party Moties had reported directly to the embassy ship, but Whitbread's and Sally's Fyunch(click)s had stayed aboard. "No point," said Whitbread's Motie. "We've been seeing the decision maker every day."

Perhaps there was a point. The cutter was crowded, and the taxi to *MacArthur* had not arrived.

"What's holding them up?" Renner said. "Lafferty, put in a call." Lafferty, the cutter's pilot, was largely unemployed these days. He used the communications beam.

"No answer, sir," he said. He sounded puzzled.

"You're sure the set's working?"

"It was an hour ago," Lafferty said. "Uh—there's a signal. It's from *Lenin,* sir."

Captain Mikhailov's face appeared on the screen. "You will please request aliens to leave this vessel," he said.

Somehow the Moties conveyed amusement, surprise, and a slightly hurt look all at once. They left with a backward look and a signaled query. Whitbread shrugged. Staley didn't. When the Moties were in the air-lock bridge, Staley closed the door behind them.

Kutuzov appeared. "Mr. Renner, you will send all personnel aboard to *Lenin.* They will wear pressure suits, and one of my boats will arrive to get them. Civilians will cross on a line and will then obey orders of my boat's pilot. They must carry sufficient air for one hour in space. Meanwhile, you will make no attempt to communicate with *MacArthur.* Is this understood?"

Renner gulped. "Aye aye, sir."

"You will not admit aliens until further notice."

"But what do I tell them, sir?" Renner asked.

"You will tell them Admiral Kutuzov is a paranoid fool, Mr. Renner. Now carry out your orders."

"Aye aye, sir." The screen went blank. Renner looked pale. "Now *he's* reading minds—"

"Kevin, what's going on here?" Sally demanded. "Get us up in the middle of the night, rush us up here— Now Rod won't answer us, and the Admiral wants us to risk our lives and offend the Moties." She sounded very much like Senator Fowler's niece; an Imperial lady who had tried to cooperate with the Navy and now had had enough.

Dr. Horvath was even more indignant. "I will not be a party to this, Mr. Renner. I have no intention of putting on a pressure suit."

"Lenin's moving alongside *MacArthur,"* Whitbread said casually. He stared out the view port. "The Admiral has her ringed with boats—I think somebody's carrying a line over."

Everyone turned to the view ports. Lafferty focused the cutter's telescope and flashed the results on the ship's bridge screens. After a while figures in space suits began moving along lines toward *Lenin*'s boats, which then moved away to let others take their places.

"They're abandoning *MacArthur*," Staley said wonderingly. He looked up, his angular face contorted. "And one of *Lenin*'s boats is headed this way. My lady, you'll have to hurry. I don't think there's much time."

"But I told you, I am not going," Dr. Horvath insisted.

Staley fingered his pistol. The cabin grew tense.

"Doctor, do you remember the orders Viceroy Merrill gave Admiral Kutuzov?" Renner asked carefully. "As I recall, he was to destroy *MacArthur* rather than let the Moties obtain any important information." Renner's voice was cool, almost bantering.

Horvath tried to say something else. He seemed to be having difficulty controlling his features. Finally he turned to the pressure suit locker without a word. After a moment, Sally followed him.

Horace Bury had gone to his cabin after the coffee demonstration. He liked to work late at night and sleep after lunch, and although there wasn't anything to work on at the moment, he'd kept the habit.

The ship's alarms woke him. Somebody was ordering the Marines into combat uniform. He waited, but nothing else happened for a long time. Then came the stench. It choked him horribly, and there was nothing like it in any of his memories. Distilled quintessence of machines and body odor—and it was growing stronger.

More alarms sounded. "PREPARE FOR HARD VACUUM. ALL PERSONNEL WILL DON PRESSURE SUITS. ALL MILITARY PERSONNEL WILL DON BATTLE ARMOR. PREPARE FOR HARD VACUUM."

Nabil was crying in panic. "Fool! Your suit!" Bury screamed and ran for his own. Only after he was breathing normal ship's air did he listen for the alarms again.

The voices didn't sound right. They weren't coming through the intercom, they were—shouted through the corridors. "CIVILIANS WILL ABANDON SHIP. ALL CIVILIAN PERSONNEL, PREPARE TO ABANDON SHIP."

Really. Bury almost smiled. This was a first time—was

it a drill? There were more sounds of confusion. A squad of Marines in battle armor, weapons clutched at the ready, tramped past. The smile slipped and Bury looked about to guess what possessions he might save.

There was more shouting. An officer appeared in the corridor outside and began shouting in an unnecessarily loud voice. Civilians would be leaving *MacArthur* on a line. They could take one bag each, but would require one hand free.

Beard of the Prophet! What could cause this? Had they saved the golden asteroid metal, the superconductor of heat? Certainly they would not save the precious self-cleaning percolator. What should he try to save?

The ship's gravity lessened noticeably. Flywheels inside her were rotating to take off her spin. Bury worked quickly to throw together items needed by any traveler without regard to their price. Luxuries he could buy again, but—

The miniatures. He'd have to get that air tank from D air lock. Suppose he were assigned to a different air lock?

He packed in frenzy. Two suitcases, one for Nabil to carry. Nabil moved fast enough now that he had orders. There was more confused shouting outside, and several times squads of Navy men and Marines floated past the stateroom door. They all carried weapons and wore armor.

His suit began to inflate. The ship was losing pressure, and all thought of drill or exercise left him. Some of the scientific equipment couldn't stand hard vacuum—and nobody had once come into the cabin to check his pressure suit. The Navy wouldn't risk civilian lives in drills.

An officer moved into the corridor. Bury heard the harsh voice speaking in deadly calm tones. Nabil stood uncertainly and Bury motioned to him to turn on his suit communications.

"ALL CIVILIAN PERSONNEL, GO TO YOUR NEAREST AIR LOCKS ON THE PORT FLANK," the unemotional voice said. The Navy always spoke that way when there was a real crisis. It convinced Bury utterly. "CIVILIAN EVACUATION WILL BE THROUGH PORT-SIDE LOCKS ONLY. IF YOU ARE UNSURE OF YOUR DIRECTION ASK ANY OFFICER OR RATING. PLEASE PROCEED SLOWLY. THERE IS TIME TO EVACUATE

ALL PERSONNEL." The officer floated past and turned into another corridor.

Port side? Good. Intelligently, Nabil had hidden the dummy tank in the *nearest* air lock. Praise to the Glory of Allah that had been on the port side. He motioned to his servant and began to pull himself from hand hold to hand hold along the wall. Nabil moved gracefully; he had had plenty of practice since they had been confined.

There was a confused crowd in the corridor. Behind him Bury saw a squad of Marines turn into the corridor. They faced away and fired in the direction they'd come. There was answering fire and bright blood spurted to form ever-diminishing globules as it drifted through the steel ship. The lights flickered overhead.

A petty officer floated down the corridor and fell in behind them. "Keep moving, keep moving," he muttered. "God bless the joeys."

"What are they shooting at?" Bury asked.

"Miniatures," the petty officer growled. "If they take this corridor, move out fast, Mr. Bury. The little bastards have weapons."

"Brownies?" Bury asked incredulously. "Brownies?"

"Yes, sir, the ship's got a plague o' the little sons of bitches. They changed the air plants to suit themselves . . . Get movin', sir. Please. Them joeys can't hold long."

Bury tugged at a hand hold and sailed to the end of the corridor, where he was deftly caught by an able spacer and passed around the turn. Brownies? But, they'd been cleared out of the ship . . .

There was a crowd bunched at the air lock. More civilians were coming, and now noncombatant Navy people began to add to the press. Bury pushed and clawed his way toward the air-bottle locker. Ah. It was still there. He seized the dummy and handed it to Nabil, who fastened it to Bury's suit.

"That won't be necessary, sir," an officer said. Bury realized he was hearing him through atmosphere. There was pressure here—but they hadn't come through any pressure-tight doors! The Brownies! They'd made the invisible pressure barrier that the miner had on her survey ship! He had to have it! "One never knows," Bury muttered to the officer. The man shrugged and motioned another pair into the cycling mechanism. Then it was Bury's turn. The Marine officer waved them forward.

The lock cycled. Bury touched Nabil on the shoulder and pointed. Nabil went, pulling himself along the line into the blackness outside. Blackness ahead, no stars, nothing. What was out there? Bury found himself holding his breath. Praise be to Allah, I witness that Allah is One— *No!* The dummy bottle was on his shoulders, and inside it two miniatures in suspended animation. Wealth untold! Technology beyond anything even the First Empire ever had! An endless stream of new inventions and design improvements. Only . . . just what kind of djinn bottle had he opened?

They were through the tightly controlled hole in *MacArthur's* Field. Outside was only the blackness of space— and a darker black shape ahead. Other lines led to it from other holes in *MacArthur's* Field, ano minuscule spiders darted along them. Behind Bury was another space-suited figure, and behind that, another. Nabil and the others ahead of him, and . . . His eyes were adjusting rapidly now. He could see the deep red hues of the Coal Sack, and the blot ahead must be *Lenin's* Field. Would he have to crawl through *that?* But no, there were boats outside it, and the space spiders crawled into them.

The boat was drawing near. Bury turned for a last look at *MacArthur.* In his long lifetime he had said good-by to countless temporary homes; *MacArthur* had not been the best of them. He thought of the technology that was being destroyed. The Brownie-improved machinery, the magical coffeepot. There was a twinge of regret. *MacArthur's* crew was genuinely grateful for his help with the coffee, and his demonstration to the officers had been popular. It had gone well. Perhaps in *Lenin* . . .

The air lock was tiny now. A string of refugees followed him along the line. He could not see the cutter, where his Motie would be. Would he ever see him again?

He was looking directly at the space-suited figure behind him. It had no baggage, and it was overtaking Bury because it had both hands free. The light from *Lenin* was shining on its faceplate. As Bury watched, the figure's head shifted slightly and the light shone right into the faceplate.

Bury saw at least three pairs of eyes staring back at him. He glimpsed the tiny faces.

It seemed to Bury, later, that he had never thought so fast in his life. For a heartbeat he stared at the thing coming up on him while his mind raced, and then— But the men who heard his scream said that it was the shriek of a madman, or a man being flayed alive.

Then Bury flung his suitcase at it.

He put words into his next scream. "They're in the suit! They're inside it!" He was wrenching at his back now, ripping the air tank loose. He poised the cylinder over his head, in both hands, and pitched it.

The pressure suit dodged his suitcase, clumsily. A pair of miniatures in the arms, trying to maneuver the fingers . . . it lost its hand hold, tried to pull itself back. The metal cylinder took it straight in the faceplate and shattered it.

Then space was filled with tiny struggling figures, flailing six limbs as a ghostly puff of air carried them away. Something else went with them, something football shaped, something Bury had the knowledge to recognize. That was how they had fooled the officer at the air locks. A severed human head.

Bury discovered he was floating three meters from the line. He took a deep, shuddering breath. Good: he'd thrown the right air tank. Allah was merciful.

He waited until a man-shaped thing came out of *Lenin*'s boat on backpack jets and took him in tow. The touch made him flinch. Perhaps the man wondered why Bury peered so intently into his faceplate. Perhaps not.

MacArthur lurched suddenly. Rod clawed at the intercom and shouted, "Chief Sinclair! What are you doing, Chief?"

The reply was barely audible. " 'Tis nae my doin', Captain. I hae nae control o' the altitude jets, and precious little o' anything else."

"Oh, Lord God," Blaine said. Sinclair's image faded from the screens. Other screens faded. Suddenly the bridge was dead. Rod tried alternate circuits. Nothing.

"Computer inactivated," Crawford reported. "I get nothing at all."

"Try the direct wire. Get me Cargill," Rod told his talker.

"I have him, Captain."

"Jack, what's the situation back there?"

"Bad, Skipper. I'm beseiged in here, and I don't have communications except for direct wires—not all of them." *MacArthur* lurched again as something happened aft. "Captain!" Cargill reported excitedly. "Lieutenant Piper reports the Brownies are fighting each other in the main crew kitchen! Real pitched battle!"

"Jesus, Number One, how many of those monsters do we have aboard?"

"Skipper, I don't know! Hundreds, maybe. They must have hollowed out every gun on the ship, and they've spread to everywhere else too. They're—" Cargill's voice cut off.

"Jack!" Rod shouted. "Talker, have we got an alternate line to the First Lieutenant?"

Before the Quartermaster's Mate could answer, Cargill came on the line again. "Close one, Skipper. Two armed miniatures came out of the auxiliary fire-control computer. We killed 'em."

Blaine thought furiously. He was losing all his command circuits, and he didn't know how many men he had left.

The computer was bewitched. Even if they did regain possession of *MacArthur* there was a good chance she couldn't be made spaceworthy again. "You still on, Number One?"

"Yes, sir."

"I'm going down to the air lock to talk to the Admiral. If I don't call you in fifteen minutes, abandon ship. Fifteen minutes, Jack. Mark."

"Aye aye, sir."

"And you can start rounding up the crew now. Port side only, Jack—that is, if she stays oriented where she is. The lock officers have orders to close the holes in the Field if she shifts."

Rod motioned to his bridge crew and began working his way toward the air locks. The corridors were in confusion. Yellow clouds filled several—ciphogene. He'd had hopes for ending the Motie threat with gas, but it hadn't worked and he didn't know why.

The Marines had ripped out a number of bulkheads and barricaded themselves behind the debris. They poised watchfully, weapons ready.

"Civilians out?" Rod asked the officer in charge of the lock.

"Yes, sir. Far as we know. Skipper, I had the men make one sweep through that territory, but I don't like to risk another. The Brownies are thick in civilian country—like they were living there or something."

"Maybe they were, Piper," Blaine said. He moved to the air lock and oriented his suit toward *Lenin*. The communication laser winked on, and he hung in space, holding himself steady to keep the security circuit open.

"Your situation?" Kutuzov demanded. Reluctantly, knowing what it would mean, Rod told him.

"Recommended action?" the Admiral snapped.

"*MacArthur* may never sail again, sir. I think I'll have to abandon her and scuttle as soon as I've made a sweep to rescue any trapped crewmen."

"And where will you be?"

"Leading the rescue party, sir."

"No." The voice was calm. "I accept your recommendation, Captain, but you are hereby *ordered* to abandon your ship. Log that order, Commander Borman," he added to someone on his bridge. "You will issue the order to abandon and scuttle, turn over command to your First Lieutenant, and report aboard *Lenin*'s number-two cutter. Immediately."

"Sir. Sir, I request permission to remain with my ship until my crew is safe."

"Denied, Captain," the merciless voice snapped. "I am quite aware that you have courage, Captain. Have you enough to live when you lose your command?"

"Sir—" Oh, God damn him to hell! Rod turned toward *MacArthur,* breaking the secure circuit. There was fighting at the air lock. Several miniatures had dissolved the bulkhead opposite the Marines' barricade, and the joeys were pouring fire into the gap. Blaine gritted his teeth and turned away from the battle. "Admiral, you cannot order me to leave my crew and run!"

"I cannot? You find it hard to live now, Captain? You think they will whisper about you the rest of your life, and you are afraid of that? And you tell this to *me?* Carry out your orders, Captain My Lord Blaine."

"No, sir."

"You disobey direct order, Captain?"

"I can't accept that order, sir. She's still my ship."

There was a long pause. "Your devotion to Navy tradition is admirable, Captain, but stupid. It is possible that you are only officer in Empire who can devise defense against this menace. You know more about aliens than anyone else in Fleet. That knowledge is worth more than your ship. It is worth more than every man aboard your ship, now that civilians are evacuated. I cannot allow you to die, Captain. You will leave that ship even if I am required to send new commanding officer into her."

"He'd never find me, Admiral. Excuse me, sir, I have work to do."

"Stop!" There was another pause. "Very well, Captain. I will make agreement with you. If you will stay in communication with me, I will allow you to remain aboard *MacArthur* until you have abandoned and scuttled. At instant that you are no longer in communication with me, that is moment at which you no longer command *Mac-Arthur*. Need I send Commander Borman there?"

The trouble is, Rod thought, he's right. *MacArthur's* doomed. Cargill can get the crew out as well as I can. Maybe I *do* know something important. But *she's my ship!* "I'll accept your proposition, sir. I can direct operations better from here anyway. There's no communications left on the bridge."

"Very well. I have your word, then." The circuit went dead.

Rod turned back to the air lock. The Marines had won their skirmish, and Piper was waving to him. Rod went aboard. "Commander Cargill here," the intercom said. "Skipper?"

"Yeah, Jack?"

"We're fighting our way to port side, Skipper. Sinclair's got his people ready to leave. Says he can't hold the engine rooms without reinforcements. And a runner tells me there are civilians trapped in the starboard petty officers' lounge. A Marine squad is there with them, but it's a tough fight."

"We've been ordered to abandon ship and scuttle, Number One."

"Yes, sir."

"We have to get those civilians out. Can you hold a route from bulkhead 160 forward? Maybe I can get some help in to let the scientists get that far."

"I think we can, sir. But, Captain, I can't get to the Field generator room! How do we scuttle?"

"I'll take care of that, too. Get moving, Number One."

"Aye aye, Skipper."

Scuttle. The word had an unreal sound. Rod breathed deeply. The suit air had a sharp metallic taste. Or perhaps it wasn't the air at all.

It was nearly an hour before one of *Lenin's* boats pulled alongside the cutter. They watched it approach in silence.

"Relay from *MacArthur* through *Lenin,* sir," the coxswain said. The screen lit.

The face on the screen wore Rod Blaine's features but

it wasn't his face. Sally didn't recognize him. He looked older, and the eyes were—dead. He stared at them, and they stared back. Finally Sally said it. "Rod, what's *happening?*"

Blaine looked her in the eyes, then looked away. His expression hadn't changed. He reminded Sally of something pickled in a bottle at the Imperial Museum. "Mr. Renner," the image said. "Send all personnel over the line to *Lenin*'s boat. Clear the cutter. Now all of you, you're going to get some funny orders from the boat's pilot. Obey them, exactly as given. You won't have a second chance, so *don't argue.* Just do as you're told."

"Now, just a minute," Horvath bellowed. "I—"

Rod cut him off. "Doctor, for reasons you will understand later, we are not going to explain a damned thing. Just do as you're told." He looked back to Sally. His eyes changed, just a little. Perhaps there was concern in them. Something, a tiny spark of life, came into them for a moment, anyway. She tried to smile, but failed. "Please, Sally," he said. "Do *exactly* as *Lenin*'s pilot instructs you. All right. Out. Now."

They stood immobile. Sally took a deep breath and turned toward the air lock. "Let's go," she said. She tried again to smile, but it only made her look more nervous.

The starboard air lock had been reconnected to the embassy ship. They left by the port side. *Lenin*'s boat crew had already rigged lines from the auxiliary vessel to the cutter. The boat was almost a twin for *MacArthur*'s cutter, a flat-topped lifting body with a shovel-blade reentry shield hanging below the nose.

Sally pulled herself gently along the cable to *Lenin*'s cutter, then cautiously moved through the hatch. She was halted when she entered the airlock. The mechanism cycled, and she felt pressure again.

Her suit was a woven fabric that fitted like an extra skin. A baggy protective garment covered that. The only space inside her suit that she didn't fill was the helmet that joined the skintight body stocking with a neck seal.

"It will be necessary to search you, my lady," a guttural-voiced officer said. She looked around: two armed

Marines stood in the air lock with her. Their weapons weren't aimed at her—not quite. But they stood alertly, and they were afraid.

"What *is* this?" she demanded.

"All in good time, my lady," the officer said. He assisted her in detaching the air-bottle backpack from her suit. It was thrust into a transparent plastic container. The officer looked into her helmet after he took that off, then put it in with the backpack and her coveralls. "Thank you," he muttered. "You will please now go aft. The others will join you there."

Renner and the other military personnel were treated differently. "Strip," the officer said. "Everything, if you please." The Marines did not even do them the courtesy of pointing their weapons slightly away. When they had removed everything—Renner even had to put his signet ring into the plastic container—they were sent forward. Another Marine officer indicated battle armor, and two Marines helped them into it. There were no weapons in sight now.

"Damnedest strip-tease act I ever saw," Renner said to the pilot. The coxswain nodded. "Mind telling me what it's about?"

"Your captain will explain, sir," the coxswain said.

"More Brownies!" Renner exclaimed.

"Is that it, Mr. Renner?" Whitbread asked from behind him. The midshipman was climbing into battle armor as instructed. He hadn't dared ask anyone else, but Renner was easy to talk to.

Renner shrugged. There was an air of unreality about the situation. The cutter was packed with Marines and armor—many were *MacArthur*'s Marines. Gunner Kelley watched impassively from near the air lock, and he held his weapon trained at its door.

"That's all of them," a voice announced.

"Where is Chaplain Hardy?" Renner asked.

"With the civilians, sir," the coxswain said. "A minute, please." He worked at the communications gear. The screen lit with Blaine's face.

"Secure circuit, sir," the coxswain announced.

"Thank you. Staley."

"Yes, Captain?" the senior midshipman answered.

"Mr. Staley, this cutter will shortly come alongside *Lenin*. The civilians and cutter crew except Cox'n Lafferty will transfer to the battleship, where they will be inspected by security personnel. After they have left, you will take command of *Lenin*'s number-one cutter and proceed to *MacArthur*. You will board *MacArthur* from the starboard side immediately aft of the starboard petty officers' lounge. Your purpose is to create a diversion and engage any surviving enemies in that area in order to assist a group of civilians and Marines trapped in the lounge to escape. You will send Kelley and his Marines into that lounge with pressure suits and battle armor for twenty-five men. The equipment is already aboard. Send that party forward. Commander Cargill has secured the way forward of bulkhead one six zero."

"Aye aye, sir." Staley sounded incredulous. He stood at near-rigid attention despite the absence of gravity in the cutter.

Blaine almost smiled. At least there was a twitch to his lips. "The enemy, Mister, is several hundred miniature Moties. They are armed with hand weapons. Some have gas masks. They are not well organized, but they are quite deadly. You will satisfy yourself that there are no other passengers or crew in the midships starboard section of *MacArthur*. After that mission is accomplished, you will lead a party into the midships crew mess and send out the coffeepot. But be damned sure that pot is *empty*, Mr. Staley."

"Coffeepot?" Renner said incredulously. Behind him Whitbread shook his head and murmured something to Potter.

"Coffeepot, Mr. Renner. It has been altered by the aliens, and the technique used could be of great value to the Empire. You will see other strange objects, Mr. Staley. Use your judgment about bringing them out—but under no circumstances will you send out anything that might contain a live alien. And watch the crewmen. The miniatures have killed several people, used their heads as decoys, and inhabited their battle armor. Be sure that a man in armor is a *man,* Mr. Staley. We haven't seen them try that trick with a skintight pressure suit yet, but be damned careful."

"Yessir," Staley snapped. "Can we regain control of the ship, sir?"

"No." Blaine fought visibly for control of himself. "You will not have long, Mister. Forty minutes after you enter *MacArthur,* activate all conventional destruct systems, then start the timer on that torpedo we rigged. Report to me in the main port entryway when you've got it done. Fifty-five minutes after you enter, *Lenin* will commence firing on *MacArthur* in any event. You have that?"

"Yes, sir," Horst Staley said quietly. He looked at the others. Potter and Whitbread looked back uncertainly.

"Captain," Renner said. "Sir, I remind you that I'm senior officer here."

"I know that, Renner. I have a mission for you too. You will take Chaplain Hardy back aboard *MacArthur*'s cutter and assist him in recovering any equipment or notes that might be required. Another of *Lenin*'s boats will come for that, and you will see that everything is packed into a sealed container the boat will bring."

"But—sir, I should be leading the boarding party!"

"You're not a combat officer, Renner. Do you recall what you told me at lunch yesterday?"

Renner did. "I did not tell you I was a coward," he grated.

"I'm aware of that. I am also aware that you are probably the most unpredictable officer I have. The Chaplain has been told only that there is a plague epidemic aboard *MacArthur,* and that we're going back to the Empire before it spreads to everybody. That will be the official story to the Moties. They may not believe it, but Hardy'll have a better chance of selling it to them if he believes it himself. I have to have somebody who knows the real situation along too."

"One of the midshipmen—"

"Mr. Renner, get back aboard *MacArthur*'s cutter. Staley, you have your orders."

"Aye aye, sir."

Renner departed, seething.

Three midshipmen and a dozen Marines hung from crash webbing in the main cabin of *Lenin*'s cutter. The civilians and regular crew were gone, and the boat moved away from *Lenin*'s black bulk.

"All right, Lafferty," Staley said. "Take us to *MacArthur*'s starboard side. If nothing attacks us, you will ram, aiming for the tankage complex aft of bulkhead 185."

"Aye aye, sir." Lafferty did not react noticeably. He was a big-boned man, a plainsman from Tabletop. His hair was ash-blond and very short, and his face was all planes and angles.

The crash webbing was designed for high impacts. The midshipmen hung like flies in some monstrous spider web. Staley glanced at Whitbread. Whitbread looked at Potter. Both looked away from the Marines behind them. "OK. Go," Staley ordered. The drive roared.

The real defensive hull of any warship is the Langston Field. No material object could withstand the searing heat of fusion bombs and high energy lasers. Since anything that can get past the Field and the ship's defensive fire will evaporate anything below, the hull of a warship is a relatively thin skin. It is, however, only relatively thin. A ship must be rigid enough to withstand high acceleration and jolt.

Some compartments and tanks, however, are big, and in theory can be crushed by enough impact momentum. In practice— Nobody had ever taken a combat party aboard a ship that way as far as Staley's frantically searching memory could tell him. It was in the Book, though. You *could* get aboard a crippled ship with her Field intact by ramming. Staley wondered what damn fool had first tried it.

The long black blob that enclosed *MacArthur* became a solid black wall without visible motion. Then the shovel-blade reentry shield went up. Horst watched blackness grow on the forward view screen as he peered over Lafferty's shoulder.

The cutter surged backward. An instant of cold as they passed through the Field, then the screaming of grinding metal. They stopped.

Staley unclasped his crash webbing. "Get moving," he ordered. "Kelley, cut our way through those tanks."

"Yes, sir." The Marines swept past. Two aimed a large cutting laser at the buckled metal that had once been the interior wall of a hydrogen tank. Cables stretched from the weapon back into the mangled cutter.

The tank wall collapsed, a section blown outward and narrowly missing the Marines. More air whistled out, and dead miniature Moties blew about like autumn leaves.

The corridor walls were gone. Where there had been a number of compartments there was a heap of ruins, cut-off bulkheads, surrealistic machinery, and everywhere dead miniatures. None seemed to have had pressure suits.

"Christ Almighty," Staley muttered. "OK, Kelley, get moving with those suits. Let's go." He charged forward across the ruins to the next airtight compartment door. "Shows pressure on the other side," he said. He reached into the communications box on the bulkhead and plugged in his suit mike. "Anybody there?"

"Corporal Hasner here, sir," a voice answered promptly. "Be careful back there, that area's full of miniatures."

"Not now," Staley answered. "What's your status in there?"

"Nine civilians without no suits in here, sir. Three Marines left alive. We don't know how to get them scientist people out without suits."

"We've got suits," Staley said grimly. "Can you protect the civilians until we can get through this door? We're in vacuum."

"Lord, yes, sir. Wait a minute." Something whirred. Instruments showed the pressure falling beyond the bulkhead companionway. Then the dogs turned. The door opened to reveal an armored figure inside the petty officers' mess room. Behind Hasner two other Marines trained weapons on Staley as he entered. Behind them— Staley gasped.

The civilians were at the other end of the compartment. They wore the usual white coveralls of the scientific staff. Staley recognized Dr. Blevins, the veterinarian. The civilians were chattering among themselves— "But there's no air in here!" Staley yelled.

"Not here, sir," Hasner said. He pointed. "Some kind of box thing there, makes like a curtain, Mr. Staley. Air can't get through it but we can."

Kelley growled and moved his squad into the mess room. The suits were flung to the civilians.

Staley shook his head in wonder. "Kelley. Take charge here. Get everybody forward—and take that box with you if it'll move!"

"It moves," Blevins said. He was speaking into the microphone of the helmet Kelley had passed him, but he wasn't wearing the helmet. "It can be turned on and off, too. Corporal Hasner killed some miniatures who were doing things to it."

"Fine. We'll take it," Staley snapped. "Get 'em moving, Kelley."

"Sir!" The Marine Gunner stepped gingerly through the invisible barrier. He had to push. "Like—maybe kind of like the Field, Mr. Staley. Only not so thick."

Staley growled deep in his throat and motioned to the other midshipmen. "Coffeepot," he said. He sounded as if he didn't believe it. "Lafferty. Kruppman. Janowitz. You'll come with us." He went back through the companionway to the ruins beyond.

There was a double-door airtight companionway at the other end, and Staley motioned Whitbread to open it. The dogs turned easily, and they crowded into the small air lock to peer through the thick glass into the main starboard connecting corridor.

"Looks normal enough," Whitbread whispered.

It seemed to be. They went through the air lock in two cycles and pulled themselves along the corridor walls by hand holds to the entryway into the main crew mess room.

Staley looked through the thick glass into the mess compartment. "God's teeth!"

"What is it, Horst?" Whitbread asked. He crowded his helmet against Staley's.

There were dozens of miniatures in the compartment. Most were armed with laser weapons—and they were firing at each other. There was no order to the battle. It seemed that every miniature was fighting every other, although that might have been only a first impression. The compartment drifted with a pinkish fog: Motie blood. Dead and wounded Moties flopped in an insane dance as the room winked with green-blue pencils of light.

"Not in there," Staley whispered. He remembered he was speaking through his suit radio and raised his voice. "We'd never get through that alive. Forget the coffeepot." They moved on through the corridor and searched for other human survivors.

There were none. Staley led them back toward the crew messroom. "Kruppman," he barked. "Take Janowitz and get this corridor into vacuum. Burn out bulkheads, use grenades—anything, but get it into vacuum. Then get the hell off this ship."

"Aye aye, sir." When the Marines rounded a turn in the steel corridor the midshipmen lost contact with them. The suit radios were line-of-sight only. They could still hear, though. *MacArthur* was alive with sound. High-pitched screams, the sounds of tearing metal, hums and buzzes—none of it was familiar.

"She's not ours any more," Potter murmured.

There was a *whoosh*. The corridor was in vacuum. Staley tossed a thermite grenade against the mess-room bulkhead and stepped back around a turn. Light flared briefly, and Staley charged back to fire his hand laser at the still-glowing spot on the bulkhead. The others fired with him.

The wall began to bulge, then broke through. Air whistled into the corridor, with a cloud of dead Moties. Staley turned the dogs on the companionway but nothing happened. Grimly they burned at the bulkhead until the hole was large enough to crawl into.

There was no sign of live miniatures. "Why can't we do that all over the ship?" Whitbread demanded. "We could get back in control of her . . ."

"Maybe," Staley answered. "Lafferty. Get the coffee maker and take it port side. Move, we'll cover you."

The plainsman waved and dove down the corridor in the direction the Marines had vanished. "Had we nae best be goin' wi' him?" Potter asked.

"Torpedo," Staley barked. "We've got to detonate the torpedo."

"But, Horst," Whitbread protested. "Can't we get control of the ship? I haven't seen any miniatures with vacuum suits . . ."

"They can build those magic pressure curtains," Staley reminded him. "Besides, we've got our orders." He pointed aft, and they moved ahead of him. Now that *MacArthur* was clear of humans they hurried, burning through airtight compartments and grenading the corridors beyond. Potter and Whitbread shuddered at the damage they were doing to the ship. Their weapons were not meant to be used aboard a working space craft.

The torpedoes were in place: Staley and Whitbread had been part of the work crew that welded them on either side of the Field generator. Only—the generator was gone. A hollow shell remained where it had been.

Potter was reaching for the timers that would trigger the torpedo. "Wait," Staley ordered. He found a direct wire intercom outlet and plugged his suit in. "Anyone, this is Midshipman Horst Staley in the Field generator compartment. Anyone there?"

"Aye aye, Mr. Staley," a voice answered. "A moment, sir, here's the Captain." Captain Blaine came on the line. Staley explained the situation. "The Field generator's gone, sir, but the Field seems strong as ever . . ."

There was a long pause. Then Blaine swore viciously, but cut himself off. "You're overtime, Mr. Staley. We've orders to close the holes in the Field and get aboard *Lenin*'s boats in five minutes. You'll never get out before *Lenin* opens fire."

"No, sir. What should we do?"

Blaine hesitated a moment. "I'll have to buck that one up to the Admiral. Stay right where you are."

A sudden roaring hurricane sent them scurrying for cover. There was silence, then Potter said unnecessarily, "We're under pressure. Yon Brownies must have repaired one or another door."

"Then they'll soon be here." Whitbread cursed, "Damn them anyway." They waited. "What's keeping the Captain?" Whitbread demanded. There was no possible answer, and they crouched tensely, their weapons drawn, while around them they heard *MacArthur* coming back to life. Her new masters were approaching.

"I won't leave without the middies," Rod was saying to the Admiral.

"You are certain they cannot reach after port air lock?" Kutuzov said.

"Not in ten minutes, Admiral. The Brownies have control of that part of the ship. The kids would have to fight all the way."

"Then what do you suggest?"

"Let them use the lifeboats, sir," Rod said hopefully. There were lifeboats in various parts of the ship, with a dozen not twenty meters from the Field generator compartment. Basically solid-fuel motors with inflatable cabins, they were meant only to enable a refugee to survive for a few hours in the event that the ship was damaged beyond repair—or about to explode. Either was a good description of *MacArthur*'s present status.

"The miniatures may have built recording devices and transmitters into lifeboats," Kutuzov said. "A method of giving large Moties all of *MacArthur*'s secrets." He spoke to someone else. "Do you think that possible, Chaplain?"

Blaine heard Chaplain Hardy speaking in the background. "No, sir. The miniatures are animals. I've always thought so, and the adult Moties say so, and all the evidence supports the hypothesis. They would be capable of that only if directly ordered—and, Admiral, if they've been *that* anxious to communicate with the Moties, you can be certain they've already *done* it."

"Da," Kutuzov muttered. "There is no point in sacrificing these officers for nothing. Captain Blaine, you will instruct them to use lifeboats, but caution them that no miniatures must come out with them. When they leave, you will immediately come aboard *Lenin*."

"Aye aye, sir." Rod sighed in relief and rang the intercom line to the generator compartment. "Staley: the Admiral says you can use the lifeboats. Be careful there aren't any miniatures in them, and you'll be searched before you board one of *Lenin*'s boats. Trigger the torpedoes and get away. Got that?"

"Aye aye, sir." Staley turned to the other middies. "Lifeboats," he snapped. "Let's—"

Green light winked around them. "Visors down!" Whitbread screamed. They dove behind the torpedoes while the beam swung wildly around the compartment. It slashed holes in the bulkheads, then through compartment walls beyond, finally through the hull itself. Air rushed out and the beam stopped swinging, but it remained on, pouring energy through the hull into the Field beyond.

Staley swung his sun visor up. It was fogged with silver metal deposits. He ducked carefully under the beam to look at its source.

It was a heavy hand laser. Half a dozen miniatures had been needed to carry it. Some of them, dead and dry, clung to the double hand holds.

"Let's move," Staley ordered. He inserted a key into the lock on the torpedo panel. Beside him Potter did the same thing. They turned the keys—and had ten minutes to live. Staley rushed to the intercom. "Mission accomplished, sir."

They moved through the airtight open compartment's door into the main after corridor and rushed sternward, flinging themselves from hand hold to hand hold. Null-gee races were a favorite if slightly nonregulation game with midshipmen, and they were glad of the practice they'd had. Behind them the timer would be clicking away—

"Should be here," Staley said. He blasted through an airtight door, then fired a man-sized gap through the outer hull itself. Air whistled out—the miniatures had somehow again enclosed them in the stinking atmosphere of Mote Prime even as they had come aft. Wisps of ice-crystal fog hung in the vacuum.

Potter found the lifeboat inflation controls and smashed the glass cover with his pistol butt. They stepped out of the way and waited for the lifeboats to inflate.

Instead the flooring swung up. Stored beneath the deck was a line of cones, each two meters across at the base, each about eight meters long.

"The Midnight Brownie strikes again," said Whitbread.

The cones were all identical, and fabricated from scratch. The miniatures must have worked for weeks beneath the deck, tearing up the lifeboats and other equipment to replace them with—these things. Each cone had a contoured crash chair in the big end and a flared rocket nozzle in the point.

"Look at the damn things, Potter," Staley ordered. "See if there's anywhere Brownies could hide in them." There didn't seem to be. Except for the conical hull, which was solid, everything was open framework. Potter tapped and pried while his friends stood guard.

He was looking for an opening in the cone when he caught a flicker of motion in the corner of his eye. He snatched a grenade from his belt and turned. A space suit floated—out of the corridor wall. It held a heavy laser in both hands.

Staley's nerves showed in his voice. "You! Identify yourself!"

The figure raised its weapon. Potter threw the grenade.

Intense green light lashed out through the explosion, lighting the corridor weirdly and tearing up one of the conical lifeboats. "Was it a man?" Potter cried. "Was it? The arms bent wrong! Its legs stuck straight out—what was it?"

"An enemy," Staley said. "I think we'd better get out of here. Board the boats while we've still got 'em." He climbed into the reclined contour seat of one of the undamaged cones. After a moment the others each selected a seat.

Horst found a control panel on a bar and swung it out in front of him. There were no labels anywhere. Sentient or nonsentient, all Moties seemed to be expected to solve the workings of a machine at a glance.

"I'm going to try the big square button," Staley said firmly. His voice sounded oddly hollow through the suit radio. Grimly he pushed the button.

A section of the hull blew away beneath him. The cone swung out as on a sling. Rockets flared briefly. Cold and blackness—and he was outside the Field.

Two other cones popped out of the black sea. Frantically Horst directed his suit radio toward the looming black hulk of *Lenin* no more than a kilometer away. "Midshipman Staley here! The lifeboats have been altered. There are three of us, and we're alone aboard them—"

A fourth cone popped from the blackness. Staley turned in his seat. It looked like a man—

Three hand weapons fired simultaneously. The fourth cone glowed and melted, but they fired for a long time. "One of the—uh—" Staley didn't know what to report. His circuit might not be secure.

"We have you on the screens, Midshipman," a heavily accented voice said. "Move away from *MacArthur* and wait for pickup. Did you complete your mission?"

"Yes, sir." Staley glanced at his watch. "Four minutes to go, sir."

"Then move fast, mister," the voice ordered.

But how? Staley wondered. The controls had no obvious function. While he searched frantically, his rocket fired. But what—he hadn't touched anything.

"My rocket's firing again," said Whitbread's voice. He sounded calm—much calmer than Staley felt.

"Aye, and mine," Potter added. "Never look a gift horse in the mouth. We're movin' away from yon ship."

The rumble continued. They were accelerating together at nearly a standard gee, with Mote Prime a vast green crescent to one side. On the other was the deep black of the Coal Sack, and the blacker mass of *Lenin*. The boats accelerated for a long time.

The young Russian midshipman carried himself proudly. His battle armor was spotless, and all his equipment arranged properly by the Book. "The Admiral requests that you come to the bridge," he chirped in flawless Anglic.

Rod Blaine followed listlessly. They floated through the air lock from *Lenin*'s number-two hangar deck to a flurry of salutes from Kutuzov's Marines. The full honors of a visiting captain only stirred his grief. He'd given his last orders, and he'd been the last man to leave his ship. Now he was an observer, and this was probably the last time anyone would render him boarding honors.

Everything aboard the battleship seemed too large, yet he knew it was only an illusion. With few exceptions the compartments and corridors of capital ships were standardized, and he might as well have been aboard *MacArthur*. *Lenin* was at battle stations, with all her airtight doors closed and dogged. Marines were posted at the more important passageway controls, but otherwise they saw no one, and Rod was glad of that. He could not have faced any of his former crew. Or passengers.

Lenin's bridge was enormous. She was fitted out as a flagship, and in addition to the screens and command posts for the ship herself there were a dozen couches for the Admiral's battle staff. Rod woodenly acknowledged the Admiral's greeting and sank gratefully into the Flag Captain's chair. He didn't even wonder where Commander Borman, Kutuzov's flag lieutenant and chief of staff, had gone. He was alone with the Admiral at the flag command station.

MacArthur was displayed from half a dozen views on the screens above him. The last of *Lenin*'s boats were pulling away from her. Staley must have accomplished his mission, Rod thought. Now she has only a few minutes to live. When she's gone I'll really be finished. A newly promoted captain who lost his ship on her first mission—even the Marquis' influence would not overcome that. Blind hatred for the Mote and all its inhabitants welled up inside him.

"Dammit, we ought to be able to get her back from a bunch of—of goddamn *animals!*" he blurted.

Kutuzov looked up in surprise. His craggy eyebrows came closer together in a frown, then relaxed slightly. "Da. If that is *all* they are. But suppose they are more than that? In any event is too late."

"Yes, sir. They triggered the torpedoes." Two hydrogen bombs. The Field generator would vaporize in milliseconds, and *MacArthur* would— He writhed in pain at the thought. When the screens flared, she'd be gone. He looked up suddenly. "Where are my midshipmen, Admiral?"

Kutuzov grunted. "They have decelerated to a lower orbit and are beyond the horizon. I will send a boat for them when everything is clear."

Strange, Rod thought. But they couldn't come directly to *Lenin* by the Admiral's orders, and the boats wouldn't provide any real protection when *MacArthur* exploded. What they had done was unnecessary caution since the torpedoes did not give off a large fraction of their energy in x-rays and neutrons, but it was understandable caution.

The timers twirled noiselessly to zero. Kutuzov watched grimly as another minute, and another, went past. "The torpedoes did not fire," he said accusingly.

"No, sir." Rod's misery was complete. And now—

"Captain Mikhailov. You will please prepare main battery to fire on *MacArthur*." Kutuzov turned his dark gaze to Rod. "I dislike this, Captain. Not so much as you. But I dislike it. Do you prefer to give order yourself? Captain Mikhailov, you permit?"

"Da, Admiral."

"Thank you, sir." Rod took a deep breath. A man ought to kill his own dog. "Shoot!"

Space battles are lovely to see. The ships approach like smooth black eggs, their drives radiating dazzling light.

Scintillations in the black flanks record the explosions of torpedoes that have escaped destruction from the stabbing colors of the secondary lasers. The main batteries pour energy into each other's Fields, and lines of green and ruby reflect interplanetary dust.

Gradually the Fields begin to glow. Dull red, brighter yellow, glaring green, as the Fields become charged with energy. The colored eggs are linked by red and green threads from the batteries, and the colors change.

Now three green threads linked *Lenin* and *MacArthur*. Nothing else happened. The battle cruiser did not move and made no attempt to fight back. Her Field began to glow red, shading to yellow where the beams converged amidships. When it became white it would overload and the energy stored in it would be released—inward and out. Kutuzov watched in growing puzzlement.

"Captain Mikhailov. Please take us back a klick." The lines on the Admiral's brow deepened as *Lenin*'s drive moved her gently away from *MacArthur*.

MacArthur shaded green with faintly bluish spots. The image receded on the screens. Hot spots vanished as the lasers spread slightly. A thousand kilometers away she glowed richly in the telescopes.

"Captain, are we at rest with respect to *MacArthur*?" Kutuzov asked.

"Da, Admiral."

"She appears to move closer."

"Da, Admiral. Her Field is expanding."

"Expanding?" Kutuzov turned to Rod. "You have explanation?"

"No, sir." He wanted nothing more than oblivion. Speaking was pain, awareness agony. But—he tried to think. "The Brownies must have rebuilt the generator, sir. And they always improve anything they work on."

"It seems pity to destroy it," Kutuzov muttered. "Expanded like that, with that great radiating surface, *MacArthur* would be match for any vessel in Fleet . . ."

MacArthur's Field was violet now, and huge. It filled the screens, and Kutuzov adjusted his to drop the magnification by a factor of ten. She was a great violet balloon tethered by green threads. They waited, fascinated, as ten minutes went by. Fifteen.

"No ship has ever survived that long in violet," Kutuzov muttered. "Are you still convinced we deal only with *animals*, Captain Blaine?"

"The scientists are convinced, sir. They convinced me," he added carefully. "I wish Dr. Horvath were here now."

Kutuzov grunted as if struck in the belly. "That fool. Pacifist. He would not understand what he saw." They watched in silence for another minute.

The intercom buzzed. "Admiral, there is a signal from the Mote embassy ship," the communications officer announced.

Kutuzov scowled. "Captain Blaine. You will take that call."

"I beg your pardon, sir?"

"Answer the call from the Moties. I will not speak to any alien directly."

"Aye aye, sir."

Its face was any Motie's face, but it sat uncomfortably erect, and Rod was not surprised when it announced, "I am Dr. Horvath's Fyunch(click). I have distressing news for you, Captain Blaine. And by the way, we appreciate the warning you gave us—we don't understand why you wish to destroy your ship, but if we had been alongside—"

Blaine rubbed the bridge of his nose. "We're fighting a plague. Maybe killing *MacArthur* stopped it. We can hope. Listen, we're a little busy now. What's your message?"

"Yes, of course. Captain, the three small craft which escaped from *MacArthur* have attempted reentry to Mote Prime. I am sorry, but none survived."

Lenin's bridge seemed to fog. "Reentry with lifeboats? But that's plain silly. They wouldn't—"

"No, no, they tried to land. We tracked them part way— Captain, we have recordings of them. They burned up, completely—"

"God damn it to hell! They were safe!"

"We're terribly sorry."

Kutuzov's face was a mask. He mouthed: "Recordings."

Rod nodded. He felt very tired. He told the Motie, "We would like those recordings. Are you certain that none of my young officers survived?"

"Quite certain, Captain. We are very distressed by this. Naturally, we had no idea they would attempt such a thing, and there was absolutely nothing we could do under the circumstances."

"Of course not. Thank you." Rod turned off the screen and looked back at the battle display in front of him.

Kutuzov muttered, "So there are no bodies and no wreckage. Very convenient." He touched a button on the arm of his command couch and said, "Captain Mikhailov, please send cutter to look for the midshipmen." He turned back to Rod. "There will be nothing, of course."

"You don't believe the Moties, do you, sir?" Rod asked.

"Do you, Captain?"

"I—I don't know, sir. I don't see what we can do about it."

"Nor I, Captain. The cutter will search, and will find nothing. We do not know where they attempted reentry. The planet is large. Even if they survive and are free, we could search for days and not find them. And if they are captives—they will never be found." He grunted again and spoke into his command circuit. "Mikhailov, see that the cutter searches well. And use torpedoes to destroy that vessel, if you please."

"Yes, sir." *Lenin*'s captain spoke quietly at his post on the opposite side of the big bridge. A score of torpedoes arced out toward *MacArthur*. They couldn't go *through* the Field; the stored energy there would fuse them instantly. But they exploded all at once, a perfect time-on-target salvo, and a great ripple of multicolored light swept around *MacArthur*'s violet-glowing surface. Bright white spots appeared and vanished.

"Burn-through in nine places," the gunnery officer announced.

"Burn-through into what?" Rod asked innocently. She was still his ship, and she was fighting valiantly for her life . . .

The Admiral snarled. The ship was five hundred meters inward from that hellish violet surface—the bright flashes might never have reached her, or might have missed entirely.

"Guns will continue to fire. Launch another torpedo attack," Kutuzov ordered.

Another fleet of glowing darts arced out. They exploded all across the violet shimmering surface. More white spots rippled across, and there was an expanding ripple of violet flame.

And then *MacArthur* was as she was. A violet fire balloon a full kilometer in diameter, tethered by threads of green light.

A mess steward handed Rod a cup of coffee. Absently he sipped. It tasted terrible.

"Shoot!" Kutuzov commanded. He glared at the screens in hatred. "Shoot!"

And suddenly it happened. *MacArthur*'s Field expanded enormously, turned blue, yellow—and vanished. Automatic scanners whirred and the magnification of the screens increased. The ship was there.

She glowed red, and parts had melted. She should not have been there at all. When a Field collapses, everything inside it vaporizes . . .

"They must have fried in there," Rod said mechanically.

"Da. Shoot!"

The green lights stabbed out. *MacArthur* changed, bubbled, expanded, fuming air into space. A torpedo moved almost slowly to her and exploded. Still the laser batteries fired. When Kutuzov finally ordered them off, there was nothing left but vapor.

Rod and the Admiral watched the empty screen for a long time. Finally the Admiral turned away. "Call in the boats, Captain Mikhailov. We are going home."

33 • *Planetfall*

Three smallish cones, falling. A man nested in each, like an egg in an egg cup.

Horst Staley was in the lead. He could see forward on a small square screen, but his rear view was all around him. Except for his pressure suit he was naked to space. He turned gingerly, to see two other flame-tipped cones behind him. Somewhere, far beyond the horizon, were *MacArthur* and *Lenin*. There was no chance that his suit radio would carry that far, but he turned to the hailing frequency and called anyway. There was no answer.

It had all happened so fast. The cones had fired retrorockets and by the time he had called *Lenin* it had been too late. Perhaps the signal crew had been busy with something else, perhaps he had been slow— Horst felt suddenly alone.

They continued to fall. The rockets cut off.

"Horst!" It was Whitbread's voice. Staley answered.

"Horst, these things are going to reenter!"

"Yeah. Stick with it. What else can we do?"

That did not call for an answer. In lonely silence three small cones fell toward the bright green planet below. Then: reentry.

It was not the first time for any of them. They knew the colors of the plasma field that builds before a ship's nose, colors differing according to the chemistry of the ablation shield. But this time they were practically naked to it. Would there be radiation? Heat?

Whitbread's voice reached Staley through the static. "I'm trying to think like a Brownie, and it isn't easy. They knew about our suits. They'd know how much radiation they'd stop. How much do they think we can take? And heat?"

"I've changed my mind," Staley heard Potter say. "I am not going down."

Staley tried to ignore their laughter. He was in charge

325

of three lives, and he took it seriously. He tried to relax his muscles as he waited for heat, turbulence, unfelt radiation, tumbling of the cone, discomfort and death.

Landscape streamed past him through plasma distortions. Circular seas and arcs of river. Vast stretches of city. Mountains cased in ice and cityscape, the continuous city engulfing the slopes to the snowy peaks. A long stretch of ocean; would the damn cones float? More land. The cones slowing, the features getting larger. Air whipping around them now. Boats on a lake, tiny specks, hordes of them. A stretch of green forest, sharply bounded, laced by roads.

The rim of Staley's cone opened and a ring of parachute streamed back. Staley sagged deep into the contoured seat. For a minute he saw only blue sky. Then came a bone-jarring *Thump*. He cursed in his mind. The cone teetered and toppled on its side.

Potter's voice rang in Staley's ears. "I hae found the hover controls! Look for a sliding knob near the center, if the beasties hae done the same to all. That is the thrust control, and moving the whole bloody control panel on its support tilts the rocket."

Too bad he hadn't found it sooner! Staley thought. He said, "Get near the ground and hover there. The fuel may burn out. Did you find a parachute release, Potter?"

"No. 'Tis hanging under me. Yon rocket flame must hae burned it away by now. Where are you?"

"I'm down. Let me just get loose—" Staley opened the crash webbing and tumbled out on his back. The seat was 30 cm lower within the cone. He drew his weapon and burned out a hole to examine the space below. Compressible foam filled the compartment. "When you get down, make *sure* there are no Brownies aboard the lifeboat," he ordered crisply.

"Damn! I nearly flipped over," came Whitbread's voice. "These things are tricky—"

"I see you, Jonathon!" Potter shouted. "Just hover and I'll come to you."

"Then look for my parachute," Staley ordered.

"I don't see you. We could be twenty kilometers apart. Your signal is none too strong," Whitbread answered.

Staley struggled to his feet. "First things first," he muttered. He looked the lifeboat over carefully. There was no place a miniature might have hidden and lived through reentry, but he looked again to be sure. Then he switched to hailing frequency and tried to call *Lenin*—expected no answer and got none. Suit radios operate on line of sight only and they are intentionally not very powerful, otherwise all of space would be filled with the chatter of suited men. The redesigned lifeboats had nothing resembling a radio. How did the Brownies intend for survivors to call for help?

Staley stood uncertainly, not yet adjusted to gravity. There were cultivated fields all around him, alternating rows of purple eggplant-looking bushes with chest-high crowns of dark leaves, and low bushes bright with grain. The rows went on forever in all directions.

"Still haven't spotted you yet, Horst," Whitbread reported. "This is getting us nowhere. Horst, do you see a big, low building that gleams like a mirror? It's the only building in sight."

Staley spotted it, a metal-gleaming thing beyond the horizon. It was a long walk away, but it was the only landmark in sight. "Got it."

"We'll make for that and meet you there."

"Good. Wait for me."

"Head that way, Gavin," Whitbread's voice said. "Right," came the reply. There was more chatter between the other two, and Horst Staley felt very much alone.

"Wup! My rocket's out!" Potter shouted.

Whitbread watched Potter's cone drop toward the ground. It hit point first, hesitated, and toppled into the plants. Whitbread shouted, "Gavin, are you all right?"

There were rustling sounds. Then Whitbread heard: "Oh, sometimes I get a twinge in my right elbow when the weather's nasty . . . old football injury. Get as far as you can, Jonathon. I'll meet you both at the building."

"Aye aye." Whitbread tilted the cone forward on his rocket. The building was large ahead of him.

It *was* large. At first there had been nothing to give it scale; now he had been flying toward it for ten minutes or more.

It was a dome with straight sides blending into a low, rounded roof. There were no windows, and no other features except a rectangular break that might have been a door, ridiculously small in the enormous structure. The gleam of sunlight on the roof was more than metallic; it was mirror-bright.

Whitbread flew low, traveling quite slowly. There was something awesome about the building set in the endless croplands. That more than the fear that his motor might burn out checked his first impulse to rush to the structure.

The rocket held. The miniatures might have changed the chemicals in the solid motor; no two things built by Moties were ever quite identical. Whitbread landed just outside the rectangular doorway. This close the door loomed over him. It had been dwarfed by the building.

"I'm here," he almost whispered, then laughed at himself. "There's a doorway. It's big and closed. Funny— there aren't any roads leading here, and the crops grow right up to the edge of the dome."

Staley's voice: "Perhaps planes land on the roof."

"I don't think so, Horst. The roof is *rounded*. I don't think there are ever many visitors. Must be some kind of storage. Or maybe there's a machine inside that runs itself."

"Best not fool with it. Gavin, are you all right too?"

"Aye, Horst. I'll be at yon building in half an hour. See you there."

Staley prepared for a longer hike. There were no emergency rations that he could see in the lifeboat. He thought for a while before removing his combat armor and the pressure suit under it. There weren't any secrets there. He took the helmet and dogged it onto the neck seal, then rigged it as an air filter. Then he took the radio out of the suit and slung it on his belt, first making one last attempt to contact *Lenin*. There was no answer. What else? Radio, water bag, sidearm. It would have to do.

Staley looked carefully around the horizon. There was only the one building—no chance of walking toward the wrong one. He started out toward it, glad of the low gravity, and swung easily into stride.

A half-hour later he saw the first Motie. He was practically alongside before he noticed it: a creature different from any he'd seen before, and just the height of the plants. It was working between the rows, smoothing soil with its hands, pulling out weeds to lay between the careful furrows. It watched him approach. When he came alongside it turned back to work.

The Motie was not quite a Brown. The fur patches were thicker, and more thick fur encased all three arms and the legs. The left hand was about the same as a Brown's but the right hands had five fingers each, plus a bud, and the fingers were square and short. The legs were thick and the feet large and flat. The head was a Brown's with drastically back-sloping forehead.

If Sally Fowler was right, that meant that the parietal area was almost nil. "Hello," Horst said anyway. The Motie looked back at him for a second, then pulled out a weed.

Afterwards he saw many of them. They watched him just long enough to be sure he wasn't destroying plants; then they lost interest. Horst hiked on in the bright sunshine toward the mirror-bright building. It was much farther than he had thought.

Mr. Midshipman Jonathon Whitbread waited. He had done enough of that since joining the Navy; but he was only seventeen standard years old, and at that age waiting is never really easy.

He sat near the tip of the reentry cone, high enough to bring his head above the plants. In the city the buildings had blocked his view of this world. Here he saw the entire horizon. The sky was brown all the way around, shading to something that might have had blue tinges directly overhead. Clouds roiled to the east in thick patches, and a few dirty-white cumulus scudded overhead.

The sun was just overhead too. He decided he must be near the equator, and remembered that Castle City was far to the north. He could not sense the greater width of the sun's disc, because he could not look directly at it; but it was more comfortable to look at *near* than the small sun of New Scotland.

The sense of an alien world was on him, but there was nothing to see. His eyes kept straying to the mirror-surfaced building. Presently he got up to examine the door.

It was a good ten meters high. Impressively tall to Whitbread, a gigantic thing for a Motie. But were Moties impressed by size? Whitbread thought not. The door must be functional—what was ten meters high? Heavy machinery? There was no sound at all when he put his pick-up microphone against the smooth metallic surface.

At one side of the alcove containing the door was a panel mounted on a stout spring. Behind the panel was what seemed to be a combination lock. And that was that —except that Moties expected each other to solve such puzzles at a glance. A key lock would have been a NO TRESPASSING sign. This was not.

Probably it was intended to keep out—what? Browns? Whites? Laborers and the nonsentient classes? Probably all of them. A combination lock could be thought of as a form of communication.

Potter arrived panting, his helmet nearly awash with sweat, a water bag hanging from his belt. He turned his helmet mike to activate a small speaker and cut off his radio. "I had to try the Mote Prime air for meself," he said. "Now I know. Well, what hae you found?"

Whitbread showed him. He also adjusted his own mike. No point in broadcasting everything they said.

"Um. I wish Dr. Buckman were here. Those are Motie numbers—aye, and the Mote solar system, with the dial where the Mote ought to be. Let me see'. . . ."

Whitbread watched interestedly as Potter stared at the dial. The New Scot pursed his lips, then said, "Aye. The gas giant is three point seven two times as far from the

Mote as Mote Prime. Hmmm." He reached into his shirt pocket and took out the ever-present computer box. "Umm . . . three point eight eight, base twelve. Now which way does the dial go?"

"Then, again, it might be somebody's birthday," said Whitbread. He was glad to see Gavin Potter. He was glad to see anyone human here. But the New Scot's meddling with the dials was—disturbing. Left, right, left, right, Gavin Potter turned the dials . . .

"I seem to remember Horst gave us orders concerning this building." Whitbread was uneasy.

" 'Best not fool with it.' Hardly orders. We came to learn about Moties, did we not?"

"Well . . ." It was an interesting puzzle. "Try left again," Whitbread suggested. "Hold it." Whitbread pushed the symbol representing Mote Prime. It depressed with a click. "Keep going left."

"Aye. The Motie astronomical maps show the planets going counterclockwise."

On the third digit the door began to slide upward. "It works!" Whitbread shouted.

The door slid up to a height of one and a half meters. Potter looked at Whitbread and said, "Now what?"

"You're kidding."

"We hae our orders," Potter said slowly. They sat down between the plants and looked at each other. Then they looked at the dome. There was light inside, and they could easily see under the door. There were buildings in there . . .

Staley had been walking for three hours when he saw the plane. It was high up and moving fast, and he waved at it, not expecting to be seen. He was not and he walked on.

Presently he saw the plane again. It was behind him, much lower, and he thought it had spread wings. It settled lower and vanished behind the low rolling hills where he had come down. Staley shrugged. It would find his parachute and lifeboat and see his tracks leading away. The direction should be obvious. There was nowhere else to go.

In a few minutes the plane was higher and coming straight toward him. It was moving slowly now, obviously searching. He waved again, although he had a momentary impulse to hide, which was plainly silly. He *needed* to be found, although what he would say to a Motie was not at all clear.

The plane moved past him and hovered. Jet pipes curved down and forward, and it dropped dangerously fast to settle into the plants. There were three Moties inside, and a Brown-and-white emerged quickly.

"Horst!" it called in Whitbread's voice. "Where are the others?"

Staley waved toward the rounded dome. It was still an hour's march away.

Whitbread's Motie seemed to sag. "That's torn it. Horst, are they *there* yet?"

"Sure. They're waiting for me. They've been there about three hours."

"Oh, my God. Maybe they couldn't get inside. Whitbread couldn't get inside. Come *on,* Horst." She gestured toward the plane. "You'll have to squeeze in somehow."

Another Brown-and-white was inside and the pilot was a Brown. Whitbread's Motie sang something ranging through five octaves and using at least nine tones. The other Brown-and-white gestured wildly. They made room for Staley between the contoured seats, and the Brown did things to the controls. The plane rose and shot toward the building ahead. "Maybe they didn't get in," Whitbread's Motie repeated. "Maybe."

Horst crouched uncomfortably in the speeding jet and wondered. He didn't like this at all. "What's wrong?" he asked.

Whitbread's Motie looked at him strangely. "Maybe nothing." The other two Moties said nothing at all.

Whitbread and Potter stood alone within the dome. They stared in wonder.

The dome was only a shell. A single light source very like an afternoon sun blazed halfway down its slope. Moties used that kind of illumination in many of the buildings Whitbread had seen.

Underneath the dome it was like a small city—but not quite. Nobody was home. There was no sound, no motion, no light in any of the windows. And the buildings . . .

There was no coherency to this city. The buildings jarred horribly against each other. Whitbread winced at two clean-lined many-windowed pillars framing what might have been an oversized medieval cathedral, all gingerbread, a thousand cornices guarded by what Bury's Motie had said were Motie demons.

Here were a hundred styles of architecture and at least a dozen levels of technology. Those geodesic forms could not have been built without prestressed concrete or something more sophisticated, not to mention the engineering mathematics. But this building nearest the gate was of sun-baked mud bricks. Here a rectangular solid had walls of partly silvered glass; there the walls were of gray stone, and the tiny windows had no glass in them, only shutters to seal them from the elements.

"Rain shutters. It must have been here before the dome," Potter said.

"Anyone can see that. The dome is almost new. That . . . cathedral, it might be, that cathedral in the center is so old it's about to fall apart."

"Look there. Yon parabolic-hyperboloid structure has been cantilevered out from a wall. But look at the wall!"

"Yah, it must have been part of another building. God knows how old *that* is." The wall was over a meter thick, and ragged around the edges and the top. It was made of dressed stone blocks that must have massed five hundred kilos each. Some vinelike plant had invaded it, surrounded it, permeated it to the extent that by now it must be holding the wall together.

Whitbread leaned close and peered into the vines. "No cement, Gavin. They've fitted the blocks together. And still it supports the rest of the building—which is concrete. They built to last."

"Do ye remember what Horst said about the Stone Beehive?"

"He said he could feel the age in it. Right. Right . . ."

"It must be of all different ages, this place. I think we'll find that it's a museum. A museum of architecture? And they've added to it, century after century. Finally they threw up that dome to protect it from the elements."

"Yah . . ."

"Ye sound dubious."

"That dome is two meters thick, and metal. What kind of elements . . ."

"Asteroid falls, it may be. No, that's nonsense. The asteroids were moved away eons ago."

"I think I want to have a look at that cathedral. It looks to be the oldest building here."

The cathedral was a museum right enough. Any civilized man in the Empire would have recognized it. Museums are all alike.

There were cases faced in glass, and old things within, marked by plaques with dates and printing on them. "I can read the numbers," said Potter. "Look, they're in four and five figures. And this is base twelve!"

"My Motie asked me once how old our recorded civilization is. How old is theirs, Gavin?"

"Well, their year is shorter . . . Five figures. Dating backward from some event; that's a minus sign in front of each of them. Let me see . . ." He took out his computer and scrawled quick, precise figures. "That number would be seventy-four thousand and some-odd. Jonathon, the plaques are almost new."

"Languages change. They must translate the plaques every so often."

"Yes . . . yes, I know this sign. 'Approximately.' " Potter moved swiftly from exhibit to exhibit. "Here it is again. Not here . . . but here. Jonathon, come look at this one."

It was a very old machine. Once iron, it must be rust now, all the way through. There was a sketch of what it must have looked like once. A howitzer cannon.

"Here on the plaque. This double-approximation sign means educated guesswork. I wonder how many times *that* legend has been translated?"

Room after room. They found a wide staircase leading up, the steps shallow but broad enough for human feet. Above, more rooms, more exhibits. The ceilings were low. The lighting came from lines of bulbs of incandescent filaments that came on when they entered, went out when they left. The bulbs were mounted carefully so they wouldn't mar the ceiling. The museum itself must be an exhibit.

The plaques were all alike, but the cases were all different. Whitbread did not think it strange. No two Motie artifacts were ever precisely alike. But one . . . he almost laughed.

A bubble of glass several meters long and two meters wide rested on a free-form sculpted frame of almost peach-colored metal. Both looked brand-new. There was a plaque on the frame. Inside was an ornately carved wooden box, coffin sized, bleached white by age, its lid the remains of a rusted wire grille. *It* had a plaque. Under the rusted wire, a selection of wonderfully shaped, eggshell-thin pottery, some broken, some whole. Each piece in the set had a dated plaque. "It's like nested exhibits," he said.

Potter did not laugh. "That's what it is. See here? The bubble case is about two thousand years old . . . that can't be right, can it?"

"Not unless . . ." Whitbread rubbed his class ring along the glass bubble. "They're both scratched. Artificial sapphire." He tried it on the metal. The metal scratched the stone. "I'll accept two thousand."

"But the box is around twenty-four hundred, and the pottery goes from three thousand up. Look you how the style changes. 'Tis a depiction of the rise and fall of a particular school of pottery styling."

"Do you think the wooden case came out of another museum?"

"Aye."

Whitbread did laugh then. They moved on. Presently Whitbread pointed and said, "Here, that's the same metal, isn't it?" The small two-handed weapon—it had to be a gun—carried the same date as the sapphire bubble.

Beyond that was a puzzling structure near the wall of the great dome. It was made of a vertical lacework of hexagons, each formed from steel members two meters long. There were thick plastic frames in some of the hexagons, and broken fragments in others.

Potter pointed out the gentle curve of the structure. " 'Twas another dome. A spherical dome with geodesic bracing. Not much left of it—and it wouldn a' hae covered all of the compound anyway."

"You're right. It didn't weather away, though. Look at how these members near the edge are twisted. Tornadoes? This part of the country seems flat enough."

It took Potter a moment to understand. There were no tornadoes in the rough terraformed New Scotland. He remembered his meteorology lessons and nodded. "Aye. Maybe. Maybe." Beyond the fragments of the earlier dome Potter found a framework of disintegrating metal within what might have been a plastic shell. The plastic itself looked frayed and motheaten. There were two dates on the plaque, both in five figures. The sketch next to the plaque showed a narrow ground car, primitive looking, with three seats in a row. The motor hood was open.

"Internal combustion," said Potter. "I had the idea that Mote Prime was short on fossil fuels."

"Sally had an idea on that too. Their civilization may have gone downhill when they used up all their fossil fuels. I wonder."

But the prize was behind a great glass picture window in one wall. They found themselves looking into the "steeple" past an ancient, ornately carved bronze plaque that had a smaller plaque on it.

Within the "steeple" was a rocket ship. Despite the holes in the sides and the corrosion everywhere, it still held its shape: a long, cylindrical tank, very thin-walled, with a cabin showing behind a smoothly pointed nose.

They made for the stairs. There must be another window on the first floor . . .

And there was. They knelt to look into the motor.

Potter said, "I don't quite . . ."

"NERVA style," said Whitbread. His voice was almost a whisper. "Atomic. Very early type. You send some inert fuel through a core of uranium or plutonium or the like. Fission pile, prefusion . . ."

"Are you sure?"

Whitbread looked again before he nodded. "I'm sure."

Fission had been developed after internal combustion; but there were still places in the Empire that employed internal combustion engines. Fission power was very nearly a myth, and as they stared the age of the place seemed to fall from the walls like a cloak and wrap them in silence.

The plane landed near the orange rags of a parachute and the remains of a cone. The open doorway was an accusing mouth just beyond.

Whitbread's Motie jumped from the plane and rushed over to the cone. She twittered, and the pilot bounded from the ship to join her. "They opened it," Whitbread's Motie said. "I never thought Jonathon would solve it. It must have been Potter. Horst, is there any chance at all they didn't go inside?"

Staley shook his head.

The Motie twittered to the Brown again. "Watch for aircraft, Horst," Whitbread's Motie said. She spoke to the other Brown-and-white, who left the airplane and stared at the skies.

The Brown picked up Whitbread's empty pressure suit

and armor. She worked rapidly, shaping something to take the place of the missing helmet and closing the suit top. Then she worked on the air regenerator, picking at the insides with tools from a belt pouch. The suit inflated and was set upright. Presently the Brown closed the panel and the suit was taut, like a man in vacuum. She tied lengths of line to constrict the shoulders and punched a hole at each wrist.

The empty man raised his arms to the sound of hissing air blowing out the wrist holes. The pressure dropped and the arms fell. Another spurt of hissing, and the arms rose again . . .

"That ought to do it," Whitbread's Motie said. "We set your suit up the same way, and raised the temperature to your body normal. With luck they may blast it without checking to see if you're in it."

"Blast it?"

"We sure can't count on it, though. I wish there were some way to make it fire on an aircraft . . ."

Staley shook the Motie's shoulder. The Brown stood by watching with the tiny half-smile that meant nothing at all. The equatorial sun was high overhead. "Why would anyone want to kill us?" Staley demanded.

"You're all under death sentence, Horst."

"But *why?* Is it the dome? Is there a taboo?"

"The dome, yes. Taboo, no. What do you take us for, primitives? You know too much, that's all. Dead you-name-its tell no tales. Now come on, we've got to find them and get out of here."

Whitbread's Motie stooped to get under the door. Needlessly: but Whitbread would have stooped. The other Brown-and-white followed silently, leaving the Brown standing outside, her face a perpetual gentle smile.

They saw the other midshipmen near the cathedral. Horst Staley's boots clumped hollowly as they approached. Whitbread looked up, noticed the Motie's walk, and said "Fyunch(click)?"

"Fyunch(click)."

"We've been exploring your—"

"Jonathon, we don't have time," the Motie said. The other Brown-and-white eyed them with an air of impatience.

"We're under a death sentence for trespassing." Staley said flatly. "I don't know why."

There was silence. Whitbread said, "Neither do I! This is nothing but a museum—"

"Yes," Whitbread's Motie said. "You *would* have to land *here*. It's not even bad luck. Your dumb animal miniatures must have programmed the reentry cones not to hit water or cities or mountain peaks. You were bound to come down in farm lands. Well, that's where we put museums."

"Out here? Why?" Potter asked. He sounded as if he already knew. "There are nae people here—"

"So they won't get bombed."

The silence was part of the age of the place. The Motie said, "Gavin, you aren't showing much surprise."

Potter attempted to rub his jaw. His helmet prevented it. "I don't suppose there's any chance of persuading you that we hae learned nothing?"

"Not really. You've been here three hours."

Whitbread broke in. "More like two. Horst, this place is fantastic! Museums within museums; it goes back incredibly far—is that the secret? That civilization is very old here? I don't see why you'd hide that."

"You've had a lot of wars," Potter said slowly.

The Motie bobbed her head and shoulder. "Yah."

"Big wars."

339

"Right. Also little wars."

"How many?"

"God's sake, Potter! Who counts? Thousands of Cycles. Thousands of collapses back to savagery. Crazy Eddie eternally trying to stop it. Well, I've had it. The whole decision-maker caste has turned Crazy Eddie, to my mind. They think they'll stop the pattern of Cycles by moving into space and settling other solar systems."

Horst Staley's tone was flat. As he spoke he looked carefully around the dome and his hand rested on his pistol butt. "Do they? And what is it we know too much of?"

"I'm going to tell you. And then I'm going to try to get you to your ship, alive—" She indicated the other Motie, who had stood impassively during the conversation. Whitbread's Motie whistled and hummed. "Best call her Charlie," she said. "You can't pronounce the name. Charlie represents a giver of orders who's willing to help you. Maybe. It's your only chance, anyway—"

"So what do we do now?" Staley demanded.

"We try to get to Charlie's boss. You'll be protected there. (Whistle, click, whistle.) Uh, call him King Peter. We don't have kings, but he's male now. He's one of the most powerful givers of orders, and after he talks to you he'll probably be willing to get you home."

"Probably," Horst said slowly. "Look, just what is this secret you're so afraid of?"

"Later. We've got to get moving."

Horst Staley drew his pistol. "No. Right now. Potter, is there anything in this museum that could communicate with *Lenin?* Find something."

"Aye aye—do ye think ye must hae the pistol?"

"Just find us a radio!"

"Horst, listen," Whitbread's Motie insisted. "The decision makers *know* you landed near here somewhere. If you try to communicate from here, they'll cut you off. And if you *do* get a message through, they'll destroy *Lenin.*" Staley tried to speak, but the Motie continued insistently. "Oh, yes, they can do it. It wouldn't be easy. That Field of yours is pretty powerful. But you've seen what our Engineers can come up with, and you've *never* seen what the *Warriors* can do. We've seen one of your best ships destroyed now. We know how it can be done. Do you think one little battleship can survive against fleets from both here and the asteroid stations?"

"Jesus, Horst, she may be right," Whitbread said.

"We've got to let the Admiral know." Staley seemed uncertain, but the pistol never wavered. "Potter, carry out your orders."

"You'll get a chance to call *Lenin* as soon as it's safe," Whitbread's Motie insisted. Her voice was almost shrill for a moment, then fell to a modulated tone. "Horst, believe me, it's the only way. Besides, you'll never be able to operate a communicator by yourself. You'll need our help, and we aren't going to help you do anything stupid. We've got to get *out* of here!"

The other Motie trilled. Whitbread's Motie answered, and they twittered back and forth. Whitbread's Motie translated. "If my own Master's troops don't get here, the Museum Keeper's Warriors will. I don't know where the Keeper stands on this. Charlie doesn't know either. Keepers are sterile, and they're not ambitious, but they're *very* possessive of what they already have."

"Will they bomb us?" Whitbread asked.

"Not as long as we're in here. It would wreck the museum, and museums are *important*. But the Keeper will send troops—if my own Master's don't get here first."

"Why aren't they here yet?" Staley demanded. "I don't hear anything."

"For God's sake, they may be coming already! Look, my Master—my old Master—won jurisdiction over human studies. She won't give that up, so she won't invite anybody else in. She'll try to keep the locals out of this, and since her holdings are around the Castle it'll take a while to get Warriors here. It's about two thousand kilometers."

"That plane of yours was a fast one," Staley said flatly.

"An emergency Mediator's vehicle. Masters forbid each other to use them. Your coming to our system almost started a war over jurisdiction anyway, and putting Warriors in one of those could certainly do it . . ."

"Don't your decision makers have any military planes at all?" Whitbread asked.

"Sure, but they're slower. They might drive you to cover anyway. There's a subway under this building—"

"Subway?" Staley said carefully. Everything was happening too fast. He was in command here, but he didn't know what to do.

"Of course. People do visit museums sometimes. And it'll take a while to get here by subway from the Castle. Who knows what the Keeper will be doing meantime? He might even forbid my Master's invasion. But if he does, you can be *sure* he'll kill you, to keep any other Masters from fighting here."

"Find anything, Gavin?" Staley shouted.

Potter appeared at the doorway of one of the modernistic glass-and-steel pillars. "Nothing I can operate as a communicator. Nothing I can even be sure is one. And this is all the newer stuff, Horst. Anything in the older buildings may be rusted through."

"Horst, we've got to get out of here!" Whitbread's Motie insisted again. "There's no time for talk—"

"Those Warriors could come in planes to the next station and then take the subway from there," Whitbread reminded them. "We'd better do *something*, Horst."

Staley nodded slowly. "All right. How do we leave? In your plane?"

"It won't hold all of us," Whitbread's Motie said. "But we can send two with Charlie and I could—"

"No." Staley's tone was decisive. "We stay together. Can you call a larger plane?"

"I can't even be sure that one would escape. You're probably right. It would be better to stay together. Well, there's nothing left but the subway."

"Which might be full of enemies right now." Staley thought for a moment. The dome was a bomb shelter and the mirror was a good defense against lasers. They could hole up here—but for how long? He began to feel the necessary paranoia of a soldier in enemy territory.

"Where do we have to go to get a message through to *Lenin?*" he demanded. That was obviously the first thing.

"King Peter's territory. It's a thousand kilometers, but that's the only place you could get equipment to send a message that couldn't be detected. Even that might not do it, but there's certainly nowhere else."

"And we can't go by plane—OK. Where's the subway? We'll have to set up an ambush."

"Ambush?" The Motie nodded agreement. "Of course. Horst, I'm not good at tactics. Mediators don't fight. I'm just trying to get you to Charlie's Master. *You'll* have to worry about them trying to kill us on the way. How good are your weapons?"

"Just hand weapons. Not very powerful."

"There are others in the museum. It's part of what museums are for. I don't know which ones still work."

"It's worth a try. Whitbread. Potter. Get to looking for weapons. Now where's that subway?"

The Moties looked around. Charlie evidently understood what was said, although she attempted no word of Anglic. They twittered for a moment, and Whitbread's Motie pointed. "In there." She indicated the cathedral-like building. Then she pointed at the statues of "demons" along the cornices. "Anything you see is harmless except those. They're the Warrior class, soldiers, bodyguards, police. They're killers, and they're *good* at it. If you see anything like that, run."

"Run, hell," Staley muttered. He clutched his pistol. "See you below," he called to the others. "Now what about your Brown?"

"I'll call her," Whitbread's Motie said. She trilled.

The Brown came inside carrying several somethings, which she handed to Charlie. The Moties inspected them for a moment, and Whitbread's Motie said, "You'll want these. Air filters. You can take off the helmets and wear these masks."

"Our radios—" Horst protested.

"Carry them. The Brown can work on the radios later, too. Do you really want your ears inside those damn helmets? The air bottles and filters can't last anyway."

"Thanks," Horst said. He took the filter and strapped it on. A soft cup covered his nose, and a tube led to a small cannister that attached to his belt. It was a relief to get the helmet off, but he didn't know what to do with it. Finally he tied it to his belt, where it bobbled along uncomfortably. "OK, let's get moving." It was easier to speak without the helmet, but he'd have to remember not to breathe through his mouth.

The ramp was a spiral leading down. Far down. Nothing moved in the shadowless lighting, but Staley pictured himself as a target to anyone below. He wished for grenades and a troop of Marines. Instead there was only himself and his two brother midshipmen. And the Moties. Mediators. "Mediators don't fight," Whitbread's Motie had said. Have to remember that. She acted so like Jonathon Whitbread that he had to count arms to be sure whom he was talking to, but she didn't fight. Browns didn't fight either.

He moved cautiously, leading the aliens down the spiral ramp with his pistol drawn. The ramp ended at a doorway and he paused for a moment. There was silence beyond it. Hell with it, he thought, and moved through.

He was alone in a wide cylindrical tunnel with tracks along the bottom and a smoothed ramp to one side. To his left the tunnel ended in a wall of rock. The other end seemed to stretch on forever into darkness. There were scars in the tunnel rock where ribs would have been in a giant whale.

The Motie came up behind him and saw where he was looking. "There was a linear accelerator here, before some rising civilization robbed it for metal."

"I don't see any cars. How do we get one?"

"I can call one. Any Mediator can."

"Not you, Charlie," Horst said. "Or do they know she's in the conspiracy too?"

"Horst, if we wait for a car, it'll be full of Warriors. The Keeper *knows* you opened his building. I don't know why his people aren't here yet. Probably a jurisdictional fight between him and my Master. Jurisdiction is a big thing with decision makers . . . and King Peter will be trying to keep things confused too."

"We can't escape by plane. We can't walk across the

fields. And we can't call a car," Staley said. "OK. Sketch
a subway car for me."

She drew it on Staley's hand computer screen. It was
a box on wheels, the universal space-filling shape of
vehicles that must hold as many as possible and must be
parked in limited space. "Motors here on the wheels. Controls
may be automatic—"

"Not on a war car."

"Controls here at the front, then. And the Browns and
Warriors may have made all kinds of changes. They do
that, you know . . ."

"Like armor. Armored glass and sides. Bow guns." The
three Moties stiffened and Horst listened. He heard
nothing.

"Footsteps," the Motie said, "Whitbread and Potter."

"Maybe." Staley moved catlike toward the entrance.

"Relax, Horst. I recognize the rhythms."

They had found weapons. "This one's the prize," said
Whitbread. He held up a tube with a lens in the business
end and a butt clearly meant for Motie shoulders. "I don't
know how long the power lasts, but it cut a hole all the
way through a thick stone wall. Invisible beam."

Staley took it. "That's what we need. Tell me about the
others later. Now get into the doorway and stay there."
Staley positioned himself where the passenger ramp ended,
just to one side of the tunnel entrance. Nothing would see
him until it was coming out of that tunnel. He wondered
how good Motie armor was. Would it stop an x-ray laser?
There was no sound, and he waited, impatiently.

This is silly, he told himself. But what else is there?
Suppose they come in planes and land outside the dome?
Should have closed the door and left somebody. Not too
late for that, either.

He started to turn toward the others behind him, but
then he heard it; a low humming from far down the track.
It actually relaxed him. There were no more choices to
make. Horst moved cautiously and took a better grip on
the unfamiliar weapon. The car was coming fast . . .

It was much smaller than Staley had expected: a toy of
a streetcar, whistling past him. Its wind buffeted his face.

The car stopped with a jerk, while Staley waved the gun like a magician's wand, back and forth across it. Was anything coming out the other side? No. The gun was working properly. The beam was invisible, but crisscross lines of red-hot metal lined the vehicle. He swiped the beam across the windows, where nothing showed, and along the roof, then stepped quickly out into the tunnel and fired down its length.

There was another car there. Staley ducked back to cover most of his body but continued to fire, aiming the gun at the oncoming car. How the hell would he know when the battery—or whatever it used for power—quit? A museum piece, for God's sake! The second car went past, and there were cherry-red lines across it. He swept the weapon along it, then stepped out to fire down the tunnel again. There was nothing there.

No third car. Good. Systematically he fired at the second car. Something had stopped it just behind the first —some kind of collision avoidance system? He couldn't know. He ran toward the two cars. Whitbread and Potter came out to join him.

"I told you to stay put!"

Whitbread said, "Sorry, Horst."

"This is a military situation, Mr. Whitbread. You can call me Horst when people aren't shooting at us."

"Yes, sir. I wish to point out that nobody has fired except you."

There was a smell from the cars: burning meat. The Moties came out from hiding. Staley carefully approached the cars and looked inside. "Demons," he said.

They examined the bodies with interest. Except for statues they'd never seen the type before. Compared to the Mediators and Engineers they seemed wire-thin and agile, like greyhounds next to pugs. The right arms were long, with short thick fingers and only one thumb; the other edge of the right hand was smooth with callus. The left arm was longer, with fingers like sausages. There was something under the left arm.

The demons had teeth, long and sharp, like true monsters from childhood books and half-forgotten legends.

Charlie twittered to Whitbread's Motie. When there was no answer she twittered again, more shrill, and waved at the Brown. The Engineer approached the door and began to examine it closely. Whitbread's Motie stood petrified, staring at the dead Warriors.

"Look out for booby traps!" Staley yelled. The Brown paid no attention and began to feel cautiously at the door. "Watch out!"

"They will have traps, but the Brown will see them," Charlie said very slowly. "I will tell her to be careful." The voice was precise and had no accent at all.

"You can talk," Staley said.

"Not well. It is difficult to think in your language."

"What's wrong with my Fyunch(click)?" Whitbread demanded.

Instead of answering, Charlie twittered again. The tones rose sharply. Whitbread's Motie seemed to jerk and turned toward them.

"Sorry," she said. "Those are my—Master's Warriors. Damn, damn, what am I doing?"

"Let's get in there," Staley said nervously. He raised his gun to cut through the side of the car. The Brown was still inspecting the door, very carefully, as if afraid of it.

"Allow me, sir." Whitbread must have been kidding. He was holding a thick-handled short sword. Horst watched him cut a square doorway in the metal side of the subway car with one continuous smooth, slow sweep of the blade. "It vibrates," he said. "I think."

A few smells got through their air filters. It must have been worse for the Moties, but they didn't seem to mind. They crawled inside the second car.

"You better look these over," Whitbread's Motie said. She sounded much better now. "Know your enemy." She twittered at the Brown, and it went to the controls of the car and examined them carefully, then sat in the driver's seat. She had to toss a Warrior out to do it.

"Have a look under the left arm," Whitbread's Motie said. "That's a second left arm, vestigial in most Motie subspecies. Only thing is, it's all one nail, like a—" She thought for a moment. "A hoof. It's a gutting knife. Plus enough muscle to swing it."

Whitbread and Potter grimaced. At Staley's direction they began to heave demon bodies out the hole in the side of the car. The Warriors were like twins of each other, all identical except for the cooked areas where the x-ray laser had swept through them. The feet were sheathed in sharp horn at toe and heel. One kick, backward or forward, and that would be all. The heads were small.

"Are they sentient?" Whitbread asked.

"By your standards, yes, but they aren't very inventive," Whitbread's Motie said. She sounded like Whitbread reciting lessons to the First Lieutenant, her voice very precise but without feelings. "They can fix any weapon that ever worked, but they don't tend to invent their own. Oh, and there's a Doctor form, a hybrid between the real Doctor and the Warrior. Semisentient. You should be able to guess what they look like. You'd better have the Brown look at any weapons you keep—"

Without warning the car began to move. "Where are we going?" Staley asked.

Whitbread's Motie twittered. It sounded a little like a mockingbird whistle. "That's the next city down the line . . ."

"They'll have a roadblock. Or an armed party waiting for us," Staley said. "How far is it?"

"Oh—fifty kilometers."

"Take us halfway and stop," Staley ordered.

"Yes, sir." The Motie sounded even more like Whitbread. "They've underestimated you, Horst. That's the only way I can explain this. I've never heard of a Warrior killed by anything but another Warrior. Or a Master, sometimes, not often. We fight the Warriors against each other. It's how we keep their population down."

"Ugh," Whitbread muttered. "Why not just—not breed them?"

The Motie laughed. It was a peculiarly bitter laugh, very human, and very disturbing. "Didn't any of you ever wonder what killed the Engineer aboard your ship?"

"Aye." "Of course." "Sure." They all answered together. Charlie twittered something.

"They may as well know," Whitbread's Motie said. "She died because there was nobody to get her pregnant." There was a long silence. "That's the whole secret. Don't you get it *yet?* Every variant of my species has to be made pregnant after she's been female for a while. Child, male, female, pregnancy, male, female, pregnancy, 'round and 'round. If she doesn't get pregnant in time, she dies. Even us. And we Mediators *can't* get pregnant. We're mules, sterile hybrids."

"But—" Whitbread sounded like a kid just told the truth about Santa. "How long do you live?"

"About twenty-five of your years. Fifteen years after maturity. But Engineers and Farmers and Masters—especially Masters!—have to be pregnant within a couple of our years. That Engineer you picked up must have been close to the deadline already."

They drove on in silence. "But—good Lord," Potter said carefully. "That's terrible."

" 'Terrible.' You son of a bitch. Of course it's terrible. Sally and her—"

"What's eating you?" Whitbread demanded.

"Birth control pills. We asked Sally Fowler what a human does when she doesn't want children just yet. She uses birth control pills. But nice girls don't use them. They just don't have sex," she said savagely.

The car was speeding down the tracks. Horst sat at the rear, which was now the front, staring out with his weapon poised. He turned slightly. The Moties were both glaring at the humans, their lips parted slightly to show teeth, enlarging their smile, but the bitterness of the words and tones belied the friendly looks. "They just don't have sex!" Whitbread's Motie said again. "Fyoofwuffle" (whistle)! "Now you know why we have wars. Always wars . . ."

"Population explosion," Potter said.

"Yeah. Whenever a civilization rises from savagery, Moties stop dying from starvation! You humans don't know what population pressure is! We can keep the numbers down in the lesser breeds, but what can the givers of orders do about their own numbers? The closest thing we've got to a birth control pill is infanticide!"

"And you can nae do that," Potter said. "Any such instinct would be bred out o' the race. So presently everyone is fighting for what food is left."

"Of course." Whitbread's Motie was calmer now. "The higher the civilization, the longer the period of savagery. And always there's Crazy Eddie in there pitching, trying to break the pattern of the Cycles, fouling things up worse. We're pretty close to a collapse now, gentlemen, in case you didn't notice. When you came there was a terrible fight over jurisdiction. My Master won——"

Charlie whistled and hummed for a second.

"Yeah. King Peter tried for that, but he couldn't get enough support. Wasn't sure he could win a fight with my Master. What we're doing now will probably cause that war anyway. It doesn't matter. It was bound to start soon."

"You're so crowded you grow plants on the rooftops," said Whitbread.

"Oh, that's just common sense. Like putting strips of cropland through the cities. Some always live, to start the Cycles over."

"It must be tough, carving out a civilization without even radioactives," said Whitbread. "You'd have to go direct to hydrogen fusion every time?"

"Sure. You're getting at something."

"I'm not sure what."

"Well, it's been that way for all of recorded history, a long time by your standards. Except for one period when they found radioactives in the Trojan asteroids. There were a few alive up there and they brought civilization here. The radioactives had been pretty thoroughly mined by some older civilization, but there were still some there."

"God's eyes," said Whitbread. "But——"

"Stop the car, please," Staley ordered. Whitbread's Motie twittered and the car came smoothly to a halt. "I'm getting nervous about what we're running into," Staley explained. "They *must* be waiting for us. Those soldiers we killed haven't reported in—and if those were *your* Master's men, where are the Keeper's? Anyway, I want to test the Warriors' weapons."

"Have the Brown look them over," Whitbread's Motie said. "They may be rigged."

They looked deadly, those weapons. And no two were identical. The most common type was a slug thrower, but there were also hand lasers and grenades. The butt of each weapon had been individualized. Some balanced only against the upper right shoulder, some squared against both. The gun sights differed. There were two left-handed models. Staley dimly remembered heaving out a left-handed body.

There was a rocket launcher with a fifteen-centimeter aperture. "Have her look at this," Staley said.

Whitbread's Motie handed the weapon to the Brown, accepting a slug thrower in return which she put under a bench. "This was rigged." The Brown looked at the rocket launcher and twittered. "OK," Whitbread's Motie said.

"How about the loads?" Staley passed them over. There were several different kinds, and none exactly alike. The Brown twittered again.

"The biggest rocket would explode if you tried to load it," Whitbread's Motie said. "They may have figured you right at that. Anyway, they certainly prepared enough traps. I've been assuming that the Masters think you're a kind of inept Mediator. It was what *we* thought, at first. But these traps mean they think you could kill Warriors."

"Great. I'd rather they thought we were stupid. We'd still be dead without the museum weapons. Come to that, why keep live guns in a museum?"

"You don't see the point of a museum, Horst. It's for the next rise in the Cycles. Savages come to put together another civilization. The faster they can do it, the longer it'll be before another collapse. because they'll be expanding their capabilities faster than the population. See? So the savages get their choice of a number of previous civilizations, and the weapons to put a new one into action. You noticed the lock?"

"No."

"I did," said Potter. "You need some astronomy to solve it. I presume that's to keep the savages from getting the goods before they're ready."

"Right." The Brown handed over a big-nosed rocket with a twitter. "She fixed this one. It's safe. What are you planning to do with it, Horst?"

"Pick me some more. Potter, you carry that x-ray laser. How close are we to the surface?"

"Oh. Hm. The"—Bird Whistle—"terminus is only one flight of stairs below the surface. The ground is pretty level in that region. I'd say we're three to ten meters underground."

"How close to other transportation?"

"An hour's walk to—" Bird Whistle. "Host, are you going to damage the tunnel? Do you know how long this subway has been in use?"

"No." Horst slid through the makeshift hatch in the side of the car. He walked a score of meters back the way they had come, then doubled that. The weapons could still be booby-trapped.

The tunnel was infinitely straight ahead of him. It must have been trued with a laser, then dug with something like a hot-rock boring machine.

Whitbread's Motie's voice carried down the tunnel. "Eleven thousand years!"

Staley fired.

The projectile touched the roof of the tunnel, far down. Horst curled up against the shock wave. When he raised his eyes there was considerable dirt in the tunnel.

He chose another projectile and fired it.

This time there was reddish daylight. He walked down to look at the damage. Yes, they could climb that slope.

Eleven thousand years.

"Send the car on without us," Horst said. Whitbread's Motie twittered and the Brown opened the control panel. She worked at blinding speed. Whitbread remembered a Brown asteroid miner who had lived and died eons ago, when *MacArthur* was home and Moties were a friendly, fascinating unknown.

The Brown leaped off. The car hesitated a second, then accelerated smoothly. They turned to the ramp Horst had created and climbed silently.

The world was all the shades of red as they emerged. Endless rows of crops were folding their leaves against the night. An irregular ring of plants leaned drunkenly around the hole.

Something moved among the plants. Three guns came up. The twisted thing plodded toward them . . . and Staley said, "At ease. It's a Farmer."

Whitbread's Motie moved up beside the midshipmen. She brushed dirt off her fur with all her hands. "There'll be more of those here. They may even try to smooth out the hole. Farmers aren't too bright. They don't have to be. What now, Horst?"

"We walk until we can ride. If you see planes—hmm."

"Infrared detectors," said the Motie.

"Do you have tractors in these fields? Could we grab one?" Staley asked.

"They'll be in the shed by now. They don't usually work in the dark . . . of course the Farmers may bring one to smooth out that hole."

Staley thought a moment. "Then we don't want one. Too conspicuous. Let's hope we look like Farmers on an infrared screen."

They walked. Behind them the Farmer began straightening plants and smoothing the soil around their roots. She twittered to herself, but Whitbread's Motie didn't translate. Staley idly wondered if Farmers ever *said* anything, or if they merely cursed, but he didn't want to talk just yet. He had to think.

The sky darkened. A red point glowed overhead: Murcheson's Eye. Ahead of them was the yellow city-glow of —Bird Whistle. They walked on in silence, the midshipmen alert, weapons ready, the Moties following with their torsos swiveling periodically.

By and by Staley said to the Motie, "I've been wondering what's in this for you."

"Pain. Exertion. Humiliation. Death."

"That's the point. I keep wondering why you came."

"No, you don't, Horst. You keep wondering why your Fyunch(click) didn't."

Horst looked at her. He *had* wondered that. What was his twin mind doing while demons hunted her own Fyunch(click) across a world? It brought dull pain.

"We're both duty oriented, Horst, your Fyunch(click) and I. But your Fyunch(click)'s duty is to her, let us say, her superior officer. Gavin—"

"Aye."

"I tried to talk your Fyunch(click) into coming down, but she's got this Crazy Eddie idea that we can end the Cycles by sending our surplus population to other stars. At least neither will help the others find us."

"Could they?"

"Horst, your Motie must know exactly where you are, assuming I got here; and she'll know that when she finds out about the dead Warriors."

"We'd better flip a coin the next time we get a choice. She can't predict *that*."

"She won't help. Nobody would expect a Mediator to help hunt down her own Fyunch(click)."

"But don't you *have* to obey your Master's orders?" Staley asked.

The Motie swiveled her body rapidly. It was a gesture they hadn't seen before, obviously not copied from anything human. She said, "Look. Mediators were bred to stop wars. We represent the decision makers. We speak for them. To do our job we have to have *some* independence of judgment. So the genetic engineers work at the balance.

Too much independence and we don't represent the Masters properly. We get repudiated. Wars start."

"Aye," Potter broke in. "And too little independence makes for inflexible demands, and you hae the wars anyway . . ." Potter trudged in silence for a moment. "But if obedience is a species-specific thing, then ye'll be unable simply to help us alone. Ye'll be taking us to another Master because ye hae nae choice."

Staley gripped the rocket launcher tighter. "Is this true?"

"Some," Whitbread's Motie admitted. "Not as completely as you think. But, yes, it's easier to choose among many orders than try to act with none at all."

"And what does King Peter believe should be done?" Staley demanded. "Just what are we walking into?"

The other Motie twittered. Whitbread's Motie answered. The conversation went on for many seconds, very long for Moties. The sunset light died, and Murcheson's Eye blazed a hundred times brighter than Earth's full Moon. There were no other stars in the Coal Sack. Around them the fields of plants were dark red, with sharp black shadows of infinite depth.

"Honesty," Charlie said at last. "My Master believes we must be honest with you. It is better to live by the ancient pattern of the Cycles than chance total destruction and the doom of all our descendants."

"But . . ." Potter stammered in confusion. "But why is it nae possible to colonize other stars? The Galaxy is big enough for all. You would nae attack the Empire?"

"No, no," Whitbread's Motie protested. "My own Master wants only to buy land as bases on Empire worlds, then move outside the Empire entirely. Eventually we'd be colonizing worlds around the edges of the Empire. There'd be commerce between us. I don't think we'd try to share the same planets."

"Then why—" Potter asked.

"I don't think you could build that many space craft," Whitbread interrupted.

"We'd build them on colony worlds and send them back," the Motie answered. "Hire commercial shipping from men like Bury. We could pay more than anyone else. But look—it couldn't last. The colonies would secede, so to speak. We'd have to start over with new colonies farther away. And on *every* world we settled there'd be population problems. Can you imagine what it would be like three hundred years from now?"

Whitbread tried. Ships like flying cities, millions of them. And Secession Wars, like the one that wrecked the First Empire. More and more Moties . . .

"Hundreds of Motie worlds, all trying to ship our expanding population out to newer worlds! Billions of Masters competing for territory and security! It takes *time* to use your Crazy Eddie Drive. Time and fuel to move around in each system looking for the next Crazy Eddie point. Eventually the outer edge of the Mote Sphere wouldn't be enough. We'd have to expand inward, into the Empire of Humanity."

"Um," said Whitbread. The others only looked at the Motie, then plodded onward toward the city. Staley held the big rocket launcher cradled in his arms, as if the bulk gave him comfort. Sometimes he put his hand to his holster to touch the reassuring butt of his own weapon as well.

"It'd be an easy decision to reach," Whitbread's Motie said. "There'd be jealousy."

"Of us? Of what? Birth control pills?"

"Yes."

Staley snorted.

"Even that wouldn't be the end. Eventually there would be a huge sphere of Motie-occupied systems. The center stars couldn't even *reach* the edge. They'd fight among themselves. Continual war, continually collapsing civilizations. I suspect a standard technique would be to drop an asteroid into an enemy sun and figure on resettling the planet when the flare dies down. And the sphere would keep expanding, leaving more systems in the center."

Staley said, "I'm not so sure you could whip the Empire."

"At the rate our Warriors breed? Oh, skip it. Maybe you'd wipe us out. Maybe you'd save some of us for zoos;

you sure wouldn't have to worry about us not breeding in captivity. I don't really care. There's a good chance we'd bring on a collapse just by converting too much of our industrial capacity to building space craft."

"If you're not planning war with the Empire," Staley said, "why are the three of us under death sentence?"

"Four. My Master wants my head as much as yours . . . well, maybe not. You'll be wanted for dissection."

Nobody showed surprise.

"You're under death sentence because you now have enough information to have worked this out yourselves, you and *MacArthur*'s biologists. A lot of the other Masters support the decision to kill you. They're afraid that if you escape now, your government will see us as a spreading plague, expanding through the Galaxy, eventually wiping out the Empire."

"And King Peter? He doesn't want us killed?" Staley asked. "Why not?"

The Moties twittered again. Whitbread's Motie spoke for the other one. "He may decide to kill you. I have to be honest about that. But he wants to put the djinn back in the bottle—if there's any way that humans and Moties can go back to where we were before you found our Crazy Eddie probe, he'll try it. The Cycles are better than—a whole Galaxy of Cycles!"

"And you?" Whitbread asked. "How do you see the situation?"

"As you do," the Motie said carefully. "I am qualified to judge my species dispassionately. I am not a traitor." There was a plea in the alien voice. "I am a judge. I judge that association between our species could only result in mutual envy, you for your birth control pills, us for our superior intelligence. Did you say something?"

"No."

"I judge that spreading my species across space would involve ridiculous risks and would not end the pattern of the Cycles. It would only make each collapse more terrible. We would breed faster than we could spread, until collapse came for hundreds of planets at a stroke, routinely . . ."

"But," said Potter, "ye've reached your dispassionate judgment by adopting our viewpoint—or rather, Whitbread's. You act so much like Jonathon the rest of us have to keep counting your arms. What will happen when you give up the human viewpoint? Might not your judgment—Ugh!"

The alien's left arm closed on the front of Potter's uniform, painfully tight, and drew him down until his nose was an inch from the Motie's sketched-in face. She said, "Never say that. Never think that. The survival of our civilization, any civilization, depends entirely on the justice of my class. We understand all viewpoints, and judge between them. If other Mediators come to a different conclusion from mine, that is their affair. It may be that their facts are incomplete, or their aims different. I judge on the evidence."

She released him. Potter stumbled backward. With the fingers of a right hand the Motie picked Staley's gunpoint out of her ear.

"That wasna' necessary," said Potter.

"It got your attention, didn't it? Come on, we're wasting time."

"Just a minute." Staley spoke quietly, but they all heard him easily in the night silence. "We're going to find this King Peter, who may or may not let us report to *Lenin*. That's not good enough. We've got to tell the Captain what we know."

"And how will you do that?" Whitbread's Motie asked. "I tell you, we won't help you, and you can't do it without us. I hope you don't have something stupid in mind, like threatening us with death? If that scared me, do you think I'd be *here?*"

"But—"

"Horst, get it through that military mind of yours that the *only* thing keeping *Lenin* alive is that my Master and King Peter agree on letting it live! My Master wants *Lenin* to go back with Dr. Horvath and Mr. Bury aboard. If we've analyzed you right, they'll be very persuasive. They'll argue for free trade and peaceful relationships with us—"

"Aye," Potter said thoughtfully. "And wi'out our message, there'll be nae opposition . . . why does this King Peter no call *Lenin* himsel'?"

Charlie and Whitbread's Motie twittered. Charlie answered. "He is not sure that the Empire will not come in strength to destroy the Mote worlds once you know the truth. And until he is sure . . ."

"How in God's name can he be sure of anything like that from talking to us?" Staley demanded. "I'm not sure myself. If His Majesty asked me, right now, I don't know what I'd advise—for God's sake, we're only three midshipmen from one battle cruiser. We can't speak for the Empire."

"Could we do it?" Whitbread asked. "I'm beginning to wonder if the Empire would be able to wipe you out . . ."

"Jesus, Whitbread," Staley protested.

"I mean it. By the time *Lenin* gets back and reports to Sparta, they'll have the Field. Won't you?"

Both Moties shrugged. The gestures were exactly alike —and exactly like Whitbread's shrug. "The Engineers will work on it now that they know it exists," Whitbread's Motie said. "Even without it, we've got some experience in space wars. Now come *on*. God's teeth, you don't know how close to war we are right now! If my Master thinks you've told all this to *Lenin* she'll order an attack on the ship. If King Peter isn't convinced there's a way to make you leave us alone, *he* might order it."

"And if we do no hurry, the Admiral will already hae taken *Lenin* back to New Caledonia," Potter added. "Mr. Staley, we hae nae choices at all. We find Charlie's Master before the other Masters find us. 'Tis as simple as that."

"Jonathon?" Staley asked.

"You want advice? Sir?" Whitbread's Motie clucked in disapproval. Jonathon Whitbread looked at her irritably, then grinned. "Yes, sir. I agree with Gavin. What else can we do? We can't fight a whole goddamn planet, and we're not going to build secure communications out of anything we'll find around here."

Staley lowered his weapon. "Right. Lead on, then." He

looked at his small command. "We're a damn sorry lot to be the ambassadors of the human race."

They struck out across the darkened fields toward the brightly lit city beyond.

37 • *History Lesson*

There was a three-meter-high wall around (Bird Whistle) city. It might have been stone, or a hard plastic; the structure was difficult to see in the red-black light of Murcheson's Eye. Beyond it they could see great oblong buildings. Yellow windows loomed over their heads.

"The gates will be guarded," Whitbread's Motie said.

"I'm sure," Staley muttered. "Does the Keeper live here too?"

"Yes. At the subway terminal. Keepers aren't allowed farm lands of their own. The temptation to exploit that kind of self-sufficiency might be too much even for a sterile male."

"But how do you get to *be* a Keeper?" Whitbread asked. "You're always talking about competition among Masters, but how do they compete?"

"God's eyes, Whitbread!" Staley exploded. "Look, what do we do about that wall?"

"We'll have to go through it," Whitbread's Motie said. She twittered to Charlie for a moment. "There are alarms and there'll be Warriors on guard."

"Can we go over it?"

"You'd pass through an x-ray laser, Horst."

"God's teeth. What are they so afraid of?"

"Food riots."

"So we go through it. Any one place better than another?"

The Moties shrugged with Whitbread's gestures. "Maybe half a kilometer farther. There's a fast road there."

They walked along the wall. "Well, how do they compete?" Whitbread insisted. "We've got nothing better to talk about."

Staley muttered something, but stayed close to listen.

"How do *you* compete?" Whitbread's Motie asked. "Efficiency. We have commerce, you know. Mr. Bury might be surprised at just how shrewd some of our Traders are. Partly, Masters buy responsibilities—that is, they show they can handle the job. They get other powerful givers of orders to support them. Mediators negotiate it. Contracts—promises of services to be delivered, that kind of thing—are drawn up and published. And some givers of orders work for others, you know. Never directly. But they'll have a job they take care of, and they'll consult a more powerful Master about policy. A Master gains prestige and authority when other givers of orders start asking her for advice. And of course her daughters help."

"It sounds complex," Potter said. "I think o' nae time or place similar in human history."

"It is complex," said Whitbread's Motie. "How could it be anything else? How can a decision maker be anything but independent? That's what drove Captain Blaine's Fyunch(click) insane, you know. Here was your Captain, Absolute Master on that ship—except that when whoever-it-was on *Lenin* croaked frog, Captain Blaine hopped around the bridge."

"Do you really talk about the Captain that way?" Staley asked Whitbread.

"I refuse to answer on the grounds that it might tend to get me dumped into the mass converter," Whitbread said. "Besides, we're coming to a bend in the wall . . ."

"About here, Mr. Staley," Whitbread's Motie said. "There's a road on the other side."

"Stand back." Horst raised the rocket launcher and fired. At the second explosion light showed through the wall. More lights rippled along its top. Some shone out into the fields, showing crops growing to the edge of the wall. "OK, get through fast," Staley ordered.

They went through the gap and onto a highway. Cars and larger vehicles whizzed past, missing them by centimeters as they cowered against the wall. The three Moties walked boldly into the road.

Whitbread shouted and tried to grab his Fyunch(click). She shook him off impatiently and strolled across the street. Cars missed her narrowly, cunningly dodging past the Moties without slowing at all.

On the other side the Brown-and-whites waved their left arms in an unmistakable sign: *Come on!*

Light poured through the gap in the wall. Something was out there in the fields where they'd been. Staley waved the others into the street and fired back through the gap. The rocket exploded a hundred meters away, and the light went out.

Whitbread and Potter walked across the highway. Staley loaded the last round into the rocket launcher, but saved it. Nothing was coming through the gap yet. He stepped out into the street and began to walk. Traffic whizzed past. The urge to run and dodge was overwhelming, but he moved slowly, at constant speed. A truck whipped past in a momentary hurricane. Then others. After a lifetime he reached the other side, alive.

No sidewalks. They were still in traffic, huddled against a grayish concrete-like wall.

Whitbread's Motie stepped into the street and gave a curious three-armed gesture. A long rectangular truck stopped with screeching brakes. She twittered to the drivers and the Browns immediately got out, went to the back of the truck, and began removing boxes from the cargo compartment. The traffic streamed past without slowing at all.

"That ought to do it," Whitbread's Motie said briskly. "The Warriors will be coming to investigate the hole in the wall—"

The humans got in quickly. The Brown who'd followed them patiently from the museum climbed into the right-hand driver's seat. Whitbread's Motie started for the other driver's seat, but Charlie twittered at her. The two Brown-and-whites whistled and chirped, and Charlie gestured vehemently. Finally Whitbread's Motie climbed into the cargo compartment and closed the doors. As she did the humans saw the original drivers walking slowly down the street away from the truck.

"Where are they going?" Staley asked.

"Better than that, what was the argument about?" Whitbread demanded.

"One at a time, gentlemen," Whitbread's Motie began. The truck started. It jolted hard, and there was humming from the motors and the tires. Sounds of myriads of other vehicles filtered in.

Whitbread was jammed between hard plastic boxes, with about as much room as a coffin. It reminded him unpleasantly of his situation. The others had no more room, and Jonathon wondered if they had thought of the analogy. His nose was only centimeters from the roof.

"The Browns will go to a transport pool and report that their vehicle was commandeered by a Mediator," Whitbread's Motie said. "And the argument was over who'd stay up front with the Brown. I lost."

"Why was it an argument?" Staley demanded. "Don't you trust each other?"

"I trust Charlie. She doesn't really trust me—I mean, how could she? I've walked out on my own Master. As far as she's concerned, I'm Crazy Eddie. Best to see to things herself."

"But where are we going?" Staley asked.

"To King Peter's territory. Best available way."

"We can't stay in this vehicle long," Staley said. "Once those Browns report, they'll be looking for it—you must have police. Some way to trace a stolen truck. You do have crime, don't you?"

"Not the way you think of it. There aren't really any laws—but there are givers of orders who have jurisdiction over missing property. They'll find the truck for a price. It'll take time for my Master to negotiate with them, though. First she'll have to show that I've gone insane."

"I don't suppose there's a space port here?" Whitbread asked.

"We couldn't use it anyway," Staley said flatly.

They listened to the hum of traffic for a while. Potter said, "I thought of that too. A space craft is conspicuous.

If a message would bring an attack on *Lenin,* 'tis certain we'd nae be allowed to return ourselves."

"And how are we going to get home?" Whitbread wondered aloud. He wished he hadn't asked.

" 'Tis a twice-told tale," Potter said unhappily. "We know aye more than can be allowed. And what we ken is more important than our lives, is it nae so, Mr. Staley?"

"Right."

"You never know when to give up, do you?" Whitbread's voice said from the dark. It took a moment for them to realize it was the Motie speaking. "King Peter may let you live. He may let you return to *Lenin.* If he's convinced that's best, he can arrange it. But there's no way you will send a message to that battleship without his help."

"The hell we won't," Staley said. His voice rose. "Get this through your ear flap. You've been square with us —I think. I'll be honest with you. If there's a way to get a message out, I'm going to send it."

"And after that, 'tis as God wills," Potter added.

They listened to the humming of the traffic. "You won't have the chance, Horst," Whitbread's voice said. "There's no threat you can make that would get Charlie or me to have a Brown build you the equipment you'd need. You can't use our transmitters if you could find one—even I couldn't use strange gear without a Brown to help. There might not even *be* the proper communications devices on this planet, for that matter."

"Come off it," Staley said. "You've got to have space communications, and there are only so many bands in the electromagnetic spectrum."

"Sure. But nothing stays idle here. If we need something, the Browns put it together. When it's not needed any more, they build something else out of the parts. And you want something that'll reach *Lenin* without letting anyone know you've done that."

"I'll take the chance. If we can broadcast a warning to the Admiral, he'll get the ship home." Horst was positive. *Lenin* might be only one ship, but President Class battle-wagons had defeated whole fleets before. Against Moties without the Field she'd be invincible. He wondered why he'd ever believed anything else. Back at the museum there'd been electronics parts, and they could have put together a transmitter of some kind. Now it was too late; why had he listened to the Motie?

They drove on for nearly an hour. The midshipmen were cramped, jammed between hard boxes, in the dark. Staley felt his throat tighten and was afraid to talk any more. There might be a catch in his voice, something to communicate his fears to the others, and he couldn't let them know he was as afraid as they were. He wished for something to happen, a fight, anything—

There were starts and stops. The truck jerked and turned, then came to a halt. They waited. The sliding door opened and Charlie stood framed in light.

"Don't move," she said. There were Warriors behind her, weapons ready. At least four.

Horst Staley growled in hatred. Betrayed! He reached for his pistol, but the cramped position prevented him from drawing it.

"No, Horst!" Whitbread's Motie shouted. She twittered. Charlie hummed and clacked in reply. "Don't do anything," Whitbread's Motie said. "Charlie has commandeered an aircraft. The Warriors belong to its owner. They won't interfere as long as we go straight from here to the plane."

"But who are they?" Staley demanded. He kept his grip on the pistol. The odds looked impossible—the Warriors were poised and ready, and they looked deadly and efficient.

"I told you," Whitbread's Motie said. "They're a bodyguard. All Masters have them. Nearly all, anyway. Now get out, slowly, and keep your hands off your weapons. Don't make them think you might try to attack their Master. If they get that idea, we're all dead."

Staley estimated his chances. Not good. If he had Kelley and another Marine instead of Whitbread and Potter— "OK," he said. "Do as she says." He climbed slowly out of the van.

They were in a luggage-handling area. The Warriors

stood in easy postures, leaning slightly forward on the balls of their wide, horned feet. It looked, Staley thought, like a karate stance. He caught a glimpse of motion near the wall. There were at least two more Warriors over there, under cover. Good thing he hadn't tried to fight.

The Warriors watched them carefully, falling in behind the strange procession of a Mediator, three humans, another Mediator, and a Brown. Their weapons were held at the ready, not quite pointing at anyone, and they fanned out, never bunching up.

"Will nae yon decision maker call your Master when we are gone?" Potter asked.

The Moties twittered together. The Warriors seemed to pay no attention at all. "Charlie says yes. She'll notify both my Master and King Peter. But it gets us an airplane, doesn't it?"

The decision maker's personal aircraft was a streamlined wedge attended by several Browns. Charlie twittered at them and they began removing seats, bending metal, working at almost blinding speed. Several miniatures darted through the plane. Staley saw them and cursed, but softly, hoping the Moties wouldn't know why. They stood waiting near the plane, and the Warriors watched them the whole time.

"I find this slightly unbelievable," said Whitbread. "Doesn't the owner *know* we're fugitives?"

Whitbread's Motie nodded. "But not *his* fugitives. He only runs the (Bird Whistle) airport baggage section. He wouldn't assume the prerogatives of my Master. He's also talked to the (Bird Whistle) airport manager, and they both agree they don't want my Master and King Peter fighting here. Best to have us all out of here, fast."

"Ye're the strangest creatures I hae ever imagined," Potter said. "I can no see why such anarchy does nae end in—" he stopped, embarrassed.

"It does," Whitbread's Motie said. "Given our special characteristics, it has to. But industrial feudalism works better than some things we've tried."

The Browns beckoned. When they entered the airplane there was a single Motie-shaped couch starboard aft.

Charlie's Brown went to it. Forward of that were a pair of human seats, then a human seat next to a Motie seat. Charlie and another Brown went through the cargo compartment to the pilot's section. Potter and Staley sat together without conversation, leaving Whitbread and his Motie side by side. It reminded the midshipman of a more pleasant trip that had not been very long ago.

The plane unfolded an unbelievable area of wing surface. It took off slowly, straight up. Acres of city dwindled beneath them, square kilometers of more city lights rose above the horizon. They flew over the lights, endless city stretching on and on with the great dark sweep of farm land falling far behind. Staley peered through the view port and thought he could see, away to the left, the edge of the city: beyond it was nothing, darkness, but level. More farm lands.

"You say every Master has Warriors," Whitbread said. "Why didn't we ever see any before?"

"There aren't any Warriors in Castle City," the Motie said with obvious pride.

"None?"

"None at all. Everywhere else, any holder of territory or important manager goes about with a bodyguard. Even the immature decision maker is guarded by his mother's troops. But the Warriors are too obviously what they are. My Master and the decision makers concerned with you and this Crazy Eddie idea got the others in Castle City to agree, so that you wouldn't know just how warlike we are."

Whitbread laughed. "I was thinking of Dr. Horvath."

His Motie chuckled. "He had the same idea, didn't he? Hide your paltry few wars from the peaceful Moties. They might be shocked. Did I tell you the Crazy Eddie probe started a war all by itself?"

"No. You haven't told us about any of your wars—"

"It was worse than that, actually. You can see the problem. Who gets put in charge of the launching lasers? Any Master or coalition of them will eventually use the lasers to take over more territory for his clan. If Mediators run the installation, some decision maker will take it away from them."

"You'd just give it up to the first Master who ordered you to?" Whitbread asked incredulously.

"For God's sake, Jonathon! Of course not. She'd have been ordered not to to begin with. But Mediators aren't good at tactics. We can't handle battalions of Warriors."

"Yet you govern the planet . . ."

"For the Masters. We have to. If the Masters meet to negotiate for themselves, it *always* ends up in a fight. Anyway. What finally happened was that a coalition of Whites was given command of the lasers and their children held as hostages on Mote Prime. They were all pretty old and had an adequate number of children. The Mediators lied to them about how much thrust the Crazy Eddie probe would need. From the Masters' point of view the Mediators blew up the lasers five years early. Clever, huh? Even so . . ."

"Even so, what?"

"The coalition managed to salvage a couple of lasers. They had Browns with them. They had to. Potter, you're from the system the probe was aimed at, aren't you? Your ancestors must have records of just how powerful those launching lasers were."

"Enough to outshine Murcheson's Eye. There was even a new religion started about them. We had our own wars, then—"

"They were powerful enough to take over civilization, too. What it amounts to is that the collapse came early that time, and we didn't fall all the way back to savagery. The Mediators must have planned it that way from the beginning."

"God's teeth," Whitbread muttered. "Do you always work that way?"

"What way, Jonathon?"

"Expecting everything to fall apart at any minute. *Using* the fact."

"Intelligent people do. Everyone but the Crazy Eddies. I think the classic case of the Crazy Eddie syndrome was that time machine. You saw it in one of the sculptures."

"Right."

"Some historian decided that a great turning point in history had come about two hundred years earlier. If he could interfere with that turning point, all of Motie history from that point on would be peaceful and idyllic. Can you believe it? And he could prove it, too. He had dates, old memoranda, secret treaties . . ."

"What was the event?"

"There was an—Emperor, a very powerful Master. All of her siblings had been killed and she inherited jurisdiction over an enormous territory. Her mother had persuaded the Doctors and Mediators to produce a hormone that must have been something like your birth control pills. It would stimulate a Master's body into thinking she was pregnant. Massive shots, and after that she would turn male. A sterile male. When her mother died, the Mediators had the hormone used on the Emperor."

"But you do have birth control pills then!" Whitbread said. "You can use them to control the population—"

"That's what this Crazy Eddie thought. Well, they used the hormone for something like three generations in the Empire. Stabilized the populations, all right. Not very many Masters there. Everything peaceful. Meanwhile, of course, the population explosion was happening on the other continents. The other Masters got together and invaded the Emperor's territory. They had plenty of Warriors—and plenty of Masters to control them. End of Empire. Our time machine builder had the idea she could set things up so that the Empire would control all of Mote Prime." Whitbread's Motie snorted in disgust. "It never works. How are you going to get the Masters to become sterile males? Sometimes it happens anyway, but who'd want to before having children? That's the only time the hormone can work."

"Oh."

"Right. Even if the Emperor *had* conquered all of Mote Prime and stabilized the population—and think about it, Jonathon, the only way to do that would be for the rulers to pass control on to breeders while never having any children themselves—even if they did, they'd have been attacked by the asteroid civilizations."

"But *man,* it's a *start!*" said Whitbread. "There's got to be a way—"

"I am not a man, and there doesn't got to be a way. And that's another reason I don't want contact between your species and mine. You're *all* Crazy Eddies. You think every problem has a solution."

"All human problems hae at least one final solution," Gavin Potter said softly from the seat behind them.

"Human, perhaps," the alien said. "But do Moties have souls?"

" 'Tis nae for me to say," Potter answered. He shifted uncomfortably in his seat. "I am no a spokesman for the Lord."

"It isn't for your chaplain to say either. How can you expect to find out? It would take revealed knowledge—a divine inspiration, wouldn't it? I doubt if you'll get it."

"Hae ye nae religion at all, then?" Potter asked incredulously.

"We've had thousands, Gavin. The Browns and other semisentient classes don't change theirs much, but every civilization of Masters produces something else. Mostly they're variants of transmigration of souls, with emphasis on survival through children. You can see why."

"You didn't mention Mediators," Whitbread said.

"I told you—we don't have children. There are Mediators who accept the transmigration idea. Reincarnation as Masters. That sort of thing. The closest thing to ours I've heard of in human religions is Lesser-Way Buddhism. I talked to Chaplain Hardy about this. He says Buddhists believe they can someday escape from what they call the Wheel of Life. That sounds an awful lot like the Cycles. I don't know, Jonathon. I used to think I accepted reincarnation, but—there's no knowing, is there?"

"And you hae nothing like Christianity?" Potter demanded.

"No. We've had prophecies of a Savior who'd end the Cycles, but we've had *everything,* Gavin. It's for damn sure there's been no Savior yet."

The endless city unrolled beneath them. Presently Potter leaned back in his chair and began to snore softly. Whitbread watched in amazement.

"You should sleep too," said the Motie. "You've been up too long."

"I'm too scared. You tire easier than we do—you ought to sleep."

"I'm too scared."

"Brother, now I'm really scared." Did I really call him brother? No, I called *her* brother. Hell with it. "There was more to your museum of art than we understood, wasn't there?"

"Yeah. Things we didn't want to go into detail about. Like the massacre of the Doctors. A very old event, almost legend now. Another Emperor, sort of, decided to wipe the entire Doctor breed off the planet. Damn near succeeded, too." The Motie stretched. "It's *good* to talk to you without having to lie. We weren't made to lie, Jonathon."

"Why kill off the Doctors?"

"To keep the population down, you idiot! Of course it didn't work. Some Masters kept secret stables, and after the next collapse they—"

"—were worth their weight in iridium."

"It's thought that they actually became the foundation of commerce. Like cattle on Tabletop."

The city fell behind at last, and the plane moved over oceans dark beneath the red light of Murcheson's Eye. The red star was setting, glowing balefully near the horizon, and other stars rose in the east below the inky edge of the Coal Sack.

"If they're going to shoot us down, this is the place," Staley said. "Where the crash won't hit anything. Are you sure you know where we're going?"

Whitbread's Motie shrugged. "To King Peter's jurisdiction. If we can get there." She looked back at Potter. The midshipman was curled into his seat, his mouth slightly open, gently snoring. The lights in the plane were dim and everything was peaceful, the only jarring note the rocket launcher that Staley clutched across his lap. "You ought to get some sleep too."

"Yeah." Horst leaned back in the chair and closed his eyes. His hands never relaxed their tight grip on the weapon.

"He even sleeps at attention," Whitbread said. "Or tries to. I guess Horst is as scared as we are."

"I keep wondering if any of this does any good," the alien said. "We're damned close to falling apart anyway. You missed a couple of other things in that zoo, you know. Like the food beast. A Motie variant, almost armless, unable to defend itself against us but pretty good at surviving. Another of our relatives, bred for meat in a shameful age, a long time ago . . ."

"My God." Whitbread took a deep breath. "But you wouldn't do anything like that now."

"Oh, no."

"Then why bring it up?"

"A mere statistical matter, a coincidence you may find interesting. There isn't a zoo on the planet that doesn't have breeding stock of Meats. And the herds are getting larger . . ."

"God's teeth! Don't you ever stop thinking about the next collapse?"

"No."

Murcheson's Eye had long since vanished. Now the east was blood-red in a sunrise that still startled Whitbread. Red sunrises were rare on inhabitable worlds. They passed over a chain of islands. Ahead to the west lights glowed where it was still dark. There was a cityscape like a thousand Spartas set edge to edge, crisscrossed everywhere by dark strips of cultivated land. On man's worlds they would be parks. Here they were forbidden territory, guarded by twisted demons.

Whitbread yawned and looked at the alien beside him. "I think I called you brother, some time last night."

"I know. You meant sister. Gender is important to us, too. A matter of life and death."

"I'm not sure I mean that either. I meant friend," Whitbread said with some awkwardness.

"Fyunch(click) is a closer relationship. But I am glad to be your friend," said the Motie. "I wouldn't have given up the experience of knowing you."

The silence was embarrassing. "I better wake up the others," Whitbread said softly.

The plane banked sharply and turned northwards. Whitbread's Motie looked out at the city below, across to the other side to be sure of the location of the sun, then down again. She got up and went forward into the pilot's compartment, and twittered. Charlie answered and they twittered again.

"Horst," Whitbread said. "Mr. Staley. Wake up."

Horst Staley had forced himself to sleep. He was still as rigid as a statue, the rocket launcher across his lap, his hands gripping it tightly. "Yeah?"

"I don't know. We changed course, and now—listen," Whitbread said. The Moties were still chattering. Their voices grew louder.

38 • *Final Solution*

Whitbread's Motie came back to her seat. "It's started," she said. She didn't sound like Whitbread now. She sounded like an alien. "War."

"Who?" Staley demanded.

"My Master and King Peter. The others haven't joined in yet, but they will."

"War over us?" Whitbread asked incredulously. He was ready to cry. The transformation in his Fyunch(click) was too much to bear.

"Over jurisdiction over you," the Motie corrected. She shivered, relaxed, and suddenly Whitbread's voice spoke to them from the half-smiling alien lips. "It's not too bad yet. Just Warriors, and raids. Each one wants to show the other what she *could* do, without destroying anything really valuable. There'll be a lot of pressure from the other decision makers to keep it that way. They don't want to be in a fallout pattern."

"God's teeth," said Whitbread. He gulped. "But—welcome back, brother."

"Where does that leave us?" Staley demanded. "Where do we go now?"

"A neutral place. The Castle."

"Castle?" Horst shouted. "That's your Master's territory!" His hand was very near his pistol again.

"No. Think the others would give my Master *that* much control over you? The Mediators you met were all part of my clan, but the Castle itself belongs to a sterile male decision maker. A Keeper."

Staley looked distrustful. "What do we do once we're there?"

The Motie shrugged. "Wait and see who wins. If King Peter wins, he's going to send you back to *Lenin*. Maybe this war will convince the Empire that it's better to leave us alone. Maybe you can even help us." The Motie gestured disgustedly. "Help us. He's Crazy Eddie too. There'll never be an end to the Cycles."

"Wait?" Staley muttered. "Not me, damn it. Where is this Master of yours?"

"*No!*" the Motie shouted. "Horst, I *can't* help you with something like that. Besides, you'd never get past the Warriors. They're *good,* Horst, better than your Marines; and what are you? Three junior officers with damn little experience and some weapons you got from an old museum."

Staley looked below. Castle City was ahead. He saw the space port, an open space among many, but gray, not green. Beyond it was the Castle, a spire circled by a balcony. Small as it was, it stood out among the industrial ugliness of the endless cityscape.

There was communications gear in their baggage. When Renner and the others came up, the Sailing Master had left everything but their notes and records in the Castle. He hadn't said why, but now they knew: he wanted the Moties to think they would return.

There might even be enough to build a good transmitter. Something that would reach *Lenin*. "Can we land in the street?" Staley asked.

"In the street?" The Motie blinked. "Why not? If Charlie agrees. This is her aircraft." Whitbread's Motie trilled. There were answering hums and clicks from the cockpit.

"You're sure the Castle is safe?" Staley asked. "Whitbread, do you trust the Moties?"

"I trust this one. But I may be a little prejudiced, Hor—Mr. Staley. You'll have to make your own judgment."

"Charlie says the Castle is empty, and the ban on Warriors in Castle City still holds," Whitbread's Motie said. "She also says King Peter's winning, but she's only hearing reports from her side."

"Will she land next to the Castle?" Staley asked.

"Why not? We have to buzz the street first, to warn the Browns to look up." The Motie trilled again.

The grumble of motors died to a whisper. Wings spread again, and the plane dipped lower, falling almost straight down to pull level with a swoop. It whizzed past the Castle, giving them a view of its balconies. Traffic moved below, and Staley saw a White on the pedestrian walkway across from the Castle. The Master ducked quickly into a building.

"No demons," Staley said. "Anybody see Warriors?"

"No." "Nae." "Me neither."

The plane banked sharply and fell again. Whitbread stared wide-eyed at the hard concrete sides of skyscrapers whipping past. They watched for Whites—and Warriors—but saw neither.

The plane slowed and leveled off two meters above the ground. They glided toward the Castle like a gull above waters. Staley braced himself at the windows and waited. Cars came at them and swerved around.

They were going to *hit* the Castle, he realized. Was the Brown trying to ram their way through like the cutter into *MacArthur?* The plane dropped joltingly and surged against brakes and thrust reversers. They were just beneath the Castle wall.

"Here, trade with me, Potter." Staley took the x-ray laser. "Now move out." The door wouldn't work for him and he waved at the Motie.

She threw the door wide. There was a two-meter space between wingtip and wall, making twenty-five meters in all. That wing of the aircraft had folded somehow. The Motie leaped into the street.

The humans dashed after her, with Whitbread carrying the magic sword in his left hand. The door might be locked, but it would never stand up to *that*.

The door was locked. Whitbread hefted the sword to hew through it, but his Motie waved him back. She examined a pair of dials set in the door, took one in each of the right hands, and as she twirled them turned a lever with her left arm. The door opened smoothly. "Meant to keep humans out," she said.

The entryway was empty. "Any way to barricade that damn door?" Staley asked. His voice sounded hollow, and he saw that the furnishings were gone from the room. When there was no answer, Staley handed Potter the x-ray laser. "Keep guard here. You'll need the Moties to tell if someone coming through is an enemy. Come on, Whitbread." He turned and ran for the stairs.

Whitbread followed reluctantly. Horst climbed rapidly, leaving Whitbread out of breath when they reached the floor where their rooms were. "You got something against elevators?" Whitbread demanded. "Sir?"

Staley didn't answer. The door to Renner's room stood open, and Horst dashed inside. "God damn!"

"What's the matter?" Whitbread panted. He went through the door.

The room was empty. Even the bunks were removed. There was no sign of the equipment Renner had left behind. "I was hoping to find something to talk to *Lenin* with," Staley growled. "Help me look. Maybe they stored our stuff in here somewhere."

They searched, but found nothing. On every floor it was the same: fixtures, beds, furniture, everything removed. The Castle was a hollow shell. They went back downstairs to the entryway.

"Are we alone?" Gavin Potter asked.

"Yeah," Staley replied. "And we'll starve pretty bloody quick if nothing worse. The place has been stripped."

Both Moties shrugged. "I'm a little surprised," Whitbread's Motie said. The two Moties twittered for a moment. "She doesn't know why either. It looks like the place won't be used again—"

"Well, they damn well know where we are," Staley growled. He took his helmet from his belt and connected the leads to his radio. Then he put the helmet on. *"Lenin, this is Staley. Lenin, Lenin, Lenin,* this is Midshipman Staley. Over."

"Mr. Staley, where in hell are you?" It was Captain Blaine.

"Captain! Thank God! Captain, we're holed up in— Wait one moment, sir." The Moties were twittering to each other. Whitbread's Motie tried to say something, but Staley didn't hear it. What he heard was a Motie speaking with Whitbread's voice— "Captain Blaine, sir. Where do you get your Irish Mist? Over."

"Staley, cut the goddamn comedy and report! Over."

"Sorry, sir. I really must know. You'll understand why I ask. Where do you get your Irish Mist? Over."

"Staley! I'm tired of the goddamn jokes!"

Horst took the helmet off. "It isn't the Captain," he said. "It's a Motie with the Captain's voice. One of yours?" he asked Whitbread's Motie.

"Probably. It was a stupid trick. Your Fyunch(click) would have known better. Which means she's not cooperating with my Master too well."

"There's no way to defend this place," Staley said. He looked around the entryway. It was about ten meters by thirty, and there was no furniture at all. The hangings and pictures which adorned the walls were gone. "Upstairs," Horst said. "We've got a better chance there." He led them back up to the living quarters floor, and they took positions at the end of the hall where they could cover the stairwell and elevator.

"Now what?" Whitbread asked.

"Now we wait," both Moties said in unison. A long hour passed.

The traffic sounds died away. It took them a minute to notice, then it was obvious. Nothing moved outside.

"I'll have a look," Staley said. He went to a room and peered carefully out the window, standing well inside so that he wouldn't expose himself.

Demons moved on the street below. They came forward in a twisting, flickering quick run, then suddenly raised their weapons and fired down the street. Horst turned and saw another group melting for cover; they left a third of their number dead. Battle sounds filtered through the thick windows.

"What is it, Horst?" Whitbread called. "It sounds like shots."

"It is shots. Two groups of Warriors in a battle. Over us?"

"Certainly," Whitbread's Motie answered. "You know what this means, don't you?" She sounded very resigned. When there was no answer she said, "It means the humans won't be coming back. They're gone."

Staley cried, "I don't believe it! The Admiral wouldn't leave us! He'd take on the whole damn planet—"

"No, he wouldn't, Horst," Whitbread said. "You know his orders."

Horst shook his head, but he knew Whitbread was right. He called, "Whitbread's Motie! Come here and tell me which side is which."

"No."

Horst looked around. "What do you mean, no? I need to know who to shoot at!"

"I don't want to get shot."

Whitbread's Motie was a coward! "I haven't been shot, have I? Just don't expose yourself."

Whitbread's voice said, "Horst, if you've exposed an eye, any Warrior could have shot it out. Nobody wants you dead now. They haven't used artillery, have they? But they'd shoot *me*."

"*All* right. Charlie! Come here and—"

"I will not."

Horst didn't even curse. Not cowards, but Brown-and-whites. Would his own Motie have come?

The demons had all found cover: cars parked or abandoned, doorways, the fluting along the sides of one building. They moved from cover to cover with the flickering speed of houseflies. Yet every time a Warrior fired, a Warrior died. There had not been all that much gunfire, yet two thirds of the Warriors in sight were dead. Whitbread's Motie had been right about their marksmanship. It was inhumanly accurate.

Almost below Horst's window, a dead Warrior lay with its right arms blown away. A live one waited for a lull, suddenly broke for closer cover—and the fallen one came to life. Then it happened too fast to follow: the gun flying, the two Warriors colliding like a pair of buzz saws, then flying away, broken dolls still kicking and spraying blood.

Something crashed below. There were sounds in the stairwell. Hooves clicked on marble steps. The Moties twittered. Charlie whistled, loudly, and again. There was an answering call from below, then a voice spoke in David Hardy's perfect Anglic.

"You will not be mistreated. Surrender at once."

"We've lost," Charlie said.

"My Master's troops. What will you do, Horst?"

For answer Staley crouched in a corner with the x-ray rifle aimed at the stairwell. He waved frantically at the other midshipmen to take cover.

A brown-and-white Motie turned the corner and stood in the hallway. It had Chaplain Hardy's voice, but none of his mannerisms. Only the perfect Anglic, and the resonant tones. The Mediator was unarmed. "Come now, be reasonable. Your ship has gone. Your officers believe you are dead. There is no reason to harm you. Don't get your friends killed over nothing, come out and accept our friendship."

"Go to hell!"

"What can you gain by this?" the Motie asked. "We only wish you well—"

There were sounds of firing from below. The shots rebounded through the empty rooms and hallways of the Castle. The Mediator with Hardy's voice whistled and clicked to the other Moties.

"What's she saying?" Staley demanded. He looked around: Whitbread's Motie was crouched against the wall, frozen. "Jesus, now what?"

"Leave her alone!" Whitbread shouted. He moved from his post to stand beside the Motie and put his arm on her shoulder. "What should we do?"

The battle noises moved closer, and suddenly two demons were in the hallway. Staley aimed and fired in a smooth motion, cutting down one Warrior. He began to swing the beam toward the other. The demon fired, and Staley was flung against the far wall of the corridor. More demons bounded into the hallway, and there was a burst of fire that held Staley upright for a second. His body was chewed by dragon's teeth, and he fell to lie very still.

Potter fired the rocket launcher. The shell burst at the end of the hallway. Part of the walls fell in, littering the floor with rubble and partly burying the Mediator and Warriors.

"It seems to me that no matter who wins yon fight below, we know aye more about the Langston Field than is safe," Potter said slowly. "What do ye think, Mr. Whitbread? 'Tis your command now."

Jonathon shook himself from his reverie. His Motie was stock-still, unmoving—

Potter drew his pistol and waited. There were scrabbling sounds in the hallway. The sounds of battle died away.

"Your friend is right, brother," Whitbread's Motie said. She looked at the unmoving form of Hardy's Fyunch-(click). "That one was a brother too . . ."

Potter screamed. Whitbread jerked around.

Potter stood unbelieving, his pistol gone, his arm shattered from wrist to elbow. He looked at Whitbread with eyes dull with just realized pain and said, "One of the dead ones threw a rock."

There were more Warriors in the hall, and another Mediator. They advanced slowly.

Whitbread swung the magic sword that would cut stone and metal. It came up in a backhanded arc and cut through Potter's neck—Potter, whose religion forbade suicide, as did Whitbread's. There was a burst of fire as he swung the blade at his own neck, and two clubs smashed at his shoulders. Jonathon Whitbread fell and did not move.

They did not touch him at first except to remove the weapons from his belt. They waited for a Doctor, while the rest held off King Peter's attacking forces. A Mediator spoke quickly to Charlie and offered a communicator—there was nothing left to fight for. Whitbread's Motie remained by her Fyunch(click).

The Doctor probed at Whitbread's shoulders. Although she had never had a human to dissect, she knew everything any Motie knew about human physiology, and her hands were perfectly formed to make use of a thousand Cycles of instincts. The fingers moved gently to the pulverized shoulder joints, the eyes noted that there was no spurting blood. Hands touched the spine, that marvelous organ she'd known only through models.

The fragile neck vertebrae had been snapped. "High-velocity bullets," she hummed to the waiting Mediator. "The impact has destroyed the notochord. This creature is dead."

The Doctor and two Browns worked frantically to build a blood pump to serve the brain. It was futile. The communication between Engineer and Doctor was too slow, the body was too strange, and there was too little equipment in time.

They took the body and Whitbread's Motie to the space port controlled by their Master. Charlie would be returned to King Peter, now that the war was finished. There were payments to be made, work in cleaning up after the battle, every Master who had been harmed to be satisfied; when next the humans came, there must be unity among Moties.

The Master never knew, nor did her white daughters ever suspect. But among her other daughters, the brown-

and-white *Mediators* who served her, it was whispered that one of their sisters had done that which no *Mediator* had ever done throughout all the Cycles. As the *Warriors* hurried toward this strange human, Whitbread's Motie had touched it, not with the gentle right hands, but with the powerful left.

She was executed for disobedience; and she died alone. Her sisters did not hate her, but they could not bring themselves to speak to one who had killed her own Fyunch-(click).

PART FOUR

CRAZY EDDIE'S ANSWER

39 • *Departure*

"Boats report no trace of our midshipmen, my Admiral." Captain Mikhailov's tone was both apologetic and defensive; few officers wanted to report failure to Kutuzov. The burly Admiral sat impassively in his command chair on *Lenin*'s bridge. He lifted his glass of tea and sipped, his only acknowledgment a brief grunt.

Kutuzov turned to the others grouped around him at staff posts. Rod Blaine still occupied the Flag Lieutenant's chair; he was senior to Commander Borman, and Kutuzov was punctilious about such matters.

"Eight scientists," Kutuzov said. "Eight scientists, five officers, fourteen spacers and Marines. All killed by Moties."

"Moties!" Dr. Horvath swiveled his command chair toward Kutuzov. "Admiral, nearly all those men were aboard *MacArthur* when you destroyed her. Some might still have been alive. As for the midshipmen, if they were foolish enough to try to land with lifeboats . . ." His voice trailed off as Rod turned dead eyes toward him. "Sorry, Captain. I didn't mean it that way. Truly, I am sorry. I liked those boys too. But you can't blame the Moties for what happened! The Moties have tried to help, and they can do so much for us—Admiral, when can we get back to the embassy ship?"

Kutuzov's explosive sound might have been a laugh. "Hah! Doctor, we are going home as soon as boats are secured. I thought I had made that clear."

The Science Minister pressed his lips tightly against his wide teeth. "I was hoping that you had regained your sanity." His voice was a cold, feral snarl. "Admiral, you are ruining the best hopes mankind ever had. The technology we can buy—that they'll give us!—is orders of magnitude above anything we could expect for centuries. The Moties have gone to enormous expense to make us welcome. If you hadn't forbidden us to tell them about the escaped miniatures I'm sure they'd have helped. But you had to keep your damned secrets—and because of your stupid xenophobia we lost the survey ship and most of our instruments. Now you antagonize them by going home when they planned more conferences— My God, man, if they were warlike nothing could provoke them as you have!"

"You are finished?" Kutuzov asked contemptuously.

"I'm finished for now. I won't be finished when we get back."

Kutuzov touched a button on the arm of his chair. "Captain Mikhailov, please make ready for departure to the Alderson entry point. One and one-half gravities, Captain."

"Aye aye, sir."

"You are determined to be a damn fool, then," Horvath protested. "Blaine, can't you reason with him?"

"I am determined to carry out my orders, Doctor," Kutuzov said heavily. If Horvath's threats meant anything to him, he didn't show it. The Admiral turned to Rod. "Captain, I will welcome your advice. But I will do nothing to compromise safety of this ship, and I cannot allow further personal contact with Moties. Have you suggestions, Captain Lord Blaine?"

Rod had listened to the conversation without interest, his thoughts a confused blur. What could I have done? he asked himself endlessly. There was nothing else to concern him. The Admiral might ask his advice, but that was courtesy. Rod had no command and no duties. His ship was lost, his career finished— Brooding in self-pity wasn't doing any good, though. "I do think, sir, that we should try to keep the Moties' friendship. We shouldn't make the Government's decisions . . ."

"You are saying I do that?" Kutuzov demanded.

"No, sir. But it is likely the Empire will want to trade with the Mote. As Dr. Horvath says, they have done nothing hostile."

"What of your midshipmen?"

Rod swallowed hard. "I don't know, sir. Possibly Potter or Whitbread weren't able to control their lifeboats and Staley tried a rescue. It would be like him—"

Kutuzov scowled. "Three lifeboats, Captain. All three reenter, and all three burn." He examined the displays around him. A boat was being winched into *Lenin's* hangar deck, where Marines would flood it with poison gas. No aliens would get loose in *his* flagship! "What would you like to say to Moties, Doctor?"

"I won't tell them what I'd *like* to say, Admiral," Horvath said pointedly. "I will stay with your story of plague. It's almost true, isn't it? A plague of miniatures. But, Admiral, we must leave open the possibility of a returning expedition."

"They will know you lie to them," Kutuzov said flatly. "Blaine, what of that? Is better Moties hear explanations they do not believe?"

Damn it, doesn't he know I don't want to think about Moties? Or anything else? What good is my advice? Advice from a man who lost his ship— "Admiral, I don't see what harm it would do to let Minister Horvath speak to the Moties," Rod emphasized "Minister"; not only was Horvath a ranking Council Minister, but he had powerful connections with the Humanity League, and influence in the Imperial Traders' Association as well. That combination had nearly as much clout as the Navy. "Somebody ought to talk to them, it doesn't matter much who. There's not a man aboard who can lie to his Fyunch(click)."

"Very well. Da. Captain Mikhailov, please have communications call Mote embassy ship. Dr. Horvath will speak to them."

The screens lit to show a brown-and-white half-smiling face. Rod grimaced, then glanced up quickly to confirm that his own image pickup wasn't on.

The Motie looked at Horvath. "Fyunch(click)."

"Ah. I was hoping to speak to you. We are leaving now. We must."

The Motie's expression didn't change. "That seemed obvious, but we are very distressed, Anthony. We have much more to discuss, trade agreements, rental of bases in your Empire—"

"Yes, yes, but we haven't the authority to sign treaties or trade agreements," Horvath protested. "Really, we did accomplish a lot, and now we *have* to go. There was plague on *MacArthur,* something new to our doctors, and we don't know the focal infection center or the vector. And since this ship is our only way home, the Ad—our decision makers think it best we leave while there is a full astrogation crew. We'll be back!"

"Will you come yourself?" the Motie asked.

"If at all possible. I'd love to." He had no trouble sounding sincere about *that.*

"You will be welcome. All humans will be welcome. We have great hopes for trade between our races, Anthony. There is much we can learn from each other. We have gifts as well—can you not take them on your ship?"

"Why, thank you—I—" Horvath looked at Kutuzov. The Admiral was about to explode. He shook his head violently.

"It would not be wise," Horvath said sadly. "Until we know what caused the plague, it is best we add nothing we have not already been exposed to. I'm very sorry."

"So am I, Anthony. We have noted that your engineers are—how can I put this delicately? Are not so advanced as ours in many ways. Underspecialized, perhaps. We have thought partially to remedy this with our gifts."

"I—excuse me a moment," Horvath said. He turned to Kutuzov after switching off the sound pickup. "Admiral, you cannot refuse such an opportunity! This may be the most significant event in the history of the Empire!"

The Admiral nodded slowly. His dark eyes narrowed. "It is also true that Moties in possession of Langston Field and Alderson Drive may be most significant threat in history of human race, Minister Horvath."

"I'm aware of it," Horvath snapped. He turned the sound pickup on. "I am afraid that—"

The Motie interrupted. "Anthony, can you not inspect our gifts? You may take pictures of them, learn them well enough to duplicate them later. Surely that would be no danger to persons who have been on the Mote planet itself?"

Horvath thought furiously. He *had* to have those! The pickup was switched off, and Horvath smiled thinly at the Admiral. "He's right, you know. Can't we put them in the cutter?"

Kutuzov seemed to taste sour milk. Then he nodded. Horvath turned back to the Motie in relief. "Thank you. If you will place the gifts in the cutter, we will study them on the way out and you may retrieve both the gifts and the cutter, our gift to you, at the Crazy Eddie point in two and a half weeks."

"Excellent," the Motie said warmly. "But you will not need the cutter. One of our gifts is a space craft with controls suitable for human hands and minds. The others will be aboard it."

Kutuzov looked surprised and nodded quickly. Horvath caught it with an inward smile. "That's wonderful. We will bring gifts for you on our return. We want very much to repay your hospitality—"

Admiral Kutuzov was saying something. Horvath leaned away from the screen pickup to listen. "Ask about the midshipmen," the Admiral commanded.

Horvath gulped and said, "Is there any other word about our midshipmen?"

The Motie's voice took on a pained note. "How could there be, Anthony? They were killed attempting reentry, and their craft burned away completely. We have sent you pictures, did you not receive them?"

"Uh—I didn't see them," Horvath replied. Which was true, but it didn't make saying it any easier. The damned Admiral didn't believe anything! What did he think, that the boys were captured somewhere and being tortured for information? "I'm sorry, I was instructed to ask."

"We understand. Humans are very concerned about their young decision makers. So are Moties. Our races do have much in common. It has been good to speak with you again, Anthony. We hope you will return soon."

An alarm flashed on the bridge consoles. Admiral Kutuzov frowned and listened attentively to something Horvath couldn't hear. Simultaneously a speaker announced the quartermaster's report. "Ship's boats secure, sir. Ready to depart."

The Motie had evidently overheard. She said, "The gift ship is quite capable of catching up with you, provided you do not accelerate at more than"—there was a pause as the Motie listened to something—"three of your gravities."

Horvath shot an inquiring eye at the Admiral. The officer was brooding heavily, evidently about to say something. Instead he nodded to Horvath. "One and a half of our gees for this trip," Horvath told the Motie.

"Our gifts will join you in five hours," the Motie said.

The screens flashed and Horvath's pickup went dead. Admiral Kutuzov's voice grated in the Minister's ear. "I am informed that a ship has left Mote Prime and is traveling toward Alderson point at one point seven four of our gravities. Two Mote gravities. You will please have them explain what that ship is doing." The Admiral's voice was calm enough, but the tone was imperative.

Horvath gulped and turned back to the Motie. His screen came active again. He asked hesitantly, afraid to offend them. "Do you know?" he finished.

"Certainly," the Motie replied smoothly. "I have only just learned of it myself. The Masters have sent our ambassadors to the Empire to rendezvous with you. There will be three of them, and we request that you convey them to your Imperial capital where they will represent our race. They have full authority to negotiate for us."

Kutuzov took a deep breath. He seemed about to

scream, and his face was almost purple with effort, but he only said, very quietly so that the Motie could not hear, "Tell them we must discuss this. Captain Mikhailov, accelerate when convenient."

"Aye aye, sir."

"We're leaving now," Horvath told the Motie. "I—we —must discuss the question of ambassadors. This is a surprise—I would have hoped that you would come yourself. Will there be any of our Fyunch(click)s sent as ambassadors?" He spoke rapidly as the warning tones sounded behind him.

"There will be time for any discussions needed," the Motie assured him. "And no, no Motie ambassador could identify with any individual human; all must represent our race. Surely you can understand that? The three have been selected to represent all views, and unanimously acting they can commit all Moties to an agreement. Given the plague menace, they would expect to be quarantined until you are certain they are no threat to your health—" A loud tone sounded through *Lenin*. "Farewell, Anthony. To all of you. And return soon."

The final warning horns blared and *Lenin* surged forward. Horvath stared at the blank screen as behind him the others broke into astonished chatter.

40 • *Farewell*

His Imperial Majesty's President Class battleship *Lenin* was packed, crammed to capacity and beyond with *MacArthur*'s crew and the scientists who had been aboard her. Able spacers shared hammocks in rotation with their duties. Marines slept in corridors, and officers were stuffed three and more into staterooms meant for one. There were Motie artifacts salvaged from *MacArthur* in her hangar deck, which Kutuzov insisted be kept in vacuum, constantly under guard, with inspections. There was no place aboard where the ship's company could be assembled.

If there had been an assembly point it would not have been used. *Lenin* would remain at battle stations until she left the Mote system, even during the funeral services conducted by David Hardy and *Lenin's* chaplain, George Alexis. It was not an unusual situation for either; although it was traditional for the ship's company to assemble when possible, burial services were often conducted with the ship at battle stations. As he put on a black stole and turned to the missal a rating held open for him, David Hardy reflected that he had probably conducted more requiems this way than before an assembly.

A trumpet note sounded through *Lenin.* "Ship's company, at ease," the Chief Boatswain ordered quietly.

"Eternal rest grant them, O Lord," Hardy intoned.

"And let light perpetual shine upon them," Alexis answered. Every verse and response was familiar to anyone who had been in the Navy long enough to be part of *Lenin's* crew.

"I am the Resurrection and the Life, saith the Lord. Whosoever believeth in me, though he were dead, yet shall he live: and whosoever liveth and believeth in me, shall never die."

The service went on, with the spacers responding from their duty stations, a low murmur through the ship.

"I heard a voice from Heaven saying unto me, Write. From henceforth blessed are the dead who die in the Lord: even so saith the Spirit; for they rest from their labors."

Rest, Rod thought. There's that, anyway, rest for the kids. He shivered. I've seen plenty of ships lost, and plenty of men under my command have bought it a hundred parsecs from home. Why is this one getting to me? He took a deep breath but the tightness in his chest remained unchanged.

Lights dimmed throughout *Lenin,* and the recorded voices of the Imperial Navy choir chanted a hymn in which the crewmen joined. "Day of wrath, and doom impending, David's words with Sybil's blending: Heavens and worlds in ashes ending . . ."

Sybil? Rod thought. God, that must be ancient. The hymn went on and on, ending in a burst of male voices.

Do I believe any of this? Rod wondered. Hardy does, look at his face. And Kelley, ready to launch his comrades out the torpedo tubes. Why can't I believe as they do? But I do, don't I? I always thought I did, there's got to be some purpose in this universe. Look at Bury. This isn't even his religion, but it's getting to him. Wonder what he's thinking?

Horace Bury stared intently at the torpedo tubes. Four bodies and a head! The head of a Marine the Brownies had used for a Trojan horse. Bury had seen it only once, spinning through space in a cloud of fog and shattered glass and kicking, thrashing, dying Brownies. He remembered a square jaw, a wide, slack mouth, glittering dead eyes. Allah be merciful to them, and may His legions descend on the Mote . . .

Sally's taking it better than I am, Rod thought, and she's a civilian. We both liked those boys . . . Why don't I worry about the others? Five Marines killed getting the civilians out. It wouldn't be so bad if the middies had been killed in action. I expected losses when I sent the rescue party in with the cutter. I wasn't sure the kids would ever get out of *Mac* at all. But they did, they were safe!

"Unto Almighty God we commend the souls of our brothers departed, and we commit their bodies to the deeps of space; in sure and certain hope of the resurrection unto eternal life, through our Lord Jesus Christ; at whose coming in glorious majesty to judge the worlds, the seas shall yield their dead, and the deeps give forth their burdens . . ."

Kelley pressed the keys and there was a soft *whoosh*, another—three, four, five. Only four bodies and a head recovered out of twenty-seven dead and missing.

"Ship's Company, atten-shut!"

"Shoot!"

And what will the Moties make of that? Rod wondered. Three broadsides fired off into space at nothing—except the third, which would vaporize the bodies launched a moment ago. The Admiral had insisted, and no one had argued.

Contralto trumpet notes died away as *Lenin*'s trumpeter and *MacArthur*'s ended taps in duet. The ship was still for a moment.

"Ship's company, dismissed!"

The officers moved silently away from the torpedo room. Lights brightened in the corridors and men hurried back to their action stations or their crowded rest areas. Navy routine continues, Rod thought. Funeral services are part of the Book too. There is a regulation for everything: birth aboard ship, registration of; burial, with or without bodies; and one for captains who lose their ships. The Book demands a court-martial for that one.

"Rod. Wait a minute, Rod. Please."

He stopped at Sally's call. They stood in the corridor while the other officers and crew split around them. Rod wanted to join them, to get back to the solitude of his cabin where no one would ask him what happened aboard *MacArthur*. Yet here was Sally, and something way inside wanted to talk to her, or just be close to her—

"Rod, Dr. Horvath says the Moties have sent ambassadors to meet us at the Crazy Eddie point, but Admiral Kutuzov won't let them aboard! Is that right?"

Damn! he thought. Moties again, Moties— "It's right." He turned away.

"Rod, wait! We've got to do something! Rod, where are you going?" She stared at his back as he walked rapidly away. Now what did I do? she wondered.

Blaine's door was closed but the telltale showed that it wasn't locked. Kevin Renner hesitated, then knocked. Nothing happened. He waited a moment, then knocked again.

"Come in."

Renner opened the door. It seemed strange to walk directly into Blaine's cabin: no Marine sentry on duty, none of the mysterious aura of command that surrounds a captain. "Hi, Captain. Mind if I join you?"

"No. Can I get you anything?" Blaine clearly didn't care

one way or another. He didn't look at Renner, and Kevin wondered what would happen if he took the polite offer seriously. He could ask for a drink . . .

No. Not time to push. Not just yet. Renner took a seat and looked around.

Blaine's cabin was big. It would have been a tower room if *Lenin* had been designed with a tower. There were only four men and one woman who rated cabins to themselves, and Blaine wasn't using the precious room; he looked to have been sitting in that chair for hours, probably ever since the funeral services. Certainly he hadn't changed. He'd had to borrow one of Mikhailov's dress uniforms and it didn't fit at all.

They sat silently, with Blaine staring into some internal space-time that excluded his visitor.

"I've been going over Buckman's work," Renner said at random. He had to start somewhere, and it probably shouldn't be with Moties.

"Oh? How goes it?" Blaine asked politely.

"Way over my head. He says he can prove there's a protostar forming in the Coal Sack. In a thousand years it'll be shining by its own light. Well, he can't prove it to me, because I don't have the math."

"Um."

"How are you making out?" Renner showed no indication of leaving. "Enjoying your vacation from duties?"

Blaine finally lifted haunted eyes. "Kevin, why did the kids try to do a reentry?"

"God's eyes, Captain, that's plain silly. They wouldn't have tried anything of the kind." *Jesus, he's not even thinking straight. This is going to be tougher than I thought.*

"Then you tell me what happened."

Renner looked puzzled, but obviously Blaine meant it. "Captain, the ship was lousy with Brownies—everywhere nobody was looking. They must have got to the lifeboat storage area pretty early. If you were a Motie, how would you redesign an escape craft?"

"Superbly." Blaine actually smiled. "Even a dead man couldn't pass up a straight line like that."

"You had me wondering." Renner grinned, then turned serious. "No, what I mean is, they'd redesign for every new situation. In deep space the boat would decelerate and scream for rescue. Near a gas giant it would orbit. Always automatic, mind, because the passengers could be hurt or unconscious. Near a habitable world the boat would reenter."

"Eh?" Blaine frowned. There was a spark of life in his eyes. Renner held his breath.

"Yeah, but Kevin, what went wrong? If the Brownies got to the boats they'd have designed them *right*. Besides, there'd be controls; they wouldn't *make* you reenter."

Renner shrugged. "Can you figure out Motie control panels at a glance? I can't, and I doubt that the middies could. But the Brownies would expect them to. Captain, maybe the boats weren't finished, or got damaged in a fire fight."

"Maybe—"

"Maybe a lot of things. Maybe they were designed for Brownies. The kids would have had to crowd in, rip out a dozen fifteen-centimeter Motie crash couches or something. There wasn't much time, with the torpedoes due to go in three minutes."

"Those goddamn torpedoes! The casings were probably full of Brownies and a rat ranch, if anyone had looked!"

Renner nodded. "But who'd know to look?"

"I should have."

"Why?" Renner asked it seriously. "Skipper, there's—"

"I'm not a skipper."

Aha! Renner thought. "Yes, sir. There's still not a man in the Navy who'd have looked. Nobody. *I* didn't think of it. The Tsar was satisfied with your decontamination procedure, wasn't he? Everybody was. What bloody good does it do to blame yourself for a mistake we all made?"

Blaine looked up at Renner and wondered. The Sailing Master's face was slightly red. Now why's he so stirred up? "There's another thing," Rod said. "Suppose the lifeboats were properly designed. Suppose the kids made a perfect reentry, and the Moties lied."

"I thought of that," said Renner. "Do you believe it?"

"No. But I wish I could be sure."

"You would be if you knew Moties as well as I do. Convince yourself. Study the data. We've got plenty aboard this ship, and you've got the time. You've *got* to learn about Moties, you're the Navy's heaviest expert on them."

"Me?" Rod laughed. "Kevin, I'm not an expert on anything. The first thing I've got to do when we get back is convince a court-martial—"

"Oh, rape the court-martial," Renner said impatiently. "Really, Captain, are you sitting here brooding over that formality? God's teeth!"

"And what do you suggest I brood over, Lieutenant Renner?"

Kevin grinned. Better Blaine irritated than the way he'd been. "Oh, about why Sally's so glum this afternoon—I think she's hurt because you're mad at her. About what you're going to say when Kutuzov and Horvath have it out over the Motie ambassadors. About revolts and secessions in the colony worlds, or the price of iridium, or inflation of the crown—"

"Renner, for God's sake shut up!"

Kevin's grin broadened. "—or how to get me out of your cabin. Captain, look at it this way. Suppose a court finds you guilty of negligence. Certainly nothing worse. You didn't surrender the ship to an enemy or anything. So suppose they seriously want your scalp and they hang that on you. Worse thing they could do would be ground you. They wouldn't even cashier you. So they ground you, and you resign—you're still going to be Twelfth Marquis of Crucis."

"Yeah. So what?"

"So what?" Renner was suddenly angry. His brows knitted, and one fist clenched. "So what? Look, Captain, I'm just a merchant skipper. All my family's ever been, and all we ever want to be. I put in a hitch in the Navy because we all do—maybe back home we're not so thick on Imperialism as you are in the Capital, but part of that's because we trust you aristocrats to run the show. We do our part, and we expect you characters with all the privileges to do yours!"

"Well—" Blaine looked sheepish, and a little embarrassed by Renner's outburst. "And just what do you see as my part?"

"What do you think? You're the only aristocrat in the Empire who knows a bloody thing about Moties, and you're asking me what to do? Captain, I expect you to put your arse in gear, that's what. Sir. The Empire's got to develop a sensible policy about Moties, and the Navy's influence is big— You can't let the Navy get its views from Kutuzov! You can start by thinking about those Motie ambassadors the Admiral wants to leave stranded here."

"I'll be damned. You really are worked up about this, aren't you?"

Renner grinned. "Well, maybe a little. Look, you've got time. Talk to Sally about the Moties. Go over the reports we sent up from Mote Prime. Learn about them so when the Admiral asks your advice you'll have some sensible arguments to give him. We've got to take those ambassadors back with us—"

Rod grimaced. Moties aboard another ship! Good Lord—

"And stop thinking like that," Renner said. "They won't get loose and multiply all over *Lenin*. They wouldn't have time, for that matter. Use your head, sir. The Admiral will listen to you. He's got it in for Horvath, anything Doc suggests the Tsar's going to turn down, but he'll listen to you . . ."

Rod shook his head impatiently. "You're acting as if my judgment were worth something. The evidence is against that."

"Good Lord. You're really down in the dumps, aren't you? Do you know what your officers and men think of you? Have you any idea? Hell, Captain, it's because of guys like you that I can accept the aristocracy—" Kevin stopped, embarrassed at having said more than he intended. "Look, the Tsar's got to ask your opinion. He doesn't have to take your advice, or Horvath's, but he does have to ask both of you. That's in the expedition orders—"

"How the devil do you know that?"

"Captain, my division had the job of rescuing the logs and order books from *MacArthur*, remember? They weren't marked SECRET."

"The hell they weren't."

"Well, maybe the light was bad and I didn't see the security stamps. Besides, I had to be sure they had the right books, didn't I? Anyway, Dr. Horvath knows all about that regulation. He's going to insist on a council of war before Kutuzov makes a final decision on the ambassador question."

"I see." Rod fingered the bridge of his nose. "Kevin, just who put you up to coming in here? Horvath?"

"Of course not. I thought of it myself." Renner hesitated. "I did have some encouragement, Captain." He waited for Blaine to respond, but got only a blank stare. Renner snorted. "I sometimes wonder why the aristocracy isn't extinct, the lot of you seem so stupid sometimes. Why don't you give Sally a call? She's sitting in her cabin with a bleak look and a lot of notes and books she can't get interested in right now—" Renner stood abruptly. "She could use some cheering up."

"Sally? Worried about—"

"Jee-sus Christ," Renner muttered. He turned and strode out.

41 • *Gift Ship*

Lenin moved toward the Crazy Eddie point at one and a half gees. So did the gift ship.

The gift ship was a streamlined cylinder, swollen at the many-windowed nose, like a minaret riding a fusion flame. Sally Fowler and Chaplain Hardy were highly amused. Nobody else had noticed the clumsy phallicism— or would admit to it.

Kutuzov hated the gift ship. The Motie ambassadors could be dealt with simply by following orders, but the gift ship was something else again. It had caught up with *Lenin,* taken station three kilometers away, and broadcast a cheery message, while *Lenin*'s gunners tracked it helplessly. Kutuzov had told himself it couldn't carry a large enough weapon to penetrate *Lenin*'s Field.

There was a better reason to hate that ship. It was tempting Kutuzov to violate his orders. The *MacArthur* crewmen volunteers who went over to test it were enthusiastic about everything on it. The controls resembled a Navy cutter, but the drive was a standard Motie fusion drive, long, slender stinger guiding a plasma flow at enormous efficiencies. There were other details, all of them valuable; Admiral Lavrenti Kutuzov wanted to take that ship home.

And he was afraid to let it get near his command.

After the naval officers tested it, the civilians had to go aboard. All this traffic made nonsense of the thin fiction of plague aboard *MacArthur,* and Kutuzov knew it; but at least he wouldn't have to explain it to any Motie. He didn't intend to communicate with them. Let Horvath read him the expedition orders and demand his council of war. There would be no aliens aboard *Lenin* while Kutuzov lived. That ship, though—

He looked at it floating in his screens as scientific personnel were ferried to it. They'd come to *Lenin* for the requiem services, and now hurried back to resume their studies of their new toy.

Every report showed that it was filled with marvels of enormous value to the Empire, yet how did he dare take it aboard? It was no good seeking advice. Captain Blaine might have been of help, but no, he was a broken man, doomed to sink deeper into his own failures, useless just when his advice might be needed. Horvath had blind faith in the good intentions of everything Motie. Then there was Bury, with equally blind hatred, despite all the evidence showing that the Moties were friendly and harmless.

"Probably they are," Kutuzov said aloud. Horace Bury

looked up in surprise. He had been drinking tea with the Admiral on the bridge while they watched the Motie gift ship. The Trader shot an inquiring look at the Admiral.

"Probably the Moties are friendly. Harmless," Kutuzov repeated.

"You can't believe that!" Bury protested.

Kutuzov shrugged. "As I have told the others, what I believe is of no importance. Is my task to maximize information brought back to Government. With only this ship, any chance of loss means loss of all information. But that Motie space craft would be very valuable, would it not, Your Excellency? What would you pay to the Navy for license to produce ships with that drive?"

"I would pay much more to see the Motie threat ended forever," Bury said earnestly.

"Um." The Admiral was inclined to agree. There were enough problems in the Trans-Coalsack Sector. God only knew how many colonies were revolting, how many of the outies had made common cause against the Empire; aliens were a complexity the Navy did not need. "But still— the technology. The trade possibilities. I should think you would be interested."

"We can't trust them," Bury said. He was very careful to speak calmly. The Admiral was not impressed with men unable to control their emotions. Bury understood him very well—his own father had been the same way.

"Admiral, they have killed our midshipmen. Surely you do not believe that fable about reentry? And they released those monsters on *MacArthur,* and almost succeeded in getting them aboard *Lenin.*" The Trader shuddered imperceptibly. Tiny glowing eyes. It had been that close— "Surely you will not allow these aliens into the Empire. You will not let them board your ship." Mind-reading monsters. Telepathic or not, they read minds. Bury fought to control his desperation: if even Admiral Kutuzov was beginning to believe the alien lies, what chance had the Empire? The new technology would excite the Imperial Traders Association as nothing ever had, and only the Navy had enough influence to overcome the demands for commerce the ITA would make. Beard of the Prophet, something had to be done! "I wonder if you are not being unduly influenced by Dr. Horvath?" Bury asked politely.

The Admiral scowled, and Horace Bury smiled behind his face. Horvath. That was the key, play Horvath against the Admiral. Someone had to . . .

Anthony Horvath was at that moment feeling very pleased and comfortable despite the 1.5 gee acceleration. The gift ship was roomy, and it had studied touches of luxury among its endless marvels. There was the shower, with half a dozen adjustable heads set at different angles, and a molecular sieve to reclaim the water. There were stocks of prefrozen Motie dinners which needed only the microwave ovens to make a variety of meals. Even the culinary failures were . . . interesting. There was coffee, synthetic but good, and a well-stocked wine locker.

To add to his ease, *Lenin* and Kutuzov were comfortably distant. Aboard the battleship everyone was stuffed together like cargo pods in a merchantman, crowded into cabins and sleeping in corridors, while here Horvath lolled at his ease. He drew the microphone closer and resumed dictating with another sigh of contentment. All was well with the worlds . . .

"Much of what the Moties construct has multiple purposes," he told his computer box. "This ship is an intelligence test *per se,* whether or not so intended. The Moties will learn much about our abilities by observing how long it takes our crew to control the drive properly. Their own Browns, I suspect, would have had it working perfectly in an hour, but to be fair, a Brown would have no difficulty concentrating on the telltales for days at a stretch. Humans intelligent enough for such tasks find them excruciatingly boring, and it is our own custom to have crewmen stand watches while their officers remain on call to deal with any problems. We thus respond more slowly, and require more personnel, to perform tasks that individual Moties find exceedingly simple.

"The Moties have also told us a great deal about themselves. For example, we employ humans as a backup to automatic systems, although we will often omit the automation in order to give constant employment to humans needed for emergencies but otherwise superfluous. The Moties appear deficient in computer technology, and seldom automate anything. Instead, they employ one or more subspecies as biological computers, and they seem to have an adequate supply of them. This is hardly an option left open for human use." He paused for thought and looked around the cabin.

"Ah. Then there are the statuettes." Horvath lifted one and smiled. He had them arrayed like toy soldiers on the table before him: a dozen Motie figurines of transparent plastic. Internal organs showed through in vivid color and detail. He looked at them again contentedly, then grimaced slightly. These *had* to be brought back.

Actually, he admitted to himself, they didn't. There was nothing special about the plastic, and the statuettes were recorded in every detail; any good plastic former could be programmed to turn out thousands an hour, the same way these probably were made in the first place. But they were *alien,* and they were gifts, and he wanted them for his desk, or for the New Scotland Museum. Let Sparta have copies for a change!

He could identify most of the forms at a glance: Engineer, Mediator, Master; the huge Porter form; an overmuscled Engineer with broad, stubby-fingered hands and big splayed feet, probably a Farmer. A tiny Watchmaker (damn the Brownies! twice damn the Admiral who wouldn't let the Moties help with their extermination). There was a small-headed long-fingered Physician. Next to it was the spindly Runner who seemed to be all legs—Horvath spoke to his computer box again.

"The Runner's head is small, but there is a distinctly bulging forehead. It is my belief that the Runner is nonsentient but has the verbal capacity to memorize and deliver messages. It can probably carry out simple instructions. The Runner may have evolved as a specialized message carrier before civilization reached the telephone stage, and is now kept for traditional functions rather than utility. From the brain structure it becomes fairly clear that the Brownie or Watchmaker could never have memorized or delivered messages. The parietal lobe is quite undeveloped." *That* for Kutuzov.

"These statuettes are extremely detailed. They disassemble like puzzles to reveal internal details. Although we do not yet know the function of most internal organs, we may be sure they divide differently from those of human organs, and it is possible that the Moties' conscious design philosophy of overlapping multiple functions is duplicated in their gross anatomy as well. We have identified the heart and lungs, the latter consisting of two distinct lobes of unequal size."

Chaplain Hardy braced himself in the doorway when the ship's acceleration dropped, then surged. After the engineers had steadied it he came into the lounge and sat quietly without speaking. Horvath waved and continued his dictation.

"The only area where the statuettes are vague and undifferentiated is in the reproductive organs." Horvath smiled and winked at the Chaplain. He really did feel contented. "The Moties have always been reticent about sex. These statuettes may be educational toys for children; certainly they were mass produced. If this is the case—we really must ask the Moties if we get a chance—it implies that the Motie culture shares some similarities with that of humans." Horvath frowned. Sex education for the young was a periodic thing among humanity. Sometimes it was quite explicit and widespread, and at other periods of history it was nonexistent. In the civilized portions of the Empire such things were left to books at present, but there were plenty of newly discovered planets where the whole topic was forbidden knowledge to subadolescents.

"Of course, it may be simple efficiency," Horvath continued. "Statuettes made to differentiate the sex organs would require three times as many figurines, a set for the male, another for the female, and a third for the reproductive phase itself. I note that there is a single developed mammary gland on all the forms, and I believe we were told that all Moties can suckle young." He stopped dictating and punched in codes on his computer. Words flowed across the screen. "Yes. And the single working teat is always on the right side, or at least on the side opposite the single heavy-work arm. Thus the pups may be held with the strong arm, while the right arms are available for petting and grooming; this is very logical, given the ultrasensitivity and dense sensory nerve endings in the right hands." He cleared his throat and reached for the brandy snifter, waving at Hardy to help himself.

"The single teat on the higher forms argues strongly that multiple birth must be extremely rare among the upper-caste Moties. However, litters must be common with the Watchmaker caste, at least this must be the case after the creature has produced several offspring. We can be sure that the vestigial teats down the right side of the miniature develop into working organs at some stage of their development; otherwise their numbers could not have increased so rapidly aboard *MacArthur.*" He set the box down. "How goes it, David?"

"Fairly well. That Motie toy has me fascinated. It's a game of logic, no question about it, and a very good one at that. One player selects some rule to sort the various objects into categories, and the other players attempt to deduce the rule and prove it. Very interesting."

"Ah. Perhaps Mr. Bury will want to market it."

Hardy shrugged. "The Church might buy a few—to train graduate theologians. I doubt if there'd be much mass popular interest. Too tough." He looked at the statuettes and frowned. "There seems to be at least one missing form, did you notice?"

Horvath nodded. "The nonsentient beast we saw in the zoo. The Moties wouldn't talk about it at all while we were there."

"Or afterward either," Hardy added. "I asked my Fyunch(click) but she kept changing the subject."

"Another mystery for future investigation," Horvath said. "Although we might do well to avoid the subject in the presence of Moties. We wouldn't want to ask their ambassadors, for example." He paused invitingly.

David Hardy smiled softly but didn't take the invitation.

"Well," Horvath said. "You know, there aren't many things the Moties didn't want to talk about, I wonder why they're so shy about that caste? I'm fairly sure the thing wasn't an ancestor of the other Motie forms—not an ape or monkey, so to speak."

Hardy sipped his brandy. It was very good, and he wondered where the Moties had obtained a supply for a model. This was undoubtedly a synthetic, and Hardy thought he could detect the difference, but he had to strain. "Very thoughtful of them to put this aboard." He sipped again.

"Too bad we'll have to leave all this," Horvath said. "We're doing all right with the recording, though. Holograms, x-rays, mass densities, tadon emissions, and anything that comes apart we take apart and holo the contents. Commander Sinclair has been very helpful—the Navy can be very helpful sometimes. I wish it were always so."

Hardy shrugged. "Have you thought about the problem from the Navy's view? If you guess wrong, you've lost some information. If they guess wrong, they've endangered the race."

"Bosh. One planetful of Moties? No matter how advanced they are, there just aren't *enough* Moties to threaten the Empire. You know that, David."

"I suppose, Anthony. I don't think the Moties are a threat either. On the other hand, I can't believe they're quite as simple and open as you seem to think. Of course I've had more time to think about them than you have . . ."

"Eh?" Horvath prompted. He liked Chaplain Hardy. The clergyman always had interesting stories and ideas. Of course he'd be easy to talk to, his profession demanded it, but he wasn't a typical priest—or a typical Navy blockhead either.

Hardy smiled. "I can't perform any of my regular jobs, you know. Linguistic archeology? I'll never even learn the Motie language. As to the commission the Church gave me, I doubt if there's enough evidence to decide *anything*. Ship's chaplain isn't that time-consuming—what's left but to think about Moties?" He grinned again. "And contemplate the problems the missionaries will have on the next expedition—"

"Think the Church will send a mission?"

"Why not? Certainly no theological objections I can raise. Probably useless, though . . ." Hardy chuckled. "I recall a story about missionaries in Heaven. They were discussing their former work, and one told of the thousands he'd converted. Another boasted of a whole planet of the fallen whom he had brought back to the Church. Finally they turned to this little chap at the end of the table and asked him how many souls he'd saved. 'One.' Now that story is supposed to illustrate a moral principle, but I can't help thinking that the missions to Mote Prime may produce it in, uh, real life . . ."

"David," Horvath said. There was a note of urgency in his voice. "The Church is going to be an important influence on Imperial policy regarding Moties. And I'm sure you know that the Cardinal will give great weight to your opinions when he reports to New Rome. Do you realize that what you conclude about Moties will be as influential as— Damn it, more influential. More influential than the scientific report, or perhaps even the Navy's."

"I'm aware of it." Hardy was serious. "It's influence I didn't ask for, Anthony. But I'm aware of the situation."

"All right." Horvath wasn't a pusher either. Or tried not to be, although sometimes he got carried away. Since he'd gone into scientific administration he'd had to learn to fight for his budgets, though. He sighed deeply and changed tactics. "I wish you'd help me with something right now. I'd like to take these statuettes back with us."

"Why not wish for the whole ship?" Hardy asked. "I do." He sipped his brandy again and cleared his throat. It was much easier to talk about Moties than about Imperial policies. "I noticed you were giving rather a lot of attention to the blank areas on the figures," he said mischievously.

Horvath frowned. "I did? Well, perhaps. Perhaps I did."

"You must have spent considerable time thinking about it. Didn't it strike you as odd that that's another area of Motie reticence?"

"Not really."

"It did me. It puzzles me."

Horvath shrugged, then leaned forward to pour more brandy for both of them. No point in saving it to be abandoned later. "They probably think their sex lives are none of our business. How much detail did *we* give *them?*"

"Quite a lot. I had a long and happy married life," said Chaplain Hardy. "I may not be an expert on what makes a happy love life, but I know enough to teach Moties all *they'll* ever need to know. I didn't conceal anything, and I gather Sally Fowler didn't either. After all, they're *aliens*— we're scarcely tempting them with prurient desire." Hardy grinned.

Horvath did too. "You have a point, Doctor." He nodded thoughtfully. "Tell me, David—why did the Admiral insist on blasting the bodies after the funeral?"

"Why, I should have thought that—ah. Yes. And no one protested. We didn't want aliens dissecting our comrades."

"Precisely. Nothing to hide, just squeamish about aliens dissecting dead men. One thing the Tsar and I could agree on. Now, David, could the Moties feel the same way about reproductions of themselves?"

Hardy thought about that for a moment. "Not impossible, as well you know. Plenty of human societies have felt the same way about, say, photographs. Many still do." He sipped the brandy again. "Anthony, I just don't believe it. I don't have anything better to offer, but I don't believe you've put your finger on it. What we need is a long conference with an anthropologist."

"The damned Admiral wouldn't let her come aboard," Horvath growled, but he let the anger pass quickly. "I'll bet she's still fuming."

Sally wasn't fuming. She'd exhausted her vocabulary earlier. While Hardy and Horvath and the others merrily explored the alien gifts, she had to be content with holographs and dictated reports.

Now she couldn't concentrate. She found she'd read the same paragraph five times and threw the report across the cabin. Damn Rod Blaine. He had no right to snub her like that. He had no right to get her brooding over him either.

There was a knock at her stateroom door. She opened it quickly. "Yes— Oh. Hello, Mr. Renner."

"Expecting someone else?" Renner asked slyly. "Your face fell a full klick when you saw it was me. Not very flattering."

"I'm sorry. No, I wasn't expecting anyone else. Did you say something?"

"No."

"I thought—Mr. Renner, I thought you said 'extinct.' "

"Getting any work done?" Renner asked. He glanced around her cabin. Her desk, usually orderly, was a litter of paper, diagrams, and computer printouts. One of Horvath's reports lay on the steel deck near a bulkhead. Renner twisted his lips into what might have been a half-smile.

Sally followed his gaze and blushed. "Not much," she admitted. Renner had told her he was going to visit Rod's cabin, and she waited for him to say something. And waited. Finally she gave up. "All right. I'm not getting anything done, and how is he?"

"He's a bag of broken glass."

"Oh." She was taken aback.

"Lost his ship. Of course he's in bad shape. Listen, don't let anyone tell you that losing a ship is like losing your wife. It isn't. It's a lot more like seeing your home planet destroyed."

"Is— Do you think I can do anything?"

Renner stared at her. "Extinct, I tell you. Of course there's something you can do. You can go hold his hand, for God's sake. Or just sit with him. If he can go on staring at the bulkhead with you in the room, he must have got hit in the fire fight."

"Hit? He wasn't wounded—"

"Of course not. I mean he must have got— Oh, skip it. Look, just go knock on his door, will you?" Kevin steered her out into the corridor, and without quite knowing how she found herself propelled to its end. When she looked puzzled, Renner indicated the door. "I'm going for a drink."

Well, she thought. Now merchant captains are telling the aristocracy how to be polite to each other ... There was no point in standing in the corridor. She knocked.

"Come in."

Sally entered quickly. "Hi," she said. Oh, boy. He looks awful. And that baggy uniform—something's got to be done about *that*. "Busy?"

"No. I was just thinking about something Mr. Renner said. Did you know that deep down underneath Kevin Renner really believes in the Empire?"

She looked around for a chair. No point in waiting for him to invite her. She took a seat. "He's a Navy officer, isn't he?"

"Oh, yeah, of course he *supports* the Empire or he wouldn't have taken a commission—but I mean, he really believes we know what we're doing. Amazing."

"Don't we?" she asked uncertainly. "Because if we don't, the whole human race is in big trouble."

"I remember thinking I did," Rod said. Now this was faintly ridiculous. There had to be a long list of subjects to discuss with the only girl in ten parsecs before it got to political theory. "You look nice. How do you do it? You must have lost everything."

"No, I had my travel kit. Clothes I took to the Mote, remember?" Then she couldn't help herself and laughed. "Rod, have you any idea of just how silly you look in Captain Mikhailov's uniform? You two aren't the same size in *any* dimension. Whoa! Stop it! You will not begin brooding again, Rod Blaine." She made a face.

It took a moment, but she'd won. She knew it when Rod glanced down at the huge pleats he'd tucked in the tunic so that it wouldn't be quite so much like a tent. Slowly he grinned. "I don't suppose I'll be nominated for the *Times*'s list of best-dressed men at Court, will I?"

"No." They sat in silence as she tried to think of something else to say. Now blast it, why is it hard to talk to him? Uncle Ben says I talk too much anyway, and here I can't think of a thing to say. "What was it Mr. Renner said?"

"He reminded me of my duties. I'd forgotten I still had some. But I guess he's right, life goes on, even for a captain who's lost his ship . . ." There was more silence, and the air seemed thick and heavy again.

Now what do I say? "You—you'd been with *MacArthur* a long time, hadn't you?"

"Three years. Two as exec and a year as skipper. And now she's gone— I better not get started on *that*. What have you been doing with yourself?"

"You asked me, remember. I've been studying the data from Mote Prime, and the reports on the gift ship—and thinking of what I can say that will convince the Admiral that we *have* to take the Motie ambassadors back with us. And we must convince him, Rod, we've just got to. I wish there were something else we could talk about, and there will be lots of time after we leave the Motie system." And we'll have a lot of it together, too, now that *MacArthur*'s gone. I wonder. Honestly, am I a little glad my rival's dead? Boy, I better never let him think I even suspect that about myself. "Right now, though, Rod, there's so little time, and I haven't any ideas at all—"

Blaine fingered the knot on his nose. About time you stopped being the Man of Sorrows and started acting like the future Twelfth Marquis, isn't it? "All right, Sally. Let's see what we can come up with. Provided that you let Kelley serve us dinner here."

She smiled broadly. "My lord, you have got yourself a deal."

43 • *Trader's Lament*

Horace Bury was not a happy man.

If *MacArthur*'s crew had been difficult to deal with, *Lenin*'s was an order of magnitude worse. They were Ekaterinas, Imperial fanatics, and this was a picked crew under an admiral and a captain from their home world. Even the Spartan Brotherhoods would have been easier to influence.

Bury knew all this in advance, but there was this damnable urge to dominate and control his environment under all circumstances; and he had almost nothing to work with.

His status aboard was more ambiguous than before. Captain Mikhailov and the Admiral knew that he was to remain under Blaine's personal control, not charged with any crime, but not allowed freedom either. Mikhailov had solved the problem by assigning Bury Marine servants and putting Blaine's man Kelley in charge of the Marines. Thus, whenever he left his cabin, Bury was followed through the ship.

He tried to talk to *Lenin*'s crewmen. Few would listen. Perhaps they had heard rumors of what he could offer, and were afraid that *MacArthur*'s Marines would report them. Perhaps they suspected him of treason and hated him.

A Trader needs patience, and Bury had more than most. Even so, it was hard to control himself when he could control nothing else; when there was nothing to do but sit and wait, his hair-trigger temper would flare into screaming rages and smashed furniture, but never in public. Outside his cabin Bury was calm, relaxed, a skilled conversationalist, comfortable even with—most especially with—Admiral Kutuzov.

This gave him access to *Lenin*'s officers, but they were very formal, and suddenly busy when he wanted to talk. Bury soon found that there were only three safe subjects:

card games, Moties, and tea. If *MacArthur* had been fueled by coffee, *Lenin*'s drive operated on tea; and tea drinkers are more knowledgeable about the subject than coffee drinkers. Bury's ships traded in tea as they traded in anything else men would pay for, but he was carrying none, and he did not drink it.

Thus Bury spent endless hours at the bridge table; in threes, officers of both *Lenin* and *MacArthur* were willing to sit with him in his cabin, which was always less crowded than the wardroom. It was easy to talk to *Lenin*'s officers about Moties, too—always in groups, but they were curious. After ten months in the Motie system, most had never seen a Motie. Everyone wanted to hear about aliens, and Bury was ready to tell them.

The intervals between rubbers stretched as Bury spoke animatedly of the Motie world, the Mediators who could read minds though they said they could not, the zoo, the Castle, the baronial estates with their fortified look—Bury had certainly noticed that. And the conversation would move to the dangers. The Moties had not sold weapons or even shown them, because they planned an attack and would keep its nature a surprise. They had seeded *MacArthur* with Brownies—it was almost the first act of the first Motie they'd ever encountered—and the insidiously helpful and likable beasts had seized the ship and nearly escaped with all the military secrets of the Empire. Only Admiral Kutuzov's vigilance had prevented total disaster.

And the Moties thought themselves more intelligent than humans. They saw humanity as beasts to be tamed, with gentleness if possible, but tamed, converted into another caste to serve the nearly invisible Masters.

He spoke of Moties and he hated them. Pictures flashed through his mind, sometimes at the mere thought of a Motie, and always at night when he tried to sleep. He had nightmares of a Marine space suit and battle armor. It approached from behind, and three tiny pairs of eyes glittered through the faceplate. Sometimes the dream would end in a cloud of spidery six-limbed aliens thrashing, dying in vacuum, flopping around a human head; and Bury would sleep. But sometimes the nightmare ended with Bury mute-ly screaming at *Lenin*'s guards while the suited figure entered the battleship, and Bury would wake in cold sweat. The Ekaterinas had to be warned.

They listened, but they did not believe. Bury sensed it. They had heard him screaming before he came aboard, and they had heard the screams at night; and they thought he was mad.

More than once Bury thanked Allah for Buckman. The astrophysicist was a strange person, but Bury could talk to him. At first the Marine "honor guard" that stood outside Bury's door had puzzled Buckman, but before long the scientist ignored it as he ignored most inexplicable activities of his fellow men.

Buckman had been going over the Moties' work on Murcheson's Eye and the Coal Sack. "Fine work! There are some things I want to check for myself, and I'm not sure about some of their assumptions . . . but that damned Kutuzov won't let me have *Lenin*'s telescope facilities."

"Buckman, is it possible that the Moties are more intelligent than we are?"

"Well, the ones I dealt with are brighter than most of the people I know. Take my brother-in-law . . . But you mean in general, don't you?" Buckman scratched his jaw thinking. "They could be smarter than I am. They've done some damn fine work. But they're more limited than they know. In all their million years, they've had a chance to examine only two stars close up."

Buckman's definition of intelligence was a limited one.

Bury early gave up trying to warn Buckman against the Motie threat. Buckman too thought Bury was crazy; but Buckman thought everyone was crazy.

Thank Allah for Buckman.

The other civilian scientists were friendly enough, but with the exception of Buckman they wanted just one thing from Bury: an analysis of trade possibilities with Moties. Bury could give that in six words: *Get them before they get us!* Even Kutuzov thought that judgment premature.

The Admiral listened politely enough, and Bury thought he had convinced him that the Motie ambassadors should be left behind, that only idiots like Horvath would take an enemy aboard the only ship capable of warning the Empire about the aliens; but even that wasn't certain.

It all made for a splendid opportunity for Horace Bury to practice patience. If his patience ever cracked, only Nabil knew it; and Nabil was beyond surprise.

44 • *Council of War*

There was a picture of the Emperor in *Lenin*'s wardroom. Leonidas IX stared down the length of the long steel table, and ranked on both sides of his image were Imperial flags and battle banners. Paintings of naval battles from the history of both the First and Second Empire hung on all the bulkheads, and in one corner a candle burned before an icon of St. Katherine. There was even a special ventilation system to keep it burning in zero gee.

David Hardy could never help smiling at that icon. The thought of such an image aboard a ship with that name was amusing; he supposed that either Kutuzov knew nothing of the history of communism—after all, it *had* been a very long time ago—or his Russian nationalistic sympathies overcame it. Probably the former, since to most Imperials Lenin was the name of a hero from the past, a man known by legend but not detail. There were many such: Caesar, Ivan the Terrible, Napoleon, Churchill, Stalin, Washington, Jefferson, Trotsky, all more or less contemporaries (except to careful historians). Preatomic history tends to compress when seen from far enough away.

The wardroom began to fill up as the scientists and officers entered and took their places. Marines reserved two seats, the head of the table and the plate immediately to its right, although Horvath had tried to take that seat. The Science Minister shrugged when the Marine objected with a stream of Russian, and went to the other end, where he displaced a biologist, then chased another scientist from the place to *his* right and invited David Hardy there. If the Admiral wanted to play games of prestige, let him; but Anthony Horvath knew something of that business too.

He watched as the others came in. Cargill, Sinclair, and Renner entered together. Then Sally Fowler, and Captain Blaine—odd, Horvath thought, that Blaine could now enter a crowded room with no ceremonial at all. A Marine indicated places to the left of the head of the table, but Rod and Sally sat in the middle. He can afford to, Horvath thought. He was born to his position. Well, my son will be too. My work on this expedition should be enough to get me on the next honors list . . .

"Attention!"

The officers stood, as did most of the scientists. Horvath thought for a moment and stood as well. He looked at the door, expecting the Admiral, but Captain Mikhailov was the only one there. So we have to go through this twice, Horvath thought.

The Admiral fooled him. He came in just as Mikhailov reached his seat, and muttered, "Carry on, gentlemen," so quickly that the Marine gunner had no chance to announce him. If anyone wanted to snub Kutuzov, they'd have to find another opportunity.

"Commander Borman will read from the expedition orders," Kutuzov said coldly.

" 'Section Twelve. Council of War. Paragraph One. The Vice Admiral Commanding shall seek the advice of the scientific staff and senior officers of *MacArthur* except when delay would in the Admiral's judgment, and his alone, endanger the safety of the battleship *Lenin*.

" 'Paragraph Two. If the senior scientist of this expedition shall disagree with the Vice Admiral Commanding, he may request a formal Council of War to render advice to the Admiral. The senior scientist may—' "

"That will be sufficient, Commander Borman," Kutuzov said. "Pursuant to these orders and upon formal request of Science Minister Horvath, this Council of War is convened to render advice on subject of aliens requesting passage to the Empire. Proceedings will be recorded. Minister Horvath, you may begin as you will."

Oh, wow, Sally thought. The atmosphere in here's like the chancel of St. Peter's during High Mass in New Rome. The formality ought to intimidate anyone who disagreed with Kutuzov.

"Thank you, Admiral," Horvath said politely. "Given that this may be a long session—after all, sir, we are discussing what may be the most important decision any of us will ever reach—I think refreshments might be in order. Could your people provide us with coffee, Captain Mikhailov?"

Kutuzov frowned, but there was no reason to reject the request.

It also lowered the frost level in the compartment. With stewards bustling about, and the smell of coffee and tea in the air, a lot of the frigid formality evaporated, as Horvath had intended.

"Thank you." Horvath beamed. "Now. As you know, the Moties have requested that we convey three ambassadors to the Empire. The embassy party will, I am told, have full authority to represent the Mote civilization, sign treaties of friendship and commerce, approve cooperative scientific efforts—I needn't go on. The advantages of presenting them to the Viceroy should be obvious. Are we agreed?"

There was a murmur of assent. Kutuzov sat rigid, his dark eyes narrowed behind craggy brows, the face a mask molded from ruddy clay.

"Yes," Horvath said. "I should think it quite obvious that if there is any way we can do it, we ought to extend every courtesy to the Motie ambassadors. Wouldn't you agree, Admiral Kutuzov?"

Caught in his own trap, Sally thought. This is recorded—he'll have to make sense.

"We have lost *MacArthur*," Kutuzov said gruffly. "We have only this one vessel. Dr. Horvath, were you not present at conference when Viceroy Merrill planned this expedition?"

"Yes—"

"I was not, but I have been told of it. Was it not made plain then that no aliens were to board this vessel? I speak of direct orders of Viceroy himself."

"Well—yes, sir. But the context made it very clear what he meant. There would be no aliens allowed aboard *Lenin* because it was possible they would prove hostile; thus, no matter what they did, *Lenin* would be safe. But now we know the Moties are *not* hostile. In the final expedition orders, His Highness left the decision to you; there's no prohibition like that in the order book."

"But he did leave it to me," Kutuzov said triumphantly. "I fail to see how that is different from oral instructions. Captain Blaine, you were present: Am I mistaken in impression that His Highness said 'under no circumstances' would aliens board *Lenin?*"

Rod swallowed hard. "Yes, sir, but—"

"I think this matter is finished," the Admiral said.

"Oh, no," Horvath said smoothly. "Captain Blaine, you were about to continue. Please do so."

The wardroom was still. Will he do it? Sally wondered. What can the Tsar do to him? He can make it tough for him in the Navy, but—

"I was only going to say, Admiral, that His Highness was not so much giving orders as laying out guidelines. I think that if he had intended you to be bound by them, he'd not have given you discretion, sir. He'd have put it in the order book."

Good for you, Sally cheered silently.

Kutuzov's eye slits narrowed even further. He gestured to a steward for tea.

"I think you underestimate the confidence His Highness has in your judgment," Horvath said. It sounded insincere and he knew it instantly. The point ought to have been made by someone else—Hardy, or Blaine—but Horvath had been afraid to prime them for this meeting. Both were far too independent.

The Admiral smiled. "Thank you. Perhaps he has more confidence in me than you, Doctor. So. You have demonstrated that I can act against express wishes of Viceroy. Certainly I will not do so lightly, and you have yet to

convince me of necessity. Another expedition can bring
back ambassadors."

"Will they send any after an insult like that?" Sally
blurted. Everyone looked at her. "The Moties haven't
asked for much, Admiral. And this request is so reasonable."

"You think they will be offended if we refuse?"

"I—Admiral, I don't know. They could be, yes. Very
offended."

Kutuzov nodded, as if he could understand that. "Perhaps it is lesser risk to leave them here, my lady. Commander Cargill. Have you made study I requested of
you?"

"Yes, sir." Jack Cargill spoke enthusiastically. "The
Admiral asked me to assume the Moties have the secrets
of the Drive and Field and estimate their military potential under those circumstances. I've plotted their naval
strength—" He gestured to a petty officer and a graph
appeared on the wardroom intercom screen.

Heads turned, and there was a moment of shocked
silence. Someone gasped. "That many?—"Good God!"—
"But that's bigger than the sector fleet—"

The curves rose steeply at first, showing conversion of
Motie passenger and cargo ships to navy vessels. Then
they flattened out, but began rising again.

"You can see the threat is quite high," Cargill said
smoothly. "Within two years the Moties could put together a fleet that would be a significant challenge to the
entire Imperial Navy."

"This is ridiculous," Horvath protested.

"Oh, no, sir," Cargill answered. "I was quite conservative in my estimate of their industrial capacities. We have
the neutrino readings, and a good estimate of their energy
generation—number of fusion plants, thermal output—
and I assumed efficiencies no greater than our own, although I suspect they're better than that. God knows
they've no shortage of skilled workmen."

"Where do they get the metals?" de Vandalia demanded. The geologist sounded puzzled. "They've mined

everything on the planet and, if we can believe what they told us, on the asteroids."

"Conversion of existing stuff. Luxury items. Superfluous transportation vehicles. Right now every Master has a fleet of cars and trucks that could be consolidated. They'd have to do without some things, but remember—the Moties have *all* the metals of a whole planetary system already mined out." Cargill was glib, as if he'd expected all this. "A fleet uses a lot of metal, but it's not really very much compared to an entire industrial civilization's resources."

"Oh, all right!" Horvath snapped. "I'll grant you the *capability* estimates. But how the devil can you call it a threat estimate? The Moties aren't a threat."

Cargill looked annoyed. "It's a technical term. 'Threat' in intelligence work refers to capabilities—"

"And not intentions. You've told me that before. Admiral, all this means is that we'd *better* be polite to their ambassadors, so they *won't* go all out building warships."

"That is not my interpretation," Kutuzov said. He seemed less imperious now; his voice was more smoothly modulated, whether because he wanted to convince the others or because he was more confident was not clear. "It means to me that we take every precaution to prevent Moties from obtaining secret of Langston Field."

There was more silence. Cargill's graphs were frightening in their simplicity. The Mote fleet was potentially larger than those of all the outies and rebels in the sector combined.

"Rod—is he right?" Sally asked.

"The figures are right," Blaine muttered grimly. "But— OK. Here goes." He raised his voice. "Admiral, I'm not certain we can protect the Field in any case."

Kutuzov turned toward him in silence and looked expectant.

"First, sir," Rod said carefully, "there is the risk that the Moties have already obtained that secret. From the Brownies." Pain crossed Rod's face, and he had to make an effort not to finger the bridge of his nose. "I don't believe they did, but it's possible. Second, they may have obtained it from the missing midshipmen. Both Whit-bread and Staley knew enough to give them a good start . . ."

"Aye. Mr. Potter knew more," Sinclair seconded. "He was a verra studious lad, sir."

"Or Potter, then," Rod said. "I don't believe it happened, but it could."

"Ridiculous"—"As paranoid as the Tsar"—"They're dead." Several civilians spoke at once. Sally wondered what Rod was doing, but stayed quiet.

"Finally, the Moties know the Field exists. We've all seen what they can do—frictionless surfaces, differential permeabilities, realignment of molecular structures. Look what the Brownies did with *Mac*'s generator! Frankly, Admiral, given that they know the Field is possible, it's only a question of time before their Engineers build one. Therefore, while protection of our technological secrets is important, it can't be the *only* consideration."

There was more excited chatter around the table, but the Admiral wasn't listening. He seemed to be thinking about what Rod had said.

Horvath took a breath to speak but controlled himself. Blaine had made the first visible impression on the Admiral, and Horvath was realist enough to know that anything he said would be rejected automatically. He nudged Hardy. "David, can't you say something?" he pleaded.

"We can take any precautions you like," Sally announced. "They accept the plague story, whether they believe it or not. They said their ambassadors would expect to be quarantined—surely they can't escape your security people, Admiral. And we won't have them long, you can Jump as soon as they're aboard."

"That is true," Hardy said thoughtfully. "Of course, we may irritate the Moties even more by taking their ambassadors—and never returning them."

"We wouldn't do *that!*" Horvath protested.

"We might, Anthony. Be realistic. If His Majesty decides that the Moties are dangerous and the Navy decides they know too much, they'll never be allowed to return."

"So there's no risk at all," Sally spoke quickly. "No threat to *Lenin* from Moties confined to quarantine. Admiral, I'm sure the lesser risk is to take them. That way we don't risk offending them until Prince Merrill—or His Majesty—can make decisions about the future."

"Um." Kutuzov sipped tea. His eyes showed interest. "You are persuasive, my lady. As are you, Captain Blaine." He paused. "Mr. Bury was not invited to this conference. I think it is time to hear from him. Boatswain, you will bring His Excellency to wardroom."

"Da, Admiral!"

They waited. The silence was broken by a dozen muttered conversations around the table.

"Rod, you were *brilliant*," Sally beamed. She reached under the table and squeezed his hand. "Thanks."

Bury entered, followed by the inevitable Marines. Kutuzov waved dismissal and they retired, leaving the Trader blinking at the end of the room. Cargill stood to give him his place at the table.

Bury listened attentively as Commander Borman summarized the arguments. If Bury was surprised by what he heard, he showed nothing, his expression remaining polite and interested.

"I ask for your advice, Excellency," Kutuzov said when Borman was finished. "I confess I do not want these creatures aboard this ship. Yet. Unless they are threat to safety of *Lenin* I do not believe I am justified in refusing Minister Horvath's request."

"Ah." Bury stroked his beard as he attempted to marshal his thoughts. "You are aware that in my opinion the Moties can read minds?"

"Ridiculous," snapped Horvath.

"Hardly ridiculous, Doctor," Bury said. His voice was calm and unruffled. "Improbable, perhaps, yet there is evidence of a rather unreliable human ability." Horvath started to say something but Bury continued smoothly, "Not conclusive evidence, of course, but evidence. And by reading minds I do not necessarily imply telepathy. Consider: the Moties' skill in the study of individual humans is such that they can literally play that person's role; play it so well that his friends cannot detect the difference. Only their appearance betrays them. How often have you seen ratings and Marines automatically obey the orders of a Motie mimicking an officer?"

"Make your point," Horvath said. He could hardly argue with *that;* what Bury said was common knowledge.

"Therefore: whether they do so by telepathy, or by perfect identification with human beings, they read minds. Thus they are the most persuasive creatures anyone will ever encounter. They know precisely what motivates us, and precisely what arguments to make."

"For God's sake!" Horvath exploded. "Are you saying they'll talk us into *giving* them *Lenin?*"

"Can you be certain they *can't? Certain,* Doctor?"

David Hardy cleared his throat. Everyone turned toward the Chaplain, and Hardy seemed embarrassed. Then he smiled. "I always knew study of the classics would have some practical value. Are any of you familiar with Plato's *Republic?* No, of course not. Well, on the first page, Socrates, conceded to be the most persuasive man who ever lived, is told by his friends that either Socrates will stay overnight with them, or his friends will compel him to do so by force. Socrates asks reasonably if there is not an alternative—can he not persuade them to let him go home. The reply, of course, is that he won't be able to because his friends won't listen to him."

There was a short silence.

"Oh," said Sally. *"Of course.* If the Moties never meet Admiral Kutuzov, or Captain Mikhailov—or any of *Lenin's* crew—how could they talk them into *anything?* Surely, Mr. Bury, you don't imagine they could persuade *MacArthur's* crew to mutiny?"

Bury shrugged. "My lady, with all respect, have you thought of what the Moties can offer? More wealth than exists in the Empire. Men have been corrupted by far less—"

And you've done it, too, Sally thought.

"If they're that good, why haven't they done it already?" Kevin Renner's voice was mocking, just short of insubordination. With his discharge due as soon as they returned to New Scotland, Renner could afford any action that wouldn't get him formally charged.

"Possibly they have not yet needed to do so," Bury said.

"More likely they can't do it," Renner retorted. "And if they can read minds, they've already got every secret we have. They associated with Sinclair, who knows how to fix everything in the Navy—they had a Fyunch(click) assigned to my Lord Blaine, who's got to know every political secret—"

"They were never in direct contact with Captain Blaine," Bury reminded him.

"They had Miss Fowler for as long as they needed." Renner chuckled at some interior joke. "She must know more about Empire politics than most of us. Mr. Bury, the Moties are good, but they're not *that* good, at persuasion, or at mind reading."

"I would be inclined to agree with Mr. Renner," Hardy added. "Although certainly the precautions suggested by Miss Fowler would be in order. Confine contact with the aliens to a select few: myself, for example. I doubt that they could corrupt me, but even if they could, I have no command authority. Mr. Bury, if he'll accept. Not, I suggest, Dr. Horvath or any scientist with access to complex equipment, and no ratings of Marines except under supervision both direct and by intercom. It may be rather hard on the Moties, but I think there could be little danger to *Lenin.*"

"Um. Well, Mr. Bury?" Kutuzov asked.

"But—I tell you, they're dangerous! The technological abilities are beyond belief. Allah the Merciful, who can know what they can construct from harmless items? Weapons, communications equipment, escape gear—" Bury's calm manner was evaporating and he struggled to contain himself.

"I withdraw the suggestion that Mr. Bury be given access to the Moties," Hardy said carefully. "I doubt if they would survive the experience. My apologies, Your Excellency."

Bury muttered in Arabic. Too late he realized that Hardy was a linguist.

"Oh, surely not," Hardy said with a smile. "I know my ancestry much better than *that.*"

"I can see, Admiral," Bury said, "that I have not been sufficiently persuasive. I'm sorry, because for once I have no motives but the welfare of the Empire. If I were interested only in profits—I am not slow to realize the trade potentials and the wealth to be made from the Moties. But I consider them the greatest danger the human race has ever faced."

"Da." Kutuzov spoke decisively. "On that we may possibly agree, if we add one word: potential danger, Excellency. What we consider here is lesser risk, and unless there is risk to *Lenin* I am now persuaded that lesser risk is to transport these ambassadors under conditions suggested by Chaplain Hardy. Dr. Horvath: you agree?"

"If that's the only way we can take them, yes. I think it's shameful to treat them this way—"

"Bah. Captain Blaine. Do you agree?"

Blaine stroked the bridge of his nose. "Yes, sir. Taking them is the lesser risk—if Moties are a threat, we can't prove it, and we may learn something from the ambassadors."

"My lady?"

"I agree with Dr. Horvath—"

"Thank you." Kutuzov seemed to be sucking lemons. His face puckered into near-agony. "Captain Mikhailov. You will make preparations for confinement of Moties. The fiction is risk of plague, but you will see that they cannot escape. Captain Blaine. You will inform Moties that we will take their ambassadors aboard, but it is possible they will not wish to come once they know conditions we must impose. No tools. No weapons. Baggage to be inspected and sealed, not available to them on voyage. No miniatures or other inferior castes, only ambassadors. Give them what reasons you like, but those conditions are not subject to change." He stood abruptly.

"Admiral, what about the gift ship?" Horvath asked. "Can't we take—" His voice trailed off, because there was no one to speak to. The Admiral had stalked out of the wardroom.

45 • The Crazy Eddie Jump

Kutuzov called it the Alderson point. *MacArthur*'s refugees tended to call it the Crazy Eddie point, and some of *Lenin*'s crew were catching the habit. It was above the plane of the Mote system, and usually rather hard to find. It would be no problem this time.

"Just project the path of the Motie ship until it intersects the direct line between the Mote and Murcheson's Eye," Renner told Captain Mikhailov. "You'll be close enough, sir."

"Motie astrogation is that efficient?" Mikhailov asked incredulously.

"Yah. It's enough to drive you crazy, but they can do it. Assume constant acceleration."

"There is another ship approaching that point from the Mote," Kutuzov said. He reached past Captain Mikhailov to adjust the bridge screen controls, and vectors flashed in front of them. "It will not arrive until well after we have departed."

"Fuel ship," Renner said positively. "And I'll bet anything you like that the ship carrying the ambassadors is light, transparent, and so obviously harmless that no one could suspect it of anything, sir."

"Not even me, you mean," Kutuzov said. Renner saw no smile to accompany the words. "Thank you, Mr. Renner. You will continue to assist Captain Mikhailov."

They had left the Trojan asteroids behind. Every scientist aboard wanted *Lenin*'s telescopes to examine those asteroids and the Admiral had made no objections. It was not clear whether he feared a last-minute attack from the asteroids, or shared the civilians' wish to know everything about Moties, but Buckman and the others had their chance.

Buckman soon lost interest. The asteroids were thoroughly civilized and their orbits had been shaped. They weren't worth anything at all. The others didn't share that view. They watched the light of Motie fusion drives, measured neutrino fluxes from power stations, saw flecks of light that showed a dark spectrum around the chlorophyll green band, and wondered. Huge plant farms were under domes there—it was the only possible conclusion. And on every rock large enough to see, there was the characteristic single crater proving conclusively that the asteroid had been moved.

Once Buckman regained his interest. He had been examining the asteroid orbits as a favor to Horvath. Suddenly his eyes went blank. Then he feverishly punched codes into the computer and watched the results. "Incredible."

"What's incredible?" Horvath asked patiently.

"The Stone Beehive was dead cold."

"Yes." Horvath had experience drawing information out of Buckman.

"Assume the rest of the asteroids are. I believe it. Those orbits are perfect—project them back or forward as far as you like, they'll *never* have collisions. Those things could have been up there a *long* time."

Horvath went away talking to himself. Just how old *was* that asteroid civilization? Buckman thought in stellar lifetimes! No wonder the Stone Beehive had been cold: the Moties made no orbit corrections. They just put them where they wanted them—

Well, he thought, time to get back to the gift ship. It won't be long before we have to abandon it—wonder if Blaine's making any progress?

Rod and Sally were at the moment in conference with the Admiral. They met on the bridge: to the best of Rod's knowledge, no one but the Admiral and his steward had ever seen the inside of Kutuzov's cabin. Possibly not even the Admiral, as he seemed always to be on the bridge, watching the screens like any scope dope, perpetually looking for Motie treachery.

"It is pity," Kutuzov was saying. "That ship would be valuable. But we cannot risk it aboard. Mechanisms—who knows what they are for? And with Moties here to take advantage?" Kutuzov shuddered.

"Yes, sir," Rod agreed affably. He doubted that the gift ship was any threat, but there *were* assemblies not even Sinclair could understand. "I was thinking of some of the other artifacts. Small parts. Those statuettes Chaplain Hardy is so fond of. We could seal everything in plastic, then weld it all inside grounded steel containers and strap the whole works on the hull inside the Field. If the Moties have anything that'll hurt us after those precautions, maybe it's better we don't go home."

"Um." The Admiral fingered his beard. "You believe these artifacts valuable?"

"Yes, sir." When Kutuzov said valuable, he meant something different from what Sally or Horvath implied. "The more we know about Motie technology, the better threat estimates Cargill and I can make, sir."

"Da. Captain, I wish your honest opinion. What do you think of Moties?"

Sally controlled herself with an effort. She wondered what Rod would say. He was proving to be an absolute genius at maneuvering the Admiral.

Rod shrugged. "I can agree with both Dr. Horvath and yourself, sir." When Kutuzov's eyes widened, Rod hastened to add, "They could be the greatest potential danger we have ever faced, or the greatest potential opportunity we've ever found. Or both. Either way, the more we know about them, the better—provided we take precautions against the dangers."

"Uh. Captain, I value your opinion. If I give permission, will you take personal responsibility for neutralization of any threat from Motie artifacts taken from that ship? I want more than obedience. I demand your cooperation, and your word that you will take no risks."

That isn't going to make me popular with Horvath, Rod reflected. At first the Science Minister will be glad to take *anything;* but it won't be long before he'll want something I can't be sure of. "Yes, sir. I'll go over and see to it myself. Uh—I'll need Miss Fowler."

Kutuzov's eyes narrowed. "Bah. You will be responsible for her safety."

"Of course."

"Very well. Dismissed." As Rod and Sally left the bridge, Commander Borman looked curiously at his Admiral. He wondered if he saw a grin. No, of course not. It simply wasn't possible.

If there had been an officer of higher rank than Blaine present at the time, Kutuzov might have explained, but he would not discuss a captain—and future marquis—with Borman. What he might have said, though, was, "It is worth risk of Miss Fowler to keep Blaine active. When he does not brood, he is good officer." Kutuzov might never leave the bridge, but the morale of his officers was part of his duty; and like all duties he took it seriously.

The conflicts developed immediately, of course. Horvath wanted *everything,* and assumed that Rod had merely been humoring the Admiral; when he found that Blaine took his promise seriously, the honeymoon was over. He was midway between rage and tears as Blaine's crewmen began to disassemble the gift ship, ripping apart delicate assemblies—sometimes cutting at random to prevent the possibility that the Moties had predicted what humans would do—and packing them in plastic containers.

For Rod, it was a period of useful activity again; and this time he had Sally for company. They could talk for hours when they were not working. They could drink brandy, and invite Chaplain Hardy in. Rod began to learn something of anthropology as he listened to Sally and Hardy argue over theoretical niceties of cultural development.

As they approached the Crazy Eddie point, Horvath became almost frantic. "You're as bad as the Admiral, Blaine," he charged as he watched an artificer use a cutting torch on an assembly that generated the complex field altering molecular structures in another magic coffeepot.

"We've already *got* one of those aboard *Lenin*. What harm would another do?"

"The one we have wasn't designed by Moties who knew it would go aboard the battleship," Sally answered. "And this one is different . . ."

"Everything the Moties make is different," snapped Horvath. "You're the worst of the lot—more cautious than Blaine, by God. I'd have thought you'd know better."

She smiled demurely and tossed a coin. "Better cut it there too," she told the artificer.

"Yes, miss." The spacer shifted his torch and began again.

"Bah." Horvath stamped out to find David Hardy. The Chaplain had assumed the role of peacemaker, and it was just as well; without him communications on the cutter would have ceased within hours.

The spacer finished slicing the assembly and packed it into the waiting box. He poured plastic around it and sealed the lid. "Got a steel crate outside, sir. I'll just go weld it in."

"Good. Carry on," Blaine told him. "I'll inspect it later." When the spacer had left the cabin, he turned to Sally. "You know, I never noticed, but Horvath's right. You *are* more cautious than I am. Why?"

She shrugged. "Don't worry about it."

"I won't, then."

"There's Buckman's protostar," she said. She flicked off the lights, then took his hand and led him to the viewport. "I never get tired of looking at it."

There were a few moments before their eyes adjusted and the Coal Sack was more than endless blackness. Then the reds began to show, and there was a small whirlpool of red on black.

They stood very close. They did a lot of that lately, and Rod liked it. He ran his fingers up her spine until he was scratching her gently beneath the right ear.

"You'll have to tell the Motie ambassadors pretty soon," she said. "Thought of what you'll say to them?"

"More or less. Might have been better to give them

some warning, but—well, the Admiral's way may be safer."

"I doubt if it makes any difference. It will be nice to get back where there are more stars. I wonder— Rod, what do you think the Motie ambassadors will be like?"

"No idea at all. I guess we'll know soon enough. You talk too much."

"That's what Uncle Ben tells me."

They were quiet for a long time.

"Stand by. They're coming aboard."

"OPEN HANGAR DECK HATCHES. LINE CARRIERS AWAY."

"STAND BY WINCHES."

The gig was brought down into *Lenin's* maw. Another boat stood by with the Moties' baggage; everything, even the pressure suits the Moties had worn aboard the gig, had been transferred over in a separate boat. The passenger gig landed on the steel decks with a *clunk*.

"Ship's company, ATTENTION."

"Marines, PRESENT ARMS!"

The air lock opened and a full boatswains' chorus sounded the pipes. A brown-and-white face appeared. Then another. When the two Mediators were entirely outside the gig, the third Motie emerged.

It was pure white, with silky tufts at the armpits, and there was gray around the muzzle and dotted through the torso.

"An older Master," Blaine whispered to Sally. She nodded. Cosmic ray impact on hair follicles had the same effects on Moties as on humans.

Horvath strode forward to the end of the line of Marines and side boys. "Welcome aboard," he said. "I'm very glad to see you—this is a historic moment."

"For both races, we hope," the lead Mediator replied.

"On behalf of the Navy, welcome aboard," Rod said. "I must apologize again for the quarantine precautions, but—"

"Don't worry about it," one Motie said. "I am called Jock. And this is Charlie." She indicated the other Mediator. "The names are just a convenience; you couldn't pronounce ours." She turned to the white Master and twittered, ending with "Captain Roderick Blaine and Minister Anthony Horvath," then turned back to the humans. "My Lord Minister Horvath, I present the Ambassador. He requests that you call him Ivan."

Rod bowed. He had never been face to face with a Motie, and he felt an urgent impulse to reach forward and stroke the fur. A male White.

"The honor guard will conduct you to your quarters," Rod said. "I hope they will be large enough; there are two adjacent cabins." And four cursing officers who were displaced from them, too; the ripples of that had run down through the Navy pecking order until a junior lieutenant found himself in the gun room with *Lenin*'s middies.

"One cabin would be sufficient," Charlie said calmly. "We do not need privacy. It is not one of our species' requirements." There was something familiar about Charlie's voice, and it bothered Rod.

The Moties bowed in unison, perfect copies of Court behavior; Rod wondered where they'd learned *that*. He returned the bow, as did Horvath and the others in hangar deck, then the Marines led them away, another squad falling in at the rear of the procession. Chaplain Hardy would be waiting for them in their cabins.

"A male," Sally mused.

"Interesting. The Mediators called it 'the Ambassador,' yet the Moties implied that the three had equal powers. We were told they have to act in unison to sign treaties—"

"Maybe the Mediators aren't *his* Mediators," said Sally. "I'll ask—I'm sure I'll get the chance. Rod, are you *sure* I can't go up there with them? Now?"

He grinned. "You'll get your shot. Let Hardy have his for the moment." Hangar deck was clearing rapidly now. There hadn't been a single *Lenin* crewman there, or in the boats that met the Motie ship. The baggage gig was winched into place and sealed off.

"NOW HEAR THIS. MAN YOUR JUMP STATIONS, STAND BY FOR ALDERSON DRIVE. MAN YOUR JUMP STATIONS."

"Not wasting any time, is he?" Sally said.

"None at all. We'd better hurry." He took her hand and led her toward his cabin as *Lénin* began slowing her rotation to zero gravity. "I suspect the Moties didn't need the spin," Rod said as they reached the cabin door. "But that's the Admiral. If you're going to do something, do it right—"

"STAND BY FOR ALDERSON DRIVE. MAN YOUR JUMP STATIONS."

"Come on," Rod urged. "We've just time to get the Motie cabin on the intercom." He turned the controls until the Motie quarters were in view.

Chaplain Hardy was saying, "If you need anything, there will be orderlies outside your door at all times, and that button and switch will connect directly to my cabin. I'm your official host for this trip."

Tones sounded through the ship. Hardy frowned. "I'll go to my cabin now—you'll probably prefer to be alone for the Alderson shift. And I suggest you get in your bunks and stay there until the shift is over." He caught himself before he could say anything else. His instructions were clear: the Moties learned nothing until they were out of their home system.

"Will it take long?" Jock asked.

Hardy smiled thinly. "No. Good-by, then."

"*Auf Wiedersehen,*" said Jock.

"*Auf Wiedersehen.*" David Hardy left with a puzzled look. Now just where had they learned *that?*

The bunks were wrongly proportioned, and too hard, and made no provision for individual differences among the Moties. Jock swiveled her torso and waved her lower right arm, so, indicating displeasure with the situation but surprise that things were not worse. "Obviously copied from something for a Brown." Her tones indicated positive knowledge deduced but not observed directly. The voice changed to conversational mode. "I wish we had been able to bring our own Brown."

Charlie: "I also. But we would not be trusted with a

Brown. I know." She began a new thought, but the Master spoke.

Ivan: "Was the human Master among those waiting to meet us?"

Jock: "No. Curse! So long I have tried to study him, and still I have not met him nor even heard his voice. For all of me, he may be a committee, or one Master subject to discipline from the humans. I would wager much of my anatomy that he is human."

Ivan spoke. "You will make no attempt to contact the Master of Lenin. Should we meet him, you will not become his Fyunch(click). We know what happens to the Fyunch(click)s of humans."

It was not necessary to speak in response. The Master knew he had been heard, and thus would be obeyed. He went to his bunk and looked with distaste.

Alarms rang, and human speech came through loud-speakers.

"Prepare for Crazy Eddie Drive. Final Warning," one translated. They lay on the bunks. A louder tone sounded through the ship.

Then something horrible happened.

46 • Personal and Urgent

"Rod! Rod, look at the Moties!"

"Uh?" Blaine struggled for control of his traitor body. Awareness was difficult; concentration was impossible. He looked across to Sally, then followed her gaze to the intercom screen.

The Moties were twitching uncontrollably. They'd drifted free of their bunks, and the Ambassador floated about the cabin in complete disorientation. He caromed off a bulkhead and drifted toward the other side. The two Mediators watched, unable to do anything and in trouble themselves. One cautiously reached for the Master but lost her grip on the fur. All three were drifting helplessly about the compartment.

Jock was the first to anchor herself to a hand hold. She whistled and snorted, then Charlie drifted toward the Master. She caught his fur in the left arm, and Jock, holding the bulkhead with two rights, extended his left until Charlie could grasp it. They painfully worked their way back to the bunks and Jock strapped Ivan in. They lay disconsolately, whistling and clucking.

"Shouldn't we help?" Sally asked.

Rod flexed his limbs and took a square root in his head. Then he tried two integrals and got them right. His mind was recovering enough to pay attention to Sally and the Moties. "No. Nothing we could do anyway—there's no permanent effect ever been observed, barring a few who just go insane and never get back in contact with reality."

"The Moties haven't done that," Sally said positively. "They acted purposefully, but they weren't very good at it. We recovered much quicker than they did."

"Nice to see something we're better at than Moties are. Hardy ought to show up pretty soon—it'll take him a while longer than us, though. He's older."

"ACCELERATION WARNING. STAND BY FOR ONE GRAVITY. ACCELERATION WARNING." A Mediator twittered something, and the Master responded.

Sally watched them awhile. "I guess you're right. They don't seem in too much trouble, but the Master's still a little twitchy."

A tone sounded. *Lenin* jolted, and weight returned. They were under command and headed home. Rod and Sally looked at each other and smiled. Home.

"What could you do for the Master anyway?" Rod asked.

She shrugged helplessly. "Nothing, I suppose. They're so *different*. And—Rod, what would you do if you were Imperial Ambassador to another race and they locked you in a little cabin with not one, but two spy eyes in each compartment?"

"I've been waiting for them to smash the damn things.

They saw them, of course. We didn't try to hide them. But if they said anything to Hardy we must have missed it."

"I doubt if they did. They don't act as if they care about them. Privacy 'is not one of our species' requirements,' Charlie said." Sally shuddered. "That's *really* different."

A buzzer sounded and Rod automatically turned toward his cabin door before he realized it had come over the intercom. One of the Moties walked carefully across the cabin and opened her door. Hardy came in.

"Everything all right?" he asked warily.

"You might have warned us about that," Jock said. There was no accusation in the voice; it was a simple statement of fact. "Does the Crazy Eddie Drive affect humans like that?"

"Like what?" Hardy asked innocently.

"Disorientation. Vertigo. Inability to concentrate. Muscles out of control. Nausea. Death wish."

Hardy looked surprised. Probably he was, Rod thought. The Chaplain wouldn't watch the Moties without telling them he was doing it, even though half a dozen pairs of eyes would be staring at the screens every watch. "There is an effect on humans, yes," came Hardy's voice. "Not so violent as you describe. The Drive causes disorientation and a general inability to concentrate, but the effect passes rapidly. We didn't know how it would affect you, but in all our history there have been few cases of irreversible effects, and those were all, uh, psychological."

"I see," said Charlie. "Dr. Hardy, if you will excuse us, we do not yet feel up to conversation. Perhaps in a few hours. And next time we will take your advice and be in our bunks, strapped down, and asleep, when you turn on your Crazy Eddie machine."

"I'll leave you then," Hardy said. "Could we—is there anything you require? Is the Ambassador all right?"

"He is well enough. Thank you for your concern."

Hardy left, and the Moties went back to their bunks. They twittered and whistled.

"And that," Rod said, "is that. I can think of a lot of

more interesting things to do than watch Moties lie around chattering in a language I don't understand."

And there's plenty of time to study the Moties, Sally thought. For a wonder, we don't either one of us have duties right now—and we do have privacy. "So can I," she said demurely.

Despite the cubic kilometers of yellow-hot flame around her, *Lenin* was a happy ship. Kutuzov relaxed his vigil and let the crew resume normal watches for the first time since the destruction of *MacArthur*. Although the ship was deep within a sun, she had fuel, and her problems were in the Book. Navy routine would deal with them. Even the scientists forgot their disappointment at leaving the alien system with unanswered questions: they were going home.

The only woman in ten parsecs would have been a subject for speculation under any circumstances. Fights might have started over either of two questions. *What are my/your chances with her?* and *Is she being wasted?* But Sally had clearly chosen her man. It made life easier for those who worry over such problems, and for those whose duty it is to stop fist fights.

The first night after the Jump, Kutuzov held a dinner party. It was formal, and most of the guests did not enjoy themselves much; the Admiral's table talk was confined to professional matters. However, he left early, and a much wilder party developed.

Rod and Sally stayed for three hours. Everyone wanted to talk about Moties, and Rod was surprised to find himself discussing them with only a hint of the dull pain that had formerly come over him when he thought of the aliens. Sally's enthusiasm was enough in itself—and besides, she seemed as worried about *him* as about the aliens. She had even spent hours remaking Mikhailov's extra dress uniform so that it almost fit.

When they left the party, neither Moties nor the Mote were mentioned during the hours they were together before going to their separate cabins.

The ship moved outward. Eventually the yellow beyond

the Field turned to orange, then brick-red, and *Lenin's* probes reported her Field hotter than the photosphere around her. Scientists and crew alike eagerly watched the screen, and when stars appeared against a red-black background everyone had a drink in celebration. Even the Admiral joined them, his features a broad and heavy smile.

Shortly afterward the communications officer established contact with a waiting tanker. There was also a small message sloop, fast, manned by young crewmen in perfect physical condition. Kutuzov dictated his report and sent it with two of his midshipmen, and the sloop accelerated at three gravities, racing for the Alderson point where it would Jump to the New Caledonia System and deliver the report of mankind's first contact with an alien civilization.

The tanker carried mail and nearly a year's worth of news. There had been more revolts in the sector. A former colony had allied with an armed outie system and defied the Empire. New Chicago was occupied by the Army, and although the economy was working again much of the population was resentful of Imperial paternalism. The inflation of the crown was under control. Her Imperial Majesty had given birth to a boy, Alexander, and Crown Prince Lysander was no longer the only insurance of the present Imperial line. That news was worth another celebration on *Lenin*, and it got so big that Mikhailov had to borrow *MacArthur* crewmen to man his ship.

The sloop returned with more messages masered even before the message ship could rendezvous. The Sector Capital was wild with enthusiasm, and the Viceroy was planning a gala reception for the Motie ambassadors. War Minister Armstrong sent a muted "well done" and a thousand questions.

There was also a message for Rod Blaine. He learned of it when he was summoned to Kutuzov's cabin by the Admiral's Marine orderly.

"This is probably it," Rod told Sally. "Put Blaine under arrest until he can be tried by court-martial."

"Don't be silly." She smiled encouragement. "I'll wait for you here."

"If they ever let me come back to my cabin." He turned to the Marine. "Lead on, Ivanov."

When he was let into the Admiral's cabin it was a shock. Rod had expected a bare room, functional and cold; instead it was a bewildering variety of colors, oriental carpets, tapestries on the walls, the inevitable icon and portrait of the Emperor but much more. There were even leather-bound books in a shelf above Kutuzov's desk. The Admiral indicated a Spartan rose teak chair. "Will you have tea?" he asked.

"Well—thank you, sir."

"Two glasses tea, Keemun." The steward drew them from a silver thermos shaped like an ancient Russian samovar, and served the tea in crystal cups.

"You may go. Captain Blaine, I have orders concerning you."

"Yes, sir." Rod said. He might at least have waited until I'd enjoyed the tea.

"You will be leaving this ship. As soon as the sloop makes rendezvous you are to go aboard for return to New Caledonia at maximum acceleration flight surgeon will approve."

"Yes, sir—are they *that* eager to haul me in front of a court-martial?"

Kutuzov looked puzzled. "Court-martial? I do not think so, Captain. There must be formal court of inquiry, certainly. That is in regulations. But I would be surprised if court of inquiry made charges against you."

Kutuzov turned to his elaborately carved desk. There was a message tape on the polished wood surface. "This is for you. It is marked 'personal and urgent' and doubtless it will explain."

Rod took the tape and examined it curiously.

"It is in commanding-officer code, of course," the Admiral said. "My flag secretary will assist you if you like."

"Thank you."

The Admiral used the intercom to summon a lieutenant, who fed decoding tapes into the code machine. It clattered out a thin form.

"Will that be all, Admiral?" the Lieutenant asked.

"Yes. Captain, I leave you to read your message. Good morning." Admiral and lieutenant left the cabin as the code machine continued to chatter. The message flimsy wormed out of the machine's innards.

Rod tore it off and read in growing wonder.

He read it again on his way back to his cabin. Sally stood when he came in. "Rod, that's the strangest look I've ever seen!"

"Got a letter," he said.

"Oh—news from home?"

"Sort of."

She smiled, but her voice was puzzled. "How is everyone? Your father all right?" Rod seemed very nervous and excited, but he was too cheerful to have got bad news. So what was upsetting him? It was as if he had some task to carry out, something he wanted to do but was afraid of—

"My family's fine. So is yours—you'll know about that soon enough. Senator Fowler is in New Scotland."

She looked at him incredulously. "Uncle Ben is out here? But why?"

"He says he got worried about you. Nobody to take care of you, so he had to—"

She put her tongue out at him and grabbed for the message blank. Rod dodged nimbly despite the gravity-and-a-half acceleration.

"All right," he told her. He laughed, but it was strained. "The Emperor sent him. As his personal representative, to chair an Imperial Commission to negotiate with the Moties." Rod paused. "We're both appointed to the Commission."

She looked at him blankly. Slow comprehension invaded her eyes. This was professional recognition beyond anything she'd imagined.

"Congratulations, Commissioner," Rod laughed. He caught her wrist in both hands and held her at arm's length. "The Lord President of His Majesty's Commission Extraordinary also asks me when we're getting married. I think it's a pretty fair question."

"But—I—Rod—we—" She caught her breath.

"By God, I've got you at a loss for words. Just once you're not talking." He took advantage of the opportunity to kiss her. Then again. That lasted a long time.

"I think I'd better read that letter," she said when they parted. "If you please."

"You still haven't answered your uncle's question, and I won't let you read it until you do."

"*His* question!" Her eyes flashed. "Rod Blaine, if I do marry anyone—*if*, mind you—he's going to ask me himself!"

"All right. Lady Sandra Liddell Leonovna Bright Fowler, will you marry me?" The banter was gone from his voice, and although he tried to keep his grin he lost that too. He looked like a four-year-old about to sit on Father Christmas' lap for the first time. "When we get back to New Scotland—"

"Yes, of course I'll marry you—New Scotland? Rod, your father will expect us to be married at Court. All our friends are on Sparta—"

"I think maybe you'd better read that message, sweetheart. We may not get to Sparta for a while." He handed her the flimsy and perched on the arm of the chair she sank into. "It's this part." He pointed.

FIRST REACTION HERE UNCERTAIN WHETHER TO MAKE YOU HERO OR VILLAIN STOP LOSS OF MACARTHUR NOT GREETED WITH JOY AT ADMIRALTY STOP CRANSTON EXPLODED STOP ARMSTRONG SAID QUOTE HOW IN HELL CAN ANYONE LOSE A BATTLE CRUISER CLOSE QUOTE STOP

PARAGRAPH KUTUZOV REPORT IN YOUR FAVOR STOP KUTUZOV TAKES FULL RESPONSIBILITY FOR LOSS STOP KUTUZOV REPORTS POSSIBLE SUPERIOR CASTES MOTIES COULD HAVE CLEARED MACARTHUR OF VERMIN BUT HIS DECISION RISK OF COMPROMISE OF IMPERIAL TECHNOLOGICAL SECRETS TOO GREAT STOP KUTUZOV STILL UNDECIDED EXTENT OF MOTIE THREAT BUT SUGGESTS ADMIRALTY ASSEMBLE LARGE BATTLE FLEET STOP HORVATH REPORT STATES MOTIES FRIENDLY NO FLEET NEEDED AND MOTIES QUOTE GREATEST OPPORTUNITY IN HISTORY CLOSE QUOTE STOP PROBLEM IN MY LAP STOP

"Ours too," Rod said. "Read on."

PARAGRAPH BY ORDER OF SOVEREIGN I AM NOW LORD PRESIDENT OF IMPERIAL COMMISSION EXTRAORDINARY FOR NEGOTIATING WITH ALIENS STOP BY PERSONAL DIRECTION OF HIS MAJESTY RODERICK LORD BLAINE DASH THAT IS YOU BUT YOU ALMOST BLEW IT LOSING YOUR SHIP STOP DO NOT MAKE HABIT OF THAT DASH AND LADY SANDRA BRIGHT APPOINTED COMMISSIONERS STOP COMMISSION HAS FULL AUTHORITY TO ACT IN NAME OF SOVEREIGN STOP COMMISSIONERS WILL REMAIN IN NEW SCOTLAND UNLESS ADVISABLE CONVEY ALIEN REPRESENTATIVES TO SPARTA STOP

PARAGRAPH IF COMMISSION CONCLUDES ALIENS POSE THREAT OR POTENTIAL THREAT TO EMPIRE COMMISSION WILL ACT IN CONCERT WITH VICEROY TRANSCOALSACK TO TAKE SUCH IMMEDIATE MEASURES AS SEEM ADVISABLE STOP ANY SUGGESTIONS INTERROGATIVE

PARAGRAPH ROD UNLESS THOSE MOTIES ARE SIMPLE FARMERS AND THIS PROBE MAKES ME SURE THEY AINT YOU AND SALLY ARE GOING TO BE OUT HERE A LONG TIME STOP PRESUME YOU HAVE RETAINED SANITY SO ARE ENGAGED TO SALLY STOP WHEN IS WEDDING INTERROGATIVE YOUR FATHER SENDS BLESSINGS STOP SO DO I STOP MARQUIS EXPECTS YOU TWO WILL BE MARRIED BY NEXT TIME HE SEES YOU STOP IF YOU THINK MARQUIS AND I HAVE ARRANGED THIS YOU AINT SEEN NOTHING YET STOP HIS MAJESTY APPROVES IMMEDIATE WEDDING STOP YOUR MOTHER AND EMPRESS SEND BLESSINGS STOP

"But what if I said no?" Sally demanded. "That's the most arrogant thing I've ever seen!"

"But you didn't say no. You said yes." He leaned down to kiss her hard.

She struggled away and he saw she was genuinely angry.

"Damn it." Her voice was very low and clear. "Damn. 'His Majesty approves'—God's teeth! If I turned you down now it'd be high treason!"

"I did ask first," he pointed out. "And you answered. First."

"That was clever. Oh, stop looking like a little boy.

Yes, I want to marry you. I don't much like being *commanded* to do something I wanted to do anyway."

He studied her. "You were out from under for a long time. I never was."

"What?"

"The obligations that go with the titles. First you were en route to study primitive cultures—your own free choice. I went to the Academy for my *Wanderjahr*. Then you were in the prison camp, but even in that hellhole you weren't under any authority you could *respect.*" He was choosing his words with great care. Sally was red with anger.

"Then *MacArthur*. As a guest. Under my authority then, remember? And you respected the fact to such an extent—"

"All *right,* I stowed away when we captured the Crazy Eddie probe. You know why."

"Too right. Then New Scotland, where you were practically the highest rank around. You enjoyed that, didn't you? The few people above you weren't interested in making you do anything. And on to Mote Prime, doing exactly what you wanted to do in life. You were out from under for a long time. Now you're back in the box."

"That's what it feels like."

Rod flicked the flimsy in her hand. "Arrogant as hell. Right. It jarred me, but not the way it got to you. I've been under orders for a long time. All my life."

"It's the first time you've been ordered to marry anyone, I take it."

"Yeah. But we've both been expecting something like that, haven't we? Politically, from an Empire standpoint, our marriage is just too good an alliance to pass up. We get the privileges, the property, the titles, and now the bill comes in. Blind luck we love each other, because we owe it to—"

"To whom?" she demanded.

Rod grinned helplessly. The idea was irresistibly funny. "To Kevin Renner. The Empire exists for the purpose of making it easier for Renner to play tourist. We owe this to

Renner, and we're paid well for the privilege, and he's gonna collect."

She was awed. "Does he really think that way? My God, he does! He ordered me to your cabin!"

"What? He *what?*"

She giggled. "Fantastic. We ought to ask him and see what he does. Let me finish reading this, Rod."

PARAGRAPH I HAVE DISCRETION IN NAMING OTHER MEMBERS OF COMMISSION STOP WILL EXPECT YOUR HELP STOP EVERYBODY IN FIFTY PARSECS WANTS ON COMMISSION STOP GIVEN POWERS HIS MAJESTY DELEGATED TO US DONT BLAME THEM STOP YOUR FIRST TASK IS HELPING ME TO FILL OUT COMMISSION STOP SECOND WILL BE ARRANGING EVIDENCE AND WITNESS LIST STOP

PARAGRAPH ADMIRAL KUTUZOV HAS ORDERS TO PUT YOU ABOARD MESSAGE SLOOP FOR RETURN BEST POSSIBLE SPEED TO NEW SCOTLAND STOP BRING SALLY IF YOU THINK BEST AND FLIGHT SURGEON APPROVES STOP ADMIRAL WILL ASSUME RESPONSIBILITY FOR HORACE BURY STOP GET MOVING STOP KISS SALLY FOR ME STOP BREAK BREAK REGARDS BENJAMIN BRIGHT FOWLER COMMA SENATOR OPEN PARENTHESES LORD PRESIDENT IMPERIAL COMMISSION EXTRAORDINARY ACTING FOR HIS MAJESTY LEONIDAS IX CLOSE PARENTHESES BREAK MESSAGE ENDSXX

"Am I going in the message sloop?" she asked.

"That's up to you. You're in condition. Want to?"

"Yes—there are a lot of things to arrange before the Moties get there— My God, we've got to settle things about the Moties, and there's the wedding— Rod, do you realize how big a deal the marriage of Crucis Court and the Fowler heir will be in a provincial capital? I'll need three secretaries, Uncle Ben's not going to be any use, and we've got to arrange for a reception for the Moties and— Oh, all right. Where were we?"

47 · *Homeward Bound*

Kutuzov and Mikhailov went all out in preparing for Rod and Sally's farewell dinner party. *Lenin*'s cooks worked all day to turn out a traditional Ekaterina banquet: dozens of courses, soups, pastries, roasts, stuffed grape leaves from the hydroponics farm, shish kebab, an endless stream of food; and between courses there were thimble glasses of vodka. It was impossible to talk during the meal, for as soon as one course was finished *MacArthur*'s stewards brought another; or, to give a respite for digestion, *Lenin*'s Marines performed dances transported from the Russian steppes to St. Ekaterina's hills and preserved nine hundred years by fanatics like Kutuzov.

Finally the bandsmen left and the stewards removed the dishes, leaving the guests with tea and more vodka. *Lenin*'s junior midshipman toasted the Emperor, and Captain Mikhailov toasted the Tsarevitch Alexander, while the Admiral beamed.

"He can put on quite a show when he's not scared silly," Renner whispered to Cargill. "Never thought I'd say that— Here it comes. The Tsar himself's going to give a toast. Who's left?"

The Admiral stood and lifted his glass. "I will reserve my toast for one moment," he said thickly. It was possible that the endless glasses of vodka had affected him, but no one could be certain. "Captain Blaine, when next we meet roles will be reversed. Then you must tell *me* how to deal with Moties. I do not envy you that task."

"What's Horvath scowling about?" Cargill whispered. "He looks like somebody put a frog in his bunk."

"Aye. Is it nae possible he wants a place on yon Commission?" Sinclair asked.

"Bet that's it," Renner put in. "I wouldn't mind being on it myself—"

"You and everybody else," Cargill said. "Now shut up and listen."

"There is more we must congratulate Lord Blaine about," Kutuzov was saying, "and that is why I reserve toast. Chaplain Hardy has announcement."

David Hardy stood. His smile was broad and merry. "Lady Sandra has given me the honor of formally announcing her engagement to Lord Commissioner Blaine," Hardy said. "I've already extended my private congratulations—let me be the first to give them publicly."

Everyone spoke at once, but the Admiral cut them off. "And now my toast," Kutuzov said. "To the future Marquise of Crucis."

Sally blushed as she sat while the others stood and lifted their glasses. Well, it's official now, she thought. No way to get out of it if I wanted to—not that I do, but it's so *inevitable* now . . .

"Also to Lady Commissioner," Kutuzov added. Everyone drank again. "And to Lord Commissioner. Long life and many children. May you protect our Empire when you negotiate with Moties."

"Our thanks," Rod said. "We'll do our best, and of course I'm the luckiest man alive."

"Perhaps her ladyship will speak," Kutuzov prompted.

She stood, but she could think of nothing to say. "Thank you all," she blurted and sat.

"Out of words again?" Rod asked wickedly. "And with all these people around—I've lost a rare opportunity!"

After that the formality vanished. Everyone pressed around them.

"All the happiness in the world," Cargill said. He pumped Rod's hand vigorously. "I really mean that, sir. And the Empire couldn't have made a better choice for the Commission."

"You will nae be married before we arrive?" Sinclair asked. " 'Twould nae be fair, to be married in my city wi'out me present."

"We don't quite know when," Sally told him. "But certainly not before *Lenin* gets in. You're all invited to the wedding, of course." So are the Moties, she added to herself. And I wonder what they'll make of it?

The party dissolved into a kaleidoscope of small groups with Rod and Sally at the focus. The wardroom table was lowered into the deck to give them more room as stewards circulated with coffee and tea.

"You will of course allow me to offer my congratulations," Bury told them smoothly. "And I hope you will not think I am trying to bribe you when I send a wedding gift."

"Why would anyone think that?" Sally asked innocently. "Thank you, Mr. Bury." If her first remark had been ambiguous, her smile was warm enough to cover it. Sally didn't care for Bury's reputation, but he'd been charming enough while she'd known him; if only he'd get over this insane fear of Moties!

Eventually Rod was able to move away from the center of the party. He found Dr. Horvath in a corner of the room. "You've been avoiding me all night, Doctor," Rod said affably. "I'd like to know why."

Horvath tried to smile but realized it was thin. His brows knitted for a moment, then relaxed in decision. "No point in anything but honesty. Blaine, I didn't want you on this expedition. You know why. OK, your man Renner convinced me you couldn't have done anything else about the probe. We've had our differences, but all in all I have to approve of the way you've handled the command. With your rank and experience it was inevitable that you'd be given a place on the Commission."

"I hadn't expected it," Rod answered. "In hindsight and from Sparta's viewpoint I suppose you're right. Is that why you're upset with me?"

"No," Horvath said honestly. "As I said, it was inevitable, and I don't let laws of nature upset me. But I expected a place on that Commission, Blaine. I was senior scientist on this expedition. I had to fight for every scrap of information we got. By God, if they're giving two seats to expedition members I've earned a place."

"And Sally hasn't," Rod said coldly.

"She was very useful," Horvath said. "And she's charming and bright, and of course you're hardly going to be objective about her—but honestly, Blaine, do you really equate her competence with mine?"

Rod's frown vanished. He smiled broadly, and almost laughed. Horvath's professional jealousy was neither comic nor pathetic, merely inevitable; as inevitable as his belief that the appointment questioned his competence as a scientist. "Relax, Doctor," Rod said. "Sally isn't on that Commission because of scientific ability any more than I am. The Emperor's not concerned with competence, but interest." He almost said loyalty, and that wouldn't have done at all. "In a way, your not being named immediately"—Rod emphasized that word—"is a compliment."

Horvath's brows shot up. "I beg your pardon?"

"You're a scientist, Doctor. Your whole training and really your whole philosophy of life is objectivity, right?"

"More or less," Horvath agreed. "Although since I left the laboratory—"

"You've had to fight for budgets. Even then you've been involved in politics only to help your colleagues do the things you'd do if you were free of administrative duties."

"Well—yes. Thank you. Not many people seem to realize that."

"Consequently, your dealings with Moties would be the same. Objective. Nonpolitical. But that may not be the best course for the Empire. Not that you'd be wanting in *loyalty*, Doctor, but His Majesty *knows* Sally and I put the Empire first. We've been indoctrinated that way from the day we were born. We can't even pretend to scientific objectivity where Imperial interests are concerned." And if that doesn't smooth his feathers the hell with him.

It did, though. Horvath still wasn't happy, and he obviously wasn't going to give up trying for a seat on the Commission; but he smiled and wished Rod and Sally a happy marriage. Rod excused himself and went back to Sally with a feeling of accomplishment.

"But can't we even say good-by to the Moties?" she was pleading. "Rod, can't you convince him?"

Rod looked helplessly at the Admiral.

"My lady," Kutuzov said heavily. "I do not wish to disappoint you. When Moties arrive in New Scotland they will be your concern, not mine, and you will then tell me what to do about them. Until that time, Moties are my responsibility, and I intend no changes in policies agreed before they came aboard. Dr. Hardy can deliver any message to them."

What would he do if Rod and I ordered him to let us see them? she thought. As Commissioners. But that would make a scene, and Rod seems to think the Admiral's a pretty useful man. They could never work together again if we did that. Besides, Rod might not *do* it even if I ask him to. *Don't push.*

"It's not as if these Moties were special friends," Hardy reminded her. "They've had so little contact with people I hardly know them myself. I'm sure that will change when we get to New Scotland." Hardy smiled and changed the subject. "I trust you will keep your promise and wait for *Lenin* before you're married."

"But I insist you marry us," Sally said quickly. "We'll *have* to wait for you!"

"Thank you." Hardy was going to say something else, but Kelley came purposefully across the wardroom and saluted.

"Cap'n, I've got your gear sent off to *Hermes,* and Lady Sally's as well, and them orders did say 'soonest.' "

"My conscience," Rod laughed. "But he's right. Sally, we'd better get ready." He groaned. "It's going to be tough facing three gravs after *that* dinner—"

"I must leave also," Kutuzov said. "I have dispatches to put aboard *Hermes.*" He smiled awkwardly. "Farewell, my lady. And you also, Captain. Godspeed. You have been good officer."

"Why—thank you, sir." Rod looked around the wardroom and spotted Bury across the compartment. "Kelley, the Admiral's assuming responsibility for His Excellency—"

"With your permission I will continue Gunner Kelley in command of Marine guards," Kutuzov said.

"Certainly, sir. Kelley, be damn careful when we get to

New Scotland. He may or may not try to escape. I don't have any idea of what he's got to face when we get there, but the orders are plain enough, we're to keep him in custody. He may try to bribe one of your men—"

Kelley snorted. "He'd better not."

"Yeah. Well, so long, Kelley. Don't let Nabil put a dagger in your ribs. I'll want you with me on New Scotland."

"Yes, sir. You be careful, Captain. The Marquis will kill me if something happens to you. Told me that before we left Crucis Court."

Kutuzov cleared his throat loudly. "Our guests must leave immediately," he announced. "With our final congratulations."

Rod and Sally left the wardroom to a chorus of shouts, some overloud. The party seemed destined to last a long time.

The message sloop *Hermes* was a tiny affair. Her living space was no larger than *MacArthur*'s cutter, although overall she was much bigger. Aft of the life-support systems she was tankage and engines and little else but access crawlways. They were hardly aboard before they were under way.

There was little to do in the tiny ship, and the heavy acceleration made real work impossible anyway. The surgeon's mate examined his passengers at eight-hour intervals to be sure they were able to take *Hermes'* three gees, and approved Rod's request that they get it over with sooner and boost up to 3.5 gravs. Under that weight it was better to sleep as much as possible and confine mental activities to light conversation.

Murcheson's Eye was enormous behind them when they reached the Alderson Point. An instant later, the Eye was only a bright red star against the Coal Sack. It had a small yellow mote.

They were rushed aboard a landing craft the instant *Hermes* made orbit around New Scotland. Sally barely had time to say her farewells to the sloop's crew, then they were strapped in.

"VISITORS CLEAR LANDING BOAT. PASSENGERS SECURE FOR REENTRY."

There were clunks as the air locks were closed. "Ready, sir?" the pilot called.

"Yeah—"

The retros fired. It wasn't a smooth reentry at all; the pilot was in too much of a hurry, They dropped low over New Scotland's craggy rocks and spouting geysers. When they arrived at the city they still had too much speed and the pilot had to circle twice; then the boat came in slowly, hovered, and settled on the roof landing port of Admiralty House.

"There's Uncle Ben!" Sally shouted. She rushed forward to fling herself into his arms.

Benjamin Bright Fowler was eighty standard years old, and looked it; before regeneration therapy men would have guessed he was fifty and in his prime intellectual years. They would have been right about the latter guess.

He stood 174 cm and massed ninety kilos: a portly, short man, nearly bald, with a fringe of dark hair graying around a shiny dome. He never wore a hat except in the coldest weather, and usually forgot it then.

Senator Fowler was dressed outlandishly in baggy trousers flaring over soft, polished leather boots. A knee-length and very battered camel's-hair coat covered his upper body. His clothes were very expensive and never properly cared for. His dreamy eyes that tended to water and his rumpled appearance did not make him an impressive figure, and his political enemies had more than once made the mistake of taking his looks as a sign of his abilities. Sometimes, when the occasion was important enough, he'd let his valet choose his clothes and dress him properly, and then, for a few hours at least, he looked appropriate; he was, after all, one of the most powerful men in the Empire. Usually, though, he put on the first thing he found in his wardrobe, and since he would never let his servants throw out anything he'd once liked, he often wore old clothes.

He grasped Sally in a bear hug while she kissed his forehead. Sally was taller than her uncle and was tempted to plant a kiss on the top of his head, but she knew better. Benjamin Fowler neglected his appearance and became angry if anyone reminded him of that, but actually he was a little sensitive about his baldness. He also absolutely refused to allow cosmetic physicians to do anything for it.

"Uncle Ben, I'm glad to see you!" Sally pushed herself away before he crushed a rib. Then, with mock anger: "You've been rearranging my life! Did you *know* that radiogram would make Rod propose to me?"

Senator Fowler looked puzzled. "You mean he hadn't already?" He pretended to examine Rod with microscopic care. "He looks normal enough. Must be internal damage. How are you, Rod? You look good, boy." He enfolded Rod's hand in his own. His grip was strong enough to hurt. With his left hand Fowler extracted his pocket computer from beneath the disreputable folds of his thick coat. "Sorry to rush, kids, but we're late. Come on, come on—" He turned and darted for the elevator, leaving them to follow helplessly.

They went down twelve floors and Fowler led them around twists of corridors. Marines stood guard outside a door. "Inside, inside," the Senator urged. "Can't keep all those admirals and captains waiting. Come on, Rod!"

The Marines saluted and Rod absently responded. He entered in bewilderment: a large room, paneled in dark wood, with an enormous marble table across its length. Five captains and two admirals were seated at the table. A legal officer sat at a smaller desk, and there were places for a recorder and clerks. As soon as Rod entered someone intoned, "This Court of Inquiry is now in session. Step forward and be sworn. State your name."

"Uh?"

"Your name, Captain," the Admiral at the center of the table snapped. Rod didn't recognize him; he knew only half the officers in the room. "You do know your name, don't you?"

"Yes, sir— Admiral, I wasn't told I was coming directly to a Court of Inquiry."

"You know it now. *Please state your name.*"

"Roderick Harold, Lord Blaine, Captain, Imperial Space Navy; formerly master aboard INS *MacArthur*."

"Thank you."

They shot questions at him. "Captain, when did you first learn that the miniature aliens were capable of using tools and performing useful work?" "Captain, please describe the sterilization procedures you employed." "Captain, in your judgment, did the aliens outside the ship ever know you had miniatures loose aboard your vessel?"

He answered as best he could. Sometimes one officer would ask a question, only to have another say, "That's in the report, damn it. Didn't you listen to the tapes?"

The inquiry moved at blinding speed. Suddenly it was over. "You may retire for the moment, Captain," the presiding Admiral said.

Sally and Senator Fowler were waiting in the hall. There was a young woman in kilts with a businesslike brief case standing with them.

"Miss McPherson. My new social secretary," Sally introduced her.

"Very pleased to meet you, my lord. My lady, I had best be—"

"Certainly. Thank you." McPherson left with a click of heels on marble floors. She had a nice walk. "Rod," Sally said. "Rod, do you know how many parties we've *got* to go to?"

"Parties! My God, woman, they're deciding my fate in there and you—"

"Nonsense," Senator Fowler snapped. "That was decided weeks ago. When Merrill, Cranston, Armstrong, and I listened to Kutuzov's report. There I was, your appointment from His Majesty in my pocket, and you'd gone and lost your ship! It's a good thing your Admiral's an honest man, boy. Damn good thing."

The door opened. "Captain Blaine?" a clerk called.

He entered to stand in front of the table. The Admiral held up a paper and cleared his throat.

"Unanimous findings of a special Court of Inquiry convened to examine the circumstances surrounding the loss of His Imperial Majesty's General Class battle cruiser *MacArthur*. One. This Court finds that the vessel was lost through accidental infestation by alien life forms and was properly destroyed to prevent contamination of other vessels. Two. This Court honorably acquits her master, Captain Roderick Blaine, ISN, of negligence. Three. This Court orders the surviving officers of *MacArthur* to prepare a detailed report of procedures whereby such losses can be prevented in future. Four. This Court notes that the search and sterilization of *MacArthur* was hindered by the presence of a large number of civilian scientists and their equipment property aboard, and that Minister Anthony Horvath, senior scientist, protested the sterilization and advised minimum disruption of the civilian experiments. Five. This Court notes that Captain Blaine would have been more diligent in searching his vessel except for the difficulties noted in point four; and this Court recommends no reprimand for her master. These findings being unanimous, this Court is adjourned. Captain, you may go."

"Thank you, sir."

"Yeah. That was pretty sloppy, Blaine. You know that, don't you?"

"Yes, sir." *My God, how many times have I thought about it?*

"But I doubt if anyone in the Navy could have done better. The ship must have been a madhouse with all those civilians aboard. All right, Senator, he's all yours. They're ready in Room 675."

"Good. Thank you, Admiral." Fowler hustled Blaine out of the hearing room and down the corridor to the elevator. A petty officer had one waiting.

"Now where are we going?" Rod demanded. "Six seventy-five? That's retirement!"

"Of course," the senator said. They entered the elevator. "You didn't think you could stay in the Navy and be on that Commission, did you? That's why we had to hurry that Inquiry through. Until it was on the record you couldn't be retired."

"But, Senator—"

"Ben. Call me Ben."

"Yes, sir. Ben, I don't *want* out! The Navy's my career—"

"No more." The elevator stopped and Fowler hustled Rod out. "You'd have had to leave eventually. Family's too important. Can't have the peers neglecting government to go chasing around in those ships all their lives. You knew you'd have to retire early."

"Yes, sir. After my brothers were killed there wasn't any question of it. But not yet! Look, can't they give me a leave of absence?"

"Don't be an idiot. The Motie question's going to be with us a long time. Sparta's too far away to handle it. Here we are." Fowler led him through the door.

His retirement papers were already made out. Roderick Harold, Lord Blaine: to be promoted to Rear Admiral and placed on the inactive list by order of His Imperial Majesty. "Retirement pay to be sent where, sir?"

"I beg your pardon?"

"You're entitled to retirement pay. Where do you want us to send it, my lord? To the Yeoman clerk Rod was already a civilian.

"Can I donate it to the Navy Relief Fund?"

"Yes, sir."

"Do that."

The clerk wrote rapidly. There were other questions, all trivial. The documents were made out and thrust at him, and the Yeoman held out a pen. "Just sign here, my lord."

The pen was cold in his hand. Rod didn't want to touch it.

"Come on, come on, there're a dozen appointments waiting," Senator Fowler urged. "You and Sally both. Come on, boy, sign!"

"Yes, sir." No point in delaying. There's nothing to argue about. If the Emperor himself named me to that damned Commission— He scrawled rapidly, then placed his thumb print on the papers.

A taxi whisked them through New Scotland's narrow streets. Traffic was thick and the cab had no official flags to open holes for them. It was an unusual experience for Rod to travel this way; usually he'd had Navy fliers to take him from rooftop to rooftop, and the last time in New Scotland he'd had his own gig with waiting crew. No more, no more.

"I'll have to buy a flier and get a chauffeur," Rod said. "I take it Commissioners rate an air transport license?"

"Surely. You rate anything you want," Senator Fowler said. "In fact the appointment carries a titular baronage, not that *you* need it, but it's another reason why we're getting so popular lately."

"Just how many Commissioners will there be?"

"I've got discretion on that, too. We won't want too many." The taxi lurched as the driver nearly hit a pedestrian. Fowler took out his pocket computer. "Late again. Appointments at the Palace. You'll be staying there, of course. Servant's quarters will be crowded, but we'll squeeze your man in—got anybody, or you want my secretary to arrange it?"

"Kelley's in *Lenin*. I guess he'll stay with me." Another good man lost for the Navy.

"Kelley! How is the old scoundrel?"

"He's fine."

"Glad to hear that. Your father wanted me to ask about him, now I think of it. You know that Marine's my age? I can remember him in uniform when your father was a lieutenant, and that was a *long* time ago."

"Where's Sally?" When Rod came out of 675 she had been gone. He'd been just as pleased; with his retirement papers bulging in his tunic he didn't feel much like talking.

"Out shopping for clothes, of course. You won't have to do that. One of my people got your sizes from Navy records and brought you a couple of suits. They're at the Palace."

"Ben—you're moving pretty fast, Ben," Rod said carefully.

"Have to. By the time *Lenin* orbits we need some answers. Meanwhile you've got to study the political situation out here. It's all tied together. ITA wants trade, soonest. Humanity League wants cultural exchanges, ditto. Armstrong wants his fleet to deal with outies, but he's scared of Moties. That's got to be settled before Merrill can get on with the reconquest of Trans-Coalsack. Stock markets from here to Sparta are jumpy—just what will Motie technology do to the economy? What blue-chip companies are going to get ruined? Who gets rich? And every damn bit of that's in our hands, boy. *We've* got to make the policies."

"Oof." The full impact was just hitting him. "What about Sally? And the rest of the Commission?"

"Don't be stupid. You and I *are* the Commission. Sally will do what's needed."

"You mean what you want her to do. I wouldn't be too sure of that—she's got a mind of her own."

"Think *I* don't know that? I've lived with her long enough. Hell, you're independent too. I don't expect I can dictate to you."

You've been doing a good enough job so far, Rod thought.

"You can guess about the Commission, can't you?" Ben asked pointedly. "Parliament's been concerned about Imperial prerogatives. If there's anything that's pure prerogative it's defense against aliens. But if they're peaceful and all that, Parliament wants a say in the trade deals. Emperor isn't about to turn the Motie question over to Government until we're sure what we're up against. But he can't manage this from Sparta. Can't come out here himself—boy, that *would* cause problems at the Capital. Parliament couldn't stop him from turning it over to Crown Prince Lysander, but the boy's too young. Deadlock. His Majesty's one thing, but appointed agents with Imperial powers are another. Hell, *I* don't want to give Imperial authority to anybody but the Royal Family. One man, one family, can't personally exercise too much power no matter how much they've got in theory, but give them appointed agents and it's another matter."

"What about Merrill? It's his sector."

"What about him? Same objections to him as anybody else. More. Viceroy's job is pretty carefully defined. Dealing with aliens isn't. Merrill wouldn't get too big for his britches and try to set up his own little Empire out here, but history shows one thing damn clear, you got to watch out for that. So it had to be a Commission. Parliament's not about to approve that much power for any single man, not even me. Made me chairman since I've got the votes. Put my niece on it—my brother was more popular than I am, we needed a woman, and here's Sally just been to the Mote. Fine. But I can't stay out here too long, Rod. Somebody's got to. That's you."

"I saw that coming. Why me?"

"You're a natural. Needed your old man's support to get the Commission approved anyway. Marquis is pretty popular right now. Done some good work consolidating his sector. Good war record. Besides, you're almost Royal Family. You're in line for the Throne—"

"About twenty-eighth. My sister's boy has a better claim than I do."

"Yeah, but it's not spreading the prerogative too far. The peers trust you. Baronage likes your father. Commons too, and nobody's going to think you want to be king out here, you'd lose Crucis Court. So now the problem is to find a couple of local dummies who'll take their baronages and go along with you after I leave. You'll have to find yourself a replacement before you can go home, but you'll manage that. I did." Fowler smiled beatifically.

The Palace loomed up ahead of them. Kilted guards stood outside in ceremonial uniforms, but the officer who checked their credentials against his appointment list before waving them through the gates was a Marine.

"Got to hurry," Senator Fowler said as they drove around the circular way to the bright red-and-yellow-rock steps. "Rod, if those Moties are a threat, could you order Kutuzov in there with a battle fleet?"

"Sir?"

"You heard me. What are you smiling about?"

"I had this conversation with one of my officers back at Mote Prime. Only I was in your seat. Yes, sir. I wouldn't want to, but I could. And I can answer so fast because I decided the question on the way home, otherwise I'd have had to tell you to stuff your Commission." He paused a moment. "Sally couldn't, though."

"Wouldn't expect her to. She wouldn't fight it, either. Any evidence that would make you or me order something like that would make her resign. Look, I've been over those reports until I'm deaf and blind, and I can't find much wrong—there are a few things, though. Like your middies. I'm having trouble swallowing that frog."

"So am I—"

The cab pulled up at the Palace steps and the driver opened the doors for them. Rod fished for bills to pay the fare, and he gave too large a tip because he wasn't used to riding in cabs.

"Will that be all, my lord?" the waiter asked.

Rod glanced at his pocket computer. "Yes, thank you. We're going to be late, Sally." He made no attempt to stand. "Angus—we'll have coffee. With brandy."

"Yes, my lord."

"Rod, we really will be late." Sally didn't get up either. They looked at each other and laughed. "When was the last time we had lunch together?" she asked.

"A week? Two? I don't remember. Sally, I've never been so busy in my life. Right now a main fleet action would be a relief." He grimaced. "Another party tonight. Lady Riordan. Do we have to go?"

"Uncle Ben says Baron Riordan is very influential on New Ireland, and we may need some support there."

"Then I suppose we have to." Angus arrived with coffee. Rod tasted it and sighed in satisfaction. "Angus, that is the best coffee and brandy I've ever had. Your quality has improved in the last week."

"Yes, my lord. It is reserved for you."

"For me? Sally, is this your—?"

"No." She was as puzzled as he. "Where did you get it, Angus?"

"A merchant captain personally brought it to Government House, my lady. He said it was for Lord Blaine. The chef tried it and said it was fit to serve."

"And that it is," Rod agreed enthusiastically. "Who was the captain?"

"I'll find out, my lord."

"Some officer seeker," Rod said thoughtfully after the waiter left. "Although you'd think he'd have let me know—" He glanced at his computer again. "I suppose we haven't long. We can't keep the Viceroy waiting all afternoon."

"We might as well. You and Uncle Ben won't agree to my suggestion, and—"

"Let's leave that until the conference, sweetheart." The Viceroy was demanding an immediate Commission decision on what to do about the Moties. He was only one of many. War Minister Armstrong wanted to know how large a battle fleet it would take to disarm the Moties—just in case, he said, so that Admiral Cranston's War Plans Division could go to work.

The Imperial Traders' Association insisted that everything Bury knew about trade possibilities be made available to all members. The Grand Deacon of the Church of Him wanted proof that the Moties were angels. Another Himmist faction was sure they were devils and the Empire was suppressing the information. Cardinal Randolph of the Imperial Church wanted tapes of Motie life broadcast on tri-v to finish the Himmists once and for all.

And everyone in two hundred parsecs wanted a seat on the Commission.

"At least we'll be in the same meeting," Sally said.

"Yeah." Their Palace quarters were in the same corridor but they never saw each other except at parties. During the confused blur of the past weeks Rod and Sally had seldom been in the same conferences.

Angus returned and bowed. "Captain Anderson, *Ragnarok,* my lord."

"I see. Thank you, Angus. That's an Imperial Autonetics ship, Sally."

"Then Mr. Bury sent the coffee and brandy! That was very nice of him—"

"Yeah." Rod sighed. "We really *do* have to go." They went upstairs from the executive dining room to Viceroy Merrill's working office. Senator Fowler, War Minister Armstrong, and Fleet Admiral Cranston were waiting impatiently.

"Our first lunch together in two weeks," Rod explained. "My apologies." They sounded perfunctory.

"It won't be so bad when *Lenin* gets in," Senator Fowler said. "Horvath's scientists can make most of the public appearances. They'll eat it up."

"Assuming you give them permission to appear," Prince Merrill drawled. "You haven't let your protégés say much for all the talking they've done."

"Your pardon, Highness," Admiral Cranston said. "I'm in a hurry. What do I do about *Lenin*'s arrival? The ship orbits in sixty hours, and I have to send orders to Kutuzov."

"We'd have that settled if you'd agree to my suggestion, Uncle Ben," said Sally. "Give them quarters in the Palace, assign them servants and guards, and let the *Moties* decide whom they want to see."

"She has a point, Benjie," Merrill observed. "After all, they *are* the representatives of a sovereign power. Hard to justify keeping them penned up, eh? Make a big stink, and for what?"

"Admiral Kutuzov is convinced the Moties are a threat," the War Minister said. "He says they are very persuasive. Give them a chance to speak to whom they will and there is no telling what they might do. They could make political trouble for us, Your Highness, and we do no need that."

"But you have to agree that three Moties aren't any military threat," Sally insisted.

Benjamin Fowler sighed heavily. "We've been over this before. It isn't the military threat I worry about! If we turn the Moties loose they *will* make deals. Bury's report convinces me of that. The Moties can get interest groups formed to support them. Negotiate trade agreements."

"The Commission has a veto on any agreement, Uncle Ben."

"Harder to kill a deal than see one isn't made to begin with. Look, if the Moties are everything Horvath thinks they are: peaceful, anxious to sell or give us new technology, no competition for living space—and how in hell can he know that?—no military threat, never going to ally with the outies . . ."

Admiral Cranston growled deep in his throat.

"And all the rest of it, even if they're all that and more, they are *still* problems. For one thing, their technology's going to shake up the whole Empire. We can't just turn all that loose without some plans for readjustment."

"Labor people are on to that," Merrill said dryly. "President of IF of L was in here not an hour ago demanding that we bottle up the Moties until his staff can study unemployment problems. Not *against* new technology, but wants us to be cautious. Can't say I blame him."

"The ITA isn't solid any more either," Rod added. "At Lady Malcolm's last night a couple of Traders told me they've got second thoughts about Moties." Rod fingered the lapels of his brightly colored knit tunic. Civilian clothes fit better and should have been more comfortable than Navy uniform, but they didn't *seem* more comfortable. "Damn it, I don't know what to say! I've been so busy with meaningless speeches and conferences and these goddamn parties I haven't had a chance to do any constructive thinking."

"Course, of course," Merrill soothed. "Still and all, my lord, my orders from HM are clear. I have to take the advice of your Commission. And I am still waiting for that advice. Lady Sandra—"

"Sally. Please." She'd never liked her given name, for no reason she could have told anyone.

"Lady Sally has at least offered us something. Senator, you and Blaine have to do more than protest that you don't know enough!"

"There is the small matter of my fleet," Armstrong put in. "I must know if Cranston's battleships can go back to chasing outies, or must they stand by in this corner of the sector? We'll hae more revolts if we do no show the flag in the distant provinces!"

"Same demands?" Rod asked.

"Aye. They want ships o' their own. More say in Imperial policy too, but mostly the ships. 'Tis enough to drive me mad! They hae control o' their internal affairs. They do no pay more taxes than we. When the outies stir about they shout for the Navy and we come. But these are no your problems, my lord. If we truly need ships to defend mankind from alien monsters I'll find them for you if I hae to work in MacPherson's Yards myself."

"Would almost be worthwhile if the Moties were hostile," Merrill said thoughtfully. "A real threat to the Empire would consolidate the provinces— Wonder if we could sell that story to the barons?"

"Your Highness!" Sally protested.

"Just a thought, just a thought."

"Dazzle 'em with footwork," Fowler growled. They all turned to stare at him. "It's obvious. Let the press corps have a field day. When *Lenin* gets in, we'll put on a show like New Scotland's never seen. Big reception for the Moties. Full honors. Lots of formalities, parades, reviews, tours. Conferences with the Foreign Office people. Nobody can object if the Motie public appearances are ceremonial and the Foreign Office monopolizes the rest of their time. Meanwhile, we get to work. Your Highness, we'll have advice for you as soon as possible, but Leoni —His Majesty did not send me out here to make snap judgments. Until I know more, we'll just have to make do."

49 · *Parades*

The landing boat settled on the roof of the Palace with a high-pitched whine of jets dying to a low rumble, then silence. A long roll of drums began outside. The martial sound filtered into the cabin, then blared as the entryway was opened.

David Hardy blinked into morning sunlight bright on the varicolored stones of the Palace. He sniffed fresh air with no smell of ships and men and filters, and felt the warmth of New Cal. His feet sensed solid rock below. Home!

"HONOR GUARD, ATTENTION!"

Oh, Lord, they're going all out, David thought. He squared his shoulders and moved down the ramp as cameramen focused their zoom lenses. Other naval officers and civilians followed. Dr. Horvath was the last, and when he appeared David nodded to the officer in charge.

"PRESENT ARMS!" *Snap! Crack!* Fifty pairs of white gloves made identical motions and slapped their weapons at identical times. Fifty scarlet sleeves heavy with gold braid poised in geometrical precision. The drum roll swelled louder and faster.

The Moties came down the ramp. They blinked at New Cal's sunlight. Trumpets blared a salute, them halted with the drum roll. The silence was broken only by faint traffic sounds from streets half a kilometer away. Even the newsmen on their high platform were still. The Moties swiveled their bodies rapidly about.

Curiosity! A human world at last, and humans who governed; yet what were they doing? Ahead were two lines of twenty-five Marines in rigid pose, their weapons held in what could not be a comfortable position, all identical and obviously not threatening anyone; but Ivan automatically swiveled to look behind for his Warriors.

To their right were more of these Marines but they carried noisemakers, not weapons, and several carried banners with colors dipped; three more carried weapons and a fourth held up a larger banner that was not dipped: symbols they'd seen before. Crown and spaceship, eagle, sickle-and-hammer.

Directly ahead, past the clump of people from Lenin *and* MacArthur, *were more humans in a wild array of clothing. They were obviously waiting to speak to the Moties, but they did not speak.*

"Captain Blaine and Miss Fowler," Jock twittered. "Their posture indicates that the two in front of them receive deference."

David Hardy led the Moties forward. The aliens were still wrinkling their noses, and they chattered among themselves in musical tones. "If the air is distasteful," David said, "we can build filters. I hadn't noticed that ship's air distressed you." He took another lungful of the clean precious stuff.

"No, no, it's only a bit flat and tasteless," said a Mediator. It was impossible to tell the two apart. "Then there's the extra oxygen. I think we'll need that."

"Gravity?"

"Right." The Motie squinted toward the sun. "We'll also need dark glasses."

"Certainly." They reached the end of the lines of honor guards. Hardy bowed to Merrill. Both Mediators did likewise in perfect imitation. The White stood erect for a moment, then bowed, but not so deeply as the others.

Dr. Horvath was waiting. "Prince Stefan Merrill, Viceroy to His Imperial Majesty for Trans-Coalsack Sector," Horvath announced. "Your Highness, the Ambassador from Mote Prime. He is called Ivan."

Merrill bowed formally, then indicated Benjamin Fowler. "Senator Benjamin Bright Fowler, Lord President of the Imperial Commission Extraordinary. Senator Fowler is empowered to speak with you in the name of the Emperor, and he has a message for you from His Majesty."

The Moties bowed again.

Senator Fowler had allowed his valet to dress him properly; all the billions of humanity would eventually see recordings of this meeting. He wore a dark tunic with no decoration but a small golden sunburst on the left breast, his sash was new, his trousers fit perfectly and vanished into the tops of glove-soft, gleaming boots. He thrust a black Malacca cane with carved gold head under his left arm as Rod Blaine held out a parchment.

Fowler read in his "official speeches" voice; in debates he was a firebrand, but his formal speeches were stilted. This one was no exception.

"Leonidas IX by Grace of God Emperor of Humanity to the representatives of the Mote Civilization, Greetings and Welcome. For a thousand years mankind has searched for brothers in the universe. We have dreamed of them for all our history. . . ." The message was long and formal, and the Moties listened in silence. To their left a knot of men hustled and whispered together, and there were some pointed instruments the Moties recognized as badly designed tri-v cameras. There was a forest of cameras and far too many men; why did the humans need so many to do a simple task?

Fowler finished the message. He followed the Motie gaze without turning his head. "The gentlemen of the press," he murmured. "We'll try to keep them from bothering you." Then he held up the parchment to show the Imperial Seal, and presented it to the Moties.

"They obviously expect a reply. This is one of the 'formal' events Hardy warned us of. I have no idea what to say. Have you?"

Jock: "No. But we must say something."

The Master spoke. "What have they said to us?"

"I could translate but it would be meaningless. They have welcomed us in the name of their Emperor, who appears to be an over-Master. The short, round one is Mediator to this Emperor."

"Ah. We have at last found one who can communicate. Speak to her."

"But he has said nothing!"

"Say nothing in return."

"We are very grateful for your Emperor's welcome. We believe this first meeting between intelligent races will be a historic occasion, perhaps the most important event in all our histories. We are eager to begin trade and the mutual enrichment of Moties and Mankind."

"*You sound like Horvath.*"

"*Of course. Those were his words. He used them often before the humans destroyed their lesser ship. We must know why they did that.*"

"*You will not ask until we know more of humans.*"

The Moties stood blinking in a silence that stretched embarrassingly. They obviously had no more to say.

"Doubtless you are tired from your journey," Merrill said. "You will want to rest in your quarters before the parade begins." When the Moties did not reply, Merrill waved his hand slightly. The band struck up a march and the Moties were ushered toward an elevator.

"We'll get you away from the goddamn press corps," Fowler muttered. "Can't do anything in a goldfish bowl." He turned to smile for the cameras. So did the others, and they were still smiling as the elevator door closed in the faces of the reporters who had rushed forward when they saw that the Moties were leaving.

There were no obvious spy eyes in the rooms, and the doors had inside locks. There were many rooms, all with very high ceilings. There were three rooms with what the humans thought were beds for Moties, and each of those rooms was adjoined by a room with waste disposal and washing facilities. In another room were a refrigerator, flame and microwave stoves, large stocks of food including the stores brought by the Moties, implements for eating, and equipment they did not recognize. Still another room, the largest of all, held a big polished wood table and both Motie and human chairs.

They wandered through the vast spaces.

"A tri-v screen," Jock exclaimed. *He turned the controls, and a picture appeared. It was a tape of themselves listening to the message from the Emperor. Other channels showed the same things, or men talking about the Motie arrival or—*

A big man in loose clothing was shouting. His tones and gestures indicated rage. "Devils! They must be destroyed! The Legions of Him will go forth against the Legions of Hell!"

The shouting man was cut off and replaced by another man, also in loose clothing, but this one did not shout. He spoke calmly. "You have heard the man who calls himself the Voice of Him. It is of course not necessary for me to say it, but speaking for the Church I can assure you that the Moties are neither angels nor devils; merely intelligent beings much like us. If they are a threat to humanity it is not a spiritual one, and His Majesty's servants will certainly be more than adequate to deal with them."

"Cardinal Randolph, has the Church determined the, ah, status of Moties? That is, their place in the theology of—"

"Of course not. But I can say they are hardly supernatural beings." *Cardinal Randolph laughed and so did the commentator. There was no sign of the man who had been screaming in rage.*

"Come," the Master said. *"You will have time for this later."* They went into the large room and sat at the table. Charlie brought grain from their food supply.

"You have smelled the air," Jock said. *"No industrial development. The planet must be nearly empty! Room for a billion Masters and all their dependents."*

"Too much of this sunlight would make us blind. The gravity would shorten our lives." Charlie inhaled deeply. *"But there is room and food and metal. The gravity be cursed with the sunlight. We'll take it."*

"I must have missed hearing the offer." Jock gestured

amusement. "I do not believe the three of us will take it by force."

"These humans drive me to thoughts of Crazy Eddie! Did you see? Did you hear? The Mediator for the Emperor detests the operators of the tri-v cameras, yet he makes expression of pleasure for them and implies that he may not have the power to prevent them from annoying us."

"They have given us a tri-v," the Master said.

"And it is obviously what the humans watch. There were spokesmen for many Masters. You saw." Jock indicated pleasure. "I will have many opportunities to discover how humans are ruled and how they live."

"They have given us a source of information which they do not control," the Master said. "What does this mean?"

The Mediators were silent.

"Yes," said Ivan. "If we are not successful in our mission, we will not be permitted to return." He indicated indifference. "We knew this before we left. Now it is more vital than ever that we establish trade with humans as quickly as possible; or determine that intercourse with humans is undesirable and find a way to prevent it. You must act quickly."

They knew. The Mediators who proposed their mission and the Masters who consented had recognized the time limits before they left Mote Prime. There were two: the life span of a Mediator was not long, and the Master would die at nearly the same time. The massive hormone imbalance which made him sterile and permanently male would kill him. But only mules and a sterile Keeper could be sent, for no Master would entrust any but a Keeper with this task; and only a Keeper could survive without breeding.

The span of the second time limit was not so predictable, but it was no less sure: Civilization was again doomed on the Mote. Another Cycle was turning, and *despite the inevitable Crazy Eddies there would be no halting it. After the collapse the humans would see Moties in savagery. The Race would be helpless, or nearly so; and what would the humans do then?*

No one knew and no Master would risk it.

"The humans have promised discussions of trade. I presume the Mediator will be their instrument. Also perhaps Mr. Bury or another like him." *Jock left his chair and examined the paneled walls. There were buttons concealed in filigree and he pressed one. A panel slid open to reveal another tri-v, and Jock operated it.*

"What is there to discuss?" *the Master demanded.* "We need food and land, or we must be left alone with the Cycles. We must conceal the urgency of our needs and their reasons. We have little to trade but ideas; there are no resources to expand. If humans wish durable goods they must bring us the metals to make them from."

Any drain of resources from the Mote would prolong the next collapse; and that must not be.

"The Navy's keeping it a big hush-hush, but I can tell you this, they've got technology beyond anything the First Empire ever had," *a commentator on the view screen said. He seemed awed.*

"The humans no longer possess much of what they had," *said Jock.* "Once, during the period they call the First Empire, they had food-conversion machinery of amazing efficiency. It required only power and organic matter, garbage, weeds, even deceased animals and humans. Poisons were removed or converted."

"Do you know the principles? Or how widespread was its use? Or why they no longer possess it?" *the Master demanded.*

"No. The human would not speak of it."

"I heard," *Charlie added.* "He was a rating named Dubcek, and he was attempting to conceal the obvious fact that humans have Cycles. They all do."

"*We know of their Cycles,*" Ivan said. "*Their oddly erratic Cycles.*"

"*We know what the midshipmen told us in their last hours. We know what the others have implied. We know they are in awe of the power of their First Empire, but have little admiration of their previous civilizations. Little more. Perhaps with the tri-v I can learn.*"

"*This food machine. Will others know more of it?*"

"*Yes. If we had a Brown, and with what the humans know of the principles, it is possible that—*"

"*Make me joyful beyond dreams,*" said Charlie. "*Cease to wish we had Browns.*"

"*I can't help it. I have only to lie on their couches, or sit in this chair, and somehow my thoughts turn—*"

"*A Brown would die revealingly. Two Browns would breed and breed and breed and if prevented from breeding would die revealingly. Shut up about Browns.*"

"*I will. But that one food machine would stave off any new Cycle for half a 144-years.*"

"*You will learn all you can about the machine,*" Ivan directed. "*And you will cease to speak of Browns. My couch is as badly designed as yours.*"

The grandstand was in front of the Palace gates, and it was filling with humans. More temporary structures stretched in both directions down the roadway, as far as the Moties could see from their place in the front row. Humans swarmed around and into them.

Ivan sat impassively. There was no understanding the purpose of all this, but the humans were attempting to observe the proprieties. As they left their rooms they were followed by humans with weapons, and the men did not watch the Moties; they looked unceasingly at the crowds around them. These Marines were not impressive and they would be as Meats in the hands of Warriors, but at least the human Masters had provided a bodyguard. They were trying to be polite.

The Mediators chattered as Mediators always did, and Ivan listened carefully. Much could be learned from Mediator conversations.

Jock: "These are the over-Masters of this planet, of twenty planets and more. Yet they have said that they must *do this thing. Why?*"

Charlie: "I have theories. Notice the patterns of deference as they approach their seats. Viceroy Merrill assists Sally to climb the stairs. Titles are omitted by some and always used by others, and given redundantly in full over the loudspeakers. The 'gentlemen of the press' would seem to have no status at all, yet they stop whom they please, and although the others will prevent them from going where they will, they are not punished for trying."

Jock: "What pattern do you see? I find none."

Ivan: "Have you conclusions?"

"Only interesting questions," Charlie replied.

Ivan: "Then allow me my own observations."

Jock changed to the Trailing Trojans Recent tongue. "What pattern do you see?"

Charlie answered in the same language. "I see a complex netting of obligations, but within it there is a pyramid of power. No one is truly independent, but as you near the top of the pyramid power increases enormously; however, it is seldom used to its fullest. There are lines of obligations that reach in all directions, upwards, downwards, sideways in a totally alien manner. Where no Master works directly for any other, these humans all work for each other. Viceroy Merrill answers commands from above and obligations from below. The Browns and Farmers and Warriors and Laborers demand and receive periodic accounting of the doings of their Masters."

Jock (astonishment): "It is too complex. Yet we must know or we cannot predict what the humans will do."

Charlie: "The patterns change as we look. And there is this attitude they call 'formality'—Shock!"

Jock: "Yes, I saw. The small female who ran in front

of the car. Look, the men in the car are shaken, perhaps injured. The car stopped very suddenly. What prerogatives could that female have?"

Jock: *"If that is her parent carrying her away, then she is a proto-Engineer. Except that she is a small female and they have few female Engineers, and that Master's car stopped to avoid striking her, to the detriment of the Master. Now I understand why their Fyunch(click)s go mad."*

The stand was nearly full, and Hardy returned to his place beside them. Charlie asked, "Can you explain again what is to happen here? We did not understand, and you had little time."

Hardy thought about it. Every kid knew what a parade was, but nobody ever told children; you took them to one instead. Children liked them because there were strange and wonderful things to watch. Adults—well, adults had other reasons.

He said, "A lot of men are going to walk past us in regular patterns. Some will play musical instruments. There will be vehicles carrying displays of handiwork and agriculture and art. There will be more men walking, and groups of them will be identically dressed."

"And the purpose?"

Hardy laughed. "To do you honor, and to honor each other and themselves. To display their skills." *And maybe to show their power* . . . "We've been having parades since history began, and there's no sign we're about to give them up."

"And this is one of those 'formal' events you spoke of?"

"Yes, but it's supposed to be fun too." Hardy smiled benevolently at his charges. They did look funny in their brown-and-white fur and their bulbous black goggles, held on by straps because they had no noses to support ordinary glasses. The goggles gave them an unnaturally solemn look.

Hardy glanced at a rustle behind him. The Admiralty staff were taking their places. Hardy recognized Admiral Kutuzov with Fleet Admiral Cranston.

And the Moties were chattering among themselves, their voices warbling up and down the scales, their arms flickering . . .

"It is he! It is Lenin's Master!" Jock stood upright and stared. The arms indicated surprise, joy, wonder . . .

Charlie studied the attitudes of the humans as they moved in the broken space of the grandstand. Who deferred to whom? In what fashion? The similarly dressed ones reacted predictably, and designs on their clothing gave their exact status. Blaine had once worn such clothing and while he did he fitted into the place theory would assign him. Now he did not wear it, and the patterns were different for him. Even Kutuzov had bowed to him. And yet: Charlie observed the actions of the others, and the facial attitudes, and said, "You are correct. Be cautious."

"Are you certain?" the White demanded.

"Yes! He is the one I have studied for so long, from so far away, solely from the behavior of those who took his orders. Look, the broad stripe on his sleeve, the ringed planet symbol on his chest, the deference of Lenin's Marine guards—certainly it is he. I was correct from the first, one being, and human!"

"You will cease to study him. Turn your eyes front."

"No! We must know of this type of human! This is the class they choose to command their ships of war!"

"Turn around."

"You are a Master but you are not my Master."

"Obey," said Ivan. Ivan was not good at argument.

Charlie was. As Jock twitched and stammered in internal conflict, Charlie switched to an ancient, half-forgotten language, less for concealment than to remind Jock how much they had to conceal. "If we had many Mediators the risk would be tolerable; but if you should go mad now, policy would be decided by Ivan and me alone. Your Master would not be represented."

"But the dangers that threaten our world—"

"Consider the record of your sisters. Sally Fowler's Mediator now goes about telling Masters that the world could be made perfect if they would exercise restraint in their breeding. Horace Bury's Mediator—"

"If we could learn—"

"—cannot be found. He sends letters to the most powerful Masters asking for offers should he change allegiance, and pointing out the value of information he alone possesses. Jonathon Whitbread's Mediator betrayed her Master and killed her own Fyunch(click)!" Charlie's eyes flickered to Ivan. The Master was watching but he would not understand.

Charlie changed to the common tongue. *"Captain my Lord Roderick Blaine's Mediator went Crazy Eddie. You were present. Gavin Potter's Mediator is Crazy Eddie. Sinclair's Mediator is useful in society, but quite mad."*

"This is true," said the White. *"We have placed her in charge of a project to develop force shielding such as the humans possess. She works startlingly well with Browns and uses tools herself. But with her Master and her sister Mediators she talks as if her parietal lobe were damaged."*

Jock sat down suddenly, eyes front.

"Consider the record," Charlie continued. *"Only Horst Staley's Mediator is sane by any rational standard. You must not identify with any human. Certainly this should pose no hardship. There cannot be any evolved instinct in us to identify with humans!"*

Jock changed back to Trailing Trojans Recent. *"But we are alone out here. What, then, should I be Fyunch(click) to, Ivan?"*

"You will be no human's Fyunch(click)," Ivan stated. He had heard only the concealing language change. Charlie made no answer.

Glad that's over, whatever it was, Hardy thought. The Motie conversation had lasted only half a minute, but there must have been a lot of information exchanged— and the emotional content was high. David was certain of that although he could as yet recognize only a few phrases of any Motie tongue. He had only recently become certain that there were many still in current use.

"Here come the Viceroy and the Commissioners," Hardy said. "And the bands are starting. Now you'll know what a parade is like."

It seemed to Rod that the very rock of the Palace trembled from the sound. A hundred drummers paced by in thunder, and behind them a brass band blared some march ancient in CoDominium times. The leader raised his mace and the group countermarched before the reviewing stand to polite applause. Batons swirled as girls tossed them high in the air.

"The Ambassador asks if these are Warriors," Charlie shouted.

Rod almost laughed but carefully controlled his voice. "No. This is the John Muir High School band—a youth group. Some of them may become warriors when they're older, and some of 'em will be farmers, or engineers, or—"

"Thank you." The Moties twittered.

Not that we haven't had warriors, Rod thought. With this reception sure to have the biggest tri-v audience in the history of the Empire, Merrill wasn't going to neglect the opportunity to display a glimpse of the mailed fist. It might make prospective rebels think twice. But there hadn't been much military equipment displayed, and there'd been more young girls with flowers than Marines and soldiers.

The parade was interminable. Every provincial baron had to show off; every guild, corporation, town, school, lodge—anything, they all wanted in the act and Fowler'd said let them all come.

The John Muir School band was followed by a half-battalion of Covenanter Highlander troops with kilts, more drums, and squealing bagpipes. The wild music grated on Rod's nerves but he was careful to control himself; although Covenant was on the other side of the Coal Sack the Highlanders were naturally popular on New Scotland, and all New Scots either loved or professed to love the pipes.

The Highlanders carried swords and pikes, and wore bearskin shakos nearly a meter high. Waves of bright plaids streamed from their shoulders. There was no threat visible, but the reputation of the Covenanters was threat enough; no army in the known worlds would relish tangling with them when they took off their ceremonial finery and put on body armor and battle dress; and Covenant was loyalist to the core.

"Those are warriors?" Charlie asked.

"Yes. They're part of Viceroy Merrill's ceremonial guard," Rod shouted. He stood to attention as a color party marched past, and had to make a strong effort to keep his hand from rising to the salute. Instead he took off his hat.

The parade went on: a flower-covered float from some New Irish barony; artisans' guilds displays; more troops, Friedlanders this time, marching awkwardly because they were artillerists and tankers and hadn't their vehicles. Another reminder to the provinces of just what His Majesty could send against his enemies.

"What do the Moties make of all this?" Merrill asked out of the corner of his mouth. He acknowledged the colors of another baronial float.

"Hard to say," Senator Fowler replied.

"More to the point is what the provinces will make of it," Armstrong said. "This show will be worth a visit by a battle crusier many places. And 'tis far cheaper."

"Cheaper for the government," Merrill said. "Hate to think what was spent on all this. Luckily, I didn't have to spend it."

"Rod, you can make your exit now," Senator Fowler said. "Hardy'll make your excuses to the Moties."

"Right. Thanks." Rod slipped away. Behind him he heard the sounds of the parade and the muted conversation of his friends.

"I never heard so many drums in all my life," Sally said.

"Bosh. Goes on every Birthday," Senator Fowler reminded her.

"Well, I don't have to watch *all* of it on Birthdays."

"Birthday?" Jock asked.

Rod left as Sally was trying to explain patriotic holidays and a hundred pipers tramped past in Gaelic splendor.

50 • *The Art of Negotiation*

The little group moved in angry silence. Horowitz' hostility was just short of audible as he led the way deeper underground. I am the most competent xenologist in Trans-Coalsack, he was thinking. They'll have to go to Sparta to find anyone better. And this goddamn lordling and his half-educated lady doubt my professional word.

And I have to put up with it.

There wasn't much doubt about *that*, Horowitz reflected. The University President had personally made it clear. "For God's sake, Ziggy, do what they want! This Commission is a big deal. Our whole budget, not to mention your department, is going to be affected by their reports. What if they say we don't cooperate and ask for a team from Sparta?"

So. At least these young aristocrats knew his time was valuable. He'd told them half a dozen times on the way to the labs.

They were deep underground in the Old University, walking on worn rock floors carved an age before. Murcheson himself had paced these corridors before the terraforming of New Scotland was complete, and legend had it that his ghost could still be seen prowling through the rock-walled passageways: a hooded figure with one smoldering red eye.

And just why is this so damned important anyway? Balaam's ass, why does the girl make such a big deal out of it?

The laboratory was another room quarried from living rock. Horowitz gestured imperiously and two graduate assistants opened a refrigerated container. A long table slid out.

The pilot of the Crazy Eddie probe lay disassembled on the smooth white plastic surface. Its organs were arranged in a semblance to the positions they'd had before dissection, with black lines drawn across the flayed skin to join them to points on the skin and the exploded skeleton. Light red and dark red and grayish green, improbable shapes: the components of a Motie Mediator were all the colors and textures of a man hit by a grenade. Rod felt his belly twist within him and remembered ground actions.

He winced as Sally leaned forward impatiently for a better look. Her face was set and grim—but it had been that way back at Horowitz' office.

"Now!" Horowitz exploded in triumph. His bony finger jabbed at peanut-sized slime-green nodes within the abdomen. "Here. And here. These would have been the testes. The other Motie variants have internal testes too."

"Yes—" Sally agreed.

"This small?" Horowitz asked contemptuously.

"We don't know." Sally's voice was still very serious. "There were no reproductive organs in the statuettes, and the only Moties the expedition dissected were a Brown and some miniatures. The Brown was female."

"I've seen the miniatures," Horowitz said smugly.

"Well—yes," Sally agreed. "The testes in male miniatures were big enough to see—"

"Much bigger than this in proportion. But never mind. These could not have produced sperm. I have proved it. That pilot was a mule!" Horowitz slapped the back of his hand against his open palm. "A mule!"

Sally studied the exploded Motie. She's really upset, Rod thought.

"Moties start male, then turn female," Sally mumbled, almost inaudibly. "Couldn't this one have been immature?"

"A pilot?"

"Yes, of course—" She sighed. "You're right, anyway. It was the height of a full-grown Mediator. Could it have been a freak?"

"Hah! *You* laughed at *me* when I suggested it might have been a mutation! Well, it isn't. While you were off on that jaunt we did a bit of work here. I've identified the chromosomes and gene-coding systems responsible for sexual development. This creature was a sterile hybrid of two other forms which *are* fertile." Triumph.

"That fits," Rod said. "The Moties told Renner the Mediators were a hybrid—"

"Look," Horowitz demanded. He activated a lecture screen and punched in codes. Shapes flowed across the screen. Motie chromosomes were close-packed discs connected by thin rods. There were bands and shapes on the discs—and Sally and Horowitz were speaking a language Rod didn't understand. He listened absently, then found a lab assistant making coffee. The girl sympathetically offered a cup, the other assistant joined them, and Rod was pressed for information about Moties. Again.

Half an hour later they left the university. Whatever Horowitz had said, Sally was convinced.

"Why so upset, sweetheart?" he asked. "Horowitz is right. It makes sense for the Mediators to be mules." Rod grimaced at the memory. Horowitz had pointedly added that being mules, the Mediators wouldn't be influenced by nepotism.

"But my Fyunch(click) would have told me. I'm sure she would. We *did* talk about sex and reproduction and she said—"

"What?"

"I don't remember exactly." Sally took out her pocket computer and scrawled the symbols for information recall. The gadget hummed, then changed tone to indicate it was using the car's radio system to communicate with the Palace data banks. "And I don't remember just when she said it—" She scrawled something else. "I should have used a better cross-reference system when I filed the tape."

"You'll find it. Here's the Palace—we've got a conference with the Moties after lunch. Why don't you ask them about it?"

She grinned.

"You're blushing."

Sally giggled. "Remember when the little Moties first coupled? It was the first positive indication we'd had of sex changes in adult Moties, and I went *running* down to the lounge— Dr. Horvath still thinks I'm some kind of sex maniac!"

"Want *me* to ask?"

"If I don't. But, Rod, my Fyunch(click) wouldn't lie to me. She just *wouldn't* have."

They ate in the executive dining room, and Rod ordered another brandy and coffee. He sipped and said thoughtfully, "There was a message with this—"

"Oh? Have you talked to Mr. Bury?"

"Only to thank him. The Navy's still entertaining him as a guest. No, the message was the gift itself. It told me he could send messages, even before *Lenin* made orbit."

She looked shocked. "You're right—why didn't we—"

"Too busy. By the time I thought of it, it didn't seem important enough to report, so I haven't. The question is, Sally: What *other* messages did he send, and why did he want me to know he could do it?"

She shook her head. "I'd rather try to analyze the motivations of aliens than of Mr. Bury. He's a very strange man."

"Right. But not a stupid one." He stood and helped Sally out of her chair. "Time for the conference."

They met in the Motie quarters of the Palace. This was supposed to be a working conference, and Senator Fowler was running political interference elsewhere so that Rod and Sally could ask questions.

"I'm glad you coopted Mr. Renner for the advisory staff," Sally told Rod as they got off the elevator. "He's got a—well, a *different* outlook about the Moties."

"Different. That's the word." Rod had also been assigned others from the expedition: Chaplain Hardy, Sinclair, and several scientists. Until Senator Fowler made up his mind about Dr. Horvath's request for Commission membership they couldn't use him, though; the Science Minister might refuse to become a subordinate to the Commissioners.

The Marines outside the Motie quarters snapped to attention as Rod and Sally approached. "See. You worry too much," Rod said as he acknowledged the salutes. "The Moties haven't complained about the guards."

"Complained? Jock told me the Ambassador *likes* having guards," Sally said. "I guess he's a little afraid of us."

Rod shrugged. "They watch a lot of tri-v. God knows what they think of the human race now." They entered to hear an animated conversation in progress.

"Of *course* I expected no direct evidence," Chaplain Hardy was insisting. "But although I didn't expect it, I would have been pleasantly surprised to find something concrete: scripture, or a religion similar to ours, something like that. But expect it, no."

"I still wonder what you think you could have found," Charlie said. "Were it my problem to prove that humans had souls, I shouldn't know where to begin looking."

Hardy shrugged. "Nor do I. But begin with your own beliefs—you think you possess something like an immortal soul."

"Some do, some don't," Charlie said. "Most Masters believe it. Like humans, Moties do not care to think their lives are purposeless. Or that they can and will be terminated. Hello, Sally. Rod. Please be seated."

"Thanks." Rod nodded greetings to Jock and Ivan. The Ambassador looked like a surrealist rendition of an Angora cat as he lay sprawled on the edge of a couch. The Master flicked the lower right hand, a gesture which Rod had learned meant something similar to "I see you." There were evidently other greetings, but they were reserved for other Masters: equals, not creatures with whom Mediators discussed business.

Rod activated his pocket computer to get the agenda for the day's meeting. The readout was coded to remind him of both the formal items for discussion and the questions Senator Fowler wanted answered without the Moties' knowing the questions had been asked; questions such as why the Moties hadn't ever asked about the fate of the Crazy Eddie probe. *That* one needed no code at all; Rod was as puzzled as the Senator. He was also reluctant to get the Moties asking, since he would have to explain what he'd done to the probe.

"Before we begin," Rod said. "The Foreign Office requests that you attend a reception tonight. For the baronage and some representatives of Parliament."

The Moties twittered. Ivan twittered back. "We will be honored," Jock said formally. There was no expression in the voice.

"OK. So now we're back to the same problems we've always had. Are you a threat to the Empire, and just what will your technology do to our economy."

"Oddly enough," Jock said, "the same questions concern us. Except in reverse."

"But we never seem to *settle* anything," Sally protested.

"How could we?" Hardy asked reasonably. "Assuming that the threat question is negligible, until we know what our friends will sell the economists can't predict what they'll do to us—and the Moties have the same difficulty."

"They aren't as concerned about them as we are," Renner said impatiently. "I'm with Sally. We talk a lot, but we don't get much done."

"We won't get any of it done if we don't get started." Rod looked at his computer readout. "The first item is superconductors. The physics boys are happy enough, but the econ section wants better cost data. I'm supposed to ask—" He touched the control to let the questions roll across the tiny screen.

"Are you mules?" Sally blurted.

There was silence. Hardy's eyes narrowed slightly; otherwise he didn't react. Renner lifted his left eyebrow. They stared, first at Sally, then at the Moties.

"You mean Mediators," Jock said carefully. "Yes. Of course."

There was more silence. "All of you?" Renner asked.

"Certainly. We are hybrid forms. None of you seem to like that answer. Sally, what is troubling you? Mediators were a late evolutionary development, and evolution is by groups and tribes as often as by individuals—that's true for humans too, isn't it?"

Hardy nodded. "Not only us. Most alien life forms we've found, too."

"Thank you. We assume that tribes with Mediators survived better than those without. We have never seen a fertile Mediator, but if ever there were one, she must have acted in her children's interests rather than the tribe's." The Motie shrugged. "That's all speculation, of course. Our history doesn't go back *that* far. As for me, I would like to have children, but I have always known I would not—" The Motie shrugged again. "Still, it is a pity. The sex act is the ultimate in enjoyment. We know this. We empathize all too well with Masters."

There was more silence. Hardy cleared his throat but said nothing.

"Sally, while we are speaking of Motie problems, there is something else you must know about us."

You could cut the gloom in here with a knife, Rod thought. Now just why is it so depressing that—

"Compared with your species, ours is short-lived. We three were chosen for our experience and intelligence, not our youth. We have considerably fewer than ten years to live."

"But— *No!*" Sally was visibly shaken. "All of you?"

"Yes. I would not raise such a painful topic, but we all think it wise to tell you. Your parades, these formal receptions, all of this baffles us most pleasantly. We anticipate great pleasure in solving the mystery of why you do these things. But we also must establish trade and diplomatic relations with you, and there is a definite time limit—"

"Yes," said Sally. "Yes, of course. Not even ten years!"

Jock shrugged. "Mediators live a total of twenty-five. Win a few, lose a few. You presumably have your own problems." The alien voice took on a note of grim amusement. "Such as the wars you suffer through lack of Mediators!"

The Motie looked around the conference room. There was more silence, and blank stares. "I've distressed you all. I am sorry, but it had to be said— Let us resume tomorrow, when you've had time to think about this." She uttered a high, sweet note, and Charlie and Ivan followed her through a paneled doorway into the Motie private quarters. The door closed gently behind them.

As they walked to Ivan's room Charlie twittered to the Master. They entered and closed the door; and although they were certain the room had no spy or listening devices, they spoke in a high grammar rich with poetic allusions. The humans could never decipher it.

The Master's posture was a demand for explanation.

"There was not time to consult," Jock cried. "I had to speak at once before they placed too much importance on the question."

"You told them yes," Ivan said. "You might have said no. Or maybe. Or some are, and some not . . ."

Charlie said, "You might have told them we don't discuss such things. You know humans do not like to speak openly of sexual matters."

"They can when they want to," Jock protested. "And their next request would have been that we submit to examination by their xenologists. We have already submitted to their physicians—how could we refuse now?"

Ivan: "Their xenologists would find nothing. A male would show zero sperm count, but you are female."

Charlie pantomimed ritual sorrow: Circumstances force me to disagree with you, Master. "Their original examinations were directionless. Can you say they would be less thorough now? That they would not find that all three of us suffer from hormone imbalances?" Charlie's arms moved, so, to indicate apology for reminding the Master of his sterility; moved again to indicate pressing importance. "The same imbalance that they detected in the Brown miner. Imbalances that were not present when they found the miner, but which developed before she died aboard MacArthur."

The others were suddenly quiet. Charlie continued inexorably. "They are not stupid. They may well have connected these disturbances with sexual abstinence. What have they discovered about Watchmakers? They must have had Watchmakers to examine; the miner would have brought them aboard as a matter of course."

"Curse!" Ivan assumed a pose of thought. "Would they cage the Watchmakers separately?"

Both Mediators gestured lack of knowledge. "Jock was right to answer as she did," Charlie said. "They have the body that was aboard the Crazy Eddie probe. There must have been one, and it must have been a Mediator, a young one with a long life so that he could negotiate with whomever the probe might find here."

"But our records show that Mediator would be dead," Jock said. "He must have been; the humans learned nothing from him. Curse! If only the records were complete—"

"If only the records were complete. If only we had a Brown. If only the humans would tell us what they have done with the probe. If only the humans would tell us why they destroyed MacArthur. You will cease these meaningless phrases. You must have learned them from humans." Ivan commanded with finality. "Speak of what the humans have learned from the pilot of the probe."

Charlie: "They would dissect the pilot. Their biological sciences are as advanced as ours. More advanced. They speak of genetic engineering techniques not recorded in any museum, and certainly not discovered in this Cycle. Thus we must assume their xenobiologists could learn that the pilot was sterile. Renner's Fyunch(click) told him that Mediators were hybrids."

"Crazy Eddie. Even then," Ivan said. "Now she argues incessantly with her Master." He paused, thinking, his arms waving for silence. "You have done well," he told Jock. "They would learn you are sterile in any case. It is crucial that they do not learn how important that is. Does this tell humans that Fyunch(click)s can and do lie to humans?"

Silence. Finally Jock spoke. "We do not know. Sally's Fyunch(click) spoke to her of sex, but the conversation was aboard the human ship. We have no record, only what was reported to us."

"Reported by a Crazy Eddie," Ivan said.

Jock said, "I did my utmost to distract them."

"But did you succeed?"

"Yes. It was evident in their faces."

Ivan could not read a human face, but he understood the concept: there were muscles around human eyes and mouth used for signaling emotions, like Motie gestures. Mediators could read them. "Go on."

"Direct reference to the sex act to slow their minds. Then the fact of our life spans, delivered as one might admit to having a terminal disease. Now these long-lived creatures will mourn for us."

"Well they might," said Charlie.

"They will pity us for our handicaps. They might even attempt to remedy them."

Ivan turned quickly to Jock. "Do you believe they can do so?"

"Master, no! Am I Crazy Eddie?"

Ivan relaxed. "You will consider this matter carefully. You will discuss the evidence the humans have, and what they may deduce from it. Were there not two Engineers as well as your Master aboard the embassy ship that met MacArthur?"

Jock: "Affirm."

"Curse. And how many Mediator pups when they returned?"

"I had four sisters."

"Curse!" Ivan wanted to say more; but to state the obvious would have lost Jock's loyalty forever; it might even have shocked Charlie into abnormalities. Curse! Mediators identified with Masters. They held the usual Master emotions about children.

Though sterile from an early age, Ivan was not immune to those emotions; but he knew. The children should have been spaced.

"No point in sitting here," Renner announced.

"Yeah." Rod led the way to the Commission's office suite in the Palace. Sally followed silently.

"Kelley, I think you'd better bring a round of drinks," Rod said when they were seated at the conference table. "Make mine a double."

"Aye aye, my lord." Kelley gave Rod a puzzled look. Was Lady Sally giving him problems already? And them not even married yet?

"Twenty-five years!" Sally exploded. There was bitter anger in her voice. She said it again, this time to Chaplain Hardy. "Twenty-five years?" She waited for him to explain a universe in which there was so much injustice.

"Maybe it's the price they pay for better than human intelligence," Renner said. "It's heavy."

"There are compensations," Hardy said thoughtfully. "Their intelligence. And their love of life. They talk so fast, they probably think fast as well. I expect that Moties pack a lot into their few years."

There was more silence. Kelley returned with a tray. He set down the glasses and left, his face screwed into puzzled disapproval.

Renner glanced at Rod, who was in Thinker position: elbow on chair arm, chin on closed fist, face brooding. Kevin lifted his glass. "Here's to the wake."

No one responded. Rod left his drink untouched. A man could live a good, useful life in a quarter of a century, he thought. Didn't people live about that long in preatomic days? But it couldn't be complete. I'm twenty-five now, and I haven't raised a family, or lived with a woman I love, or even begun my career in politics . . .

He watched Sally rise and pace the floor. What does she think she's doing? Is she going to solve that problem for them? If they can't, how could we?

"This isn't getting us anywhere," Renner said. He lifted

his glass again. "Look, if it doesn't upset the Mediators that they're short-lived mules, why should we—" He stopped in mid-sentence. "Mules? Then the pup Mediators on the embassy ship—must have been children of the two Browns and the hidden White."

They all looked at him. Sally stopped her pacing and took her seat again. "There were four pups when we got back to Mote Prime," she said. "Weren't there?"

"Indeed," Hardy said. He swirled brandy in his glass. "That is rather a high birth rate."

"But they've so little time," Sally protested.

"One would be a high birth rate in that ship. On that mission." Renner sounded positive. "Chaplain, what do you think of that as an ethical situation? You're going to meet a strange well-armed race. You're in a fragile toy of an unarmed ship. So you have children all over the place . . ."

"I see your point," said David Hardy. "But I'll want to think about it. Perhaps—"

He was interrupted by fists slamming on the table. Two fists. Sally's "God's teeth!" She seized the stylus and scribbled symbols on the face of her computer. It hummed and flashed. "We were waiting for the transfer ship. I *know* I didn't misunderstand. I *couldn't* have."

Hardy looked puzzlement at Sally. Renner looked a question at Rod. Rod shrugged and watched his girl. "Her Motie never told her they were mules," he explained to the others.

The computer hummed again. Sally nodded and keyed in instructions. A screen on the back wall lit to show Sally Fowler, eight months younger, talking to a brown-and-white alien. The voices were eerily identical.

Motie: But you marry to raise children. Who raises children born without marriage?

Sally: There are charities.

Motie: I take it *you've* never—

Sally: No, of course not.

The living Sally was almost blushing, but her face remained grim.

Motie: How not? I don't mean *why* not, I mean *how?*

Sally: Well—you know that men and women have to have sexual relations to make a baby, the same as you—I've examined you pretty thoroughly . . .

"Perhaps not thoroughly enough," Hardy commented.

"Apparently not," Sally said. "Shh."

Motie: Pills? How do they work? Hormones?

Sally: That's right.

Motie: But a proper woman doesn't use them.

Sally: No.

Motie: When will you get married?

Sally: When I find the right man . . . I may have found him already.

Someone was chuckling. Sally looked around, to see Rod looking beatifically unconcerned, Hardy smiling gently, and Renner laughing. She looked curses at the Sailing Master, but he obstinately refused to vanish in black smoke.

Motie: Then why don't you marry him?

Sally: I don't want to jump into anything. "Marry in haste, repent at leisure." I can get married any time. Well, any time within the next five years. I'll be something of a spinster if I'm not married by then.

Motie: Spinster?

Sally: People would think it odd. What if a Motie doesn't want children?

Motie: We don't have sexual relations.

There were various clunks, and the screen went blank.

"The literal truth," she mused. " 'We don't have sexual relations.' They don't either, but not by choice."

"Really?" David Hardy sounded puzzled. "The statement in context with the question is highly misleading . . ."

"She didn't want to talk about it any more," Sally insisted. "And no wonder. I just misunderstood, that's all."

"I never misunderstood my Motie," Renner said. "Sometimes she understood me all too well . . ."

"Look. Let's drop it."

"The day we went down to Mote Prime. You'd known

each other for months," Renner mused. "Chaplain, what do you think?"

"If I understand you properly, the same as you."

"Just what are you hinting at, *Mr*. Renner? I said let's drop it." The Lady Sandra was incensed. Rod steeled himself for what was coming: ice or explosion, or both.

"I'm not hinting it, Sally," Renner said with sudden decision. "I'm saying it. Your Motie lied to you. Deliberately and with forethought."

"Nonsense. She was embarrassed—"

Hardy shook his head slightly. It was a tiny motion, but it stopped Sally. She looked at the priest. "I think," David said, "I can recall only one occasion when a Motie was embarrassed. It was at the Museum. And all of them acted the same way there—nothing like your Fyunch-(click) did just now, Sally. I'm afraid it's very probable that Kevin is right."

"And for what reason?" Sally insisted. "Just why would my—almost my sister—why would she lie to me? About that?"

There was silence. Sally nodded in satisfaction. She couldn't snap at Chaplain Hardy; not that she had that much respect for his office, but for him. Renner was another matter. "You will tell me if you find an answer to that question, *Mr*. Renner."

"Yah. Sure." Renner's expression made him look oddly like Buckman: Bury would have recognized it at once. He had barely heard her.

They left the glittering ballroom as soon as they could. Behind them a costumed orchestra played waltzes, while the Moties were introduced to a seemingly endless line. There were provincial barons, Parliament leaders, traders, people with friends in the protocol office, and assorted party crashers. Everyone wanted to see the Moties.

Rod took Sally's hand as they walked through deserted Palace corridors toward their quarters. An ancient waltz faded hollowly behind them.

"They've so little time to live, and we're wasting it with —that," Sally muttered. "Rod, it's not fair!"

"Part of their mission, sweetheart. What good would it do them to agree with us if we can't hold the baronage? Even with the Throne behind us we're safer playing the political game. And so are they."

"I suppose." She stopped him and leaned against his shoulder. The Hooded Man was fully risen, black against the stars, watching them through the stone arches. A fountain splashed in the courtyard below. They stood that way in the deserted corridor for a long time.

"I do love you," she whispered. "How can you put up with me?"

"That's pretty easy." He bent down to kiss her, desisted when there was no response.

"Rod, I'm so embarrassed . . . how am I ever going to apologize to Kevin?"

"To *Kevin?* You're kidding. Have you ever seen Renner apologize to anyone? Just forget it. Talk as if it had never happened next time you see him."

"But he was *right*—you knew, didn't you? You knew it then!"

He started her walking again. Their footsteps echoed through the corridors. Even in the dim lights the rock walls flashed iridescent colors as they moved. Then a wall blocked the smoldering gaze of the Hooded Man, and they were at the stairs.

"I suspected it then. Just from the reports and the brief relationship I had with *my* Motie. After you left this afternoon I did some checking. They lied to you."

"But why, Rod? I can't understand it—" They climbed another flight in silence.

"You aren't going to like the answer," Rod said as they reached their floor. "She was a Mediator. Mediators represent Masters. She was ordered to lie to you."

"But why? What possible reason could they have for concealing that they were mules?"

"I wish I knew." Or that I didn't know, he thought. But there was no point in telling Sally until he was sure. "Don't take it so hard, sweetheart. We lied to them, too."

They reached his door and he put his hand on the identiplate. The door swung open to reveal Kelley, tunic unfastened, sprawled in an easy chair. The Marine leaped to his feet.

"Good God, Kelley. I've told you not to wait up for me. Go to bed."

"Important message, my lord. Senator Fowler will be here later. He asks you to wait for him. Wanted to be sure you got the message, my lord."

"Yeah." Rod's voice was lemon-sour. "OK. I got the message. Thanks."

"I'll stay to serve you."

"No, you won't. No sense in everybody staying up all night. Get out of here." Rod watched the Marine vanish into the corridor. When he was gone Sally giggled loudly. "I don't see what's so damned funny," Rod snapped.

"He was protecting my reputation," Sally laughed. "What if you hadn't got the message and Uncle Ben came chargin' in here and we—"

"Yeah. Want a drink?"

"With Uncle Ben coming in a few minutes? Waste of good liquor. I'm going to bed." She smiled sweetly. "Don't stay up too late."

"Wench." He took her shoulders and kissed her. Then again. "I could set the door so he can't get in—"

"Good night, Rod."

He watched until she was inside her own suite across the hall from his, then went back inside to the bar. It had been a long dull evening, with only the thought of leaving the party early to look forward to.

"Damn!" he said aloud. He tossed off a brimming glass of New Aberdeen Highland Cream. "God damn it to hell!"

Senator Fowler and a preoccupied Kevin Renner came in after Rod had poured his second drink. "Sorry about the hour, Rod," Fowler said perfunctorily. "Kevin tells me something interesting happened today—"

"He did, uh? And he suggested this conference, right?" When Benjamin Fowler nodded, Rod turned to his former sailing master. "I'll fix you for this, you—"

"We haven't got time for games," Fowler said. "Got any more of that Scotch?"

"Yeah." Rod poured for both of them, tossed off his drink, and poured himself another. "Have a seat, Ben. You too, Mr. Renner. I won't apologize for letting the servants go to bed—"

"Oh, that's all right," Renner said. He lapsed back into whatever reverie was consuming him, sank into a chair, then grinned in astonishment. He'd never been in a massage chair before, and obviously enjoyed it.

"OK," Senator Fowler said. "Tell me what *you* think happened this afternoon."

"I'll show it to you." Rod manipulated his pocket computer and the wall screen came on. The picture was not good; it had been recorded by a small camera built into a decoration on Rod's tunic, and the viewpoint was limited. The sound was excellent, though.

Fowler watched in silence. "Let's see that again," he said. Rod obligingly ran the conference once more. While Fowler and Renner watched he went to the bar, decided against another Scotch, and poured himself coffee.

"Now just why do you think this was so all-fired important?" Fowler demanded.

Kevin Renner shrugged. "It's the first proof we have that they lie to us. What else haven't they told us?"

"Hell, they haven't told us much of anything," Fowler said. "And was that a lie?"

"Yeah," Rod said quietly. "By implication, anyway. It wasn't misunderstanding. I've checked on that. We've got too many records of conversations where the Moties implied something false, realized they'd done it from watching our reactions, and corrected themselves. No. That Motie deliberately encouraged Sally to believe something that isn't true."

"But what the hell does it do for us to know Mediators don't have kids?" Fowler demanded.

"It tells us two Browns and a White had four children," Renner said slowly. "On a small ship. In space. Under dangerous conditions. Not to mention crowded."

"Yeah." Ben Fowler stood and removed his dress tunic. The shirt underneath was old, very soft, and carefully patched in three places. "Rod, just what do Moties think of their kids?" Fowler asked. "Maybe they think they're nothing much until they can talk. Expendable."

"Wrong," said Renner.

"The tactful way," Rod said quietly, "the polite way to disagree with the Senator would be to say, 'That turns out not to be the case.' "

Renner's face lit up. "Hey. I like that. Anyway, the Senator's wrong. The Moties think everything of their children. The only religion they ever told me about teaches that their souls divide to enter their children. They practically worship the little darlings."

"Uh." Fowler held out his glass for a refill. He scowled impatiently. "Could it be they like 'em so much they have kids whenever they get the chance?"

"Possible," Rod said. "And from that the threat is obvious. But—"

"But exactly," Fowler said. "Then that planet's got to be *crowded*. Which it was. Which means the Moties have got population pressure problems like we've *never* had . . ."

"Presumably they can control them," Rod said carefully. "Because if they can't— They've been cooped up in that system a long time."

"With what results?" Fowler demanded. "What do we know of Motie history?"

"Not a lot," Renner said. "They've been civilized a long time. Really long. They were moving asteroids in bunches at least ten thousand years ago. I'm almost afraid to think how much history they've had." Kevin wriggled in the chair to get the full effects of the massage. "So they've had plenty of time to solve their population problems. Just from the time they launched that Crazy Eddie probe to now they could have filled up the planet. They didn't, so they can control population . . ."

"But they don't want to," Ben announced. "And what does that mean? If they get out here into the Empire, how long before they outnumber us?" Senator Fowler toyed thoughtfully with a worn spot on his shirt. "Maybe that's what they're trying to hide. High birth rate and a lack of desire to do anything about it." He stood in sudden decision, no longer pensive. "Rod, get your people looking into this. I want everything we've got about Motie history."

"Yes, sir," Rod said unhappily. *And what is this going to do to Sally when we get it? Because—*

"You sound like the prosecutor in a murder trial," Renner said. "Good Lord, Senator, they've got a *long* history. Of course they've solved the population pressure problem."

"Fine. How?" Fowler snapped.

"I don't know. Ask 'em," said Renner.

"I intend to. But since we know they can and do lie to us— Now just why would that surprise a politician?" Ben wondered. "Anyway. Now that we know that, I want to have my ducks in a row before I go in there and confront the Moties."

"The opportunities for trade are fabulous," Jock announced. The arms indicated excitement. "These humans are indescribably inefficient in the use of their resources. They have no instinct for complex tools."

"None?" demanded Ivan.

"None that I have seen." Jock indicated the tri-v. "They must train their young in every trade. Many of the programs on this set are for that purpose."

"They have time to learn," Charlie reflected. "They live very long. Longer than any Master."

"Yes, but what a waste. They have no Browns, and no Watchmakers—"

Ivan interrupted. "You are certain they have no Watchmakers?"

"Yes. We saw no signs on the ships, nor have there been any on the tri-v, nor are there the expected products of Watchmakers. There are no individualized personal items—"

"I have seen such. The guards who attended us on Lenin carried such and many wore such footgear."

"Made by our own Watchmakers—"

"Precisely," said Ivan. "Now we know why they destroyed MacArthur. And why they fear us."

The Mediators jabbered excitedly until Ivan cut them off again. "You agree?" He asked in the tone commanding information to be confirmed.

"Yes!" they said in unison. Charlie spoke rapidly, drowning Jock out. "The Brown miner they took aboard would have carried a breeding pair of Watchmakers. The humans know nothing of Watchmakers and would have allowed them to escape. And given free run of the ship and much time to adapt to it—"

"Yet we were told they have Watchmakers," Ivan said.

Jock took a pose indicating memory recall. After a second he said, "No. Sally allowed us to assume that they have them. When her Fyunch(click) suggested that human Watchmakers were large, Sally agreed."

"And the midshipmen seemed startled when we spoke of them regarding construction of their lifeboats," Charlie said flatly. "Yes. You are certainly correct."

There was silence. Ivan thought. Then he said, "They know we have a prolific subspecies. You will reflect on this."

"They fear that we deliberately caused the destruction of MacArthur," Charlie said. "Curse! If only they had told us. We could have told them of the dangers, and the humans would have nothing to fear. Curse! Why did the universe arrange that the first Motie they met was a Brown?"

"They said MacArthur was infested with plague," Jock mused. "And so it was, although we did not believe them. A plague of Watchmakers. Yet. If they truly believe we deliberately destroyed their ship, or allowed it to be destroyed, why have they not said so? Why did they not ask?"

"They conceal their vulnerabilities," said Charlie. "And they never admit defeat. Even in their final minutes the midshipmen refused to surrender."

There was silence. Ivan spoke. "The humans did not wish us to know there were Watchmakers aboard until they had killed them. They were certain they could do that. Then, after, they did not wish us to know Watchmakers could destroy their ships."

"Fools!" Charlie shouted. "Watchmakers given time to adapt can destroy any ship. They contribute greatly to a collapse. If they were not so useful we would have them exterminated."

"That's been done," Jock said. He gestured dry humor. "With the usual result. Another Master kept hers—"

"Silence," Ivan demanded. "They fear us. Speak of that."

"Do you know of what the humans call 'fiction'?" Charlie asked. "Deliberately constructed legends. Both those who hear and those who tell them know they are false."

Ivan and Jock indicated they were familiar with the concept.

"There was a tri-v program last evening. It was fiction as are many of the broadcasts. This one was called 'Istvan Dies.' When it was completed the commentator spoke as if the major action of the story were true."

"I did not see," Jock said. "Viceroy Merrill wished me to meet some Traders before the reception for the Barons. Curse! These endless formalities consume our time and we learn nothing from them."

"I did not tell you of this program," Charlie said. "The principal actor portrayed a man obviously intended to be Admiral Kutuzov."

Jock signaled astonishment and lament for lost opportunities.

"You have a point?" Ivan demanded.

"Yes. The story was one of conflicting motives. The admiral in command did not wish to do what he did. There was war between humans: between the Empire and those outies they fear so greatly."

"Could we not come to terms with the outies?" Jock demanded.

"How?" Ivan said. "They control all access to us. If they suspect we would ever do so, they would do anything to prevent it. Do not even think of such things. Tell me of your program."

"In this war there was revolt of a planet. Other planets would soon revolt. What was a small war could become a *very large war, with many planets involved. The admiral detected a way to prevent that, and decided it was his duty. With five ships like* Lenin *he killed all life on a planet inhabited by ten millions of humans."*

There was long silence.

"They are able to do this?" Ivan demanded.

"I believe so," Charlie answered. "I am not a Brown to be certain, but—"

"You will reflect on this. Remember that they fear us. Recall that they now know we have a prolific subspecies. Recall also that from study of the probe they placed this man in charge of the expedition to our system. Fear for your Masters and your sisters." Ivan went to his chamber. After a long time the Mediators began to speak rapidly, but very softly.

52 • *Options*

Heavy clouds raced across New Scotland skies. They parted to let New Cal's bright rays slant warmingly into the paneled conference room. Bright objects flashed momentarily before the windows polarized. Outside there were deep shadows in the Palace grounds, but the sunlight was yet bright in the narrow streets where government offices emptied for the day. Kilted crowds jostled and milled as the sector bureaucracy hurried home to their families, a drink, and tri-v.

Rod Blaine stared moodily through the windows. Down below a pretty secretary hurried out of the Palace, so frantic to reach a people-mover that she nearly bowled over a senior clerk. An important date, Rod thought. And the clerk will have a family . . . all those people. My responsibility, and that may be just too damn bad for the Moties.

There was a bustle of activity behind him. "You got arrangements for feedin' the Moties?" Kelley demanded.

"Yes, sir," a steward answered. "The chef would like

to do something with that mush they eat, though—spices, something. He don't feel right, just putting meat and grain in a pot and boilin' it."

"He can get artistic some other time. The Commissioners don't want anything fancy tonight. Just be able to feed 'em all if they want it." Kelley glanced at the magic coffeepot to be sure it was full, then glared at an empty space next to it. "Where's the goddamn chocolate?" he demanded.

"It's comin', Mr. Kelley," the steward said defensively.

"Right. See that it's here before the Moties come in. That'll be an hour." Kelley glanced at the wall clock. "OK. I guess we're ready. But make sure of that chocolate."

Since they'd discovered it aboard *Lenin* the Moties had become addicted to hot chocolate. It was one of the few human beverages they liked; but the *way* they liked it! Kelley shuddered. Butter he could understand. They put butter in chocolate aboard the Limey ships. But a drop of machine oil in every cup?

"Ready for us, Kelley?" Rod asked.

"Yes, my lord," Kelley assured him. He took his place at the bar and pressed a button to signal that the conference could begin. Somethin' botherin' the boss, he decided. Not his girl, either. Glad I don't have his problems.

A door opened and the Commission staff came in, followed by several of Horvath's scientists. They took seats along one side of the inlaid table and laid their pocket computers in front of them. There were soft hums as they tested their linkup with the Palace computer system.

Horvath and Senator Fowler were still arguing as they entered. "Doctor, it takes time to process these things—"

"Why?" Horvath demanded. "I know you don't have to check with Sparta."

"All right. It takes *me* time to make up my mind, then," Fowler said irritably. "Look: I'll see what I can do for you next Birthday. You had a gong coming even before the Mote expedition. But, damn it, Doctor, I'm not sure you're temperamentally suited for a seat on—" He broke off as heads turned toward them. "We'll finish this later."

"All right." Horvath looked around the room and went to a seat directly across from Ben's. There was a quick reshuffle as the Science Minister arranged his staff on his side of the table.

Others came in—Kevin Renner, Chaplain Hardy, both still in Navy uniform. A secretary. Stewards entered and there was more confusion as Kelley sent coffee around.

Rod frowned as he took his seat, then smiled as Sally entered hastily. "Sorry I'm late," she panted. "There was—"

"We haven't started yet," Rod told her. He indicated a place next to his.

"What's all this about?" she asked quietly. There was something in Rod's manner that worried her, and she studied him carefully. "Why is Uncle Ben so interested in Motie history? Just what happened last night?"

"You'll see. The Senator's about to start." *And I hope it'll be all right, sweetheart, but I doubt it. What happens to us after this?* Rod turned grimly to the conference. *I wonder what my Fyunch(click) is doing now? It'd be nice to send a representative to this and—*

"Let's get moving," Senator Fowler said brusquely. "This meeting of the Lords Commissioners Extraordinary representing His Imperial Majesty to the inhabitants of the Mote System is convened. Please write your names and the organizations you represent." There was a second of silence broken by the soft hums of the computer links.

"We've got a lot to cover," the Senator continued. "Last night it became obvious *that* the Moties lie to us about certain critical matters—"

"No more than we've done to them," Dr. Horvath interrupted. *Blast! I have to control myself better than that. The point must be made, but if the Senator gets really irritated—*

"It's *what* they lie about that concerns us, Doctor," Fowler said smoothly. He paused a moment, and power seemed to gather around him. The dumpy old man in baggy clothing vanished. The Prime Minister spoke.

"Look, all of you, I like things informal. If you've got something to say, spit it out. But let me finish my sentences first." There was a thin smile, wintry cold. "Anybody else you can interrupt, if you're big enough. Now, Dr. Horvath, just what are the Moties hiding from us?"

Anthony Horvath ran his slim fingers through thinning hair. "I need more time, Senator. Until this morning it hadn't occurred to me that the Moties were hiding *anything.*" He glanced nervously at Chaplain Hardy, but the priest said nothing.

"It was a bit of a surprise to all of us," Fowler said. "But we've got evidence that Moties breed at a godawful rate. The question is, could we *make* them keep their numbers down if they don't want to? Rod, could the Moties have been hiding weapons from us?"

Rod shrugged. "In a whole system? Ben, they could hide damn near anything they wanted to."

"But they are utterly unwarlike," Horvath protested. "Senator, I am as concerned for the safety of the Empire as anyone in this room. I take my duties as a Sector Minister quite seriously, I assure you."

You're not assurin' us, you're talkin' for the record, Kelley thought. Cap'n Blaine knows it, too. What's botherin' the boss? He looks like he does before an action.

"—no evidence of warlike activities among the Moties," Horvath finished.

"That turns out not to be the case," Renner put in. "Doc, I like Moties as well as you do, but something produced the Mediators."

"Oh, well, yes," Horvath said easily. "In their prehistory they must have fought like lions. The analogy is quite apt, by the way. The territorial instinct shows up still —in their architecture and in their social organization, for example. But the combats were a long time ago."

"Just how long?" Senator Fowler asked.

Horvath looked uncomfortable. "Possibly a million years."

There was silence. Sally shook her head sadly. Cooped up in one tiny system for a million years—a million *civilized* years! The *patience* they must have learned!

"No wars in all the time since?" Fowler asked. "Really?"

"Yes, damn it, they've had wars," Horvath answered. "At least two of the kind that Earth went through at the close of the CoDominium period. But that was a long time ago!" He had to raise his voice to carry across Sally's startled gasp. There were mutters around the table.

"One of those was enough to make Earth damn near uninhabitable," Ben Fowler said slowly. "How long ago are you talking about? Million years again?"

Horvath said, "Hundreds of thousands, at least."

"Thousands, probably," Chaplain Hardy said carefully. "Or less. Sally, have you revised your estimates of the age of that primitive civilization you dug up?"

Sally didn't answer either. There was an uncomfortable silence.

"For the record, Father Hardy," Senator Fowler asked, "are you here as Commission staff?"

"No, sir. Cardinal Randolph has asked me to represent the Church to the Commission."

"Thank you."

There was more silence.

"They had nowhere to go," Anthony Horvath said. He shrugged nervously. Someone giggled, then fell silent when Horvath continued. "It's obvious that their first wars were a very long time ago, in the million-year range. It shows in their development. Dr. Horowitz has examined the expedition biological findings and—well, you tell them, Sigmund."

Horowitz smiled in triumph. "When I first examined the probe pilot I thought it might be a mutation. I was right. They are mutations, only it all happened a long time ago. The original animal life on Mote Prime is bilaterally symmetric, as on Earth and nearly everywhere. The first asymmetric Motie must have been a drastic mutation. Couldn't have been as well developed as the present forms, either. Why didn't it die out? Because there were deliberate efforts to obtain the asymmetric form, I think. And because everything else was mutating also. The competition for survival was low."

"But that means they had civilization when the present forms developed," Sally said. "Is that possible?"

Horowitz smiled again.

"What about the Eye?" Sally asked. "It must have irradiated the Mote system when it went supergiant."

"Too long ago," Horvath said. "We checked. After all, we've got the equivalent of five hundred years' observation of the Eye in data from our explorer ships, and it checks with the information the Moties gave Midshipman Potter. The Eye's been a supergiant for six million years or more, and the Moties haven't had their present form anything like that long."

"Oh," said Sally. "But then what caused the—"

"Wars," Horowitz announced. "General increase in radiation levels, planet-wide. Coupled with deliberate genetic selection."

Sally nodded reluctantly. "All right—they had atomic wars. So did we. If the CoDominium hadn't developed the Alderson Drive we'd have exterminated ourselves on Earth." She didn't like the answer, though. It was hard to accept. "Couldn't there have been another dominant species that killed itself off, and the Moties developed later?"

"No," Horvath said carefully. "Your own work, Lady Sally: you've shown just how well adapted the Motie form is to using tools. The mutation must have been a tool user to begin with—or was controlled by tool users. Or both."

"That's one war," Senator Fowler said. "The one that created the Moties as we see 'em. You said two."

Horvath nodded sadly. "Yes, sir. The presently evolved Moties must have fought with atomic weapons. Later there was another period of radiation that split the species into all those castes—both the civilized forms and the animals. Plus intermediates like Watchmakers." Horvath looked apologetically at Blaine, but there was no sign of emotion.

Sigmund Horowitz cleared his throat. He was clearly enjoying this. "I believe the Browns were the original form. When the Whites became dominant they bred the other subspecies to their own uses. Controlled evolution again, you see. But some forms evolved by themselves."

"Then the asymmetric animals are not ancestors to Moties?" Senator Fowler asked curiously.

"No." Horowitz rubbed his hands together and fingered his pocket computer in anticipation. "They are degenerate forms—I can show you the gene mechanisms."

"That won't be necessary," Senator Fowler said hastily. "So we have two wars. Presumably the Mediators could have been bred in the second one—"

"Better make it three wars," Renner put in. "Even if we assume they ran out of radioactives in the second one."

"Why?" Sally demanded.

"You saw the planet. Then there's the adaptation to space," Renner said. He looked expectantly at Horvath and Horowitz.

Horowitz' triumphant grin was even broader now. "Your work again, my lady. The Moties are so well adapted to space that you wondered if they'd evolved there. They did." The xenobiologist nodded emphatically. "But not until they'd had a long evolutionary period on the planet itself. Want me to review the evidence? Physiological mechanisms that adjust to low pressure and no gravity, intuitive astrogation—"

"I believe you," Sally said quietly.

"Mars!" Rod Blaine shouted. Everyone looked at him. "Mars. Is that what you're thinking, Kevin?"

Renner nodded. He seemed to be a man in conflict, his mind racing ahead and not liking what it found. "Sure," he said. "They fought at least one war with asteroids. Just look at the surface of Mote Prime, all torn by overlapping circular craters. It must have damn near wiped out the planet. It scared the survivors so much they moved all the asteroids out to where they couldn't be used that way again—"

"But the war killed off most of the higher life on the planet," Horowitz finished. "After a long time the planet was repopulated by Moties who'd adapted to space."

"But a very long time ago," Dr. Horvath protested. "The asteroid craters are cold and the orbits are stable. All this happened long ago."

Horvath didn't seem very comfortable with his conclusions, and Rod scratched a note. Not good enough, Rod thought. But—there must be *some* explanation . . .

"But they could still fight with asteroids," Horvath continued. "If they wanted to. It would take more energy, but as long as they're in the system they can be moved. We've no evidence of recent wars, and what has all this to do with us anyway? They used to fight, they evolved the Mediators to stop it, and it worked. Now they don't fight any more."

"Maybe," Senator Fowler grunted. "And maybe not."

"They didn't fight *us*," Horvath insisted.

"Battle cruiser got destroyed," Fowler said. "OK, spare me the explanations. There's the midshipmen, and yeah, I've heard all the stories about them. The fact is, Dr. Horvath, if Moties fight each other you know damn well one faction's going to pick up allies among the outies and rebels. Hell, they might even *encourage* revolts, and by God's teeth we don't need that! There's another thing bothers me, too—have they got a planetary government?"

There was more silence.

"Well, Sally?" the Senator demanded. "It's your field."

"They— Well, they have a kind of planetary government, Jurisdiction. A Master or a group of them takes jurisdiction over something and the rest go along."

Ben Fowler scowled at his niece. "Hell, we don't even let *humans* wander around the universe until they've got planetary governments. Can't you just see some Motie colony deciding to help a faction back home on Mote Prime?" He looked around the table and scowled again. "Damn it, don't all of you look at me like that. You'd think I wanted to shoot Father Christmas! I want trade with the Moties, but let's not forget the Prime Directive of the Empire."

"We need more time," Horvath protested. "You can't decide anything right now!"

"We don't have the time," Rod said quietly. "You must be aware of the pressures, Doctor. You helped create them. Every interest group in this sector is demanding immediate action." Rod had been getting daily calls from the Humanity League, and he was certain that Minister Horvath had been feeding information to the group.

"What's bothering you is the potential birth rate," Horvath said. "I'm sure you realize that they *must* be able to control their population. They'd not have survived this long if they couldn't."

"But they may not *want* to," Fowler said. "Could we *make* them do it? Rod, has your Commander Cargill done any more work on that threat estimate?"

"Refinements only, Senator. His original calculations hold up pretty well."

"So it'd take a big fleet operation to compel the Moties —and that's with their present resources. What kind of problems are we handing our grandchildren if we help 'em get colonies?"

"You can't prevent them from getting out now," Horvath protested. "Capt—My Lord Blaine's analysis proved that. They'll eventually get the Langston Field, and they'll come out. We *must* have friendly relations with them before then. I say let's start trading with them right now and work out our problems as they come up. We can't solve everything at once."

"That's your recommendation?" Fowler asked.

"Yes, sir. Mine, the Humanity League's, the Imperial Traders—"

"Not all of 'em," Rod interrupted. "Their local council's divided. A sizable minority wants nothing to do with Moties."

"So they're in industries that will be ruined by Motie technology," Horvath said with a shrug. "We can handle that problem. Senator, the Moties will inevitably develop *something* that gets them out of their system. We should get them so bound to the Empire that their interests are ours before it happens."

"Or take 'em into the Empire and be done with it," Fowler muttered. "I thought of that one last night. If they can't control their population, we can do it for them—"

"But we know they can," Horvath protested. "We've proved they've been civilized a *long* time in one system. They've learned—" He stopped for a moment, then con-

tinued excitedly. "Has it occurred to you that they may
have population allotments? The Moties on that expedition ship may have been required to have their children
at a certain time, or not at all. So they had them aboard
ship."

"Hmm," Fowler said. His scowl vanished. "Maybe
you've got something there. We'll—*I'll*—ask the Moties
when they come in. Dr. Hardy, you've been sitting there
like a man about to be hanged in low gravity. What's got
you upset?"

"Rats," the Chaplain said carefully.

Horvath looked around quickly, then nodded in submission. "They disturbed you also, David?"

"Of course. Can you find the file, or must I?"

"I have it," Horvath sighed. He scrawled numbers on
the face of his pocket computer. It hummed and the wall
screens lit . . .

. . . a Motie city, struck by disaster. Cars overturned
and rusted through littered broken streets. Crashed aircraft
were imbedded in the ruins of fire-scorched buildings.
Weeds grew from cracks in the pavement. In the center of
the picture was a sloping mound of rubble, and a hundred
small black shapes darted and swarmed over it.

"It's not what it looks like. It's one floor of the Motie
zoo," Horvath explained. He touched his controls and the
image zoomed closer to focus on a single black shape
which grew until the outlines were fuzzy: a pointed, rat-
like face, with wicked teeth. But it was not a rat.

It had one membranous ear, and five limbs. The foremost limb on the right side was not a fifth paw; it was a
long and agile arm, tipped with claws like hooked daggers.

"Ah," Horowitz exclaimed. He looked accusingly at
Horvath. "You didn't show me this one . . . more wars,
eh? One of the wars must have wiped out so much life that
ecological niches were left empty. But this— Did you get
a specimen?"

"Unfortunately no."

"What did it degenerate from?" Horowitz asked wonderingly. "A long step from the intelligent Motie to—to

that. Is there a Motie caste you have not shown me? Something similar to that?"

"No, of course not," Sally said.

"No one would breed selectively for those things," Horowitz mused. "It must have been natural selection—" He smiled in satisfaction. "More proof, if it were needed. One of their wars almost depopulated their planet. And for a very long time, too."

"Yah," Renner said quickly. "So while these things took over Mote Prime the civilized Moties were out in the asteroids. They must have bred out there for generations, Whites and Browns and Watchmakers and maybe some things we didn't see because we didn't get to the asteroid civilization."

"But a long time ago, again," said Horvath. "Very long— Dr. Buckman's work on asteroid orbits—well. Perhaps the Mediators were evolved in space before they resettled the planet. You can see they were needed."

"Which makes the Whites as warlike now as then," Senator Fowler pointed out.

"Now they have Mediators, Uncle Ben," Sally reminded him.

"Yeah. And maybe they've solved their population pressure— Doctor, get that goddamn thing off the screen! It gives me the willies. Why the *hell* would anyone put a ruined city in a zoo anyway?"

The feral image vanished and everyone seemed relieved. "They explained that." Horvath seemed almost cheerful again. "Some of their forms evolved for cities. A thorough zoo would have to include them."

"*Ruined* cities?"

"Maybe to remind them of what happens when they don't listen to the Mediators," Sally said quietly. "A horrible example to keep them scared of war."

"It'd do it, too," Renner said. He shuddered slightly.

"Let's sum this up. The Moties are due in a few minutes," Senator Fowler said. "One. The potential reproductive rate is enormous, and the Moties are willing to have kids in places we wouldn't.

"Two. The Moties lied in a way that concealed their high birth-rate potential.

"Three. Moties have had wars. At least three big ones. Maybe more.

"Four. They've been around a long time. *Really* long. That argues that they've got their population under control. We don't know *how* they do it. but it might tie in to why they have kids on dangerous missions. We have to ask. OK so far?"

There was a chorus of muttered assents. "Now to options. First, we could take Dr. Horvath's advice and negotiate trade agreements. The Moties have asked for permanent stations, and the right to look for and settle on uncolonized worlds inside the Empire and beyond. They don't insist on the interior space, but they'd like stuff we don't use, such as asteroids and terraformable rocks. They offer a lot in exchange."

He paused for comments, but there weren't any. Everyone was content to let the Senator do the summation for the record.

"Now that course of action means turning the Moties loose. Once they have bases where we don't control access to them, outies and rebels are certain to dicker with the Moties. We have to outdicker, and it's possible that being generous now will get their gratitude later. Immediate agreement has the support of Commissioner Sandra Bright Fowler. We still OK so far?"

There were more nods and yeses. A few of the scientists looked curiously at Sally. Dr. Horvath gave her an encouraging smile.

"Second option. We take the Moties into the Empire. Install a governor general, at least on any Mote colony, possibly on Mote Prime itself. This would be expensive, and we don't know what happens if the Moties try to resist. Their military potential is damn high."

"I think that would be terribly unwise," Anthony Horvath said. "I can't believe the Moties would submit easily, and—"

"Yeah. I'm trying to lay out the possibilities, Doctor. Now that you've entered your objection I may as well state that this plan has the tentative approval of the War Ministry and most of the Colonial Office people. No Commissioners yet, but I intend to put it to the Moties as a possibility. Hell, they might *want* in."

"Well, if they voluntarily enter the Empire, I'd support the action," Horvath said.

"So would I," Sally added.

Ben Fowler screwed his heavy features into a mask of contemplation. "Me, I don't think it would work," he mused. "We generally govern through locals. Now just what reward can we promise for cooperation with us against a conspiracy by their whole race? But we'll ask them."

Fowler straightened in his chair. The amused, thoughtful smile vanished. "Possibility three. The hoof-and-mouth disease remedy."

There were gasps. Horvath's lips were tightly drawn and he took a deep breath. "Does that mean what I think, Senator?"

"Yeah. If there isn't any hoof-and-mouth disease, there won't be any. If there aren't any Moties, there won't be a Motie problem."

David Hardy's voice was low but very firm. "The Church would object to that very strongly, Senator. With every means we have."

"I'm aware of that, Father. I'm aware of the Humanity League's feeling too. As a matter of fact, unprovoked extermination isn't a real alternative. Not that we can't physically do it, but politically, no. Unless the Moties are a direct and immediate threat to the Empire."

"Which they aren't," Horvath said positively. "They're an opportunity. I wish I could make you *see* that."

"Doc, I may see things as well as you do. Ever think of that? Now those are the possibilities. Are we ready for the Moties, or has anybody got something else to bring up?"

Rod took a deep breath and glanced at Sally. She's not going to like this— "Senator, have we forgotten Sally's dig? Where she found a primitive civilization not more than a thousand years old? How were the Moties primitive so recently?"

More silence. "Had to be wars, didn't it?" Rod asked.

"No," Sally said. "I've thought about that—the Moties have zoos, right? Couldn't I have found—well, a reservation for primitives? We have them all over the Empire, cultural preserves for people who don't want to be part of technological civilization—"

"After a million years of civilization?" Renner asked. "Lady Sally, do you really *believe* that?"

She shrugged. "They're aliens."

"I hadn't forgotten it," Ben Fowler said. "OK, let's discuss it. Sally, your notion's silly. You know what happened, they moved the asteroids around so long ago the pits are cold. Then, about the time of the CoDominium, they blasted themselves into a new Stone Age. Doesn't argue too strong they've learned not to fight, does it?"

"We did the same thing then," Sally said. "Or would have, if we'd been trapped in a single system."

"Yeah," Fowler answered. "And if I was a Commissioner for a Motie Empire, I wouldn't let humans wander around space without a keeper. Anything else?"

"Yes, sir," Rod told him. "Sally, I don't like this, but—"

"Get on with it," Fowler growled.

"Yes, sir." Am I losing her because of Moties? But I can't just forget it. "Dr. Horvath, you seemed very uncomfortable after we agreed that the Moties have been civilized for millennia. Why?"

"Well—no reason, actually—except—well, I need to do more checking, that's all."

"As Science Minister, you're responsible for technological forecasts, aren't you?" Rod asked.

"Yes," Horvath admitted unhappily.

"Where do we stand with respect to the First Empire?"

"We haven't caught up with them yet. We'll get there in another century."

"And where would we be if there hadn't been the Secession Wars? If the old Empire'd been going along without interruption?"

Horvath shrugged. "You're probably right, my lord. Yes. It bothered me also. Senator, what Commissioner

Blaine implies is that the Moties aren't advanced enough to have had civilization for a million years. Or even ten thousand. Possibly not for a thousand."

"Yet we *know* they moved those asteroids at least ten thousand years ago," Renner exclaimed. His voice showed excitement and wonder. "They must have recolonized the Mote about the same time the Alderson Drive was developed on Earth! The Moties aren't really much older than we are!"

"There's another explanation," Father Hardy pointed out. "They recolonized much earlier than that—and they have a new set of wars every millennium."

"Or even more often," Senator Fowler added softly. "And if that's the case, we know how they control their population, don't we? Well, Dr. Horvath? What's your advice now?"

"I—I don't know," the Science Minister stammered unhappily. He picked at his nails, realized he was doing it, and laid his hands on the table where they wandered like small wounded animals. "I think we have to be sure."

"So do I," the Senator told him. "But it wouldn't hurt to —Rod, tomorrow you'll work with the Admiralty."

"I remind you, Senator, that the Church will forbid any member to take part in the extermination of the Moties," Hardy said carefully.

"That's pretty close to treason, Father."

"Perhaps. It's also true."

"Anyway, it wasn't what I had in mind. Maybe we have to take the Moties into the Empire. Whether they like it or not. Maybe they'll submit without a fight if we go in there with a big enough fleet."

"And if they don't?" Hardy asked.

Senator Fowler didn't answer.

Rod looked at Sally, then around the table, finally at the paneled walls.

It's such an ordinary room, he thought. There's nothing special about the people in it either. And right here, in this stupid little conference room on a barely habitable planet, we've got to decide the fate of a race that may be a million years older than we are.

The Moties aren't going to surrender. If they're what we think they are, they won't be beaten either. But there's only the one planet and some asteroids. If they're gone . . .

"Kelley, you can bring the Moties in now," Senator Fowler said.

The last of New Cal's dying rays fell into the room. The Palace grounds outside turned purple in shadow.

53 • *The Djinn*

They were following their escorts through the Palace corridors. As they walked, Jock spoke to the Ambassador.

"Something has changed. This Marine who summoned us looks at us differently. As might a Warrior at another Warrior."

They entered the conference room. A sea of human faces— "Yes," Jock said. "Much is different. We must be on guard."

"What may they know?" Ivan demanded.

Jock indicated lack of knowledge. "Some fear us. Others pity us. All try to hide their changed emotional state."

The Marine conducted them to badly designed couches at one end of a large conference table. "Humans are addicted to these tables," Charlie twittered. "Sometimes the shape of them is very important, for reasons I have been unable to know."

There were the meaningless greetings the humans called "formalities": insincere inquiries into the state of health, nebulous benedictions and hopes for past well-being; all compensations for the lack of human Mediators. Charlie attended to these as Jock continued to speak to the Master.

"The human at the opposite end of the table is an unimportant clerk. On our two-hand side at the center is the power. The Emperor's Mediator has reached some decision. Lord Blaine reluctantly shares it. Sally disagrees, very much, but is unable to argue. She wishes for reasons to object. We may need to find them for her. Opposite the

Emperor's Mediator are the scientists, and they share Sally's emotions. They do not feel as involved in the decision as she. The others are of no importance except the priest. I am still unable to determine his importance, but it has increased since last we saw him. He may be more dangerous to us than all the rest—"

"Can he understand our language?" Ivan demanded.

"Not if we speak rapidly and with formal grammar. He detects elementary emotional content, and is aware that we are exchanging much information in a short time."

"Find out what disturbs the humans." Ivan curled on his couch and surveyed the room with distaste. Keepers sometimes spoke directly with Mediators from many Masters, but it was never a pleasant experience. All negotiation with humans was painfully slow. Their thoughts crept like liquid helium, and often they had no conception of their own interests.

But he could not simply instruct the Mediators. They were unstable, increasingly so. They must be controlled directly. And the Race must be preserved . . .

"This meeting may be more pleasant than the others," Charlie said.

Senator Fowler looked startled. "Why do you say that?"

"From your expression you are determined to achieve decisions at this meeting," Charlie answered. "You have told us that the meeting will be long, lasting even through dinner. Your tri-v tells us that you are under great pressure to conclude an agreement with us. We are slowly learning your ways, and coming to enjoy them; but our training, our whole reason for existence, is to reach agreements. So far you have been careful to avoid them."

"Blunt enough," Fowler muttered. And intended to put us a bit ill at ease, wasn't it, my friend? You're smooth. "We need information first. About your history."

"Ah." Charlie hesitated only a second, but she saw the signals Jock gestured, and the Master's finger movements. "You are concerned about our wars?"

"Damn right," Senator Fowler agreed. "You hid damn near your whole history. Lied about what you did tell us."

There were mutters of disapproval. Dr. Horvath shot

Fowler a disgusted look. Didn't the man know anything about negotiations? But of course he did, which made such rudeness even more puzzling . . .

Charlie gave a human shrug. "As you did with us, Senator. Our history: very well. Like you humans, we have had periods of warfare. Often over religions. Our last great wars were several of your centuries ago—since that time we have managed to control ourselves. But we have rebellions from time to time. Masters much like your outies, who place independence ahead of the good of the race. It is then necessary to fight them—"

"Why didn't you just admit that in the first place?" Rod demanded.

The Motie shrugged again. "What did we know of you? Until you gave us the tri-v and let us see you as you are, what *could* we know? And we are as ashamed of our conflicts as many of you are of yours. You must understand, nearly all Mediators serve Masters who have no connection with war. We were instructed to assure you of our peaceful intentions toward your race. Our internal conflicts did not seem to be any of your business."

"So you hid your weapons?" Rod asked.

Charlie looked to Jock. The other Mediator answered. "Those we have. We are inhabitants of a single star system, my lord. We have no racial enemies and few resources to devote to naval vessels—our military forces, such as they are, are more similar to your police than to your Navy and Marines." The Motie's gentle smile said nothing more, but somehow conveyed another thought: They would be fools to let the humans know how much or how little armament they had.

Sally smiled happily. "I told you, Uncle Ben—"

Senator Fowler nodded. "One other little point, Charlie. Just how often do your reproductive castes breed, anyway?"

It was Jock who answered. When Charlie hesitated, David Hardy watched with interest—was there communication by gesture? "When they are allowed to," the alien said smoothly. "Don't yours?"

"Eh?"

"You control your populations through economic incentives and forced emigration. Neither alternative is available to us, yet our reproductive drives are no less strong than yours. Our Masters breed when they can."

"You mean you have legal mechanisms to restrict population?" Horvath asked.

"Essentially yes."

"And why didn't you say that before?" Senator Fowler demanded.

"You didn't ask."

Dr. Horvath was grinning now. So was Sally. Relief showed around the room. Except—

"You deliberately misled Lady Sally," Chaplain Hardy said carefully. "Please tell me why."

"That Mediator served Jock's Master," Charlie answered. "She should speak to you of this. And please excuse us, I must tell the Ambassador what has been said." Charlie twittered.

"Jock, you must take great care. We have won their sympathy. They want reasons to believe us. These humans have almost as much empathy as Mediators when they are in the proper mood, but they can change instantly."

"I have listened," Ivan said. "Do what you can to reassure these humans. If we are ever once away from their control we will be useful to all of them, and we will be an economic necessity to powerful groups of humans."

"She felt the truth would upset you," Jock answered. "I am not sure what was said. It was not discussed with me. We do not often discuss sex and reproduction within our family groups and almost never beyond them. The subject is— You do not have the emotion. It is similar to embarrassment but not identical. And you must realize how closely a Mediator will identify with her Fyunch(click). Lady Sally does not easily discuss sexual matters, nor does she enjoy doing so; her Mediator would feel the same emotions, and would know that the sterility of Mediators would upset Sally if she knew—as it did, when you learned of it. I say all this, but I do not know for certain: the matter was never thought important."

"All that suspicion," Sally said. "Just to spare me. I'm glad we cleared it up."

The Motie shrugged. "Despite our abilities, some misunderstandings between alien species are inevitable. Remember the toilet doors?"

"Yes." Sally could see what Ben Fowler was going to ask next. She spoke quickly to cut him off. "Now that we've got that straight, just what *do* your Masters do when they don't want children yet?" She felt a rush of blood and suspected her cheeks were growing red. Dr. Horvath eyed her curiously. Lecherous old man, she thought. Of course that isn't really being fair to him.

The Moties twittered for a moment. "Abstinence is common," Jock said. "We also have chemical and hormonal methods like yours. Do you wish the mechanics discussed here?"

"I'm more interested in the incentives," Senator Fowler said heavily. "What happens to Masters, or Browns, or whatever, if they start having children every six months?"

"Would you not define that as an action placing independence as more important than the interests of the race?" Jock asked.

"Yeah."

"So do we."

"And that's how you get wars started," Dr. Horvath concluded. "Senator, with all respect I think we've got the answers to our questions. The Moties control their populations. When individuals fail to go along, there's conflict. Sometimes that leads to wars. Just how is this different from humans?"

Benjamin Fowler laughed. "Doctor, you keep asking me to see your point of view, which is based on ethics. You never see mine, which isn't. I never claimed the human race was superior to Moties—in ethics, or intelligence, or anything else. I only claim it's my race, and I'm charged with protecting human interests." He turned back to the Moties. "Now that you've seen us in operation," Fowler continued, "what do you think of our Empire?"

Jock chuckled. "Senator, what do you expect me to say? You have us in your power—the three of us, and all of our people. Your warships control the Crazy Eddie point leading to our system. You could presumably exterminate us, and I've heard speeches demanding just that on your tri-v . . ."

"Not from anyone important," Anthony Horvath protested. "From nuts and cranks—"

"Certainly. But it was said. Thus any answer I give to the Senator's question will be what I believe he wants to hear. How could it be otherwise?"

"Well said," Ivan twittered. "Humans appear to respect admission of truth contrary to interests. In this case they inevitably would know anyway. But take care."

"Trust my skills, Master. Note that most have relaxed. Only the clergyman and the naval officer called Renner are not satisfied. The Emperor's Mediator is now undecided, and when we came into this room he had decided against us."

Charlie: "I am fearful. Would it not be best to tell them all, now that they know so much? How can we long keep our Cycles and our reproductive patterns secret? My Master wished to tell them all—"

"You will be silent and allow Jock to speak to the humans. Defer questions which upset you to her."

"I will, Master. I was instructed to obey you. But I am still of the opinion that my Master was correct."

"And if he has assessed the humans incorrectly?" Jock asked. "If they see us as a threat to their descendants? May they not destroy us all now, while they are able?"

"Silence. Speak to the humans."

"The Ambassador points out that as the Empire is both the most powerful association of humans and the group closest to our home, it is to our interest to be in alliance with your Empire, regardless of our opinions. We're surrounded."

"And that's a fact," Sally agreed. "Uncle Ben, how long does this go on? We have the draft agreements worked out by the economics technicians. Can't we get to the details of that?"

Fowler was not satisfied. It showed in the set of his heavy jowls, the tense shoulders. There was trouble in the

Empire without Moties. Add Motie technology in the hands of outies and rebels, and anything could happen.

"There is a draft agreement," Senator Fowler said carefully. "Before we put that to you, I've another proposition. Have you any interest in joining the Empire? As a Class One system member, for example? You'd have home rule, representation on Sparta, and access to most of the Imperial markets."

"We have considered it. It would take time to work out details—"

"No," Senator Fowler said positively. "That's the one thing it won't take. Your pardon, but we have no intention of letting your Engineers invent the Field and construct a war fleet. The first condition would be immediate admission of Imperial observers to every point in your system."

"Disarmament. Trust in your good intentions," Jock said. "Would you submit to such terms?"

"I haven't been asked to," Ben said. "You have."

"I said they would make this offer," Charlie twittered.

"We cannot accept," Ivan answered flatly. "We would be helpless. Assume the humans are sincere. Assume the Empire would not destroy us when our true nature became obvious. Can we believe that many generations from now the Empire will be ruled by benevolence? It is a risk we cannot take. The Race must be assured of survival."

"There is no assurance!"

"We must get out of our system and into the universe. When we are firmly established in many systems the humans will not dare attack any of them," Jock said. Her gestures showed impatience.

"You are convinced that we cannot accept this offer?" Charlie asked.

Jock: "We have discussed this before. The humans will be thorough. They will want to disarm the Warriors. Before that happens, the Masters will fight. There will be war precisely when the humans expect it. They are not fools, and their naval officers are afraid of us. Overwhelming force would back up the observers. If we pretend to accept, they will feel justified in destroying us: remember the fate of human planets in rebellion. This offer cannot even buy time."

"Then give the answer we agreed upon," commanded Ivan.

"The Ambassador regrets that any such agreement would exceed his authority. We can speak for all the Moties, but only within certain limits; placing our entire race at your mercy is beyond them."

"You can't blame them for that," Dr. Horvath said. "Be reasonable, Senator."

"I'm trying to be reasonable and I didn't blame them. I made them an offer, that's all." He turned back to the aliens. "Planets have been brought into the Empire against their will. They don't get anything like the privileges I offered you—"

Jock shrugged. "I cannot say what the Masters would do if you attempted conquest of our system. I suspect they would fight."

"You'd lose," Senator Fowler said flatly.

"We'd hate that."

"And in losing you might suck up so much of our strength that *we'd* lose most of this sector. Set the unification drive back a century, maybe. Conquest is expensive." Senator Fowler didn't add that sterilization wasn't; but the unspoken thought hung heavily in the brightly lit room.

"Can we make a counteroffer?" Jock said. "Allow us to set up production centers on uninhabitable worlds. We will terraform them: for every world you give us, we will terraform another for you. As to the economic dislocations, you can form companies to hold a monopoly on trade with us. Part of the stock could be sold publicly. The balance could be held to be given as compensation to the companies and workers displaced by our competition. I think you would find that this would minimize the disadvantages of our new technology, while giving you all the benefits."

"Brilliant," Horvath exclaimed. "Just what my staff is working on right now. You would agree to this? Trade with no one but authorized companies and the Imperial Government?"

"Certainly. We would also pay the Empire for naval protection of our colony worlds—we have no desire to keep fleets in your parts of space. You could inspect the colony shipyards to be certain."

"And the home world?" Fowler asked.

"Contact between Mote Prime and the Empire would be minimal, I presume. Your representatives would be welcome, but we would not wish to see your warships near our homes—I may as well tell you, we were very much concerned over that battleship in orbit about our planet. It was obvious that it carried weapons that could make Mote Prime nearly uninhabitable. We submitted, even invited you closer, precisely to show you that we have little to hide. We are no threat to your Empire, my lords. You are a threat to us, as you well know. Yet I think we can agree to our mutual advantage—and our mutual safety—without unduly straining either race's trust in the benevolence of the other."

"And you'll terraform one planet for us for every one you take over?" Horvath asked. He thought of the advantages: incalculable. Few stellar systems had more than one inhabitable world. Interstellar trade was hideously expensive compared with interplanetary travel, but terraforming operations were even more costly.

"Is that not enough?" Jock asked. "Surely you appreciate our position. We have now only one planet, some asteroids, and a gas giant which is beyond even our ability to make habitable. It is worth an enormous investment in resources to double what we have available. I say this because it is obvious, although I am told that your trading procedure does not usually include admission of disadvantages. On the other hand—" The Motie looked curiously at her three hands. The humans did likewise and there was laughter. Which was the *other* hand for a Motie? "Your uninhabitable planets in suitable orbits must not be of much value to you, or you would have terraformed them yourselves. You get, then, something for nothing, where we get a great deal for great effort. Surely a fair bargain?"

"Damn good tor the Navy," Rod said. "Practically a new fleet paid for by the Moties . . ."

"Hold it," Senator Fowler said. "We're haggling over the price when we haven't decided what we are yet."

Jock shrugged. "I made you an offer, that's all." His imitation of the Senator's voice and mannerisms brought laughter. Ben Fowler frowned for a moment, then laughed with the others.

"Well," Fowler said. "Don't know that everything's settled, but I do know I'm gettin' hungry. Kelley, bring our guests some of that chocolate and ring down for dinner. We may as well be comfortable while we finish this discussion."

54 • *Out of the Bottle*

"It is close," Jock reported. "Almost the Senator agrees. Sally already has."

"And Blaine?" Ivan demanded.

"He will do as the Senator wishes, although he would rather agree with Sally. He likes us, and he sees an advantage for the Navy. It is unfortunate that his Fyunch(click) went insane; she would be of great use here."

"Can it work?" Charlie asked. "Jock, how can it work? Before the new colonies are established, the Imperials will see us as we are. They will visit our system, and they will know. And then?"

"They will never know," Jock said. "Their own Navy will prevent it. There will be visits by unarmed ships, but they will risk no more naval vessels. Can we not deceive a few ships full of humans? They can never speak our language. We will have time to prepare for them. We will never let them see Warriors. How will they learn? Meanwhile the colonies will be established. The humans can have no conception of how quickly we can establish colonies, or how quickly they will be able to build ships. We will be in a much better bargaining position then, in contact with many humans—and we can offer them anything they want. We will have allies, and we will be spread far enough that not even the Empire could exterminate us. If they cannot do it with certainty they will not attempt it. That is how these humans think."

The Marine brought them the drink humans called chocolate, and they drank with pleasure. Humans were omnivores like Moties, but the flavors humans preferred were generally tasteless. Chocolate, though: that was excellent, and with extra hydrocarbons to simulate the waters of the home world, it was incomparable.

"What alternatives have we?" Jock demanded. "What would they do if we told them everything? Would they not dispatch their fleet to destroy us all and save their descendants from our threat?"

"I approve this agreement," Ivan said. "Your Master will also."

"Perhaps," Charlie said. She thought, falling into a pose that excluded the world around her. She was the Master— "I can agree," she said. "It is better than I had hoped. But the danger!"

"There has been danger since the humans first came to the Mote system," Jock said. "It is less now than before."

Ivan observed carefully. The Mediators were excited. The strain had been great, and despite their outward control they were close to the edge. It was not part of his nature to wish for what could not be, but he hoped that the efforts to breed a more stable Mediator would succeed; it was difficult to work with creatures who might suddenly see an unreal universe and make judgments based on it. The pattern was always the same. First they wished for the impossible. Then they worked toward it, still knowing it to be impossible. Finally they acted as if the impossible could be achieved, and let that unreality influence every act. It was more common with Mediators than any other class, but it happened to Masters also.

These Mediators were close to the edge, but they would last. The Race would be preserved. It must be.

* * *

"A thousand crowns for your thoughts," Sally said. Her eyes twinkled with happiness—and relief.

Rod turned from the window to grin at her. The room was large, and the others were gathered near the bar, except for Hardy, who sat near the Moties listening to their chatter as if he might understand a word or two. Rod and Sally were effectively alone. "You're very generous," he said.

"I can afford it. I'll pay you just after the wedding . . ."

"With the income from Crucis Court. I haven't got it yet, don't be so anxious to kill Dad off. We may be living on his generosity for years."

"What were you thinking about? You look so serious."

"How I'm going to vote on this if the Senator won't agree."

She nodded soberly. "I thought so—"

"I could lose you over this, couldn't I?"

"I don't know, Rod. I guess it would depend on *why* you rejected their offer. And what you agreed to in its place. But you aren't going to reject it, are you? What's wrong with what they propose?"

Rod stared at the drink in his hand. It was some kind of nonalcoholic gup Kelley had brought; the meeting was too important for Scotch. "Nothing wrong, maybe. It's the maybe, Sally. Look out there." He pointed to New Scotland's streets.

There were few people at this hour. Theater and dinner goers. Sightseers come to view the Palace after dark. Sailors with their girls. Covenanter guardsmen in kilts and bearskins standing rigidly at the sentry box near the driveway entrance. "If we're wrong, their kids are dead."

"If we're wrong, the Navy takes it on the chin," Sally said slowly. "Rod, what if the Moties come out, and in twenty years they've settled a dozen planets. Built ships. Threaten the Empire? The Navy can still handle them . . . you won't have to, but it could be done."

"Sure about that? I'm not. I'm not sure we could defeat them now. Exterminate them, yeah, but whip them? And twenty years from now? What would the butcher's bill be?

New Scotland for sure. It's in their way. What other worlds would go?"

"What have we got for choices?" she asked. "I— Rod, I worry about our kids too. But what can we do? You can't make war on the Moties because they *might* be a threat someday!"

"No, of course not. Here's dinner. And I'm sorry I spoiled your happy mood."

They were all laughing before the dinner ended. The Moties put on a show: imitations of New Scotland's most famous tri-v personalities. In minutes they had everyone at the table gasping helplessly.

"How do you do it?" David Hardy asked between fits of laughter.

"We have been studying your humor," Charlie answered. "We subtly exaggerate certain characteristics. The cumulative effect should be amusing if our theory was correct; apparently it was."

Horvath said, "You can make a fortune as entertainers no matter what else you have to trade."

"That, at least, will have little effect on your economy. We will require your aid in scheduling release of our technology, however."

Horvath nodded gravely. "I'm glad you appreciate the problem. If we just dump everything you have on the market, it would make chaos out of the market—"

"Believe me, Doctor, we have no desire to make problems for you. If you see us as an opportunity, think of how we see you! To be free of the Mote system after all these centuries! Out of the bottle! Our gratitude is unbounded."

"Just how old are you?" David Hardy asked.

The Motie shrugged. "We have fragments of records that indicate times a hundred thousand years ago, Dr. Hardy. The asteroids were already in place then. Others may be older, but we can't read them. Our real history starts perhaps ten thousand years ago."

"And you've had collapses of civilization since then?" Hardy asked.

"Certainly. Entrapped in that system? How could it be otherwise?"

"Do you have records of the asteroid war?" Renner asked.

Jock frowned. Her face wasn't suited for it, but the gesture conveyed distaste. "Legends only. We have— They are much like your songs, or epic poems. Linguistic devices to make memorization easier. I do not think they are translatable, but—" The Motie paused for a moment. It was as if she were frozen into the position she'd happened to be in when she decided to think. Then:

> "It is cold and the food is gone,
>   the demons rove the land.
> Our sisters die and the waters boil,
>   for the demons make the skies fall."

The alien paused grimly. "I'm afraid that's not very good, but it's all I can do."

"It's good enough," Hardy said. "We have such poetry too. Stories of lost civilizations, disasters in our prehistory. We can trace most of them to a volcanic explosion about forty-five hundred years ago. As a matter of fact, that seems to be when men got the idea that God might intervene in their affairs. Directly, as opposed to creating cycles and seasons and such."

"An interesting theory—but doesn't it upset your religious beliefs?"

"No, why should it? Can't God as easily arrange a natural event to produce a desirable effect as He could upset the laws of nature? In fact, which is the more miraculous, a tidal wave just when it is needed, or a supernatural once-only event? But I don't think you have time to discuss theology with me. Senator Fowler seems to have finished his dinner. So if you'll excuse me, I'll be away a few minutes, and I think we'll get started again—"

Ben Fowler took Rod and Sally to a small office behind the conference room. "Well?" he demanded.

"I'm on record," Sally said.

"Yeah. Rod?"

"We've got to do *something*, Senator. The pressure's getting out of hand."

"Yeah," Ben said. "Damn it, I need a drink. Rod?"

"Thanks, I pass."

"Well, if I can't think straight with a good belt of Scotch in me the Empire's already collapsed." He fumbled through the desk until he found a bottle, sneered at the brand, and poured a stiff drink into a used coffee cup. "One thing puzzles me. Why isn't the ITA making more trouble? I expected them to give us the most pressure, and they're quiet. Thank God for what favors we have." He tossed off half the cup and sighed.

"What harm does it do to agree now?" Sally asked. "We can change our minds if we find out anything new—"

"Like hell, kitten," Ben said. "Once something specific is in the works, the sharp boys'll think how to make a crown out of it, and after they've got money invested—I thought you learned more about elementary politics than that. What do they teach in the university nowadays? Rod, I'm still waiting for something out of you."

Rod fingered his bent nose. "Ben, we can't stall much longer. The Moties must know that—they may even cut their offer once they see just how much pressure we're under. I say let's do it."

"You do, huh. You'll make your wife happy anyway."

"He's not doing it for me!" Sally insisted. "You stop teasing him."

"Yeah." The Senator scratched his bald spot for a moment. Then he drained his cup and set it down. "Got to check one or two things. Probably be okay. If they are— I guess the Moties have a deal. Let's go in."

Jock gestured rapture and excitement. "They are ready to agree! We are saved!"

Ivan eyed the Mediator coldly. "You will restrain yourself. There is much to do yet."

"I know. But we are saved. Charlie, is it not so?"

Charlie studied the humans. The faces, the postures— "Yes. But the Senator remains unconvinced, and Blaine is afraid, and—Jock, study Renner."

"You are so cold! Can you not rejoice with me? We are saved!"

"Study Renner."

"Yes . . . I know that look. He wears it playing poker,

when his down card is an unexpected one. It does not help us. But he has no power, Charlie! A wanderer with no sense of reponsibility!"

"Perhaps. We juggle priceless eggs in variable gravity. I am afraid. I will taste fear until I die."

55 • *Renner's Hole Card*

Senator Fowler sat heavily and looked around the table. The look was enough to still the chatter and get everyone's attention. "I guess we know what we are all after," he said. "Now comes haggling over the price. Let's get the principles set, uh? First and foremost. You agree not to arm your colonies and to let us inspect 'em to be sure they aren't armed?"

"Yes," Jock said positively. She twittered to the Master. "The Ambassador agrees. Provided that the Empire will, for a price, protect our colonies from your enemies."

"We'll certainly do that. Next. You agree to restrict trade to companies chartered by the Imperium?"

"Yes."

"Well, that's the main points," Fowler announced. "We're ready for the small stuff. Who's first?"

"Can I ask what kind of colony they'll set up?" said Renner.

"Eh? Sure."

"Thank you. Will you be bringing representatives of all your classes?"

"Yes . . ." Jock hesitated. "All that are relevant to the conditions, Mr. Renner. We'd hardly take Farmers to a nonterraformed rock until the Engineers had built a dome."

"Yeah. Well, I was wondering, because of this." He fumbled with his pocket computer and the screens lit. They showed an oddly distorted New Cal, a brilliant flash, then darkness. "Woops. Wrong place. That was when the probe fired on Captain Blaine's ship."

"Ah?" Jock said. He twittered to the others. They answered. "We had wondered what was the fate of the probe. Frankly, we believed you had destroyed it, and thus we did not wish to ask—"

"You're close," Renner said. More images flashed on the screen. The light sail was rippling. "This is just before they shot at us."

"But the probe would not have fired on you," Jock protested.

"It did. Thought we were a meteor, I guess," Rod answered. "Anyway—"

Black shapes flowed across the screen. The sail rippled, flashed, and they were gone. Renner backed the tape until the silhouettes were stark against the light, then stopped the film.

"I must warn you," Jock said. "We know little about the probe. It is not our specialty, and we had no chance to study the records before we left Mote Prime."

Senator Fowler frowned. "Just what are you getting at, Mr. Renner?"

"Well, sir, I wondered about the images." Renner took a light pointer from a recess in the table. "These are various Motie classes, aren't they?"

Jock seemed hesitant. "They appear to be."

"Sure they are. That's a Brown, right? And a Doctor."

"Right." The light pointer moved. "Runner," Jock said. "And a Master . . ."

"There's a Watchmaker." Rod almost spat it. He couldn't hide his distaste. "The next one looks like a Farmer. Hard to tell from a Brown but—" His voice went suddenly uneasy. "Renner, I don't recognize that next one."

There was silence. The pointer hovered over a misshapen shadow, longer and leaner than a Brown, with what seemed to be thorns at the knees and heels and elbows.

"We saw them once before," Renner said. His voice was almost automatic now. Like a man walking through a graveyard on a bet. Or the point man advancing over the hill into enemy territory. Emotionless, determined, rigidly under control. It wasn't like Renner at all.

The screen divided, and another image appeared: the time-machine sculpture from the museum in Castle City. What looked like a junk-art sculpture of electronic parts was surrounded by things bearing weapons.

At his first sight of Ivan, Rod had felt an embarrassingly strong urge to stroke the Ambassador's silky fur. His impulse now was equally strong: he wanted to be in karate stance. The sculpted things showed in far too much detail. They grew daggers at every point, they looked hard as steel and stood like coiled springs, and any one of them would have left a Marine combat instructor looking as if he'd been dropped into a mowing machine. And what was that under the big left arm, like a broad-bladed knife half-concealed?

"Ah," said Jock, "a demon. I suppose they must have been dolls representing our species. Like the statuettes, to make it easier for the Mediator to talk about us."

"All of those?" Rod's voice was pure wonder. "A ship-load of full-sized mockups?"

"We don't know they were full-sized, do we?" asked Jock.

"Fine. Assume they were mockups," Renner said. He went on relentlessly. "They were still models of living Motie classes. Except this one. Why would that one be in the group? Why bring a demon with the rest?"

There was no answer.

"Thank you, Kevin," Rod said slowly. He didn't dare look at Sally. "Jock, is this or is it not a Motie class?"

"There's more, Captain," Renner said. "Look real close at the Farmer. Now that we know what to look for."

The image wasn't very clear, little more than a fuzzy-edged silhouette; but the bulge was unmistakable on the full profile view.

"She's pregnant," Sally exclaimed. "Why didn't I think of that! A pregnant statuette? But— Jock, what does this mean?"

"Yeah," Rod asked coldly.

But it was impossible to get Jock's attention.

"Stop! Say no more!" Ivan commanded.

"What would I say?" Jock wailed. "The idiots took a Warrior! We are finished, finished, when moments ago we had the universe in our hand!' The Motie's powerful left hand closed crushingly on air.

"Silence. Control yourself. Now. Charlie, tell me what you know of the probe. How was it built?"

Charlie gestured contempt interrupted by respect. "It should be obvious. The probe builders knew an alien species inhabited this star. They knew nothing more. Thus they must have assumed the species resembled ours, if not in appearance, then in the essentials."

"Cycles. They must have assumed Cycles," Ivan mused. "We had yet to know that all races are not condemned to the Cycles."

"Precisely," said Charlie. "The hypothetical species had survived. It was intelligent. They would have no more control of their breeding than we, since such control is not a survival characteristic. Thus the probe was launched in the belief that this star's people would be in collapse when the probe arrived."

"So." Ivan thought for a moment. "The Crazy Eddies put pregnant females of every class aboard. Idiots!"

"Give them credit. They did their best," said Charlie. "The probe must have been rigged to dump the passengers into the sun the instant it was hailed by a space-traveling civilization. If the hypothetical aliens were that advanced, they would find, not an attempt to take over their planet with the light sail as a weapon, but a Mediator sent on a peaceful errand." Charlie paused for thought. "An accidentally dead Mediator. The probe would have been set to kill her, so the aliens would learn as little as possible. You are a Master: is this not what you would do?"

"Am I also Crazy Eddie, to launch the probe at all? The strategy did not work. Now we must tell these humans something."

"I say tell them all," Charlie said. "What else can we do? We are caught in our own lies."

"Wait," Ivan commanded. Only seconds had passed, but Jock was normal again. The humans were staring *curiously.* "*We must say something momentous. Hardy knows we are excited. True?*"

"*Yes,*" *Charlie gestured.*

"*What discovery could so have excited us?*"

"*Trust me,*" *Jock said quickly.* "*We may yet be saved.* Demon worshipers! We told you we have no racial enemies, and this is true; but there is a religious faction, secret, which makes gods of the time demons. They are vicious, and very dangerous. They must have seized the probe before it left the asteroid belt. Secretly, perhaps—"

"Then the passengers and crew were alive?" Rod asked.

Charlie shrugged. "I believe so. They must have committed suicide. Who knows why? Possibly they thought we had developed a faster-than-light drive and were waiting for them. What did you do when you approached them?"

"Sent messages in most human languages," Rod answered. "You're sure they were alive?"

"How would we know?" Jock asked. "Do not be concerned about *them.*" The voice was filled with contempt. "They were not proper representatives of our race. Their rituals include sacrifice of sentient classes."

"Just how many of these demon worshipers are there?" Hardy asked. "I was never told of them."

"We are not proud of their existence," Jock answered. "Did you tell us of outies? Of the excesses of Sauron System? Are you pleased that we know humans are capable of such things?"

There were embarrassed murmurs.

"Damn," Rod said quietly. "They were alive after all— after all that distance." The thought was bitter.

"You are distressed," Jock said. "We are pleased that you did not speak to them before you met us. Your expedition would have been of quite a different character if you had—"

She stopped, watching curiously. Dr. Sigmund Horowitz had risen from his seat and was bent against the screen, examining the time-machine picture. He fingered the screen controls to enlarge one of the demon statuettes. The silhouette from the probe faded, leaving half the screen blank, then another picture came on and grew and grew—

a sharp-fanged, rat-faced creature squatting on a pile of rubble.

"Aha!" Horowitz shouted in triumph. "I wondered what the ancestry of the rats could be! Degenerate forms of this . . ." He turned to the Moties. There was nothing in his manner but curiosity, as if he'd paid no attention to the conversation before. "What do you use this caste for?" he asked. "Soldiers, aren't they? Have to be. What else would they be good for?"

"No. They are only myths."

"Balderdash. Demons with weapons? Father Hardy, can you imagine devils carrying blast rifles?" Horowitz fingered the controls again and the probe silhouette appeared. "Abraham's Beard! That's no statue. Come now, this is a Motie subspecies. Why do you hide it? Fascinating— I've never seen anything so well adapted for . . ." Horowitz' voice trailed off.

"A Warrior caste," Ben Fowler said slowly. "I don't wonder that you hid it from us. Dr. Horowitz, would you suppose that—creature—is as prolific as we know the other Moties can be?"

"Why not?"

"But I tell you the demons are legendary," Jock insisted. "The poem. Dr. Hardy, you recall the poem? These are the creatures who made the skies fall . . ."

"I believe that," Hardy said. "I'm not sure I believe they're extinct. You keep their feral descendants in zoos. Anthony, I put a hypothetical question to you: If the Moties have a very prolific caste devoted to warfare; their Masters have pride in independence similar to terran lions; they have had several disastrous wars; and they are hopelessly trapped in a single planetary system: what is the most reasonable projection of their history?"

Horvath shuddered. So did the others. "Like—*MacArthur*," Horvath answered sadly. "Cooperation among Masters must break down when population pressures become severe enough . . . *if* that's really a current caste, David."

"But I tell you again, they are legendary demons," Jock protested.

"I'm afraid we don't believe everything you tell us," Hardy said. There was deep sadness in his voice. "Not that I ever accepted everything you said. Priests hear a lot of lies. But I always did wonder what you were hiding. It would have been better if you'd shown us some kind of military or police forces. But you couldn't, could you? They were—" he gestured at the screen. "Those."

"Rod," Senator Fowler said. "You look pretty grim."

"Yes, sir. I was thinking what it would be like to fight a race that's bred Warriors for ten thousand years. Those things must be adapted to space warfare too. Give the Moties Field technology, and—Ben, I don't think we could beat them! It'd be like trying to fight millions of Sauron cyborgs! Hell, the couple of thousand they had were enough to keep the war going for years!"

Sally listened helplessly. "But what if Jock's telling the truth? Couldn't she be right? There was a Warrior caste, it's extinct now, and outlaw Moties—want to bring them back."

"Easy enough to find out," Fowler muttered. "And best done fast, before the Motie Browns build a fleet that could stop us."

"If they haven't already," Rod muttered. "They work so fast. They rebuilt the embassy ship while it was on its way to *MacArthur*. A complete overhaul, with two Browns and some Watchmakers. I think Commander Cargill's threat estimate may be a bit conservative, Senator."

"Even if it isn't," said Renner, "we still have to picture every ship captained and crewed by Admiral Kutuzov."

"Right. Okay, Jock. You see our situation," said the Senator.

"Not really." The Motie was crouched forward and looked very alien.

"I'll spell it out. We don't have the resources to fight a million critters evolved for warfare. Maybe we'd win, maybe not. If you keep those things around, it's because you need 'em; your system's too crowded to keep useless mouths. If you need 'em, you fight wars."

"I see," Jock said carefully.

"No, you don't," the Senator growled. "You know something about Sauron System, but not enough. Jock, if you Moties breed Warrior castes, our people are goin' to identify you with Saurons, and I don't think you appreciate just how much the Empire hated them and their superman ideas."

"What will you do?" Jock asked.

"Take a look at your system. A *real* look."

"And if you find Warriors?"

"We don't need to look, do we?" Senator Fowler demanded. "You know we'll find 'em." He sighed heavily. His pause for thought was very short—no more than a second. Then he stood and went to the view screen, walking slowly, like a juggernaut—

"What will we do? Can we not stop him?" Jock wailed.

Ivan remained calm. "It would do no good, and you could not do it. That Marine is no Warrior, but he is armed and his hand is on his weapon. He fears us."

"But—"

"Listen."

"Conference call," Fowler told the Palace operator. "I want Prince Merrill and War Minister Armstrong. Personally, and I don't give a damn where they are. I want 'em now."

"Yes, Senator." The girl was young, and frightened by the Senator's manner. She fumbled with her equipment, and the room was still for a time.

Minister Armstrong was in his office. His tunic was missing and his shirt unbuttoned. Papers littered his desk. He looked up in irritation, saw who was calling, and muttered, "Aye?"

"A moment," Fowler said brusquely. "I'm getting the Viceroy on a conference circuit." There was another long wait.

His Highness came on; the screen showed his face only. He seemed breathless. "Yes, Senator?"

"Your Highness, you have seen my Commission from the Emperor?"

"Yes."

"You accept my authority in all matters having to do with the aliens?"

"Of course."

"As representative of His Imperial Majesty I order you to assemble the sector battle fleet as quickly as possible. You will place Admiral Kutuzov in command to await my orders."

There was more silence on the screens. An irritating babble filled the conference room. Ben gestured imperiously for silence and it cut off.

"As a matter of form, Senator," Merrill said carefully, "I will require confirmation of that order from another member of the Commission."

"Yeah. Rod."

And here it is, Rod thought. He didn't dare look at Sally. A race of Warriors? Independent Masters? We can't let them get out into human space. We wouldn't last a century.

The Moties are frozen stiff. They know what we'll find. Unrestricted breeding and demons. Every nightmare every kid ever had . . . but I *like* Moties. No. I like the Mediators. I've never known any of the others. And the Mediators don't control the Mote civilization. Carefully he looked down at Sally. She was as unmoving as the Moties. Rod drew in a deep breath.

"Your Highness, I approve."

56 • Last Hope

Their quarters seemed small now, despite the high ceilings. Nothing had changed. There were all the delicacies the Empire could find to put in their kitchen. A single push on a button would summon a dozen, a hundred servants. The Marines in the corridor outside were polite and respectful.

And they were trapped. Somewhere at the edges of

New Cal's system, at a base called Dagda, the Empire's warships were summoned; and when they had arrived . . .

"They will not kill them all," Charlie gibbered.

"But they will." Jock's voice was a wail, quavering.

"The Warriors will fight. The Navy will lose ships. And Kutuzov will be in command. Will he risk his ships to spare any of us? Or will he reduce our planet to iridescent slag?"

"The asteroids as well?" Charlie whimpered. "Yes. There has never been a Cycle in which both were gone. Master, we must do something! We cannot allow this! If we had been truthful with them—"

"Their fleet would even now be on its way instead of merely ordered to assemble," Jock said contemptuously. "It was so close! I had them!" Three fingers the size of knackwurst closed, empty. "They were ready to agree, and then—and then—" She whimpered on the edge of madness but recoiled from the brink. "There must be something we can do."

"Tell them all," Charlie said. "What harm can it do? Now they see us as evil. At least we can explain why we lied to them."

"Think of what we can offer them," Ivan ordered. "Consider their interests and think of ways to protect them without destroying the Race."

"Help them?" Jock asked.

"Of course. Help them to be safe from us."

"It is the Warriors they fear. Would the Masters agree to kill all the Warriors? We could then join the Empire."

"Crazy Eddie!" Charlie screamed. "And how many Masters would keep Warrior breeding stock?"

"It has been attempted before," Ivan said. "Think of something else."

"Can we make them believe we cannot build the Fields?" Charlie asked.

"To what end? They will know soon enough. No. They will not enter our system again until their fleet is ready, and then they will take it all. A dozen battleships. If that fleet enters our system, the Warriors will fight and the

Race will die. They must not send it. THEY MUST NOT!"

Jock used a half-forgotten tongue, not known to Masters. "He is nearly insane."

"As are we." Charlie wriggled in bitter, silent Motie laughter. "Pity the Master. His fears are our own, plus the fear that we will go mad. Without us he would be mute, watching the fleet assemble, unable to say a word in protest."

"Think!" Ivan ordered. "They are sending Kutuzov. He destroyed a human planet—what mercy will he show to aliens? Think! Think or the Race is doomed!"

As Sally entered Rod's office she heard him speaking into the phone. He hadn't seen her. For a moment she hesitated, then stood motionless, listening.

"I agree, Lavrenti. The asteroid civilization must be covered in the first sweep. It may even be their prime naval base."

"I do not like to divide fleet," the heavily accented voice said from the phone. "You give me two missions, Lord Blaine. They are not compatible. To fall upon Moties and cripple them without warning—yes, that is possible. To invite their attack before we react—that will cost lives and ships we cannot spare."

"You'll plan it that way nonetheless."

"Yes, my lord. My officers will bring you preliminary plans in the morning. They will also bring you loss estimates. What officer do you suggest I place in command of decoy vessel, my lord? Classmate of yours? Stranger? I await your suggestions."

"Damn it!"

"Please excuse my impertinence, my lord. Your commands will be obeyed."

The screen went dark. Rod sat staring at its blank face until Sally came in and sat across from him. The Warrior statuettes were vivid behind his eyes.

"You heard?"

"Some of it—is it really that bad?"

Rod shrugged. "Depends on what we're up against. It's

one thing to go in shooting, blast our way in and saturate the planet and asteroids with hellburners. But to send the fleet in, give the Moties warning of what we're up to, and wait for them to attack us? The first hostile move could be from the laser cannon that launched the probe!"

She looked at him miserably. "Why do we have to do it at all? Why can't we just let them alone?"

"So that one of these days they can come out here and chop up our grandkids?"

"Why does it have to be us?"

"It was, though. Tell me, Sally, is there any doubt about it? About what the Moties really are?"

"They're not monsters!"

"No. Just our enemies."

She shook her head sadly. "So what will happen?"

"The fleet goes in. We demand they surrender to the Empire. Maybe they accept, maybe not. If they do, suicide crews go in to supervise the disarmament. If they fight, the fleet attacks."

"Who— Who's going to land on Mote Prime? Who'll be in charge of the— *No!* Rod, I can't let you *do* that!"

"Who else could it be? Me, Cargill, Sandy Sinclair— *MacArthur*'s old crew will land. Maybe they'll really surrender. Somebody's got to give them that chance."

"Rod, I—"

"Can we have the wedding soon? There's no heir to either of our families."

"No use," said Charlie. "Taste the irony. For millions of years we have been in a bottle. Its shape has shaped our species to our detriment. Now we have found the opening, and now the Navy pours through to burn our worlds."

Jock sneered, "How vivid and poetic are your images!"

"How fortunate we are to enjoy your constructive advice! You—" Charlie stopped suddenly. Jock's walk had turned—strange. She paced with her hands twisted uncomfortably behind her, head bent forward, feet close together to render her stance as precarious as a human's.

Charlie recognized Kutuzov. *She made a peremptory shushing motion to stop Ivan from commenting.*

"I need a human word," said Jock. "We never heard it, but they must have it. Summon a servant," *she snapped in Kutuzov's voice, and Charlie leaped to obey.*

Senator Fowler sat at a small desk in the office next to the Commission conference room. A large bottle of New Aberdeen Highland Cream stood on the otherwise bare oak desk. The door opened and Dr. Horvath came in. He stood expectantly.

"Drink?" Fowler asked.

"No, thank you."

"Want to get down to it, eh. Right. Your application for membership on this Commission is denied."

Horvath stood rigid. "I see."

"I doubt it. Sit down." Fowler took a glass from the desk drawer and poured. "Here, hold this anyway. Pretend you're drinking with me. Tony, I'm doing you a favor."

"I do not see it that way."

"Don't, eh? Look. The Commission's going to exterminate the Moties. Just what's that going to do for you? You *want* to be part of that decision?"

"Exterminate? But I thought the orders were to bring them into the Empire."

"Sure. Can't do anything else. Political pressure's too big to just go in and wipe 'em out. So I got to let the Moties draw some blood. Including the father of the only heir I'll ever have." Fowler's lips were tightly drawn. "They'll fight, Doc. I just hope they don't make a phony surrender offer first, so Rod'll have a chance. You really want to be part of that?"

"I see . . . I guess I really do see. Thank you."

"You're welcome." Fowler reached into his tunic and took out a small box. He opened it for a second to look inside, closed it, and scaled it across the desk to Horvath. "There. That's yours."

Dr. Horvath opened it and saw a ring with a large blank green stone.

"You can carve a baron's crest on that next Birthday," Fowler said. "Do not bind the mouths and all that. Satisfied?"

"Yes. Very. Thank you, Senator."

"No thanks needed. You're a good man, Tony. OK, let's get in there and see what the Moties want."

The conference room was nearly filled. The Commissioners, staff, Horvath's scientists, Hardy, Renner—and Admiral Kutuzov.

Senator Fowler took his seat. "Lords Commissioners representing His Imperial Majesty are now convened. Write your names and organizations." He paused briefly as they scrawled on their computers. "The Moties have requested this meeting. They didn't say why. Anybody got anything to bring up before they get here? No? OK, Kelley, bring 'em in."

The Moties were silent as they took their places at the end of the table. They looked very alien; the human mimicry was gone. The permanent smiles were still painted on, and the fur was combed sleek and shiny.

"Your ball," the Senator said. "I may as well tell you we're unlikely to believe anything you say."

"There will be no more lies," Charlie said. Even the voice was different; the Mediator sounded alien, not like a blend of all the voices the Moties had ever heard, but with a distinct—

Rod couldn't trace it. Not an accent. It was almost perfection, the ideal of Anglic.

"The time for lies is finished. My Master thought so from the beginning, but Jock's Master was given jurisdiction over negotiations with humans. As you were given such jurisdiction for your Emperor."

"Faction fight, eh?" Fowler said. "Pity we didn't meet your boss. A bit late now, isn't it?"

"Perhaps. But I will now represent him. You may call him King Peter if you like; the midshipmen did."

"What?" Rod stood at his seat, and the chair fell backward to crash to the floor. "When?"

"Just before they were killed by Warriors," Charlie said. "Attacking me will gain you no information, my lord; and it was not my Master's Warriors who killed them. Those who did were ordered to take them alive, but the midshipmen would not surrender."

Rod carefully retrieved his chair and sat. "No. Horst wouldn't," he muttered.

"Nor would Whitbread. Nor Potter. You may be as proud of them as you wish, Lord Blaine. Their last moments were in the finest traditions of the Imperial Service." There was no trace of irony in the alien voice.

"And just why did you murder those boys?" Sally demanded. "Rod, I'm sorry. I—I'm sorry, that's all."

"It wasn't your fault. The lady asked you a question, Charlie."

"They had discovered the truth about us. Their landing boats took them to a museum. Not one of the places of amusement that we allowed you to visit. This one has a more serious purpose." Charlie spoke on, in a low voice. She described the museum and the battle there, the flight across Mote Prime, the beginning of the war between Motie factions, and the landing in the street outside the Castle. She told of the final battle.

"My own Warriors lost," she finished. "Had they won, King Peter would have sent the midshipmen back to you. But once they were dead—it seemed better to attempt to deceive you."

"Lord God," Rod whispered. "So that's your secret. And we had all the clues, but—"

Someone was murmuring across the room. Chaplain Hardy. *"Requiem aeternam donum est, Domine, et lux perpetuae . . ."*

"Just how the hell do you think telling us this will help you?" Senator Fowler asked.

Charlie shrugged. "If you're going to exterminate us, you may as well know why. I'm trying to explain that the Masters will not surrender. King Peter might, but he doesn't control Mote Prime, much less the asteroid civilization. Someone will fight."

"As I predicted, my lords," Kutuzov said heavily. "And men and ships sent to accept surrender will be doomed.

Perhaps Fleet as well. If we enter Mote System, it must be in full attack."

"Oh, boy," Senator Fowler muttered. "Yeah. I see your plan. You think we can't order an unprovoked attack, and maybe we *won't* send in a suicide mission first. Well, you read us wrong, Charlie. It'll mean my head, maybe, but all you've convinced me of is to give the Admiral his way. Sorry, Father, but that's the way I see it."

The Senator's voice crackled across the room. "Admiral Kutuzov. You will hold your fleet in readiness, and it will accept no communications from any source without my prior approval. And I mean *any* source. Understood?"

"Aye aye, Senator." Kutuzov raised a communicator to his lips. "Mikhailov. Da." He spoke fluid syllables. "It is done, Senator."

"I have not finished," Charlie said. "You have another alternative."

"And what's that?" Fowler demanded.

"Blockade."

57 • *All the Skills of Treason*

They stood for a long time on the balcony outside Rod's suite. Faint sounds of a city after dark floated up to them. The Hooded Man rose high in the sky, his baleful red eye watching them with indifference: two human lovers, who would send squadrons of ships into the Eye itself and keep them there, until they too passed away . . .

"It doesn't look very big," Sally murmured. She moved her head against his shoulder and felt his arms tighten around her. "Just a fleck of yellow in Murcheson's Eye. Rod, will it work?"

"The blockade? Sure. We worked out the plan at Fleet Battle Ops. Jack Cargill set it up: a squadron inside the Eye itself to take advantage of the Jump shock. The Moties don't know about that, and their ships won't be under command for minutes at best. If they try to send them through on automatic it just makes it worse."

She shivered against him. "That wasn't really what I meant. The whole plan—will it work?"

"What choices have we?"

"None. And I'm glad you agree. I couldn't live with you if— I couldn't, that's all."

"Yeah." And that makes me grateful to the Moties for thinking up this scheme, because we can't let the Moties get out. A galactic plague—and there are only two remedies for that kind of plague. Quarantine and extermination. At least we've got a choice.

"They're—" She stopped and looked up at him. "I'm afraid to talk to you about it. Rod, I couldn't live with *myself* if we had to—if the blockade won't work."

He didn't say anything. There was a shouted laugh from somewhere beyond the Palace grounds. It sounded like children.

"They'll get past that squadron in the star," Sally said. Her voice was tightly controlled.

"Sure. And past the mines Sandy Sinclair's designing too. But where can they go, Sally? There's only one exit from the Eye system, they don't know where it is, and there'll be a battle group waiting for them when they find it. Meanwhile they've been inside a star. No place to dissipate energy. Probably damaged. There's nothing you can think of that we haven't considered. That blockade's *tight*. I couldn't approve it otherwise."

She relaxed again and leaned against his chest. His arms encircled her. They watched the Hooded Man and his imperfect eye.

"They won't come out," Rod said.

"And they're still trapped. After a million years . . . what will we be like in a million years?" she wondered. "Like them? There's something basic we don't understand about Moties. A fatalistic streak I can't even comprehend. After a few failures they may even just—give up."

He shrugged. "We'll keep the blockade anyway. Then, in about fifty years, we'll go in and see what things are like. If they've collapsed as thoroughly as Charlie predicts, we can take them into the Empire."

"And then what?"

"I don't know. We'll have to think of something."

"Yes." She drew away from him and turned excitedly. "I know! Rod, we have to really look at the problem. For the Moties. We can help them."

He looked at her wonderingly. "I think the best brains in the Empire are likely to be working on it."

"Yes, but for the Empire. Not for the Moties. We need—an Institute. Something controlled by people who *know* the Moties. Something outside of politics. And we can do it. We're rich enough . . ."

"Eh?"

"We can't spend half of what we have between us." She dashed past him and into his suite, then through it and across the corridor to her own. Rod followed to see her burrowing among the stacks of wedding gifts that littered the large rose-teak table in her entry hall. She grunted in satisfaction when she found her pocket computer.

Now should I be irritated? Rod thought. I think I'd better learn to be happy when she's like this. I'll have a long time to do it. "The Moties have been working on their problem awhile," he reminded her.

She looked up with faint irritation. "Pooh. They don't see things the way we do. Fatalism, remember? And they've had nobody to force them into adopting any solutions they do think up." She went back to scribbling notes. "We'll need Horowitz, of course. And he says there's a good man on Sparta, we'll have to send for him. Dr. Hardy. We'll want him."

He regarded her with awe and wonder. "When you get going, you move." And I better move with you if I'm going to have you around all my life. Wonder what it's like to live with a whirlwind? "You'll have Father Hardy if you want him. The Cardinal's assigned him to the Motie problem—and I think His Eminence has something bigger in store. Hardy could have been a bishop long ago but he doesn't have the normal share of miterosis. Now I don't think he's got much choice. First apostolic delegate to an alien race, or something."

"Then the Board will be you and me, Dr. Horvath, Father Hardy—and Ivan."

"Ivan?" But why not? And as long as we're doing this, we may as well do it right. We'll need a good executive director. Sally's no use as an administrator, and I won't have time. Horvath, maybe. "Sally, do you know just how much we're up against? The biology problem: how to turn a female to male without pregnancy or permanent sterility. But even if you find something, how do we get the Moties to *use* it?"

She wasn't really listening. "We'll find a way. We're pretty good at governing—"

"We can hardly govern a *human* empire!"

"But we do, don't we? Somehow." She pushed a stack of gaily wrapped packages aside to make more room. A large box almost fell and Rod had to catch it as Sally continued to scrawl notes into her computer's memory bank. "Now just what's the code for *Imperial Men and Women of Science?*" she asked. "There's a man on Meiji who's done some really good work in genetic engineering, and I can't remember his name . . ."

Rod sighed heavily. "I'll look him up for you. But there's one condition."

"What's that?" She looked up in curiosity.

"You finish this up by next week, because, Sally, if you take that pocket computer on our honeymoon, I'll throw the goddamn thing into the mass converter!"

She laughed, but Rod didn't feel reassured at all. Oh. Well. The computers weren't expensive. He could buy her a new one when they got back. In fact, maybe he ought to make a deal with Bury; he might need the things in shipload lots if they were ever going to have a family . . .

Horace Bury followed the Marine guards through the Palace, pointedly ignoring the other Marines who'd fallen in behind him. His face was calm, and only a close study of his eyes could show the despair that bored through him.

As Allah wills, he sighed, and wondered that he no

longer resented the thought. Perhaps there would be comfort in submission . . . there was little else to console him. The Marines had brought his servant and all his baggage down on the landing ship, and then separated him from Nabil at the Palace roof. Before they did, Nabil had wispered his message: Jonas Stone's confession was even now reaching the Palace.

Stone was still on New Chicago, but whatever he had told Naval Intelligence was important enough to be put on a message sloop. Nabil's informant didn't know what the rebel leader had said, but Bury did, as surely as if he could read the coded tapes. The message would be brief, and it would contain death by hanging for Horace Bury.

So this is the end of it all. The Empire acts swiftly against treason: a few days, a few weeks. No more. There is no chance to escape. The Marines are polite, but very alert. They have been warned, and there are many of them, too many. One might accept a bribe, but not when his comrades are watching.

As Allah wills. But it is a pity. Had I not been so concerned with the aliens, had I not done the Empire's work with the Traders, I would long since have escaped. Levant is large. But I would have had to leave New Scotland, and it is here the decisions will be made—what point to escape when the aliens may destroy us all?

The Marine Sergeant conducted him to an ornate conference room and held open the door until Bury went inside. Then, incredibly, the guards retired. There were only two men in the room with him.

"Good morning, my lord," Bury said to Rod Blaine. His words were even and smooth, but his mouth felt dry, and there was a sharp taste in the back of his throat as he bowed to the other man. "I have not been introduced to Senator Fowler, but of course his face is known to everyone in the Empire. Good morning, Senator."

Fowler nodded without rising from his seat at the big conference table. "Good morning, Excellency. Good of you to come. Have a seat, won't you?" He waved to a place opposite his.

"Thank you." Bury took the indicated chair. Then more

astonishment, as Blaine brought coffee. Bury sniffed carefully and recognized it as a blend he had sent to the Palace chef for Blaine's use.

In the Name of Allah. They are playing games with me, but to what end? He felt rage mingled with fear, but no hope at all. And a wild, bubbling laugh rose in his throat.

"Just so we know where we stand, Excellency," Fowler said. He waved, and Blaine activated a wall screen. The bulky features of Jonas Stone loomed out into the ornately paneled room. There was sweat on the brow and along the cheekbones, and Stone's voice alternately boomed and pleaded.

Bury listened impassively, his lip curled in contempt for Stone's weakness. There was no doubt at all: the Navy had more than enough evidence to send him to a traitor's death. Still the smile did not fade from Bury's lips. He would give them no satisfaction. He would not plead.

Eventually the tape ended. Fowler waved again and the rebel leader's image vanished. "Nobody's seen that but the three of us, Excellency," Fowler said carefully.

But no. What do they want? Is there hope after all?

"I don't know that it needs discussing," the Senator continued. "Me, I'd rather talk about Moties."

"Ah," said Bury. The tiny sound almost stuck in his throat. And do you wish to deal, or do you taunt me with the final horror? He swallowed coffee to moisten his tongue before he spoke. "I am sure that the Senator is aware of my views. I consider Moties the greatest threat humans have ever faced." He looked at the two men opposite him, but there was nothing to be read in their faces.

"We agree," Blaine said.

Quickly, while hope rose in Bury's eyes, Fowler added, "There's not much question about it. They're locked into a permanent state of population explosion followed by total war. If they ever get out of their system— Bury, they've got a soldier subspecies that puts the Saurons to shame. Hell, you've seen them."

Blaine did things to his pocket computer and another picture appeared: the time-machine sculpture.

"Those? But my Motie said they—" Bury stopped himself in realization. Then he laughed: the laugh of a man who has nothing more to lose. "*My* Motie."

"Precisely." The Senator smiled faintly. "I can't say we have much trust in your Motie. Bury, even if it were only the miniatures that got loose, we could lose whole worlds. They breed like bacteria. Nothing big enough to see breeds like that. But you know."

"Yes." Bury gathered himself with difficulty. His face smoothed, but behind his eyes was a myriad of glittering tiny eyes. Splendor of Allah! I almost brought them out myself! Praise and glory to the One who is merciful . . .

"Dammit, stop shivering," Fowler commanded.

"My apologies. You will doubtless have heard of my encounter with miniatures." He glanced at Blaine and envied his external calm. Miniatures could be no less unpleasant to the commander of *MacArthur*. "I am pleased to hear that the Empire recognizes the dangers."

"Yeah. We're going to blockade the Moties. Bottle 'em up in their own system."

"Would it not be better to exterminate them while we can?" Bury asked quietly. The voice was calm, but his dark eyes blazed.

"How?"

Bury nodded. "There would be political difficulties, of course. But I could find men to take an expedition to Mote Prime, and given the proper orders—"

Fowler gestured dismissal. "I've got my own *agents provocateurs* if I need 'em."

"Mine would be considerably less valuable." Bury looked pointedly at Blaine.

"Yeah." Fowler said nothing more for a moment, and Blaine stiffened visibly. Then the Senator continued. "Better or worse, Trader, we've decided on the blockade. Government's shaky enough without being accused of genocide. Besides, I don't know as I like the idea of unprovoked attack on intelligent beings. We'll do it this way."

"But the threat!" Bury leaned forward, unmindful of the fanatical gleam in his eyes. He knew he was close to madness, but he no longer cared. "Do you think you have locked the djinn away because the cork is back in the bottle? What if another generation does not see the Moties as we do? What if they let the djinn loose again? Glory of Allah! Picture swarms of their ships. They pour into the Empire, each commanded by things that look like *that* and think like Admiral Kutuzov! Specialized Warriors more than the equals of Sauron Death's-heads! And you will let them live? I tell you they must be destroyed . . ."

No! Men are never persuaded simply because they must believe. They will not listen when— Visibly he relaxed. "I see that you have decided. How may I be of assistance?" *Or do you wish anything of me at all? Is this a game?*

"I think you already have," Blaine said. He lifted his coffee and sipped. "And I thank you for the gift."

"Blockade's about the most expensive kind of naval action there is," Fowler mused. "Never very popular either."

"Ah." Bury felt the tension die within him. They held his life, but they needed him—perhaps he could keep far more than his life. "You are concerned about the Imperial Traders' Association."

"Exactly." There was no reading Fowler's expression.

Relief. For this I will build a mosque. It would make my father gloriously happy, and who knows? Perhaps Allah exists after all. That bubbling laugh was still there in his throat, but he knew that if he began he would never stop. "I have already pointed out to my colleagues the disadvantages of unrestricted trade with Moties. I have had my share of success, although too many Traders are like the neighbor who followed Aladdin into the magician's cave. Incalculable wealth glitters more brightly than the dangers."

"Yeah. But can you hold 'em? Find out who intends to sabotage us and squash their schemes?"

Bury shrugged. "With some assistance. It will be very expensive. I assume I will have the use of secret funds . . ."

Fowler grinned evilly. "Rod, what else was it Stone said? Something about—"

"It will not be necessary to bring up that man's ravings," Bury protested. "I believe I have sufficient wealth." He shuddered. What would he have when this was done? Fowler wouldn't care if he bled Bury to death. "If there is something that requires resources beyond mine—"

"We'll discuss it then," Fowler said. "There will be, too. For instance, this blockade's going to suck up a lot of resources Merrill thought he'd have for the unification of Trans-Coalsack. Now it seems to me a smart Trader might just have a few contacts among the rebels. Might even be able to persuade 'em to our point of view. I don't know how that would work, of course."

"I see."

Fowler nodded. "Thought you might. Rod, take that tape and see it's put in a good safe place, will you? I doubt if we'll be needing it again."

"Yes, sir." Rod did things to his pocket computer. The machine hummed: a tiny whine that signaled a new kind of life for Horace Bury.

There will be no evasions, Bury thought. Fowler will accept only results, not excuses; and my life will be at stake in this game. It will not be easy to be this man's political agent. Yet what choice is there? On Levant I could only wait in fear. At least this way I will know how they are dealing with the Moties . . . and perhaps change their policies as well.

"One more thing," the Senator said. He gestured and Rod Blaine went to the office door. Kevin Renner entered.

It was the first time any of them had seen the Sailing Master in civilian clothing. Renner had chosen bright plaid trousers and an even brighter tunic. His sash was some silklike material that looked natural but probably was synthetic. Soft boots, jewelry; in short, he looked like most of Bury's successful merchant captains. Trader and shipmaster eyed each other wonderingly.

"Yes, sir?" Renner asked.

"Bit premature, aren't you, Kevin?" Rod asked. "Your discharge isn't effective until this afternoon."

Renner grinned. "Didn't think the Provost would mind. And it sure feels good. Morning, Excellency."

"You know Trader Bury, then," Fowler said. "Good enough, since you'll be seeing a lot of each other."

"Uh?" Renner's face took on a wary look.

"The Senator means," Rod explained, "that he'd like to ask you a favor. Kevin, do you recall the terms of your enlistment?"

"Sure."

"Four years, or the duration of a Class One Imperial emergency, or the duration of a formal war," Rod said. "Oh, by the way, the Senator has declared the Motie situation a Class One emergency."

"Now wait a minute!" Renner shouted. "You can't do that to me!"

"Yes, I can," said Fowler.

Renner sagged into a chair. "Oh, my God. Well, you are the expert."

"Haven't made it public yet," Senator Fowler said. "Wouldn't want to panic anybody. But you've been officially notified now." Fowler waited for that to sink in. "Of course, we might have an alternative for you."

"Bless you."

"Bitter, aren't you?" Rod said. He was cheerful. Renner hated him.

"You did us a good piece of work, Renner," Fowler said. "Empire's grateful. *I'm* grateful. You know, I brought a hatful of blank Imperial patents when I came out . . . how'd you like to be a baron come next Birthday?"

"Oh, no! Not me! I've put in my time!"

"But surely you'd find the privileges enjoyable," Rod said.

"Damn! So I should have waited until morning to bring the Senator to your room. I *knew* I should have waited. No, sir, you'll not make any aristocrat out of Kevin Renner! I've got too much of the universe to explore! I don't have time for all the work . . ."

"It might spoil your carefree life," Senator Fowler said. "Anyway, it wouldn't be so easy to arrange. Jealousy and such. But you're *too* useful, Mr. Renner, and there *is* the Class One emergency."

"But—but . . ."

"Civilian ship captain," Fowler said. "With a knighthood. And an understanding of the Motie problem. Yep, you're just what we need."

"I haven't got any knighthood."

"You will. You can't turn *that* down. Mr. Bury'll insist that his personal pilot have at least the St. Michael and St. George. Won't you, Excellency?"

Bury winced. It was inevitable that the Empire would assign men to watch him, and they would want a man who could talk to the merchant captains. But this—harlequin? Beard of the Prophet, the man would be intolerable! Horace sighed to the inevitable. At least he was an intelligent harlequin. Perhaps he would even be useful. "I think Sir Kevin would be an admirable man to command my personal ship," Bury said smoothly. There was only a trace of distaste in the voice. "Welcome to Imperial Autonetics, Sir Kevin."

"But—" Renner looked around the room for help, but there wasn't any. Rod Blaine was holding a paper—what was it? Renner's discharge! As Kevin watched, Blaine tore the document to shreds.

"All right, dammit!" Renner could see no mercy from *them*. "But as a civilian!"

"Oh, sure," Fowler agreed. "Well, you'll hold a commission in Naval Intelligence, but it won't show."

"God's navel." The phrase gave Bury a start. Renner grinned. "What's the matter, Excellency? God doesn't have a navel?"

"I foresee interesting times," Bury said slowly. "For both of us."

58 · *And Maybe the Horse Will Sing*

Bright sunlight sparkled on the Palace roof. Fleecy, impossibly white clouds scudded overhead, but there was only a gentle breeze across the landing deck. The sunlight felt very warm and pleasant.

An admiral and two captains stood at the entryway to a landing boat. They faced a small group of civilians, three aliens wearing dark goggles, and four armed Marines. The Admiral carefully ignored the Moties and their escort as he bowed to the civilians. "Your pardon, my lady. My lord. It appears I will not be present at wedding after all. Not that I will be missed, but I regret taking your friends so soon." He indicated the two captains and bowed again. "I leave them to make farewells."

"Good luck, Admiral," Rod said quietly. "Godspeed."

"Thank you, my lord," Kutuzov said. He turned and entered the boat.

"I will never understand that man," Sally said.

"You are correct." Jock's voice was bluntly factual.

Sally looked at the alien in surprise before turning to the other officers. She extended her hand. "Good luck, Jack. Sandy."

"You too, Sally." Cargill glanced at the braid on his sleeves. The four rings of a post captain were bright and new. "Thanks for getting me a ship, Rod. I thought I was stuck in BattleOps forever."

"Thank the Admiral," Rod answered. "I recommended you but he decided. Sandy's the one who'll have to sweat. He'll be in the flagship."

Sinclair shrugged. "As Engineer of the Fleet I expect to put in time aboard other ships," he said. "Best observation point for new tricks'll be inside the Eye. So I'll be wi' this Sassenach, and that's nae bad thing. It would no do to hae his ship come apart."

Cargill ignored him. "Sorry to miss the wedding, Sally. I intend to claim a guest's privilege, though." He leaned forward to brush Sally's cheek with his lips. "If you get tired of him, there are other captains in the Navy."

"Aye," Sinclair agreed. "And my commission was signed two minutes before Cargill's. You will no forget that, Jack."

"How can I? You just remember that *Patton*'s *my* ship. We'd best be off, Skipper. The rendezvous' going to be tricky as it is. Good-by, Jock. Charlie." Cargill hesitated, then saluted awkwardly.

"Farewell," Charlie answered. Ivan twittered, and Jock added, "The Ambassador wishes you Godspeed and good luck."

"I wish I could be sure you meant that," Cargill said.

"Of course we mean it," said Charlie. "We want you to feel *safe*."

Cargill turned away looking thoughtful. He climbed aboard the boat. Sinclair followed and the ratings closed the entryway. Engines whined, and humans and Moties retreated into a shelter. They watched in silence as the boat lifted from the roof and vanished into the bright skies.

"It will work," Jock said.

"You do read minds, don't you?" Rod asked. He stared off into the sky but there was nothing to see but clouds.

"Of course it's going to work," Sally said. Her voice was emphatic.

"I think I understand you humans at last," Charlie told them. "Have you ever read your ancient histories?"

Rod and Sally looked blankly at the Motie. "No."

"Dr. Hardy showed us a key passage," Charlie said. He waited as the elevator arrived. Two Marines entered, and after the Moties and humans were inside, the others followed. Charlie continued the story as if armed guards were not present. "One of your most ancient writers, a historian named Herodotus, tells of a thief who was to be executed. As he was taken away he made a bargain with the king: in one year he would teach the king's favorite horse to sing hymns."

"Yes?" Sally prompted. She seemed puzzled and looked anxiously at Charlie. He seemed calm enough, but Dr. Hardy said he was worried about the aliens . . .

"The other prisoners watched the thief singing to the horse and laughed. 'You will not succeed,' they told him. 'No one can.' To which the thief replied, 'I have a year, and who knows what might happen in that time. The king might die. The horse might die. I might die. And perhaps the horse will learn to sing.'"

There was polite laughter. "I didn't tell it very well," Charlie said. "I wasn't trying to be humorous anyway.

That story made me realize at last just how *alien* you humans are."

There was an embarrassed silence. As the elevator stopped Jock asked, "How goes your Institute?"

"Fine. We've already sent for some of the department heads." She laughed, embarrassed. "I have to work fast: Rod won't let me think about the Institute after the wedding. You are coming, aren't you?"

The Mediators shrugged in unison, and one looked at the Marines. "We will be delighted if we are allowed to attend," Jock answered. "But we have no gifts for you. There is no Brown to make them."

"We'll get along without," Rod said. The elevator door stood open, but they waited for two of the Marines to inspect the corridor.

"Thank you for allowing me to meet Admiral Kutuzov," Jock said. "I have waited to speak with him since our embassy ship arrived alongside *MacArthur*."

Rod looked at the aliens in wonder. Jock's conversation with Kutuzov had been brief, and one of the most important questions the Motie had asked was "Do you like lemon in tea?"

They're so damned civilized and likable, and because of that they're going to spend the few years they've got left under guard while the Information Office blackguards them and their race. We've even hired a writer to script a play on the last hours of my midshipmen.

"It was little enough to do," Rod said. "We—"

"Yes. You can't let us go home." Charlie's voice changed to that of a New Scot youth. "We know aye more about humans than is safe." She gestured smoothly to the Marines. Two walked ahead into the hall, and the Moties followed. The other guards closed behind, and the procession marched through the corridor until they reached the Motie quarters. The elevator door closed softly.

Epilogue

Defiant lay nearly motionless in space at the outer fringes of the Murcheson System. There were other ships grouped around her in battle formation, and off to starboard hung *Lenin* like a swollen black egg. At least half the main battle fleet was in readiness at all times, and somewhere down in the red hell of the Eye other ships circled and waited. *Defiant* had just completed a tour with the Crazy Eddie Squadron.

That term was very nearly official. The men tended to use a lot of Motie terms. When a man won a big hand at poker he was likely to shout "Fyunch(click)!" And yet, Captain Herb Colvin mused, most of us have never seen a Motie. We hardly see their ships: just targets, helpless after transition.

A few had made it out of the Eye, but every one had been so badly damaged that it was hardly spaceworthy. There was always plenty of time to warn the ships outside the Eye that another Motie was on the way—if the Eye hadn't killed them first.

The last few ships had emerged from the Crazy Eddie point at initial velocities up to a thousand km per second. How the hell could the Moties hit a Jump point at such speeds? Ships within the Eye couldn't catch them. They didn't need to, with the Motie crews—and autopilots—helpless in Jump shock and unable to decelerate. The fleeing black blobs had run up through the rainbow and exploded every time. Where the Moties used their unique expanding fields, they exploded sooner, picking up heat faster from the yellow-hot photosphere.

Herb Colvin laid down the latest report on Motie tricks and technology. He'd written a lot of it himself, and it all added up to hopeless odds against the Moties. They couldn't beat ships that didn't have to carry an Alderson Drive, ships on station and waiting for Moties who still didn't suspect the Jump disorientation . . . he could almost feel sorry for them.

Colvin took a bottle from the cabinet on the bulkhead of his patrol cabin and poured expertly despite the Coriolis forces. He carried his glass to his chair and sank into it. A packet of mail lay on his desk, the most recent letter from his wife already ripped open so that he could be sure there was nothing wrong at home. Now he could read the letters in order. He raised his glass to Grace's picture on the desk.

She hadn't heard much from New Chicago, but things were all right there the last time her sister had written. Mail service to New Scotland was slow. The house she'd found was outside the New Scot defensive system, but she wouldn't worry because Herb had told her the Moties couldn't get through. She'd taken a lease for the whole three years they'd be out here.

Herb nodded in agreement. That would save money—three years on this blockade, then home, where he'd be Commodore of New Chicago's Home Fleet. Put the Alderson engines back in *Defiant:* she'd be flagship when he took her home. A few years on blockade service was a small price to pay for the concessions the Empire offered.

It took the Moties to do it, Herb thought. Without them we'd still be fighting. There were still worlds outside the Empire and always would be, but in Trans-Coalsack unification was proceeding smoothly and there was more jawboning than fighting. The Moties did that for us, anyway.

A name caught Herb Colvin's eye. Lord Roderick Blaine, Chairman of the Imperial Commission Extraordinary— Colvin looked up at the bulkhead to see the familiar spot where *Defiant* had been patched following her battle with *MacArthur*. Blaine's prize crew had done that, and a pretty good job it was. He's a competent man, Colvin admitted reluctantly. But heredity's still a hell of a way to choose leaders. The rebel democracy in New Chicago hadn't done too well either. He went back to Grace's letter.

My Lord Blaine had a new heir, his second. And Grace was helping out at this Institute Lady Blaine had set up.

His wife was excited because she often talked with Lady Sally and had even been invited out to the manor house to see the children . . .

The letter went on, and Colvin dutifully read it, but it was an effort. Would she never get tired of gushing about the aristocracy? *We'll never agree on politics,* he decided and looked up fondly at her picture again. *Lord, I miss you—*

Chimes sounded through the ship and Herb stuffed the letters into his desk. It was time to go to work; tomorrow Commodore Cargill would come aboard for Fleet inspection. Herb rubbed his hands in anticipation. This time he'd show the Imperials just how a ship ought to be run. The winner of this inspection would get extra time ashore next leave, and he intended to have that for his crew.

As he stood a small yellow-white point of light flashed through the view port. *One of these days,* Herb thought. *Someday we're going in there.* With all the talent the Empire's got working on the problem we'll find a way to govern the Moties.

And what will we call ourselves then? he wondered. *The Empire of Man and Motie?* He grinned and went out to inspect his ship.

Blaine Manor was large, with sheltered gardens overhung with trees to protect their eyes from the bright sun. Their quarters were very comfortable, and the Mediators had become accustomed to the ever present Marine guards. Ivan, as always, treated them as he would his own Warriors.

There was work. They had daily conferences with the Institute scientists, and for the Mediators there were the Blaine children. The oldest could speak a few words of Language and could read gestures as well as a young Master.

They were comfortable, but still it was a cage; and at nights they saw the brilliant red Eye and its tiny Mote. The Coal Sack was high in the night sky. It looked like a hooded Master blind in one eye.

"I fear," said Jock. "For my family, my civilization, my species, and my world."

"That's right, think large thoughts," said Charlie. "Why waste your mighty brain on little things? Look you—" Her voice and posture changed; she would speak of serious matters. "We've done what we can. This Institute of Sally's is a trivial fiasco, but we continue to cooperate. We show how friendly and harmless and honest we are. And meanwhile the blockade works and it will always work. There's not a hole in it."

"There is," said Jock. "No human seems to consider that the Masters might reach the Empire through normal space."

"There is no hole," Charlie repeated. She shifted two arms for emphasis. "No breach before the next collapse. Curse! Who could build another Crazy Eddie probe before the famines begin? And where would they send it? Here, into their fleets?" She signaled contempt. "Perhaps into the Coal Sack, toward the heart of the Empire? Have you thought of the launching lasers—far greater to compensate for the dust in the Coal Sack? No. We have done what we can, and the Cycles have begun again."

"Then what can we anticipate?" Jock's right arms were folded, his left extended and open: ready for attack, and thus projecting rhetorical mercilessness. "There may be unsuccessful attempts to penetrate the blockade. Wasted effort. The collapse will be hastened. Then, a long period in which the Empire can half forget that we exist.

"New technologies rise, warlike as rising technologies are always. They would know of humanity. Perhaps they can preserve or reinvent the Field. When they reach the height of their power, before the decline, they will breed Warriors and come forth conquering everything: Mote Prime, asteroids, all. And on to the Empire."

Charlie listened after a hurried glance at the Master. Ivan lay impassive, listening to the chatter of the Mediators as Masters often did, and it was impossible to know what he thought.

"Conquest," Jock said. "But the more progress they make against the Empire, the more thoroughly will the

Empire retaliate. They have numbers. For all their talk of limiting populations, they have numbers and all of space. Until we can escape human space entirely and breed, they will always have the numbers. They bottle us up until we overbreed, and then collapse. And with the next collapse —extermination!"

Charlie's knees were against her belly, right arms pulled tight against her chest, left arm protecting her head. An infant about to be born into a cruel world. Her voice was muffled. *"If you had better ideas, you should have raised them."*

"No. There are no better ideas."

"We bought time. Hundreds of years of time. Sally and her silly Institute will have hundreds of years to study the problem we raise for humans. Who knows, perhaps the horse will learn to sing hymns."

"Would you bet on it?"

Charlie looked out of the curve of her arm. *"At these odds? Curse, yes!"*

"Crazy Eddie!"

"Yes. A Crazy Eddie solution. What else is there? One way or another, the Cycles end now. Crazy Eddie has won his eternal war against the Cycles."

Jock looked to Ivan and met a shrug. Charlie had gone Crazy Eddie. It hardly mattered now; it was, in fact, a fine and enviable madness, this delusion that all questions have answers, and nothing is beyond the reach of a strong left arm.

They would never know. They would not live that long. But they had bought time; the Blaines knew what they must find, and their children would grow up to know Moties as more than a legend. Two generations of power would not hate Moties.

If anyone could teach a horse to sing hymns, it would be a trained Mediator.